TALES
of a
LONG NIGHT

A NOVEL BY
Alfred Döblin

Translated from the German by Robert and Rita Kimber

FROMM INTERNATIONAL PUBLISHING CORPORATION
New York

Printed in the United States of America

First U.S. Edition

Library of Congress Cataloging in Publication Data

Döblin, Alfred, 1878-1957.
Tales of a long night.
I. Title.
PT2607.035H313   1984   833'.912   84-18798

ISBN 0-88064-016-2
ISBN 0-88064-017-0 (pbk.)

10 9 8 7 6 5 4 3 2

Contents

❄ BOOK THREE

❄ BOOK FOUR

❄ BOOK FIVE

BOOK ONE

The Homecoming

THEY brought him back. It would not be his lot to set foot on the Asian continent.

At dawn, five days after the convoy had passed through the Panama Canal, two Japanese kamikaze planes hurtled down on his ship. The first one angled down out of a wall of clouds, glided through the soft mist that lay on the gently rocking ocean, grazed the ship's bridge, bored through the deck, and, screeching and spewing flames, ripped huge holes in the ship's hull. Hungry water flooded in. Mattresses and boards stuffed into the holes gave the crew time enough to make repairs and drag away the wounded.

Then the second kamikaze plane hit. The human bomb, plummeting vertically out of the heavy cloud that was passing by overhead like a pregnant cow, slashed through the deck and burrowed into the engine room.

He was tossed up into the air like a doll, flipping and twisting head over heels, flying in flames and black clouds with chunks of machinery, metal fragments, splinters of wood, with corpses, the wounded, and severed limbs. Nothing was conscious in that hot maelstrom.

The cruiser was gutted. The survivors in the crew, with help from a neighboring ship, moved every body with any sign of life in it over to another cruiser. They found him, far from the site of the explosion, on a dark, metal stairway he had tumbled down.

The water gurgled peacefully and somnolently around the ships as they continued on their eastward course. The pregnant cow overhead moved heavily on. She had put a long way behind her and had a still longer one to go.

In the belly of the cruiser, in the operating room, strong electric lights were burning. In the passageways and in the prep room the stretchers piled up, laden with the half-cremated, the mutilated, young creatures that were still breathing but no longer had the appearance of human beings. Their swift, hot flight through the air had stripped them of that.

3

His left leg was gone. The surgeons trimmed away the scraps of bone and flesh, removed pieces of wood and metal from his arms and shoulders, cleaned the gaping flesh wound on his back. They were able to work with minimal anesthetic. Shock had made him almost impervious to pain. A transfusion before surgery, another during it, then the other drugs, sulfa, penicillin. He had had tetanus shots earlier.

When they took him off the table his pulse was stable. He was breathing evenly, shallowly, and felt cool to the touch.

Two days later all the survivors who were fit enough to travel were flown westward across the ocean and set down on the warm Pacific coast of America.

Hospitals on hills covered with palm trees took them in. Here their terrors could abate.

A large city spread out flat below them. Its buildings crept up the hillsides. Colorful, blossoming gardens surrounded opulent homes, garages, and blue swimming pools. Cars streamed inaudibly along the well-groomed boulevards. There were broad business streets where buses and trolleys rolled by, chairs and benches full of people lounging in green parks. Women crossed the street and looked into gleaming show windows full of clothes, shoes, hats, jewelry. It was hot. People were eating ice cream in the drugstores and dropping nickels in the jukeboxes at their tables. Soft, crooning jazz.

He did not respond to any questions. He was like these people on the street. He had walked, a twenty-year-old man, some weeks ago on leave, through a huge, strange city, London, had bought a newspaper on a street corner and, while walking, a cigarette in his mouth, had looked at the latest war news. He had driven a military vehicle and stopped in front of a store where he had bought some items of civilian clothing for after the war, ties and gloves. Nor did he forget flowers for his mother, his young, elegant mother, intensely fragrant, deep red carnations.

His pale yellow face showed no sign of mental activity. It was as smooth and unwrinkled as an infant's. It flushed red when his temperature climbed; his eyes glistened. No sound, not a groan from his dry mouth.

Then he was well enough to be transported to the East Coast with some other wounded, traveling, in one of those endless hospital trains, to Boston, where an English hospital ship was waiting to take them back to their European homeland.

The war in Europe was over by now. He had had a part in it from the very beginning, in an antiaircraft unit during the blitz, in the signal corps, in the preparations for D day. He fought in Normandy and in the thrust through France and Belgium. At his own request he received orders for the Far East as forces were gathering for the attack on Japan.

There was nothing more to fear on the Atlantic Ocean. It was summer. One beautiful day followed on another. The big ship that was taking him home rocked softly. The massive black vessel rose and fell peacefully.

The horizon rose, fell. The ship was picked up, slid down into the trough. The engines hummed in its belly. The wounded lay next to each other in rows on the deck, protected from the wind.

It was in the afternoon of an unusually calm day when a shrill, penetrating scream rose from one of the beds on the deck, the kind of scream that someone who is about to be murdered would produce. The scream cracked and became a long, clear wail. It raised havoc on the deck. The wounded called out for nurses and medics. People came running from all directions.

The amputee Edward Allison lay gasping on his bed, bluish red in the face, as if he were suffocating, tore at his blankets, and had ripped off some of his dressings. He smashed ferociously at the footboard with his sound leg and tossed from right to left, from left to right in his battle with an invisible opponent he was trying to escape. Immense fear lay on his face. His eyes were rolled up, showing nothing but white. His lips trembled, his teeth chattered, drops of sweat on his forehead.

He did not answer the nurses and doctors that were holding him. The battle resumed with renewed strength. He screamed at his enemy in an unknown language. Fear grew. His attendants gave him a shot as they struggled with him. They carried him quickly off the deck to spare his companions any further distress. Almost everyone here had had horrible experiences. Many patients were trembling already. Panic could spread through the whole ship like wildfire.

Below, he remained quiet. His eyes moved, watching everything that went on around him.

When the ship neared Europe and he was lying on deck again, his attendants pointed out the first seagulls to him and made him aware of the excitement on board. The ship sailed past islands. Small boats came into view. And suddenly, after a meal he had let the nurse spoon into him without putting up any resistance, he was changed, lying there with large, troubled, questioning eyes. And look: He moved his lips.

A nurse came up to him. He whispered something. She bent over him. He whispered: "What's going on? Where am I?"

"On a ship. We're almost home. We can already see land." He stared at her. "What land?"

"England, Mr. Allison."

"Who is Mr. Allison?"

She touched his shoulder. "You. The man lying here. You are Mr. Edward Allison. Come on now, let me settle you comfortably."

"Who is Edward Allison?"

"There, look at that dark line. We're arriving. In five hours we can go on land."

And in the time it took her to run gleefully to the doctor to report this change in her patient's condition and then to return with the doctor, he had stretched out in the bed and was lying quiet and immobile again, had slipped back into the abyss, had the smooth, empty face of an infant, like a natural object, a tree trunk, the surface of a pond.

He occupied a white hospital room, was back on European soil, not wondrous Asia which he had longed for. His family was notified.

Alice, his mother, had a slim face with regular features. She could look young with a girlish sweetness. Her gaze was open, deep, and penetrating. If she did not press her lips together, as she often did, giving her face a sharp expression, her mouth was soft and full. She was slender, trim, light on her feet, and moved slowly. When she had learned of Edward's wounds, she had shut herself up in her room for weeks on end and seemed sunk in apathy whenever she came out. Now she waved the telegram in the air, announced the news, and laughed and cried by turns. She began that same day to get the house ready for him, to decorate his room—and to drop down into a chair again and again, crying to herself. The family soon learned that Edward would be transferred to a sanitarium whose director was a frequent guest in the Allison household. Alice sat in her room and waited, as if blessed.

Kathleen, the daughter, three years younger than Edward, a serious, sober girl who had served in the ambulance corps during the war, watched her mother and asked questions of her. Kathleen was surprised at the response the news evoked in her mother. She thought her mother ridiculous. And now Alice began primping. Kathleen saw that she had a young, interesting mother, a different kind of woman from herself. Her mother smiled a lot. She was no doubt practicing the smile she would use to welcome Edward. What a disgusting display. What a fuss over a wound. Other mothers showed some pride and courage.

As always, Kathleen's father did not interfere with his wife. He behaved, Kathleen thought, in a dignified way. He sat in his library on the second floor, heavy, immobile, a fat man, this distinguished writer who had made a name for himself as a journalist and travel reporter. He had then turned to fiction, humorous sketches, short stories that publishers and newspapers fought over tooth and nail and that had made him a wealthy man. Even before the war had begun, he had left his London residence for this country house, his summer quarters.

Alice was standing on the platform with Kathleen when her son was carried off the hospital train. His stretcher, wrapped in blankets, was placed on a dolly and quickly rolled away. His mother didn't even get a chance to put her flowers on the stretcher. Then she sent him flowers every day in the sanitarium. But why couldn't she visit him? Finally she received permission, but all she would be allowed to do was look into his room through a window in the door.

The two of them, Alice and Kathleen, climbed out of the carriage. The mother, pale, ran up the steps. Kathleen, as if apologizing for her mother's behavior, followed at an exaggeratedly slow pace. The wide entry hall with its linoleum floor opened onto a waiting room. Dr. King, a tall, broad-shouldered man with sparse gray-white hair, soon appeared and warmly offered both hands to his visitors. But instead of immediately taking them to Edward, he settled himself heavily in a wicker chair, lit a cigar, and began a conversation that dragged on until the mother could bear it no longer and asked with a pained smile that she now be permitted her promised look into Edward's room.

"Besides, if I can't speak with him, why can't I at least go into his room and take his hand? I promise not to say a word."

"You mustn't for his sake, my dear Mrs. Allison. I can't predict what kind of effect on him the sight of his mother, contact with the old domestic milieu, memories—even without words—will have. Quite frankly, I'd prefer to postpone that experiment until later."

"Is he very weak, Doctor?"

"I'm sure you'll understand, after everything that has happened to him. We're most concerned about his psychic condition. We haven't begun treatment yet. It will be hard on you to see him. From time to time he is in the grip of certain fantasies."

Alice felt her throat close up.

"Fantasies? What do you mean? What does he say? What does he look like?"

"Like a sick man."

A nurse was standing in the doorway. The doctor signaled to her.

"This is Gertrude, his nurse. These are the ladies I mentioned, Nurse, his mother and sister. Let them have a look through the window in the door."

Alice seized the doctor's hand. "Oh, God, Doctor, why all this fuss?"

The doctor said good-bye. The mother hesitated. Kathleen got up with a shrug of her shoulders and went along with the nurse. Her mother followed slowly.

To the left a row of windows looking out onto the grounds, to the right one padded door after another. The nurse stopped in front of a room, put her index finger to her mouth, and quietly opened the padded door.

They stayed outside. Even Kathleen felt her heart pounding. The nurse motioned to them to come into the dark hallway. Alice, unable to follow, clung to the wall. Kathleen slipped inside. She pressed her face against the small, square window. After half a minute she scurried out, took her mother by the hand, and whispered, "He's lying with his back to the door. All I could see was his head. Come on, Mother. Go on in."

Now she felt sorry for her mother.

"I will," Alice said. With her head lowered, she slipped by the other two and stepped to the window.

In this room lay her son.

It was a bright, simple hospital room, but in it lay her son.

It was a room that had walls and solid objects in it and that was part of the building it was in, but it was part of her, too. In it lay her son.

She looked into the room and saw:

He was lying with his face to the window and his back to the door where his mother stood and called silently to him.

He must have felt her presence. He began to move, to turn over. He rolled onto his back and lay stretched out, his face toward the ceiling. Now the head with the mussed brown hair turned to the right. His face turned slowly toward the door. His head rose slightly from the pillow. Two eyes looked over at the window in the door.

Alice had on a charming, girlish outfit. She was wearing a light green summer dress. She had put on a wide straw hat over her loose hair and wore flowers at her breast. Her hands trembled in white gloves that reached to her elbows, her fingers crushing the violets she wanted to give him.

He lay there. His lips moved. The corners of his mouth quivered.

— Out of the clouds, the first plane. It bored through the deck, tore holes in the ship's hull.

The second straight down. It smashed, thundered, through the deck, exploded, and pulverized the engine room so that the ship, its guts torn, emitted a horrifying animal bellowing. A geyser shot up, carrying planks, smokestacks, and men with it, rolled everything up in bales of black smoke, a darting red flame in the troop quarters. Chunks of metal, bodies, torn limbs, rained down on the sea, pattering lightly. The sea licked its lips. Fire faced over the ship. Death leaned over and picked up his spoils.

Edward's mouth was open. Moaning. Moaning. His head sank back onto the pillow.

But now something strange moved over his face. His features grew tense, the lips pressed together, the eyes squeezed shut. And an evil, vicious expression slowly took shape, alternating with one of fear, immense fear. Now came rage and despair, one following on the heels of the other. He raised his arms to protect his face. The man ground his teeth together, bared them.

Alice was wearing a red leather belt around her slim waist. Her hand let the crushed violets fall. She tried to pull her handkerchief from the belt and press it against her mouth.

When that horrible expression appeared on the face inside—but this was her son, Edward—she pressed closer to the door, against the window. Did she want to break in, come to his aid?

The dreadful expression stayed for a long time. The eyes opened, cast a look full of hate and pain toward the door.

Alice's arms flew up into the air. Her knees gave way. As she sank to the floor, as if wanting to sit down, the nurse grabbed her by the shoulders, bent over, and picked her up.

Kathleen had gone back out into the hallway so that she would not have to watch her mother struggle helplessly with her feelings. She followed anxiously behind the nurse, her mother's broad straw hat in her hand. In the waiting room, on the black leather sofa, Alice came to, sat up with a start, looked from one to the other and back, stared into space, and asked for her purse.

She smoothed her hair and powdered her face. Her hands were shaking; around her mouth, too, there was a strange twitching. She stood up.

"Please, you needn't worry about me. I felt faint. I've caused you a lot of trouble."

She asked the nurse to give her regards to the doctor and left with a nod, her step as springy as when she had come. Without taking her daughter's arm she went to the door and down the steps of the sanitarium to where her carriage was waiting, an old-fashioned country carriage drawn by two black horses.

In the Clinic

SHE reported to Gordon Allison, her husband, that the sight of Edward had been a real shock to her. His illness had taken more of a toll on him than she would have expected. But, she added, they could count on complete recovery. The doctor had already treated many cases like this. Edward was receiving excellent care in the sanitarium. And in a few weeks his family would be able to speak with him.

Although, as she had noted, he was in good hands in the sanitarium, she urged with great persistence that he be discharged from it. Yes, she wanted to have him. She would not be dissuaded by the arguments of the medical director and his assistants. She kept coming back again and again to the "beneficial atmosphere of the home." She could not grasp that someone in Edward's condition would not even notice that atmosphere. Every few days she reappeared at the sanitarium and harassed the doctor again.

Her daughter did not come with her anymore. She was annoyed with her mother and made fun of her: as if Edward were a baby that had to be in his mother's care. He had, after all, been in the war, in both the European and the Pacific theaters, and had managed without his mother. Then, too, Kathleen was watching what went on around her closely and felt that her mother was putting on a show. With her husband, at table, and with guests, Alice was excessively cheerful. But if anyone happened upon her in her favorite spot by the fence in the garden where she could look down on the street, she would be there hunched over, lost in thought and staring off into space. She had not been her old self ever since Edward entered the sanitarium.

She was guarding some secret.

The doctors would not let Edward go home. They were determined to cure him.

In the weeks before, doctors had rescued his maimed, fever-ridden

10

body from the jaws of death. Now, like the angels in the legend who gathered around the bed of the sleeping King Salomon to guard his dreams, other doctors surrounded his bed and struggled to cure his soul.

In the thundering explosion on the cruiser, while his body was being torn apart, riddled with shrapnel, tossed up in smoke and flame and sent flying, his consciousness had been extinguished, his soul paralyzed. The fear of annihilation had driven it off into the death it had almost suffered in reality. It had played dead, as a hunted animal sometimes will, and it had still not shaken off this simulated rigidity of death.

Why was Edward clinging to death? What was he hiding from, and why had he dug himself in behind that fearful "No" that was on his face every day and that had made Alice faint?

Death has an easy time of it in the world. He finds lots of tools to work with and entryways to come in by. But what is someone to do who wants to aid the cause of life? He has no crushing bombs, kamikaze planes, land mines, at his disposal. How is he to blow the annihilating thunder away from the ears of this mute man, relax his rigid limbs, and wipe that "No" from his face?

The doctors squared off against the artillerymen and munitions makers in Edward's past. They slowly tunneled under the ramparts his soul had thrown up around itself. They breached the walls it was hiding behind.

There was a drug then that the doctors could use to creep up on a man's soul. It was called Pentothal, a soporific, which, injected into the bloodstream, induced narcosis but then left the patient in a peculiar semiconscious state. He lay still and listened; he understood, and the doctors could communicate with him as with someone in hypnosis. He could remember and could speak about things he would otherwise keep to himself. With this tool the doctors could approach the completely mute and gloweringly unapproachable Edward.

Everything went as it was supposed to. Dr. King broke through Edward's defenses at the very first attempt.

The medical director, this tall, heavy, white-haired man with slack-skinned cheeks and slightly trembling lips, sat in his white doctor's coat on a chair next to Edward's bed.

The doctor told the dreaming man on the bed that he was crossing the sea, the Pacific Ocean. (The doctor repeated what he had heard from Edward and from others about Edward's disastrous journey.) The ship was making good time. The sea was calm. They had been under-way for four days.

Edward repeated what he heard, speaking softly, slowly, in a sleepy, nasal voice:

"The sea is calm. We're making good time. If the Jap planes will only leave us alone. I don't trust this quiet. Everybody else is acting as if they aren't worried. I've got an uneasy feeling. We have antiaircraft guns but not enough fighter planes."

The doctor: "Come on, stop worrying. Another big aircraft carrier just joined the convoy yesterday."

"That's news to me. Where's it supposed to be?"

"I'll show it to you later. You can't see it in this fog."

Edward mumbled and started talking again:

"I can't stand the sea, especially this one. The glare makes me sick. — You hear that? Here they come again."

"Those are our planes."

"Can't you hear? They're shooting. We don't have any fighters. Where the hell are those new planes hiding?"

"The shooting's stopped already."

Edward fell silent. Suddenly his face reddened. He started chewing someone out.

"What are you doing here, Jonny? Always following me around. You have no business on deck."

"Who is Jonny?"

"He's always following me. I promised his father I'd watch out for him. The kid is eighteen, he says. He's probably just sixteen. He adopted me in Belgium and hasn't let go since. His father used to be a consul in Shanghai. Their house in Birmingham is loaded with dragons, pagodas, swords, porcelain, even medicines, all kinds of stuff. Pretty nice. He liked that stuff. Me, too."

He began to sob. "He was the best chess player on board, that kid. He was supposed to have stayed below. Somebody must have told him we were having a game on deck, so he came up."

He cried loudly and tossed his head back and forth. He sat up and wanted to get out of bed. The doctor had to ring for a nurse. Together, they held the dreaming man until he lay still again. Tears ran down his reddened cheeks.

The doctor wakened him.

"You were asleep."

Edward touched his face. "It's hot. I've been sweating."

He took the towel the doctor handed him and dried his face. He stared dully into space.

Then the doctor started to tell him what he had said in his half-waking state.

Edward said lightly:

"We were escorting a convoy to Asia. It was supposed to go to Burma. And just as we were—"

He didn't get any further than that. He lost his train of thought. He tried to pick it up. He struggled. His face darkened, his eyes opened wide. He looked past the doctor. His arms, which he had moved freely before, were pressed close to his body. His fingers were clenched, his nails digging into his palms.

And soon he was unapproachable again, braced to fight, to defend himself.

The doctors made renewed attacks on the fortress.

Once when Edward was in a semiconscious state, the doctor brought up the chess game, which Edward had never mentioned again.

In his agitation, Edward began stuttering:

"I have to find him. He was sitting on the other side of the table."

"Where is the table?"

"Blown to pieces, the chairs, nothing left. Ah, ah—"

Then he screamed out:

"There's something under the chair. It's his uniform. Oh, God, oh, God. Jonny, what's happened? Get up, Jonny. Come on, come on, will you? I told you to stay below. Get up. Help me. He can't get up."

"Is he moving?"

Edward whimpered. His fingers dug into the doctor's arm, which was pressing him back down onto his bed. Suddenly—and without waking—he threw himself to one side and vomited in a single spasm.

The doctor held a glass of water to his mouth. He swallowed, mumbling and grunting as he lay back.

"There's a head. A sailor's hat. Everything helter-skelter. They may not belong together."

Then the words boiled up:

"I kept telling you you were underestimating the kamikaze bombers. They're as bad as the long-range bombers. Where are you taking him? Wait for the doctor. It's a crime to treat people like this. You can't be sure that he's dead. Dead, dead, Jonny dead. Stinking world, blast it to pieces. There they go with him."

After a pause:

"Jonny, what will I do? What will I tell your father? I shook his hand and said, 'You can depend on me. I'll keep an eye on him. If he doesn't come back, I won't either.' He had no business coming up on deck with us."

The doctor: "He could have been hit if he'd been somewhere else. Don't blame yourself. This is war. Anybody can get it."

Edward: "I wanted to get away, far away. And then he came with his talk about China. — I've had a bellyful of your Europe."

"What has Europe done to you? You're an Englishman."

"Goddamn Europe. If only it were destroyed."

Pause.

The doctor: "You've had some bad experiences?"

"I've had enough of Europe. But nobody can say that I didn't do my part. Father makes a lot of my heroism. What does he know about war?"

Pause.

The doctor: "We're moving. It's on fire. Watch out. We'll help."

Edward screamed: "Don't move. You back there. Take cover! Take cover! Medics. My hands? Oh, that doesn't matter. Fire has never been any big problem for us. Just a routine shipboard fire. Now all our fliers are up, a day too late. — Where have they taken him? There they are, lying next to each other. Horrible."

He cried quietly to himself.

"You were good friends?"

"That was some fine life we led. We didn't care about anything. When things get too awful nothing bothers you anymore. We had nerves of steel. We carried out our orders. In Belgium and Germany people sat in their villages, cooked, knitted, did their laundry. What did they know about the world? We were in our element. Jonny had great ambitions."

"Women?"

Edward laughed: "He treated them like poodles. They had to 'sit up and beg.' They were good for relaxation."

It was clear. He thought about his dead friend a lot; he partially identified with Jonny, this cheerful comrade who personified everything he loved. That was why he clung to him, followed him into the land of the dead, played the dead man himself. But along with that were these obscure reproaches and accusations against Europe, against his homeland. He had turned his back on his country; he did not want to return to it.

*   *   *

Edward stayed in the clinic for months. His condition improved in every way. How strange that he never gave a thought to his lost leg. He patiently let his dressings be changed. It seemed to amuse him that he had something that interested the doctors and nurses.

Now his mother and Kathleen were allowed to visit.

A bomb had fallen on his ship and done all this to him in a matter of seconds.

He came home. The bomb kept falling.

Alice stood by his bed. He received her with coolness, reserve.

He watched her closely.

She put flowers on his table. He thanked her as a stranger would and watched her.

The mother and sister left. Kathleen felt sorry for her mother.

"I want to take him home," Alice decided on her next visit. The doctor had no fundamental objections. But the question remained whether the home atmosphere would be beneficial.

"What could possibly be wrong with it?" Alice sighed.

"You can see for yourself, Alice, how he is. He doesn't want to take any medications. He can't rest; he's constantly awake. I sometimes have the feeling that he uses staying awake as a defense against falling back into rigidity. That's why he's devouring books. He's on an inner quest, searching for something; he doesn't know what. But he has to search. It's a compulsion. Hypnosis hasn't been any help."

"Give him to me," Alice begged.

The doctor looked at her. "He'll press you hard. People in this condition are implacable."

"Give him to me, Doctor."

The doctor drew in his lower lip, sniffed, and looked down at the floor. He had an idea. The Allisons' house was nearby. He could keep an eye on the case.

"I'll see what he says himself," the doctor answered. Alice's eyes opened wide.

"Yes, ask him. I'll wait here."

Her gaze followed him as he left the room. She hadn't moved an inch when he came back. Edward had asked for a day to think it over.

"I'll be back tomorrow morning."

On his next morning's rounds, Dr. King asked Edward if he wanted to go home. Edward still hadn't made a decision.

For the first time, he asked the doctor a question.

"What do you advise? Should I go?"

"What's keeping you from saying yes?"

"Nothing." But then he added, "Do I have to? Should I? Why?"

"Your mother would like it. There's no other reason."

"Mother would like to have me at home? Did she say so?"

"Every time she's been here."

"How did she ask? Out of politeness—because it's the proper thing to do?"

"I don't think so. It didn't sound that way to me."

"How did it sound? Why should I go? What's going on here?"

"Would you like to go? After all, she is your mother."

Edward looked squarely at the doctor and searched in his face. He folded his arms and thought. He looked up at the ceiling, over to the window, looked around in the large room.

"And I'll have my old room?"

"I'm sure of it."

Now, with Edward so open to him, the doctor risked a question: "Can you tell me what it is that's troubling you about this move? Maybe then I could advise you better."

"You know that I've been away from home for years. A lot has happened in that time. I wanted to become a completely different person. I never wanted to come back at all."

"Not even to your mother?"

He nervously rubbed his hands together on the covers and didn't answer. Then he made up his mind.

"Tell her I'll come."

He called the doctor back. "She said it several times? And she really meant it?"

"Your mother has no reason to say things to me that she doesn't really mean. And as I've said, I had a very different impression."

"That she is inviting me, that she is asking me to come?"

"Exactly. She asked urgently that you come, and that's what she has been asking ever since you arrived here. I just haven't told you."

Edward whispered hastily, "Is she coming today?"

"She's already here."

"Tell her I'll come."

He was suddenly excited.

—"Do you realize," the doctor said to Alice, "that you're in for a hard time of it? Quite apart from his instability and the fact that he needs somebody all the time. When soldiers come back from the front, they always have accounts to settle with their homeland."

"You know how well we get along together, Doctor."

"Yes, of course. But you never know. Perhaps you got along too well with him."

"Oh, come on, you and your psychoanalytical nonsense. Just give him to me, for God's sake. Why not? Why are you tormenting me like this? I almost lost him. I almost died with him. Give him back to me."

She cried.

The white-haired man leaned over her chair and patted both her hands.

"You shall have him, Alice. The very reason why I wanted to keep him was that I didn't want to torment you."

"He won't torment me if he's with me. He can't torment me. My poor boy torment me? Ridiculous."

In the House of Allison

AND so Edward Allison—after Normandy, after France, Belgium, and Germany, after the Pacific Ocean—returned to his parents' home, alive but crippled, very grave, tense, and reserved, as if he were entering a danger zone.

This handsome country house, the property of Gordon Allison, had, like its owner, gone untouched by the war. Gordon Allison had moved out here in early 1939, before the war began, bringing everything he cared about with him. When the war actually broke out, he congratulated himself on his prudence, especially during the heavy bombardments of London and Coventry and during the evacuation.

When the ambulance with the Red Cross flag on it drove up the poplar-lined drive, Alice quickly drew the window curtains, ran to her door, locked it, turned back into her room as if she were looking for something, then kneeled down at her bed.

"Merciful God, Mother of God, to whom I pray, stand by me.

"You have seen how I lay before you here, on my knees, my face to the floor, and how I called on you again and again through those long years for help or for the patience to endure. I could not understand what was happening to me when he, too, my only son, was taken from me—until I learned that he was coming back. And now I have him. He's here. But look: He is searching. And, like me, he can't rest.

"You saw, Mother of God, how I cried because I did not understand. Now I do understand. You are sending him to me. You are sending him into my home as my helper. This medallion I'm holding in my hand still bears the kisses I pressed on your image when I began to grasp what you meant to do—that you would send him back to me, and so ill, and that he should regain his health here with me.

"But now I'm afraid again. He's here. Merciful God, where are you leading me? Did I do the right thing? God, protect our home, protect us all. Do not abandon me. God, stand by me. My life is about to take a new turn. I don't know what will happen.

"I've taken a chance. Have I done right? Forgive me. I had to do it. I wanted to do it. You know that. Now it's happened. You heard my prayers. He is here. Mother of God, did I do wrong to get into this? You are the truth, dear God. All I want is the truth, and I want justice. A bolt of lightning has struck me. Did you cast that bolt? Have pity on me, merciful God. Stand by us all."

She ran to her old mahogany dresser, poked around in it, and found in a drawer a gold chain with a black stone cross on it. She pressed it to her, kissed it, fell to her knees again, and begged for help.

Scarcely breathing, she listened at the door, the chain still in her hand. Men's slow, heavy steps, a maid's voice: "Down this hall and then left to the open door."

A muffled sound; they had set the stretcher down. Whispered words now; they were carrying him to his bed. From him, nothing. The heavy steps again in the hall. The maid's voice: "I'll get Mrs. Allison."

Alice pressed the chain to her lips, stuck it back in its place, and opened the door.

"Mrs. Allison," the maid called.

In the peaceful house Edward lay in his old room on the ground floor. A door opened onto the garden. He could see the rose bushes, the yellow, red, and white roses, the wilted ones, the tulip bed, the carnations, the constantly changing sky, and, beyond, hills with chestnut trees. Complete peace. Here a man could become well again.

He put up with things for a few days. His mother was overjoyed to have him home. She sat at his bedside for hours at a time and held his hand. He remained reticent and often sent her away (he had a nurse)—didn't she have anything to attend to in the house?

"Let me be, Edward. Believe me, I have nothing to do. Allow me this pleasure."

She watched him anxiously. Would he have spells of that strange state he had been in before? In these days, nothing.

But the restlessness gradually came over him again. One thing had passed; something else took its place. He was unaware of what was going on in him, but something lay hidden there; it manifested itself in a different form. Like a stone that falls into a pond: It sinks and is no longer visible, but the rings from it can still be seen on the surface.

The questions he would ask! The things he wanted to know! About people from yesterday, from the day before. Kathleen had to laugh sometimes when he asked about these unimportant people who had disappeared ages ago, like a certain milliner who often came to the house in London ten or fifteen years back. And what had become of a certain hunchbacked tutor, Marray. They called him Marks. Was he still alive?

New nurses had to be called in. None of them could put up with him. One tried to be strict. She did her job, read, and said nothing. She ordered him to read and sleep, too. Didn't he realize that other people had a right to a little peace, too? Whereupon he really did quiet down, but only to talk at his mother more tenaciously than ever the next time she appeared, not letting her go. They had to set up a regular schedule. Every family member had to put aside a certain time for him each day. Oh, it was wearing. He was a tyrant. But they did it.

Weeks passed. In the early fall Edward's condition improved.

He was given crutches. He was to practice with them and move around in the house.

GORDON Allison, the father, sat heavily in his spacious armchair in his library, his head tilted to the left as far as the rolls of fat on his short neck would permit. This was his study, which he left only to eat, to sleep, and to take occasional strolls through the house.

He was a friendly man, dissipated in his own corpulence, who took the position that wars, seen in the light of world history, recur among human beings from time to time like the flu, typhus, scarlet fever, and that no cure had yet been found for them. We would do well to accept wars as a given and to do what we can to make their course less virulent.

Armed with this view, he participated in the First World War and came through unscathed. He weathered the second one equally well, retreating instantly to his country house, far from cities and centers of population; and so there was nothing to report about him in connection with the war. By his own fireside, in his massive, custom-made armchair, he had survived, unharmed, dramatic catastrophes at sea, breakthroughs on the front, various amphibious landings, D day.

He had no difficulty in mastering the newspapers, magazines, and extra editions of the papers that were laid on his smoking table at noon and in the evening. He could either hold the mute paper and the printer's ink in front of his eyes, or he could put them aside, just as he pleased. They were powerless and so harmless as to be pathetic. They were no different from the radio next to his armchair. Every hour it overflowed with reports that would annoy him and that he did not want to hear. Occasionally he would tap into it so that he could revel in his own power and security. He saw the radio tremble and nearly burst with its need to communicate. Then he took pity on it, reached for the knob, gave the radio a chance to blow off steam for fifteen seconds. It flung out a few words, meaningless words torn out of context. It screamed something (a big moment for the radio). But he did not let it finish, no, not a chance. There were limits to his pity. His fingers were already turning the knob, and some dance music puffed out of the speaker like a cloud of cigarette smoke. The news had been forced to retreat, was far off by now, not visible even with a telescope. Smirking, Gordon Allison leaned back in his chair, puffed at his pipe, and petted the subdued device. It wasn't so hard to get along with after all.

Who or what could get at Gordon Allison?

His children were no pleasure to him now. You could see that quickly enough. Edward, his son, had marched off briskly to war with two legs and come back with only one, and with a troublesome war neurosis that defied medical treatment. And Kathleen suffered from gastritis. Neither condition spoke well for war. Edward and Kathleen often came to him and sat down with him.

During the war Gordon Allison had supported every loan. He wrote letters and sent packages to the front. He developed a nobleness of mind that was almost superhuman. His name appeared on many appeals to the public. This increased his popularity. He came down, as he put it, "out of his ivory tower." Later, when this kind of enthusiasm began to wear on him, the heroic letter writer turned to more philosophical encouragement of the troops at the front. He pillaged his library, from Homer and Pindar to Burke and Wellington, amassing a lexicon of stoic bon mots. He offered fortification for the heart. He snatched up everything that showed how men could triumph over suffering, and he scattered this instruction about in his essays. When he later read in print what he had said, he was deeply moved.

Now it so happened that Kathleen, who was every bit her father's daughter, swore by his doctrine and, when the war was over, brought his collected letters and articles home in a handsome box. Her unhappy father had been obliged to give her this box himself. Now he wished that a small, localized fire would break out in his house and destroy the box, or that thieves would come and, carefully avoiding other objects, find their way to this box and steal it (on the assumption that it contained jewels). But when the box was neither destroyed by fire nor stolen by thieves, Gordon Allison wished that Kathleen would at least lose the key. She did not lose it. Now his son came home. It would be incorrect to say that the father had gone out of his way to lure the son into his house. Kathleen noted that her father had taken on this unpleasant task because her mother had wanted to have her Edward at home.

Gordon Allison rarely visited his son in his room, and he never did so alone. He clearly wanted to shield himself from embarrassing questions. He did not succeed in this. Edward could not be avoided, His persistence was pathological. He probed and probed, oblivious to the pain he was causing those he interrogated. His illness explained his behavior, but that knowledge did not make this behavior any more tolerable. Edward, the tyrant, would sit somewhere with a vague expression on his face, or he would thump up to someone, say thank you if the person inquired about his health, and even at this point in the encounter one could see from his wrinkled forehead that he was formulating a question in his mind. Then he would come up with a bizarre question that was of no concern to anyone, not even him, and no answer he received made his face brighten. Every question he asked obviously missed the mark, but this did not prevent him from drawing his bow again and again. A mysterious sphinx in him moved his lips but did not let him formulate the right sentence.

Gradually, his questions began to circle around one ill-defined theme: Who was to blame for the war? It was understandable that a poor wounded veteran would wonder about that. But what did it have to do with the House of Allison? And why did Edward bring this particular concern to his father, of all people, who was so clearly blameless for the war?

The phlegmatic Gordon Allison was not pleased. He found himself buttonholed and drawn into complex, abstract discussions. He had to take part in these discussions even though he hated any kind of discussion and especially political ones, in which laughter was not permitted. He contradicted himself. He suffered. He looked about him for aid. He was subjected to cross-examination, a trial in his own house. And as he confessed with a sigh to his confidante, the young Kathleen, he was distressed by the unchanging expression of torment on Edward's face, by the whole sickroom atmosphere he had brought with him. Oh, why hadn't they left him with Dr. King in the clinic? Does a sick man regain his health by making healthy people sick?

With time it became clear to Gordon that Edward had a hypothesis: Certain people were responsible for the war and for his misfortune. The task at hand, then, was to find out precisely who was to blame for all that mass slaughter and misery. This was a hopelessly childish view that Gordon Allison, who was older and more reasonable, felt obliged to oppose yet one that he could not refute, because, as he said, he lacked the necessary eloquence.

On one occasion when his son Edward was harrying him mercilessly again (oh, Gordon thought, if only my house in London were not damaged, I would flee and dig myself in in my studio, or I could go to the doctor and have him puncture my eardrums so that I couldn't hear anymore—but then Edward could give me his questions in writing), Gordon, the father, this desperate man, had an idea.

Sitting together with the two tormenting spirits he himself had sired, sitting in his library, which he could not close off with iron bars, he decided to meet the enemy attack head-on.

"I'm an escapist," Gordon Allison sighed, wiping his forehead. He wiped his neck and the back of his neck, too. "I will remain an escapist," he announced, "and I think that recent events do not disprove my views but only confirm them. Here you are, my son. To my joy, you have come home from the war, but you are missing a leg. And here sits your sister, Kathleen. She is wearing her military decorations on her apron, and her mother tells me that she even wears them on her pajamas at night. But on the footstool in front of my dear Kathleen there is no cool lemonade, such as the rest of us are enjoying. She has hot tea and a white medication, which she hopes will convince her stomach to leave her in peace."

"A result of the war, and nothing but," Kathleen interjected sharply, "and it's not just in my head, Father."

"You'll get a disability pension. But let me speak quite openly: The state should thank you for your efforts but give you nothing more, no, not a thing, so that you'll learn your lesson once and for all and not lead your country into disaster again."

Dumbfounded, Kathleen let the straw in her stomach medicine drop.

Delighted by this reaction, the fat pacifist continued: "One thing that is obvious, that you will never be able to change, and that a glance into the streets should prove to you: You may be the younger generation, and you never cease to complain about me, but you are not a young generation. My dear son and you, dear Kathleen, you have come out of your schools and universities burdened with moldy old stuff, rags that someone has sold you and that you put on and wear."

The father groaned and dropped his handkerchief. His daughter picked it up; he thanked her. "I'm terribly fond of both of you, but the sight of you and your monotonous arguments make my blood boil. How can anybody be so young in years and so strong and at the same time think as anachronistically as you do? How can anybody study medicine, build a motor, and still think the way his ancient ancestors did, walk around, so to speak, with greaves on and a spear in his hand. That raises my hackles."

Kathleen: "Father, if we hadn't picked up a spear you probably wouldn't be sitting here right now."

He nodded thoughtfully: "I know. I'd be in a cemetery. And not even in our family grave here but somewhere else. Maybe I would have been dragged off to some foreign country."

"Oh, Father," the daughter smiled, "you would have stayed here. Why would anyone drag you off?"

"I'm harmless, I know. Or do you mean that nobody would haul me off because I'm too heavy?"

Kathleen: "Cargo space in wartime is always valuable."

The father: "They would have taken me seriously. Over there I wouldn't have died a natural death. I would have lost more than a leg. They would have stood me up against a wall, and 'bang, bang,' your kindly father would have been dead and gone."

Kathleen glanced ironically at him: "What would our kindly father have done to earn himself this hero's death?"

He lay comfortably in his armchair and studied the ceiling: "A famous general of the First World War, which you are too young to remember, devised what seemed to be a very shrewd maneuver to hasten the end of that conflict. The Russians were still living under the czar at that time, and the general I have in mind, a certain General Ludendorff, had the bright idea (and it was a truly military idea, which is to say an idea profoundly lacking in awareness) of letting the Russian revolutionaries who were living abroad return to Russia to undermine the morale of the Russian army and so further Ludendorff's own ends. The repatriated revolutionaries carried the plan out, though not, we might say, altogether to the general's pleasure and satisfaction. For once the revolutionaries had undermined Russian morale, they decided to stay in the business and undermine some other morales, such as German morale, as well. The upshot was that the czar's army collapsed, which was all to the good for Ludendorff, but then his own people drove him out of power in turn."

Gordon Allison fell silent, leaving his listeners unclear about his meaning. Kathleen broke her father's silence.

"In other words, if you set a trap for somebody else, you're likely to get caught in it yourself."

Her father made an impatient gesture:

"That's not the point. The general thought these revolutionaries were harmless because they didn't have any troops, cannons, airplanes, and whatnot. Therefore, he thought, he could safely let them go about their business. But they had a powerful weapon at their disposal. They could think and speak. They knew something. They convinced others because they were convinced themselves, and one man they convinced became a thousand, a thousand became millions. . . ."

This was how Gordon Allison, who was seeking a route of escape, smuggled in his grand scheme, which was to tell stories instead of discuss issues. He wanted to avoid further cross-examinations by fleeing to territory where he felt confident of himself. His children asked him just how he pictured going about this. He had already given his idea some thought, and he suggested that the family should gather in the evening, alone or with guests and friends (for the subject matter at hand was too broad to be kept within the bounds of a single family and should not be allowed to sink to the level of familial quibbling). And in this undisturbed atmosphere, they should try—seriously, calmly, and objectively—to uncover the truth about the question before them, the truth that Edward had recently demanded so urgently, as if up to now only untruth had been available. Yes, each one of them should put his cards on the table.

In this solution Gordon Allison hoped to find comfort.

"It's your opinion, Edward, that all of us here in this house have been keeping you in the dark. You think we lack candidness. Let's take the bull by the horns."

"I never said that," Edward objected.

"Well, in any case, I am at your disposal, and I declare my innocence. I am prepared, together with you and Kathleen and any third or fourth who wants to join us, to search out the truth, the pure, undisguised, and complete truth."

"That is generous of you, Father," Kathleen praised him.

"I would like, in my own way, to steer our discussion away from mere abstraction and come closer to the truth. which is indeed, as Edward suggests, inextricably tied in with people, with human fates, and which cannot be separated from them. But how can we do this? That is the question. As the first in line, I plan to develop my view by means of an example, a story. I want to tell a story and see if it is convincing. Then the rest of you can tell your stories, though if you prefer, you can choose some other method."

23 ALICE was amazed when her children brought her this news. "Whose idea is this?"

Kathleen laughed. "We kept pestering Father until he came up with it."

Alice turned to Edward. "How about you, Eddy. Do you want to do this? Will you—enjoy it?"

"First tell me what you think, Mother."

"Oh, I don't know," she hesitated. "Father hasn't told stories for a long time. I can hardly recall when it was he last sat down with you to tell stories—probably a long time ago when Kathleen was still small. In any case, it's nice of him to think of this. We have to thank him."

Edward: "I like the idea. An effort on his part."

Alice: "Yes, Eddy. Your father is doing it for your sake. This isn't typical behavior for him. He's doing it for you."

"Excuse me, Mother. Should I ask him not to do it? What do you want, Mother?"

He looked at her. What a pained look. She lowered her eyes.

"Do what you like, Eddy. Do what you think is best."

"I say yes. Is that all right with you, Mother?"

"Yes."

Dr. King, the clinic director, was due for a visit at this time. He checked the condition of his former patient, the son of his friend Gordon. The doctor learned of the plan to use stories to entertain Edward, who was still overly wakeful and restless and who cast about the house like a bloodhound; a parlor game in which everyone would take part.

The doctor thumped his walking stick on the floor (he was with Gordon in the library) and sniffed, a sign of surprise and interest.

"Well, well, so you want to tell stories. Who came up with this idea?"

Gordon spoke: "I wanted to put an end to this eternal abstract haggling over guilt and responsibility. I wanted to deal with concrete cases."

"We all know you can spin a yarn all right. It's your profession."

The doctor rested his chin on the silver handle of his stick and looked up at his friend.

"He'll put the screws to you, Gordon."

"I know. I've known that for a long time. He's strangely mistrustful. What do I have to hide? I know he'll put the pressure on me, and that's precisely why I want to challenge him, get his pathological, unarticulated accusations out in the open, and be done with them. Am I responsible for his condition? How so? Did I send him off to war? He should bear his wound bravely and accept it as an honor, as a decoration, the way other men do."

The doctor: "What kind of questions is he asking? Just about the war?"

"That's just a front. He's after people who are supposed to be guilty of something or other."

"Who is he putting the finger on, you or Alice?"

Gordon's face darkened, and he didn't answer.

The doctor: "That's the way patients of this kind are. You mustn't let it bother you. They ask about the strangest things."

"I can't oblige him. I haven't reached the age yet when people reveal all and write their memoirs. Alice is thirty-eight."

"Age has nothing to do with it. So you want to tell stories."

"Yes. That'll at least keep him quiet. I'll tell a story. He goes snuffling around in the house. He wasn't like that before. I realize he's a sick man, but this is his parents' house. This is no garbage can where he can scrounge for bones."

"Don't get stirred up, Gordon."

"You should have kept him in the clinic. A family can't cope with something like this. I know Alice is behind it all, but she clearly didn't realize what she was getting into. What does he want? Whose hide is he after? The family's? Mine? I have the feeling he's stalking me and wants to lead me into a trap. Can you understand that? Did I drop the bomb that landed on his ship? Did I—I ask you again—send him off to war? You know yourself that he insisted on going. If he hadn't enlisted they would have happily let him continue his studies. A country needs people after a war, too. I'd like to talk this over with him in detail and in my own way, Ben. I want to make my point of view clear, but with someone else there to keep a check on what I say. He sits there across from me like a district attorney. I don't deserve this from him."

The doctor placated him.

"You mustn't reproach him. Do you know yet what story you want to tell?"

"I'm still thinking about that."

"Take your time. Whatever it is I'm sure it will interest everybody you invite to hear it."

As Dr. King left he expressed his regrets that he would not be able to attend the story sessions from the beginning. But he would come as soon as time permitted.

Allison accompanied him into the hallway and whispered proudly: "I mean to tell him, first, what is of interest to any thinking person these days and, second—without being overly explicit—what any father who means well by his son should tell him by way of enlightenment about things like marriage, love, family. I'll be fulfilling a certain parental duty there, toward Kathleen as well."

Dr. King: "I hope you don't get stage fright."

The two men laughed as they parted.

Lord Crenshaw's Adventure

HIS name was Gordon Allison. But everyone called him Lord Crenshaw.

His friends had given him this title, taking it from a Hollywood street and bus line of the same name, which, by a complex route, links La Brea Avenue with the endless Wilshire Boulevard.

In one of Gordon Allison's earliest stories a lord was sitting in this Crenshaw bus late one evening, meaning to go somewhere in Hollywood. Such a hushed, mysterious atmosphere prevailed in the dimly lit bus that the lord, who may well have had a few drinks, fell asleep and, on being wakened at the end of the line, had to be asked to leave the now empty bus.

He preferred, however, to make a return trip in the same bus so that he could come fully to his senses again. Then he made the entire journey once more until, at the end—or the beginning—of the line, the driver began to wonder about him and drew him into conversation, suspecting that this elegant gentleman might well be a criminal who was hoping to elude his pursuers this way.

A lady joined the conversation: It seemed to her that she had dined with this gentleman the evening before. The gentleman was asked where he wanted to go; and when he could not, or would not, answer, further questions were put to him: Where did he live? And, finally: What was his name? What was his profession?

At a loss for words (he seemed driven into a corner), the stranger clutched at a straw and called himself Lord Crenshaw. The name "Crenshaw" had stuck in his mind after he had glanced at the sign on the bus. The "Lord" was his own embellishment.

Once the general derisive laughter had faded away in the dark night in front of the bus, the gentleman underwent further interrogation at the police station; and after he had been released and taken to a nearby hotel (there was no evidence against him, and he had enough money with him,

though no papers revealing his identity), the police kept him under surveillance, giving him an opportunity to recall who he really was.

The story became increasingly entangled. Wherever the gentleman
went in search of himself, always very well-heeled, and claimed that
people knew him, in hotels, restaurants, cafés, and in some nightclubs,
he was rebuffed. But strange things happened. His consciousness gradually took on a chameleonlike quality. It adapted itself to whomever he
was dealing with. The lord snapped up suggestions and learned parts
easily. He was obviously pleased to have finally arrived at his destination and caught up with his identity. But these gains were short-lived.
His Crenshaw bus moved on.

Before long he had gathered an entire retinue, both men and women,
who all claimed, most of them untruthfully, to know him, to have
known him under various names, to have lived with him here and there,
in the eastern United States, in Europe (one woman went as far as
Morocco), and to have letters from him, which they would produce.
The gentleman had, it appeared, led every single one of these lives
without forfeiting one iota of his elegance and vigor. But he could not
remember any of them (or said he could not). And so he tried to get by
under a different persona. He remained the anonymous, the totally in-
scrutable Lord Crenshaw.

The police, who always have a large selection of unsolved crimes in
stock, confronted him with a number of witnesses. The uncanny fellow
managed to slither out of every trap. Nothing could be proved against
him. The only sure thing the police had on him was his fingerprints.
With them to go on they could at least pin the man down when he
emerged from his next metamorphosis as a still different butterfly.

On one occasion he happened into a film studio in the southern part
of Los Angeles, arriving just as a thriller was being made. His lordship
grew restless watching the filming. A new turn was in the making, and
before long he had asked to play a certain role in the film.

The film director had been briefed (a detective was always on the
lord's heels; reporters were instantly on the spot; a sensational new
wrinkle in the Crenshaw affair promised headlines for tomorrow's papers). The director let him play the part but, of course, took no film.
Crenshaw did not know the script and made up, on his own, a different
role than it called for. The other actors, at a nod from the director
(actually from the detective), played along with him.

The film called for the kidnapping of an actress. The getaway car stood ready. The lord tossed the young woman into it and drove off with her. She screamed. Everyone laughed. The reporters scribbled notes and took pictures like mad.

Off he raced, leaving the studio lot behind, and disappeared for good. Yes, after abducting the young woman, Lord Crenshaw disappeared from the scene, completely, mysteriously, just as he had come upon it.

The police sat there with their set of fingerprints.

Imposters turned up later, imitating Crenshaw for the publicity. People were amused; people were afraid; people laughed and talked about the story. Only the police were bitter and kept hoping to track the man down someday.

But some people claimed there was no mask to tear off in Crenshaw's case. There simply were people with multiple personalities.

And so some of Gordon Allison's friends and acquaintances had named him after this shady figure, having once heard Alice, his young, charming, distinguished wife, address him as "Lord Crenshaw" at a party.

(Perhaps she was the young woman Lord Crenshaw had kidnapped and disappeared with forever?) In any case, the name amounted to a kind of judgment on Gordon; and over the Allison family ruled a mysterious figure with interchangeable personalities.

Gordon Allison sat heavily—his listeners gathered once or twice each week—in his library (invaded by many people now and so deprived of its hermetic isolation), sat in his massive armchair, his legs planted like pillars on the floor.

At the first evening gathering, he greeted the circle—his family, reinforced by friends. He announced the plan and purpose of this meeting and explained its character.

"We will begin peacefully, and everyone will present his point of view in a large or small example, in a story, because that is the best way to argue a case without wounding others. We will talk; we will debate; we will learn. But no one should let himself fall slave to his own opinion. He that has eyes to see, let him see. He that has ears to hear, let him hear. Our motto is: Follow attentively and willingly. We expect you all to show patience and forbearance for your neighbor, even if you don't understand his position. If we don't proceed this way, we'll be combatants who sit on their horses and race across the battlefield but shoot right on by each other without engaging their opponents at all."

Since no remarks were forthcoming from anyone else, he began the story telling himself.

We need not describe the arena—the spacious, old-fashioned den and library of a country house, equipped with a couch, chairs, bay windows, and tables—nor the combatants. The head of the household we already know. Family and guests are gathered around him. We will introduce them when they go into action. Various lamps along the walls, behind the master of the house a floor lamp with a yellow cloth shade, throwing its light on the table next to him.

Anyone who saw Lord Crenshaw sitting there in his chair by the fireplace, saw the great mass of him, this uncanny, incomprehensible man, himself out of touch with his own personality (or perhaps thoroughly in touch with it?), this Lord Crenshaw, heavy with personas, anyone would think: What a mountain, a living mountain of fat, flesh, and skin. He was wearing a wide, pale blue bathrobe cinched with a belt. On his small feet he wore blue socks and embroidered yellow slippers. Fat had wreaked havoc on the man. He had fought this enemy for decades, but in the last ten years he had given up the struggle.

And his fat was crushing him, just as the serpents of Lerna had crushed Laocoon and his sons. It surrounded him, enclosed him, locked him away in armor plate, and drove him so far back behind his soft masses that anyone who saw him in his bedlike armchair saw not him, Crenshaw-Allison, but the wall he was behind.

His voice emerged from him unchanged, not bloated. But all his gestures were slowed down, distorted, drawn out, like a picture of a bird flying over a pond. Plato says that the human soul lives in the body as in a prison, and he offers various reasons for this debilitation of the human soul. But however that may be: In Crenshaw-Allison's case, the sentencing, the imprisonment, was visible. For what? Who had condemned him? His ridiculous blubber had overpowered him and dealt with him like leprosy, which grossly distorts the face and makes it immobile and buries tender, cheerful, and querulous souls alike behind the grisly features of a lion.

In front of and around Gordon Allison, Alice and his two children; Alice, as always, the youngest of all, so trim, fine featured; a delicate skin; wide, bright eyes. Fat had not altered her face. But was it her face? Edward lay on the sofa, thrown down there by his suffering. Kathleen, on a footstool, suspicious.

Looking at their heavy host in his armchair (they admired the writer), his guests thought: Lucky for us that we're not like him; we carry nothing around with us that is not part of us. Such were their thoughts. They thought they knew who they were. But did they? Perhaps they, too, like the Lord Crenshaw of the story, were riding in a huge bus, had forgotten who they were, and were trying to catch up with themselves.

Crenshaw-Allison began to speak.

The Princess of Tripoli

IN olden times there lived a man—"

"Oh, Father," Kathleen interrupted, "don't go reviving that man from olden times. Let him be dead. He must be dead by now."

"Of course he's dead, Kathleen. I'm just about to bring him back to life."

"Don't do it, Father. There are so many people alive already."

The son from the sofa: "Kathleen, let him talk. Fair play, you know."

Lord Crenshaw thanked him and continued.

"There once lived in France, in Provence, a long time ago a knight and troubadour by the name of Jaufie Rudel de Blaia. Pilgrims returning from Antioch had told him about the virtue and beauty of the Princess of Tripoli, and even though he had never seen her, he was in love with her. He wrote poems about her and celebrated her in song.

"And it so happened, after he had been doing this in his homeland for some time, that such a yearning for the princess possessed him, such an irresistible longing to declare his love to her, that he took up the cross, it being the time of the Crusades, and set out for the Holy Land and to her. The Holy Sepulcher, though, was far from his mind. His pilgrimage was to the Princess of Tripoli, whom he had never seen, our Jaufie Rudel de Blaia.

"But just as he had failed to think about the Holy Sepulcher or the Moslems, so, too, he had failed to think about the long voyage by sea. He fell ill underway, and when his ship finally arrived, he lay there sick, mute, like a dead man.

"He was carried to an inn in the city. This was Tripoli, the city he had longed to visit these many years, the city he had sung of, pining away for love of the heavenly, virtuous princess whose name he did not know but whose image he carried in his heart, the princess he had to find if ever he was to be at peace. And he lay now in an unfamiliar room

34

surrounded by strangers, closed his eyes, opened them, and asked, 'Where am I? What has happened to me?'

"The princess heard about him. She learned of the pilgrim, the knightly troubadour, who had taken up the cross and traveled across the sea not to conquer the Holy Sepulcher and massacre the Saracens but for the sake of her beauty and virtue, to lay his love at her feet.

"She came to the inn and had him carried to her palace. Her doctors attended him. His eyes brightened. His voice grew audible. He saw the woman he worshiped: Griselda Barbe of Tripoli.

"He whispered his poems to her.

"She held the dying man. She kissed his lips. She closed the eyes that had lived long enough to behold her.

"She had him buried in the Templars' residence in Tripoli. Her kiss and a state burial were all she could give him.

"But just as he had remained devoted to her all the long years before he set out to search for her, refusing to give up until he had found her, so she held to him and never abandoned him. She entered a cloister. There she waited for that moment when her senses would fade and he would step out of the shadows and come to her bedside to bend over her and kiss her."

Quiet. Lord Crenshaw took a deep breath and let his chin fall on his chest. (Oh, to be able to do that—to at least have that in death.)

He went on:

"This story is often told and has become part of our literature. You know it from Swinburne."

Edward had been placed on the sofa near the fireplace. He lay stretched out there, his face turned to the storyteller, cushions at his back, both his crutches leaning against a chair. The red light of the fire that fell on his father from the side played over him. Now it leapt and trembled; now it poured a glow over his head, torso, and arms as if a crucible had been emptied out on them. Sometimes he lay in darkness and disappeared. His face had shrunk during his illness. It had followed the lead of his inner life and drawn in on itself. His eyes were only half-open. He murmured, "I know the story."

Kathleen in a clear voice: "Me, too."

The father was pleased. "Swinburne says:

There lived a singer in France of old
By the tideless dolorous midland sea."

Kathleen: "And the ending . . .

> *. . . and her close lips touched him and clung*
> *Once, and grew one with his lips for a space;*
> *And so drew back, and the man was dead."*

Lord Crenshaw spread his arms out. "These lines have stuck with me for decades, and I've given a lot of thought and research to this story. I gradually realized that I was dealing with a tale that has been handed down through the centuries and has been daubed over in the course of time, like an old painting that is so dimmed by layers of shellac that we have trouble seeing the original anymore. That's what I wanted to get at."

Edward: "What did you find, Father?"

"Not so fast, Eddy. We all have time, and especially we storytellers. Stopwatches will begin to work only after the last storyteller is dead. I didn't find anything. You can't find anything about Jaufie in books. But you can put your head to work, and people then were the same as they are today. We can imagine what the real story was that has been picked up in the romantic ballad of troubadour Jaufie and his princess.

"To get at the truth, I gave my imagination free rein, yes, my imagination. You find that strange, using imagination to find the truth. Imagination is usually associated with the fabrication of castles in the air, with illusion. But I've been of a different persuasion for a long time. For me, the imagination has a special function. In the hands of a dreamer it produces daydreams, something between sleep and wakefulness. But in the hands of the wakeful, it takes us beyond flat, everyday wakefulness."

Edward: "No need to defend the imagination. Tell us what it revealed to you."

Kathleen: "No, Edward, now it's my turn to say 'Not so fast.' You surely don't mean to say, Father, that you want to steal reality from us."

Lord Crenshaw bellowed: "How could I manage that? To steal your precious reality! The point is that reality is very stupid sometimes, and we ought to help it out a little."

His tone was sarcastic, triumphant, and challenging. He was warming to his work.

"I purposely chose this touching story, this story that—if you'll forgive me for saying so—positively oozes sentimentality (the quality that obviously helped preserve it over the centuries), I chose this story to show you how and what genuine reality is and what can be made out of it. No, it is I who want to deal in reality."

Again the murmuring voice from the sofa: "Go ahead, Father. Tell us what your reality looks like."

And again a protest from Kathleen: "No, I say. Why should he? Swinburne's story is true. Why should it not be? You said yourself you never found anything to prove it wasn't. Sentimentality—I don't think I'm sentimental. Are you against love? What do you have against love?"

Lord Crenshaw shook his head slowly. "The stuff a man has to put up with from his children! Me? Against love? We've gotten on the wrong track here. We're not talking about love. We're trying to find out what the truth behind this maudlin ballad is."

Kathleen pleaded, "But it is true."

While the lord smiled at her amiably and nodded without saying a word, Edward said urgently, "Kathleen, we don't want to argue."

His sister meekly folded her hands in her lap. The father continued to regard her with his friendly smile.

"It takes time for us to realize what kind of world we humans live in, what a remarkable world we, together with that other so-called reality, add up to. We think we are in the saddle, that we are riding; later things look different. Sometimes we have the image of a spider and a web, but we aren't the spider. We're the flies struggling in the web."

He opened the top button of his robe, loosened the belt, and let himself go.

The words poured out of him.

"It was the time of the troubadours in southern France, in Provence. It was the time of the Crusades, feudal lords, knights, armor, tournaments, and of one undivided Christian faith.

"In this time, at the castle of his father, de Blaia, Jaufie Rudel grew up as the only child of a man and a woman who were a match for each other. The husband was strong and coarse, and so was his wife. But he surpassed her in both these qualities, and she must have realized that, and so she had submitted to him and become his wife. The husband also had working to his advantage the powers due the master of the house by law, and in the rough and ready customs of those times a wife was not exempt from those powers.

"And so de Blaia the elder often beat up his noble spouse. And during one such exercise of his rights as lord of the household, he robbed her upper jaw of several teeth. This deformed her mouth and made it less attractive. There were no false teeth then. The wife, who used to go by the peaceful name of Valentine, did not forget this injury, and it did not make her any the milder.

"At this time our little Rudel romped around with the children of the village and was cared for and supervised by a dreamy monk. Frail and unlike his parents as he was, he took more pleasure in the company of the easygoing and clever Barnabas than he did in the soldiering and falconry his father had in mind for him. The so-called laws of genetics play mysterious tricks on us. The families of Rudel's father and mother had never produced anything but sturdy figures, all of them bursting with joie de vivre, combativeness, and courage. But Rudel, Pierre and Valentine's son, nearly disappeared in his page's armor and dragged his lance sadly, like a carpenter hauling on a heavy beam, and he sometimes even tripped over it.

"Nor, as the pious Barnabas sadly admitted, was young Rudel intellectually promising, and this caused his vexed and disappointed father to take the boy more forcefully under his wing than ever. The poor, obviously untalented son was allowed so little free time that to save himself he resorted to that dismal art of women: playing sick.

"He was genuinely sick a lot, too. It did his stomach no good that, as a page, he had to accompany his father to outlying castles and eat and drink to excess there to prove his masculinity. From time to time, then, he would be confined to his room for a couple of weeks. And with the approval and discreet protection of Barnabas, he received visits from the village boys and girls and recovered from his page's life. Valentine, the malcontent and much abused mother, saw through Rudel's illnesses, but she shielded him anyway because, hard as she was, she was not as hard as her husband; and, furthermore, it was an action taken against the father, the brutal Pierre, and she wanted to have young Rudel on her side in her marital conflict."

The son on the sofa had gradually slipped down from the cushions and was lying flat on his back, completely in the dark, his gaze on the ceiling where lights played with the shadows. His arms lay crossed on his chest. He listened with only one ear, for he was hearing something else that absorbed him completely. That is why he had slid down from the cushions under the play of light on the ceiling. He gave no outward sign of what he was feeling.

He bent down, in spirit, to the floor and stammered the words he had read in the Psalms:

"My soul is among lions: and I lie even among them that are set on fire, even the sons of men, whose teeth are spears and arrows, and their tongue a sharp sword. They have prepared a net for my steps; my soul is bowed down."

His consciousness grew dim; he slipped away on the thread of a melody sung by an alto voice.

It was a long time ago, a trivial matter. If I had then, if I had . . . But no one knew, no one had any strength. You went along with him, you went along with her.

How many things called me, how many ran past me and turned to look back. Many things were still possible then.

A lizard, a basilisk, the long, quick tongue.

He drew back, frightened.

Flames rose up. A column of fire rose high in the air, ash, shrapnel. And something came flying down, stretched its arms out, a human creature threw itself on his chest, drew him to it. Someone cried out, called to him to come, a woman's voice?

Lord Crenshaw, a living mountain of fat and flesh, sitting near the fireplace and close to the sofa where Edward lay, lifted his arm and continued his story:

"Now the pope at that time was a powerful man, Urban II, a Frenchman. He had lived in the monastery at Cluny. Messengers from Emperor Alexis of Byzantium came to him in Piacenza, and what they had to tell about affairs in the Holy Land so disturbed Urban II that he traveled to Clermont in France to hold a council about this dreadful situation. Nobility of high and low rank, clergy and laity, soon came to Clermont in droves, and the pope spoke to them:

"'O, you people of the Franks, you people, chosen and loved of God, who pours out glory over many of your works and deeds—you rulers over all nations, powerful because of the location of your country and because of the honor in which you hold the Holy Church—rise up, you people of the Franks! Follow the example of your glorious ancestors and inspire your homeland to glorious deeds. Think of the war fought by Charlemagne, think of Louis and of the others who destroyed the realms of the heathens and spread the rule of the Holy Church to their lands.'

"He denounced the depravity of the Turks and exhorted the nobles, high and low, the clergy and the laity, the knights and the noblemen, in fatherly tones.

"'Don't ask for time to take care of your family affairs. Do not let your worldly possessions hold you back. Rise up and take courage! The land you inhabit is surrounded by mountains and bordered by the sea. It is too small for you. You cannot prosper here. As you all well know, this land barely provides you with your basic needs.

"'And so I spur you on to wrest the land of the Holy Sepulcher from the villainous heathen and make it your own. For to whom—if you will recall—was this land of milk and honey promised and granted by God Almighty? To the children of Israel, to them and to no others, was it given. And its capital is Jerusalem, which is, as everyone knows, the center, the navel of the world.'

"And now, since he felt that the bait he had offered was not quite sufficient, he addressed some massive threats to the knights, whom he was particularly keen to convince:

"'You knights, you conceited, vainglorious men, you, who tear each other apart in civil wars, you robbers of widows' (yes, he said that), 'you oppressors of children' (that, too) 'you—guilty of murder and blasphemy' (he let them have it, they blanched) '—you are drawn to corpses and the din of battle. You have only one choice: Either you give up your claims to knighthood, or you answer my call and become knights of Christ, battling to win the Holy Sepulcher.'

"Our Pierre de Blaia, Blaia the elder, did not attend this council. But Peter the Hermit soon appeared, spreading Urban's message throughout the land.

"Now, what was there to keep Pierre at his castle? Valentine, his pugnacious wife, perhaps? Or his son, who (let us not mince words) was clearly growing against the grain of the family? Or the castle? No, he could, in good conscience, leave his castle and his son to his faithful Valentine, and his Valentine he could leave to herself.

"His speculations proved correct. He could not remember when Valentine had ever been as solicitous and affectionate with him as she was from the moment when he revealed to her that he meant to take up the cross and travel to the Holy Land to do battle with the Moslems.

"And when one foggy morning soon thereafter he set out with his small retinue and rode down from the castle into the valley and when Valentine stood on the drawbridge with young Rudel, she was overcome with unexpected feelings. Sorrowful and tender she felt, and she cried, and she continued to cry when she went back inside the castle. She herself did not know why.

"Slowly and solemnly they rode off down below, their lances high, their pennants snapping in the wind. And slowly and solemnly they sang a crusader's song. Already they had ceased to inhabit and rule over this land.

"Young Rudel let his mother cry. And then, unsentimental and resolute as children are, he drew the obvious conclusion: His father's departure had improved his own situation. The poor innocent! He would soon enough realize that he had gone from the frying pan into the fire.

"At first his mother, Valentine, was too busy to concern herself with him. She inspected her holdings and found that her husband, who had succumbed to such a sudden fit of piety, her absent husband had woefully neglected his lands; that is, he had not exploited them as mercilessly as was his due. That is, preoccupied with his feuds, tournaments, and banquets, he had not fleeced and squeezed the peasants or had not fleeced and squeezed them enough. He had even gone into debt to finance his crusade, and at outrageous interest. The more his wife, who at first rode about her lands in high spirits, probed into the mess her husband had left behind, the more truculent she became. And she swore that when her noble Pierre returned—if he ever did return—she would give him the dressing down of his life.

"But he did not come back. In a war many men must die; it may be me, it may be you. She waited a long time. Many did return years later, but no one from Pierre's entire retinue returned, nor did Pierre himself.

"In the meantime Jaufie grew up. He took part in all the exercises and games that were expected of a knight in the making, but he was happiest spending his time at the foot of the mountain in the village of Conci where minstrels lived among the peasants. These artists offered to join first one knight's following, then another's, and they displayed their skills at church festivals and other celebrations. Here Jaufie felt at home and safe, safe from his father at first and now from his mother. Here there were no rules and no noble society. His parental home had spoiled his taste for such things.

"The monastery of the worthy monk Barnabas was close by. The monk understood his pupil. He would gladly have trained Rudel for the ecclesiastical life since the secular one of a knight did not suit the boy at all. But Barnabas could not persuade his charge. He had to be satisfied with teaching Jaufie to write, to sing, and to play the lute; and, also, he had to make up alibis for him whenever the boy lingered too long among the villagers in Conci. With many a sigh, Barnabas acquiesced in all this, even though much happened of which he did not approve. It did not escape his attention, for instance, that Jaufie spent a lot of time in the house and in the fields of a certain peasant, not, however, for the peasant's sake but for that of his grown daughter Gertraude, who was also known as Petite Lay because she had learned and sung songs as a very small child. And this Circe seduced the young lord of the castle, or so his troubled teacher thought.

"It was true that Jaufie and Petite Lay kept each other's company, but the nature of their bond was not quite what Barnabas imagined it to be. She was a young, black-haired, black-eyed girl who received the visits of the young lord with respect and humility and allowed him to accompany her and help her in the fields. But Jaufie's attention caused her great fear, as it did her father and mother, too; for they might all suffer for it. They might lose everything they had if Valentine, the mistress of Blaia, ever got wind of her son's doings. Did Petite Lay love the young lord? It never occurred to her to ask herself that question. Also, her situation made it very difficult for her to ever discuss this alone with him. Not only her parents stood between them but also the young people of the village, who ridiculed Petite Lay for her high ambitions.

"Indeed, as time passed they boycotted her more and more. And one time the jealous peasant boys had themselves some sport with the young master of Blaia when they caught him on the way to their village and terrified him with threats. They also thought they could put an end to his visits in the village by spreading the rumor among the servants at the castle that Jaufie and Petite Lay were secretly married and were living together as man and wife. This almost cost the rumormongers their lives, so harshly did the noble Valentine, who was also judge and jury over the territory, have them whipped. But she let no word of this affair reach Jaufie. She talked it over with the monk, who told her that the young lord had to be able to move about freely in the territory he would one day rule over and that he had to be protected from young ruffians who did not respect legitimate authority. Valentine could not have agreed more. Also, it served her purposes nicely if her son, Jaufie, who would inherit the family holdings, entertained himself with other things and did not interfere with her conduct of government.

"There are many beautiful things in Provence, and it was here that Jaufie and Petite Lay enjoyed each other's company. No, it was not a marriage; together they made up for the happy childhood they had not had. Petite Lay had not been able to be happy below in the village, and Jaufie had not been happy in the castle.

"Now, she was his wandering castle, and he was the lord who watched over it.

"This castle had ramparts and moats. Its creator had built it on jagged cliffs and decorated it with delicate battlements, with oriels and gardens. But anyone who tried to take it with weapons of war would fail. He might be able to burn it down with flaming arrows, but only someone who knew the password could conquer it. Then the gate would open; the drawbridge would lower. Who knew the password? To whom did the mistress of this castle reveal it?

≈ "WHEN Jaufie had grown to young manhood, a count in this area, the brother of the still missing lord of Blaia, decided to dub a number of young noblemen knights at Easter. Among them was Jaufie Rudel. It seemed at first that the count's motive for this ceremony was to create a large retinue for his own pilgrimage to the Holy Land. What misery for our Jaufie! He dutifully confessed to the pious Barnabas what he was thinking and what the pious man already knew anyhow, namely, that he wanted to flee before the solemn event on Easter Monday. But Barnabas would not let him off the hook; and so on that day, that dreadful day—on which, however, everything went off just as it should—Jaufie was dubbed a knight, a noble knight, against his will.

"'Won't you take up a spiritual calling after all, Jaufie?' the worried Barnabas asked. 'Won't you renounce the world?' He knew, of course, what the answer would be.

"'No,' stammered the frightened youth.

"'Then become a knight in God's name. Take this upon yourself, and stand by your oath.'

"At the count's castle Jaufie went through the same ceremony as the others. Fully armed, he watched through the night. Then he was dressed in white, set in a tub, stripped of his shirt, and bathed. Finally, he was taken to Mass and dubbed a knight: 'Remember that you are now a knight, a defender of the order and the empire.'

"His sword was buckled on him. He was a knight now and knew that something would happen soon, but he still didn't know what. But he was on his guard. Legally, he was entitled to take over the governance of his father's lands, but he didn't dare raise this delicate issue with his mother, Valentine. She continued to rule in the name of her crusading Pierre, and was, as we know, a woman to be reckoned with.

"And because young Jaufie enjoyed wandering around proudly with his sword on, what do you think the proud Valentine decided to do, Valentine, for whom one knight had been quite enough and who had had her hands full to get quit of him? She decided that she, too, would become a knight. She would not play second fiddle to her son. For at that time women, too, could become knights, chevaliers. That part of France must have produced a remarkably rugged breed of women in those days. The ruling king, Sancho of Castile, had founded an order for them, and so the no longer youthful Valentine was knighted and could thereafter, whenever she was not wielding a cooking spoon or rattling down to the wine cellar with her keys, buckle on her sword, her knight's sword.

"Jaufie was astonished when his mother set off for Castile 'to attend to some business,' as she told him. He needn't fear, she said. She would be back in three weeks. And in three weeks she did indeed reappear, now on a white horse, just like the one he had ridden himself when he was knighted. She wore a helmet and carried a lance with a pennant on it, and she had—he could not believe his eyes—a sword at her waist. Two weeks later, as she had promised her son before her departure, she put on a great festival, a festival to celebrate not just his attainment of knighthood but—unusual as this may have been—hers as well.

"Now it became clear to young Jaufie that his mother meant to rob him of his inheritance, and meek and patient though he was, this roused his ire.

"And he fretted and wracked his brain, trying to think what to do. He recalled that as a knight he had sworn to defend the right and to avenge injustice. Did that not apply to injustice he himself suffered? He got no encouragement in this from old Barnabas, who feared the worst and claimed that the injustice one experienced oneself was not meant, but only the injustice that others suffered. Injustice that we ourselves suffer is there to be borne. Would Jaufie attack his own mother, to whom he owed so much? And the wise monk let fall some other remarks to remind Jaufie how free his mother had left him to pursue his amusements in the village and how much leniency and maternal understanding she had shown in the face of certain difficulties relating to the village of Conci and to Petite Lay.

"'But things can't go on this way,' Jaufie rebelled. 'Where will we wind up? One of these days she may throw me right out of the castle.'

"'Why would she do that, my son? You are not demanding. You are no great expense to her.'

"Something had to be done. Of that much Jaufie remained certain after his rather unproductive talk with his wise adviser. The most likely thing that occurred to him to do was spend a lot of money. It was, after all, his money.

"Now when the young knight told the knightly Valentine he intended to deck himself out elegantly in the latest French and Moorish style— not only himself but also his horses and some pages and squires, and on top of that he needed dogs and falcons and servants to attend to them— he did not meet with a refusal from his noble mother. Far from it. She did not reach for her sword but for her purse and said, to young Jaufie's amazement and horror: 'At last.' And it made him all the more nervous when she embraced him and called not 'Rudel' but 'My son,' something she had never done as long as he could remember.

"Uneasy after this dismaying reception, he scuttled off to his Barnabas, who congratulated him; and since this felicitation was of no help to him, he moved on to the village of Conci, to Petite Lay's house, to tell her what had happened.

"Petite Lay's brother, by the by, had at first taken part in the attacks on Jaufie; but in the meantime, having found Jaufie a friendly and decent fellow, he had been won over to the young knight's side. Now this brother had learned nothing but a few minstrel's skills, but he still knew a great deal about the ways of the world and considerably more than Jaufie did. It was he Jaufie first confided in: 'What's up with my mother? Why is she so pleased that I want to spend a lot of money? There's something unnatural about this.'

"The flaxen-headed peasant: 'Nothing unnatural at all. She just wants to marry you off.'

"'Me?'

"'Marry you off to a noblewoman, as befits your class. She wants you out of the house at no expense to herself.'

"Jaufie, in astonished admiration, pressed his hand. 'You are smarter than Barnabas.'

"'Barnabas knows as much as I do, Jaufie. He just won't come out and say it.'

"'So what should I do?' the knight asked his oracle.

"Girart—that was the young peasant's name—was silent for a while; then a broad grin spread across his face, and he said, wise as he was, 'You'd do better to ask Petite Lay.'

"She was lying in her bed in the next room. A cow had kicked her in the leg. The leg had swollen up, and manure from this same cow had been applied to the swelling as a poultice. The medication lay under the blanket, hidden from Jaufie's view. But he could smell it; and Petite Lay, blushing beet red, explained what it was. He had a hard time putting up with the stench. It pained him that this creature, fresh as the dew, had to undergo a treatment that could give off such an odor. It unsettled him so much that, instead of asking her advice, he took flight. And what did he do next? He bearded the lion and had a talk with Mama. Their exchange was the friendliest imaginable. Jaufie was amazed to find his mother so affable. He had never seen or heard her this way before. Nor did she hide from him, when he finally got around to asking her, what she had meant recently with those mysterious words 'At last' when he had revealed his plan to her to equip himself in keeping with the times and his station. She said she was aware of what had gone on in Conci, but it did not pain her. Up till now Jaufie had been an immature youngster and had not yet partaken of the things of his class. Now, at last, she said, he was taking pleasure in them. He had left childish things behind and was ready for love befitting a man and a knight."

Lord Crenshaw Comes Around to His Theme

SURE of himself, comfortable in his chair, Lord Crenshaw took pleasure in pouring his story out over the little assembly that lay mute in the half darkness.

Now he hitched himself up in his chair and made this announcement:

"This brings us to the chapter that prompted me to tell that ballad of old before. Yes, because of the customs of this period and because of the unnatural but irresistible power that products of fantasy hold over people, that is why I am telling the story of Jaufie Rudel de Blaia, of whom it is said that he took up the cross and died in the arms of his lady, whom he had never seen before but of whom he had sung time and again.

"The women of this epoch (I'm speaking of the members of the aristocracy) scored a remarkable coup. The troubadour tradition originated with them and was (you needn't be so surprised) a women's-rights movement. The men, the knights, were hard and strong, the women, too. The women, as we have seen from one example, constituted an assemblage of humanity that could hold its own in the best of company. The noble princess Eleanor of Aquitaine served as their standard bearer and leader in the struggle for their rights.

"Eleanor, who would later become Queen of England, took part in a crusade with her husband, Louis VII of France. And how did she go to the Holy War? Wearing a helmet and armor. Her banner went before her, surrounded by pugnacious women, young female knights of Eleanor's stamp. Arriving in Palestine, she fought tirelessly and like a man. But not to be outdone in anything and to give her sex its due, she also rushed into innumerable love affairs, enriching them with the resounding and romantic history of her experiences in the Holy Land. A young unbeliever, a Saracen in the service of the sultan Nureddin, is said to

47

have stood especially high in her favor. We know nothing about this emir, but of one thing we are certain: Eleanor knew quality when she saw it.

"As Duchess of Normandy, acting, as always, out of both love and a heroic nature (a whole, a harmonious person), she founded the first court of love.

"From then on, anyone unhappy in love and bemoaning his condition could find comfort here.

"We have all heard in school the name of the French troubadour who celebrated Eleanor in song: Bertrand de Ventadour. She was already far away in England, where she had followed King Henry II, while Bertrand was still singing of the nightingale at his window that waked him in the morning and reminded him of Eleanor. Under her leadership the women of this era managed to acquire men's rights, the rights of their husbands. It was accepted practice and in good taste for married women of the upper class to have a liaison with a knight, to love him, and to be praised in his songs. This arrangement was felt to be less objectionable than the liaison of a prince with his mistress in later centuries.

"What our Valentine de Blaia was planning, then, when she so willingly offered young Jaufie all the money she had readily available was this: Her Jaufie, a talented singer and lute player who had occasionally entertained her own gatherings with his compositions, was to become a troubadour, a knight armed with sword and lyre. What a marvelous thing, a troubadour! What glory his songs lent to his name, and how interesting and feared a fellow he could become, for a singing knight who traveled with his pages and squires from castle to castle could also spread rumors and dispense honors. He was a writer, a poet, and a wandering reporter. He did not sing just about Charlemagne, Charles Martell, and the bold Roland.

"Jaufie was in a pickle. He was able to sing, compose songs, and play the lute all right, but he would have to go wandering from court to court. He didn't like the unsettled life of a troubadour. And, most important: Of whom would he sing? The little peasant girl of Conci, Petite Lay? She was out of the question. And why? Let's take a look at the Rules for Troubadours.

"According to paragraph 1 of the Laws of Love, marriage is no excuse for rejecting a lover. In paragraph 3 it is clearly stated that no one may have two lovers at once. Paragraph 4 asserts that the intensity of love never remains constant. It increases one minute and decreases the next. Paragraph 23 informs anyone who didn't already know it that a person in love doesn't eat or sleep much and that (paragraph 24) a lover's every act ends in thoughts of his (her) beloved. In paragraph 31 we find the magnanimous proposition that nothing need prevent a lady from being loved by two knights at once. Similarly, one knight may make himself available to two ladies as an object of adoration (though here, it seems to me, we find ourselves in contradiction with paragraph 3).

"But however that may be: These rules apply only and exclusively to ladies, to noblewomen, and to knights. Not a single paragraph had anything to say about the clever, sweet, and poor Petite Lay, although, as far as Jaufie was concerned, she surpassed any ladies of his acquaintance in beauty and virtue, not to mention cleverness. There was no place for Petite Lay, who lived and worked at the foot of the hill below the castle and was never in a bad mood and was true to him and never gave a peasant lad so much as the time of day.

"'Oh, will this never end,' Jaufie sighed to her.

"Things grew worse. He had no choice. He could not go back, and finally he said to himself, and then tentatively to Petite Lay: Why not ride around to the courts?

"Petite Lay was proud of him. There were painful scenes when they didn't speak to each other. He became angry with her and jealous because she urged him to go. But she was able to placate him: She didn't want to see his gifts go to waste. And what was so difficult about falling in love with some beautiful noblewoman, she wanted to know. His heart was surely big enough for that, and she would be happy if he would keep a small corner of it reserved for her.

"This kind of talk pained him. She was tormenting him. But she stood firm: He should go.

"Sometimes he thought she had a lover in the village. But one glance into her good, intelligent face reassured him.

"Then he asked her advice on whom he should love. She should give it some thought. She said she would, and because her brother was one of Jaufie's minstrels she arranged (disguised as a man) to ride around with Jaufie to the castles and inspect all the noblewomen. Finally, at a tournament at Courtoie Castle, she seized Jaufie's hand, looked at him decisively, and announced: 'Jaufie, there she is.'

"Her words stabbed at his heart. He felt that she was rejecting him, wanted to leave him on a mere whim, out of feminine cruelty. He would have been pleased beyond words to continue traveling and riding with her (he had at last gotten her away from her wretched village) under the pretext of searching out the queen of his heart. But now he realized there had been no pretext. She had been in earnest.

"Rosamunde de Courtoie was her choice.

"She had good taste. Rosamunde was a glorious creature. A woman? An adolescent, an almost-adult girl. Fresh from her parents' house, she sat at the tournament beside her massive, bearded husband, a bull of a man, the feared knight Robert de Courtoie, and eagerly watched the games that he was putting on for her. She, this tender bud of a girl, this sweet feminine treasure next to Courtoie, wore exquisite clothes, a different outfit every day, works of art that competed with her natural beauty but, because they could not begin to rival it, only served to heighten it, oriental fabrics with fantastically brilliant Saracen patterns, imports that the Crusades had brought into the country. The olive-skinned Count Robert had himself come back from the Crusades with two Saracen captives who served as the young Rosamunde's bodyguards or, to be more exact, as her warders.

"Anyone who saw Rosamunde on the grandstand in front of the castle, saw her next to the count who was exhibiting his possession, basking in his glory—Rosamunde, enveloped and hidden in all her brocade grandeur, covered with embroidered tigers and snakes and lotus plants—anyone who saw her could not but notice how helplessly, submissively, childishly, and sweetly she acquiesced in everything, looking here, then there, apparently not knowing what to make of it all. Every now and then, though, when everyone else's attention was riveted on a fight, one could observe how her delicate white hands, which she was obliged to decorate with heavy rings—there was no part of her body on which Robert had not put his seal, the brand of a convict—flew involuntarily to her bare throat and how she folded them under her chin as though in prayer, and as her head sank wearily under the burden of her tiaralike headdress, her fine jewel of a face faded and became empty, and the corners of her mouth trembled.

"What was she dreaming of? What did her lips, which moved ever so slightly from time to time, entrust to the air? And only to the air, for it was certain that no human ear would ever hear those words.

"Jaufie had appeared at Robert and Rosamunde's court and taken part in a singing competition, also in the tournament; and, as always, Petite Lay served as his squire. Jaufie was trotting next to her outside the ring when she patted his horse's neck, reached over to him, and said out of the blue, 'I think she's it, Jaufie.'

"That was the start of a long talk that lasted all the way back to Blaia and Conci and didn't even end then, and it was not Petite Lay who kept bringing up the subject again and again. She already knew what the conclusion had to be: Jaufie, she's it.

"What a violation of his nature this all was. How painful for Petite Lay. But neither of them could get the better of this plague. Indeed, how should they? Custom was the omnipotent tyrant of the times. It demanded that Jaufie court a noblewoman, and Petite Lay was intelligent and clear-headed enough to appoint herself custom's advocate. She reached this decision calmly. She had seen it coming for a long time, and that is why she had ridden along from one castle to the next as his minstrel (not just for that reason, of course. She also wanted to be with him). She wanted to be at his side in every phase of this battle that was hers as well as his. Her visits to the castles opened her eyes completely. She saw what a court was, a knight; and what she was. What was she doing to her Jaufie? She had debated with herself and decided she would let nothing take him from her. And then another time she had decided she had to let him go. Today she kissed him again and cried on his shoulder, but only a little, and before he could ask her what was wrong, her eyes were dry, and she was laughing and cheering him up.

"But when she saw the beautiful Rosamunde on the grandstand at Courtoie Castle, all her pain was dispelled. Petite Lay stood before Rosamunde as before the image of a saint, and in all that crowd her eyes saw only her.

"Never had a human being inspired such feelings of closeness in her, of yielding, of self-abandon. Not even Jaufie (although she was not conscious of this) had touched her so deeply. What was it she was feeling: love, compassion, respect. She stood in the crowd; time passed in a dreamlike ecstasy. She slept at the castle that night but slept very little. Unable to calm down, she kept thinking about that bewitching figure in her sumptuous robes. It became clear to her as they rode away—and bliss filled her when suddenly she confronted the idea that this woman was for Jaufie—it was clear that Rosamunde, none other than Rosamunde, would command Jaufie's heart.

"Now they talked in Blaia and in Conci, then in Conci and in Blaia. She remained deaf to all Jaufie's objections. And Jaufie began to sense some bond between Petite Lay herself and the mistress of Courtoie, for the girl's words were filled with a mysterious urgency.

"Hesitatingly he gave in to her, was astonished by her, and wanted to set off on this adventure to please her. (In his heart he was jealous.)

"How Petite Lay embraced him in her little house the evening he decided to win Rosamunde's love.

"'Oh, Jaufie, how wonderful' (Tears sprang to her eyes.) 'How I love you.' The thought she kept to herself: And how I envy you. If only I were a man who could sing her praises.

"And something the subtle Petite Lay did not let herself admit (but we will not keep it secret) was that she wanted to put Jaufie's love to a test, wanted to tempt him. She wanted to fight her own private tournament with this most beautiful and most elegant of noblewomen.

"So what happened? Things you're unlikely to find in the history of any other troubadour: A troubadour composes love songs to a lady that his own true love presents to him; and she, the lover herself, helps him write his impassioned verses to that other woman.

"Now it so happened that Petite Lay, this dapper young minstrel, was standing near Rosamunde once after a tournament and Rosamunde's gaze fell on this slim, handsome minstrel who stared raptly at her. Rosamunde blushed. She looked away, then looked back again. And later she sent one of her maidservants to find out who this handsome minstrel was. Petite Lay realized immediately that the messenger came from Rosamunde, and she asked the servant to ask her mistress, in complete secrecy, if she would take it amiss if he (she) paid her his respects. Nothing could make him (her) happier than to spend a minute in her presence. Petite Lay assumed an aristocratic name.

"That evening, when the men were drinking together, she was led in secret to Rosamunde's chambers. And now the young noblewoman could look at leisure into the enticing face of this page while Petite Lay dissolved in joy at her feet. The handsome page spoke in a whisper so his voice would not betray him. Rosamunde's disconcertion grew, and Petite Lay sensed that the chambermaid would soon leave the room, that the beautiful stranger would soon yield to her desire to kiss her, so rapturously did she gaze at her lips. Never in her life had Rosamunde seen a page like this one.

"A struggle broke out in Petite Lay when Rosamunde reached for her hands and shut the door behind her. They were alone. Petite Lay had come here for Jaufie's sake—or why had she come and assumed a false name? She didn't know. But then she did know. Mad as it was, she wanted to woo Rosamunde and put her to the test not just for Jaufie's sake. She wanted to court her herself.

"The young page was in turmoil. When he sighed and looked up questioningly and smiled to himself at the strangeness of it all, it was as good as done: Rosamunde saw that shy smile. The page did not dare; she did not dare either; but then all their doubts were swept away in the long, thirsty kiss the young noblewoman pressed on his lips.

"And what happened next? Yes, that's the way people are, and that's how nature subdues them and bewitches them, and all their thoughts fade away to nothing.

"While the page was embracing the noblewoman—the lady who was covering his face with kisses—Petite Lay thought not at all about Jaufie or her sex. She was all love and joy and rapture and infinite amazement and bliss and gratitude that this had been given to her. She could scarcely move.

"This scene could not last long. Rosamunde released her, ran to her table, and pressed a small, colored handkerchief into the hand of the page who stood there dumbfounded, his face aglow, his eyes gleaming. Without embracing again, they whispered a few words. The page felt his way down the dark stairs. Then he was outdoors.

"An hour long Jaufie searched for his accustomed companion. She kept herself hidden on a hill behind the castle, trying to collect herself; but she couldn't, and now what would happen? She had to go back to Jaufie. Should she tell him everything? She could not bring herself to do that. The joy of those kisses and embraces was still flowing through her body. Her mouth opened, her face grew radiant as she recalled those brief minutes that heaven had showered down on her. And she saw clearly that she had fallen into a trap. She had wanted to woo Rosamunde for Jaufie and had succumbed to her herself. Did she want to court her for Jaufie at all anymore? No, she did not, for Jaufie was her rival.

"She laughed as she sat under a tree. She saw her dear, innocent Jaufie before her. Once again she was the clever, clearheaded Petite Lay, who had gotten herself into a difficult game. She was not afraid to play it out. It challenged her, it animated her: Jaufie—her rival. But Jaufie didn't want to play at all. Oh, she sighed, if I were Jaufie I'd have won already.

"Then, in high spirits, she went down to the castle. (From time to time she stood still and lowered her head. Joy pulsed through her; she trembled; Rosamunde has bewitched me.) And she felt for Rosamunde's fine, batiste handkerchief which she had in her belt, and she thrust it into her bosom. But she could not stand having it there, and

she put it back into her belt, but there it could be seen. So back again to
her breast. Now I'm lost, totally lost.

"What delight she brought to Jaufie, who had been worried about
her. He had not seen his Petite Lay so entrancing for a long time. He
walked back with her to the woods. How she caressed him, this victorious deceiver. How she was intoxicating him he could not know. The
fact was they were three. The intoxication Rosamunde had inspired was
overflowing onto him.

"Under plaintive protest he let her go. This had to be. She laughed
and rapped him on the mouth and pulled his ears. She had never been
like this. She had blossomed in the space of an hour. Puzzled, his heart
pounding, he walked back alongside her. Who was this next to him?
Who was his page, this peasant girl Petite Lay? She was a woman all of
a sudden. His Petite Lay was a woman.

"They rode back to Conci and Blaia, Rosamunde's handkerchief on
Petite Lay's breast.

"Petite Lay remained in Rosamunde's spell, and her yearning for
Rosamunde gave her no rest in Conci, but how could she go to
Courtoie, to the castle, to her, without him? She put pressure on him.
They wrote poems together. Jaufie wrote well. He could hold his own
with the competition. But what force found its way into his songs now,
what a sweet glow emanated from them. Petite Lay wrote verses to
Rosamunde. She spoke in jest (but her heart tembled when she spoke
such words aloud): 'We sing to Rosamunde of Courtoie, Rosamunde
the sweet, the only Rosamunde, a heavenly flower in the garden of
earth.'

"He 'How you praise her. You want to tempt me. You want to drive
me into her arms.'

"She: 'Into heaven, Jaufie. I've seen her, after all. Only a woman can
know what another woman is. I think only a woman can truly love another woman.'

"He (not understanding): 'You mustn't say that, Petite Lay, my joy.
We are knights. We, too, know how to love tenderly and virtuously.'

"She (condescendingly): 'What do you mean, "virtuously"?'

"'With honor and respect, and with no other motive than to serve
our beloved.'

"She: (Oh, this frenzy—this longing to be near her! She has bewitched me. What is happening to me? I can't make sense of anything.)

"They wrote together, wrote Petite Lay's songs to Rosamunde. The noble lady was delighted with them. No other suitor could hold a candle to Jaufie de Blaia. During their visits to Courtoie, Petite Lay sometimes stole—oh, how seldom—to her mistress's chamber; precious, pilfered minutes. Petite Lay worshiped her mistress, kissed her feet. The lady was delighted by this tempestuous adoration and enjoyed her double conquest of Knight Jaufie and of the handsome page who served him.

"And when Jaufie realized that his songs had reached their mark, he was jubilant; and with her woman's intuition, Petite Lay could tell that he, Jaufie, was thoroughly hooked now. She knew this because Jaufie no longer wanted to take her to the singing contests at Courtoie. It had not escaped the young knight's attention that during the competitions his noble lady looked more at Petite Lay, his handsome page, than at him.

"Oh, how hurt Petite Lay was when Jaufie, using some lame excuse, left her behind in Conci for the first time. This was her own doing: She had written his love songs, and now he was leaving her at home. She wept out of rage and longing.

"But when Jaufie rode off with the others for the second and third time, she cried no more over her lovely mistress. She began to hate her instead. All she saw now was how eagerly he rode off and how happy he was when he came back. That sly Rosamunde who was stealing her Jaufie away! What a treacherous creature, married to Robert, a powerful knight, and fooling around secretly first with her, the page Petite Lay, and, as if that weren't enough, carrying on with Jaufie now, too. So that's what noblewomen were like. Lecherous creatures of luxury.

"She wondered how she could tear her Jaufie away from the clutches of this siren.

"She didn't have to think for long, for Sir Robert took action.

"Jaufie had finally taken Petite Lay with him again to Courtoie Castle, and she lost no time in storming the ladies' chambers. There was a passionate reunion; Petite Lay did not tear herself away as quickly as she should have. She meant to call her mistress to account and break with her, but she was unable to find the first words. Her nerve failed her.

"Then a hubbub arose in the house. Robert's men were clattering up the front and back stairs. Someone had been whispering in his ear, and he thought that his wife was receiving Jaufie de Blaia, whose success with Rosamunde had been quite enough to enrage him.

"A terrified confidante of Rosamunde's rushed into the room, bringing women's clothes for Petite Lay. The handsome page realized the moment of truth had come. He tore his cap off, and her black hair tumbled from the top of her head and down over her ears and shoulders. He opened his shirt. Oh, the soft bosom, the lovely, tender woman's arms.

"The two women stood stock still. Petite Lay gratefully accepted the clothes from the maid and pulled them on. Smiling calmly, a challenge in her eye, she buckled the silver belt. The maid, who had recovered her composure, stuffed the page's clothes in a closet.

"When the knight stormed into the room, he found three women sitting at their embroidery, and Petite Lay was explaining to the other two in a high woman's voice what pattern and colors to use in the border.

"Robert walked around them, eyeing them suspiciously. But they went on embroidering. He looked at Petite Lay and ordered her to stand up. She screamed when, before Rosamunde's eyes, he shamelessly felt her breasts. She could do nothing but put up with it when he seized her arm in an iron grip. Rosamunde fled to the window.

"After searching the room, the knight left. The lady told her maid to leave. Alone with the unmasked page, she slapped Petite Lay and spit at her, her face twisted with fury. 'Canaille! Canaille!' was all she could say. The girl took it, not even moving when Rosamunde kicked her.

"When Rosamunde sat on a stool, buried her face in her hands, and neither said anything nor drove Petite Lay out, the girl knew why the poor, precious prisoner was crying. She came to her side, stroked her hair, embraced her, yes, embraced this lonely, abandoned creature who did not protest Petite Lay's caresses.

"'Come back,' Rosamunde begged. 'Don't leave me alone.' Petite Lay secretly laid the handkerchief that her mistress had given her on the table and left when she saw that sweet, ecstatic expression returning to her face again.

"But the knight gave no peace. The results of his search had left him dissatisfied. He was convinced that Jaufie had visited his wife and had then managed to hide. Nor had he been pleased by the presence of that strange woman.

"'Don't go to Courtoie,' Petite Lay begged Jaufie. He thought she was just jealous, and he went. Her songs had won him his lady. He came back, beaming more and more each time. He rose still higher in Rosamunde's favor. She clung to him now. He appeared less and less often in Conci, in Petite Lay's house. She saw him ride off with his minstrels. The cheerful racket they made when they came back in the night wakened her.

"'Do without, just do without,' she said to herself. 'You stupid peasant girl, what did you expect?' But another voice in her said bitterly: He goes there and kisses her and leaves me alone.

"But let us turn to that mighty knight Robert and his two Saracens. A troubadour's love was, of course, not only legal but also a noble thing. Still, it is not hard to understand how a husband might not be altogether pleased by a troubadour's attentions to his wife. Robert felt (but given the circumstances he was not allowed to say so) that for all the legality of it he was still being cuckolded. The misery of his situation was that the relationship between troubadour and noblewoman was so honorable and socially acceptable that he could not object to it without losing face. The issue had been aired in public debate on April 29, 1174.

"'Can true love exist between marriage partners?'

"Husbands had to swallow all this without complaint. And at the Countess of Champagne's court of love all those poor sinners guilty of marriage were given this to hear:

"'We do hereby solemnly declare that we concur in the opinion of those here present, namely, that love is unable to exert its power over married people. For lovers voluntarily grant each other anything and everything and are not prompted by utilitarian motives. Married people, on the other hand, are duty bound to submit to the desires of their partners and not to deny the other anything. It is obvious that no real love can exist under such conditions. Let this decision and opinion, reached after careful thought and consultation with many noblewomen, stand from this day forward as law.'

"After a celebration at Courtoie Castle, some troubadours who happened to be present had read the whole of this judgment to the master of the house, Sir Robert, commenting on it and gleefully rubbing his nose in it. He listened, glowering. The whole world was against him. So he began thinking what other means he could find to defend his rights (yes, his rights) and maintain his claim on the tender flower, the much admired Rosamunde, his precious legal possession. Jaufie de Blaia, the young knight troubadour, had obviously won out in the contest for Rosamunde. Robert suffered the tortures of the damned every time Jaufie appeared at his castle. Jaufie had escaped him once. That would not happen a second time.

"Then Robert gave a men's evening at his castle, but no troubadours were invited. And as soon as everyone was sufficiently warmed with wine, Robert began to speak personally and touched on men's sacred rights that young freebooters were trampling underfoot, a frightening development that would have grave consequences. Whereupon this man-to-man talk turned to acts of self-help; and, with appropriate horror and pleasure, the story of Monsieur de Roussillon was told, a man with a wife named Soremunde, a sweet creature whose sweetness, it seemed to him, however, had been sampled by others.

"And once, after Monsieur de Roussillon had been hunting with Soremunde's lover, he sat down to table with her and served up a tender roasted and peppered meat that she ate with pleasure.

"'Do you know what you have just eaten, Soremunde?'

"'Tender meat, my lord.'

"'It must have tasted better to you than anything in the world, Soremunde. It was the heart of Guillem de Cabustuy.'

"She fell unconscious to the floor. But when she got up again, she said, 'Indeed, it tasted so good that I never want to eat anything again.' And she went to the window and jumped out.

"All the men at Robert's table listened to this story with pleasure. They lent Robert encouragement.

"Two days later Jaufie did not return from a trip. His minstrels reported that three masked robbers had attacked them in the forest. The robbers had struck Jaufie down, then carried him off.

"The search party Valentine de Blaia sent out found him unconscious in a gorge. All his equipment was smashed; his sword lay broken by his side. The ribbons Rosamunde had awarded him were gone.

"He was delivered home, with broken ribs, to the proud, speechless Valentine. She grasped the situation immediately. It was just like him. He had been treated like a traveling merchant. She felt not a trace of pity for him. She was ashamed, for him and for herself.

"She entered Jaufie's sickroom only once.

"Sir Robert arranged things so that news of what had happened reached Rosamunde's ears. And one of her maids had to bring back to her a ribbon she had given Jaufie. It was dirty.

"The young woman took this blow quietly. Noblewomen from the area came to visit her. These ladies, a kind of secret organization, discussed the case. What possible actions could these ladies take against Robert, the brutal husband? The same ones that a union, an association of industrialists, can take today against uncooperative members of their organizations: various degrees of boycott, social defamation, ostracism.

Rosamunde was interrogated. She revealed no details, but the ladies acted on their own initiative.

"The customs of the times showed their power. They were a force to be reckoned with. All visits to Courtoie ceased. Fewer and fewer invitations came. Sir Robert went around in a funk. No one appeared to drink, eat, or fight. There was no one to whom he could show off his riches and his greatest treasure, Rosamunde. Soon the rumor was that Sir Robert was considering a conciliatory mission to Blaia and intended to hang his Saracens, who had attacked Jaufie. The ladies were jubilant.

"Then, unexpectedly, Lady Rosamunde of Courtoie appeared at the palace of the Countess of Champagne, requested that a meeting of the court of love be convened, and, at the meeting, pulled out a piece of parchment which, when read by a man summoned for that purpose, was found to say:

"'Paragraph 18: Courage and accomplishment are the only qualities that make a knight worthy of a lady's love.'

"'And in this respect,' the otherwise so reserved Lady of Courtoie testified, 'I have grave doubts about Sir Jaufie. It distresses me to have to say this, but how can an honorable knight permit a ribbon given him by his lady to be taken from him, besmirched with dirt from the road, and then sent back to his lady? Why, if prevented himself, did he not commission others to join together in defense of my honor and send its detractors to me for punishment?'

"The ladies were not prepared for this. Indeed, since they were fighting on Jaufie's side, it amounted to a stab in the back. But while they were giving their dismayed consideration to paragraph 18, Lady Rosamunde had a second paragraph read aloud, number 17. Lady Rosamunde smiled her most discreet smile at it, and the ladies' high court broke into a smile, too.

"The paragraph said: A new love fully banishes the old.

"And the marvelous lady received the congratulations of all the others, whom she had won over with this persuasive argument.

"And when a diplomatically gifted lady was given the delicate mission of riding to the troubadour Jaufie de Blaia to assure him of the sympathy of all the ladies meeting at the moment at the Countess of Champagne's palace and, at this same opportunity, to convey to him everything else he should know (so that he would not ask the court for further support nor be surprised when the sanctions against Sir Robert were lifted), when this lady, a veritable female ambassadress, arrived at the castle of Blaia, she found a recovered Sir Jaufie among his minstrels in the castle courtyard and in the best of spirits. They sang and played, and Jaufie, a composer and conductor as well as a poet and lute player, was trying out a new song with them. He, too, was singing a new song. And the ambassadress, this formal official, who did not want to interrupt, stood by, took her ease on the grass, and listened to learn who it was that Sir Jaufie sang of now.

"And what do you know? It was a new lady. A new lady, a new knight: blessed land of Provence!

"It was a happy day at Blaia Castle. Guests had come to congratulate Jaufie on the recovery of his health and added their good wishes on his recently chosen but as yet unannounced new love (see paragraph 17).

"And who was the lucky one? A lady who lived not in Roussillon nor in Catalonia nor in Aragon nor in Provence nor anywhere at all in France. She was not known in Spain or England or in Germany or the Netherlands either. In fact, no one at all had ever seen her, not even Sir Jaufie. She was the Princess of Tripoli.

"Was she a living human being?

"Or a figure in a dream, a dream figure."

Jaufie Goes to Tripoli with Petite Lay

THE sybaritic figure by the fireplace looked pensively into the room where his audience sat comfortably, listening.

Alice, his slim, delicate wife; Edward, the romantic, skeptical warrior and veteran in the shadows on the sofa—was he listening?—Kathleen, his daughter, sitting up straight, her clear, gray eyes attentive, focused on her father.

And farther back in the dimly lit room, the guests; one, his head propped up by an elbow on the end table, immobile, as if not there; another, an American traveling through, settled here in an armchair, his long legs stretched out in front of him, his arms hanging left and right over the armrests and down to the rug (he let the story pour down his gullet, as it were, like a drink); and then near the wall a devoted elderly lady who kept her black hat on, Miss Virginia, a teacher; and way back in the corner under a bust of Socrates, two solid gentlemen who occasionally whispered to each other.

Lord Crenshaw paused. His story was approaching its high point, and he reveled in what he would soon reveal to his listeners. He let his tale spread out on all sides like a flock of grazing sheep, but when he thought the time ripe, his dogs would run off barking, and he would have the flock together again.

"Yes," Lord Crenshaw sighed, "a dream figure, that's all the Princess of Tripoli was. To the puzzlement of the castles near and far, this was the woman the recuperated Jaufie de Blaia celebrated in his songs.

"The noblewomen might justifiably have felt insulted that he scorned living flesh and blood, namely, them; but, finally, the course Jaufie was pursuing now was both the noblest and boldest imaginable, and for that he could be forgiven all.

"Lady Rosamunde had gotten out of the affair gracefully without appearing cruel yet retaining her right to an admirer. Citing the authority of paragraph 18, she was bestowing her favor on another knight.

"But our curly-haired Petite Lay—not Jaufie, who never had bright ideas—had been no less clever. She had been frightened to death when her faithless friend was carried unconscious into the castle (she had seen this coming). She nursed him, she alone, and was all kindness to him. She consoled him, and she managed to arrange things so that no noblewoman would ever steal her Jaufie from her again. How? I've already told you. Since custom required that a knight and troubadour pay homage to a lady, she suggested that Jaufie honor this custom in the breach by choosing the Princess of Tripoli as his mistress. She also advised him not to try winning back his honor by force of arms. She suggested instead that he challenge his enemies and put them to shame by choosing as his mistress a lady who far surpassed all others but who (this she only implied, but he understood completely) was so unknown that no other knight would be likely to dispute his claim to her. He could say anything he liked about her, and no one would contest it. Why make a fuss about a lady in the moon?

"'How about the Princess of Tripoli?' piped up the clever Petite Lay at his bedside. She had heard of such a lady.

"'Where is Tripoli?' moaned the downcast knight who wanted nothing more than to crawl off out of the world's sight.

"'I don't know, my dear. In Africa, I think.'

"'Now you want to send me off to Africa,' Jaufie whimpered.

"'Maybe it's somewhere else. Who knows?'

"'Sweet Petite Lay, let me get my health back first.'

"'You don't have to go there. All you have to do is serve her. From afar. It's absolutely painless. She may even be dead.'

"'What?' the innocent knight said in amazement.

"'She probably is dead because people are forever dying young in Africa with all those lions and snakes around. There are huge flying fish, too, that get in women's hair and then fly off with them. That's probably how she died. You know, some sad, premature death. Nobody knows where she's buried.'

"'Then what use is she to me?'

"'You can write songs to her, worship her. Is that so hard to understand, my sweet? You and I will sit down together and sing her praises, just the way you sang of that fickle Rosamunde, in the same meter, everything just the same except that this woman will suit you better' (and me, too, she thought to herself). 'There are two possibilities. Either she's alive, or she's dead. If she's dead, then she can't make any trouble or be untrue to you. And if she's alive, she'll never even hear about you way off there in Africa.'

"'And what's in this for me, dear girl?'

"'A cultured knight of the late twelfth century asks me what's in it for him? First, Jaufie Rudel, you will have fulfilled your obligation to society; and, second . . .'

"'And second?'

"She looked at him tenderly and kissed his dumb, battered face, 'And, second, you can love me.'

"He pressed his physician to him as fervently as his wounds allowed.

"Without releasing her, he asked, 'But won't people think I'm crazy for adoring someone I've never seen?'

"'You're a troubadour, a poet. You sing about her from morning to night. It's the noblest, most high-minded thing you can do for the very reason that it's so farfetched.' (Don't press me so hard, Jaufie. You're getting too close for comfort.) 'Nobody knows her, not even you, but who is to say what's crazy and what's normal for a poet. Do you want people to think you're normal?'

"Jaufie stammered, 'That's the last thing I want.'

"'You see?' She freed herself from his embrace but kept his hand in hers. 'What lady would even want a normal knight? You—inspired by the highest ideals—will range through the wide, the widest of worlds. That is, you'll sit in your room and write poems with me.'

"He raised a few technical objections. People would insist that he go on a pilgrimage to the princess to lay his love at her feet. Petite Lay dismissed this by saying, first, that there was no such place as Tripoli and, second, that the princess was long since dead of poisonous snakes and flying fish. That was obvious.

"And so our battered knight recovered. And when he could mount his horse again, he set off on his rounds of the castles, and no one opposed him when he appeared at singing contests with his warm, lovely songs in praise of an absent lady. No one envied him this sublime, ascetic pleasure.

"We next see Jaufie, accompanied by his minstrels, at the court of the King of Aragon, where everyone was delighted with this paragon of virtue who longed for an unknown lady in far Tripoli. During Jaufie's visits at the king's court, he learned through conversations there that Tripoli was not on the moon at all but in the kingdom of Antioch, and someone at the court of Aragon even claimed (to Petite Lay's horror) that the Princess of Tripoli was alive and well and wandering around in the city. This news worried her troubadour, too. It appeared the princess had not succumbed to a poisonous snake after all, even though there was in fact an abundance of them there (how had she managed to evade them?), nor had she been devoured by a cooperative lion or carried away by a helpful flying fish who had built her a nest in a tree and now lived there with her in perfect harmony.

"After hearing this disagreeable news, Petite Lay was eager to leave the court of Aragon. But she had drawn the attention of some courtiers. Jaufie had won praise for the bold innovation of adding a female voice to his choir, and it was inevitable that someone would play up to this clever and attractive young woman familiar with the ways of nobility. But she wanted to be off, for the rumor was going around that Jaufie, who lived and sang for the princess and the princess alone, longed to see his distant love and that he had already made plans for the journey. But this was nothing but a malicious rumor spread by a high-ranking personage who, infatuated with Petite Lay, wanted to send Jaufie off on his travels and take his place in Petite Lay's affections.

"Jaufie and Petite Lay fled. But rumor had run faster than they. At Blaia Castle a delighted Valentine had nothing but praise for her son's boldness. The matter was settled. He would travel to Antioch. (Once again Valentine was happy to rid herself of a male relation.)

"Jaufie smiled and groaned.

"He rode about the countryside to escape his mother, who, unasked by him, was making preparations for his journey and brooked no opposition from him. But the instant he began to sing of the princess in Tripoli, his listeners were overcome with emotion: So this was the knight who surpassed all others in passion and nobility, who loved a lady he had only heard of, and who pined away in such overpowering love (one could see from his face how he suffered) that now, delicate as his health was, nothing could hold him back from the long journey to Tripoli. And he received one ribbon after another from the softest and whitest of hands. His pilgrimage called. Their thoughts would go with him.

"This was, as one can imagine, the low ebb of Jaufie's relationship with Petite Lay. She cried her eyes out. He blamed her for the whole mess (and rightly, she had to admit). It was she who had cooked up this story about Tripoli back then after his disaster with Robert and Rosamunde. She had duped him with her talk about lions and flying fish. Nobody had actually seen the princess; but, apparently blessed with the physical constitution of a bear, the lady seemed to have survived the upheavals of war. Petite Lay gnashed her teeth: The princess must be a witch. What other explanation was there? She, Petite Lay, would kill her.

"Ha! Jaufie said scornfully. How would she even get there? For under no circumstances was he going to Tripoli. He had no business at all with this princess. She was Petite Lay's private responsibility. Petite Lay could figure out how to deal with her. His job was to write poems.

"Friends who came to visit him at Blaia and hear his latest songs heaped ecstatic praise on him not only for his wonderful verses but also for the seriousness behind them, a seriousness so profound, his friends had heard, that it compelled him to undertake this horribly arduous journey.

"'Can't a man just write poems,' Jaufie roared, 'without you people babbling platitudes about "seriousness" and "true feeling"? What kind of cloddish ideas do you have about poets anyhow?'

"Yes, they had their cloddish ideas, and they meant to stick by them. For these philistines, there was no such thing as pure poetry. Jaufie squirmed on the hook.

Then, when he received an invitation from the court of Aragon because the king and queen wanted to see this troubadour, this crowning glory of all troubadours, before he set sail for Tripoli, when this happened Jaufie knew his fate was sealed. Petite Lay knew it, too. She had fought bravely and well for her friend; now they wanted to take him from her.

"They rode home from the king's court in silence. Then they stood face to face in Petite Lay's garden in Conci. Jaufie, who was holding on to his horse's bridle, said roughly that he meant to stop for just a minute. All he wanted to tell her was that he would accept his lot, but here their ways would part. She had brought this misery down on him.

"She responded as coldly as he had spoken: 'I'll go with you. We'll suffer the same fate.'

"'I don't need you. Besides, if this is the way it has to be, I'll marry the Princess of Tripoli. Maybe I'll become King of Tripoli. This is what you've gotten me into.'

"He left. Everything was over between them.

"He asked Pater Barnabas what language was spoken in Tripoli. He wanted to prepare his acceptance speech for when he assumed the throne. Barnabas said that Latin was spoken everywhere in the world. He shouldn't worry if he made a few mistakes. That wouldn't be unusual for a king.

"Jaufie pressed him further. Would he have to marry the princess, he asked, if he meant to become King of Tripoli?

"This question amazed the pious old man. Hadn't Jaufie celebrated her in song? He owed his fame to her.

"'But now I've had enough of her,' Jaufie bellowed. 'I wish I'd never seen her—I mean never heard of her.'

"There was no way out. It had to be. But the moment this became clear, Petite Lay disappeared and could not be found. Her brother Gottfried, who was also one of Jaufie's minstrels, told him this, mentioning, too, that she had left a message with Pater Barnabas. Jaufie went to the monk. He told him he wanted to see Petite Lay to vent his ire on her. Otherwise, he had no need of her. But the idea of taking the long, fearsome journey without her was unbearable for him.

"Shaking his head pensively, Barnabas reported that the fearless and unwomanly Petite Lay had gone on foot to a nearby castle where she knew a certain knight of the king happened to be staying, and this knight had taken her to Aragon on the invitation of a high personage there.

"Having delivered this intelligence, the monk pressed Jaufie's hand warmly. Jaufie went numb. The devil! It was she who had driven him to this horrible journey into the unknown, and now she was saving her own skin and would amuse herself nicely at the court of Aragon. It was a conspiracy. The plotters were sending him to Tripoli to get rid of him. But they wouldn't get away with it.

"He saddled up his horse and was off to Aragon. They had a tête-à-tête. She was wearing a noblewoman's dress already, one that had been given her, as she calmly announced to Jaufie. She looked absolutely ravishing.

"'Given to you? What for? Who gave it to you? And what did you give in return?'

"She ignored all his questions and told him how pleased and grateful she was that he had made this visit to Aragon before leaving on his journey. She promised to use her connections at court to make his journey as pleasant as possible. She could name any number of way stations and inns, and she could recommend good highways, too, not to mention trustworthy people to whom he could turn in case of emergency. She would give him appropriate letters of introduction.

"He flew into a rage. He didn't want to go at all.

"'Then stay home,' Petite Lay graciously advised him.

"'I can't. You know that.'

"'Then what can I do for you?' She was behaving like a grand patroness, and her words implied that some powerful nobleman stood behind her.

"Jaufie had to spent a long, anxious week to win from her what he could have had earlier at a much cheaper price. Yes, she would go with him. She wanted to go with him. She had, of course, known very well that he would come to get her. And under no circumstances would she have let him go alone.

"'But,' she explained, acting the grande dame, 'what is love without struggle? Paragraph 8 in the Laws of Love says: Jealousy makes the heart grow fonder.'

"AT Blaia preparations for the journey were completed. Pater Barnabas blessed the travelers—Jaufie and his troupe, Petite Lay among them. The son took leave of his mother, Valentine, who many years before had accompanied another of her men, the rough-hewn Pierre, to the swaying castle bridge (and had watched, without pain, as he passed out of sight).

"First there were long miles to cover on horseback. Then the journey became a sea voyage. Jaufie looked at the sea with horror, how it lay there, shining and glittering like a snake, making its small, treacherous movements. He had often sung of the malice and the dangers of the sea, painting them for his listeners. The aesthete in him thought he had come to terms with the sea. But now he had the real sea before him.

"He stood on the shore and said to himself:

"My sea is more powerful, more varied, more interesting, than you. You are ponderous and boring. You think length and breadth are quite enough. I'm not impressed by them. My sea is quick as lightning, a decisive character that has borrowed some qualities from us human beings. My sea, if it could look at you, would laugh at you, you fat, stupid water snake.

"In vain he talked. He had to go out on it, out into it. He had to board the ship. Still another of his failings was fear of water. He had to board the ship with his pages, his horses, and—his only comfort—Petite Lay. The instant they were on board he told her what he thought about the sea, the real sea. She mustn't believe that this was the real sea. It was a liquid lie, an imitation, the effort of an overinflated talent that tried to make up in size what it lacked in intuition.

"She calmed him down and agreed with him completely, but that didn't alter the fact that they were sailing. Grimly, he sat down by a mast and turned his back on this irksome giant. But they were sailing, and the ship rocked. That was the vengeance of the sea, this peasant ruffian. Jaufie leaned over and gagged, disgusted by this encounter that was being forced on him. His sea rolled and raged and tossed waves heavenward, but no one would ever dream of throwing up because of a verbal storm.

"He suffered. He was desperately seasick. And then on top of that a dysentery epidemic broke out on board. The crew was unperturbed. They knew such things happened.

"Mediterranean women, some of them gypsies, came on board to travel from one port to the next. And when Jaufie became so ill that Petite Lay feared he might die, she summoned a gypsy who had various potions at her disposal.

"She appeared in an imposing, though dirty, costume, a parrot on her shoulder, a magic wand in one hand, several paper bags in the other. Since Jaufie was in a bad state, he turned to her with great hopes. She rapped on the walls of his cabin and burned pieces of paper taken from the bags. She gave each piece of paper a name, and when she had burned it, she said, 'Now it's gone.' She meant the illness.

"But for some reason (why, I don't know) the illness did not feel she was talking to it. The gypsy explained that she was working systematically. She began by disposing of the minor illnesses; then she would ambush the major one in one swift attack. However that may be, Jaufie did not recover during the first consultation, logical as he thought the procedure to be. So he asked her if she had any more paper with her. She was sorry, but for the moment it was all gone. Oh, he said, he had lots of paper. And he pointed to the pile of his manuscripts next to his bed. She picked one up and looked at it to see if it had healing powers. What she saw was a page covered with writing, a poem to the Princess of Tripoli.

"'Oh,' the sorceress cried, 'the Princess of Tripoli. Do you want to see her? Many men have come to see her.'

"'Why didn't one of them marry her?' Jaufie growled.

"The sorceress said, with overtones of mystery, that she would rather not say anything more right now. But it was good that Jaufie had told her he was going to the princess. That had a bearing on his illness.

"To that Jaufie gave his woeful assent: Had it not been for her, he never would have boarded this ship.

"'You see? But now I'll do everything I can to cure you. I live in Tripoli, too, although,' she added coyly, 'I myself do not serve the princess. But if that lady of high station learned I had not cured you, it would go badly for me.'

"Now that was a happy coincidence, finding this particular physician.

She gave Jaufie some powders to swallow. They didn't help his dysentery. She burned several more diseases, but she missed the right one again. She confessed that some diseases had difficult names, and you had to get the pronunciation right. But in the end they all yielded to her. She asked for some more paper. He pointed to his collected works.

"'How can I burn these? You'll have to give them to her. She reads everything. She gets bundles of manuscripts with every ship that comes in. She already has a library, and she has an office with several women who catalog her manuscripts.'

"'What?' Jaufie asked, amazed. 'Lots of them are sent to her?'

"'For years now. Court officials are sent out every year and go to Italy, Greece, Spain, to spread word of her virtue, beauty, and so forth. She organized a whole royal department for this purpose.'

"Jaufie's hair stood on end. He could hardly tell up from down anymore. He stammered (oh, what a good thing that Petite Lay was not present to hear all this): 'A whole department? A big organization?'

"The sorceress, full of admiration, said yes. 'The princess understands this kind of thing. She knows the world better than I do.'

"Jaufie was beginning to think anything was possible now and asked whether the princess wasn't perhaps a gypsy or sorceress, too.

"She waved his question aside. 'Get better first. Then you'll find out.'

"Then he had to swallow another powder, and she burned a lot of paper. But Jaufie was so embarrassed by what the sorceress had told him about the princess that he kept it to himself and didn't reveal it even to Petite Lay.

"And when the sorceress reappeared, after the last powder had had an effect completely contrary to the expected one, he asked her innocently what else she was able to do.

"She said she didn't mean to brag, but there were very few things she couldn't do. She waved a new paper bag in the air, the parrot on her shoulder screamed mystical words, and she thumped her green staff on the floor. Could she disappear? Jaufie asked her.

"'Make myself invisible?'

"The patient nodded. 'Absolutely invisible.'

"In response, she produced a great cloud of smoke and called from the doorway (perhaps she was already outside), 'Can you see me?'

"'No,' he answered gleefully.

"The next day (they were nearing the coast), she pointed to her staff and said she could transform anything with it.

"'That doesn't impress me,' murmured the pessimistic Jaufie. 'The princess can do that, too. She transformed me into a donkey.'

"The transforming she had in mind had to do with his purse. She wanted to transform it, or at least three ducats from it, from his money into her money. He gave her the coins, with the request that she do her transforming of them outside and, at the same time, make herself disappear.

"He noted with satisfaction during the last days of the voyage that she had succeeded in this latter experiment.

"Jaufie still lay sick, and the rumor went around on board that he would die—yes, he whom longing for the Princess of Tripoli had driven across the sea would die before he saw the object of his praise.

"But he was still alive when the ship reached port, and he was carried to a knights' inn. And word that he had just arrived, that he was on the verge of death, and was lying in the inn spread through the city and finally reached the princess, who sent gifts and a doctor and, through a messenger, let him know how delighted she was to have him near. News of him had come to her. There was nothing she desired more fervently than that he regain his health and come to her.

"Morose and mistrustful, Jaufie received this message and didn't know what to do next. Petite Lay didn't know what to do either. For in the city she had heard of strange doings of the kind the ship's sorceress had reported, yet she could get no precise information. This much seemed clear, though: Jaufie had had many predecessors. But what had become of them no one knew."

Jaufie Sees His Father Again

⊠ "JAUFIE had been lying in the inn for three weeks—presumably deathly ill, in reality long since recovered, and suffering only from sheer terror of his adored lady—when Petite Lay came running in one evening to tell him that an older knight had been hanging around in the courtyard of the inn and inquiring in detail about Jaufie and his plans. No one in the inn knew the man. His imposing retinue had waited in the street. He had said he would come back the next morning to see Jaufie.

"He appeared at an early hour. He wore a heavy gray beard, and his speech revealed that he originally came from France. Like many in this country, however, he wore Saracen clothing and carried Saracen weapons. This man could not hear enough about France, and he was curious about Jaufie and Petite Lay's personal lives, too. He inquired about knights who lived in the vicinity of Blaia and about how things were going in the castles.

"He asked in such great detail about Jaufie's own castle that Jaufie grew anxious, fearing the man had been sent by the princess to get his property if he died. It was remarkable what a lively interest the graybeard knight took in everything they told him. He knew their country clear to the Pyrenees and described first this estate, then that one. He was particularly keen about the ladies. He made crude, obscene remarks about them in Petite Lay's presence. This violated the code of knightly behavior, and Jaufie was embarrassed by it. Finally, when the stranger used somewhat milder but still obscene and animalistic terms in asking about Jaufie's own mother, the formidable Lady Valentine, Jaufie could not contain his outrage any longer.

"The old knight, his curved Saracen sword on his knees, responded jovially. 'Don't work yourself up over expressions like that, Jaufie. I've used similar words with her before, and in your presence, too. And sometimes I didn't stop at words. I am, you see, your father, Pierre.'

71

"Petite Lay fled the room instantly, the old knight's roaring laughter following on her heels. 'And I saw you in your cradle, too.'

"He called her, but she stayed out of sight. Neither she nor Jaufie had any reason to fear the gray knight (who lived near the city), for he had come with the best intentions, which he now revealed to his son.

"First, he had wanted to see Jaufie to get an idea of what he was like and how he had developed, for Jaufie had been a problem child for his father. But now, as Pierre could see, the boy was quite in order except for his lovesick yodeling, which went against the gray knight's grain. If he, Pierre, had been at home, he would have kept his son away from that. Drooling over women was no fit occupation for a man and a knight.

"His second and main motive was to enlighten the utterly naive Jaufie, whose poems had evoked much loud laughter in Antioch, about the Princess of Tripoli, for what could Jaufie know of her?

"Our young hero sat on the edge of his bed, downcast and full of evil forebodings, and thanked his father for coming. He knew very little about the princess, but he was eager to hear more. To speak quite openly, he said, he had learned aboard ship some startling, indeed, some embarrassing things about her from a local sorceress who had afterwards disappeared.

"'What, for example?' his father encouraged him. 'Did you talk with a gypsy? Was she carrying a staff?'

"'She burned a lot of paper to cure me, a pile of my songs to the princess.'

"'And what did she say?'

"'That the princess has an office at court, a central bureau, that circulates rumors about her, and that she sends out emissaries who spread word of her beauty, her virtue—'

"'And her wealth.'

"'Yes, and other things, too, all to lure knights.'

"The old knight: 'Who think they will become kings of Tripoli.'

"The son lowered his gaze. 'That's right, my father.'

"'But there's more, my son. That isn't all there is to know, and I can tell you the rest because I made the princess's acquaintance fifteen years ago.'

"'Fifteen years ago? But she was still a child then.'

"The older man laughed and laughed. 'Her, a child? It's you who are the child, my son.'

"Then he told his son the whole story.

" 'This woman is the grandmother of one of the first knights who came to this country and wrested it from the heathens. And when our knight returned to England—'

" 'She's from England?' Jaufie wailed.

" 'That, too, my son. But as I was saying: After he had conquered this country, he went home to settle accounts with some enemies there and to fetch some valuables he did not want to leave there. Now at his castle at home lived his grandmother, who had made a lot of trouble for him in the past. This woman had reached a venerable age, as is only fitting for the grandmother of a grown knight and crusader. Most crusaders' grandmothers, and their mothers, too, were dead; but this one was still alive and would not die and lived at our knight's castle in England. She had outlived his own wife and been hard on the servants. I have often observed that people who are able to do much ill to others without tiring or feeling regret live to be very old. So it was with this woman. Abusing, deceiving, and oppressing others kept her fit.

" 'When she realized that her grandson had come home to divest himself of his holdings and perhaps even to dismiss his servants, she became uneasy. How could she live without a large household to boss around and servants to tyrannize? This was a threat to her health. She did not take it sitting down.

" 'She learned from others (for her grandson did not dare reveal his plans to his grandmother) that the knight wanted to return to Antioch. This could have been the end of her (but was instead the end of him). She insisted on seeing him and then explaining to him that she had to go to Antioch because of the climate. She could not tolerate English fog anymore. Jaufie, my son, we here in Antioch have never noticed that the climate was particularly pleasant, but it may be that compared with England's it is good. At any rate, she did not let her grandson wriggle out of her grasp. He warned her that she was accustomed to the English fog and would never survive even the trip to the English coast. She would not be dissuaded. They set out. She survived the land journey. He said she would not survive the voyage at sea. She survived it.'

" 'She didn't get seasick?'

" 'She was the only one on board who didn't. She tended her grandson who was prostrated with seasickness.'

" 'Just as I was.'

"The father: 'He settled her in Tripoli, in his castle. Because we are victors and conquerors in this land, Jaufie, we can get servants cheap and lots of them. We are the undisputed masters in this country. The knight, the grandson I'm speaking of, established her in his castle, and she was soon back at her old ways, bossing and bullying people just as she had in England. Things went off without a hitch for her. She did not grow weaker. Her sport kept her strong. The knight, her grandson, died of malaria. Malaria didn't dare touch her.

"'Now that she was alone in her castle and running things her way, she hit on an idea that the climate and the Bible had suggested to her. I know all about this, my son, for—but you'll hear about that soon enough.

"'The climate here makes people friendly, especially toward the opposite sex. This friendliness sometimes takes surprising forms and, in my opinion, is responsible for the founding of the Mohammedan faith. Anyhow, the grandmother succumbed to the influence of the climate. One would have thought it wouldn't take with someone her age anymore, but it took.

"'You may say, Jaufie, that if someone is ninety or a hundred or a hundred and ten and this happens to him, nothing much will come of it. Don't you believe it. This great-grandmother managed famously. She put the youngest, most beautiful competition to shame. I don't know how she became Princess of Tripoli. People say that there used to be a native prince of Tripoli. She married him and, of course, outlived him. This marriage had not been enough for her.'

"'Did she murder him?' the troubadour whispered.

"'Probably, no doubt in some unnatural way. But I'd like to tell you what the ideas were that she got from the Bible. The passage is in the first book of Kings, chapter 1. There you'll find these lines:

"'Verse 1: Now King David was old and stricken in years; and they covered him with clothes, but he gat no heat.

"'Verse 2: Wherefore his servants said unto him, Let there be sought for my lord the king a young virgin: and let her stand before the king, and let her cherish him, and let her lie in thy bosom, that my lord the king may get heat.

"'Verse 3: So they sought for a fair damsel throughout all the coasts of Israel, and found Abishag a Shunammite, and brought her to the king.

"'Verse 4: And the damsel was very fair, and cherished the king, and ministered to him: but the king knew her not.'

"The gray knight read the text from a paper that he had drawn out of the neck of his chain mail.

"'She gave me this piece of paper when I visited her for the first time.'

"The knight looked into space with a dreamy gaze. Jaufie asked him, 'What did she look like, Father?'

"'She had tried baths and goat's blood first. Then sheep's blood. Then she tried pelts from freshly skinned kittens. Then she ate the entrails of pregnant bitches. And when she found that none of this helped and she had gone through the entire animal, vegetable, and mineral kingdoms to make herself young or at least younger or at least to keep from getting older—when all that had failed, she turned to human beings.'

"'For God's sake,' the troubadour trembled. 'She slaughters human beings?'

"'Not in any crass way, but slaughter them she does. To put it simply: She demands love.'

"Jaufie felt cold chills run down his spine. 'Horrible. How old is she?'

"'You have written songs to her, my son. How old is she? Nobody knows. Everything about her is kept secret. You might think that she died years ago. But from the fact that her office is still working and the card catalog growing and that knights, troubadours keep coming, we have to conclude that she's still alive.

"'Before I got to know her there were two noblemen with her. Both of them wanted a soft life. Everything here is in firm ownership, and to get what you want you have to resort to the sword. These two wanted to be the princess's heirs. Each one figured a year would do it. Both of them lasted only half a year.

"'Then the first one fled. He wandered around the countryside, was afraid of people and lazy as a lapdog. He didn't dare go back to his old friends; and reduced to idiocy, he apparently starved to death. The other was already crazy when she let him go. He was a big fellow who rattled around inside his armor like a skeleton and had such a mad look in his eye that it gave you the creeps. Eventually, he ran amok with a dagger, killed a dozen people or so, and had to be beaten to death.

"'I was next in line. Yes, me. I was in desperate straits at that point, and I hadn't been here very long. Otherwise I never would have gone to her. I'd already heard something about her. But, Jaufie, what I went through then—'

"The young troubadour stroked his father's hand sympathetically: 'If I had only known. I would have come to help you—'

"'You were still small. I thought I could come into property easily and become Prince of Tripoli. For that, I would put up with her for a while. But she wanted to take my life to prolong her own disgraceful one. She wanted to live forever.'

"'Dreadful woman!'

"The gray knight: 'I wasn't afraid. I knew how to deal with women. I won't say anything about your mother. It was because of her that I came here in the first place. That says enough. But this one demanded love. My experience had taught me to adopt a certain aloofness with women. I had to throw my experience overboard and start all over again, as it were. And not only that: It wasn't enough that I kissed her—the memory of it fills me with horror. I forced myself to kiss a mummy with my own live lips, but worse yet: The mummy returned my kiss. Yet it wasn't enough that I kissed her. I had to embrace her, too. To encourage me, she gave me that paper I just read to you, Old Testament, first book of Kings, chapter 1, verses 1 through 4, about aged King David and the Shunammite Abishag. She called me Abishag and insisted that I call her David. She also put on a pair of pants she took from one of my pages.'

"'And you put up with that, Father?'

"'With what, my son? That she wore pants?'

"'No, that she called you Abishag.'

"'You can see for yourself, Jaufie, how enervating this climate is, and then I was willing to go to any lengths to not have to return to Blaia Castle. Yes, I let her call me Abishag. Sometimes she would call me that in front of the servants. That gave her particular pleasure because she could see how much it annoyed me. She tried to dress me up in women's clothes. The very thought of it made her blood race. I did what she wanted and thought she would decline rapidly now. She would die in my arms. It would have been easy to strangle her. But I thought: That's unnecessary. She can't last more than another few weeks. But my presence and the fact that she could torment me gave her new life.

"'When I finally realized that, my son Jaufie, I began to hate this woman who was humiliating me as I have never hated any woman before and as no one should ever hate another human being. May God in his mercy forgive me, for he must know how such hate was possible.'

"The gray knight was silent for a moment.

"Jaufie: 'So you left her then?'

"'Yes. It was the boldest venture of my life. I wouldn't have the nerve for it now. As Abishag, I left her palace one evening and wandered through the streets of Tripoli. I had on women's clothes, a veil and whatnot. I couldn't even walk naturally anymore. She had brought me to that. People snatched at me. They laughed at my act. But I thought I really was Abishag. Imagine. That's how low I had sunk. Another month and I would have gone as crazy as my predecessors.

"'After me, the Princess of Tripoli had about ten more knights who all came from far away. A sly Levantine, a businessman, had established himself in the palace. He was making a fortune on her because he realized what she was after: to live forever, at the cost of others. It was this Levantine who gave her the idea that you fell for, my son, the idea of setting up an advertising office, spreading the word through troubadours' songs, and all the rest. But it is thanks to this idea that I am seeing you again now. And though I never would have dreamed it in my wildest dreams,' he said, bursting into laughter, 'here you are following in my footsteps.'

"'I'm a troubadour, Father, and only as a troubadour have I sung her praises.'

"'She's not interested in your praise, Jaufie. Her office takes care of that. She employs highly qualified old writers who write the poems about her that are then sent around in the world. But that you have come here in person, a young knight—'

"'Father, she will never lay eyes on me!'"

How the Wily Jaufie Escaped
the Princess

"AFTER this talk with his father, Jaufie had no choice but to consult with Petite Lay and his troupe and to tell them (after swearing them to secrecy) what a dastardly deception he had fallen prey to and what frightful news his father had brought him.

"The little troupe of Frankish minstrels sat dejectedly around their troubadour and could not believe what they were hearing. Jaufie sat dejectedly, too, for he could not imagine how he could ever return home after this fiasco. Should he try to find himself another noblewoman there (for he was, after all, a troubadour and had to have a lady)?

"Petite Lay, who was responsible for all this, was not dejected. She sang gleefully, 'Home, home!' and embraced Jaufie in front of everyone and kissed him. It was a far different kiss from the one the harpy had in store for him.

"Only Gottfried, her brother, grasped the situation: The princess would not let them go. She could not permit it. It would be a mortal affront in the eyes of the whole world if Jaufie went away without paying suit to her.

"Petite Lay: What could the witch do to stop them?

"Gottfried: 'Catch us at sea, bring us back, and take vengeance on us.'

"What should they do? Jaufie suggested asking his father for knights to escort them.

"Gottfried: They would refuse to do battle with the princess's men. Besides, after Jaufie had praised the princess to the heavens from afar, it really was an insult to her and an exposure of her if he took to his heels once he was near her.

"Jaufie: Well, what should he do? Under no conditions would he visit her in her palace. And he flew into a rage (he was afraid) when Petite

Lay—just to vex him—suggested he do that. But when he pointed out that it was not he who had insulted and deceived the princess but she who had insulted and deceived him and all of them as well, the discussion took a fresh turn.

"Gottfried said: 'You're right, Jaufie. She's made fools of us. She'll have to pay for it.' And Gottfried knew right off exactly how to get back at her.

"'Jaufie will not go to the palace. That much is clear. We can't give her that satisfaction. Jaufie and you, Petite Lay, will stay in the inn and keep out of sight. I'll play Sir Jaufie! No objections, Jaufie! I beg you, leave this to me. I'll lie on my sickbed for a few days; then I'll get up and go to the palace.'

"Jaufie: 'And then what?'"

"Gottfried: 'Are you agreed?'"

"Jaufie: 'What do you have up your sleeve? I don't like this.'"

"'Let me handle it. First, I'll get you off the hook. You're my master; I'm in your service. Second, I'll make her pay for this. I swear it. I'll take care of that witch.'

"He shouted this sentence. He may have been only a minstrel, but his honor had been sullied.

"Then Petite Lay and her brother had a long talk, and everything was settled. Gottfried, as Sir Jaufie, took to his sickbed. The princess was itching to receive her knight, and he, to punish her.

"What Jaufie and Petite Lay should have done now was prepare for the journey and set sail with the next ship. They could then wait in an Italian port for Gottfried and the others to return. But they couldn't stand to be so far away from the action. Disguised as Gottfried and his sister, they hung around in a cheap inn nearby and awaited developments.

"They wandered through the noisy, narrow, dirty streets of the city and visited the gray knight, whom they found in his elegant quarters. He met them in the courtyard and embraced his son. He was delighted to have snatched this prey from the tigress's claws. But he had his doubts about the new plan.

"'The princess is dreadful,' he said. 'Don't neglect to pray for poor Gottfried every day.'

"He refused to let the pair go away. They had to go to his chambers and tell him more about Aragon and Blaia and Roussillon.

"'It's a real satisfaction to me,' he said, 'to hear all this firsthand. I can see now how wise I was to leave the Occident behind. I took up the cross, thinking I would atone for my sins. That was not granted to me, nor to many others. But though we did not win that prize for our pains and our fierce battles against the heathen, we have been rewarded in other ways. The holy cities and the land are not the only things we took away from them—'

"He laughed contentedly. Petite Lay sat opposite him. He winked at her. She realized he was alluding to something that had to do with women, and she asked him boldly and openly: 'Well? Aren't you going to tell us what you mean? Or isn't it fit for women's ears?'

"'On the contrary, it's especially fit for women's ears. I'm pleased to be able to speak of this with a girl from the Occident. We have changed our ways, those of us who have settled here. We have no troubadours and courts of love. Here a woman is what she originally was, a rib taken from man. And that's why she serves him and is available to him in such numbers. My child,' he said to Petite Lay, 'you can't imagine what a relief that is to the sorely tried heart of a European man.'

"Jaufie had a serious look on his face. He felt how peculiar his relationship was to his father, that is, to this knight who had suddenly turned up in his life and whom he remembered only vaguely as a dangerous monster. Jaufie was coming to like his father more and more. As a child, he must have misjudged him. But why these constant attacks on the troubadours and on the courts of love, to which he, Jaufie, owed allegiance?

"'I don't mean to offend you, my son. You are a docile type, but you do not understand the world's ways.'

"Now Petite Lay took offense, and Jaufie had to pick up his lute and sing one of his famous songs. His performance drew gales of laughter from his father.

"'No,' he said when Petite Lay exploded with anger; and he cut a horizontal line in the air with his hand, 'we don't have that kind of stuff here, and you won't be able to import it either. Live here for five years, and the scales will fall from your eyes.'

"He lived very contentedly here, and he did not want to hurt the feelings of these two wanderers from another world. He invited them, if time permitted, to come to his castle; and at the evening meal he introduced them to an agreeable young knight, an Italian, who offered to accompany them to his homeland. They agreed to everything (but were not intending to keep their word). Jaufie took leave of his father.

"And Jaufie asked his father, to whom he owed his salvation, whether he wouldn't travel to Europe with them.

"'We have only one life, my son, and we mustn't twist it out of shape.'

"The princess's knights and courtiers fetched Gottfried with great ceremony and rode to the palace with him. There, in the princess's absence, speeches were given, followed by a grand celebration complete with music and feasting that went on into the night. Gottfried was thoroughly delighted, and he was beginning to feel that the sea voyage had been worth the trouble after all. There wasn't a castle anywhere in Provence that could put on a party to equal this. He and his fellow minstrels, who were now acting the part of his troupe, were put up in the palace as the princess's guests.

"The decor in the palace was oriental. Gottfried and his troupe felt they had been dropped into the world of *A Thousand and One Nights*. The next day at noon, some courtiers and veiled ladies appeared to pay their respects to the pseudotroubadour. They accompanied Gottfried, who was growing uneasy and was making signs to that effect to his colleagues, to the princess's chambers. They told him he would now meet the woman for whom he had so passionately yearned and who herself felt such fond longing for him, her troubadour.

"In a throne room, under a purple baldachin, sat a high personage heavily veiled, which was nothing unusual in the Orient. Gottfried was permitted to approach her. Kneeling, he kissed her glove; then he could get up and, at a signal from the lord steward, begin singing.

"He sang a number of songs with great verve. He could sing as well as Jaufie.

"The lady on the throne whispered something, and a servant gave Gottfried a strong wine. He drank and kept on singing. Next he received a gold chain. Another glass of strong wine followed, and he sang some more.

"While he sat resting and was handed still another glass, an invisible women's choir sang. Next, odalisques appeared and danced.

"Gottfried, who was sweating and in high spirits by now, was delighted by them. That's what the princess must look like, he thought. Soon he would dance with her.

"But because the princess was so pleased with his songs, he had to dig deeper into his repertoire. He even repeated a few numbers, but no one seemed to mind.

"He was offered more wine. He happily accepted. Everything was spinning around him already. He told the lord steward that he had gone through his entire repertoire. That gentleman, who had not understood what Gottfried had said, nodded amiably. The princess gave no sign of weariness.

"'Does she understand French?' Gottfried asked.

"'Very little, like me. Besides, she has a tin ear and is hard of hearing.'

"That annoyed Gottfried, who felt that his artistry was being undervalued. He put his lute aside and began improvising, singing whatever came into his head, peasant songs, drinking songs, all of the most dubious sort. And because the southern wine was having its effect, he felt an urge to kick up his heels, and he began leaping and spinning about, whooping and yodeling in peasant style, in short, having a wonderful time. He was utterly delighted with the whole affair. He flung his arms around the lord steward and forced him to dance a few turns with him.

"He was a tremendous hit with the courtiers. He had, of course, completely forgotten that he was supposed to be Sir Jaufie. That couldn't have concerned him less. He was in seventh heaven.

"It was broad daylight when he woke up in an ornately furnished room and found himself in a soft bed and a fragrant nightshirt. He sat up and reconstructed the previous day, the conclusion of which he could not remember. Someone had undressed him, bathed him, and put him to bed. He looked at his hands, his legs, his feet. They had even anointed him with oil. Who had done this? Probably some odalisques, he thought. Wonderful. He explored the room and immediately found a basket with wine in it. There were goblets on the table. He uncorked a bottle and braced himself with a drink, for this would be a day of high adventure.

"He made his presence known with a few yodels, and an odalisque like the ones he had seen the day before instantly appeared in the doorway and asked politely what he would like. Instead of ringing for service here, he realized, one need only yodel.

"The cheerful fellow from Provence found this odalisque very attractive, and he asked her if she had danced yesterday, what her name was, and if she liked it here at the palace. As for himself, he would like something hot to drink and some fresh rolls.

"She brought them to his bed, into which he had retired again because all he had on was a silken nightshirt. As he continued to praise her, she stood there shyly but came closer when he asked her to. Then she sat down to eat and drink with him.

"Gottfried found life at the palace wonderful. His anger toward the princess had evaporated. He chatted away with the odalisque about this and that and eventually asked her how it was that she could stay with him in his room so long and not be disturbed by the supervising staff.

"'Who would possibly disturb us?'

"He: 'Just imagine if the door should suddenly open and the princess were standing there.'

"'But I am the princess.'

"He let go of her.

"'Who did you think I was?'

"He: 'An odalisque. One who danced yesterday.'

"She: 'But of course not. None of them would be allowed near you.'

"He was thoroughly devastated by this honor. He looked at her again. 'I thought you were from England. But you speak—I'm not quite sure.'

"She: 'Me? From England? Perhaps one of my forebears came from there, some distant ancestress.'

"'Oh, so you're her granddaughter, or great-granddaughter?' He scratched his head. 'I've heard all kinds of stories. You're supposed to be ancient. You lure troubadours here to seduce them and rejuvenate yourself from them.'

"She laughed and sprang around the room in her baggy odalisque's pants.

"'Don't you think I'm young enough? Should I turn into a child?'

"The jolly minstrel thought: Then I have no choice but to believe that her experiments with my predecessors were successful. She actually has made herself young. A fantastic person. But just to be sure he asked again:

"'So you really are—cross your heart and hope to die—the Princess of Tripoli, the ruling princess?'

"She threw herself into his arms. 'Yes and yes again, my one and only troubadour, my Jaufie de Blaia, my husband. How long I have yearned for you!'

"He was terribly embarrassed when she kissed him frantically and would not let him go.

"This was all meant for Jaufie. But what could he do? It's the bold man who carries off the prize.

"He spent a wonderful morning, a long day lovely as a dream.

"About noon she gave him a beating because she claimed he was not tender enough in his attentions to princesses. He begged her pardon. Everything has to be learned.

"But because she forgave him instantly and was kind and decent, indeed, sincerely affectionate with him, not at all given to the strictness of princesses, our good Gottfried thought it unjust to conceal his true identity and carry a lie into a relationship that had commenced so happily. He therefore asked permission to confess a secret. She had to swear not to reveal it to anyone, not even to her lord steward.

"She agreed without hesitation.

"He was not, he said, Sir Jaufie de Blaia. Jaufie had not dared come to the palace for fear of the princess, who was rumored to be old as time. He was just Gottfried, one of Jaufie's minstrels.

"She: 'And you were brave enough to come here, and you don't believe that silly tale?'

"He: 'No, I don't believe it.'

"Impressed by his boldness and cleverness, she embraced him blissfully. Then she sat down on the carpet and looked up at him thoughtfully. 'And who put this hoax over on you, this story about an ancient princess?'

"Gottfried hesitated, but since he had told her one thing, why not tell her another?

"'It was Jaufie's father.'

"'Well, well,' she said, 'his father. He's a clever man. He must know what he's talking about.'

"'But you are young, Princess.'

"Now, he thought, she will tell me how she managed to make herself young. He didn't want to hear the bloody details, and he hoped she'd keep them to herself. She spoke slowly.

"'Of course I'm young. Because I'm not the princess anymore than you are Jaufie.'

"He jumped out of bed. She dodged him. From the door she said: 'Yaahh, yaahh.' He retreated to his bed and said in a businesslike tone: 'I'd like my things, please.'

"She frolicked about. He begged. 'Now you'll give me away?'

"She flew to him, embraced him, and ran out of the room. Oh, these odalisques were lovely! Who needs a princess? He would happily make do with an odalisque.

"To his surprise she appeared again the next day at noon after he had been served a princely meal, and she entertained him as she had the day before. He considered asking the lady simply to follow him to his hotel. He would get everything ready for the trip to Europe.

"She sat on his lap, rocked back and forth, and looked at him from under her eyelashes in such a way that his heart melted. 'Would you like me to come?'

"He didn't hesitate a second. 'Yes.'

"She: 'It won't work, dearest. Because of the princess.'

"'Oh.'

"'You still have to deal with her. She's the main course. I'm just the hors d'oeuvres.'

"'Tell her I eat nothing but hors d'oeuvres. Doctor's orders. Only hors d'oeuvres, three times a day.'

"She jumped up from his lap, changed her tone, and gave him an arrogant look. 'My friend, you don't seem to have grasped the situation. No man is permitted into her presence unless he has proved his undying love for her.'

"'But I never wrote a single song about her.'

"'You'd better keep that to yourself.'

"Anger rose up in our rough-hewn Gottfried. 'Oh, stop it, Suleika. Even Jaufie, who is a knight and a famous troubadour, never wrote a song for her.'

"'What do you mean?'

"'Not for this princess.'

"'Poppycock, dear boy. What a lame argument that is. The whole charm of his suit was that it was directed at a completely unknown, possibly even nonexistent woman. That is the height of poetry, the highest pinnacle that the emotion of love has ever reached. Wonderful, to love so completely abstractly, without any object at all for one's affections. But after what you've told me, I don't admire him at all anymore. First he puts on a great show for all the world to see, then sends you in his place.'

"'I volunteered,' Gottfried murmured. He'd gotten himself in a pretty fix.

"The odalisque turned to leave. He asked when he would see the princess.

"'Patience, my friend.'

"When nothing happened in the next two days, Gottfried thought of taking to his heels, but then he remembered his master, Jaufie, and what he had promised his comrades who were conspiring with him now in the palace courtyard and whom he kept up to date on developments. Furthermore, he couldn't flee, and if he attempted it and his deception were discovered, the whole business would discredit Jaufie's name.

"So Gottfried sat tight until he was taken to the princess.

"He found himself in a dimly lit, musky-smelling room, standing before a creature that might have been human and was packed into a wide chair. It interested him not at all who or what that was. He was no archaeologist.

"He noticed at the top, where the head was, two red, glassy eyes. He was surprised that a human being could have eyes like that. They occur in some animals, especially in fish. The creature had thin white-lashes.

"He gradually made out other details: a face that seemed covered with tightly stretched leather and had been painted red and yellow. Maybe the whole thing is made out of wood, he thought as he studied it closely.

"Tufts of white hair sprouted from the chin. She seemed to have no mouth. Not surprising, Gottfried thought. Nobody in that condition eats anymore.

"Below the chin came articles of clothing, a garish odalisque costume, wide odalisque trousers. Around the figure's head was wound a white turban with a ruby clasp on the front of it.

"Now the eyes of the immobile mask, small as a doll's face, blinked. From time to time a lady-in-waiting bent over it and wiped a tear from it.

"This was the apparition Gottfried the minstrel saw before him. He had reached the object of Jaufie's desires.

"Someone had brought his lute along behind him. Now it was given to him, and he was asked to favor the company with a song, but today only one.

"The singing did him good. It gave him courage. It brought him back to himself.

"Then the mask signaled him to come closer.

"But he didn't come.

"He couldn't.

"Though he had been asked not to continue, he strummed his lute and sang again. Soon he felt in form, and he bellowed away without lute accompaniment.

"Knights rushed him and held on to him. They reasoned with him. They tried to calm him. This kind of reaction was nothing new to them. But he would not be calmed. He struggled against them. He broke loose for a second and threw his instrument at the feet of the princess, in front of whom a lady-in-waiting had stationed herself. The princess was carried out. The knights overpowered Gottfried.

"He was lying in his room, bound and seething with anger, when he heard footsteps: his hors d'oeuvre, the odalisque. She bent over him and whispered that he needn't fear. No harm would come to him. If the princess had had her way, his throat would be slit already, and she would have what she wanted in the first place: fresh human blood to bathe in. But her advisers had warned against this. She mustn't go too far.

"'What should I do? What will they do with me? I'm tied hand and foot.'

"'They'll take you to her. If she threatens you, smash the window out. Her room is on the outside wall. You'll roll down the hill. No harm will come to you.'

"'I'm tied hand and foot.'

"'Don't be afraid.'

"They soon carried him to the princess's chambers on a litter. It was all he could do to keep from screaming underway, for he feared he would be slaughtered. But then he remembered what his odalisque had told him.

"Now he saw the princess move. She held herself stiff, made tiny steps to come and sit next to the litter where he lay bound. She sent everyone, men and women alike, out of the room.

"He shrieked like a stuck pig, for he saw that she had a small dagger in her right hand. She motioned to him, and he quieted down. With a barely audible voice, she said:

"'I had you tied because I wanted to speak with you alone, and I was afraid you would attack me.'

"'I can't move,' he said between clenched teeth.

"'What harm have I done you? You sang my praises. Read this paper I'm putting down next to you.'

"'I know what it is already. King David and the Shunammite.'

"'Right. Someone has told you. It's there in the Bible. There's nothing frightening about it. Years ago I was as young and beautiful and full of charms as the noble lady celebrated in your songs. I was that lady, and when I heard your songs—my emissaries brought them to me—I said: This man knows about me. I look like an old woman, a witch that people turn from in disgust. But you know that's not who I am. You know that evil old age has transformed me into a witch.'

"She sobbed.

"Our good Gottfried: 'Turn me loose.'

"She: 'I am the noblewoman you worship. Deep inside, that's who I am. Save me, Jaufie Rudel de Blaia. I've put all my hopes in you. One man after another has deceived me.'

"Gottfried was tempted to tell her that she was talking to the wrong man: It was not he who had sung her praises.

"'You detest me. You see only my external form, which I hate, too. No one has mercy on me.'

"Her tone changed. She stared past him with glassy eyes.

"'They all hate me. They fear me. I am evil. Why should I be otherwise? They all hope I'll die. But I don't want to die. I won't die.'

"'We all have to die. That's our fate.'

"'That's not true. In the past people lived five hundred years, a thousand years. Embrace me. Warm me. I'm freezing. You are young. Give me some of your youth. They're letting me dry out. If you press your lips on my ice-cold ones, I will take fire again. I fight against death from morning till night. Help me. Will you be my knight? I will be your young princess. You promised me. Now you should keep your promise.'

"Her hands trembled heavily. She was leaning forward. He feared she might fall over him. He lay defenseless against this vampire.

"'I—' (don't want to, he wanted to say, but he caught himself in time) 'I'll give you my answer. But first untie me.'

"She picked up her dagger. As her hands neared his body, they stopped their trembling, and she cut the ropes without so much as scratching him.

"He sprang up, did a few deep-knee bends, stretched (Gottfried's manners were not knightly), and said to himself: Your time has come, you Satan's grandmother. Now just where is this window my hors d'oeuvre told me about.

"He quickly spotted it, and only five paces from her, he let loose. 'I promised you something? You're a liar. Your palace is a death trap. How many men do you have on your conscience, you monster?'

"The creature seemed amused. Its eyes gleamed. It spoke in crisp tones: 'Plenty. Who cares about animals like you that get born by the tens of thousands every year?'

"She let a small bell fall to the floor. It rang. The door sprang open instantly, and armed men raced in.

"Gottfried threw two chairs in their path. With a single leap he reached the window and dove through it, tumbled down the whole height of the wall, rolled over a tolerably smooth drop, and hid in the wall footings. The princess's men ran past him. He slept the night through and was at Jaufie's inn the next morning.

*   *   *

"The news of what had happened—the minstrel troupe was still at the palace—roused all the knights in Jaufie's quarters. Jaufie sent for his father, who arrived that same evening with a large contingent of armed men. In the morning they went to the palace. The gray knight swore he would take vengeance now both for himself and for others. His herald announced before the palace gates: 'The Princess of Tripoli, who has affronted all knighthood, deserves to die.'

"The herald threw down a gauntlet and drew back.

"A herald appeared on the palace walls, blew a fanfare, and asked in what way the princess had affronted knighthood.

"The herald outside: She had lured a knight to the palace with lies, made dishonorable demands of him, bound him, and threatened him with death.

"A long pause set in. Then the chains of the drawbridge rattled, and a detachment of knights trotted out. Their leader picked up the gauntlet with the point of his lance. The battle was on. The princess's knights had to retreat before superior power. They tried to close the gates behind them, but the enemy followed too quickly on their heels.

"The witch, who called herself a princess and who was so old that she was no longer living her own life but the lives of many others whom she had murdered, was found in her chamber, totally abandoned and dressed in an odalisque's finery. To the astonishment of her captors, who tore the colorful, billowing clothing from her body, her garments did not conceal a mummy but a white, fat, puffy female body with heavy arms and legs. Its skin was oddly bespattered with blood. The avengers slashed at her thighs with whips. Her blood spurted. It was so hot that it burned the men.

"But the truth is that if that horrible painted mummy's head had not sat atop this voluptuous body with its swelling breasts, the men would have been overcome with lust and given way to it.

"They set her naked on a goat and led her through the streets of the city to prison.

"In prison her body melted away. The judges made haste with the trial, for she was clearly dying. Her prodigious age was finally claiming her.

"She was subjected to the test of fire and failed it, whereupon she cursed the court and was burned alive over a small fire.

"The story has it that something frightful occurred during the execution. I will pass this information on, though I cannot vouch for the truth of it. Her white, puffy body, chained to an iron spit, suddenly flared up like tinder, popping lightly like an exploding pea pod, and disappeared in a greenish flame. And from this flame poured something that looked like smoke but that shrieked, laughed, howled, and rushed at the bystanders, who scattered before it. They were so busy with headlong flight that they could not report accurately on the incident, but spectators who were watching from the safe distance of rooftops were agreed that there were several beings that appeared there in the roiling fire and smoke. A huge, pot-bellied, thick-thighed, long-haired woman leapt and raged in the middle and dragged along with her the others who were trying to escape from her. The demonic horde raced across the market square and down a street toward the sea. People in the streets threw themselves to the ground.

"Jaufie's great adventure was over. Jaufie was so happy to be going home again that he didn't give any thought to the dilemma that would face him there anew: Whom would he choose as his lady now, having failed in love both at home and abroad?

"His Petite Lay, in the crannies of her heart and in her worldly little head, had this problem already solved. On arriving home she shepherded Sir Jaufie and her brother, Gottfried, who had proved his courage in Tripoli, to the court of Aragon. She was able to convince the count, who admired her greatly, to make Jaufie one of his courtiers, though Jaufie was not particularly eager to mix with his Provençal friends right away.

"And it came about by virtue of the king's authority that Petite Lay herself and the bold Gottfried—her brother and Jaufie's rescuer—were elevated to the nobility.

"And it also came about that after the death of his mother, Valentine, Jaufie became master of Blaia Castle and sang the praises of other ladies no more. The mistress of his heart, Petite Lay, yes, she herself was his lady; and an elegant, clever, and much celebrated lady she was. Many noble knights took part in tournaments for her, sang of her, and served her, all as prescribed by appropriate paragraphs in the code of love.

"But the strange thing that I have to report at the end of this story, the moral of the story, as it were, is that Sir Jaufie de Blaia lived together with his clever Petite Lay in Provence in an altogether visible, palpable, bodily form. But the world refused to accept that reality. A rumor had preceded him home from Tripoli, and rumor proved stronger than his physical presence. And the rumor that has outlived Sir Jaufie and his Petite Lay and that is still bandied about today says:

"There lived once upon a time at Blaia Castle a troubadour by the name of Jaufie Rudel. He sang of a noble lady in distant Antioch. He had heard of her beauty and virtue, and he was consumed with longing for her. He wrote poems, he sang, he fought tournaments for her. Finally, overcome with yearning, he took up the cross and traveled to her. But on the way he fell ill and was on the verge of death when he arrived in Tripoli. The princess came to his inn, took him in her arms. He saw her before he died. She kissed his lips. She gave him a prince's burial. And then she went into a cloister."

BOOK TWO

The Mother on Montmartre

THAT was Lord Crenshaw's long story, which had run into weeks in the telling, his unexpectedly opulent contribution to the entertainment and edification of his son, Edward. The lord talked his way deeper and deeper into his story. Everyone had long since forgotten what he was driving at, but he couldn't stop. And the longer Gordon Allison talked, the more he fascinated his listeners, who could not quite account for what it was about his tale that riveted their attention.

But now he was done. He had abdicated. He yielded the floor. He had done his part. He could add nothing more.

Alice visited her son in his room on a stormy November day. She pretended to look out the window. The wind, mixed with rain, was tearing the last leaves off the trees.

That's the way it was with me. I had lost hope, for years no hope. I'd taken the wrong road. I'd known it for a long time. I couldn't find my way. There were barriers and roadblocks everywhere. I couldn't move. I had no present, no future, only a past.

How the wind flings the leaves down. Is there no help in this life? Is it possible that Alice Mackenzie will ever awaken to life again? Oh, what a lost creature I am!

Edward from his bed: "How lovely it is, the way the dry leaves fall. The trees will soon be bare."

"And why is that lovely, Eddy?"

"The garden becomes clear, like handwriting. You can read it.— It really was good that I came home, Mother."

To hear that from his lips. She could have sobbed.

"The way Father tells stories. He never told stories before."

"You know, Edward, that all he does is write."

"But he's able to speak now. And how, Mother! Have you noticed?"

"He did it beautifully. We all enjoyed it. You, too, apparently."

"Why do you think that?"

Alice: "All anyone had to do was look at you. The way you listened. You didn't want to miss a word. It seems we've done the right thing after all."

"Yes, it was the right thing, to speak."

She was on the alert now.

"Mother, I never had the feeling I was a weakling. I wasn't exactly the greatest athlete, but I could hold my own in fencing, swimming, in sprinting, too."

"Of course you could, Son."

He looked sharply into her face.

"Well, if I wasn't like that, why does he run me down?"

"Edward, I don't know what you're talking about."

He: "And another thing. He goes away and leaves the mother alone."

She took a deep breath. She pushed her chair back. "I don't understand. It was only a story."

He mumbled something and stared at her again.

She: "You must realize, Edward, that he was just telling a story to entertain you."

He looked at her suspiciously.

She stood up.

He: "Why don't you tell me the truth, Mother?"

She: "What truth, Eddy?"

"Mother, what is it he was telling there? Why that story?"

"He never left me, Edward. We've always lived together."

She took his head in her hands: "Eddy, are you a child who goes to the theater and thinks everything he sees there is real?"

"You could help me. Since then, since the ship, everything in me is so tangled up that I'm not at all sure I even exist. I'm afraid. I can't make sense of anything. Mother, I'm your son, and you brought me into this world. But I died. The doctors brought me back from death, but only halfway, and you have to bring me back into the world all over again."

She sobbed aloud. "I want to. If I only knew how."

"Don't cry, Mother. You will help me. I know you will."

She hugged him tight (my ally, my helper, I won't abandon you), then ran from the room.

She threw her arms up in the air, a burning torch.

*   *   *

But he called her back; he forced her to stay with him. She shut the door. He asked, "And what story will you tell me?"

She trembled.

"I don't know. What do you think I should tell you?"

He wouldn't let her off the hook.

"Tell what you know."

"I don't know anything."

But her eyes denied that; and the mother, this delicate Alice, began to speak.

"When the war was over and I didn't hear anything from you, I went to France to look for you. I wandered around in Paris and was often on Montmartre. I saw lots of people there. I want to tell you about a mother who was waiting for her son on Montmartre.

"And there stood a woman on the steps. And that was Paris, harsh sunlight on the stone steps to Sacré-Coeur on Montmartre.

"The heat was overpowering. Not many people were on the street. In the church gardens children were playing. Women and men out of work were reading their papers and talking.

"She stood against the stone banister on the steps and did not go down them to sit on a bench in the shade.

"She stood there and looked down the street. Sometimes she would go down a step, but even then she never stopped looking at the street.

"She waited.

"For the war was over.

"The prisoners were expected home from the camps, the camps with the evil-sounding names, where they had been kept since that year of horror.

"The war was over. We were told we had won. Who could feel joy? The prisoners were to come home. The reunited would weep together.

"She stood on the steps to Sacré-Coeur in Paris and looked out on the bright street. This is where he would come. That's what they had agreed. If anything happened to one of them, if one of them were tossed up here or there and the old address was no good anymore, then they would meet at Montmartre.

"For Montmartre, at whose foot you were born, will still be standing, and the white church rising up over Paris, the one we used to visit every time we went to Paris.

"There, my son, I will stand after the war and wait for you if I have not heard from you for a long time.

"Depend on it. I'll be standing there. For our fields may be devastated, our village burned, and all of us evacuated, who knows to where. We have to agree on a meeting place where we can't miss each other. And that place will be Montmartre, beneath the Church of the Sacred Heart.

"And there she stood patiently, patiently. Attempts to trace him had yielded nothing. But there could be thousands of reasons for that.

"Philippe Chardron—there's nothing in our files under that name. He is not among the living and not among the dead. That's why we now have him filed among those many thousands of men whose whereabouts are unknown.

"You're absolutely right, my dear woman. Those people have gone somewhere. Somewhere for sure. The missing must certainly be somewhere. A man weighing sixty, seventy kilos can't just disappear into thin air like a drop of dew, a raindrop in the sun. They can't all have intentionally dropped from sight or gone into hiding. Why should they turn their backs on their country and go somewhere else, to Russia, for example. Why should Philippe Chardron choose to become Petrov Ivankovich or Cesare Pontine or Friedrich August Schulze? Such shenanigans are possible in a few isolated cases, but by and large we can dismiss that possibility.

"There are many reasons why a soldier's return can be delayed under present conditions, no need to rehearse them all. You can figure out for yourself what most of them are. So what we'd recommend, my good woman, is patience. We have noted his name, regiment, battalion, company, and the number on his dog tags. You see? Here it all is in a special file folder under the letter C. We'll have everything we need right at hand if we get word of him.

"And remember this: Once we open a file on a man and have all the information on him together, it doesn't take long before he turns up. It's a curious thing. You'd be amazed. Sometimes it takes only a few weeks, sometimes a few months or longer, but it works. It's like putting a little cheese in a trap. The mouse smells it, and before you know it, you've got him.

"This is the kind of consolation the various offices doled out to the woman. And wherever she went she left a piece of paper with a number, with or without a file cover, and the paper was stuck into one of hundreds of folders and put in its proper place on the wall. The walls were covered from top to bottom with folders and cardboard cartons. There were so many of them that shelves had to be set up in the room, and visitors had to wind between them to reach the room in back. The shelves made the room dark, but over each set of them an electric light was burning, a light of hope. It burned for all those names in the files and for everyone who had brought one of those names here and left his or her own name as well.

"So the woman made her rounds of the various offices. I've done this for my Philippe, she thought. And before he goes to Montmartre he'll stop here and find his name on file and where I'm living and that I'm still alive and that I haven't forgotten him.

"And when she was outside and turned to face the low, gray building, it did not seem so alien to her anymore. For now there was something of her Philippe in it. True, he was not living there, but a bit of him was living there, too. A place was reserved for him there, and she had done her maternal duty. She would come back again soon to see what the situation was.

"This gave her new courage, and in better spirits she went home for the noon and evening hours to the poor room she had rented in the city. And every soldier she met had something of her son, Philippe Chardron, about him.

"The soldiers were like bees that buzzed about over a field of blossoms and swept down first on this blossom, then on that one, searching in each flower for the honey that had been put there especially for them. And this whole vast Paris was just such a field, and just such a flower was waiting for her Philippe Chardron. Mind what I say, my boy. Your mother has not forgotten you. Buzz, buzz, little bees, buzz.

"The days passed, the weeks passed. The mother was not driven by that avid hope of the adventurer who has thought a plan through and expects to find a vein of gold in a certain spot and attacks that spot and digs and burrows and finds nothing. His hopes are dashed. His disappointment sends him into a rage. He bites his knuckles in fury. The mother was no adventurer.

"She waited the way a farmer waits for rain. He knows his fields; he has tilled them. He knows that the seed lies ready in the loose soil. But the rain does not come. The soil needs rain. The skies are there to yield rain, and the farmer plows and harrows and plants seed because he knows the rain will come. Everything is geared to this rain that he has every right to count on. He waits for this essential link in the chain. There can be bad times and droughts—they are rare—but he will live. He has worked. He knows it will rain.

"The mother stood and waited this same way. She had prepared her fields. She knew the soil would bear fruit.

"Sometimes she left her airy lookout on Montmartre and went down into the teeming city without visiting an office. She went to listen and to hear what was happening to others. And to do this (and to drown out, too, a voice in her that sometimes made itself heard without her doing, a pain, a horrible, intolerable pain that made her suddenly burst into tears and sob—but why, for goodness' sake?), she mingled in the crowds, stood in those places along the Seine where flowers are sold, and wandered along the quais, seeking.

"She could go to the railroad stations, too. People were coming back from the East and the North and from the South, too, because the war had extended to other parts of the earth and scattered people everywhere. Yes, trains still kept arriving and bringing people home to the city. Loaded with luggage, they spilled out of the muggy coaches they had been traveling in day and night, and some squatted there still half-asleep and didn't realize they had arrived at their destination. And some were not at their destination. They wanted to go somewhere else. They kept on sleeping because they thought the train would move on after a short stop. But everybody had to get out, everybody out of the muggy coaches. The coaches would stay in Paris. They had to be aired and cleaned and would then be shunted about, and no one knew yet which direction they would head in next or when or from which platform. So everybody out, every last man, bag and baggage.

"Many of them settled down on the platform, intending to go on sleeping. But they were roused and herded into the waiting rooms and into sleeping rooms that had served that same purpose in the war years. There, in those halls crowded with metal double-decker cots and snoring people, the newcomers threw themselves down on the mattresses, too, and fell asleep and snored and waited for their trains.

"Unusual things were going on at the railroad stations. Stretcher-bearers shoved their way through the masses of soldiers, struggling toward the ambulances. Who was that there on the stretcher? Somebody wanted to know. Where were they going with him? Ask at the hospital. At which hospital? How could anyone find out what he needed to know?

"Prisoners of war were coming back, but there were civilians, too, some of whom may have been soldiers who had already turned in their uniforms, perhaps in some camp or another where their civilian clothes had been sent. Or perhaps they had stored their clothes there before they went to the front. There were displaced persons, too, the forced laborers, but Philippe wasn't one of them. He was a regular soldier and didn't have to do forced labor for anyone. So many people, soldiers and civilians, men and women. It was pointless to look at them all.

"Chance just might play into her hands, of course. She might just turn around, and there Philippe would be. He might just be that man over there at the newsstand who is picking out a paper, folding it, shoving it in his pocket, and turning to come toward you now.

"There are other ways to go about it, too. You walk along as if you had nothing on your mind, stroll through the station, stop in front of the posted schedule, and study the arrival and departure times. You can never know who'll be standing next to you. If you want to catch fish, you have to make a lot of casts and try a lot of different places. The important thing in fishing is to be patient. Who knows how many fish swim by, and nothing happens. Then finally the rod tip arches, the line goes taut, and you've got a fish.

"Oh, no, the mother did not get discouraged. If a fisherman can be patient enough to catch some little fish, how much more patient will a mother be who is searching and waiting for her only beloved son?

"She had patience. She knew she had sowed her seed. The rain would come.

"Her son had kept birds and goldfish. The goldfish had died a long time ago, and she had not put any new ones in the tank. She had brought with her to Paris the bird cage with the two cheerful green finches in it, and she fed them and took care of them, for him. And whenever she came back home from one of her searches, the birds fluttered their greeting to her. What excitement, twittering and chattering, cries of joy. And she brought them fresh water and filled their food dishes and scattered clean sand in the cage. And then she began to talk to them and tell them about her day. She didn't bring them any sad news; she just told them this and that, what all she had seen. The birds responded with a friendly peep peep, and the mother told them whatever else came to her mind that she thought might be of interest to these small creatures and that they would understand.

"For example, that it was hotter outside, much hotter than here in the room, but it was stuffy in here, and she had to open the window wide. She hoped the people upstairs wouldn't choose just this minute to throw down the dust from their rugs. And she told them what had gone on at the railroad stations today and how many people and animals and cars had squeezed their way onto the square at the station. They would hardly believe the size of the crowd. And everybody doing something. She'd love to know what each one was up to and where he was going and why they were all in such a hurry. Only the people sitting in front of the cafés allowed themselves a few minutes of peace to drink an aperitif and smoke a cigarette. They were the only reasonable ones. The rest were all after something and wanting something, always off to a different street, a different square. That's why there's such confusion on the streets, people running every which way, and the police have to keep some kind of order. The policemen carry little white sticks in their hands and signal when you can cross the street. The people on this side want to go to the other side, and the ones on the other side want to come to this side. They want to be on the side you're just leaving. And sometimes you think you should follow them and see what's there and what they're looking for. But they just move on or climb onto a bus.

"That's the way people run around in Paris, and because everyone knows that, some have opened shops in lots of the streets, with show windows and displays to tempt the passersby to stop for a second and take a look and come in and buy something. There are lovely things, but most of them are too expensive. And then the people move on. Eventually they sit down for a drink and a snack, for all this running around is bound to be tiring.

"But because there are so many people, you don't meet anyone you're looking for. Only the officials sit still in their offices, during the hours that are noted on their doors. Inside, quiet reigns, and many people are waiting there. Everything is written down. You can inquire there. The hope of finding something out exists.

"They had nothing new about our Philippe. But they know me now and are very friendly to me. Some other women I know came, too. We all know each other, the women and the officials. Sometimes there are new faces. The old guard pounces on the newcomer and asks her a million questions, and the talk flies back and forth because the newcomer has a million questions, too, and still doesn't know how things stand for the others. They tell her what papers she needs and what line to stand in, and we show her the high shelves and the hundreds of boxes where all the records are kept. The officials offer their advice and tell her to be patient: You come and complain. We're here week after week. What can we do? —

"The birds drank their water from their dishes. They peeped and swallowed and thanked her for everything she told them. They whistled and exchanged opinions about the news they had just heard. Then they sat quietly next to each other to think it all over, to digest it well, and after a while they shoved their heads under their wings and fell asleep.

"She had to keep going out among people to listen, to ask, to search, to see—to wait and not lose heart—but then to lose heart despite herself now and then and to pull herself together again because you've got to keep your head about you and because the man at the office had told someone else that it was premature to say anything final about the fate of a missing and as yet untraceable person. It was much too early for that and would continue to be too early for a long time yet to come. He might, for example, be lying in a hospital somewhere and have forgotten his name, his dog-tag number, everything. That happened. He wouldn't know who he was. There were cases where some men had gotten married in some other part of the world even though they were already married. And still others and still others yet . . .

"And this official, this gentleman they all knew, announced this in a very loud voice so that not just this one woman but all the others who had come looking for missing relatives would hear it, too. The officials were clearly doing what they could, but it had to be understood that even if the women stormed their offices, they couldn't give out any more information than they themselves had.

"But we're not interested in storming the offices. What do we care about the offices? All we want is our son. We want our son.

"The old woman stood on the steps to the Sacré-Coeur Church, on the steps of Montmartre in Paris, looked down on the glaring, sunlit street where an occasional pedestrian dragged himself along. In the church garden down below, children were playing, men and women talking, some of them smoking, some reading papers.

"The woman saw this and felt and thought: How hard, how difficult it is to bear a child. It is not easy to carry a child and bring it into the world. It is not easy either to find one again if you've lost it. Philippe, my Philippe, has slipped away from me. I feel as if I had to give birth to him again. It hurts, the labor pains. Oh, it's hard.

"People stand around on the streets and talk. Yes, some managed to escape from the prison camps. Then they joined the maquis.— They say your son was a brave boy (of course Philippe was a brave boy!). You see what I mean. Many of them joined the maquis to get back at the Nazis. And then, and then . . .

"— What do you mean, 'then'? —

"It was just like war. Men fought. Who knows what happened to them? Some were captured by the Nazis or the militia.

"— And then? What is this 'then'? How does it concern me? —

"I'm telling you this just so you'll know what all the possibilities are. But you can imagine what happened to somebody they caught for a second time.

"— How does this concern me? —

"She hides in her room, plugs her ears, and curses the people who tell her these stories. For stories like that, once told, keep telling themselves over and over again in your head, your heart, and twist your heart into a knot.

"My son, they didn't catch you. You didn't run into their hands. Somebody could just as well say that you went to Africa in a plane and are still in the Foreign Legion because you don't know where to go. But Philippe does know where I live and what we had planned to do if we couldn't locate each other.

"My husband has been dead for fifteen years, and I have no daughter, and Philippe is my only son. What are they doing to me? What are they doing? Why do they want to take my son, Philippe, from me?

"How can you tell the moment when faith begins to crumble? When does doubt find a foothold in the soul? It can't be that the house just starts to tilt and lean of its own accord. Something has gone wrong in its foundation. What can make faith begin to crumble?

"She says to herself:

"'They're just putting me off. They're giving us the runaround. Lots of women have stopped coming. I see lots of new faces. Either their sons have been found, or they've given up. But what about me, me? What will I do? Shall I give up?

"'If I, if I don't find Philippe, if he doesn't come back, then I'm finished, Louise Chardron is washed up. I don't want to think about it; it can't be; for then I would be finished.'

"And the days start bringing nothing but fear. They were not like earlier days when she would go out to look here, ask there, to watch, to take up her post. The days were no longer simple and empty. You could put into them what you liked.

"Oh, no. They waked you with a gnashing and baring of teeth. They did it to show you—early in the morning, when it was still quiet out-side—that a new day was beginning. And then they filled sacks with gravel and rusty scrap metal, and they dumped it on the ground in front of you with a terrible racket, to frighten you, to make you even more frightened than you already are, and to drive you off, to shove you aside so that you'll run away, and it didn't bother them any that the stones and metal fell on your feet.

"Not even in the evening did they show the slightest consideration, and they went on rattling and banging even though the rest of the house was quiet as death, and you sat and thought and looked at his birds. You leap up, you beg, you scream: Watch what you're doing! Are you crazy? They dump their load, their trash, down on you. They want to bury you, suffocate you, until you fall down on your bed and cry. And they do the same thing over and over again every day, cause you so much pain, start up fresh again every day the minute they wake you with their grinding and crushing.

"I don't want to wait at the church anymore. My bones are weary. I want to spend the day sitting in my room and lying down and going only now and then to Montmartre, only now and then. I want to lie down and spend a little time with his beloved birds and listen to them. There is something of him in them.

"But here I am at the church again. It's evening and cooler now. Why have I come here? What point is there in dragging myself up here and waiting hour after hour the way I have for months now, waiting for him when I don't even know—whether he is perhaps—

"Why do I keep up this daydream? Why do I keep on kidding myself?

"He won't come. He won't come. You know that. You stand here like a tree in the fall, your bare branches stretched out to the air, to the sun, but the tree has no more leaves. What can its bare branches do?

"Just stand here. Just stand.

"And she stood, standing up straight. She kept her eyes closed for a long time, and it looked as if she had fallen asleep standing up, but she was not asleep. She was standing there waiting for her son who lay ill and wounded somewhere and wanted to come to her, wanted to come so much but couldn't because he was so far away.

"He talked to her about old times, and sometimes he was only seven years old, and she was taking him to school, and sometimes he was older, and she was proud of him, and when his father died he was her whole comfort and support. He worked in the fields and did everything. And Sundays they went to church, and no one cut a finer figure than he. And in the afternoon the neighbors came, and they chatted about this and that, and the young people went dancing.

"She opened her eyes and looked off into the distance. The city was fading in a silvery mist.

"How can a mother and her child be separated?

"They are together, they are one. And no more than your heart can fall out of your chest can a child be torn away from its mother. And when I stand here or sit in my room—you are there just as I am.

"I draw you to me when I take in a breath of air. And you, you come to me, you cling to me, because you cannot exist without me either.

"And then she was in her room again to watch the birds. They fluttered; she fed them again; she threw herself onto the bed—to sleep, to face another day.

"I can't go on.

"I can't bear it anymore.

"In Paris, when the cease-fire came and the long war was over, lots of people started picking up their lives again. Some decided to celebrate first; others wanted to get right at repairing their houses. Some came back from abroad, looked over the damage, climbed around and cursed. But there were many, too, who were searching.

"A white church stood on the hill, a shining cloud that had come down from the skies, stood in Paris above the streets. It could be seen from far off. It seemed to fly across the sky above the city.

"The hill Montmartre, the church Sacré-Coeur. A careworn mother stands there week after week.

"She stands there until her heart breaks.

"Expect nothing more.

"Expect nothing more.

"This is the end, the bitter end."

In Praise of Imagination

THE guests were different each time. Edward always lay on his sofa in the half darkness. Lord Crenshaw, descended from his throne, the man who constantly assumed and shed new guises, now free of his heavy burden, tramped around among his guests, his face aglow with triumph.

Beaming, he stopped at Edward's sofa, held out his hand (why?), and took the hand offered in return. Edward looked up at him out of narrowed eyes. The father moved on.

Dr. King, the clinic director, wearing a black frock coat, sat near Edward. He sat next to Alice and confirmed her view that Edward seemed much better. He looked much fresher and much less nervous, the doctor observed. The course of treatment they were following—an artistic one, which was only right and meet in Gordon Allison's house—reminded him of that passage in the Bible where the singer David is summoned to cheer up the melancholy Saul. Alice gave the doctor a grateful look.

"That came to my mind, too, Doctor. He lies there, and we gather around him to exorcise his demons. The Bible says: 'An evil spirit from the Lord troubled him. And Saul's servants said unto him, Behold now, an evil spirit from God troubleth thee. Let our lord now command thy servants, which are before thee, to seek out a man, who is a cunning player on an harp: and it shall come to pass, when the evil spirit from God is upon thee, that he shall play with his hand, and thou shalt be well. And Saul said unto his servants, Provide me now a man that can play well, and bring him to me. And David came to Saul. And it came to pass, when the evil spirit from God was upon Saul, that David took an harp, and played with his hand; so Saul was refreshed, and was well, and the evil spirit departed from him.'"

Alice moved closer to the tall physician, who bent his head down to hear what she was whispering.

"I recited that to him."

"And what did he say?"

"He didn't altogether agree, but he didn't object either. He liked the expression 'the evil spirit from God' and asked if I had made it up. I said no; it came from the Bible. That set him thinking, and he repeated the phrase: 'the evil spirit from God.' He thought it astonishing that God could send an evil spirit."

"And what was your response, Alice?"

"Tell me what the answer is, Doctor. Can God really send an evil spirit?"

The doctor considered for a moment. "I don't feel competent to say. But for anyone who goes by the Bible, the answer is written there as you gave it: 'an evil spirit from God.'"

"Yes, a spirit that tempts, that tests. That is awful. But Edward, what is there about Edward that needs to be tested? Saul was evil, envious, jealous. But Edward—"

The doctor: "This was your idea, Alice. Medicine looks at these things differently."

Alice said no more. (An evil spirit in him that gives him no peace? There is—no evil spirit, no. I know this spirit. I know about it.)

She gave a start. Lord Crenshaw stood before them. The doctor rose and shook his hand. "I was just telling Alice what a fine touch you displayed in your story. Best of all, there was nothing contemporary about it."

"Exactly, Doctor. Everybody today wants something cheerful and colorful but the truth as well."

Edward spoke up from his sofa (I'm flying like a vulture over a black canyon and would like to dive down into it. My brain is blasted away, pulverized into atoms. I have to put myself back together again. Watch out, Edward, watch out! Don't be afraid). Edward called over: "Won't someone see to my friend MacLyne? He's come in on the middle of things."

Kathleen: "Don't worry, Eddy. You're more or less familiar with the story, aren't you, Bob?"

MacLyne, a friend of Edward and Kathleen's, was an awkward, red-cheeked fellow with long hair, a painter, who, at the beginning of the evening before he sat down, had done his duty by the sandwiches, drunk his punch, and engaged in such animated conversation with everyone in sight that the group had settled somewhat later than usual around Lord Crenshaw and the fireplace. And when everyone finally was gathered around the fireplace and focused on the calm, animated figure in the armchair, MacLyne kept his silence unwillingly and ran his hand nervously through his hair and looked to the left and right attempting to catch someone's eye. He liked to talk and was looking for a partner. But the man in the armchair held everyone's attention. So Bob struck his sails, sank back defeated in his chair, and stared at the toes of his boots, picked lint from his pants, and wound up chewing on his knuckles.

Now he assured everyone eagerly that he knew the story, that Kathleen had told it to him. He was completely up to date.

The group had drawn together. Edward, a cushion at his back, half sitting up, began. "And now, Father, I'd like to add something to your story. I assume you wanted to illustrate something. What have we learned?"

Kathleen, the daughter, ladylike tonight with a carefully upswept hairdo, a silver comb in the back, a short black dress, a gold medallion on her breast, a white lace collar and white lace cuffs, applauded.

Lord Crenshaw: "Ideas and customs can become so all-pervasive and put people through such paces that they are no longer people. That's what this story shows. Everything Jaufie did went against nature. He couldn't bring himself to do the utterly obvious. He saw through everything but didn't fight it. What won out in the end was rumor. It made a legend of him, even in his own lifetime. He could protest all he liked; Petite Lay could laugh; but they had been reduced to a jelly fit for spreading on a bread-and-butter ballad."

Edward: "But we exist. We can't just be shoved aside."

"I understand what you're saying, Eddy, but my view is that we have been fully transformed into dream figures and creatures of fable."

Edward: "Was it as dream figures, as creatures of fable, that we went to war?"

The father: "The war is behind us. Why shouldn't we call a spade a spade now? Why go to a lot of trouble and claim things that will not stand up to scrutiny? Some speak grandly of individuals who 'caused' the war. Others ascribe it to the operation of natural laws. The economy was responsible for it. But who or what is the economy? A number of commodities, tons of coal, oil fields, mines. What can commodities possibly want? Coal is incapable of wanting anything. It has weight. We do with it what we like. Man plays with it. He is the master of all things. And so we're left with the question: Who is man?"

Lord Crenshaw paused.

Kathleen swung her slim arm: "Yes, who is man, Father? You called him the master of all things."

Now the painter mumbled something. "My long-held conviction: Everything is mere fantasy. We shouldn't kid ourselves. Calculations are never right. Anything is possible. The war could just as well have taken a completely different course."

After this mysterious announcement, the painter retired into himself again and stared at the toe of his polished black boot, the focal point of his meditation.

Edward to his father: "And what is behind imagination? Who does the dreaming?"

Gordon: "I don't know."

"If things are the way you say they are, Father, it must be a demon. That makes us mere objects, without powers of reason, that are controlled by irrational forces. Or objects with reason that are controlled by irrational forces."

He trembled. Something was closing in on him. He clenched his teeth together.

"I didn't want to pain you, Son. We are in search of the truth."

"Yes, tell me the truth. Only it can help."

Alice was frightened. Edward was speaking in the tormented tone he had used that morning. She touched Gordon's arm. He turned to her and read her glance.

Edward: "I'd like to tell a story, too, if I may. It is short. About a lion and a lake. I just remembered it. Someone told it to me once."

He lay down and squeezed his arms, which were shaking slightly, against his body. "'The Lion and His Reflection.' There once lived a lion on a mountain. The mountain was called Mondora. The lion's name—I've forgotten that. He ruled over all the animals, he, their king. They all fled before him.

"Now on this mountain of Mondora there was a glassy pond the lion went to when he was thirsty. And whenever he drank, he disturbed the water. The mirror of the pond was ruffled, and so the lion could not see himself in it.

"But one time he crept up to it. And instead of drinking right away, he stretched out next to it and extended his fearsome, kingly head out over the surface and let his tongue play above the mirror. And, behold, he caught sight of something in front of him, beneath him.

"Out of the water emerged a huge head, a thick, heavy, blood-red, thirsting tongue, a frightful tongue. The lion jumped back. Then, out of fear, he lay absolutely still. He waited. Pulling his hind legs up under his belly, he raised himself slightly, his feet firmly planted in the sand, ready to spring.

"Nothing happened. He got up slowly, drew back. And now, a few yards away from the pond, he roared, roared over the water, to challenge the creature hiding there.

"Nothing stirred. He crept up to the shore of the pond again, carefully leaned out over it—and look there: The thing emerged from the depths again, huge, monstrous, dreadful, and stood eye to eye with him. Who was it? Who came stalking up so silently from below, took notice of him, and wanted to tangle with him?

"He lay still, eye to eye with his opponent, and waited. The other did nothing.

"Who was living down there, hiding in the water he drank from every day?

"The lion tried the same tactics once again. Once again he drew back, stood up. Once again he raised his fearsome head and roared horribly. His whole body was trembling. But he did not creep up on the pond again. He trotted back to the edge of the forest and crouched there. He listened, looked, and when nothing moved, he made a swift, desperate rush and leapt, made a huge leap at his enemy's throat.

"He splashed into the water.

"He hurled himself forward, could not catch or seize his opponent, struck out at him and felt for him, this enemy who was evading him, and thrashed about and grabbed for him and swallowed water and couldn't find him or catch him. And sank in the water.

"The water closed over him."

A pause. A long pause.

The son's clear voice from the sofa: "Now I know why I forgot the lion's name. I was the lion myself."

Silence.

The doctor was about to say something to change the subject when the statue of fat on the throne spoke up. "Then you and I agree, Eddy. Wo do battle with our own illusions."

But Edward moaned, his face turned toward the ceiling. He moaned louder and louder. The black surface of the pond, the water, closed over him.

Alice had squeezed herself in next to him. She took both his hands. Kathleen began a loud conversation.

In the corner of the library were seated two gentlemen who made use of their isolated position in the semidarkness to whisper back and forth and exchange opinions from one armchair to the other behind the curtain of smoke they themselves were producing. One of them, Edwin Garrick, was a judge, a bony, serious man with bushy gray eyebrows. He said to his neighbor, "Edward still isn't quite himself. And what do you think about our friend Allison? I suspect it wasn't pure coincidence that we were seated under the bust of the wise Socrates. I don't know, Lunn, whether you share my impressions, but I feel moved to roll out some plain common sense against Gordon Allison. What manner of nonsense is Lord Crenshaw talking here anyhow? This just isn't his way. Him and his theorizing and this contrived stuff. His story was enjoyable, even though it was too long. If he publishes it, I'll show him where to cut it. But his philosophy—worthless from beginning to end."

Lunn—Judge Garrick's companion, the both of them old friends of Lord Crenshaw—a man of medium height and with a gray mustache, was a high-ranking railroad official, now retired, and a man of patience. He said with good humor, "Garrick, Crenshaw does this all the time. He starts somewhere, and then he doesn't know where to go next. He needs a switchman. His trains are almost always on the wrong tracks and then have to stop soon. That's why he's at home with short stories, or perhaps one should say short circuit stories. If he made them any longer they'd be disasters."

"Well, at least he's done now, thank God."

"You think so? He'll just stop until he's put his finger on what went wrong. Then he'll tell another story. He bails himself out of any and all nonsense by telling another story, which calls for still another story in turn."

"Everything is fantasy! Do you think he's doing the boy any good with that stuff? Edward seems to be overindulging in fantasy as it is."

Lunn: "Tell that to Crenshaw."

Kathleen had, in the meantime, asked the momentarily unengaged painter whether painting had changed much in recent years and, if so, how. No question could have pleased the painter more. The inane young man threw himself into it as into a swimming pool. Since Allison had fallen silent, he immediately saw himself as the center of attention and began to speak and to present his point of view, to explain what his point of view was. Perhaps not everyone would share this point of view, but it was the clearest and most rational one, as everyone would see. What, in short, is painting? A matter of colors and surfaces. That says it all, and whatsoever says more than that cometh of evil. This is true of painting even more than of music. Music is proud of its artificiality, the fact that its system of scales, harmonies, dissonances, was created by men, proud that it functions in an intellectual sphere where reality cannot follow it. Music is art and nothing else, art, sovereign, autonomous art. The same is true of painting.

Why is it true of painting? (No one had asked. He acted as if someone had put the question to him, encouraging him to speak on. But, in all truth, no one encouraged him, and so he charged into the fray, sparring with himself before bewildered spectators.)

Why is it true of painting? What did we use to think ("I say 'we,' meaning both great and unknown painters, and I do not exclude the greatest here"—all this flowed from the red-cheeked painter and seemed prepared in advance, ready to deliver) what did we use to think the painter's task was? The same one that Shakespeare assigned to dramatists: to hold a mirror up to nature.

"A mirror," the cloddish fellow laughed, "Eddy has just told us a story about a mirror. He hit the nail on the head with it. A mirror is nothing. A mirror can accomplish nothing at all. A mirror is foolishness. And painting proves this (and here I agree with my friend Edward completely). Should painting imitate nature, this same nature we have quite enough of already? The very thing we want, the thing we need, is nonnature, not a duplicate, not another artificial nature."

Then, to cite examples, he babbled on about beets and goose drumsticks of which there appeared not to be enough in nature, for artists had reproduced them in oil or pastels and hung them in salons so that we would not have to go without them a single minute.

The uninhibited painter was finally shut off by a long-legged, black-haired man who was present for the first time this evening and who, in order to rest his skeleton with any comfort, had to extend it from the periphery of the circle into the center. This man, the member of parliament from the district, announced loudly and from the bottom of his heart, "Well, now, we have done our duty and sung the praises of imagination quite long enough. Let's get back to the stories. I would hope someone will have something more to tell."

*   *   *

Kathleen had been invited to spend two days with friends nearby. Edward became restless; he wanted to see her. She was given the message. She was not happy about having to come home. This was impossible. Edward was behaving like a child who had to have his own way. Her parents indulged his every whim. She wanted to go right to Edward and tell him this, but her mother held her back. She didn't let Kathleen go to him until the next day.

He was brooding but was pleased that she was back. She told him about her visit.

"How strange all this sounds," he said, his hands behind his head, "how strange. I feel like I'm living on the moon. I was reading *Gulliver's Travels* yesterday. I feel like Gulliver."

She giggled. "Among the giants or the Lilliputians?"

"I don't know."

"I'll bet, Edward, that you're the giant Gulliver among the Lilliputians."

"Is that how I look? — Tell me, Kathleen: Did Father tell you stories often?"

"You know the answer to that as well as I do. It's been a long time since he did."

"You must have been six or eight years old."

She smiled. "As late as my twelfth birthday he sat for a whole afternoon with me and told me a novel that was wonderfully funny. I laughed, and he did, too. Sometimes he laughed so hard he couldn't speak anymore. He gave up the story telling later, I'm sorry to say. He said I was old enough to read books then."

"Reading books isn't as interesting."

"Nowhere near, Edward. You could see that on the evenings he was telling his story. I enjoy it so much when Father tells stories. Then he's really himself. Otherwise he sits shut away in his room. We shouldn't let him get away with that. We should prod him to come out and speak more often. If I were his wife, I would hide his pencils and pens and every last scrap of paper and not let him into his study."

"He wouldn't stand for that."

"He'd be bored to death. That would be good. Then he'd think up something else to do. Oh, Edward," she said softly, "what a pity it was for Father that this house wasn't bombed to smithereens, too. That would have been good for him. He would have stood there in despair, of course. He would have been a terrible nuisance for a while. But then he would have begun to look around and see how other people managed and how they were doing. It would have waked him up."

"Other people would have invited him to their places, you mean?"

"Yes. This way, he sits here, and that's why he's stagnating. That's why he keeps getting fatter. It's awful how fat he is, don't you think?"

"He seems not to want to go out. Why is that, do you suppose?"

"Laziness, sheer laziness. And Mother lets him have his way. He wouldn't get away with that with me."

"How did you find his story?"

"Wonderful. A novel in installments. And I loved the way he got so caught up in the story that he forgot what the point of it was. You noticed that, too, didn't you?"

"So you think we haven't gotten anywhere at all?"

She laughed. "Oh, yes, we have. Now we know precisely what he's after. He wants to convince us that everybody is like him, which is to say, lazy. The only character in his story who acted on his own was the old knight who walked out on his dragon of a wife. Everything else was dictated by fate. Or it was supposed to be fate, but it was really just Father."

"And what do you think yourself, Kathleen?"

"We have been out in the world, Edward. We know all about 'fate.' People have to make decisions and act. If you stand there and do nothing and let the good Lord take care of things, your enemies will take care of them first, and then you're finished. I saw that happen time and again. It's a terrible thing if you think somebody else will relieve you of having to act. Some doctors gawk at a wounded man and don't know what to do and don't act. Others know what to do right off. One glance and they go to work, and everything goes fine."

He was puzzled. "If Father enjoys talking so much and so long, why does he lock himself up in his library?"

She laughed. "Out of laziness, I tell you. And because nobody drives him out. All the praise he has gotten has paralyzed him. Every fan letter he gets nails him down a little bit more. And every passing year adds a few more pounds."

"Why does Mother let him do this?"

"To be perfectly honest, because she has no energy herself. She'd rather bite her own tongue off than say anything to him. They talk together very little about anything—a typical old married couple."

She pulled closer to the head of the bed and whispered to him. "They're just rusting away, Edward. I had a very different sense of them before the war. We four used to be a real family. I never saw Mother as one entity and Father as another. I saw the family as a unit. When I came back home and you were still away, I was genuinely shocked. So this was Father, and this was Mother? It was crazy. Where was our family? I couldn't piece together a family out of that.''

"Go on."

"I found my way back into things. Some kind of connections got made. But something is gone, and it'll never come back. We're older, and we see things more clearly. What are our parents like? Take Father. He sits up there and writes. Mother plays the fay. You must be aware that I used to envy her. I wanted to be a fay, too. I'm such a coarse type. But now I don't want that anymore. It's too old-fashioned for me. And then the way she was about you. When she first heard what had happened to you and then when she got the telegram saying you were coming home—well, she's been all aflutter ever since. She's behaved strangely, very strangely, believe me. When we were allowed to look into your room for the first time, she literally fainted.''

"Why?"

"You still weren't yourself. The nurse said you had glanced over at the little window in the door, and Mother was terrified. The nurse had to carry her out to the waiting room. You know what I think? When parents get older, they become dependent on their children. The Oedipus complex in reverse. Fathers cling to daughters, mothers to sons.''

"You and your psychologizing!"

"After that she sat in the garden for hours and brooded."

"Brooded? What about?"

"She doesn't seem to notice at all anymore that Father is still here, too. That irritates me. It enrages me. Don't be angry with me. I haven't let on to her. I've sat down with her a lot and comforted her. She was very nice on those occasions. We're both women, after all. I felt that Mother was accepting me as a woman for the first time. I thought she would pour her heart out to me. But she won't. She is no elf, Edward. She may have been that for me at one time. Do you think she ever really was one? She's still amazingly young. She doesn't just look young. She really *is* young. What has she talked about with you?''

"Nothing. She's just chatted about one thing and another."

The Story of the Page Who Lost His Ring

AT the beginning of the next session, after the general conversation had subsided, one of the two men kept in the semidark beneath Socrates—it was the jovial railroad man, Lunn—announced to the company: "Before Lord Crenshaw began his story we had agreed—at his own suggestion—not to discuss things but to tell stories and let each listener draw his or her own conclusions from them. We had spoken about the war, about the causes of the war, and that has faded into the background, which I do not regret in the least. As for myself, if any discussion at all is to take place, I'm in favor of wise pronouncements that say nothing. A house is a house, and an ox is an ox, and any statement that claims more than that cometh from evil. Furthermore, if someone says a house is not a house, or an ox is not an ox, then I can make my peace with that, too."

His bony neighbor with the bushy eyebrows, the judge, seconded him and put in his own vote in a deep bass voice.

"At the risk of being accused of advocating the most commonplace common sense, I have to say for my own part that I put no faith in the omnipotence, indeed, the tyranny of the imagination. Of course I have no imagination. But we all know in principle what it is. Our fantasies have completely private origins and no bearing whatsoever on world history, thank God. Our fantasies spring from a specific physical and mental state. We can understand dreams only if we know the individual who dreamed them. I should add, of course, that what I have just said does not apply to the poetic imagination."

Lord Crenshaw bowed. "I'm grateful to you for this concession."

The silly painter was fussing with his heavy red necktie, had a red face, and looked as if he was about to say something. But he had so much to say that he got none of it out.

The beanpole of an MP, who was traveling through and here at Crenshaw's invitation, busied himself redeploying his legs. His hair, which fell into disarray when he ran his hands up through it from the back (which he often did to give his arms something to do because he didn't know what else to do with them, neither the right nor the left one, for if he crossed them on his chest, which was as bony as his arms, he suffered from this clash of bone on bone, but if he let them hang down on the floor, they splayed out and made him look like an ape), his hair had been badly tinted and displayed a whole spectrum of iridescence ranging from a natural gray-white through a pale blue to a burgeoning green. This MP released his voice from its high, stark tower, and it made the following confession: "I'm not in the story-telling business, though I am sometimes accused of making things up—"

"And justly accused!" Lord Crenshaw interjected.

"Thank you," the MP continued. "One thing we can agree on in any case, Gordon, is that you poets have imagination, but you don't let anyone else look behind the scenes."

Gordon Allison laughed and shook his head. "You and your analyzing. To hell with literary historians and psychologists. What we write, we write."

The judge growled: "So it seems to you."

A clear, high woman's voice spoke up. "May I tell another story from the same period in which young Jaufie and his Petite Lay lived? Perhaps it will bring us a little further."

"Tell away!" the judge cried out enthusiastically. Lunn applauded.

The MP heaved his long limbs around and stretched out his neck so that he could inspect this self-effacing figure behind him to his right. Having done so, he folded up again. Kathleen smiled at her former teacher. Gray hair, a thin, fine-featured face, a small, lean woman wearing an unobtrusive cloth hat and a gold watch on a chain around her neck. Now Miss Virginia took off her leather gloves. She was urged to move her chair more toward the center of the circle, which she did under great protest. Now she sat opposite Gordon Allison as if under a spotlight. She was clearly regretting her offer now. Alice and Kathleen whispered encouragement to her. Her unusually clear voice trembled:

"Mr. Allison's idea of calling the courts of love and the troubadour code a medieval women's-rights movement is a good one, but what bothers me about it, if I understand him correctly, is that he thinks such movements or trends of the times come upon people from outside and that they themselves have nothing to do with creating them."

"Oh, no," Crenshaw's voice boomed out, "they do contribute to them. I said as much."

The maiden lady was stopped in her tracks. The voice of the easygoing Lunn: "Go on with your story. And no interrupting, Allison. Remember, fair play."

The elder Allison smiled upon him from on high.

Miss Virginia, who was still working at her black leather gloves: "This is the story of a page who was riding to a tournament and lost his ring on the way.

"Once upon a time a page was riding to a tournament. And as he rode along he started thinking about his opponents, and he was so caught up in his thoughts, so possessed by the idea that he was in combat right now, that he spurred his horse, seated his lance, and, in full gallop, ran into a tree. The bold dreamer went flying to the ground. His horse ran off. He had all he could do to gather himself up again. Then he lured his horse back, calmed it down, and remounted.

"In astonishment, he examined the oak that had done this to him, and he rode round and round it. It was a placid tree, a simple tree, living unto itself. Here, in its natural place, it grew out of the ground and had intended and accomplished nothing more than to stand here.

"The wiser for this insight, the page set off again, and as he settled his helmet more firmly on his head, he noticed that his head was throbbing and that the birds in the forest were singing loudly and with some apparent message—yes, loudly and with a very urgent message. But what were they saying? Amidst this song, which he felt was directed at him, he trotted slowly on under the trees and thought about the young lady whom he adored and for whom he meant to fight and win. But when he remembered his fall, he felt afraid and rode still slower and looked down at his hand. Her ring was still there. He had at least not lost the ring she had given him.

"His horse suddenly stopped, and the page was again mystified. They were standing in front of a small forest chapel. The door was open, and on the roof small birds were singing a loud concert.

"Then the page thought it would be a good idea—in view of his fall and in view of the coming tournament—to dismount and say a prayer inside.

"And when he entered the chapel and kneeled at the altar rail with his hands folded before him, his gaze fell again on the ring, which, for some strange reason, was worrying him; and when he had ended his prayers, he decided to entrust his ring to this chapel until after the tournament. He took the ring from his finger and laid it on one of the small metal trays that held burning candles. Then he lit a fresh candle, put his ring in this new tray, and let wax drip on it to keep it from falling from the tray or from being taken.

"As he did this, it seemed to him that Mary, who was present in the form of a small wooden statue, was watching him and following his every move. He looked up at her, the dripping candle in his hand. The drops of wax had already buried the ring. And she was so beautiful, this Mary, that his heart beat stronger. And he felt ashamed that he had worried about the ring and that he had buried it here in wax as he had. He put the candle down, scraped the wax off the ring, and polished it bright again with the palm of his hand. As he did this he looked around to see if anyone was watching him from behind.

"And as he stood there with the ring, not knowing what to do next, lo, the statue smiled at him so sweetly, so warmly, that he knew right then he should give Mary his ring.

"And he reached for her right hand, which she held before her breast; and without being at all surprised at how simple it was, he found he could easily slip his ring onto a finger of the soft, pliable left hand she held out to him.

"And as he took a step back and gazed ecstatically at the figure of Mary, who now wore his ring on her finger, she closed her fingers, raised the hand again, and placed it firmly next to the other hand at her breast.

"Before his very eyes this happened.

"Overwhelmed, he fell to his knees, crossed himself, and whispered a prayer. He did not dare look up. But finally he had to stand up and make sure whether he had really seen what he thought he had seen. And there her hand lay, firmly at her breast. His ring on her finger flashed in the candlelight. Then he was struck with panic: He had to wear that ring at the tournament. Could he take it off her hand?

"He screwed up his courage, whispered a prayer, begged for forgiveness—and had a go at it. He reached for her arm. He reached for her hand. The arm remained firmly in place. He pulled, he yanked, and suddenly he realized with horror what he was doing and ran outside, minus the ring.

"Outdoors, he looked at his hand, his empty finger; incredulous, he ran back in. The statue was standing in its place. Mary held her hand clasped to her breast. She refused to return his ring.

"His horse was whinnying outside. He had to go to the tournament. Distraught, he rode on.

"He lost at the tournament, as he expected he would.

"And that evening when he was returning through the forest, anger over his ill fate rose up in him, and he felt compelled to try again with the statue and get his ring back. For if misfortune insisted that he lose in battle, then he needn't suffer on top of that the loss of his ring, the ring of his beloved, who had nothing to do with this run of bad luck.

"But the closer he came to the chapel, the slower his horse went, refusing to respond to the spurs. Slowly the animal carried him to the chapel, the door of which, even now in the dark of evening, stood open again; and a white light shone out of it onto the path. There his horse carried him.

"It was a bluish white light and did not come from the candles, as the page thought it did. It was the brightness of day, of a cloudless sky; and standing there in the doorway, as he spurred his horse to race on by, was Mary herself, surrounded by the light of noon, and she was looking at the horseman. The horse lowered its head and stopped. Mary had opened her mouth to speak but said nothing. She held out both her hands as if inviting the page to come nearer.

"But his terror was so great that he kicked at his horse and stabbed it with his spurs, and when it refused to move, he leapt off it and ran away as fast as he could in his armor, stopping only after half an hour when he could run no more.

"And then his horse appeared. It came up next to him, and he was able to ride home, utterly downcast.

"He sought out his friends and told the story to all of them. Some didn't believe it. Others were worried about him and advised him to ask himself what he had done or failed to do that had made Mary call him.

"But he said over and over again: Nothing, nothing. He had, of course, had some strange experiences on the way to the tournament: his running into a tree with his lance and the way the birds in the trees seemed to be conspiring against him with their songs. And as far as the blessed Virgin, our beloved Lady, was concerned, he had in no way offended her. On the contrary, he had felt such a great love for her, indeed, such a profound and sometimes overwhelming love, that he had felt compelled from the bottom of his heart to put his ring on her finger.

"'On her finger? Why? Like an engagement ring?'

"'Exactly,' he confessed, 'that's just how I felt at that moment. Great happiness swept over me when I made that decision and asked her to accept the ring from me, and she did.'

"'Then you have plighted your troth to her. How can you expect to get the ring back?'

"Only then did the page understand what had happened. He left his friends and wept ceaselessly in his room.

"'What have I done?' he wailed. 'Why must I lose my youth and my happiness and the love of my lady because my horse happened to run me into a tree and the birds lured me into a chapel? I wanted to put my ring down there because ill luck had befallen me and I didn't want to lose the ring, and so I put it on the candle tray and buried it in wax. And Mary's statue was so beautiful that I thought I could put the ring on her finger. She seemed to be asking me to do it. She opened her hand, but then her hand refused to give my golden ring back.'

"After he had brooded over this for a few days and struggled with himself, he bought a sharp knife and a small woodworking plane and rode off into the forest with them, for he could not allow the statue to keep his ring and prevent him from ever entering his beloved lady's presence again.

"He told no one about his plan, and no one ever found out afterwards what had actually happened. He was found bloody and unconscious in the forest near the chapel. His horse, which had been running around free, drew the attention of some passersby to him. When he regained consciousness and searched through his pockets and his traveling bag, he found neither the knife nor the plane.

"He felt deep remorse over his dastardly plan; but after confessing it, he was much relieved and felt he could now yield to his bride's pleas and prepare for their wedding.

"And that he did. All his friends and relatives appeared for the great day. They ate and drank and danced on into the night. The page had breathed not a word to his bride about the strange happenings that still troubled his mind. He had had a new ring made that looked just like the first one.

"But what terror came over him when, during the last dance, his bride stood still, looked at one of his hands, then the other, drew him under a lamp to make sure she had seen aright, and then said, 'Where is my bridegroom's ring?'

"'I—I—must have lost it while we were dancing—yes, while we were dancing, for I had it before.'

"They waited until the dance was over. She comforted him in his deep distress. With a sinking heart, he sat at the boisterous table, in the hall resounding with laughter, with trumpet and fiddle music. The dance ended. The servants swept the hall, but they could not find the ring. Where could it have rolled to? His face was filled with great sadness.

"And then they stole away to the nuptial chamber upstairs. And lying with her, he forgot all else.

"It was dark.

"The drums, the stamping of feet, the whooping downstairs reached their ears. She had taken his head in her arms to press it passionately against her breast.

"His eye was drawn past her neck to the wall where a streak of light had just happened to fall, probably cast there from the carriage of some departing guests.

"But it was Mary who stepped out of the wall, looking just as she had in the doorway of the chapel, bathed in a bluish midday light, her mouth open. She did not speak, but both her hands were stretched out to him; and though she remained mute, she was no less stern and reproachful for that. At that moment the dance music faded, and the twittering and shrieking and singing of birds could be heard, so loud that his ears rang with it, and he sat up to chase the birds away.

"But they were too far away from his bed. He meant to sit up, snatch his jacket from the floor where it was lying, and toss it at the birds. Then Mary stepped away from the wall, scared the birds off, and stood next to the bed. He tore his head from his bride's arms and sat up.

"Mary was wearing a long robe closed in front. She had a small golden crown in her hair, and on her feet were red Morocco-leather shoes with bells on them. She opened the robe and, with a roguish smile on her face, showed the page the ring she was wearing on her finger just where he had placed it. Then she reached into a pocket of her robe and pulled out something that she shook in her hand without revealing it. He was to guess what it was. She opened her hand. There on her palm was the second lost ring.

"And then she reached deep down into the pocket with her left hand, and what did she bring up this time? A plane and a small, sharp knife. She tossed them back and forth in her hands without harming herself and then dropped them back in her pocket.

"How was it that she suddenly appeared next to him on the pillow and that his lips neared her foot? Now, all of a sudden, she wore no shoes, and as his lips drew near her skin, such immeasurable sweetness and bliss flowed through him that he fainted and lay there motionless.

"His bride began shaking and poking him. 'Oh, stop it, dearest. You're fretting too much about that ring. I'll have a new one made for you. What matters is that you are here with me, now and for all eternity.'

"She drew him to her.

"'If I have the love that is in your heart, then I am happy; and that love will live in my heart, too, and can never be lost to us. It is the most faithful guardian the two of us can have. It never sleeps, not even when we are asleep. It knows that we need it to watch over us and keep harm from us.'

"'No harm will befall us,' said the vacillating page, who reveled in the taste of her words and kisses and was enchanted by them. 'Yes, just as you are mine, dearest heart, so I am yours.'

"But no sooner had he said this than another voice made itself heard. 'You hypocrite, you liar, will you betray me thus? Go your way then. Here, take your ring and the other one as well. And take your knife and plane, too.'

"Huge black birds—ravens, magpies, owls—struck at his face with their wings. They croaked horribly. He tore himself from his bride's arms, sighed. 'Oh, no, do not leave me, most gracious Lady. I will do whatever you command. I kneel before you.'

"'And will you obey me day and night now? Will heavenly love and no other watch in you day and night? Will you live under my cloak until day and night are no more?'

"He swore he would.

"She asked, 'And who am I? Your prince, your knight, your noble lady?'

"'The blessed Mary, my heaven on earth and my eternal paradise.'

"The page stood by his bed and dressed himself. But he did not buckle on his sword. Hot tears poured down his cheeks. He was deaf to his bride's questions and complaints.

"And then he dried his face and sat down next to her on the bed and told her everything, about his ride through the forest, about the tree he ran into, about the birds and the chapel and how he wanted to hide his ring but how Mary interfered and how he gave her his ring but then didn't know what to do, for he already had a betrothed, and how she would not give the ring back. Now Mary had just appeared to him in this chamber. He asked his beloved bride to release him forever and for all time. Then they both kneeled by the bed, prayed, cried a lot, and were kind to each other until the cocks crowed.

"Then he took his leave of her and rode off happily, from one wedding to another, to his wedding with the blessed Mary, to whom he then dedicated every hour of his life in the monastery."

And What if There Were Such a Thing as a Human Being?

THE first sound to be heard after the small lady with the clear voice had finished was the scraping of a chair on the floor in the Socrates corner. Then a door creaked. The railroad official Lunn was fleeing the room to spare himself the discussion. His neighbor with the massive eyebrows, Garrick, went on puffing his pipe and waited to see what would come next.

"A touching story," intoned Lord Crenshaw.

Miss Virginia felt compelled to add a moral.

"We see from this story that comes from Jaufie's time and the time of the troubadours how deeply rooted in human nature pure love is, the kind of tender, idealistic love that puts a woman on a pedestal and comes straight from the heart. It originates in us, and we bring it to the surface. A women's-rights movement? I don't think so. It was more a matter of human emotion, of a higher, purer, deeper meeting of man and woman."

"That may be," Lord Crenshaw conceded. "But if we take a closer look at things, no, if we look at them from a greater distance, they will perhaps look quite different."

Kathleen: "It was a nice story, Father. Do you really think everybody is like your old gray knight who went to the Holy Land just to get himself a harem?"

Everyone laughed, Lord Crenshaw more heartily than anyone.

Kathleen: "I don't think you were listening, Father. If Virginia's story is right, it proves you wrong; for it says the new feeling did not stand above people, subduing them with the force of an imposed morality, but rather arose from them. And the new morality, the new era, represented simply—a new humanity."

125

The lonesome pipe smoker in the Socrates corner applauded.

But Lord Crenshaw raised his arms. "My view is not popular. I know you don't care for passivity. You're young; you want to act, want to have a hand in things. But I see what lies above and behind things, what deliberately stays hidden so that it won't deprive you of the pleasure of thinking it is you yourselves who act and make history. The whole point of my long story about Jaufie is that people do not do what they want to do, not what is in their own true interest. They resolutely ignore their real interests. They do not put a high value on their own real, natural impulses. They give themselves up to fantasies. They trust a bunch of ready-made ideas they pick up from others more than their own decisions. And then, once they've sold themselves down the river this way—don't laugh now—only then do they feel, in their misery, content."

Edward: "Doesn't that amount to saying that we're something like phantoms?"

Gordon: "All it means, Edward, is that humans don't have their own welfare at heart. Imagination is their burden and their punishment. Under no circumstances will they stay in the place nature has assigned them. They get itchy there. They find their place unworthy of them. They want to rise above it. Imagination sets them at odds with the world around them. Common sense, reason, insight are empty words to them."

James: "That's all well and good, but remarkable coming from a poet. I, the poet claims, see the murderous omnipotence of the imagination. You, my listeners, have to take cognizance of it. You have to see beyond imagination so that you won't deceive yourselves into thinking it is you who act and make history."

Edward: "So we're left with history minus human beings!"

Gordon: "Minus so-called free and independent actions.— Action: a word that is as grand as it is obscure."

Edward: "What do you mean?"

Gordon: "An obscure word. I've struggled with it a lot in creating characters in my books. Are they really the steam that powers the engine, or aren't they rather cogs, levers in the machinery?"

Edward: "So we do not act? So we're not even on the stage at all?"

Lord Crenshaw squinted. Then he said gloomily: "We know nothing of ourselves. I sometimes have the feeling that we are puppets. Whoever holds the strings is behind the scenes, far off, in the clouds."

Edward: "Puppets. You'd go that far, would you?"

"The longer you live, the clearer this becomes to you. You have more and more distance on yourself. You give up. You're no match for whatever it is there behind the scenes."

How dramatically the huge, glowing figure near the fireplace had changed in these few minutes. Dejected, all the starch gone out of him, Gordon Allison stretched his legs and stared blankly into space.

Edward: "So the fact of the matter is that human beings don't exist."

"You've put your finger on it. That's the be all and end all of wisdom. And if you find that a pity—well, so do I."

Edward: "And what if there were such a thing as a human being?"

"There isn't, Edward. Take my word for it."

When Alice knocked at Edward's door the next morning and went in, he was sitting up in bed; but at the sight of her he flung himself back down again, as if he were angry. She had his breakfast tray in her hand and put it on his table: "Edward."

He had pulled the covers over his head.

"What have I done, Edward?"

He threw the covers back.

"Why do you come all the time? Why doesn't Father come? Why hasn't he come once, not a single time? Do you realize that he hasn't been in my room one single time since I've been home?"

"He came a couple of times the first few weeks."

"With the doctor. Not once has he found his way here of his own accord."

"But I'll come as often as you like, Edward. I'll be a positive nuisance to you. And Kathleen comes, too."

"Why doesn't he dare to come?"

"It's hard for him to move about. He has his habits."

"He just doesn't have any time for his son."

"We've been going to his study for weeks now, and he has been telling his story for you, for you alone. Why is it so important that he come to your room?"

Edward took her hands, looked at her piercingly.

"Mother, he wants to deceive me. That's what he wants. But he won't succeed. Maybe he wants to fool himself. He won't succeed at that either. He is afraid. Why is he afraid of me?" He squeezed Alice's hands. "Bring him here to me. I want to sit down with him, face to face. We'll hash out our problem together."

"What is this all about, for heaven's sake?"

"I came back from the war minus more than just my stupid, torn-off leg. I came back without myself. My soul was stolen from me, too. I know Father's story about Lord Crenshaw who can't find his identity. He doesn't find his true self, but every now and then he finds something. I have nothing, nothing but a vacuum and always this awful fear, and then dreams about people attacking me. Do you call that living? You've got to help me. If you can, you've got to help me."

"Edward, my dear, my beloved son, you are sick. We didn't make you sick."

"You're giving yourself away, Mother."

"What do you mean by that, Edward? You're mad."

His eyes followed her as she went to the window.

"You're in league with him, Mother. Against me. Now he's lying, saying we don't exist at all. We're just puppets."

She wrung her hands.

"You see your son suffering, and you don't come to his aid. You had me come here. Why did you do it?"

She sat down in a wicker chair near the window and buried her face in her hands. "How can I help? Dear Father in heaven, how can I help?"

She moaned: "My dear son, my poor boy, what can I do? I'll gladly make any sacrifice you ask of me."

"You just say that. You don't really go out of your way the least bit. You know that yourself. That's why you come to see me all the time. You make some puny gesture in the right direction, then you sit there and contemplate the matter for a while and kid yourself into thinking you've done all you can. And he, he doesn't let anything get near him. And he's so frightened, Mother, so frightened, so empty. What's the matter with him? What's the matter with both of you?"

Stunned, she looked at him: "Nothing, Edward."

"What does he mean when he says we're victims of our imaginations? He isn't happy. Since when? Since I came into the house?"

"Edward, he is friendlier than ever. He spends more time with Kathleen and me than he used to. And he wants to hear every day in great detail how you are."

"That's called reconnaissance. He's sending his patrols out. He wants to know how secure his own position is."

In despair she walked up and down in front of his bed.

"I'm hurting you, Mother. Forgive me."

*   *   *

On the day after this conversation, Gordon Allison came to Alice with a request. While she was in his room arranging and dusting books and magazines, he stood at the open window and sometimes went out onto the balcony and took some fresh snow in his hand. Then he asked her permission to say something. He said he would have no objections if they put an end to their story-telling sessions.

He looked tired and run down. Alice thought it out of the question to stop the evening gatherings. She asked him to consider what kind of an impression that would make on Edward.

"Why? What is he getting out of them? Are they supposedly doing him some good?"

She asked him to sit down, and she shut the window.

He: "Tell him I'm exhausted. The evenings wear me out. You know, Alice, how foreign this kind of socializing is to me."

"We're doing it for Edward."

"Ask the doctor if he can't think of something different."

"Gordon, Edward himself wants to do it."

"Then please count me out."

"I don't mean to press you, Gordon, but is it Edward's manner that wears you down? He's sick."

"I know he is. But I don't understand the kind of sickness he has. And the doctor can't explain it to me either. You must realize yourself that he's getting on everybody's nerves. I tell myself to put up with it. I have amends to make to him. There's a lot I neglected to do in the past. And I hoped I could make it up to him."

"I'm happy to hear that, Gordon. That makes me very happy."

"So we should continue? Do we have to, Alice?"

She said under her breath: "Yes."

"Can't you let him know that I'm glad to have him here with us—he mustn't have the slightest doubt about that—but that I find certain aspects of his behavior very wearing, his way of asking questions and so on?"

"I can't say that to him. I can't even wish that."

"Wish what?"

"That he would stop struggling the way he is. It's his illness, and this is his way of fighting it."

Gordon, angrily: "What's all this chatter about clarity and truth? I flatly reject the insinuation that unclarity and untruth prevail here in this house. Is my house a den of thieves?"

"Gordon!"

"Let him come out in the open with his accusations, and I won't hide anything from him. Tell him that. It's up to you. Otherwise you'll be to blame."

"To blame?"

"To blame for—how can I say it?—for undermining our domestic peace, which I daresay is of some consequence to you, too."

"Is war between us the price we have to pay for his cure?"

Gordon: "Ask yourself that question. Talk to him. He doesn't listen to me. I don't have any credit with him. I never have had any, and I still don't. I'd hoped that I might someday."

Alice sat thinking for a long time.

"Come to the evenings, Gordon. I beg you. As a favor to me. Do it for my sake."

Her fingernails were digging into her palms. He was standing in front of her, searching for her eyes with his own. She managed to get control of herself. She looked up at him, her face open to him.

"So that's what you want, Alice? That's what you want from me?"

She stood up to his sad, uneasy gaze: "Yes."

His eyes scanned her face: "It's very hard."

"Do it, Gordon."

James Mackenzie

THE four of them were not alone in Gordon Allison's house at the time. The mild, quiet Alice, who floated wraithlike about the house, had felt compelled to appeal to her brother, James Mackenzie, who lived in X and worked as a director of a department in the university library there. She had asked him to come for a visit. And so this bachelor professor was now living in the house. He had taken a leave of absence to complete a study on the ancient Celts.

Alice had long, heated discussions with him in the guest room, in her boudoir, or, weather permitting, in the garden (not, however, where Edward could see them).

Professor Mackenzie, four years older than Alice and similar to her in build, in the fineness of his features, in his obliging manner, listened attentively, as he always did, and was cautious in his statements. He was a well-to-do man of the world who had selected his esoteric field out of enthusiasm for it and so he would have something to do. He responded to his sister's preoccupations as one would expect an educated man to respond to such things. He reassured her and believed not a word of what she told him about Edward and his illness. A female diagnosis. He had been away traveling a lot; he knew his sister and brother-in-law's home only superficially. Furthermore, he had a horror of family affairs. What Alice was saying struck him as totally bizarre. Strange what his sister could come up with. But she had always had a poetic nature not quite of this world. She had let herself become infected with her son's hysteria.

What stuff the delicate, refined Alice was revealing here, or thought she had to invent. In any case, his sister's fabrications proved her to be a true woman, a category he had never assigned her to before. She had always had an aesthetic, imaginative streak; that's why she had been so taken with Gordon Allison. But now she was projecting her fantasies onto reality, spinning some yarn around Gordon and Edward. James

131

was glad he was not in Gordon's shoes. As with all myths, this expert
noted, the actual events that gave rise to them lay far in the past.
Therefore, he suggested to his sister, her memory was deceiving her.
The facts of the matter were quite different from what she remembered.
Who could ever know what actually happened without documentation?
And then why bother? They had obviously put these problems behind
them, cured those illnesses.

Then she turned to Edward. James thought her psychological assess-
ment ridiculous. This kind of psychologizing had assumed epidemic proportions these days; she should not waste his time with such twaddle.
And taking the boy into the house: "You brought him here, Alice.
What on earth did you think you were doing?"

"You talk the way Gordon does. I thought you would be on my
side."

"So tell me, why did you bring him here? He was well cared for in
the clinic, and here he makes the rest of you sick."

"He does not. On the contrary. You don't understand at all. Besides,
I wanted to have him. It was my decision, and I'll stick by it."

He shrugged his shoulders. There you are. The poetic impulse has
subsided in her, so now she does her poetizing on living flesh. Poor
Gordon.

She pressed her handkerchief to her eyes. She could see he was not
going to let anything rob him of his equanimity.

Difficult weeks for Alice. She was back at the beginning again. Had
she chosen the right path? Should she follow it? Should she—risk her
life? But heaven had sent her this sign, Edward, her son, who was seeking the truth, who wanted everything clear and above board. He was
suffering from untruth, just as she had suffered from it.

Alice lived in horrible turmoil during these weeks after she realized
that James would fail her and that she was alone. If she did not act this
time, when would she?

She cried and prayed like a girl. She begged for illumination. Sometimes when she woke in the morning, she found the same litany running
through her mind: What am I doing? What is it I want to do? Am I
dreaming? Why don't I give Edward up, send him back to the clinic?
Why am I destroying my own peace of mind and Gordon's and everyone else's? This is mad, satanic. Satan is tempting me.

Contrite, she got up and spoke prayers of repentance.

And then she found herself sitting in a chair, thinking, her fists clenched: Edward is making me ill. But all she needed to do was let her guard down for an instant and thoughts of hatred and vengeance boiled up in her again, screaming and howling: freedom, truth, clarity!

And Alice trembled with delight. She felt strong again.

This is what Alice was going through, a woman feeling her way toward the turning point of her life.

Gordon Finds Some Allies

ALICE had turned away Gordon's attempt—and it was an attempt often repeated—to lock the door to his library and bury himself in his work, even in the evening. The talk wandered without direction. Everyone seemed pleased to be able to talk freely (though still within the bounds of society's rules).

Gordon, having made a major contribution—and one duly recognized as such—with his story, felt a need for rest. Pleading exhaustion, he asked for and received the company's permission to leave the room when he felt the need to; and when he was present and took part, he spoke in subdued and kindly tones. He was displaying, in his own style, a wisdom and mildness that asked others to display these same qualities in return. The evenings passed in normal, almost cozy small talk.

That changed one evening, however, when the painter MacLyne appeared, late, as usual, and remarked that the conversation was flowing on unchecked by a story. Then he sat down next to Kathleen, greeted Lord Crenshaw (who gave him a friendly nod), and dubbed himself "king of the illusionists."

"Yes," he went on to explain, "we are illusionists. We don't kid ourselves. There's no such thing as seriousness."

He was in high spirits. He had, as he announced, just received a commission from a well-known steel magnate to decorate his nearby country house with some murals.

"He has given me an absolutely free hand. He knows my paintings, and I've explained my principles to him. I presented them to him as the only truly advanced and enlightened principles there are, and he agreed with me. The man has had enough of his cannons. We can all see well enough what the result of shooting and air raids is. So I'll be doing murals for his mansion. He said he wants it to be his monastery to which he can retire later, leaving his work completely behind."

Gordon Allison: "What is he manufacturing now?"

134

MacLyne: "Vacuum cleaners and things like that, parts for machines. No cannons, no rifles, none of that stuff anymore."

Gordon, politely: "There's no demand for them at the moment."

"That may be. But nothing obliges him to have my kind of murals in his house. He could just as well get himself some classical or religious paintings. He has enough money to buy original classics. But he has become a convinced illusionist. He said to me in his office: 'Nobody can pull the wool over my eyes. Everything is image, propaganda. Everything is thought up by certain people. It doesn't much matter what you choose to do. There's no such thing as a rational direction or order that everyone can adhere to. And when people are at loggerheads and at one another's throats, it's force of arms that decides who's right. Sad but true.' He was much relieved when I told him about illusionism."

One might have expected that Crenshaw would have been interested and pleased to find a disciple. But Allison did not take the bait. He murmured, "Hmm, hmm," and asked whether the industrialist was commissioning MacLyne to do some murals for his factory, too.

"I said his house."

Allison: "I know. But if he's a convert to illusionism, then you should urge him to have illusionistic murals in his factory, too. He should convert his workers. I'd like to know how he'd react to this suggestion."

MacLyne, stupid and amazed:

"Why put murals in factories?"

Gordon: "The workers look at the pictures, and somebody explains them to the workers if they don't understand them."

"And then?"

Gordon looked around the room and beamed. "And then you wait and see what will happen." He laughed heartily. "To tell you the truth: The workers will not understand the pictures and your explanation of them even less. And if they finally do come to understand them, ha ha, then they'll be so busy laughing—the way I am right now—that they won't be able to work."

Bewildered, MacLyne looked around him helplessly: "But didn't you say yourself, Mr. Allison—"

Allison interrupted him harshly: "What did I say? I said nothing, MacLyne. I swear to you I said nothing. And if you think you heard me say anything even faintly resembling what you've been saying, then you've heard very wrong."

MacLyne: "But I didn't hear wrong, Mr. Allison. You said, you told—"

"My young friend, whatever I said, whatever I told, please leave it said and told. I did not preach any illusionism. What I offered was an insight, an awareness that is not so easy to come by. It was, first, not illusionism and, second, nothing you can use to paint walls with, especially not in the mansion of this patron of the arts whom we all know quite well and who made all his money producing cannons as fast as he could. Have I, ladies and gentlemen, preached anything of the kind?"

"No," the assembly responded, and then proceeded to tear the painter apart mercilessly. They ridiculed him without pity. They refused to listen to him—until finally he threw in the towel and, to general applause, turned his attention to the platter of cakes.

With a nudge from Alice, Kathleen joined him. That comforted him, and he tried to clarify for her what Lord Crenshaw didn't seem to have grasped correctly. For as far as abstract painting was concerned, that is to say, nonimitative painting . . . Kathleen understood what her duty was, and armed with tea and cake, she retired with him to a corner of the room.

With that, the incident seemed to be over, and the evening that had begun so pleasantly as an uncomplicated gathering for tea and cakes would have run its peaceful course if—one hesitates to say as a grand finale—a gentleman who had come as the doctor's guest had not put in his two cents' worth. Up to now this short, fat, woolly-headed, comical-looking, asthmatic man had done nothing but gasp for breath and consume large quantities of tea and cake. But now, as the evening was nearing its end, he seemed to have something on his mind that he had to unburden himself of. He made whispered inquiries of the doctor about certain guests but could not make up his mind to speak for a long time. Neither Lord Crenshaw nor Edward stirred.

Finally, when it had become quite late indeed, he could contain himself no longer and began speaking in a rapid and precise monotone. He wanted to come back to the debate over illusionism, he said. Illusionism was passivism, and passivism was no route to knowledge. "How could it be? Wars and revolutions, how could passivism explain their origins? Because the passivist is nothing but a spectator, he thinks they simply come and go. Of course they come and go. But what fuels them and how they arise doesn't interest the passivist. All he cares about is his own unreal idea of them. But wars, revolutions, and all social changes have very specific material causes. And with them our complacent illusionist wants nothing to do. Foxy as he is, he is not as completely the illusionist as he would have us believe. He knows there are certain things he'd best not look at too closely. Anyone who makes a living from a given social order will avoid casting a bright light on it. Mysticism, a partial or total obscuring of the facts, philosophy, mythology—these suit his purposes better. And illusionism belongs in this category."

In the corner where Kathleen had led the painter, she held him firmly by the arm and said, "Let's stay here. They're not talking about illusionism anymore."

MacLyne gulped down the cake that she was stuffing into him; then he burst out with a question: Were the speaker's remarks meant to apply to abstract, nonimitative painting, too?

The asthmatic, pugnacious gentleman: "I'm not familiar with that kind of painting. But if there is such a thing, then my remarks apply to it, too. If it exists, it would be a prize example of reactionary behavior. Removing objects from the world is about as far as you can go in that direction."

"We do it for artistic reasons, to make art free and pure."

"You'd do better to shoot yourself. Then you'd be absolutely free."

MacLyne: "I don't follow you. Excuse me, but what was your name?"

The man, unflustered: "Roddy O'Dowall. I'll explain what I mean, Mr.—what was your name?"

"MacLyne."

"Let me tell you, Mr. MacLyne, that poets, artists, and philosophers have always been in league to perpetuate rotten social orders from which they have profited. They do it of their own accord or on commission from cannon manufacturers, as you informed us earlier. There are any number of ways you can explain and glorify the society we live in to give it the appearance of strength and solidity. You can, for example, direct attention away from it and toward heaven if there is too much on earth that is unpleasant to look at, and so on. Or you can do away with things, objects, altogether and make the world completely empty the way your painting apparently does. Nothing but colors and lines; that, of course, is the epitome. You'll do very nicely with that stuff, Mr. MacLyne. But, if you'll forgive me for saying so, it is the height of comedy and, forgive me again, of hypocrisy."

The painter, coldly: "I stand for an artistic principle. I'm not destroyed by criticisms like yours."

O'Dowall: "I know. You are liberating art from the five senses, from concepts, from things. That's why I said before that an even more radical approach would be to shoot yourself. Then you wouldn't have to deal with color either.''

"But I want color. Color is what's most important to me.''

"Most important to you? For what?''

"For painting a picture. For creating a work of art.''

O'Dowall: "With color? Nobody will object too strenuously to that. Why not paint walls with bright colors instead of papering them? You can even dress up in all the colors of the rainbow, though we usually do that only at costume balls. It's fun and creates a festive atmosphere. But you're talking about something else. You're talking about art and intelligence. If that's art, then we're all artists. What does your kind of art have to do with intelligence? How can it have anything to do with it? Intelligence is deliberately excluded from it. Your art that consists of nothing but colors stimulates the retina only and goes no farther. Titillation for aesthetes and spectators who don't want to be bothered with anything more. It is art par excellence for two types of people: the totally disinterested, such as the tenured, the pensioned, the retired, who have already feathered their nests and have no further reason for living; and, on the other hand, for the totally interested, people like your cannon king who wants to see the world hollowed out from the inside so nobody will watch too closely what he's up to. What you do is just fine with them, your line and color stuff, your gravy without meat and potatoes. Or in literature, any kind of far-fetched story that has nothing to do with anybody's life is fine, too, just so long as it doesn't ask why people have to work for less than subsistence wages, why they have to live in substandard housing, why there are wars and air raids on our cities.

"As for the abstract, the pure art you talk about, Mr. MacLyne, I've run into proponents of it before. They haven't been able to hawk their ideas with me around. All you have to do is step on these sensitive fellows' toes, and they start shrieking and betraying their bad consciences.''

The painter cast outraged glances around the circle (he looked to Lord Crenshaw, too, but the lord, probably not yet clear himself about how to turn away this attack, merely folded his arms), and when no one came to his aid, MacLyne hissed, "You don't hear me shrieking, Mr. O'Dowall. And I don't have a bad conscience either. I just don't see things as simplistically as you do.''

The new social critic gestured toward the immobile master of the house:

"Mr. Allison knows what I'm talking about. He unmasked your patron, the steel maker, when he pointed out the inconsistency in owning cannon factories and having a house decorated with your murals. But the inconsistency is only superficial. In reality, cannon factories and illusionism make the best of bedfellows."

The room fell silent. Everyone stared into his teacup. Neither the tone nor the subject of the debate was appropriate here. Throats were cleared. Short, fat Roddy O'Dowall saw that he had done what he had set out to do, and he took his leave.

Then Alice and Kathleen, one after the other, went up to Gordon Allison, who sat strangely absorbed in his own thoughts, all trace of good cheer gone.

Because I Want Honesty

BUT the image of his father sitting there, lost in thought, twiddling his thumbs, stayed with Edward in his room. It followed him into the night. Lost in thought, he sat there, looking at no one.

But how right he is to turn his back on crass reality.

My friends, my dead friends, my comrades, the silent dead—torn away from trees, from breathing, from eating and drinking, from life in your bodies, from life with us—you are not dead. We submerge ourselves in your world, a spirit world. Father said it. He didn't know how truly he spoke.

Will I find them again? Am I not in touch with them again when I think about them?

What does that mean: to think about them? Perhaps nothing more than to draw near them. I keep them with me.

Oh, if only I could remain true to you forever! Is loyalty forbidden to us? Meetings in spirit. Dreams are not dreams; for nothing exists, nothing can enter into our lives except in the form of thought; and thought borders on dream.

Again Edward saw his father sitting there. Kathleen and his mother hovered over him.

How defeated he is. Why is he so defeated? Because he is defenseless, and that after starting off so grandly.

An odd idea: Truth and being are rooted in thought.

What joy it is, then, to think about them, those no longer with us, and to call to them and be together with them. Dead but not gone. I can invite them, and they appear. Oh, I will celebrate them.

And secretly, without letting anyone else know, Edward celebrated his dead friends in the following days. He cultivated something like Chinese ancestor worship but without all the self-effacing ritual. His was a friendly, cordial welcoming of guests, marked by attentiveness and hospitality.

140

This gave him a firmer equilibrium. He became calmer and more alert.

And at the next evening gathering, after the guests had settled in with some preliminary small talk, Edward asked his mother to move the tall floor lamp by the wall closer to him. He had brought something this evening. The group's attention turned to him.

Once the lamp stood at the son's head and the bright light fell onto his couch, the young, broad-shouldered man, aided by his mother, cautiously raised himself up on the sofa. Now, with Edward in the spotlight, people noticed for the first time that he was wearing his hair rather long and was sprouting a small beard. He had a strange look about him. He bore a striking resemblance to his mother. The broad, low forehead he may have had from his father. Now, with the one foot left to him, he felt about tentatively on the floor until he found the place he wanted for it. With strangely jerky and imprecise motions Edward tucked the blanket that covered his lower body in around him. His mother pulled it together behind his back.

"I've understood only now what Father was saying: We are utterly helpless; we don't know what we are doing. We think we act; indeed, we want to act, but in reality we do not act at all. We do not accomplish what we set out to do. And then he explained, too, what it is that acts instead of us: fantasies, ideas, prevailing intellectual systems that take on the form of custom in a given period. Have I understood you correctly, Father?"

Gordon was all attention now and signaled approval to his son with both hands: "Absolutely. Better than I understood myself."

He laughed; the others joined in. The mother sat bent over, her left elbow on her knee, her forehead resting in her hand, her eyes on the floor.

"But I can't accept this view. Something is missing in it. Father pointed an accusing finger at that pathetic steel and cannon magnate who wants to delude himself and evade responsibility for his actions. Responsibility has no place in his theory. But aren't we responsible beings, Father?"

Lord Crenshaw sighed and cast a kindly look around him. "Ask the others, Son. I can't answer that. All I can say is how things look to me. We try to explain them as best we can."

Edward wrinkled his brow.

His mother jumped up and shoved a cushion under his left arm, which he was using to prevent himself from tilting over. She hitched him closer to the armrest of the sofa. He was holding a slim blue volume in his hand.

"What counts is that we get to the truth. Even if the truth devours us. But I don't think the truth can harm us.— How do we get at the truth? I found among my books this little volume by the nineteenth-century Danish theologian Kierkegaard. The book has been standing on my shelves for a long time. I bought it once but then never looked at it. But now I've been reading in it. It confirms my views. And since I lack the imagination to tell a story, may I read two pages from this book?"

The guests all agreed. They were delighted to see him so lively. What a fresh, brisk breeze was blowing toward them now out of the war. The world had experienced fire and air raids, flight, fear, and pain. All that lay on people, a heavy, dreary burden, a mass they had to carry. They dragged themselves around under it and were crippled by it. But no one could say what it was they were carrying or why or what in the world it was that kept ailing them. They had managed so far. They were so dulled and depressed that they could not even ask the right question, this key question that affected them all.

Edward, returned from the war, almost dead but saved after all, a young man with the beginnings of a full brown beard, sat before them, palpable, credible. And with refreshing, implacable honesty, he asked this question of them and of himself. They hung on his words.

"This Kierkegaard, as the foreword says, got into a battle with the Protestant church in his country in 1855. And in this battle he wrote:

"'What do I want? Quite simply: I want honesty. I am not a Christian severity as opposed to a Christian leniency.

"'By no means. I am neither leniency nor severity. I am—a human honesty. The leniency which is the common Christianity in the land I want to place alongside of the New Testament in order to see how these two are related to one another.

"'Then, if it appears, if I or another can prove, that it can be maintained face to face with the New Testament, then with the greatest joy will I agree to it.

"'But one thing I will not do, not for anything in the world. I will not by suppression, or by performing tricks, try to produce the impression that the ordinary Christianity in the land and the Christianity of the New Testament are alike.

"'Behold, this it is I do not want. And why not? Well, because I want honesty.'"

When Edward paused momentarily and let the book he was holding up in front of him drop to his knees, Mr. O'Dowall's matter-of-fact voice broke the intent silence.

"What does all this effort on behalf of Christianity, an effort by the by that I personally find quite pointless, have to do with our questions about passivity and about the obfuscation of objective fact?"

"Mr. O'Dowall," Kathleen snapped at him, "Edward has the floor."

Mr. O'Dowall, as if he hadn't heard her: "The question of honesty has no place at all in our discussion. We take for granted that every one of us forms his judgments according to his best knowledge and in keeping with his conscience."

Edward nodded. "You're right, absolutely right. And now I'd like to read the conclusion Kierkegaard comes to. It will be of interest to everyone, regardless of his basic position. Kierkegaard wants the truth at any price. He won't tolerate any kind of blinders. He insists on the truth even if it means the ruination of the church. He refuses to bargain away his obligations, the obligations and privileges that are his birthright. He says he does not want to create the impression that Christianity in his country is like the Christianity of the New Testament.

"'Behold, this it is I do not want. And why not? Well, because I want honesty.

"'Or, if you wish me to talk in another way—well then, it is because I believe that, if possibly even the very extremest softening down of Christianity may hold good in the judgment of eternity, it is impossible that it should hold good when even artful tricks are employed to gloss over the difference between the Christianity of the New Testament and this softened form.

"'What I mean is this:

"'If a man is known for his graciousness—very well then, let me venture to ask him to forgive me all my debt; but even though his grace were divine grace, this is too much to ask, if I will not even be truthful about how great the debt is.

"'And this in my opinion is the falsification of which official Christianity is guilty: It does not frankly and unreservedly make known the Christian requirement—perhaps because it is afraid people would shudder to see at what a distance from it we are living, without being able to claim that in the remotest way our life might be called an effort in the direction of fulfilling the requirement.

"'Or (merely to take one example of what is everywhere present in the New Testament): When Christ requires us to save our life eternally and to hate our own life in this world, is there then a single one among us whose life in the remotest degree could be called even the weakest effort in this direction? And perhaps there are thousands of "Christians" in the land who are not so much as aware of this requirement. So then we "Christians" are living, and are loving our life, just in the ordinary human sense.'"

Edward glanced over at Mr. O'Dowall.

"I'd like to check with you, Mr. O'Dowall, to see if you want to interject something here. Since honesty is what we're after, I want to be sure you get a fair hearing."

"Thank you. I am not the only person in the world who advocates the position I do. We do not talk about the demands of Christianity but rather the demands of society. In society—and I needn't rehearse any proof of this—Christianity represents a single, ideological source of power that has produced a specific organization within society, namely, the church, the churches. But whether Christianity or one of the churches requires this or that is clearly a matter that has to be left to the members of that organization to decide for themselves. Whether Christianity makes demands and what demands it makes are matters of indifference to nonbelievers. I would therefore suggest that we dispense with this detour and speak concretely about war and the causes of war, that we get our feet on the ground again. That is my suggestion. It is practical; it lies within our capabilities; it is immensely instructive, indeed, necessary. We must by all means prevent our inquiry into war guilt and the causes of war from being sidetracked into the blind alley of sermonizing."

Kathleen protested softly but energetically. "But we all want Edward to continue reading. We already know what you think."

Mr. O'Dowall snorted scornfully.

Mr. O'Dowall made an angry face.

Edward: "Kierkegaard doesn't preach any sermons. He takes the question of responsibility, of guilt, seriously, no matter what the area of concern is. With your permission, I'll read some more. Perhaps my point will become even clearer.

"'If then by "grace" God will nevertheless regard us as Christians, one thing at least must be required: that we, being precisely aware of the requirement, have a true conception of how infinitely great is the grace that is showed us. "Grace" cannot possibly stretch so far, one thing it must never be used for, it must never be used to suppress or to diminish the requirement.

"'Honesty to Christianity demands that one call to mind the Christian requirement of poverty, which is not a capricious whim of Christianity, but is because only in poverty can it be truly served.'"

Edward interrupted his reading here. "And now comes a passage that will impress everyone, one that cuts to the quick; for this Kierkegaard is no true believer of the kind I suspect some here think him to be. He is like us, someone who analyzes and questions and analyzes again and subjects everything to the tribunal of his conscience, his razor-sharp intelligence, and his struggling soul. You can present him with anything you like. He'll walk around it, feel of it, rap on it, put his ear to it. Sometimes he reminds you of Socrates in his directness and clarity. But the difference between him and Socrates is in the passionateness of his inquiry. Kierkegaard has a special kind of honesty that cannot be mollified and cannot be satisfied with any answer but does not bog down in resignation either, in having to go without answers. He presses on as though possessed even though he knows his efforts will come to naught. The way Kierkegaard leaps from question to question, jumps down from one to another, calls any answer he gets into doubt, the way he leaps on and accomplishes nothing and knows nothing—that has something of fear about it, something of vertigo, something of a fall into an abyss."

(Alice turned around and caught Kathleen's glance. They both understood that in this portrait of the restless questioner Edward was portraying himself.)

"His passion," Edward continued, "can take any number of directions. It is conscience, our Christian conscience, that we carry within us like spiritual viscera—stomach, intestines, spleen, liver—without even realizing it. What makes this passion so restless that it can never be satisfied is something like the Fall, a burning guilt that cannot be extinguished and that cannot be swept aside, a guilt that is part of our nature and was unknown to old Socrates. This passion of the conscience" (Edward did not let up. He pressed on and on. Alice got up, horrified, and slipped away toward the door. She couldn't stand any more.) "This passion, as I see it, has two roots in Kierkegaard; and that is why the conscience is so important in him and in everyone like him, why it's so caustic, so crimson, so bitingly paprika red. The conscience wants, first of all, to find the truth, the whole truth, and spread out every fiber of the soul before it so as to hide nothing from it, so as to be bleached by it, I'm tempted to say. And then what it wants, what it wants next, is to run away, run head over heels. Yes, that's another aspect of conscience. To run from sinfulness, from the unbearable burden of original sin. Why do we search so frantically? To hide the fact that we have already found something. It is so obvious. We know that all we have to do is take one small step, just reach out and pick the truth up. But we don't dare touch it."

Edward mumbled something.

O'Dowall's unsubtle voice: "And what is this truth we need only pick up?"

Alice whispered sharply from the doorway: "Don't bother him, for God's sake. Let him speak."

Edward: "What was the small step Kierkegaard had to take? To believe."

He said "Hmm" a couple of times and reached for his book again.

"Kierkegaard writes, 'I want honesty.

"'If that is what the human race or this generation wants, if it will honorably, honestly, openly, frankly, directly rebel against Christianity, if it will say to God, "We can but we will not subject ourselves to this power"—but note that this must be done honorably, honestly, openly, frankly, directly—very well then, strange as it may seem, I am with them; for honesty is what I want.

"'For this honesty I am ready to take the risk.

"'Just suppose the case, suppose that quite literally I were to become a sacrifice: I would not even in that case be a sacrifice for Christianity, but because I wanted honesty.

"'Yea, this I know, that it has His consent that in a world of Christians there is one man who says, "I dare not call myself a Christian, but I want honesty, and I will venture unto the end."'"

Now Edward, who had held himself upright quite well, closed the book very slowly. It slid down the blanket and onto the rug. His mother shoved the lamp far back from him. And Edward lay in the darkness again, leaning sideways and held by his mother. She carefully helped him lie down.

Silence.

The father: "And how far did this honesty make him go? What did he risk for it?"

Edward's voice from the darkness: "He died in a hospital. He had some friends and disciples. One or the other of them left the church. Later, I read, his work drew a great deal of attention, and he has been a major influence on theologians."

The asthmatic materialist, the adversary: "On theologians. On whom else? You said he lived in the mid–nineteenth century. Since then mankind has produced two world wars, which shows that his impact was minimal. And why was it minimal? That's easy. An appeal for honesty cannot influence history any more than Mr. MacLyne's colorful paintings on factory walls can influence manufacturing or even manufacturers for that matter. People listen to the appeal, then go about their business. Why? Because things are stronger than we are and than what we think about them. A factory has its inherent laws. The workers want to make a living; they have families to feed. The factory owner wants to earn a living and, on top of that, make money and expand his plant. The technicians have their special skills, and they want to make use of them. They perfect this or that method, and before you know it you have new products. And the market is ready to absorb them. There are buyers, sellers, and middlemen, all doing their jobs, and there are advertising and newspapers, huge concerns with hundreds of employees and machines that have to be kept working. There are printers, typesetters, distribution offices, newsboys. That is only a small fragment, only a sketch of the 'thing' that thought has to cope with. What use is 'honesty' up against odds like that?"

Alice's brother, the elegant Professor Mackenzie, spoke in tones tinged with irony. "And that is nothing compared with the state, which is shored up by government, the royal house in power for centuries, the army, the civil service, Parliament with both its houses, and the entire nation with its hundreds of agencies, its police, its courts and churches. What kind of dent can honesty make on all that, Edward?"

O'Dowall, the adversary, spoke the epilogue. "Kierkegaard found out himself. He died, and a few of his friends left the church. Then, not much later, at the turn of the century, electricity was commercially developed. The face of the world was changed, by electricity, not by honesty. The economy experienced an incredible boom. We entered the era of full-scale industrial capitalism and its imperialistic phase, and two world wars followed."

Edward, as everyone looked toward him expectantly: "And now we're sitting here, waiting for the sequel, the next world war. Our role is to wait. I've read that the physicists and chemists are already preparing our fate in their laboratories. The mysterious gods of old have been replaced by knowledgeable people from our midst."

Gordon's weary voice: "And what do you want, Edward?"

"Honesty. The physicists and chemists aren't the only people in the world. The old gods have been dethroned, the ones who supposedly shaped our fate. But it wasn't they who shaped it. Now it seems to be the physicists and chemists' turn to claim the honor due the gods. They appear to be regarded as an earthly Providence, but they are not Providence. They are people like you and me. At last the gods have actually come down to earth where we can get a good look at them and throw a monkey wrench in their works. But Kierkegaard wants knowledge and honesty. And he wants to know so that he can act. Speaking is a kind of action, too. He knows life, and he wants to have an effect on it—at least on that part of it that touches him directly—and not admit of any fates. He feels bound by conscience to do that. And now the question I would ask both schools of thought represented here, the school of fantasy and the school of things, is: Is there really such a thing as a human being? Or is he like the lion on Mount Mondora who threw himself into the water and did battle with an insubstantial phantom, a reflection that mocked him. What are we all about?"

It was terrible to hear him, for what the others had said could be taken as theoretical discussion. But here a man spoke from the heart.

He was skirting an abyss (everyone could see that), and he was calling for help. And as this listener, then that one, heard him, they trembled not for him but for themselves.

Everyone sat locked in the silence in which no answer to his question came. Perhaps it only seemed long. Alice stepped in. She sat down next to Edward and whispered with him. Then the others moved and broke the spell. The adversary, the materialist, could have said: There we have a confirmation of my thesis. The word, a true and honest word, was spoken among us, but we disregarded it. For behold, the word was spoken at a tea party made up of six to eight people in Gordon Allison's house; and despite the word this tea party remained a tea party by virtue of the ambience, the tea, the cakes, and the conviviality. All that devoured the honest word, and the guests were soon chatting again and happily rattling their teaspoons. And Kathleen went around the room offering cigarettes.

At the Cathedral in Naumburg

EDWARD gave his mother no peace. He continued his interrogation. What had made her go to France? Why had she gone looking for him? What for? In what way could he help her?

She was evasive. But she had to say something, so she began to tell about the mother who stood by the cathedral in Naumburg.

"I went to Germany, too, to look for you.

"And here, too, an old woman is standing near a church. But this is not Montmartre. This is a defeated country, a small city. The Cathedral of Naumburg in Germany. She has been standing for a long time. Now she goes to a bench on the street and sits there, her scarf tied on her head. On the square in front of her and on the broad streets people are passing through. Why is she sitting here? She has no appointment to meet anyone.

"The people continue to stream by, marching in huge columns, some in small, stray groups, soldiers and civilians.

"Polish workers, Russian workers are going home. They are leaving; they pass through the city. Men in unfamiliar uniforms, French prisoners of war, they are going home, they are leaving.

"And who will come back to this country? To this country, like every other country? They were taken from here to Poland and Russia; in swamps and ice and snow they were shot, frozen to death. They were put on ships, in U-boats. Were they captured? Were they drowned? They were taken to Italy and Africa, into the heat, into the desert. Were they left lying in the sand, dead of thirst, dehydration? The world is a harsh place. The war lasted a long time.

"The woman is sitting on the bench, her scarf on her head. The war lasted a long time. We lost it. That's why the foreigners are leaving. They're leaving us alone. And now what will happen?

"There are already foreign soldiers in the city. People say: They're giving the orders now. There is no more Germany. We lost.

"Let them give orders. We've sacrificed everything we had. What more can anyone do to us?

"People come and sit down with the woman. She says:

"'I had three sons. One of them came back blind from the first war. He's dead now. The other two were killed in this war. They can be glad they're not coming back.'

"'We will not forget our heroes.'

"'Why were they taken off to these wars? Whose idea was it? Can you tell me? There has to be a reason for everything. My boys believed what they were told. They screamed victory, nothing but victory, and even from the front they wrote of nothing but victory. And now?'

"'What now?'

"'Were my boys supposed to have thought about the war? Did they start it? Did anyone ask their opinion? They had to obey orders and keep their mouths shut. Sir, you are trying to console me, but you can't console yourself. Tell me, sir, who was responsible for the war?'

"'What a question, for heaven's sake! The fatherland called. We followed our Führer!'

"'The kaiser in the first war, and we lost. The Führer in the second, and we lost again. Nobody asked my blind, dead son, or my other two either. But it was all right for them to go out and die.'

"'The fatherland.'

"'That's me, too. I'm the fatherland, too. And my boys are the fatherland.'

"'Where does that kind of talk get us? You don't know what you're saying. If we still had the Party, you'd be—'

"'I know. I'd be hanged. Little people are supposed to shut up. The fatherland is only the big shots. And now, sir, we're supposed to rebuild your houses for you so that you can sit back down at your tables and run our lives for us again.'

"She sat there. She watched the people passing by with their carts and sacks and packs, and she thought, full of hate: 'You're getting what you deserve. Even now you're still too dumb to see what's been done to you, you pigs. War is the right place for you. You deserve to be slaughtered.'

"And because the woman was sitting by the church, she had the idea, in her rage, of going inside and consulting the man in the pulpit whose sermons she had heard during the war, at first with her two sons, whom this same man had baptized and confirmed. What she had to say would be of particular interest to him, for he had been a great booster of the war effort.

"She was led into the sacristy, and the minister soon came out, and they sat down together.

"But she had hardly begun to speak when the old man sighed and, as she went on, shook his head.

"'Yes,' he said, 'it is our fault. The Lord is punishing us. Our sins are being visited upon us.'

"She stuck by her guns and insisted on knowing what she was to blame for, for no one had asked her. No one asked her son in the first war or her two younger sons in the second.

"'We are guilty, my good woman, all of us together. That is why we are being so sorely tried.'

"She screamed: 'I'm not guilty. If you're guilty, then you're guilty, but not me. It was you who stood up there in the pulpit and preached war to us. We just sat down below and listened.'

"He: 'I spoke as I had to to my congregation. We have a fatherland invested by God and authority over us, and we owe it loyalty and obedience.'

"'That's what you said, Pastor.'

"'Yes, and?'

"'Go out onto the street and look around. Read the papers. What have they brought us to, your God-given authority and obedience and whatnot? Where are we now? And you were the one who kept telling us to keep our mouths shut.'

"'You didn't have to listen.'

"'A fine minister you are. Who are we supposed to turn to?'

"'I think it's time you left.'

"'Sure, take the easy way out. You're a criminal, Pastor, a murderer.'

"'Get out.'

"'You won't say that to the Lord God in heaven.'

"She couldn't put this encounter behind her. She couldn't just let it be that she had gone into the sacristy and been thrown out. That was a strange kind of justice that lets the criminal, the guilty one, have the last word and takes the plaintiff by the scruff of his neck and throws him out the door.

"And so this mother began—this prosecutor not in official robes but in the skirts of a poor woman, a prosecutor without legal paragraphs in her head but with rage and pain in her heart—she began her search, acting as both police and prosecutor at once; and she sought out in their houses, one after the other, the people she suspected of being the guilty ones, the collaborators, the stooges, the opportunists.

"She went to the house of an industrialist whose signature had appeared on every wartime appeal to patriotism. She had to knock and ring for a long time at this handsome house before a kind of gardener finally appeared at the door and asked what she wanted. Surely she could see that no one was at home.

"'Where is the elegant gentleman who used to put in his appearance everywhere?'

"'He's in Switzerland. And what business is that of yours? What do you want?'

"'Well, well, not here, huh? Up and gone, and his lovely family, too, his lovely wife and his lovely children. All off for some skiing in the mountains, right?'

"'There's nobody home. And there's no begging allowed.'

"'All of them gone. I might have known. All of them abroad and very nicely fixed. They didn't take us along. They left us behind in the muck. We can stay here and lie in the bed they made for us. Tell me, what kind of a fool are you that you stoop low enough to play porter and watchdog for them?'

"'Clear out, or I'll call the police.'

"That's what he said to the mother, this pathetic man who was wearing a gardener's apron and had a spade in his hand. She wanted to hit him in the face, but he was just stupid and understood nothing. He hadn't understood anything in his whole life; and his elegant boss, that crook, had put him here for that very reason. Idiots like that were quite useful.

"Take a good look at him. You were an idiot like that yourself once.

"And she went on her way, this wandering angel of justice, pain and rage in her heart; and she was moved to take on one of those bigwigs who called themselves labor leaders and had run unions. Their last noteworthy contribution had been in the Workers' Front.

"It took a long time here, too, before anyone came to the door. The person inside wasn't taking any chances and had left the door chain in place. A woman's voice asked who was there and what they wanted. The mother gave her name. The woman still refused to let her in until she pressed very hard and said she had an urgent message to deliver. Then the woman inside unhooked the chain and let the mother into the hallway. Finally a man appeared. He had been sleeping and was in the process of putting his jacket on. His face was red, either from sleeping or from his agitation.

"The mother said it would be better not to stay in the hallway or everybody on the stairs would hear what they were saying.

"In the sitting room the mother asked the man for his ideas about things. There were no newspapers now, no way to get reliable information. Couldn't he share his views on what was going on out there?

"The broad-shouldered man had his jacket only halfway on. The other half of him stood there in his suspenders and looked first at the mother, then at his wife, then back at the mother again. He asked what in the world she was talking about.

"'You should be able to figure that out yourself. I've just told you. You were a big spokesman in the Workers' Front, and it was you who came and took my two sons out of the factory. The police don't seem to have paid you any surprise visits yet. So as long as you're still running around loose, I'd like to ask you what you think now about everything that's gone on so that I can make some sense out of it.'

"The fat man pulled his left arm out of his jacket and stood there in his shirt-sleeves, looking from the one woman to the other.

"'Did somebody send you here to ask me these questions?'

"'Of course somebody sent me. I'd never have had the nerve to come here on my own and call on an important man like you. There are thousands of us down there, and we want to know what's going to become of us now that everything is turned topsy-turvy. This question should be of special interest to you.'

"'Why?'

"'Because you are partially responsible for it. We wanted to ask what you think about it all now that the party is over. And what excuses you can make for yourself.'

"The fat man chewed on his mustache.

"'Where are the others?'

"'They're all waiting downstairs. They'll come up soon, one after the other. I'm just the first in line.'

"Then the man was afraid and ran into the next room and locked the door behind him. And his wife gave the mother such a hefty shove that she flew out into the hallway; and in the hall a second shove sent her out the apartment door. Then the man's wife shut that door, too, and slid the chain in place.

"The mother screamed: 'We'll get both of you!'

"Then she stomped down the stairs.

"Outside, in front of the house, she wondered whom she should turn to next as she watched the droves pass by in their rags.

"Then she had the good luck to happen on some soldiers who were hobbling out of a hospital with their canes and crutches.

"'How much disability pay will you get? Will they let you stay in the hospital a while?'

"'We don't know.'

"'And what will you do afterwards? When they throw you out of the hospital?'

"'We told you. We don't know. Who can know that? Things don't look good.'

"'You've noticed that, too, have you? So now you'll shuffle around in town and take the air and think that God's in his heaven and all's right with the world.'

"'What do you want with us?'

"'I just want to ask you what you think you're doing. After all, you've fought for your fatherland. Haven't you realized yet that you were sold a bill of goods? Go settle accounts with everybody who sat at home, the dogs. Just look at them. They may be your own father and mother.'

"'You better shut up,' the soldiers growled. 'We've heard enough out of you.'

"'No,' she said, 'this is just the beginning.'

"They turned their backs on the woman and left her standing there.

"'You'll get what's coming to you soon, you old witch.'

"Then she approached some people who were standing in a line, and they were people just like her, women with scarves on their heads, with empty shopping bags, all of them pale, lethargic, and depressed.

"She wanted to explain to them what crimes had been committed, and that they should get busy identifying the guilty parties. Everything had to be exposed, every last hypocrite unmasked. Rub their noses in their own filth.

"Most of the women agreed with her, but others didn't respond at all and said they were just waiting here and would be glad to get something, and they didn't care about much else, and in the end that's what they all said, and they turned their backs on her just as the soldiers had.

"She realized that no one would listen to her here. But where would anyone listen to her? It just couldn't be that everyone was as dulled and dead as these people. Surely you should be allowed to get at the bottom of a business that had cost you your sons? Are these human beings, or are they animals?

"She was in a fury. To whom should she turn? Was there no justice? She wanted to leave, to go anywhere else.

"But before she set off she took another look at the people standing here. Then a man came along and shoved her into the line. She stood locked in place there and said nothing.

"She couldn't get away. The people were frantic; they wanted potatoes, jam; and some of them were cursing. But most of them just pushed and jostled, weary and miserable. They were so defeated and dulled that they couldn't even complain anymore. They crowded around the trough and fought for a mouthful of food.

"She saw a bony old face next to her, a deaf man with a trembling head. He had no teeth and made sucking sounds with his lips and gums. A woman was shoved out of line and fought to get her place back. It was like a shipwreck. Everyone wanted to get into the lifeboats, but the waves tossed wildly, the wind blew, and there were only a few boats. Take me aboard, too!

"And the mother's rage and hatred subsided.

"She wrung her hands in despair. Tears came to her eyes. She could have shrieked and wailed. But she didn't. She just wept quietly, and no one noticed her.

"I am like them. See what you are like. We are all destitute, hungry, lost. There is no one who takes pity on us. Our hearts have been torn from our bodies. I don't believe in anything anymore, not in anything at all.

"So she stood in line with the others. They all waited for a dab of jam and a few potatoes, she with them. And she gnashed her teeth and cried out for justice. Her eyes were dry.

"And when she got her jam and potatoes, she went home and ate. And then she went back to the church—she didn't know where else to go—and began kicking at the door.

"And she cried and sobbed loudly, for what she was doing was so stupid, but it was all she could do: kick against the church door and show them inside what she thought about everything.

"Then she thought about Luther, and she said, 'That was the Reformation, and this is how Luther nailed his theses to the door, and this is how I'll nail mine on, too. One, two, three, four . . . They've got to listen, these people I'm talking to; they've got to sit up and listen.'

"She drummed furiously on the church door.

"She kicked at it with her feet and screamed, this frantic, helpless human being."

"And how did it end?" Edward, the tireless interrogator, asked.

Alice tried to get away again, but finally she came and sat down with him. And this is what she told him, her face glowing with joy.

In Heaven—The Archangel Michael

23 "THE mother pounded on the church door with her hands and feet and posted her theses there.

"And when night fell, the door creaked open, and a bright, white light poured over her.

"She sank to the ground.

"For as the clamor of battle rose to heaven, the last to hear it was he whose job it was to hear and to pay attention to such clamor, Saint Michael, whose name means: Who-is-like-God?

"He had, trusting in the goodness and omnipotence that stood behind him, fallen asleep on the steps of the heavenly throne. There he lay, tall and powerful as he was, on his back, in full armor, his sword on the ground near his open left hand. His helmet with its frightful plume, the mere sight of which can kill, had fallen backwards off his head, rolled down the steps, and was now rocking there, its massive opening turned up. It kept rocking and would not stand still because some diminutive angels had settled on its rim and were playing there. In the crown of the helmet, though, lay two more who had fallen blissfully asleep to the music of the heavenly choirs.

"Breaking in upon this idyll now came Saint Michael's patrols, his messengers, uneasy and anxious because the war on earth would not end and was taking on increasingly dreadful forms. They saw their master lying there and felt obliged (understandably, in view of the urgent situation) to submit a report. They spoke quietly. They spoke loudly. They spoke individually and in chorus. He slept on. Saint Michael slept like a suckling babe, or at least like one that is content and sated; for sated he certainly was, replete in his trust in the eternally All-Powerful.

"The patrol, made up of simple fellows, had immense respect for him. They even respected his sleep, for they knew everything he had accomplished, starting back in Paradise, where he had driven out mankind's sinful Ur-ancestors, and on through his mighty battle with Satan

156

for the body of Moses somewhat later. For Satan had wanted to make off with the body of this prophet and put it in a grave to prevent mankind from falling into idolatry and worshiping the grave. Saint Michael wrested the body from Satan after a frightful battle and took it away, where to, no one knows (none of which, of course, kept mankind from making other idols to worship).

"Since their great general, the hero Michael, was sleeping, there remained nothing for his scouts from earth to do, after they had screamed themselves hoarse, but to loaf around the heavenly gates and see how long Michael might sleep. The first thing they did was chase away the little angels that were seesawing on Michael's helmet; and the two who were sleeping inside it they pulled out by the legs, oblivious to their cries of protest. Then they rattled and banged around the imperturbable sleeper for so long that the other archangels on the steps of the throne noticed them and asked them what they thought they were doing.

"The scouts couldn't have been more pleased, and they began to relate, noisily and excitedly, what was going on on earth. It all began with the Nazis. They were of King Nebuchadnezzar's breed, the king who ultimately had to eat grass; and they had banded together with some others and had made colossal advances, but then a certain Churchill had turned up in England, and in America a Franklin Delano Roosevelt, and the Russians had held their ground. And some of the scouts were yelling so loudly about Stalingrad, about Petrograd, and about Moscow, and others were yelling so loudly about Tobruk and General Montgomery that the archangels covered their ears and didn't take their hands away again until these fellows, these scouts, had fallen silent. They had gotten the point: This war was a colossal war. Since they personally had nothing to do with wars, they asked the scouts what should be done.

"The scouts: They didn't know either, but no matter what else was done, Saint Michael had to be wakened. The archangels agreed, for he was their specialist for wars. But the difficult question of how to wake him remained.

"Saint Gabriel and Saint Raphael conferred—Saint Gabriel, in Latin: fortitudo Dei; it was he who had announced the Incarnation; Saint Raphael, mild, generous—they eyed their brother Michael pensively and could not decide whether to wake him or not to wake him. Either choice could have disastrous consequences. So it was a good thing that there were not just these two archangels in addition to the sleeping Michael but a few others, such as Uriel and Raguel, Sariel and Jeramiel, who, though not as well known, were of equal rank. The two

aforementioned indecisive dignitaries took these others into their confidence, and of these four, two recommended taking an immediate vote;
for their number was seven, and they couldn't help coming up with a
clear answer. Two others, however (Sariel and Jeramiel), had an idea
that struck them all as prudent. Whatever they decided to do, they
should take Michael's sword away first. For he would be furious no
matter what, furious that they had not wakened him to report the turmoil on earth or equally furious simply because they had wakened him.
That always evoked scenes from him.

"So the six archangels resolved to table the larger issue and, for the
time being, to concentrate on the limited task of taking Michael's sword
away. Pooling their strength, they set to work immediately. Like dogs
they worked, prying, heaving, shoving, with 'Altogether now' and
'Hup' and 'Hut.' The stocky Uriel had made himself lead horse and had
had the upper part of the sword laid on his back and was tugging away
on it, his arms locked behind his back, when the handle slipped out of
the unfortunate angel's grasp and the whole massive weapon tumbled
down onto the foot of the sleeping Michael.

"This strongest of archangels sat up instantly. The panicked conspirators tried to flee back to their usual places and act as if nothing had
happened. But it was too late.

"'What's going on here?' Michael bellowed after them. He reached
for his sword. He thought someone was invading heaven and they were
running from the enemy.

"'Nothing, nothing at all,' whispered Raphael, who was the first to
approach him. He smiled his chummiest smile and rubbed his hands
together. 'Oh, nothing, dear Saint Michael. We were just taking a little
exercise, a little exercise, that's all. It seems you were sleeping. Did you
sleep well, Saint Michael?'

"He looked uncertainly from one to the other. They were all re-
grouping around him now, one after the other, smiling at him with
feigned tenderness. 'Did you sleep well, Saint Michael?'

"But then they could contain themselves no longer and burst out
laughing in a great roar of laughter. That, of course, puzzled Michael.

"'What's going on here? Will somebody speak up?'

"Saint Gabriel could not keep up the comedy any longer, and he
said, 'Michael, what we have to tell you is that things are a terrible mess
on earth.'

"'A terrible mess on earth? Then I better go back to sleep for a good
long time.'

"And he seized his sword, which was in his way, and wanted to put it aside so he could lie down. Then, being in the rotten mood he was, he noticed that an ornament on the handle—a memento of his guard duty at Paradise—had been crushed flat and was hanging loose. He ran his fingers over the damaged part and eyed his colleagues suspiciously.

"'Somebody's been fooling around here.'

"'Oh,' Gabriel asked, 'is there something wrong with your sword? We're sorry to hear that, really sorry.'

"Raphael: 'Truly sorry. I hope the damage can be easily repaired.'

"Now Michael flew into a rage. Something was afoot here after all. They wanted to put something over on him. They had been tinkering with his sword; that's why they had all run away before. He had caught them red-handed as they were trying to pry his medal of honor off his sword.

"We should note here (parenthetically) that there was no general agreement in heaven about the real role Michael had played in Paradise. Some felt, and sometimes intimated as much, that it had not been his job at all to drive the people out of Paradise. On the contrary, he had been commissioned with keeping them in the garden and not letting them out. It had been Satan who wanted to lure them out, and in the end he did manage to lure them out onto the earth. And after the fact, Michael took up his totally useless post before the gates of Paradise and strutted proudly up and down there without realizing that he had been duped, indeed, that his presence prevented the people from returning. That was one version of the story. Opinion had it that the very highest authority had blamed Michael for all the subsequent trouble human beings had caused; for in Paradise, where they had been under close supervision, none of it would ever have happened. That Michael was now burdened with the endless trouble human beings and their wars caused him was a punishment for his earlier negligence. But none of this prevented him from having a valuable medal made that would recall his laudable service before the gates of an empty Paradise.

"Reminded of this history by his comrades' whisperings, he sprang up fiercely and stood there, powerful and towering over everyone else. His friends didn't move a muscle. Would he dare to have at them?

"But Gabriel, who had the mellowest voice, approached Michael with fear in his heart and said, 'Brother, we admire your strength. You are the most powerful of us, and you are so strong that we sometimes fear you might suffer the same fate as the heathen Hercules: You could, with the friendliest of intentions, lay your hand on our heads and squash our skulls.'

"Michael was flattered. But he still asked: 'All right, out with the truth. Who tried to tear the medal off my sword?'

"Gabriel: 'No one, Brother, no one. Who of us would ever dream of robbing a veteran, a tried and tested warrior like you, of his well-deserved medals? No one. Things aren't what you think. Let me clear them up for you.'

"And here Gabriel signaled to the scouts and patrols that were lurking timidly in the background. They did not come forward until Michael himself noticed them, noticed them with some astonishment, and whistled to them. He bellowed, 'What? Them, here? That crew? They have no business being here.'

"They trembled and said nothing.

"He: 'Who ordered you to come here?'

"'Calm yourself, Michael,' Raphael put in. 'They came of their own accord. They've been hanging around here quite a while now, waiting to report to you. But you were asleep.'

"Michael stretched his mighty arms out level with the ground. 'They should leave me alone with their stupid reports. I've had enough of earth. I'm going to apply for another planet. First, this shady lot goes absent without leave; second, they creep around here where they have no business; and, third, they try to steal my medal!'

"'Not so, Michael, Brother Michael,' Raphael, Gabriel, Uriel, Sariel, and Jeramiel all said at once, 'they had nothing to do with your medal. We wanted to wake you up, and that's when the accident happened. Listen to what we're saying: They have something of great importance to tell you. You're urgently needed.'

"'Where?'

"'On earth.'

"He wrung his hands in horror. He slapped his hand to his forehead. 'Not another word about earth!'

"They went on.

"'Dear Brother, the Second World War has broken out. It's already fully underway. It has a full head of steam up. We can't let things go on like this. And you are our only expert in earth affairs.'

"'Gentlemen, what have I let myself in for,' Michael moaned.

"'And because we feared a violent reaction on your part if we came to you with another problem like this, we decided not to take your sword—no, not by any means—but merely to remove it from your immediate vicinity while you were sleeping so that you would not harm yourself on it when you awoke. But it is so heavy, Brother Michael! Oh, how heavy your sword is, Brother Michael! You can be sure that no one will ever steal it from you. We struggled terribly, the five of us here before you, I—Gabriel—Raphael and Uriel, Sariel and Jeramiel. We couldn't manage. Uriel, the strongest of us all, had it up on his back. But then it slipped off and fell on your foot.'

"Michael shook his head. 'On my foot? I didn't notice anything.'

"It pleased the genial warrior that they had had such trouble with his sword. And he felt moved to show them straightaway how easy it was to handle. He sent it slashing through the air, tossed it from one hand to the other. They stood at a respectful distance. While he was going through his motions he asked, 'Who is this heathen Hercules who crushed people's skulls?'

"They said, 'An incredibly strong man who lived in ancient times, a very famous hero.'

"'Who killed him?'

"'Oh, that was all a long time ago,' Raphael said offhand. They wanted to get down to business, that is, to the war on earth. But Michael's sporting instincts had been wakened.

"'Who is Hercules? Who knows anything about Hercules?' Michael repeated as he kept practicing with his sword, swinging it tirelessly. The scouts in the background, who could not see how they would ever get through to him with their message, threw up their hands toward heaven, quite pointlessly, of course, for they already were in heaven. To babble about Hercules at a time like this!

"It turned out that the unassuming Jeramiel knew something about Hercules. He was a mild, dreamy soul. He found some good in everything, and at difficult moments or merely as a diversion, he enjoyed recounting past events for his own and his companions' benefit. He was a walking card file. The others knew that if Jeramiel once began talking he would not stop, and they tried to silence him by calling his attention to Saint Michael's inopportune athletic performance.

"But Michael had noticed that Jeramiel had opened his mouth, and he called out to him, 'Well, then, who is this Hercules, Jeramiel? Who is stronger than I am?'

"'Stronger than you? No one, Michael. Just remember who Hercules had backing him up. A certain Jupiter or Zeus, a fly-by-night deity if there ever was one, and a bunch of other two-bit gods.'

"'You don't have to keep spitting out new names, Jeramiel. I want to know about Hercules. What all did he do?'

"'Hercules—he strangled two serpents to death when he was still a baby in his cradle.'

"'Two serpents?' Michael tossed his sword gleefully into the air. 'What's so great about strangling two serpents? Is that supposed to be a heroic deed?'

"'There's more. There was the Lernean lion, for example, a monster of a lion, a pack of lions all rolled into one. Everybody warned Hercules to leave this lion alone. But he went off into the woods. He dragged the monster out of his lair, grabbed it by the ruff, and strangled it as elegantly as he had strangled the two serpents when he was a baby.'

"These tales put Michael in the best of moods. He buckled on his sword and said to the others, who obligingly joined in his laughter, 'Just listen to that. Examples of Hercules' strength.'

"Jeramiel: 'There was a serpent with seven heads living in the swamps of Lerna then. Hercules took his sword and cut all seven of them off, but they all grew right back again. So then he took a torch and cauterized the cuts, and no new heads grew.'

"'Marvelous,' Michael said scornfully, 'this guy seems to have had a thing about snakes. But you know, that business with the torch, that's not so dumb.'

"'And then a giant crab turned up to give him trouble. It was as big as a cow, and it bit his foot. He stomped its pincers to pieces, one after the other. He'd just about finished it off when it ran away into the sky and hid from him among the stars, and we can still see it today as the constellation Cancer.'

"The other angels burst out laughing. Michael didn't know whether this was all for real or just a joke, but he laughed along with the others. Now the intimidated scouts began creeping slowly into view again.

"'What else?' Michael asked.

"The learned Jeramiel thought for a moment. 'Well, there's the Augean stable. A man named Augeas, a king, had all sorts of animals: oxen, cows, calves, pigs, chickens, pheasants, doves, every kind of creature you can imagine.'

"Michael: 'A pig farmer.'

"'A king.'

"Michael: 'Funny kind of king with cows and pigs for subjects.'

"'No, he just raised the animals on the side. But he didn't have anybody to clean his stable for him, and that's why it had gotten to be such a horrendous mess. The animals reproduced hand over fist, and so did the manure.'

"'Stop!' cried Michael, who was beginning to get the point. 'So Hercules did the job for him.'

"'Right.'

"'And you dare compare me with this cesspool cleaner?'

"'Cesspool here, cesspool there, Michael, it's colossal what he did. Just imagine hauling off a pile of manure ten miles long, ten miles wide, and I don't know how many feet high.'

"'I don't want to haul it off.'

"'In those days, Michael, it was a top-priority problem. Nowadays we'd never let things get so far out of hand in the first place.'

"Raphael: 'Nowadays we'd use the manure as fertilizer and cart it away a truckload at a time.'

"The archangels chatted on in this fashion while the scouts listened intently from nearby.

"Michael had lost track of what this was all about and asked suddenly, 'What does this have to do with me?'

"Jeramiel, in his modest way: 'I thought it might interest you. It's relevant to your question about Hercules.'

"But Michael had suddenly rediscovered his scouts and bellowed, 'What are they doing here? I've already asked that once before.'

"Gabriel: 'They wanted to tell you what's happening on earth. They've been here a long time. You were asleep. As we were about to wake you, your sword fell down, and the medal on it was knocked loose.'

"Now, finally, Michael's scouts had his full attention.

"'All right, boys. On the double! Come on in a little closer, right up close now. How dare you leave your posts without orders, without my personal permission! Don't you know what defection of duty is, you deserters?'

"They fell down on their faces before him and begged for mercy. And while the other archangels calmed the furious Saint Michael down, the scouts, with their faces to the ground (in consequence of which he understood only half of what they said and they had to repeat everything), began to tell the whole, dismal history of what was happening on earth.

"Michael gradually calmed down. He sat on a step and began to ask them specific questions. They immediately rattled out answers, everyone speaking at once. Every now and then he had to ask for silence so that he could digest everything they told him. One told about Danzig and Poland, another about Denmark and Norway, a third about Belgium, Holland, France, a fourth about England. It was staggering. A fifth even told about Japan and the kamikaze planes. Pilots were diving down onto warships in the Pacific and blowing themselves up with their targets.

"The scouts had to allow a long pause at this point. Michael always needed a lot of time to think his way into things: men who, together with their bombs, dropped themselves straight down out of the air onto warships and exploded. He found that technically intriguing.

"Everyone sat and stood around a while.

"Finally Michael raised his head, his face troubled, his brow wrinkled, melancholy. 'And all this time I was asleep? What immersed me in sleep?'

"He stood up, stretched. He put his sword in front of him. He was dreaming still.

"The archangels kept talking to him, trying to bring him out of his dream. Raphael asked if he hadn't heard the thunder of the blitz over London.

"He laughed proudly, 'No.'

"At this point the heavens moved. A voice sounded: 'Michael!'

"Everything changed.

"The archangels turned their faces toward the throne.

"Then there was silence.

"The heavenly music resumed, swelled to full volume again. Michael stood there gleaming, his face dark as thunder, his lion's mane shaking. He leaned over, clapped his helmet onto his head, fastened the chin strap. He stabbed his naked sword straight up into the air.

"He leapt onto his black charger. At the head of his legions he thundered out of the heavens. He flashed down on the earth like lightning.

"His name: Michael, 'Who-is-like-God?' His task: to show mankind that God lives.

"Wherever he appeared he threw his sword into the balance. He created confusion wherever he wanted to. He created the good and the bad breaks.

"The battles came to an end.

"A woman stands in front of the church door and nails her theses to it with her hands and with her feet.

"Then the door flew open.

"The angel who came out, on foot, leading his weary horse behind him by its reins, was Michael, Who-is-like-God.

"The light emanating from his sword could kill. But it infused her with strength. She had fallen down; she could get up.

"She felt so strong that she almost asked Saint Michael for his horse and weapons so that she herself could ride off to claim the justice that was her due.

"But he gave the mother neither horse nor sword. For as we know, others had already tried their hand at the sword without success."

Thus spoke Alice. Her face was aglow. She embraced her son. Then she stood up, gleaming like a torch, her arms upraised, and fled from the room.

Professor Mackenzie's Words of Wisdom

KATHLEEN came to Edward's room with a serious expression on her face, sat down with him, but instead of speaking she lowered her head and seemed to be waiting for him to speak. He reached for her hand. Then she began.

"I can't listen to these people. You're the only one who says anything. I can't understand Father. And Mother has changed, too. Why doesn't she say what she means?"

"Does that pain you, Kathleen?"

"Doesn't it you?"

She looked sadly into her lap, at her folded hands. She whispered: "Has Mother been in to see you yet? Yes? Then I'll tell you something. Perhaps you know it already. You were still away when I came home. It was the same house, but I didn't feel at home in it. I didn't say anything to them, but I was beside myself. So this is what a marriage comes to. I remembered us all as a family before. It was Father and Mother and you and me, the children. But I never really saw our parents. During the war I became more independent, and now I have some distance on them and see them from outside, something I'd never done before. And I've found—"

She sighed deeply.

Edward: "What have you found?"

She shook her head. "I can't find my place. I don't fit in anymore. It gets harder and harder for me. Sure, some ties are still there, but things aren't the same."

She sighed. "Excuse me, Edward. Forgive me, please. I don't know who I should go to."

Edward: "Please stay."

"I don't want to brew up some conspiracy against our parents. I'd

just like to hear what you think. It pains me to see them this way.
Father buries himself in his library, writes and writes, gets mail, receives visitors. He's like some kind of official in the house. And he's
getting that way more and more. And Mother floats around the house
like a fairy. She is every inch a lady, helpful and obliging. Oh, Edward,
if you only knew how jealous of Mother I used to be because she is so
delicate and elegant and I'm so down to earth and ungainly. She used to
give us a lot of attention. Now she is tense, off somewhere else. She
doesn't talk much. I find it incomprehensible, awful. What's going on,
Edward? Do you understand it?"

"Mother talks to me some."

Kathleen: "Yes, sometimes. But what she says. None of it's right. It's
as if our parents were having an eternal fight that they don't bring out
into the open."

"Have you seen anything specific? What?"

Kathleen: "It's just a feeling I have. I'm glad that you're better. You
can't know, Edward, how Mother was before, how anxious she was.
That in itself was strange enough. It was out of character for Mother.
She tried to hide it, too, but I could tell anyway. You can't imagine how
things were here when you finally came back. You wouldn't have recognized Mother. I tell you it was unnatural. I can imagine how Mother
feels, Edward, but this—. And then you were back, and we could visit
you in the clinic. They wouldn't let us into your room. All we could do
was look through the little window in the door."

"You saw me?"

"Yes, didn't you know? You weren't well at all. The doctors didn't
want to excite you. I looked in first. You were lying with your back to
the door. And then Mother looked in. The nurse said you had turned to
face the door. Mother fainted. The nurse had to carry her out to the
waiting room. What is this, Edward? This crazy hyperemotionalism!
Mother was not herself again afterwards."

"Seeing somebody lying there like that can be pretty upsetting. Did I
say anything? What did I say?"

"You didn't say anything. I would have heard it."

"Then I must have looked bad."

"So it seems. But to be so terrified. And then to be upset for weeks
afterwards. Edward, you're lying here most of the time. You can't see
much. Something isn't right in this house."

"I'll ask Mother about it."

Kathleen: "She won't tell you the truth."

*   *   *

"I wanted to interrupt him, Alice," Gordon Allison repeated in his wife's room. He had come to find her. "It gave me the creeps. Where does he get these ideas? Who's keeping him from his honesty? And aren't we doing everything we can for him? Is our concern, our love for him dishonest? What does he want?"

Alice sank into an armchair. "I don't know."

"You'll have to speak to the doctor about it. It worries me. What can we do to calm him, Alice?"

"I don't know, Gordon."

"I saw it coming. We don't know how to deal with him. His stay here with us isn't helping him."

"Gordon, why start that again?"

"If he were alone, in his room, then all right—I wouldn't be affected. But now he's moving around, lying on the sofa. Alice, it's more than I can take."

"He is our son, Gordon."

"I want to work. I can't. I have no peace of mind anymore."

"I don't either, Gordon. But is it really so terrible if you don't work for a while?"

"You've always had something against my work."

"Never against your writing, just the way you go at it. I don't need to go into that again."

"It's the way I am."

"You're not doing anyone any good this way, Gordon."

"Now you want to start harassing me, too?"

She whispered: "You weren't always this way. Edward sees through it all."

He stood up angrily.

"You see? He can't stay. Now you're attacking me because I'm writing. Alice, something has to change around here."

She whispered, "I agree."

He went out the door.

She had asked her brother, the elegant and clever Mackenzie, to talk with Edward. The imperturbable gentleman sighed at first. Then he consented.

Actually, he was taking something of an interest in Edward. The boy pleased him more and more. A few times he told the patient about past things and events Edward had asked about, things about their home, the family. Mackenzie indulged these whims. An odd thing: A young man takes part in earth-shaking events in world history, hits the beaches on D day, sees the German front crumble, then sets sail against Japan, surrounded by death and destruction, and survives a bombing attack. Back home again he finds nothing more pressing to do than involve himself in family life and develop an interest in his family, an interest that, for an outsider, can't but have something of the comic about it. Moreover, his interest in the family was much greater than it had been, for as far as James Mackenzie could recall, Edward had kept himself aloof in the past. Kathleen, not he, had been the family child. Now, it seemed, he wanted to make up for that, was experiencing a delayed rivalry with his sister.

Now, after the Kierkegaard evening, James was sitting in Edward's room. Alice had bedded her patient down in a deck chair that faced out onto the snow-covered garden.

Edward (who had again made secret offerings to his dead friends, true to his comrades, the silent dead, torn away from snow, torn away from trees, torn away from breathing, from eating and drinking, but not torn away from life), Edward pointed to the garden.

"How true this is, Uncle. True means present. I don't want to see it debated away."

"I'm glad to hear that, my boy."

"I envy your being able to tramp around in the snow."

"You'll be able to, too. Everything out there is waiting for you to come back. The snow, the rain, the warm summer later on, the flowers, everything will receive you with redoubled joy. No, I envy you, Eddy. I envy you your return. You were ill, and that meant absence. Just watch how everything will reach out to you and welcome the prodigal son back."

"You love nature, Uncle?"

"Nature? The whole world, my boy, life. You think that I'm a book-worm because I leaf through books in libraries and archives. Books are something special, of course. They're not just the paper, the paper or parchment on which a text is printed or painted. Not at all. It's a mystery, my boy, how the spirit can lie encapsuled for centuries, millennia, in letters, in signs, and can reside in books, and as long as the books remain closed, everything is quiet in the house. You see nothing and hear nothing, although if you put your ear to it you'll hear a buzzing inside. But once you open the book, then you enter into a banquet hall;

everything is brightly lit, full of movement and talk. And the most remote times are present and come to greet you."

"You *are* a bookworm, Uncle."

"Granted. But I love nature, too, the snow, the trees, the mystery of
the seasons and how they affect us and how we move with them. It's a
wonderful thing to be part of nature, Edward. Yes, it's wonderful, as a
human being, a tree, an animal, to partake of this one great life. I've
been particularly conscious of this when I've been traveling. When the
landscape around me changed, I'd think: I've never realized before how
large my house is."

"Strange. I've never felt that."

"I didn't have much truck with this sort of thing when I was young
either. We isolate ourselves first, and we break down those walls only
slowly. We open ourselves up slowly, and that is a process of self-relin-
quishment, a flowing over into the other, into the world. Its beauties
lure us out of ourselves. It coaxes us away from our small, stupid egos."

Edward listened. The professor, his face illuminated by light from the
snow, was leaning his head on the back of the chair in a proud and quiet
pose, showing a noble profile, a firm, small mouth.

"I brought that idea and many other good ones back from a trip to
India," he said. "Even if we aren't able to put such ideas into action,
it's still worthwhile to recall them. They leave their mark on
us regardless, and move us in new directions. I've memorized certain
teachings and schooled myself on them the way one would on the contemplation of classical statuary. Listen to one of these proverbs. It
speaks about the state of enlightenment, and how do we achieve enlightenment? Through the relinquishment of self we mentioned earlier,
the flowing over of the one into the other. From duality—I and world—
we come to unity. Listen to what the proverb says:

"'Each of us is identical with universal life. Each of us lives face to
face with universal life. Each of us receives the overflowing mercy of
holiness. Life is not a sea of illness, birth, old age, death, no vale of
tears. It is Sakhavati, the land of bliss. For in it our spirit is completely
transformed, free of envy and hate, anger, ambition; it is not overpowered by grief and despair.'

"For years now, Eddy, I have refreshed myself every day with words
like these."

"Tell me more, Uncle. This is all strange to me."

"You like it. I'm glad. But first a small aside: You read Kierkegaard
to us. That was good. He wants the truth. You want the truth. You

insist on honesty. But how can you reach truth if your will is shot through with passion? The first step is to release tension, to relax."

"The first step is to release tension?"

"We've come a long way if we even notice our tension, the convulsions of our ego and its desires. We have to rid ourselves of them to achieve liberation. And that liberation orders our attitude toward the world. Our actions, even if they don't attain the ultimate heights, nonetheless become more intelligent and mature, more worthy of us. A maxim I enjoy a lot says: When a traveler returns home from a long journey to distant lands, his friends and relatives welcome him. Similarly, when a man who has lived a just life travels from this world to the next, his own good deeds receive him there just as friends receive a beloved friend on his return home."

Edward and James Mackenzie, Alice's brother, lay quietly in the light reflected from the snow in the garden. The wind whistled by now and then, blowing loose snow from the branches outside and tossing it against the windows. The branches, black now, whipped up and down, mourning the loss of their precious robes.

"You never got to know any women, Uncle?"

Alice's brother, not taken aback, murmured, "Women, yes. But the woman, no. Fate spared me that, fate or my own nature."

"I hadn't realized before how much like Mother you are."

"Eddy, you see everything differently now. You didn't use to talk with me much, or with anybody else. I had the impression you didn't like any of us. I was sorry, because I liked you. Your shy ways—you were always gloomy and off to one side—touched me. But you didn't let anybody near you. That was a convulsion, a cramping of the ego. Now that you've traveled over half the globe and met war and death and the devil face to face, you're seeing all kinds of things, including me."

"What is a family, Uncle?"

"Let's look at the snow, shall we? Look at the snow, Eddy."

Nothing was happening outside. The snow lay in soft waves, untouched by any human foot. It covered the tree trunks on one side; the other side was bare. Strange, these black strips in the white, as if writing were emerging on paper. But the whiteness, the snow, was not a blanket. It was a soundless element, from somewhere else, that had joined the ground and the trees and laid itself evenly over them and spoke to them. And they listened.

"I've never seen you before," said the tree. "Who are you?"

"We're the snow, the snow."

"Where do you come from? What do you want?"

"We're the snow, the snow. You know us. We come often. You forget us over the summer."

"What do you want?"

"Do you like us?"

"You're so light, Snow, Snow. You're so light. Come near my roots."

"Why?"

"You're so soft. I want to pet you. I can't feel anything with my branches."

"What do you want to do to us, Tree, Tree? You want to melt us. You want to put us in your mouth. Leave us alone."

The professor turned to Edward. "We mustn't let any words come between us and things. Our words, our concepts, all these preconceived notions, get in the way. They prevent contact with things. We have to get to the point where we can push words aside. That opens the way to things."

"And then what becomes of us?"

"Then we give up much of our ego, of our bad ego. You'll have enough left."

"So it's a purification. And where is my ego? I have to ask you questions the way I did with Father and during that long conversation about illusionism. How do I reach my true self?"

"The first thing is not to be so restless."

"If I'm not restless, I can't search. And how can you help being restless if you're tormented and have to ask questions all the time and aren't in possession of yourself?"

"Your illness, Eddy. It's getting better."

"It's not an illness. I dispute that."

"Eddy, let yourself go. Look at the snow. Let things come to you."

Edward didn't answer anymore. He looked mutely into the garden, but not, as the professor wanted him to, to hand himself over to the white surface.

What kind of a house have I landed in? Each person here is a craftier deceiver than the other. The one wants to fool me as much as the other, as if they were in league. He's determined to rob me of my consciousness. I'm not supposed to ask questions. I'm just supposed to lie here and gawk at things. I'm supposed to ask things to become one with me. Why should the snow become one with me? To cover me up even more? They're all trying to lead me a wild goose chase. I see what you're up to.

I feel like Hamlet. People lie to him. They try to distract him. They finally send him off on a journey because they're afraid of him, because he knows what has really happened.

I don't know. No ghost from Hades has appeared to me to entrust me with his frightful secret. Nobody speaks to me. I just have inklings. They betray themselves much too clearly.

Edward turned to the professor.

"What do you think about Hamlet, Uncle? Have you ever studied him?"

"No more than any other Englishman."

"Isn't it marvelous the way he persists and keeps digging and thinking? Because he knows something? And how they try to deceive him and throw him off the track. But it's he who holds all the cards."

"That's true, Eddy." (What is he driving at?)

"It would be wonderful, Uncle, if you would tell us the story of Hamlet sometime."

(What's he got up his sleeve? What does he want with Hamlet? Maybe Alice has been telling him some of her fantasies. That would be criminal.)

"I couldn't tell you any more than anyone else could, Eddy. Have you forgotten the story?"

"I know only the rough outlines. Tell me, Uncle, how would the whole thing have come out if the father's ghost had not risen up out of the ground at the beginning and told his son everything? Hamlet surely suspected something. Or not? He had already done some investigating."

"It would probably have gone just the way it does in the play."

"No, it would have been different. In the play he wants vengeance right away, wants to punish his father's murderers. He already knows what happened. The ghost on the battlements just fills in the details. It's his father's ghost that demands vengeance so that he can find peace, for justice must be done. Now in my version I'm assuming Hamlet doesn't know for sure. He just has an inkling, a feeling. He has some clues, certain reasons for suspicion."

James: "He wouldn't rush into such a major undertaking that could prove dangerous for him on the basis of such a vague feeling."

"Let's assume he wants to, he has to. We can invent a conflict that compels him to. Now, how does he proceed? How does he go about solving the case? He keeps falling back into his doubts and uncertainties, of course. He doesn't have things as easy as the hero of the original play. His opponents will certainly encourage his uncertainty because they are benefiting from the new state of affairs. So he has a thick wall in front of him and has to breach it."

James: "Has to, Edward? I ask again: Why does he have to?"

"It would be the storyteller's job to make this plausible somehow. Hamlet has only inklings at first. It would be a real challenge for a storyteller, but an interesting and timely challenge: Hamlet under modern circumstances. For just as Oedipus, Faust, and Don Quixote never become dated, Hamlet does not become dated either." (He spoke craftily, trying to draw the clever professor to his bait.)

James: "So we would have as the three main characters the two parents and the son. Someone has to set the son in motion."

Edward: "Someone or something or both, as you like. In any case, the son has to be driven and allow no one any peace because he can't find any peace himself. How does he proceed? How does he get at the truth? Who supplies him with information? Uncle, I'd like to make a suggestion: Do it the way Father did with his story about Jaufie and the gray knight who left his house, his wife, and his son in the lurch. Tell us about Hamlet, but minus the appearance of the ghost."

James ran a hand over his forehead but did not answer.

Edward: "You could take a different approach, too. Start with a Hamlet who is returning from abroad, from the university at Wittenberg or from a campaign with young Fortinbras. His father is dead, has been dead a long time. They had sent Hamlet to Wittenberg because they were afraid of him. But now he is back."

"And knows nothing."

"Knows nothing, but knows that he knows nothing and wants to know."

"Eddy, you should tell about this Hamlet. You seem to be much more at home in the material than I am."

"I'd like you to do it. Tell it the way any good storyteller should, one thing after another, from beginning to end: how things used to be in the house of the royal couple, how they treated Hamlet, what role he played at home—until something evil, something revolting, something horrible, unspeakable, happened, unbeknownst to him, something disgusting, if you like, that allows him no peace, like the dishonoring of his mother, or worse yet, his mother's acquiescence in her dishonor."

James Mackenzie held his hands over his ears. "Awful. Stop. That would be your story. Please don't take it amiss, but I couldn't make up that story. I wouldn't even want to hear it."

Edward, undaunted: "So what do you think, Uncle? I invite you to try it. You're a man of the world; you've seen and heard a lot."

(Oh, I understand you, my dear Edward. She has driven you crazy with her chatter. What a woman, my sister Alice. I never would have believed it. Now I understand Medea. She kills her own children to satisfy her desire for vengeance.)

Edward, after a pause: "Uncle, you will tell us the story of Hamlet. I demand it of you. I insist."

The professor pulled out his watch.

Edward: Could he count on the Hamlet story?

The professor: They had begun so nicely with words of old Indian wisdom, with contemplation of the snow, with muteness, and with the idea that we have to break through that artificial barrier that the brain constructs between us and things, and now there was to be more talk after all, and even more talk after that.

Edward: "As a favor to me."

The professor sighed, shook Edward's hand, and rolled his eyes heavenward.

Professor Mackenzie Introduces His Story

AS soon as Edward could get hold of his mother he hung on to her and interrogated her about when the family had first learned he had been wounded and just what they had heard.

"And how did you all respond? Father, Kathleen, and you?"

She: Edward could well imagine. "Father was terribly upset, asked two, three times if it was really true, if there was any hope. He was standing next to me when the telegram arrived. He sat down, had tears in his eyes, and buried his face in his hands."

"Father had tears in his eyes?"

"It hit him hard. He didn't say anything; it crumpled him like a punch to the stomach."

Edward: "That was the bomb."

Alice: "What did you say?"

Edward: "Just a thought."

Alice: "And then he stayed in his study for the next few days."

Edward: "And worked, as usual."

Alice: "I can't say for sure anymore. Those were such dreadful days."

Edward: "It was very hard for you?"

She looked down at the floor.

Edward: "My question surprises you. I'm just asking. Did you and Father talk about me then? Did he comfort you?"

"What strange questions, Edward."

He: "Kathleen told me you were very withdrawn then. You sat alone in the garden a lot."

"Sorrow is something you bear alone."

Pause.

Edward: "You visited me in the clinic. It upset you a lot. Why? You knew I was sick."

Alice: "It's quite a different thing when you actually see someone."

Edward: "And what was so different? I was pale, skinny, of course. What did you say to me?"

"We couldn't go in. Kathleen and I stood at the door and could only look through the little window in it."

"And?"

"We saw you."

Edward: "You fainted."

Alice: "Did Kathleen tell you that? It wasn't right of her to tell you that."

"But it's true."

Alice: "It wasn't right of her. Yes, I fainted. What an awful reunion that was, Eddy. What a reunion."

"Because I was so sick."

"And now you're here. With me, Eddy."

She kissed him on both cheeks and remained seated next to him. Her eyes shone with joy.

"And now you won't run away anymore."

He stroked her hand. How lovely Mother looks. How devoted to me she is. I've never seen her like this with Father.

THE evening arrived when James Mackenzie was to tell his story. Edward, acting without Mackenzie's approval, had spread the word that his uncle would tell *Hamlet*. This news drew a prompt and vehement response from his mother. She objected. That play of Shakespeare's got on her nerves. She didn't like it at all. She asked him not to insist on *Hamlet*. He shook his head and was left feeling upset when she, for her part, came out with a resigned "Oh, God."

On this evening as on all others, Lord Crenshaw sat in his armchair, an imposing figure. He leaned his right elbow on his knee, and his chin rested in the palm of his right hand, and he sat there contentedly, his back bent, looking out toward his guests. His ears and cheeks glowed red. The room was too warm. But he would not let anyone open a window.

The evening began with general conversation. The teacher, Miss Virginia, who had contributed the story of the page and his ring, drew Dr. King into a corner (they were both old friends of the family) and whispered with him.

"Will these sessions continue for a long time yet, Doctor?"

"That depends on the circumstances. Why do you ask?"

"Well, I think, Doctor, at the last meeting—weren't you taken aback by Edward's behavior?"

Dr. King: "I don't know why I should have been."

"Didn't you see how agitated he was? We all noticed it."

Dr. King: "Oh, that was to be expected."

"What? What was to be expected?"

"That he would get worked up. Things that are important, very important to us excite us."

"But I ask you, Doctor, this aggressiveness in Edward, this wildness—it strikes me like a kind of rage. We surely can't go on driving him into such states."

Dr. King: "Oh, we're not driving him. It is—how shall I say?—simply his illness running its course. As a consequence of his inquiry, of his inner process of enlightenment, he will fall into these states of excitement with increasing ease and violence. Things will get worse, and we may reach a point where we will in fact have to stop these discussions. Or perhaps he'll shy away on his own because he doesn't want to go any further, because he's afraid, and then we'll have to find a new approach. We'll just have to wait and see."

"You mean to let things go on this way, Doctor? I beg you not to. Just look at Gordon Allison, how it's affecting him. I'm in this house a lot. The tone, the whole mood has changed. Gordon has become totally depressed. Alice looks horribly troubled and tense. She asked her brother to come. She doesn't know if she's doing the right thing. Perhaps she's considering sending Edward away again."

"Oh? She hasn't said a word about that to me."

"We should suggest it to her. This business is grinding her down. Her face has such a hard expression; she never looked that way before. Oh, I know Alice. What kind of person is she becoming? Sometimes she frightens me. Can't you see that, Doctor?"

"Nothing has happened, Miss Virginia. You have to have strong nerves to sit out a cure like this. We're not telling fairy tales à la *Thousand and One Nights* here."

"You're the only one of us with nerves like that, Doctor."

He raised his hands in resignation.

The old teacher: "What is it you really mean to do here, Doctor? It was my understanding that Edward was ill, excitable, and restless because of his war wounds and that we were going to help him calm down. That's why everyone was to tell a story, just as in *A Thousand and One Nights*. Gordon Allison did a wonderful job. But then I began to get a very different feeling. And then what was it Edward was driving at the other night? It didn't sound sick. He wanted honesty, truth. He wants to know something. He seems to feel there's something obscure here that needs to be cleared up."

The doctor: "It does look that way, doesn't it?"

"Then what use are our stories from the Middle Ages and whatnot? Take him to the clinic with you and work everything through with him and help him, scientifically, to find the clarity he needs. You have the methods at your disposal. He wants some kind of truth. How can he find it here, under these conditions? What help to him can our stories be?"

"Don't worry. He'll find his truth."

"My God, how? And at what price? Can't you see how everyone here is suffering?"

"You're exaggerating. Remember that I'm here, too. I'll keep an even closer eye on things."

"Doctor, watching won't help. You've got to take him away. The truth—I can't imagine what it could be. What kind of truth, for heaven's sake? He'll find what he thinks to be the truth."

Dr. King looked at her thoughtfully.

"Is there any other kind of truth? Do you know any other? But at least in this case we'll know whether he finds the truth or not. We'll have proof positive, which is to say, if he finds it, he'll be cured."

The circle was starting to form. The doctor stood up. The graying teacher trotted along beside the giant.

"Is there really no other method besides this one? It seems so inhuman to me."

The doctor leaned over and whispered to her, "You never would have made a doctor, Miss Virginia."

The guests took their places.

Alice's brother, James Mackenzie, had the floor. He did not keep his listeners waiting. He had come to a decision quickly after his talk with Edward. He would not tell Hamlet's story, and so he would not comply with Edward's request. But he wanted to speak, wanted to relate a story that would show the company something different, namely, Lord Crenshaw as he really was.

Edward and Alice are not seeing him aright. Edward is secretly attacking him. Alice has brought me here to take sides with her, but she's deluding herself.

James Mackenzie had a weakness for Gordon, his brother-in-law, this man swollen with his own energies to outlandish dimensions. Gordon reminded James of the Indian god Shiva. He was a primal, corpulent creature that wallowed contentedly in his writing like a wild animal in a swamp. James liked the man. And when, after his talk with Edward, he took down his Shakespeare and leafed through *Hamlet* and let his imagination range, he hit on *King Lear*. Lear, that would be something up Gordon Allison's alley, the figure of the old knight from the Jaufie story again, but this time in center stage and in a setting appropriate to him.

James Mackenzie was immediately taken with the idea. Besides, his Celtic studies had made him very familiar with the Lear story. And so he began to ponder, to speculate. He kept himself hidden in the house for a day, two days, so that he would have a little peace. Alice's dark, nearly immobile face strengthened his resolve to fight on Gordon's side and give both her and Edward a true picture of him.

James Mackenzie, the elegant professor with the nobly chiseled features, began:

"I will tell of Hamlet, but not until later. With your permission, Edward, I'd like to tell a different story first."

"We have time, Uncle. Do as you like."

"Thank you. Ever since Lord Crenshaw told us about the young knight Jaufie (and what happened to him at home and in Antioch, things that have been reported very differently in the legend as it has come down to us), I've been mulling over another story that is quite similar in some respects. It's a story that Shakespeare found and made a play from. But, as in the case of Jaufie and Petite Lay, we do not know what really is behind this story, not, at any rate, from the facts as we have them.

"Lord Crenshaw told us about a family, about a son in particular, and focused his attention on this son, if I may put it that way. The gray knight, the father, he placed more in the background. I'd like to proceed differently. I'd like to tell you about a different kind of father and a different fate. My story is about King Lear."

"Ah," Lord Crenshaw said, "now there's an idea, James. We can play a fugue together. I introduce the subject, and you provide the answer."

Mackenzie: "Let me add another point. We all know Shakespeare's play, this great, horrifying, crushing drama with its central figure of the aged king who is torn apart by his family. But is this figure the real King Lear? It is a powerful drama. But if we take away the theatrical elements and trappings, the theatrical distortions essential to a heroic drama, what remains? Lord Crenshaw—beyond any doubt the master storyteller among us—has, by his example, given me the courage to ask this question. Who, in reality, was King Lear? I gave some study to this question in the past, but that was a long time ago. Now I've picked it up again and looked through my old notes. Some information was available in Gordon's library, and I've had to make do with what I've found here.

"One source tells us that Lir (it was spelled this way here) was none other than the world-renowned water god, Neptune. Yes, the fellow with the trident, Poseidon. And Lir's three daughters represented three kinds of winds, two storm winds and a light breeze, a zephyr, all of which fits in astonishingly well with the characters of the king's daughters as we know them. But this theory doesn't take us further than that. We want to know, too, for example, what moved Lear to divide up his territory among his daughters as he did and what precipitated the horrible events that followed. Unfortunately, this legend offers no enlightenment on that score, none whatsoever.

"What is it about Lear's story, as we know it and as Shakespeare presents it to us, that is so troublesome? That a father, who is a king and is therefore not only high-minded and clever but also knows how to cope with human wickedness and craftiness—otherwise he would not have become king—that this man divides up his kingdom so blindly that he is soon robbed and turned out to wander off onto a heath in storm and rain and into a life-threatening and melodramatic situation. How can this be possible? Only because the king has become old and senile.

"King Lear, if we think this old version through logically, lost his mental faculties in his old age and gave away everything to his family, retaining only some mere snippets for himself. You know that peasant proverb: Whoever gives his children bread and then himself doth go unfed, that man deserves to be beaten dead. — Lear must not have known this saying. They pitilessly take him for all he's worth. His is the story of an utter dupe. Just imagine it on the stage. The laughter begins the minute Lear appears before his solemnly assembled, loot-hungry, piously devious family to reveal to them the plan his weakened gray matter has devised to punish him with, namely, the plan to give them all he has. The family takes it all in: The cock is crowing; he's ripe to be plucked. They catch on quickly. The family reveals itself in all its glory. He notices nothing, not yet. He is fooled by their crocodile tears. They agree to everything he says. He is happy; he has found peace—or so it

seems to him—in the bosom of his family. Bit by bit they strip him of
his remaining property, using one new ruse after another; and in this
process his stupidity achieves heroic dimensions. No one feels sorry for
this poor dullard. His relatives simply laugh at him and wonder what he
will do next. He has elevated stupidity into a competence.

"Finally they have had enough of him. One daughter after the other
finds she hasn't a room for him anymore. The old fool is in the way. He
wastes the servants' time babbling with them. The daughters dress him
down. They leave it to the servants to take him his meals, or not to take
them, as they choose. He used to have a jester to keep him company, a
kind of adjutant. He no longer needs a fool, for he is fool enough himself. And then one day he decides that he has had his fill of the castle.
He winds up on the street, and that becomes his element now.

"He lives among the village poor, the tramps, the wastrels; and behold, he is happy. Here he amounts to something. And why not? What
was a vice in the castle is a virtue here. He talks endlessly about his
past, his wars, his great deeds, about his daughters and how he divided
his property among them. This is all new to his listeners. They have
time. They laugh; they laugh. Strangers listen, encourage him to speak.
They give him money. He earns a living with his garrulousness. Because
he draws crowds he does wonders for the beggars' business. They are
wild about him, and in this way his story spreads among the people, an
incredible, hair-raising, tear-jerking tale, reeking of injustice, injustice
that cries to heaven.

"And if old King Lear is not dead, then he is still alive today."

So ended James Mackenzie's first run at his Lear story. His presenta-
tion had created a warm, cozy atmosphere reminiscent of the Jaufie
evenings.

Alice was full of praise for her brother and asked him whether there
was any basis in fact for the version of Lear's story that he had just told.
But the bushy-browed Judge Garrick seated beneath the bust of Socrates objected. The story was unlikely and could hardly have happened
that way in reality, for if a royal family in olden times found itself with a
senile fool like that at its head, it did not take long before the pathetic
creature was given a grand heave-ho out of the family circle, one that
transported him, before he knew what was happening, from this vale of
tears into a better world.

Mackenzie agreed, and that was why he had designated this story
only a preliminary tale.

"So let's abandon the thesis, conceivable though it remains, that it was senility that brought King Lear to divide up his lands among his heirs and so to saw off the limb he was sitting on. Let's assume instead that the story of King Lear was not an episode in a medical history, not the final stage of a decline into senility. We will take him altogether seriously as a normal human being, as a king in full possession of his mental faculties. Let's not make things easy for ourselves. We, too, want to look reality in the face.

"There are some daughters, all of them endowed with human, all too human qualities; there is a normal king, their father, and a division of an inheritance takes place. These three factors are given. How can we bring them together: the king, his three human, all too human daughters, and the divided inheritance? Indeed, what prompted our mentally competent Lear to even think of dividing up his realm in the first place, and among these daughters whom he knew very well? I want to present this powerful figure to you, and my story is meant as a counterweight to Lord Crenshaw's tale of Jaufie and Petite Lay. This man harbors no illusions. He does not let ideas and customs lead him around by the nose. He is every inch King Lear, and he is in a position where he can afford to be. So now I'll relate the life of a man who was not the least bit susceptible to illusions and fantasies."

The Story of King Lear

Part One

"THERE once ruled in the gray past on the British Isles a king by the name of Lear, who was more than a match in brutality for any of his vassals, and for his daughters and sons-in-law as well. This royal family bore the stamp of Lear through and through. Each was like the other; none was better than the other, though of course each thought himself the best, the one true exception.

"Lear ruled over them all with an iron hand. He was not king for nothing. He fleeced his relatives and subjects alike for all they were worth. He extorted money from them, and thought it his good right to do so. Among the kingly attributes he refused to relinquish was the opposite of miserliness, that is, extravagance. He squandered his wealth, and once he had thrown it all away, he availed himself of other people's. Nothing lasted long with him. Wealth evaporated in his hands like a drop of water on a hot griddle. He demanded, extorted, and conquered others' property so he could turn right around and throw it away again. Such was the metabolism of King Lear, and from it resulted his eventful, stormy, and happy life.

"This spendthrift on the throne never knew, of course, whether he owned anything or what it was. By rights we shouldn't even use the word 'ownership' in connection with him. He never owned anything. Do we own the air we breathe in and out? He was so proud, so kingly, that he never lowered himself to owning things. He let everything pass through him and by him. He clung to nothing and wedded himself to nothing, and in this way property fulfilled its function for him.

"It therefore mattered little to him that most of his money wound up in the pockets of swindlers, and anyone who was called to his court lived in luxury and pretty much as he pleased. Everyone should have what he wanted. At Lear's court at least, no one should go in need or have to exert himself.

"Lear was pious in his own way, and he said, 'Because it lies in human nature that not all of us can live in happiness and joy, then there should be at least some who do to demonstrate that they are striving toward heavenly bliss.'

"He was, by the way, also a man who did not, on principle, allow any monasteries to exist in his realm. His reasoning was that monks who fasted and castigated themselves scorned heaven's gifts and were therefore blasphemers.

"For years now, this all-out playboy had been at the mercy of moneylenders. In days past he had gone campaigning to rid himself of his debts. But as he grew older and more given to his comforts, the only time he mounted a horse was to go hunting, and his debts grew astronomically.

"As far as the king's age in this critical period is concerned, we shouldn't have any exaggerated notions: He was in his late forties. He was a broad, solidly built man with a brown beard that was trimmed in court style and showed not a single gray hair. He was without a wife, a widower. For the ten years before his wife Reginald's death, he had had a model marriage with her. In those days the sycophants, usurers, and thieves did not have a free hand at his court, for the departed Reginald controlled the king's purse and kept it shut tight. She knew how to handle Lear, and he did what she said. He saw to it that people honored her as the queen and followed her instructions. But she left him three troublesome daughters.

"And when the period of mourning was over, concerned relatives advised the king, in the interest of his young daughters who were now motherless, to remarry. These advisers had excellent matches to offer; and he, King Lear, himself the best match of all, dutifully studied all the candidates presented to him; but, still under Reginald's spell, he decided to accept none of them. He pleaded unending grief. His allegiance to his dear departed remained unbroken. Seductive and trustworthy ladies were smuggled into his castle. He came through all these adventures unmarried. He was an ascetic, at least as far as marriage was concerned. And soon no more ladies would volunteer for these trysts. He had emerged victorious from this engagement. He had fought and won the decisive battle, both for himself and for his kingdom.

"He remained single, our king Lear. There was no Queen Lear. This robust man on the throne was to have many descendants, but none who bore his name underwent the same fate as he, namely, that posterity stole his life away from him, just as it did troubadour Jaufie's, leaving him not King Lear anymore but a tattered, bedraggled, white-bearded monster that shook its mane and spooked about on a stormy heath, moaning and raging horribly.

"But heaven, earth, and underworld in those days knew that the real King Lear intensely disliked being caught out in the rain and therefore traveled heaths only in full gallop. What reason would this richly dressed gentleman have had to go in for such outdoor amusements and to let his hair grow? No, he did not wear a mane. That went against his nature.

"He lived higher and higher on the hog, every year a little higher still. His subjects had no cause to rejoice. They slaved to come up with the taxes his overseers imposed on them. He kept countless horses and dressed in the most opulent French style. Wondrous things were told of goings-on held at his various palaces and castles, of festivities that degenerated into drinking bouts days long in duration. And there were the ladies, too, of course, his favorites, whom he was careful to keep apart in diverse locations and who lived in castles he did his best to keep elegantly furnished.

"Word has come down to us of his three daughters, offspring of his legitimate but, alas!, brief marriage with the rigorous Reginald. I do not want to shock anyone with a tally of the sons and daughters that sprang from his loins thereafter, bearing witness to his joie de vivre. Were there a hundred, as some claim? Or were there two hundred? In any case, he did not depopulate the lands. He did his best to close the gaps that his wars and his sorties for loot had created, this rough-hewn man whom not even the later kings of Poland or Saxony would ever eclipse.

"We can easily imagine how he got into financial troubles. He rejected war as a way out of them not because he was peacefully inclined but because he found war too strenuous. Furthermore, he found that the expenses of war, which involved the participation of other playboys as deeply in debt as he—it was only natural that one King Lear called several dozen more of his kind into existence—ate up any income it generated. He sensed he was in trouble. Those close to him knew it. But they let no word of it leak to the outside world.

"Do you think His Majesty let himself be led astray by facts and so put an end to His Majesty's hopelessly dissolute way of life? Then you don't know His Majesty, King Lear! He listened to one suggestion after another, hearing some quite reasonable ones among them. But he perceived himself as Lear, who was impervious to worry.

"There are some Celtic legends that are of interest in this context. One tells of divine bulls and hogs, another of an equine divinity called Epona.

"In pictures that have come down to us we find Epona as a peasant girl wearing braids and seated between colts. She is feeding the young horses. Then there are tales about wild boars. There must have been lots of them in that wooded hill country, enough to make themselves a scourge on the countryside.

"There was one wild boar of massive size. It was a dragonlike monster, something like the Lernean lions on whose account Hercules and the gods were alerted. Now the gods in charge on our British Isles at that time were Manannan and Mod. These gods had some powerful dogs, dangerous hunting dogs, whose job it was to help the gods exercise their local power and meet the demands put on them. Once the huge boar realized that a plot against his life was afoot, he jumped into the ocean and swam off to find safety. Mod and Manannan's dogs swam after him. They met in the water. The dogs attacked, barked, and bit. They hung like bloodsucking parasites on the frightful, bulky, black monster that foamed at the mouth and emitted muffled roars. He dove underwater. The dogs let him go. He resurfaced, and they were at him again. They hung on his throat, his lips, his belly. They sprang onto his head from behind and tried to blind him by scratching at his eyes. But what they did not know was that the monster had a third eye in the back of its head.

"Bellowing and screeching, the boar tore one dog after another to pieces in this battle, in the seething water. At the end, two struggling dogs were left clamped in his huge maw, and he held them underwater until there was no sign of life left in them. Then, bleeding from his gaping wounds, the monster boar climbed up on land, on the so-called Pig Island where his young were living. He meant to warn them of the danger and gather them together to flee.

"But Mod had already been at work on this island. With his spear and with sharp boulders he had crushed the whole brood in front of their cave where they had been playing. With a chunk of mountain that he had brought from twenty miles away, he had trapped the mother sow in her cave and rendered her powerless to help her children. As Hermindran, this moaning beast dripping water and blood, came up from the beach to rest in his cave, he discovered the mutilated bodies of his offspring. And as the boar stood there in a fury, shrieking horribly, and tossing his head from side to side—blood ran from both the eyes in his forehead, the eyeballs hung down to his jaws—not knowing where to turn, the god Mod appeared before him.

"The battle between these two, the boar Hermindran and the god Mod, has never been described. Mod was an old god who, it appears, had gotten wind of the approach of Christianity and was therefore ready to abdicate. It is said that he had listened, incognito, to missionaries and decided on his own to convert, but he didn't know how to go about it. For he usually wandered about in the mountains in the form of a wild horse and had never noticed from the sermons that the missionaries had addressed horses, too. He thought everything they said was directed only at people. He could have inquired, but he still had too grandiose an idea of himself to stoop to that. The business with Hermindran cropped up while he was in this state of doubt. The timing was wonderful. Now he had something to do. He could get over his feeling of having come down in the world and take out his anger on somebody. Besides, trampling wild boars was part of his job.

"He waited near the cave for the boar. He heard the monster bellowing and noticed, to his dismay, that the dogs he had sent out to chase the monster down were not in evidence. Old Mod, in the guise he liked best, that of a horse, left the clearing where had stationed himself to intercept Hermindran and trotted off to find his dogs and, one way or another, to finish off the boar.

"The woods, grown up to brush and saplings, were very dense. A wild boar can manage fine in that kind of growth, a horse less so, and especially not a gigantic horse such as the god Mod naturally was. Then, too, he was old, and his twinges of conscience and his reflections on the missionaries' teachings had made him even weaker and more fumbling. He trotted along as a horse, but he had a long white beard growing on his chin, and that impeded his progress in the thick woods. The beard caught on branches, and these same branches tore at his magnificent mane, leaving it in tatters. Using his size and weight as well as kicking with his hoofs, he smashed down whole trees. This wild-boar forest was in league with its master, the boar Hermindran.

"And now the old god Mod had made his way through to Hermindran. The boar had already heard Mod crashing through the forest, but in his rage and fury he did not retreat an inch from where his children had been slaughtered, and he was trying to make his way into the cave that the god had blocked off with the huge rock and from which the muffled squeals of the mother sow were coming. Mod emerged from the woods and stood facing this ferocious male animal. He could see that Hermindran had been in a fight. Not only was he bathed in the blood that was running from his flanks but he had also taken up a strange, puzzling stance. He stood with his back to his attacker. Mod noticed this with hate and pleasure. His dogs were not there; they had succumbed to Hermindran; but the boar's position told Mod that the dogs had torn out his eyes. He could see only with the eye in the back of his head and so could not make full use of his most dangerous weapon, his tusks.

"With a leap that was not exactly first class but that was powerful enough to do the job, Mod sprang toward the monster crouched in the midst of his slaughtered brood. But he lost his footing and crashed to the ground, hooves in the air. The blood had made the ground slippery, and on top of that he had stumbled on one of the many small corpses.

"A peculiar battle took place now between the old, unsteady horse god and the horrible, half-blind, bleeding boar. I'll spare you the details, but you should know that there were times when things looked bad indeed for the god. The reports that have come down to us say that the only way Mod managed to emerge victorious was by invoking the aid of the missionaries' god. At a particularly critical moment in the fight when the still incredibly powerful monster had caught Mod on his tusks and lifted him right up, Mod had put out his call, asking for help first in a collegial manner, from god to god, as it were, but then willing to subject himself to the newcomer. At that point Mod was able to break away from Hermindran's tusks and slide off the boar's back. Miraculously, he was on his feet again before the boar could turn around on the difficult terrain. The giant horse now delivered a dozen of his fearful kicks to various parts of the monster's anatomy, to his flanks, his back, his head, depending on which way the now staggering, stumbling monster turned.

"And at the end, when Hermindran, apparently lifeless and nothing but a horribly mutilated lump of meat (he had been at a disadvantage from the start with tusks that pointed forward and an eye that looked backwards), at the end when the boar tried his last desperate trick, rising up suddenly under the horse, toppling him over, and throwing himself upon Mod once more, all Mod needed to do was overcome his revulsion for this beast and bite into the boar's neck, slicing his carotid arteries.

"The animal's blood, steaming hot, poured out over him in rhythmic spurts. Mod accepted it as the last sacrifice made to him."

Part Two

Mackenzie reached for his teacup. Kathleen jumped up and refilled it for him. Lord Crenshaw seemed very pleased.

"Answer a couple of questions for me, James. First, since I'm assuming this is the end of the wild boar episode, what became of the god Mod? Did the missionaries baptize him? Can you fill in the details for me?"

"Later, Gordon. That would hold us up now. I suggest that we go into the circumstances of Mod's conversion at another time."

He gave his brother-in-law a cheerful wave of the hand.

Lord Crenshaw: "And my second question, which has to do only with narrative technique: What is the link between this Celtic tale and King Lear?"

"You'll see, Gordon. Since Edward said we have plenty of time, I've expanded a bit on this image, this likeness of King Lear. I meant the story as a simile for King Lear and his behavior. In the eyes of his people, Lear soon appeared to be the raging wild boar Hermindran. Once he stopped going to war and had finished grazing even the richest neighboring lands bare, he devoted himself to hunting with a passion that knew no bounds. He was immoderate in everything; he showed no regard for anyone or anything. Hundreds of hunters and dogs and horses took part in the king's hunts. He stampeded through any and every field, the planted and the fallow alike. He destroyed grain fields, gardens, and orchards. Lear ravaged his own country.

"Then someone in his country reacted and decided to deal with this wild boar. It was not a god but a human being, not a warrior but a woman. And here my story begins.

"This woman was of the lower nobility but from knightly lineage, and she had no reason to be well disposed toward the king. For on one of His Majesty's earlier campaigns to replenish the royal coffers, her husband had lost his life. She had resolved, for her own part, not to go as far as her dead husband had in her own displays of fealty.

"And after Lear and his hordes had hunted through her lands a few times, leaving chaos in their path, she blocked access to her property on all sides, ramming sharpened poles diagonally into the ground with their points facing outward, so that any horses or dogs that tried to invade would be injured or possibly even killed. She also had traps and pitfalls set here and there on her borders. Thus prepared she awaited the return of the royal hunt, which is to say, the king's next attack on her property.

"Lear's hunters soon poured onto her land and swept across it. Some of them were left by the wayside, sprawled out next to their downed and wounded horses on the hilly, difficult terrain. Their companions rode on oblivious to them. Accidents, even fatal ones, were everyday occurrences during these entertainments of Lear's. Not until the hunters had returned home did word get around that some of their number were missing and that a certain noblewoman had set pitfalls on her land. The hunters resolved to get to the bottom of this affair.

"And so, not long thereafter, this wild, field-rending, seed-trampling hunt, these riders, horses, and dogs, this collective wild boar, Hermindran redivivus, stormed onto that fenced and defended turf again. They had not penetrated very far into it before someone realized that the king, none other than the king, was missing. A moment ago he had been with them. Now they saw only his riderless horse. He was, to the horror of the hunt, nowhere to be seen, nowhere to be found.

"Why to their horror, we might ask. If the truth be known, for one reason and one reason only: The hunters knew that from the moment he was missing among them they were doomed. Without his presence they were nothing but a pack of thieves, a horde of criminals, extortionists, and rowdies. If they did not find the king soon, they ran the risk of being lynched, either right away or when they returned home.

"Anxious hours of searching. Some ladies who belonged to the party took this opportunity to disappear into the brush, rats leaving the sinking ship.

"What had happened? You have no doubt guessed. His Majesty had fallen into the hands of our resolute noblewoman. Lear had tumbled into an especially well-designed pitfall that had been lined with manure and brambles. His horse had unseated him, gotten to its feet, and run off. But Lear was left lying in the pit. Some of the lady's peasants eventually heard Lear's howls of pain and rage—his horse had given him a parting kick in the chest—and came to peer down into the pit with unconcealed glee. There, thrashing around in the manure, pleading and bellowing, was a dandified, good-for-nothing courtier. The roar the fellow made was music to these farmers' ears. They did not recognize the king.

"When he screamed at them to help him, said he was Lear, the king, they held their sides laughing. He was mistaken, they told him, if he thought they would as much as lift a finger for Lear. He would have to come up with something better than that. They took their time, plenty of time. But then, finally, they fetched a ladder from a hay wagon and pulled poor Lear out. They dealt with him just as their mistress had instructed them to. Paying no attention to their captive's protests and complaints, they tied his hands securely behind his back, left his hat lying in the manure pit despite Lear's bellowings—the hat was decorated with valuable pearls—and drove him amidst hootings and proddings to the manor house, where their mistress, who recognized the king immediately, stood waiting on the veranda.

"As the peasants led the ill-smelling huntsman up the veranda steps, he screeched that he would see every last one of them broken on the wheel and hanged. He looked a fright with manure and twigs in his beard, his hair, and on his torn coat. His nose was bleeding, and the blood poured down his jacket in a thick stream. Blood was running down over his left eye, too. Grimacing, he shook his head to try to clear his vision.

"The lady did not dream of untying him. Other reasons aside, she noticed that he was carrying a hunting knife on his belt. Her men gave him a superficial cleaning on the veranda; then she opened the heavy oaken door of her house and let him go in before her. She shut the door behind her.

"The wounded boar stood with his back to the door. His left eye was glued shut with blood. His right glared at her murderously. Without a word, she took the knife from his belt and kept it in her hand. He followed her every move, his head drawn down between his shoulders. He was afraid.

"Again he screamed that he was Lear, the king. But, out of sheer terror, he stopped his yelping. She seemed ready to murder him. He was alone.

"He watched her face as a dog does. The lady spoke. He breathed easier. She didn't recognize him. She thought he was a courtier.

"She called him every name he deserved but had never had to hear before. He learned what people thought of him and his court. She called him a bandit in the service of a robber chief.

"— What crime had he committed? murmured Lear.

"— He had hunted over her fields and land! Didn't that make him a trespasser, and didn't she have the right, having caught him red-handed, to hang him from the roof beams?

"Lear's rage, now that he had grasped his situation, was gone. No royal outrage remained, only unmitigated fear.

"This nasty person wandered up and down in front of him with his hunting knife. It had occurred to him to charge her and knock her down. But what would he have gained. His hands were tied too tightly. He tugged and yanked at his bonds, keeping his hands hidden from her view, but without success.

"She ordered him to step away from the door and then walked around him with the knife. He turned with her. It was like a nightmare. He was afraid she would stab him from behind.

"She sat down on a stool some distance from him and, to ward off the stench emanating from him, held a handkerchief to her nose. She asked him what he would do if he were in her place. Did he have guts enough to pass judgment on himself, he, a vassal to such a robber, such a villainous king?

"Then, in his fear of death, Lear humbled himself. He mumbled something she didn't understand, whereupon she demanded a clear answer. Was he not ashamed of himself? Did he regret what he had done? Would he cease his heinous actions?

"And King Lear stammered: Yes, yes, he was sorry. He hadn't known.

"'You just followed him, you say? You thought you had to follow him?'

"'Yes,' he choked out. He accepted the role of the courtier that she assigned to him. He wanted to dupe her. She would let him go; then he would see to the rest. She forced him to beg for his life. He did everything she asked.

"She played the situation for all it was worth. She came up to him with the knife time and again, making him think each time that he had just drawn his last breath. She checked to see that he was still firmly tied. He whimpered and was ashamed that he whimpered to arouse her pity.

"Then she began a polite conversation. She asked how long he had known this king, where he came from, why he had gone to court. She drove him into one lie after another. Sometimes it seemed to him she was making fun of him and knew very well who he was. But that was just a passing thought prompted by a certain mocking tone he detected in her voice occasionally. Yes, that's the way it sounded. But then she adopted an ingenuous tone again as she continued to subject him to the most humiliating interrogation imaginable.

"When she had been at this a while and seemed satisfied with what she had accomplished, he asked her to free his hands. He was not feeling well, he said. And, indeed, he tottered against the wall. She shoved a chair toward him and cut the harsh rope, stepped back, and watched as he hung his manure-bedecked head, rubbed his filthy hands together, and brushed the manure from his jacket.

"Now, to his amazement, she turned from him and left the room. He stood up instantly, moved his arms, took two steps to the door, and pressed down the latch. The door was not locked. He could leave. But perhaps there were peasants waiting outside. He could not come to a decision.

"Then a door across the room opened. The noblewoman appeared, carrying a washbasin in her hands. She put it in front of him on the chair he had left and invited him to clean himself. She closed the door behind him with the remark that the whole world didn't have to watch him wash. Then she brought towels and a second washbasin because she felt his beard needed a little more attention. Finally, she herself carried everything away. During these procedures the two exchanged few words.

"When he was feeling tolerably well refurbished and had sunk heavily into an armchair in the corner, she appeared with a pitcher of beer and a mug. He took the mug with some uncertainty and sniffed at the beer she had poured for him. He looked at her suspiciously, then he drank, drank greedily. She refilled his mug. He gestured to her to join him; but, with a stern face, she rejected his invitation.

"After this Lear held his head up and asked what was to happen next. He asked her to release him, promising to make good any damages she had suffered.

"'You pay me anything? I want nothing from you. What can you compensate me for? I want none of the tainted money Lear pays you.'

"He felt a retort rise to his lips, but fear kept him from speaking.

"She asked again whether he held an office at court or was merely another courtier. He mumbled that he was a nobleman, as he had already told her. She: Then he should tell the king what had happened to him here. He should make clear to the king and everyone else at court that she, the noblewoman, was not alone, that there were others, many others, who thought as she did, if not worse, about him and his government. The king had better watch his step. That's what the courtier should tell him.

"Lear, with a doubtful smile: Is that what she really wanted him to do? That could prove dangerous.

"She: 'On any estate in the country that the king ravages, he will suffer what you have here today, except that if we catch the king himself things will go even worse for him.'

"Lear sat there a while, struck speechless by what he had heard. Then he took hold of himself and stood up, this wounded boar. He solemnly swore to carry out her command.

"'I am letting you go on your knight's word of honor that you will come back here in two weeks to the day and report to me what the king's answer is.'

"He pushed out into the fresh air. He felt as if he were suffocating. He wanted to strike someone dead, or run his knife into his own throat.

"She accompanied him onto the veranda and had a saddled horse brought to him from her own stables. He could use it until his return. She rode with him to the border of her lands.

"It should come as no surprise that Lear then wandered around in the woods for hours after this, trying to regain his composure. The lust for murder did not leave him. Finally, he guided his horse onto the road that led to his castle and was soon discovered by horsemen from his court who were casting about in search of him. He said he had taken a fall and lain unconscious for a while. They were so delighted to have found him that they didn't press him for details. He struck them as being still dazed from his fall. He had no need for acting.

"The incident continued to gnaw at Lear for days with undiminished ferocity. Then he came out of his funk and was his old self again, to all appearances. He traveled about, ate, drank, gambled, and rode. But there remained a terrible rage inside him that he tried to overcome this way.

"He could think of nothing but that outrageous incident. The woman would have to be disposed of. That would have been easy to do. His troops would carry out any order he gave them. But that wasn't the way to do it. He wanted real revenge; and it had to be his on the very day she had appointed. He grew sick with impatience.

"And then the day came. Lear gathered a small troop of horsemen, and without betraying his plan even to the captain, he rode with them to that estate where more than his life had been taken from him.

"At the border, before the beams and stones that rose up like battlements there, he stopped and had his trumpeter request passage for him, the king, and his retinue.

"The lady soon appeared on horseback, dismounted at the sight of her visitors, and curtsied low before the king who remained in his saddle on the far side of the wall. She immediately ordered that way be made for him to enter.

"As the troop of horsemen slowly rode in, she approached the king, who reined in his horse, and told him how honored she was at his visit. Then she galloped off ahead, acting as his runner to her home.

"While the captain and his men rested under some trees before the manor house, Lear slowly climbed the veranda steps and entered the house through the door she held open for him.

"The large room was familiar to him. With great ceremony she led him to the seat of honor at the fireplace. She herself retired respectfully to the table. When she wanted to call her servants, he stopped her. He gnashed his teeth.

"Silence for minutes on end. He broke it with three words.

"'Here I am.'

"She curtsied low.

"He, in his chair, his hand on his sword: 'You recognize me?'

"She curtsied again: 'You are the king, my lord.'

"He: 'Two weeks ago—'

"She gave him a puzzled look.

"He: 'Two weeks ago, you remember—'

"She: 'I do not know of what my lord speaks.'

"Canaille! Now she's afraid. She's acting as if she doesn't remember.

"'When I was here two weeks ago to this very day I solemnly swore to come back here again.'

"'My lord, you have never entered my house before. This is the first time you have thus honored me.'

"He leaned forward, red faced with rage at this impudence.

"'The first time you have honored me, you, you—'

"She kneeled before him: 'I don't understand why you are angry with me.'

"He tore at his beard: 'Why? Why?'

"She looked up at him, her eyes sad and serious.

"What was going on? Didn't she recognize him? Had his clothes, his manner, changed his appearance so much? He looked around the hall to reassure himself that it was not he who was mistaken.

"He told her to stand up and come nearer. She should pull her chair up closer to him. He had to trap this snake. The matter required it.

"'You remember: Two weeks ago I was hunting here in this area.'

"'As you say, my king.'

"'Then something happened—'

"He fixed his eyes on her and waited. Not a muscle twitched in her open, innocent face. She did not turn away from his gaze. Was it humanly possible to lie with such aplomb? Apparently it was. If this were just any ordinary case, the woman would have to undergo a test of fire.

"He: 'And then it happened that—'

"Again he did not complete his sentence. He was amazed. He was not prepared for this.

" 'Did anyone come into your house then?'

" 'While you were hunting? No one, my lord. I would have known. Or do you mean that someone snuck into the house when I wasn't here? And hid here? Someone you were pursuing? I'll call my servants. They told me nothing of it.'

"He: No, she should stay where she was. — Now that was the limit. He thought he must be dreaming. Was she ill? She didn't look it, this robust, clever woman with the clear eyes. Since she was forbidden to get up, she looked around her in the room.

" 'I found nothing changed, nothing missing. What could anyone have wanted from me?'

"His hand fell away from the grip of his sword. He resettled himself in his chair. She was dressed just as she had been two weeks ago. He checked carefully and found he was right. She was wearing the same cap on her blonde hair, had the same pink, fresh face, the same energetic mouth; he even remembered the red pimple above the left corner of her mouth that she touched occasionally with her finger. This woman who had stood him up against the door two weeks ago, against this very door, this woman who had taken his hunting knife and circled around him so that he had to turn like a monkey because he was afraid she might run the knife into his neck from behind, this woman who then cut the bonds on his hands only to heap horrendous insults upon him afterwards, this noblewoman about whom he had gathered considerable intelligence, Lady Imogen Persh, whose father his own father had elevated to a knight—this woman was trying to dupe him, adding one more crime to the ones she had already committed. She wanted to throw him off the track. It had apparently dawned on her after the fact how scandalously she had treated him. And now she thought he was falling for her little ruse.

"Then she said to the king: Even if he had come to her house by mistake and the unexpected honor of his visit was due, unfortunately, only to this error, still, after the long, dusty ride from the capital, he should rest here and, like his companions, not refuse a drink. She did not want it said that the king, her lord, had entered her house but refused her hospitality.

"Everything she said just raised the ante higher. She was pushing to the limit, and playing her role brilliantly, surely much better than he had played his when he stood before her pretending to be his own courtier.

"And then he had an inspiration, an illumination: Perhaps it wouldn't be a bad idea to play along with her. Perhaps she was cleverer than he was. It was altogether possible that she hadn't recognized him two weeks ago (his fall, the manure, his torn clothes may well have rendered him an unkingly figure; she had never seen him before; all the nobles who hunted with him wore clothing similar to his). For the time being, at any rate, and under these circumstances, perhaps the most practical thing both parties could do was to pretend the entire incident had never occurred. Oh, what a shrewd woman! But was that really what she was up to? He decided to play along with her, eager to see how things would turn out, skeptical, bewildered by this strange, unexpected, fortunate turn of events. He would play along, with some doubts, because he now felt ridiculous and humiliated in a different way, felt like a beggar who accepted what was thrown to him. For perhaps she knew what he was thinking and was just giving him an easy way out.

"His hand, as he let all this roll over him—it seemed to him he was no longer in his own skin, that he was dreaming—dropped down to his belt now and then. He was repeatedly on the verge of exploding. Finally, to pinch himself, as it were, and convince himself of his own existence, he rose noisily to his feet, stood in front of his chair, a threatening figure, this King Lear, Hermindran, the ferocious wild boar— who he no longer was.

"She rose with him, smiled tenderly and submissively. Just look how she can smile if she chooses to. And this is the woman who humiliated me so and caused me these weeks of anguish.

"She curtsied ceremoniously, crossing her arms, oddly enough, across her breast as a Moslem does. What was going through her head? Did she think she had won?

"She went to the wall and struck a gong. Her maids came in, peasant women decked out in festive clothes. They had changed to their finery once the word had spread that the king had come to visit. At their lady's instructions, they set the large table in the hall, brought in pitchers, distributed bouquets on the table.

"Without Lear acting at all—he remained standing before his chair, immobile—the scene had changed. He let it happen. Once again, the woman had seized the initiative. He had no choice but to play along.

"But not until she was sitting across from him at table—all the doors were open; outside in front of the house and under the trees his men were drinking and flirting with peasant women—did he realize what had happened and what she had accomplished (and she did not betray herself with so much as the flicker of an eyelash; she was a lady of the lower nobility who, with visible pride, indeed, with something like bliss, was entertaining her king): She had rescued him. She had saved his life.

"And he felt calm now. He could laugh. He was his old self. Several times, while the company was eating, drinking, and talking, he became pensive and doubtful (it was and remained an outrageous situation, like a horse that keeps throwing you off), and he would bring the conversation around to that fateful hunt again (fearful that she might recant on everything). But she did not change her position. Her expression remained unruffled. And finally she turned the tables and asked him to come clean and tell her what he had been looking for in her house during her absence and how he had gotten in. For no one had seen him or told her a thing. Had he disguised himself?

"Here was an out for him: He could have said yes, revealed all, and seen what her reaction would be. It was up to him now. It was his move. But he didn't dare to make it. He breathed a sigh of relief when she did not press him for an answer.

"Lear left soon (meaning to prevent any other untoward incidents). He left in a state that is hard to describe, a mixture of admiration, gratitude, incredulity, in such confusion that before she could mount her horse, he had raced away from her at the head of his troop. And why? So that once he had passed the barrier he could laugh, laugh uproariously and endlessly, drawing his captain next to him into his laughter and infecting his other horsemen with it. Everyone laughed; they all laughed. The king had had a wonderful time; he had found the lady a lot of fun.

"Lear didn't know why he had to laugh so uncontrollably, as a schoolboy will when laughing has been forbidden. As he traveled home to his castle, he whooped his confusion away. He had fooled the lady; it was funny beyond words; he was saved: She had not recognized him. All it had taken was different clothes, different circumstances. An addled female brain. He could have ridden right back and embraced her for it.

"But in the coming days he gave little thought to the warnings the lady had given him. He had recovered his balance. He was the old Lear. He carried on as before, if not worse.

"About this time, as often happened at major courts and especially at those where a lot of partying and drinking went on, a wandering theatrical troupe appeared at Lear's court and offered its services. This was an unusual troupe, a very good one, carefully managed by a director, an odd, extravagant actor who had fallen into disfavor with Lear some time ago because he understood his work too well. For what else could one do in plays, if they were to be effective, than capture the mood of the people and reflect conditions in society and in the state as they were? But what the people thought about Lear pleased him no better when he heard it in songs and on the stage than when Lady Imogen Persh told him the same things face to face.

"But the bald-headed theater director Jack Johnson continued to practice his trade as his trade should be practiced. He was, therefore, a thorn in Lear's side. Johnson was a dreadful type who had something of a bull-headed Brutus about him. But, to Lear's regret, Johnson was not a republican, in which case Lear could have had him arrested. No, on the contrary—and this was the most intolerable thing about the fel-low—he was a monarchist, but his ideas of what a ruler should be could not help striking Lear as insulting criticism. In the plays that this chap concocted, along with others in his troupe—and rumor had it that he was aided and abetted by certain intelligent enemies of the king, some of them among the sovereign's closest associates—in these plays the bald-headed old bird held up to the king an ideal ruler that was Lear's direct opposite, a ruler who was a model for his subjects, impeccable in his integrity, moderate, a family man who practiced justice and tended his subjects as a shepherd does his flock.

"For a while Lear had been indifferent to the Greek and Roman plays the troupe had adapted and then served up to him, but then their meaning became too clear. His Majesty summoned Mr. Jack Johnson to an interview: If he, the king, and his people were in need of enlighten-ment and instruction, they had any number of clergymen and school-teachers at their disposal. It was a player's job to distract and entertain. He should not meddle in other people's work. They could do without that. And if director Johnson did not stop producing plays that posed as farces and comedies but were full of barbs and idiotic allusions, he would find himself without a royal subsidy, and he could see how well he would fare then.

"Whereupon Johnson's troupe packed their bundles, climbed into their wagons, and left without a word.

"All this had happened years ago. Now Johnson had reappeared, and it seemed he was hoping to find fair weather at court. Since it was known that Lear personally handled everything having to do with the theater and entertainments in his state, Johnson was taken, immediately upon his arrival in the city, before Lear, who was to decide whether the man should be granted a concession and, possibly, even a subsidy.

"Our obstinate Jack Johnson—the king's aides could see that at a glance—had not changed in the meantime. He had, if anything, become even more serious, gloomy, a real undertaker type. It gave Lear's lord steward great pleasure to admit this rare bird to the king's presence. The inhabitants of the king's antechamber were anticipating an extraordinary happening, namely, that a human creature without wings would fly from one door to another and land on the court pavement, a bold and unusual experiment made all the more intriguing by the fact that the guinea pig was an actor who could be expected to make all kinds of faces expressing astonishment, dismay, pain, just what no one could know in advance.

"Johnson did not fly, not on his way in nor on his way out. He walked in stiffly on his long legs, stern and arrogant, altogether the man he was, the man no one at court liked; and he shuffled out again, lost in thought, his chin up, not wasting a glance on the king's officials.

"Inside, he had gotten right down to business and explained his new repertory to the king without any mention of the past. He reported the size and nature of his troupe and offered the king a series of exciting and instructive subsidized performances at the castle and in the city. Lear, who was, as always, irritated by Johnson's stress on the didactic, had the director summarize the plots of a few of these plays for him, pronounced them run-of-the-mill and boring, and claimed, as he had before, that they came under the jurisdiction of religious and educational authorities and that Johnson would have to seek approval through the appropriate channels. Still, Lear encouraged the director to tell him still more about his plans.

"The stubborn man who stood before the king, his hat clamped between his knees, promptly took this bait and ran with it. Lear was not, of course, the least bit interested in Johnson's plays. He had had a sudden inspiration. As Johnson had rattled on, and still was rattling on, about various roles, actors, and actresses, the king saw before his eyes his Imogen Persh, this figure who preoccupied him, who had his soul in her spell, who tormented him to the depths of his being yet at the same time filled him with admiration.

"What did he want? He saw it clearly as he sat listening to the babbling of this preacher in clown's clothing: He wanted to violate her. Yes, he wanted to humiliate her as a woman, just as she had humiliated him. He wanted vengeance (his soul boiled up in him again). And this was vengeance that would cut deep: to bring her to court and cast her among the whores, among the scum that this Johnson brought with him.

"Lear finally interrupted Johnson and began a cordial conversation with him. He invited the fellow to take a seat. Because Johnson was reluctant, Lear himself had to place a chair for him. Then Johnson was seated and obliged to listen. He had to be drawn into the plot.

"Could private citizens, dilettantes, be any good as actors? Lear asked. — Why not? Johnson replied. He had turned up excellent actors here and there, people who had a natural talent and didn't know it. Some could imitate just about anything without any training at all.

"Lear: 'Is that so? Imitate just about anything. Assume all kinds of roles. You can teach them and bring them to the point where they can imitate various figures.'

"Johnson confirmed that.

"'That has endless possibilities,' Lear growled, and Johnson went on talking. And though Lear sat there in a daydream, listening to Johnson with only one ear, some details from the man's chatter were not lost on him; for example, some names, the names of feudal lords in his country with whom he was on poor terms and whom he occasionally had to drag to his court by brute force. Johnson's troupe had played for these lords. Johnson reported this innocently, or impudently, which was more his style. The fellow was in cahoots with all those rebels. I've got to put an end to these goings-on, Lear said to himself. I could throw this wretch in jail, but I won't. I'll use him to bring her here. He is just the person, this moralizing sourpuss. I won't bring her here by force. Let her come and be here. Let her walk into the trap. Then (he burst out laughing in his thoughts) she'll get hers. I'll do with her just what she did with me.

"He stood up, went around the table, stood in front of Johnson, and gave him a powerful slap on the shoulder, as if he had just had an idea.

"'I've got a job for you, old chap. You need to get some new ideas. I don't like your plays, as you well know. I don't like the people you associate with and perform for either. I'm going to send you to the country.'

"That was out of the question, said the sober, imperturbable Johnson.

"'You need new ideas, you upstart, do you hear? New themes, new material.'

"'I'm familiar with peasants,' Johnson said scornfully.

"'Not familiar enough,' Lear insisted. 'Peasant life has a lot to offer for the theater. Think of all the different animals, the soil, the trees, all of nature. That will give you ideas.'

"'I can't see how,' Johnson persisted.

"Lear was equally stubborn: 'Besides, I know somebody out in the country. He could be a great asset to the theater, both through his ideas and his own participation. An enrichment of our theatrical life. The individual I have in mind is a landowner and has, I know, a great deal of respect for me, unlike those people you mentioned earlier and that you've visited. For once, Johnson, you should get to know some people who have a high opinion of me, a very high opinion, people who see in me the king I really am. I insist that you go there and let yourself be enlightened. You should hear that side of the story, too. You have to hear both sides. That is only just.'

"Johnson, who was uncomfortable sitting before the king and whose hat, whose only hat had fallen to the floor (the king was trampling on it heedlessly as he walked up and down), Johnson, who wanted to get up and rescue his hat, was forced back into his chair by Lear and obliged to hear what the king, with both feet planted on Johnson's hat, had to tell him.

"'She is a proponent of absolute monarchy.'

"'She?'

"'The person I've been telling you about. She is the widow of one of my bravest knights. He was killed in the last war.' (I can't remember the fellow at all.) 'After this painful loss, after his heroic death in the cause of his country, she retired to the stillness of nature, where she has been pursuing her ideas. She recently sent me some samples of them. Very interesting. You'd be interested in them, Johnson.'

"Johnson, resigned (there was no more hope for his hat now): 'So I'm supposed to go there.'

"'Her name is Imogen Persh. Her husband is dead, as I mentioned before. Give her my best regards and some gifts my lord steward will send along with you. You'll engage her in profitable conversation for two or three days. I'll make up your losses for any performances you have to cancel. Then you'll invite her to the court.'

"'I'm supposed to invite her to court?'

"'That will come about naturally in the course of your talks with her. You'll know when the appropriate moment presents itself. But, in any case, Johnson, you'll bring her back. I'm depending on it. Do you understand?'

"Lear stepped back, finally releasing Johnson's crushed hat. Johnson picked it up, then dusted and reshaped it. He had understood.

"'You will bring her here!' Lear roared.

"'I understand,' Johnson replied in some fright. Then he was sent on his way.

"And just as sour and dignified as he had been on his entrance, so he was as he passed out through the expectant and disappointed antechamber. There was no heave-ho, no wingless flight, no grimacings, no landing on the pavement. Nothing splatted to the ground or moaned.

"He was and remained an unpleasant fellow.

"Johnson's bitter path began. Not until he was underway in the carriage the king had made available to him did he realize that he had to be totally out of his senses if he did what Lear had ordered him to do: fetch the king a new lover. He, Johnson, pimping for King Lear! He, joining Lear's toadies and stooges!

"How had all this come about anyhow? The business with the hat, Lear standing on it, had thrown Johnson off balance. And then Lear had sent him away before he could respond. Johnson's head worked slowly.

"He was on the verge of jumping out of the carriage, going back, and throwing Lear's vile assignment back in his face. He should find someone else to do his dirty work. But just then he arrived. The servants with the gifts got out. They were standing before a strange barrier. The driver yelled at the peasants on the other side, and some of them came running.

"Johnson peered around him, looking for some escape. But he was surrounded. The peasants had already opened a passage for him, and someone was already riding toward him, a woman. It was too late. He set out on his path, his path of suffering.

"The rider asked what he wanted. He gave his name and, pointing to the people with him, said they had been sent by Lear, the king. The rider, astounded, had him repeat what he had said. She couldn't believe it, and he could understand why. He did not look the royal emissary. He explained his position to her. Then, in silence, they traveled a road barricaded at many points and came to the large manor house. The servants with the gifts waited on the veranda; that is, they were supposed to wait. What they had in fact done was simply put the gifts on the ground and leave. They did not go out of their way for this actor.

"Inside, the lady immediately asked what his message was. She treated this Johnson the way a traveling actor, a tall, bald-headed, aging, ill-dressed man, deserved to be treated. The lady saw this whole business as an insult to her, if Lear was in fact behind it. But she was still not certain of that.

"Johnson, for his part, had been so busy being angry with himself and thinking what a jackass he had been to accept this mission that he had not prepared himself for this meeting and stood here now like a bumpkin, turned his ruined hat in his hands, and fumbled for words. He destroyed his own credibility all the more. As a director, he would have declared himself incapable of this role.

"Because of his suspicious behavior, the conversation turned into an interrogation, and that was all to the good. In the course of it he gradually recovered himself. He could organize his thoughts, make his points; he became the old Johnson. The lady made such a favorable impression on him that he could not come right out and reveal Lear's evil intentions toward her. It was impossible for him. Johnson, who was so unyielding, stubborn, and firm when it came to principles, was, in everyday dealings, at the mercy of circumstances. He could not bring himself to pain this lady. He could not tell her what a vile plot Lear was hatching against her. He could not rescue her in the simplest possible way: He could not give her a plain, straightforward warning. No, he had to keep things to himself and make himself Lear's henchman (oh, how he suffered, hoping, though, to make it up to her soon, somehow, sometime), this Lear to whose court he had gone (how could he have dreamed of it?) to warn him to mend his ways, for he was standing on the brink of an abyss—and here Johnson was wooing him a new lover!

"She was a remarkable person. This judge of human nature could see that right away. She deserved to have a king—a real king—look upon her with favor.

"Once he had told her, with some embarrassment, that he was the director of a traveling theater company and had mentioned some of the plays in his repertory, she knew who he was. She had seen him years before. He told her that having already had a successful appearance in the capital in the past, he was now planning to set up his stage there again for a few weeks, and he had so notified Lear. Lear had made his appearance conditional on his introducing a certain new tone into his presentations; and since he, Johnson, was not sure he could make such changes on the spur of the moment, he himself had suggested that he take some time to look around elsewhere. It was at this point that the king had recommended—quite out of the blue but without any objections to Johnson's proposal—that Johnson make use of this opportunity to visit Lady Persh and to take her some gifts as an expression of the king's gratitude for the cordial reception she had recently afforded him.

"'And why, if the king, who did in fact appear here a few weeks ago, is so good as to remember me and send a token of his regard, why did he send you? He has hundreds of couriers, knights, and courtiers.'

"Johnson muttered helplessly: He couldn't say. (He wanted to spare this lady, but he was insulting her. He shouldn't have come, but here he was. Oh, my eternal concessions, my compromises—will I never change?)

"She wanted to know the details of his talk with Lear. The tone of the interrogation grew harsher. Johnson suffered and felt guilty. Shouldn't he just come out with the truth? He fell back on his imagination and, sighing, recounted something of his ill-fated encounter with the king. He had told Lear about his plays in which he meant to hold a mirror up to society. Apropos of that, Lear had started to speak of nature and its beauties, and had mentioned that he had met Lady Persh out here in the country.

"Her face lit up: 'And then what?'

"He recalled what he could. (Because of that silly business with his hat, much had escaped him at the time; but now bits and pieces of the conversation were coming back to him.)

"'And because the king does not think too highly of me—he finds my understanding of monarchy too rigid—he suggested I come here and learn from Lady Persh, so to speak.'

"She: 'So that you would develop a higher opinion of him?'

"The ice was broken. She laughed for a minute, then became pensive, alert, and asked Johnson to take a seat. She warmed up. She sat across from him at the table, and since she knew little about his plays, he had to tell her about them. The dour director was as if transformed. He played parts for her. He was her ally, and she was so delighted with him that she invited him to stay—yes, he simply must stay. How embarrassing. He had still not touched on his message from the king, and how could he come out with it now, lying to her and leading her into a trap, after she had taken him in so warmly?

"She asked if he had noticed the barriers on the borders of her land. They protected her property against the ravages of the royal hunt.

"He, sadly: Exactly his point. Someone had to hold a mirror up to the king. He didn't know what was going on in his own country.

"She: 'Does one of the dukes support you?'

"'Nobody bribes me.'

"'Would you go so far as—to kill the king?'

"'I'm an actor. I write plays. I don't murder people.'

"She raised her eyebrows in an ironic look: 'Don't you understand? You inspire others to murder him. What a strange lot you men are!'

"Then she switched to a lighter tone. 'So you'll stay here a few days as my guest. I'm grateful to the king for sending you here so that you can learn my views about the monarchical principle. You obviously pushed things too far with Lear!'

"'It is your job to educate me.'

"'But that he chose me of all people, a woman as uneducated as I who can't read or write.'

"'He obviously wasn't concerned about reading and writing.'

"He remained, and she proved to be a woman of the most pleasing ways, charming Johnson with her wit, skepticism, and agreeable nature. But she was not easy to see through. And that evening as he stretched out to go to sleep in the guest room, he said to himself: Here I am an old misogynist, writer, and actor. Why is she trying so hard to win me over? What help can I be to her against Lear? Does she really want to kill the king? There are signs that she does. Maybe I'm supposed to help her, a conspiracy.

"Johnson sat straight up in bed: 'Do I want to do that?'

"He answered his own question with a clear 'No' and lay back down again.

"He rode out into the fields with her, kept her company, watched her. Now protecting the king was uppermost in his mind. They talked about everything under the sun, not ignoring nations and governments, kings and the obligations of kings. The old actor had fallen head over heels in love with this lady. He was determined, once he was alone again, to write a poem about her, perhaps even a play. She wouldn't make a bad stage character at all. And then he recalled the king asking him whether dilettantes could be any good in the theater. So Lear had had the same thought himself.

"Really a good idea of Lear's, to bring her to court, to have her there to study.

"In short: Johnson, this old bear, wanted to take her along for himself. He didn't keep that to himself for long, and on the second day he said as much to her. She laughed. Was that Lear's idea?

"He admitted it was.

"'He instructed you to invite me? Why didn't you say so right away?'

"Johnson, chagrined: 'I didn't dare. You surely would have said no.'

"'And now? Now I won't?'

"He was ashamed and sad, Icarus fallen from the clouds.

"She asked what was going on at court these days.

"He: Nothing new. People gambled, fought tournaments, hunted, went to parties and banquets.

"'And you, Johnson, are there to provide still more entertainment?'

"'I'm no clown. We're not a circus.'

"'My, what a proud bunch you are.'

"He spent a sleepless night under her roof. He didn't think about the king. He would so much have liked to take her with him. On their last day together they were in high spirits. She was delightful, seemed to have forgotten everything. Their mood at parting was warm and cheerful.

"For one whole, long day the actor wandered around in the capital without calling on the king. He didn't dare present himself to Lear in his state of disarray. Finally, he couldn't put it off any longer. And there he stood before the king who looked at him through narrowed eyes and stroked his beard.

"'So, my friend where is she?'

"He lied: She wasn't well. She had been in bed and had gotten up only at certain times to keep him company. He conveyed her humble thanks for the gifts and her special gratitude for the invitation, which, to her regret, she could not accept because of her indisposition.

"Lear asked how she had been on the last day of Johnson's visit and what his impression of her had been.

"That was the signal for a eulogy. Lear remained seated during this hymn of praise. Then he wandered around the room and circled the actor, giving him searching looks. He burst out laughing and tapped the bald man on the forehead. 'You liked her!'

"Johnson realized he had given himself away. Lear shook his fists.

"'You've betrayed me, you old goat!'

"Johnson offered a stuttering protest: He had not said a word more than he should have.

"'Then why didn't she come, scoundrel? I want her here, you understand? You were supposed to bring her. Instead you—'

"He took his riding crop and rained down blows on Johnson, who ran for the door.

"And so the old, stiff-legged actor ran out through the antechamber, giving the king's officials there the show they had hoped for at his first visit.

"On that same afternoon, while Johnson's troupe, which had just assembled its stage, was tearing it down again and loading it on the carts, Johnson, who was supervising the work, was summoned before Lear. When he played deaf, two courtiers seized him and led him off to the castle. His wailing actors and actresses trailed along behind. He had told them what had happened, and they feared the worst.

"Lear, the fierce boar, stood in his chamber and glared at the actor. Had he really invited Lady Persh? Second, had he given her the gifts? Third, had she refused the invitation?

"Johnson, again in control of himself, said yes to all three questions.

"'Why,' Lear asked, 'when I, the king, had invited her, did she say no? Can you explain that?'

"Johnson: 'She knows your court. She is a woman.'

"'You have a lot of courage, Johnson.'

"Johnson's face remained calm and cold. Furious, Lear walked back and forth.

"'She has the same opinion of me that you do, hmm?'

"'You know that perfectly well.'

"Lear looked down at his riding crop but did not reach for it.

"'Yes, I know, you wretch. You can go.'

"But as Johnson was leaving, Lear followed on his heels and bellowed into the antechamber: 'Catch him, and beat him until he can't stand up.'

"Soon after, the king summoned his cousin and confidant, an older man living in the capital. Completely beside himself with rage, the king told this man he needed his advice. He had learned of a frightful plot against his life. All the conspirators were known to him. What did his cousin think he should do?

"When Lear mentioned Lady Persh, the prince, Lear's cousin, was not surprised. He advised Lear to strike.

"That evening the lady was seized on her estate, bound, thrown into a coach, and brought to the king's castle."

Part Three

THE ABDICATION

"Lear went to see her. He looked dreadful, consumed by rage. He carried a knife at his belt.

"'They tied you?'

"'Yes.'

"'You accept my gifts, but you plot to murder me.'

"'I am my king's vassal and protect him as best I can.'

"'You want to get rid of me. You've said it to my face.'

"'I—to you? When?'

"The old game. He'd had a bellyful of it.

"'There are two Imogens in your house, hmm? You have a sister living with you who looks just like you!'

"'I have no sister. Why does my king ask?'

"'I know you have no sister.'

"The old game. I'll teach her a lesson this time.

"'I'm going to do something to you so you'll know what's what. I'm going to rape. you'

"'My king would not do that.'

"'Kiss me!' he shrieked.

"She lowered her head.

"'I can't kiss you. Free my hands first.'

"He stepped behind her and cut the ropes.

"She rubbed her hands together, then looked at the king, put her left arm around his shoulder, pressed her mouth on his, and with her right hand took away his dagger and let it fall to the floor. Then she embraced the king again and said, as she released him, 'Now do with me what you will.'

"He went to the door, came back, picked up his dagger, and left her alone.

"She was held captive for many weeks after Johnson, who was no longer of any interest to the king, had left with his troupe.

"The king's affairs were in shambles at the time. The treasury was empty. Lear fumed and cried, 'Treachery!'

"And because he had already squeezed all he could from his vassals, he decided to turn to his daughters. It was a blessing that his all too brief marriage had given him daughters who had become the wives of wealthy dukes. They could help him out, he thought. His cousin undertook the mission, but with no success. They did not want to put their money in this leaky purse. Lear cursed them for 'degenerate women' who did not want to help their father, who was in need, get back onto his feet. And in truth they did not.

"The king brooded at his castle. He could not put the rich lands of his sons-in-law out of his mind. The plotting against him increased.

"'Retire to private life,' the cousin advised. 'As regent I can give you what you need.'

"Lear would have none of that. He talked with Imogen, who had been given a living room as her cell.

"'You'll be able to celebrate your triumph soon, Imogen. I'm going to abdicate.'

"She drew back into a corner of her small chamber. 'That's not true. I don't believe you.'

"'I'll have to do it. Will you still want to kill me when I'm not king anymore?'

"She came toward him and looked him in the eye. 'So you've reached that point? You've finally done it. Now you should be happy. — Somebody really should kill you.'

"'Why now?'

"She imitated him: 'Why now?'

"How she despised him. This was the woman who had had him bound.

"'Why don't you tell me what I should do instead?'

"She hissed back at him: 'Abdicate. Abdicate.' She stood before him like a Fury. 'And your abdication will accomplish nothing.'

"He didn't know what to make of this madwoman. He slipped out as she ranted on.

"He had his own key to her chamber. Outside he looked around. He was glad that no one had heard what she had dared to say to him.

"He remained sensual, untamed, and crafty. He didn't dream of abdicating. In a consultation with his cousin and his advisers he came up with the idea of dividing his property among his daughters in exchange for an appropriate sum. But the king's title that he had inherited from his ancestors, that he wanted to retain. The members of the royal council responded to this bizarre idea with embarrassed silence. Since he seemed unwilling to admit the facts himself, they finally had to tell him there was nothing left to divide.

"He laughed cynically, 'I know, I know, gentlemen. But you forget: I have immense reserves—of debts.'

"They joined in his laughter, taking his remark for another of Lear's jokes. But they didn't know their big-hearted king. He didn't waste time in discussion. He simply acted without their assistance.

"Word got around that he had sent messengers to his ducal relatives and scheduled a special session of the royal council. People were saying (with great relief) that he meant to retire from government.

"And so he did, in one respect.

"In another, he meant to deceive his family.

"Many tales have been told about the ensuing events. This is what really happened.

"Lear, who had dealt with his creditors both directly and through middlemen and who had even managed to get a new loan by implying he had some grand financial scheme in the works (which silenced his creditors on the subject of his debts), Lear announced at the special meeting of the royal council that he would retire as head of state. He had decided to devote himself to private life (something he had been considering for a long time), not because he felt himself to be too old but because he thought, having carried the heavy burden of his office for so many years, that he had a right to a personal life, to some peace and pleasure. In former days kings in his situation had often gone into monasteries. He meant to do the same but not right away, not at the moment. He wanted to relax first, to feel free of the burden of government, and to collect himself.

"It was a sentimental, touching speech sprinkled with pathos and reeking of lies and hypocrisy from beginning to end; and as he spoke the king watched his audience's reactions carefully. His most recent financial dealings had made him vulnerable. The shameless way his foreign creditors treated him and the high interest they demanded had unsettled him. He had his back to the wall; he was defenseless.

"His audience in the royal council consisted of two groups: his three daughters, who, with their dukes, had finally put in an appearance, and the regular members of the council, the already initiated. This main group could not believe their ears when they heard Lear carry on this way. They knew nothing of his arrangements with his creditors. They couldn't know yet exactly what he was after, but they were impressed by how he set about it. The sly fox.

"And now the king resorted to the ruse you are all familiar with. He began, with painfully obvious hypocrisy, to play the concerned father. When it came time for him to leave this world, he said—a sinner, like all flesh, and he the worst sinner of all—he wanted, at the least, to feel certain that he had provided for his children and fulfilled his obligations as a father.

"'I will leave my house,' this bloated figure said, his voice cracking, this man enraged by the exorbitant interest he had had to grant his creditors so that they would give him a new loan and keep their mouths shut. 'I will leave you alone, my children. Do not think ill of me. I want to put away from me my lands and all my property, all my earthly possessions, movable and immovable, and divide them among you, and all I ask is that, for the brief period before I enter a monastery to finish my days in prayer and repentance, you take me in and care for me in a manner commensurate with my kingly rank and my love for you.

"'And just as love moves me to divide my property among you, so you shall receive in proportion to your love for me.

"'Look here' (he had mounted a detailed map of his realm on the wall). 'These blue lines divide my kingdom into three parts. The size, number of inhabitants, and the wealth of the parts are noted here in the margin. Show me now how much you love me. The measure of your love will determine what you receive. Open your hearts, and send me off into the loneliness of my old age with the gift of your love. Speak, my daughters, you who will be my sole support in the world for a short while.

"'Do not hesitate to pour out your hearts. Love between man and wife may be shy and hide itself, but love between parents and children can come out into the open. Everyone rejoices in it. We have often been apart, my daughters. But that does not matter. Nothing is as firmly and deeply rooted as love between parent and child.'

"The daughters—three in number, two married to dukes, the youngest still at home and therefore particularly well acquainted with her father—found this whole performance in the worst possible taste. Everyone present knew that Lear had never given them any attention. He had seen them rarely even when they were small children, and, in later years, only on official occasions. There was not another father of their acquaintance who behaved toward his family as their father did toward them. As a consequence, they were all against him. And now he came with this talk about love, put on this show in front of everyone, as if the others didn't know very well how things stood. Now that he was aware of the unrest in his kingdom he wanted to quietly disappear, and so he had arranged this scene to put himself in the spotlight as a good father and noble ruler.

"What enraged them the most, though, was his making the division of his kingdom among them dependent on their avowals of love for him, a shameless display whose only purpose was to humiliate them.

"But they had to rise to the bait, for the ducal husbands were sitting right there, watching to see which of the three would come out the winner. The order of the day was stop at nothing. All that mattered here was to babble and come out on top, open your mouth and let as much love run out as the king can handle. They could settle accounts with him later.

"Done with his oratory, the king looked from one daughter to the other, obviously pleased with himself. All three sat there; all three hated him. He knew what they were feeling, and he reveled in their discomfort.

"As each of them sat looking expectantly at the other, he suggested they speak in the order of their ages. He spoke with a voice of honey. He wiped one last tear from his eye.

"I don't know whether the two older daughters said exactly what has come down to us in the reports we have. Distortions may have crept in in the form of additions, slips of the pen, and so forth. It's quite possible that both of them did in fact speak with the same grandiloquence, the same far-fetched images and similes we are familiar with from their speeches. What else can you do if you have nothing to say?

"Lear took great delight in watching them squirm. They could have thrown the ink pots on the table in his face, but instead they had to outdo themselves in sweet talk. They had to offer him love, more love than all of the British Isles put together could produce.

"Then he stood up, tapped on his map, took a pointer and was about to show them what their portions would be when it occurred to him that Goneril, the youngest daughter, had not spoken yet (he had already come to his decisions anyway). He apologized, went back to his throne with his pointer in his hand, and, wielding it like a scepter, signaled to Goneril with it.

"'Now it's your turn, Goneril.'

"He was a bit uneasy as he said this, for Goneril was dangerous. She sat there the way she occasionally sat at table in the castle, both elbows planted on the table, her head in her hands, her eyes looking down at the tabletop, perhaps at the ink pot across from her, with the idea of throwing it at him. With Goneril anything was possible. She didn't speak. She balked. He encouraged her, lovingly but now very much on edge.

"Suddenly, when he pressed her again, she raised her arms off the table, shoved her chair back, and yelled at him across the table. She'd had enough. She wouldn't have anything to do with this farce Her head, with its disorderly black hair, was thrust toward him. She did everything but stick out her tongue. She stood there for a second like a small Fury, then tossed her chair aside and stormed out. This scene had often been acted out between Lear and Goneril before, at varying levels of violence. He usually put up with her insults (most of which were justified). Now he couldn't afford that. He had to be offended, no matter what. It was too bad that Goneril couldn't contain herself and keep her mouth shut on this occasion at least. She spoiled all his fun. He could see the other two sisters and their fat husbands beaming.

"Sighing, he stood up. He left the stick he had used to point at Goneril lying on the table. Somebody handed it to him. Reluctantly, he divided his kingdom."

Part Four

KING LEAR'S DECLINE AND FALL

"And so he became a king without a country. By treaty with his two ducal sons-in-law he had negotiated himself a place to live and an ample income. How they got the money that was coming to them was their own lookout. He was particularly pleased to have outwitted his creditors, who had been out to fleece him. They wouldn't be able to squeeze a penny out of his hard-nosed sons-in-law.

"His unhappy heirs, on whom Lear's creditors pounced instantaneously, realized quickly enough what kind of pig they had bought in a poke.

"One of the first official acts of the duke who had taken over Lear's castle was to empty all the dungeons. When Lear heard of this, he protested, claiming his son-in-law was turning a pack of murderers loose on his heels. But his say didn't count for anything anymore, and so Imogen Persh was set free.

"Lear was enjoying his new position. Things were going his way, so far. He had a castle in every region of his country, was free of debts, and had plenty of money, so far. His court finances had been trimmed back very little, and his court, supported by the two dukes, exceeded their own in opulence. To Lear's astonishment, the dukes were not happy about that. As we have often seen before, Lear was, for all his shrewdness, naive, indeed, blind. He had swindled them. They would take vengeance. He would wind up with the short end of the stick.

"When the first year was over and Lear, with his entire retinue, was moving to his second daughter's castle, he was given no escort. This change of quarters had nothing regal about it. Who was there to greet him? Who yielded the highways to him? He and his followers had to pull off to the side of the road when the son-in-law he was leaving, with no other motive than to humiliate Lear, rode out to the hunt and demanded the entire roadway for himself.

"The reception he got at his other daughter's, who was no more willing than her husband to greet their guest, did not bode well for the future. Since Lear would be living near his old capital here, he immediately requested reinforcements for his retinue to help protect him from murderers. His daughter, to whom he made this request and who kept him waiting in her antechamber for days on end, was not very tactful with her father, who still bore the title of king. He would be safest, she told him, in the empty dungeons of his former residence, which were now at his disposal. Such was the cordial tone that now marked Lear's relationship with his children. Its advantage over the one that prevailed at the division of the legacy was its honesty.

"It was under these dismal circumstances at the second castle that Lear one day received a visit from Johnson, the theater director who had, in vain, held up the mirror of the drama to Lear in the past and whom the king had treated so high-handedly. The tall, bald-headed actor, this Brutus, was now gloomier than ever. He walked along in his tattered coat like fate itself. But Lear was pleased to see this dismal figure: He reminded him of old times. The titular king had, however, despite his naivete, noticed a few things, one being that he was at the end of his rope.

"As before, he had the actor tell him what plays he had in his repertory. Some new ones and the old ones. In the serious ones, the Greek and Roman tragedies, the theme was still 'The Regent and the State,' the arbitrary and tyrannical regent.

"This time Lear listened. He suddenly realized that this man had a high opinion of monarchs. He was an anchor. He was a friend. Lear could pour out his heart to him.

"We know that Johnson was an idealist, a man ready to glorify what he admired, a man with heart. He had once seen this king in power. Now Lear stood here humbled, abandoned by his family, rejected, without advisers, surrounded by inferior types. Now Lear was turning to him, the shabby actor. Johnson found the situation tragic.

"With feeling (and amazement, indeed, with pity), Lear saw what an effect his plaints had had on this honest man of the people. He had not, as he recalled, treated Johnson well in the past. Only dogs displayed this peculiar devotion and loyalty. These qualities were totally absent in his courtiers, who were abandoning him in droves.

"But this dog by the name of Johnson pleased Lear. And the crafty king, who, like a cat, always landed on his feet, began thinking as he listened to the actor present arguments Lear had never been able to tolerate before: If all the old ties were broken, if his daughters and sons-in-law treated him as he deserved, then what still remained in his arsenal was the monarchical principle. And he had this fanatical actor, too. Johnson could make something of the situation, stir up a popular movement, a rebellion against the dukes. Marvelous! It would not be hard to fan the flames of such a movement with slogans like 'Save our rightful ruler from his degenerate daughters' and so on.

"He discussed his plan with Johnson, who didn't understand right away what the king was driving at. But then the dreaded day came when the greatest part of the titular king's retinue abandoned him because he could neither pay them nor supply their basic needs and when, after a furious family scene about this matter, his daughter and her husband showed him the door.

"And King Lear traveled the highway in a small peasant's wagon, accompanied by a half-dozen loyal followers, Johnson among them. His troupe had remained behind at the castle and was giving another performance without him.

"A good thing it was summer. The party could sleep outdoors and had brought food along. Johnson rode back to the capital in the morning and alerted his troupe. Now he finally grasped the situation and seized on Lear's desperate plan. It was just his cup of tea. He told his troupe what had happened to the king and what he was now condemned to suffer: begging for his food and sleeping outdoors. Johnson told his actors to take this material, to make some couplets, songs, and ballads of it that could be incorporated into the play they were doing, and to present their new lines and lyrics with feeling. It was true, of course, that the king had not been a very popular ruler, but they mustn't let that bother them now. The masses had no memory, and they were a sentimental lot that could be easily moved. The actors should pull out all the stops and write some stirring stuff about a rejected, helpless king that fate had tumbled from the throne and who was now forced to wander about in wind and weather, in storm and fog, decrying his plight to the skies, here today, there tomorrow, obliged to stand at crossroads, begging his bread.

"The actors and actresses were taken with the idea. When Johnson returned to the little group of picnickers in the forest, all that was left of Lear's once mighty retinue, and told Lear what he had done, the king found the plan splendid, just what he had had in mind. But he had not the slightest intention of spending even a single night in wind and weather, storm and fog, etc. His director, Johnson, had best be clear about that. Lear declared himself unsuited for martyr roles.

"Johnson was sympathetic but also felt obliged to remind the king of the wish he had occasionally expressed about entering a monastery. 'Later,' Lear answered, 'after due preparation. A step like that shouldn't be taken in haste.'

"The group had not moved by evening. It was raining and storming. Lear refused to go back to the capital and beg for shelter. Besides, the road was a sea of mud. They were, in short, stuck. There was no choice but for Lear, and two others who could squeeze in with him, to sleep in the cart. The others huddled outside under trees. The rain did not let up until morning. Lear was in a towering rage. He hurled threats at the whole world. Not another day of this living in the great outdoors. His companions were frightened of him. They drove on and housed him with a peasant for at least the rest of that day. Lear continued to rant.

"Johnson tried to impress on him that in terms of their propaganda campaign this vagabond existence was a gold mine. Johnson knew of a desolate, dreary heath not far away where there were witches and God knows what else. Robbers and lepers went into hiding there. Owls and wildcats ran around there. It was the ideal place for a king who was challenging the world. Lear should stay there for a week, a week at the least. Everyone would have to admit that if something like that were possible, that if a king could be driven to such lengths, then something was rotten in the state.

"Lear didn't bite. No arguments could convince him. Indeed, this suggestion shook his confidence in Johnson. He wondered whether Johnson wasn't a republican after all and didn't just want to kill him. Why should he go to this heath if all Johnson needed was propaganda material? Johnson could write what he pleased; his troupe could play anything they liked on their stage. Lear didn't have to expose himself to such hardships on that account. No, one night outdoors had been enough.

"Johnson finally realized he could not drag Lear about at will. The only solution was to find him some secret lodging and then go about spreading the necessary rumors. Johnson knew right where he would house Lear. It was only an hour's journey from here, at Lady Persh's. And so, without revealing his plan to anyone, he took one of the wagon horses and rode out to visit her. He explained the situation to her: They were both monarchists, defenders of the principle of an ideal king. They had to do something for Lear, if not out of brotherly love, then in the interest of their cause. Lear, Johnson went on, should live secretly on Lady Persh's estate while Johnson and his company spread the myth of King Lear about the country: Lear, the king, abandoned by his children to whom he had granted their legacy while he was still alive, is driven out onto the street by them, driven out into wind and weather, into storm and rain on the blustery heath. He is forced to live among rabble, among criminals, fools, madmen, among dogs, cats, and owls.

"The lady, in icy tones: 'Why doesn't he do just that? It's an excellent idea, very powerful. Did you suggest that to him?'

"'He won't do it. He won't go to the heath.'

"'Then we can't help him. Go back and tell him we insist on the heath. Without the heath there's nothing we can do for him.'

"'He realizes that himself. But he says it would be much simpler just to spread the story, the myth, without his actually going to the heath. He can sit peacefully somewhere and wait for our propaganda to have its effect.'

"Imogen was amazed at Johnson: 'And you'll go along with that? What is it you want to do? Do you really want to reinstate him as king? Haven't you had enough of him? Am I supposed to barricade my property again to keep him out? And you think I'm going to help you, me, after he kept me locked up for months?'

"Johnson hadn't known that. Oh, he said, he was sorry to hear that. But now he didn't know what to do next.

"Disheartened, he was about to leave. But Imogen stopped him. He had to sit down. She sat thinking at the table for a long time, her forehead down on it toward the end of her meditation. Finally she started up, shook herself, jumped up from her chair, and had her old open expression. And she came over to Johnson, put out her hand, and squeezed his warmly for a long time. 'All right, let him come.'

"He could have fallen down on his knees before her. He kissed her hand.

"'You always were a faithful animal, and you always will be,' she laughed. Lear had told him that, too.

"He misunderstood her completely, our good Johnson. Those were harsh times.

"Triumphantly Johnson led the pathetic little royal party up the road to Imogen's estate. Hungry and wet, they hobbled and trotted slowly along. Lear's retinue, which now consisted of only three old men (the rest had all disappeared), were quartered with Imogen's servants.

"When the enraged king, cutting a sad figure, came in, she did not close the door behind him right away.

"'You know, Lear, whose house you are entering?'

"He cringed as from a blow when she omitted the king's title. The water dripped from him. Pitifully he looked over at her.

"'I ask for lodging.'

"'Johnson has already told you that I will take you in. It's been a while since we last saw each other. The last time we met I was your captive, and you wanted to rape me.'

"He mumbled and didn't move. She shook herself, stood at the table with her back to him, then came toward him again, changed now, as she had been with Johnson, cheerful and open. She took his heavy, wet coat, offered him a chair and brought him warm beer. He drank and drank. She watched. He wolfed down the bread she gave him. Then two of her manservants came in and led him up a small stairway. She followed them.

"Those were harsh times. She did to him what he had done to her. On the top floor, in a room to the rear of the house, she locked him in. He roared with rage after he had gone inside and she had bolted the door on him.

"'You're locking me in.'

"She: 'This is where you'll stay, Lear.'

"He screamed: 'Treachery! Treachery!'

"She listened with pleasure.

"He could bellow all he wanted in his room. Downstairs, Johnson held his ears. He interceded for Lear.

"She said: 'Johnson, you really are a dog.'

"When he ranted—she never entered his room without her manservants—she remained cold and impassive. She stood mute as his imprecations rained down on her. But after a few weeks, when he began to sit quietly in his cell, the scene changed. She went in alone. Their conversations were brief. He could see she despised him. But still, it was some contact with a human being. Sometimes he cried to himself, wailed loudly in the afternoon when the day seemed too long for him, and hoped she would come or Johnson would visit him. And so he lived in a kind of delirium.

"Finally she came and sat down with him, her contempt visible in the set of her mouth. She looked at him. She took obvious pleasure in what she saw. He was breaking down physically; his beard was streaked with gray. She asked him how he pictured the future. The dukes were searching for him. It was only a matter of time before one of them would assume the throne. No one spoke of Lear anymore.

"He nodded lethargically. Where was Johnson?

"'He's on the road. He has to earn a living for himself and his troupe.'

"Lear had developed the habit of mumbling inaudibly to himself. She asked, 'What did you say?'

"He: 'Thank you for coming.'

"'Are you thirsty? Does someone bring you beer now and then? Would you like to take a walk outside?'

"He squinted at her fearfully: 'You want to be rid of me?' And he began to snivel softly.

"'All I asked was if you wanted some air. I'll send someone up to help you freshen up.'

"Holding on to the arm of a manservant, he went down the winding stairs and sat under a tree in the orchard behind the house. He didn't lift his head off his chest. Tears ran down his cheeks. Lear wept for Lear.

"When she jumped down from her horse and tapped him on the shoulder, he started with fright. She thought he should have a barber come. A warm bath would do him good, too. She gave appropriate instructions to the servant sitting with him.

"Lear did not go back to his cell but was quartered now in the large, bright guest room on the top floor. He could have gone in and out at will, but he didn't move. His only excursions were to the window to look out on the fields. Then he returned to his place at the table near the bird cage.

"He recovered slowly. Johnson came and sat with him. Lear pulled himself together and took a walk with him in the fields. Johnson spoke respectfully and treated Lear like his king. Lear spoke very little, but he did convince the actor to spend the entire day with him. Then, at Johnson's doing, other people began coming to the estate to visit the king. They came secretly and never called Lear by name. The lady of the estate brought them to him. He knew none of them. Not one was from his former court. They were of the lower nobility, like Imogen. They came respectfully to pay their homage to him, as one would to a king in exile. Lear began to carry his head higher. He paid more attention to his appearance. The lady put two of her servants at his disposal. He often called for Johnson, whom he advertised as his plenipotentiary. He occasionally put in a request to Imogen to summon Johnson. But the message came back to him that Johnson and his troupe were not available at the moment. He was working at the court of one of the dukes. That was a bitter pill for Lear, but he could not pay Johnson himself.

"Then he was feeling in good enough form that he wanted to speak with Imogen. He saw her only rarely. One day she had one of his servants ask him if he would do her the honor of dining with her. When he accepted, she sent up some gifts: new clothes and linens, also some flowers and cologne. Decked out in this finery, he went downstairs to the hall of which he had such bitter memories from the past. A servant followed him, carrying the flowers that had been sent up to him.

"When his heavy tread sounded on the steps, she was standing at the foot of the stairs curtsying to him. He saw her from above and hesitated, then, worried, went on down the stairs. He had an old grudge against this hall. Now he was standing before her. She turned and preceded him to the door of the hall, then let him pass through ahead of her. He had taken the flowers from the servant, and he gave them to her.

"She played the same game with him that she had played when he returned to see her two weeks after his first disastrous meeting with her. She was all innocence. She acted as if she didn't know he had been her captive, that she had insulted him, locked him up, and mistreated him for months on end.

"Now she stood there, this woman who had done all that to him, and was the picture of innocence and humility. She did not betray herself with a single sign. Those were harsh times.

"Wide-eyed, he took in this creature who was sitting across from him at table, eating with him, and making small talk. He saw a hard woman who was more than a match for him, a fist that crushed him. He couldn't make head nor tail of things.

"The thought ran through his head: I was king for a long time. I ruled over thousands. What is going on here? — Hermindran, the fierce wild boar, must have felt the same way. Two of his eyes were already torn out and hung down from their bloody sockets. With his third eye, he saw the god Mod, the giant horse that was pounding him with his hooves.

"When they left the table and he was about to go upstairs, she told him that the entire house was at his disposal. For as long as he stayed with her, she would take up her quarters in the back rooms. He protested. She reminded him that he, the king, was a guest in her home. What would his guests think of her if they saw him so unroyally received and unable to make use of even her small manor house?

"And so it was. Lear occupied Lady Imogen Persh's manor house. He remained in hiding, a king in exile, but his supporters, disguised as peasants, merchants, and beggars, visited him in ever greater numbers. They were taken to Lady Imogen, who acted as his lord steward and privy councillor.

"Things are never so bad in a country that they can't get worse. Lear's kingdom found that out after his abdication. The king had left a rotten administration and financial chaos behind him. The dukes had to take drastic measures to create order again and liquidate the state's immense debt. They had had a reputation as skinflints and misers before they came to power. Now they were able to fill their own purses again with the high taxes they demanded, but the country could not get back on its feet. The people started thinking: Lear may have been intractable but he couldn't be accused of stinginess. He took what he wanted, he extorted funds, he ravaged the land, but for all that people managed to save a little here, a little there. But the dukes were merciless and methodical in collecting huge sums, even resorting to armed commissars to help them.

"And so it happened that people began to speak well of King Lear the minute the dukes started clearing away the wreckage Lear had left behind him. People began to feel nostalgic for the good old days under Lear.

Lear's emissaries—headed by Lady Persh and Johnson—went about their work. Rumor had it that even the earlier abuses were, indirectly, the fault of the dukes, Lear's sons-in-law, and of his daughters; for the daughters had made Lear pay out large portions of their inheritances in advance, and that is what had ruined the state's finances. When Lear had been desperate for sources of income, he had—according to this version of the story—turned, with all paternal trust, to his daughters themselves for loans. They granted them to him, but at horrendous terms. They fleeced him so badly that he was left with no choice but to abdicate. And that's what the daughters had been after all along.

"And so—just as with troubadour Jaufie—a myth was born, in this case the myth of King Lear, the good, sore abused father. Some of this news reached Lear in Lady Persh's manor house. 'Well, well,' he said, and raised no objections to his rehabilitation.

"It had finally penetrated to him that Imogen had been his salvation. Hour after hour, day after day, he thought about how he would reward her once he was back in power. You mustn't think, of course, when you hear that, that the old Lear was dead. He was still alive, at least at those moments when he dreamed of his new kingly glory, imagining huge festivals and banquets, and hunts, too, just like the ones of old. Funny, he thought, they never learn. I was their king once before. You'd think they'd know me by now. I wouldn't trust myself an inch. With pity for his subjects, he could tell already that he would disappoint them, disappoint them bitterly. If only things were that far along.

"He saw a lot of Imogen in these days, asked her to join him at table, walked and rode with her through the fields without ever leaving her estate. She was not his kind of woman any more than that uncompromising Brutus, the director Johnson and Lear's propaganda chief, was his kind of man. But both of them could bring him to heel. He had great respect for her particularly. He ranked her even above his dead wife. Imogen was far cleverer than the dead queen. He admired Imogen; and sometimes, when he took stock of how he had come back to life, he overflowed with gratitude toward her, this woman who had caused him no little pain, too, which he had not forgotten and had no intention of forgetting.

"Unrest among the people grew. Delegations came to visit Lear. Oh ho, the old reprobate thought, it looks as if I'll be king again soon.

"The king became quite lively in these weeks, and as we all know, one of the requirements of Lear's liveliness was the company of women. And because he was no longer surrounded by the loose and cheerful ladies of his past, we can well imagine where he directed his friendly, searching, affectionate gaze. But while the only consenting partner that had mattered in Lear's past amours had been Lear himself, love with Imogen required the consent of two.

"He tried to sidle up to her on walks. She drove him off fiercely. She was His Majesty's humble servant, but a servant at some distance and armed with a formidable set of quills. Lear was in despair. But he could not desist. If he was to win her, he would have to assume her ways. Those were the conditions she set. This wooing of Imogen represented Lear's only serious enterprise during his exile. The effort proved to have rejuvenating powers. It made him more flexible and lively.

"His transformation delighted the rigid dogmatist Johnson, who was now bringing his theatrical talents to bear on politics and treating them like a big stage production. And Lear said to him on one occasion, when the mime was telling him how the monarchical idea was gaining ground and how large numbers of the bourgeoisie, the peasantry, and the nobility were rallying to it and how opposition to the dukes was growing—on this occasion Lear said that the actor was a conjurer. He was winning followers for him, the king, and drawing them away from the dukes and Lear's wicked daughters. And how was he doing this? With wars, battles, head-on attacks? No, with talk, with ideas, with fantasy, with images, with the monarchical idea. Johnson was not capable of throwing a spear, but by merely shaking it and threatening his foes with it, he achieved more than others could by actually casting it.

"Lear laughed uproariously. But Johnson thought this only right and meet and not funny at all.

"And a little later—things had progressed apace; the seed Johnson had sown was almost full grown now—the two happened to be speaking again about Johnson's inventive and imaginative tactics, but this time in Imogen's presence. They were in the hall of the manor house; and Lear, putting on his most solemn face, bid his bold champion, the director Johnson, who had introduced the new weapon of mind and fantasy into the fray, kneel down before him, the king. Which Johnson did.

"And Lear told him, as he kneeled there, that he meant to reward him for his service to the crown by elevating him to the nobility. And so he dubbed him a knight and gave him, whom he had previously called only Bill or William, a new name. Because of his abilities to influence people with the power of his imagination, to terrify them with his lion's roar, and to win battles merely by shouting and by rattling his weapons, Lear dubbed him William—not William the Screecher but William the Spearshaker, William Shakespeare, a name that the actor, rising after the ceremony with his usual serious mien, accepted.

"'No one will ever have cause to laugh at that name,' he promised the king, 'not now or in the future.'

"This theater director William Shakespeare was the first and only man that Lear raised to the nobility while in exile. The second person he elevated to higher rank was, as we can easily guess, his jailer, Imogen Persh, who had seen him at his weakest but who did not let the distinction of her new rank keep her from showing him her teeth.

"During the campaign leading to the restoration of the monarchy, the actor Shakespeare wrote his play *King Lear,* though not in exactly the same version that has come down to us. For his purposes, neither the real king (whom he knew all too well) nor a relatively young king were of much use. He chose as his father of several wily daughters an old man with a flowing white beard, a noble king who, after years of peaceful governance, had abdicated in his daughters' favor and who became a helpless, wandering beggar after his heirs had robbed him of his last penny.

"The play begins with that grandiose, grandiloquent family scene, the division of the kingdom. Shakespeare's imagination is powerful here, but it had to be especially powerful, indeed violent, because it played havoc with the truth, turning it completely on its head. *King Lear* demonstrates in exemplary fashion the magic powers of the imagination, how it can change, transform, how, with its appearance of reality, it can dissolve old, solid reality, proving it not so solid after all.

"Johnson-Shakespeare fabricated as he jolly well pleased. He gave his imagination its freest reign, of course, in the heath scene. Our Lear, with his aversion for foul weather, would never have let himself in for that. The touching scene with Cordelia was not, of course, part of the original propaganda play.

"Now let's bring our tale to its end. The dukes, blind and blundering as they were, did everything in their power to sabotage their own cause and smooth Lear's path back to the throne. There were uprisings both large and small. Tax collectors were murdered. Lear's propaganda soothed the insurgents' consciences. And then heaven spoke its judgment: There was no rain. The drought was disastrous. The year's crops were destroyed. The pretender to the throne profited from all this.

"Lear returned to his castle. He thought it only right to bring Lady Imogen with him. Everyone who wished him well and had had a part in his restoration advised him to do so. He followed their advice with divided feelings. He knew he would be up against a strict regime. But he had no choice. He put his hopes in his craftiness. The king was back on the throne, but Lear was there, too.

"And then he began, first on the sly, then openly, to rebel against the myth that was devouring and enslaving him. Former friends of both sexes who had made it through the bad times reappeared timidly and furtively. Lear complained to them, just as timidly and furtively, that he was king only by the grace of his backers and that his hands were tied.

"He sat on the throne. What was he hoping for? That he might become his own boss again and do just as he had in the past? Life moves forward; nothing repeats itself.

"Fanatics had brought him back to power. They were also his downfall. They killed him at a banquet after it had become clear to them what his intentions were.

"Imogen herself was behind the plot. She had guided him and supported him. She had, despite herself, developed a genuine feeling for him. She struggled to win him over to her ways; she compromised herself often, all to no avail. His death brought her no joy. And in the unrest following on it, she, too, was killed.

"An actor and playwright of a later age picked up this ancient but still powerful drama by the propagandist William Shakespeare and adapted it for his (and our) stage. This man, who, for all I know, was named Smith but who called himself Shakespeare, wrote a lot of plays himself and drew on other people's work as well.

"And so this *King Lear* has come down to us—the story or, if you will, the tragedy of a wild boar from Celtic times who could not find a god to tame him."

BOOK THREE

Can a Wild Boar Be Tamed?

THAT was the long story of King Lear—or of Queen Lear—that James Mackenzie, the elegant professor, Alice's brother, had offered the company, the third story, after the one about the troubadour and the one about the page and his ring. Mackenzie should, of course, in accordance with his nephew's wish, have told *Hamlet*. But he shied away from it. Early on, between sections of his story, Edward reminded him of his promise. But he always got back the answer: "Later. Let me finish with this first." And now he was finished.

The master of the house, Lord Crenshaw, was much pleased and moved by the contribution of his guest and brother-in-law. He congratulated him and, to the surprise of many present, asserted that his thesis seemed to be gaining ground in their company, the thesis that "reality" as we imagine it does not exist but is always in the sway of images and fantasies. Indeed, we could go even further and say it is image and fantasy, independent of individual human wills, that shape the world. What Gordon Allison found particularly moving in Lear's story was how the victim, Lear, resisted the alien monarchical idea that was out to devour him.

The guests let him talk. Then the small, sad voice of the teacher spoke up. "Did Lear really have to come to this end? Was there no turning around for him, no salvation? He behaved so decently in his first marriage."

Gordon Allison answered: "Who could have saved him? A woman perhaps? Lady Persh, for instance? She did her best, but he wouldn't cooperate."

He laughed loudly.

Gordon: "He was the man he was."

James Mackenzie, the teller of the story, confirmed Gordon's view: "He clearly couldn't be tamed."

Edward: "If I understand you correctly, Lear was a wild boar from

231

birth on, a wild boar through and through by nature, by birth. And so he was free of guilt."

James: "He was responsible for what he did. There's no way around that."

Edward: "Even though he was what he was by nature?"

James: "He abused his power. He didn't hold himself in check. He thought it was his good right not to have to hold himself in check. And so he got his comeuppance."

"And rightly so? That was inevitable?"

James: "I think so."

Then Edward turned his gaze on Lord Crenshaw, Gordon Allison, his father. He had followed Edward's conversation with James with keen attention. When Edward looked at him, Gordon Allison quickly turned his head aside. But their eyes met for a second, a moment. Eye to eye, they took each other's measure.

Edward: All they that take the sword shall perish with the sword.

Gordon Allison: Who is this I've taken into my house?

Gordon's face quivered. Anger surged up in him. A wave of rage swept through his brain.

Alice sat next to her son, watching him and her husband.

Gordon rose and left the room.

The workings of nature are mysterious. Edward carried in him a strange and terrifying image that kept eluding his intelligence. That image was the goal of his questioning and searching, but he didn't know what questions he should ask or why he should ask them. His questioning might be leading him onto the wrong track; but, though he didn't realize it, he was being driven on in a clear direction.

That image had been working secretly yet powerfully in him ever since it had found its way into his soul. The bomb had shaken the framework of his soul; the force of fear spread and manifested itself in his movements. He trembled. But he did more than tremble.

He often suffered from nausea. He vomited and ate poorly. The family consulted with the clinic director. Dr. King talked with Edward as he had before.

"How do you account for this, Edward? You must know. What's behind it?"

Edward said the nausea overcame him suddenly. He had to vomit.

"Nausea from what? What makes you feel sick? A situation, an event? What event?"

Edward stuck by his answer: He didn't know. But his answer was not convincing. The doctor was skeptical. His patient was evading him.

Edward made some random remarks that the doctor followed carefully. Then, after Edward had steered the conversation around to the clinic, the nurses there, and how his former nurse was and whether she still had the same rooms she had then, at that point he asked:

"Why didn't you let anyone visit me in my room when I first came to the clinic?"

"We never do. It wouldn't have been beneficial either for you or for the visitor."

"You know, Doctor, that I want to be completely open."

"You have to be. You mustn't keep anything to yourself. Otherwise you'll never make any headway with your problems."

"I know." (I know myself how to deal with my problems. No doctor can do that for me.) "Something that bothers me is that Mother fainted in front of my door. Kathleen told me. Did I look so awful?"

Then the doctor, whom the nurse had informed about the incident, reminded Edward that he had often told him, during his stay at the clinic, about the malevolent, threatening, and anxious feelings he was suffering from. Edward had apparently forgotten that.

Edward was surprised. He really could not remember that the doctor had ever said such things to him. The old man nodded.

"You've even forgotten that I talked to you about them. Seeing you, the expression on your face frightened your mother, and she fainted."

"How did I look?"

The doctor: "It's strange that I have to keep telling you that and that you always forget it again instantly. We should make an experiment to see how long it takes before it fades from your memory again."

"So what did she see in my face?"

"Fear, and a strange, ferocious rage. You bared your teeth. Sometimes you raised your arm to strike a blow or defend yourself."

"A battle scene."

The doctor: "An awful one. As you remember we were able to break through your superficial fears in the Pentothal treatments. We traced them back to certain experiences that were accessible to you. But we didn't get near the real fears, the totally repressed stuff that goes way back."

Edward stared in front of him. "I don't mean to hold anything back. We'll get to the bottom of this."

"How?"

"I don't know. But we will."

The fierce, angry expression on his face reminded the doctor of the one he had just described to his patient. Edward continued to stare into space.

The doctor: "You have a clue?"

"I think so."

The doctor: "Can you give me an idea what it is?"

Edward stood up slowly and looked at the doctor with that same malevolent grimace on his face.

"No."

He picked up his crutches, started to leave, then turned his head.

"Why do you want to know?"

He thumped off angrily.

Mackenzie's Mild Therapy

JAMES Mackenzie came into his nephew's room.

Mackenzie: "You led me astray, my lad. I should have known better than to follow the bad boys when they egged me on. I've been watching you these past weeks on our story-telling evenings. You were so tense. And I had hoped—vain hope!—to entertain and distract you."

Edward laughed and shook his head.

Mackenzie: "Well?"

"Forgive me, but you're like puppies who don't have their eyes open yet, the way you romp around and roll on your backs and sides. Seriously, Uncle, don't you know what you were telling us?"

Mackenzie sighed: "You and your ideas, Edward. You see things that aren't there. You keep digging and digging. When will you stop?"

"I can't stop. I can't."

Mackenzie: "I can't, you say. Why not? You pride yourself on it. Why? Why are you searching so hard for 'the truth'? There's no snow outside today. If there were, I'd make my old suggestion again: Let it be. Let's not talk anymore. Let's conduct our dialogue with things and leave ourselves out of it for a change. You have a sarcastic look on your face. You don't think much of my idea. But believe me, what a great disfavor we do each other. We treat one another so badly. The one instructs the other, and no one really knows what's right. A dog or a horse, reasonable animals, what kind of conversations do you think they have with each other? A dog runs around and sniffs and sits down and lets people go on by him. He believes in what he smells and what he sees. He eats and drinks and tastes what he eats. If he's hungry he goes looking for food. He doesn't understand a word, but he can interpret every sound that comes from your mouth. He is at home in the world of gesture. And where are we at home, with our words and concepts!"

235

"You want us to stop thinking, Uncle. But other people will think."

"What kind of argument is that? Every insect comes from the hand of the Creator better equipped for life than human beings are. Not to mention the flowers, the trees, the grass. Look at the trees. They are. At any and every moment, without reservation, they are. The rain falls on them. What happens when the rain falls on them? What do they do? The rain soaks into the ground. Their roots in the ground notice it. The roots are designed by nature to do that. They have pores for it, and when the water comes, it goes into the pores, and the roots swallow; the tree drinks. It knows when it has drunk enough. The pores close. The roots won't absorb any more."

"A tree is a machine."

Mackenzie: "Just the opposite. A machine is like a tree. I'm serious. The only reason we produce machines, the only real reason why we work at all is because it's in our nature. How would we have ever come on such ideas ourselves? In that respect at least we listen and obey and are connected to the rest of creation. We would have been wiped out long ago if we'd ever harbored any doubts in that respect."

Edward: "So what is it you're trying to say?"

Mackenzie: "On the British Isles ruled this tyrant, this King Lear, and he was like a wild boar and acknowledged only himself and his pleasures, his power and glory. He hardly knew his children, didn't even know later how many he had, and they never knew what it was to have a father. He was sufficient unto himself. He saw no one but himself. He devastated his land because it was in his nature to devastate and because he enjoyed leaving trails of destruction behind him. Do you see what that amounts to and what I meant to say with it, especially to you? That's the ego, and that's what the ego is like. In Lear you have an image for our ravenous, insatiable ego. It does not want to blend with anything. It wants to be unique, unmistakable. It does not seek harmony. 'I' can count only to one. It is never part of a chord.

"What was Lear to his country? A ruler? A parasite. A cancer. The country knew what ailed it. There were people who knew what health was. The lady, Queen Lear, tried to tame him. But in the old legend, the god Mod knew better what had to be done. No attempts at reform. Just wipe the beast out and clear the way for recovery."

Edward experienced the same feelings every time Mackenzie came to talk with him. Edward received him coolly, grew angry with him, then wound up interested in what he had to say. He raised his arms and stretched in his chair.

"All right, Uncle James, come clean with me. Why are you telling me all this? What are you driving at? I interpret your story very differently."

"Tell me your interpretation."

Edward licked his lips (aha, you want to pull it out of me; now you're afraid): "Another time."

"Suit yourself."

"You're not angry with me, Uncle?"

"I just hope I haven't supplied more grist for your mill. I wanted to do just the opposite. Are you listening, Eddy, or am I delivering a monologue? Or are you laughing at me? Listen, I've been here for several months now, watching you and your family, which is also my family. And I don't think you're treating yourself well. And because you're not treating yourself well, you're harming the others, too. That saddens me; and, as you know, I'm not much given to sadness. I usually live for myself, or I travel. But now Alice, your mother—and my sister—has invited me to be with you all, to keep you company, to keep her company. Now I, too, am learning what a 'family' is. I'm getting to know you. And, if you'll forgive me for saying so, I don't like the direction you're taking, Edward, so hotheaded—and pigheaded."

"Pigheaded? Strange that you pick that word. So that makes me the wild boar?"

"No, Eddy, it's not you I object to but your direction. Why do you think I told you all about the snow and the rain and the roots? What do you think my reasoning was when you pressed me to tell *Hamlet* and I said to myself that I'd rather tell about this raging wild boar that goes berserk, rooting about and tearing up the land? The image of the wild boar came to me first; Lear occurred to me later. Then I put the two together."

"Have you actually known people like him?"

Mackenzie: "Lots of them. You read from Kierkegaard. That was a wonderful, stimulating evening. You were fully alive, and I could see you very clearly, Edward. I'd been somewhat afraid of you till then— you laugh, but it's true—because I thought you were sick. I'm an unfortunate creature in that respect: I'm one of those people who are afraid of sickness and the sick. It is, I know, a stupidly atavistic throwback. Suddenly, on that evening, I saw you sitting there with your little book, filling the role of this Kierkegaard of whom I heard but whom I had avoided like the plague. And you were reading him aloud. 'Honesty, I want honesty.' I can still hear the way you said it: 'Because I want honesty. I'm willing to risk something for this honesty.' I could see it in your face. You were willing to risk something. Then came a passage about sacrifice. 'And if I should be sacrificed, literally sacrificed, then I would not be a sacrifice to Christianity but to honesty, because it is honesty I want.'"

"That's what I said. That's Kierkegaard."

"That is the wild boar."

"But, but—"

Mackenzie: "Yes, Edward, that's how I see it. And I saw, too, that we have misunderstood you, that you are not sick."

Edward's features stiffened.

Mackenzie: "I know that you're not sick. You're—forgive me—possessed. You're running wild and destroying yourself in the process. This hunger for truth, Eddy, how I've come to hate it, 'honesty' and 'frankness.' All those noble words people hide behind when they run amok are a curse. We have to 'know'—we destroy the world, rob existence of its meaning. We have to root around in existence and sniff at every single thing, tear it apart and devour it, rather than be patient and feel ourselves in the right place.

"Eddy, what is the difference between the way of life that I, an experienced old man, am urging on you and your own? People like you want to become something, and you will become it. But you are not, and you never will be. You will never achieve being. And the worst of it is, you don't even want to. Yes, that's precisely what you don't want."

Edward sat motionless.

Mackenzie: "Are you listening?" Mackenzie, in a low, friendly tone, drawing him out: "Silence is a good thing. Does a stick of wood talk when you throw it on the fire? It falls—there it is—and then it bursts into flame—that is its way. It is never going. It has always arrived."

When Edward remained silent, Mackenzie touched his hand. He wanted to add something. But then he ws struck by Edward's strange posture, the way his fingers were spread out and one hand raised in an unnatural, incomprehensible gesture.

Mackenzie peered into Edward's face; it was immobile.

But no, something was beginning to show in it. A wild expression slowly began to form in it, fear, overpowering fear. Edward gnashed his teeth, bared them. He moaned. A nightmare? His arms were raised, his hands in front of his face, his head turned aside as if he expected a blow.

"Edward, Eddy, for God's sake."

This was one of those attacks Alice had told him about, but it was far worse than Mackenzie had imagined.

"Wake up, lad."

He shook Edward.

The arms sank. Edward raised his head, which he had lowered onto his chest. His face relaxed. He took a deep breath. He opened his eyes.

Mackenzie: "What are you up to?"

Edward looked about him hesitantly.

Mackenzie tried to make him laugh.

"Were you dreaming in broad daylight? Did you sleep badly? Am I boring you?"

Now Edward began to smile. Mackenzie stayed a few minutes longer but was glad he could hand things over to his sister, Alice, who arrived just then with the coffee tray and started chatting with Edward.

Edward sat up quickly when they were both gone.

They're all trying to sell me a bill of goods. One says I'm sick, and all I have to do is wait a while and I'll get well. Just sit tight.

The other whispers in my ear that I'm healthy but possessed. Maybe he's right. At any rate, I'm not crazy.

They shouldn't think they can fool me, coming up with a diagnosis to "cure" me. In the first place, it won't work. The doctors have found that out already. And in the second, that shouldn't come as a surprise to anyone because my concerns are of a different nature. That's why they don't yield to the doctors. A stone doesn't burn in a fire built with straw.

So how do they rid themselves of this irritation?

One of them makes a wide detour around it, such a wide detour that the very size of it casts suspicion on him. Life, some old sayings tell us, is but a dream. And if life really is a dream, then why all the fuss? Besides, it's not even our own dream, of course not, because we're dream figures ourselves. A monster is sleeping somewhere, and we're just some notions of his. A demon dreams about human beings and bombs and artillery fire, and afterwards I'm missing a leg. At any rate, we humans are comfortably blameless.

The whole business is ridiculous. It's obvious. Fear inspires crazy ideas. With our knees knocking together we produce our bald-faced lies. Because the murderer can't deny his crime, he claims that neither he nor his victim exists.

Or we say we're not guilty. It's society's fault.

And then, to top it all off, we have Uncle James, our clever professor, a worldly-wise world traveler, which is to say a man who takes life easy. He says leave well enough alone. The fact of the matter is that evil resides in you yourself. Well, that's progress. And then he recommends a simple process of self-evasion and escape: Transform yourself into a stick of wood! With a little effort and good will you'll manage it. A stick of wood simply is, no doubt about that; and it's neither good nor evil, nor does it suffer pangs of conscience. When you throw it into the stove it doesn't object, and it isn't afraid. Oh, what bliss, what bliss to be a stick of firewood.

There are other choices, of course. You can become a raindrop, become one with it, assume its nature. In any case, you shut off your consciousness, no ego, no will, no thinking, no desiring—then true existence can begin.

Why? Because we make consciousness and will into cancers that eat away at being. The cure is to transform yourself back into a tree or an animal, metamorphosis in reverse, the theory of evolution stood on its head.

I get the picture. I'm the wild boar who is devastating himself and his surroundings here.

Edward sat in his chair and was in good spirits. He drank the rest of his coffee in slow sips. He broke off a piece of cookie and let it melt in his mouth.

My doctor is on the right track and has his hunches. But he wants to keep this whole business just between him and me and bury it. My life is supposed to take place in my consultations with him. He wants to cure me of a complex. That's what he'd like. You pay your doctor's bills, go home, and everything is taken care of. Oh, no, Doctor, we won't get anywhere that way. Your motto is: Don't rock the boat. You hear that same motto from the people who, for what reason I don't know, get the brilliant idea now and then to send a few million other people to their death. Not themselves, of course. They stay at home and are outraged if the heating system doesn't work.

They use the telephone to send people to the Arctic, where they freeze to death, or to the Sahara, where they die of thirst, or they send them overseas into mine fields, artillery fire, and bomber attacks. That's called historical necessity.

What good luck for mankind that it has bombs and artillery to fall back on. They make life worth living (for some people). They make for an exciting game. You can move other people around. You have pawns and rooks and knights on your board. How simple that makes the world. That's your anonymous god and his nightmare. But it's not the god who experiences the nightmare. He leaves that to everybody else.

He is not without awareness; he is not nascent, dozing nature; he is no nirvana. Far from it—he thinks, he speculates, he plays. And life has its charms—for him.

Edward sat in his chair, cheerful, expansive.

It was still pouring outside. The black tree trunks and the black, twisted branches were awash in the water. The rain formed a glasslike curtain that twisted, distorted the trees waving in the wind. Looking at the rain, Edward laughed. When had Edward ever been in such a good mood? Mackenzie had been good for him:

Old friend, drenching rain, you're there before the door, and I won't let you in. You're condemned. Here I sit. Right, I'm playing Luther. Here I sit; I cannot do otherwise. God help me. Amen. I won't let you in. I wouldn't dream of conversing with you. I lose myself in you? Ha!

Edward rocked with laughter. Then he fell serious; his mood changed. He stared into space. He felt something in his limbs.

It seems I had one of my fits. He was tapping on my hand and sitting so close to me, looked a bit pale, too. It seems I frightened him.

He gave himself up to his thoughts.

That business the doctor told me. Why didn't Mother tell me about it? A horror scene, a horror. Whatever it is in me sits there as if in a box. The lid has snapped shut, and no one has the key.

The horror the scene emanated set his thoughts wandering again. He was grinning to himself again.

Not so bad that I've got this thing, whatever it is—and that it makes me sick. Otherwise they'd be protected and wouldn't let me poke around. Blessed sickness. There's a mole at work in me, making me into a mole myself.

I'm suffering from mole disease and have turned into a mole that tunnels under the ground and chews on the roots that push up their pretty plants.

The trouble they're taking to get in my way—and how badly they're botching it. They give themselves away and talk out of school all the time. They're just the opposite of me. The truth leaks out of them as if out of a leaky barrel, and they don't even know it. My poor keg is sealed and bunged up tight. It holds on to its miserable riches.

Edward fell asleep. Alice came to look in on him. She saw the sleeper. He had a good, gentle expression on his face. How she loved him.

She tiptoed out.

When he woke up refreshed from an hour's nap, it was still raining. At first he thought of calling for someone. Then he reconsidered and decided to luxuriate in his chair and meditate. He picked up his old train of thought.

First there is Father. He was going to tell the version of things he had cooked up to suit himself. I lay on the sofa and listened. His tall tale amounted to nothing. He told about Mother and himself. He distorted, he lied. And that passes for the poetic imagination. The gray knight leaves her in the lurch, goes off on a crusade. What airs he gives himself! On a crusade! And then he slanders Mother to boot.

And I, who was I? A weakling, something not deserving of attention, a child on the fringes of the marriage. That's his view of the case. The witnesses are called. Professor James Mackenzie, brother of the wife, uncle of the plaintiff, comes to the stand. What do you have to contribute? Mackenzie is a case himself. The witness does not want to testify. The defendant rushes in to protest his innocence. But the court sees through his offer and notices how filthy the water is that he has used to wash himself clean. James Mackenzie, a different case, a caricature, everything he does turns out different from what he plans and wants. He forgets what he's about, talks, thinks he is concealing himself and others but really reveals all in the process. That's James Mackenzie for you, the well-intentioned brother who wants to help. He relates the obscure case of a mythical, majestic king and reduces it to a comic sketch. He has us expecting to hear about a king who cheats his relatives. Sounds harmless enough, doesn't it? But behind it all is the harsh, painful story of the wild boar and of the god that can cope with the boar only by killing him. Perhaps some dimwit or another is reminded of Hercules and his twelve deeds. But I'm not one of those dimwits. I do as Kathleen does. I look around the room.

The truth!

It's a funny thing about the truth, my friends. It can't be shoved under the rug. How happy I'd be to get rid of it, to send it packing back to Dr. King in the clinic.

The king: "I like him not, nor stands it safe with us to let his madness range. Therefore prepare you. I your commission will forthwith dispatch."

Guildenstern: "We will ourselves provide. Most holy and religious fear it is to keep those many many bodies safe that live and feed upon your Majesty."

"Arm you, I pray you, to this speedy voyage."

And so he goes with them, is shipwrecked, and comes back. Ha, ha. I won't go away in the first place. No, I'll stay right here. They'll have to deal with me. Times have changed. This isn't a royal house, and it's not Denmark. We're in England, in a humane age, an age of world wars, too, of course. Ah, well, time marches on.

Let's see now, what was it Professor James Mackenzie said? What was the essence of his story? Let's see: It was the story of a man, a degenerate, an act of violence, a rape that either happened or didn't happen.

Edward twisted around in his chair, turned pale, lowered his head between his knees. It didn't help. The vomit burst out of him. He wiped his mouth, shut his eyes, exhausted.

Disgusting.

But I won't get anywhere this way. If thy right hand offend thee, cut it off.

He rang.

Alice's Blue Summer Dress

23 NO one failed to notice. He was better. But the improvement in his physical health brought consequences with it that were not to everyone's liking. Edward could wander around in the house on his crutches, go upstairs slowly, and make visits. Now he could intrude upon the household physically.

Now his crutches banged and thudded in the hallways and on the stairs. His artificial leg stamped and creaked—Edward the wanderer. The restless spirit searched, pried, questioned, listened.

He invaded his father's study. He went upstairs from his room, went down the corridor, and opened the library door without knocking, as if it were his own room. He greeted his father casually and sat down somewhere. He didn't initiate a conversation. If his father asked if he wanted something, he said no. Sometimes he just shook his head, sat still, and was there. It was unclear what he wanted.

Gordon Allison acted as if he were writing or reading. He had been working erratically for weeks now. He had begun to emancipate himself from his big armchair. He had begun doing something he kept secret from the others (Kathleen would have been pleased if she had known): He was marching back and forth on his thick rug. He sat down only to take a breather. He stood at the window and looked out. His study had a large balcony. Every once in a while Gordon felt the urge to go outside. The only place he could go was onto the balcony, but that would attract attention. He didn't dare do it, though his study sometimes felt so confining to him he thought he would suffocate.

Gordon Allison was not enjoying his work anymore. Writing disgusted him. He almost welcomed Edward's visits. Let him come, let him come.

He listened for the thumping of Edward's artificial leg, noted with satisfaction that it was coming closer, and prepared himself for Edward's visit.

244

The two sat together: the son, who felt compelled to be near his father (he wanted to enter his aura; he felt calmer there), and the father, who dug himself in behind his immense desk, armed and ready to fight, or so it felt to him.

The two sometimes sat this way for two hours until Edward hitched himself to his feet, nodded to his father, and stamped out of the room.

Although his general condition improved, his trembling got worse, sometimes taking the form of violent shivering which he tried in vain to control. And he developed an odd propensity for childish pursuits. It irritated him if people called attention to this. He shrank, as it were, into a small child. One of the ways this inclination manifested itself was in expeditions to the attic where he uncovered things that delighted him, old toys, for example, wooden railroad cars. He ran them around on their tracks, and he could not tear himself away from these games. They touched him in some deep way. Here he felt strangely content. He poked and banged around in the attic for hours on end until his mother came and drove him out. But he soon returned to his strange paradise, and Alice had no choice but to send chairs and cushions up for him to prevent him from sitting on splintery crates.

Among ancient, broken-down pieces of furniture that had gathered there, among the dutifully preserved souvenirs of family celebrations, among school books, school satchels, sports equipment, Edward sat in the half dark (there was only one dim bulb in the whole large room) and read cowboy-and-Indian stories in a tattered paperback or played with building blocks, carefully building on the lid of a crate a bridge, a castle, a church, attentive, absorbed, deeply satisfied.

Alice sat down next to him. He took no notice of her.

His pleasure was visible on his face. She said, when he stopped for a moment and looked up at her, that she would long ago have thrown away these things that he was enjoying so much. They were still here only because his father had protested whenever she wanted to throw them out. He was attached to some of them.

"Which ones?" Edward asked.

"He used to be a journalist, and he has articles, newspapers, manuscripts, and drafts from that time in the trunks and cupboards. He hasn't come up here for years, but he won't let a thing go."

"How do you know, Mother, that he doesn't come up here sometimes. Maybe he comes up when you're not home."

"What an odd thought, Edward."

"He comes and gets a sheet of paper or a draft without your knowledge. How could you know? Then he works with it. It stimulates him. He doesn't say so. But then he doesn't talk to anybody about what he's doing."

"Yes, he does draw a curtain around his work. But if I ask him he'll sometimes tell me something. He actually likes me to ask."

"And do you do him that favor? Do you ask?"

"Sometimes."

"You're not interested in his work?"

"I feel it's better to leave him alone. It could disturb him if I asked."

"You haven't known for a long time what he's been writing?"

"But Edward, the minute one of his books is published I have a copy."

"That's not what I mean, Mother. You don't read it. I know you read other things."

"Edward, come now. We all have our individual tastes. After all, he doesn't write just to please me."

Edward: "I don't know. If I were a writer's wife I would always read and keep up with what my husband wrote—just to be in touch with him, if for no other reason."

"My dear boy, what do you know about artists and their marriages? I suspect there are very few artists who let their wives in on their work, and there are very few wives who are interested in their husbands' work."

"Why aren't they?"

"Why aren't they? Why should they be? If a man goes to an office, does his wife follow him? What about a shoemaker or a tailor? Is his wife interested in the shoes or suits he makes? You think it's not the same thing. For a wife, it is."

"It's not the same. You know that, Mother."

"You're dreadful, Edward. You don't accept what anyone says."

"If it's true I accept it."

After a pause, she pleaded with him.

"What shall I say now?"

"What you think."

"He used to involve me in his work earlier and told me a lot about it. Later, I have to admit, I wasn't interested. And finally we both took it for granted that we wouldn't speak about it."

"That's the way it was."

Alice: "Yes."

Edward: "He used to talk. Maybe he would talk now, too. Nobody forced him to tell us that long story he told us last fall. He'd talk now, too."

"But why, Edward? If he wants to keep his own counsel. I tell you lots of artists are like that. I let him be."

"You let him be."

"Yes."

"You feel you're doing him a favor."

"He retires into his work like a hermit. I know he's content in his isolation. He needs it."

"He needs it? What for?"

"I don't know. He needs it. And that's why I leave him alone."

Edward: "Maybe he needs it, maybe he doesn't. At any rate, he's got it. But where has it gotten him. Fantasy is all he has now. He doesn't believe in any reality anymore. That's his theory. He sees everything from afar and doesn't participate. Nothing moves him. It's surprising that he still writes at all."

Her eyes lit up. "It wouldn't be bad if he stopped writing someday."

"Why should he?"

"To face up to himself. To face up to the world."

"You want vengeance? You hate him, Mother?"

Alice: "I wish he would come out of himself—but no, I don't wish that either. I wished it before. But no more. Not for a long time. He's found some kind of peace. I let him have it."

Edward: "You hate him. He left you. He threw you over."

She laughed out loud: "Edward, what nonsense! Threw me over!"

Edward: "You let him take that path. He told us about the woman who let her gray knight go off. You should have followed him. Who drove him off? It's awful, it's terrible to see how he sits there at his desk and writes and writes, amusing books, adventure stories, and we make big circles around him. What if he died tomorrow, and we found him dead at his desk? Would anyone mourn him? Tell me what you think, Mother."

She had covered her face with her hands. She lifted her left arm and signaled him to stop. "Stop, I beg you, Edward."

He waited. When she raised her head, Edward started up again. "His stories are light. He likes mysteries. He never depicts us and our society the way writers like Balzac, Zola, Galsworthy did. What is it he's doing? He chooses his material deliberately. Whom does he confront, whom does he speak with, from whom is he shutting himself off?"

"Please, Edward, let him be. He's living his life. He's spun his web, and he's content in it."

"There. You've said it yourself. Do you realize that? If he's content, or, in your words, if he's spun his web—. Mother, if a spider sits in its web and has drunk its fill on others' blood should we just let it be?"

She held her hands over her ears, then put an arm in front of her eyes.

"This is awful, intolerable."

Before he could ask any more questions, she was gone.

When Gordon Allison heard his son stomping upstairs to the attic, he would often follow him, unobserved. He wanted to know what Edward was doing there.

The attic was large. Near the entrance there was a storeroom. From this dark storage area where lumber was kept, Gordon Allison could look into the attic area through the wide cracks between the wallboards. He had climbed to his hiding place this time when Edward and Alice had talked. He closed the door and sat on the pile of boards. After Edward had thumped around in the room a while, his mother joined him. Gordon eavesdropped on their conversation. When his son had left, he crept back to his library, which used to be the room where he worked.

Edward in his room.

— Now I'm the spider. Except I'm not full of blood. I'm a starved spider. I've spun a thread, and I'm waiting for a fly to get tangled in it.

I'm not well. I don't like my trembling. Maybe I'll develop other symptoms. But it's worth it to be sick. What if I weren't sick or if I had never been sick at all? How far along would I be then? How would things stand for me, for this family?

What truth—what degree of hypocrisy.

(He hesitated as he thought about that.)

How would things stand. They all seem to be content, including Mother.

(He couldn't get any further.)

So I'm robbing them of their tranquility. I'm disturbing the peace of the house. Father doesn't want anyone prodding at him. Mother is on the fence and finds me a nuisance. Kathleen is in good spirits. That leaves me.

(He couldn't get any further. The trembling started. It suddenly became so violent that he had to hurry to his bed to keep from being thrown to the floor. During the next half hour, he couldn't focus on a single thought. When he was lying quietly again and looking out the window, he remembered the attic and his talk with his mother.)

Mother wants to scare me off. Domestic peace—but she doesn't want it either. What does she want? Why won't she help me?

One day on the stairs Edward ran into the old spinster, Miss Virginia Graves, Kathleen's former teacher. Kathleen and her mother had gone off to visit some friends. Gordon Allison was in his study.

Edward dragged her into his room and made her a cup of tea. She wanted to leave, but he wouldn't let her go.

He complained of loneliness. She stayed. She was pleased to see him so lively and open, and she was touched by his attentiveness. He poured her a second cup of tea. Virginia Graves watched him and remarked that he reminded her of his mother, yes, of Alice, when she was his age. She had had the same friendly way about her. And she had been a regular dancing doll, too.

"What an expression, a 'dancing doll.' Mother, a dancing doll?"

"She loved to dance. She almost became a dancer. Didn't you know that, Edward? She never speaks of it. Perhaps she still regrets she didn't follow through with it. She was genuinely talented. She could do anything—draw, write poems, sing, but she was particularly good at dancing. I can still recall her poems. I think some of them were published, in Sunday literary sections. Alice's mother kept them. Everyone was proud of your mother. She was the prodigy of the family."

"I'd like to read them, those poems of Mother's."

"She had a lot of imagination. She was given to emotion and rapture. All young girls were, back then. Nowadays they wanted to go to university and earn money."

The maiden lady waxed elegiac.

Edward: "Did Mother keep those poems? Perhaps she gave some to Father?"

"She did, certainly. I know it for a fact. He soft-soaped her into giving him some. The talk was that the only reason she was interested in Gordon Allison, who already had a bit of a reputation, was to get famous herself. But people said that kind of thing because they couldn't quite understand how she could fall for this serious, gloomy, taciturn fellow. Believe it or not, that's how your father used to be. Now he is jolly, open to people. His marriage with Alice has been good for him.

But Alice Mackenzie was really wonderful. So sunny, so cheerful, child-like, an elf, and her talents. The whole Mackenzie household, where there were always concerts and plays and birthday parties and other celebrations, the whole house revolved around her. She was born on Sunday. Sunday's child is fair and wise and good and gay."

"And Father?"

"Father—he was there, too, at the parties. As was I. It was a lovely, open house. But of course—"

She pulled her chair closer to Edward's; she whispered; she was glad she could entertain him.

"But of course Alice's mother was very religious. In a corner of her bedroom, behind a curtain I embroidered for her, she had a regular altar to Mary. And Alice had a patron saint. She had a picture of her about as large as my hand hanging over the dresser in her room. I can't remember anymore which saint it was. I always had to bring her red and white carnations, nice fragrant ones whenever I came to visit. Then we put them in vases and set them on the dresser under the picture, a round little picture on a gold background."

"Mother prayed to her patron saint?"

"She was her intercessor. I had to pray, too, even though I'm not so religious. Her name—the saint's name, now I've got it—was Dorothea, no, Theodora. That's what it was. Then when Alice got to know Gordon Allison and was engaged to him she gave all that up. Mr. Allison was not religious. He had traveled so much, seen so much. Then everything became much quieter at the Mackenzies'. It's strange how the whole atmosphere of the house changed then."

"What are you thinking about in particular, Miss Virginia? Tell me. We have lots of time."

"How it came about that the whole house changed so much. We all expected them to get engaged. We all saw it coming, but we couldn't believe it. Some people thought it impossible."

"Why? Was Father so different?"

"It's all so far back. I haven't thought about it for a long time, but I can still see it all before me. Alice changed then. Too bad we don't have any pictures from that period. You can't imagine the change that came over her. He was strict with her. I guess she was supposed to give up her frivolous ways. There was much about her that displeased him. She wanted to conform to his wishes. I often came upon them in the middle of a quarrel. I thought they would break the engagement. But she was determined to marry him. She defended her decision to her mother. Her mother didn't like him. Alice could have had a more elegant husband of finer feelings. Lots of them. All she had to do was take her pick. Instead, she chose Gordon Allison.''

"You couldn't understand it either?"

"Nobody could understand it. She gave up so much for his sake.''

"Her patron saint, too.''

"She must have loved him a lot, with real passion, to have sacrificed so much for him. It's hard to imagine. A genuine love, a love like you have never seen before. Her mother used to complain that an evil fate was at work. It simply overwhelmed Alice. As if it had been preordained. And for all that she was lightness, cheer, and graciousness personified.''

Edward: "There are sides of people we don't see.''

"That's true, Mr. Edward. Her patron saint, I can still remember how Alice took leave of her. As long as Alice was still living at home, unmarried, she would stand in front of the picture sometimes, for a long while, and she would bring flowers. Then, after the wedding, she moved in with Gordon Allison, and I helped her take some small items to her new apartment. I stood with her in the pale blue room, the room of her girlhood, and we looked at each other. 'I don't want to take much with me,' she said. 'I'd like the room to stay the way it is.' I said, 'We'll just take the essentials, Alice.' We packed a few linens and one book and another, and then we came to the old picture, a small, oval picture, simply and colorfully painted on Byzantine gold. She took it down from the nail. She sat down with it, held it for a long time, for a very long time on her lap, and looked at it. Oh, Edward, how she looked at it. I stood quietly beside her. I knew what she was feeling.

"Gordon was not religious. She didn't want to take the picture to his home. She held it in her closed hand and cried. I had to comfort her, and I told her I would take the picture and would always keep a flower in front of it. She was pleased with that idea but finally decided she would leave the picture where it was. It should remain in its old place.

"I said, 'But Alice, then there won't be anyone to look at it. And who knows what will become of it.'

"'Leave it here, Virginia. That's what I want. Leave it here.'

"And she kissed it, and I kissed it, too. And she hung it back on the nail. And then we left.''

Edward: "Mother hasn't let on that she is religious. She's adjusted herself to suit Father. Was she ashamed to be religious? What do you think?''

The old teacher, in a soft voice: "I keep thinking of things now that I had forgotten. That's what comes of your being so curious, Edward, and wanting to know everything. I have to laugh when I think how things were in the Mackenzie household then, with Alice, and how Gordon turned up, and how everything changed so dramatically and incredibly. But then bit by bit things settled in very nicely after all. That's the way life is, Edward. You'll see what I mean. There was Mr. Allison, and we could hardly believe that he had come on Alice's account. No, we believed it all right because so many came on her account. People flocked to her, and she always needed lots of young people around her—Alice's mother had been the same way. But that she was interested in him, and how she could be . . . To tell the truth, I still can't understand it. I had to help her a lot then to see that nobody disturbed her rendezvous with Gordon. I didn't want to do it, particularly if I had to fend off her mother. But she kept after me, she implored me, she cried.

"She was already devoted to him.

"But why, I asked myself. I had the impression, we all did, that they weren't suited to each other. And besides that, I could see that it wasn't good for her. She couldn't handle it. Until she said to me once when I told her in all seriousness that I couldn't go along with this anymore. Do what I would, this business with Gordon would have to be her affair and hers alone. When I told her that, she said she had 'a mission' to accomplish with him."

"A mission? What did she mean?"

"A task. A duty. That was Alice for you. She'd always been like that, energy and imagination. How she got that idea I don't know. By then she'd already lost much of her cheerfulness and gaiety. There was something threatening about her sometimes. Her mother asked me about it, but I couldn't explain it either."

Edward: "She had lost herself to him."

"That must have been it. But she couldn't handle it. She accepted her situation but didn't accept it either. It remained a real conflict in her. And so she talked herself into this missionary role. And she stuck by it. She spoke about it to no one but me, and I had to swear not to breathe a word of it to anyone else. Oh, that was a hard time for me, such a responsibility, but she was so inflexible. No one could have made any headway against her. Her brother, James, had inklings sometimes, but I kept my mouth shut and played dumb. He said it really wasn't so mysterious. There were lots of women who found demonic men of just Gordon's type irresistible."

Edward: "Did he do anything about it?"

"James do anything! He just said 'hmm,' shrugged his shoulders, and went his way. Even then he called Gordon a wild boar because he was so coarse and grim. Even then. He once teased his sister at tea, asking if she thought she was strong enough to tame a wild boar. That's the story of Lear that he told us. She'd set herself the task of taming him, I think, or she had fantasized herself in that role, and to a certain extent she succeeded in it. But . . . "

"Well? What do you mean, 'but'?"

"It wasn't right for her. It demanded more strength than she had. Her heart wasn't in it."

Edward: "You can't know that, Miss Virginia."

"I know Alice. It appealed to her as an adventure. Or—something else as well: She took it on herself. She is deeply religious at heart. And when she saw him and he came to her as he was, she took that task on herself. A saint's task. But it proved very hard for her. How she changed then, our joyful Alice!

"She got downright snappy with me whenever I meddled in her relationship with Gordon. Her mother pushed me into it time and again. Then I gave up when Alice threatened she would turn away from us all if we got in her way."

Miss Virginia, after a pause: "She is stubborn. She had her mind set on it."

Edward: "But surely she didn't make herself miserable just on a whim."

"Oh, your mother is proud, Edward. You can't imagine."

"And then what?"

Miss Virginia: "Everything fell into place."

Edward: "She cursed herself for it afterwards."

Miss Virginia, startled: "How can you say that, Edward?"

Edward: "She had only one thought afterwards: to take vengeance on him."

Miss Virginia, horrified: "But Gordon didn't do anything to her. How can you say that?"

Edward: "He did everything imaginable to her."

Miss Virginia: "But she could have stayed away from him. Are you reproaching me for not stopping her, you, Edward?"

He mumbled, he smiled disparagingly. "Yes, I am, I, her son."

He was feeling ill; he swallowed. He blew out a breath of air and rubbed his lips.

Could have stayed away . . . I could have stayed away from everything in me, too, the fear and everything else, "stayed away." But it won't stay away from me. Hell won't stay away from you. And especially not if you've chosen it yourself. Oh, my poor mother. She is my mother. How can a child and a mother be any closer?

Miss Virginia looked at him uneasily. She spoke again after a while.

"Edward, you're a grown man now, and you will probably stay here in this house quite a while yet, at least as long as you're still ill. And it's a good thing that you know the people in this house better than you did before. For children today, their parents' house is only a way station. You say, Edward, that your mother accommodated herself to her situation. I know Alice Mackenzie; and believe me, accommodation is the last thing you can accuse her of."

The old spinster giggled. "Alice is not an easy customer. She's no pushover for anyone. To tell the truth, I'm pleased about that, about our women's solidarity. When she married I promised to stick by her. And I've stuck."

And Miss Virginia smiled impishly over her teacup and thought about (but did not mention) the second's services she had performed for her pupil and mistress over the years, in consultations, in carrying various secret missives back and forth, in delivering certain messages, in all kinds of sentry and surveillance duties. And Miss Virginia raised her head and smiled at Edward, the son of her Alice, looked at him with half-shut eyes, and said what was going through her mind.

"Do you remember the little story I told about the page and his ring? That's the way men are. They want submission and helpmeets for their work and their lives. But a woman wants only one thing: love. And that's what she clings to. And even if it's the ruination of her she clings to love. If her husband is too strong and strict, then the woman turns to her child. That's why your mother loves you, Edward. Believe me, you are good for her. You're Gordon Allison, but without the quills."

When Dr. King turned up one day, Alice intercepted him and drew him off in a corner. He had to wait a long time for her to say what was on her mind. She had changed a lot. She spoke, of course, about Edward.

"How does he look?" the doctor wanted to know. "Is he withdrawn, dreamy?"

"He's lively. And friendly, too, sometimes—a little too friendly."

"Is he affectionate?"

"Affectionate, yes, like a child. He plays."

"That worries you?"

"Yes. And how. But why should it worry me? I know that he's ill."

She cried. She didn't expect an answer. She just spoke to be able to speak.

"Doctor, we're so lucky that he has come back; I'm so thankful. But in this condition. Can't you help me?"

"In what way, Alice?"

"Edward acts like a child. I've noticed it; we all have. Kathleen jokes about it. I have to keep her from laughing at him to his face."

"What are your feelings about it? It makes you uneasy?"

She sat quietly with her face in her hands. "I'm so happy to have him here. Is it somehow my fault that he's the way he is? Tell me, Doctor, am I bad for him? I don't know what to do next, how I should act toward him." (She did not confess, did not confess; she did not come out of herself.)

He waited. She wanted to speak but then backed off again from what she really needed to say.

"In the months he was first home I had the feeling he didn't care whether it was me or someone else who came and talked with him. All that mattered was that he heard someone talk and that someone answered him. Now he won't let me go. He follows me all over the house. It embarrasses me, especially with Kathleen and my husband."

"What does Gordon say?"

"He smiles, of course. I've put a great burden on him, on all of us. You advised me against it. Now—. But I've got to make the best of it."

"Of what?"

"Will things go on this way with Edward, Doctor?"

The doctor sat in front of her, his hands folded on his knees. He was thinking.

"Alice, don't you want to send him back to me in the clinic after all? Shouldn't we consider the experiment here as done and finished?"

She started: "What do you mean!"

"I want to take him off your hands."

She went to the window and stood with her back to him. When she turned around again, she had made her decision.

"Thank you, Doctor. You've been a great help. You are always a great help. No, I want to keep him here."

"Think about it some more. You can come to me anytime, Alice, if things don't—work out."

She hung on to his fur coat. When he had buttoned it, she flung

herself briefly, her eyes closed, on the chest of the solemn old man who
was looking down on her.

When Alice goes into the kitchen at noontime what does Edward do?
He follows her. He pokes around in the cabinets—one mustn't interfere
with him—and he finally finds what he's looking for: an apron. As a
child he used to help his mother in the kitchen. He puts on the apron
and explains: "I need something to do."

He often helps do the dishes. His mother and the maid go out to
straighten up the dining room. Seated on a stool next to the pile of
dishes, he works contentedly alone.

Kathleen happened to glance into the kitchen once and see him
there. She kept out of his sight and slipped away quietly.

In her room she sat down at her desk, confused, troubled. What was
she thinking?

Suddenly she recalled an old scene. She and Edward were traveling
to the shore in the summer. She was supposed to have gone hiking with
her father. He had started to put on weight, and Alice had tried to push
her into going with him because she was an athletic type. But she realized what her mother's real motive was. Alice wanted to have Edward
to herself at the shore. Now it was starting all over again.

What do I care? Edward is sick. But he's making the most of it.

Her jealousy—of which she was terribly ashamed but which she could
not rid herself of—drove her to keep a close watch on her mother and
Edward. And her watchfulness was justified, she found. In the evenings
Alice accompanied her son to his room at bedtime and gave him a
"good-night kiss." The door was open. Kathleen could see in.

She felt dizzy. She found this outrageous. It tormented her so much
that she couldn't go to sleep.

Her room was on the ground floor next to Edward's. She left her
door open at night—why?—to hear whether her mother visited him
later, too, and when. But then why shouldn't she? Edward was sick,
and he didn't have a nurse anymore.

Sometimes, when Kathleen had lain in bed for an hour, waiting and
listening, she would get up in a rage to close and lock her door. Those
two were no concern of hers. Let them do whatever they liked. She was
furious with herself: Now I'm getting childish in the head, too. Idiotic
family entanglements. You go through the war only to be dragged
through this muck again. Probably the best thing to do is just leave.

*   *   *

Edward visited his mother in her room. He didn't sit with his father anymore. He looked into her closets.

She had to show him her hats, coats, and dresses. They talked about clothes in general: about fabrics, and how hard it was to come by this one or that, and how exorbitant the prices were. He was interested in shoes, too. He often remarked that people used to dress more carefully and with better taste.

Then they started looking at old books with pictures in them and at the family photo albums.

He looked at these photos hungrily. Once he had discovered the albums he could not tear himself away from them. He wanted to take pictures out of them and put them up in his room, family pictures from fifteen and twenty years ago. He was particularly taken with an old picture of Alice.

"Look! That's you, Mother, the most beautiful woman I've ever seen."

"Edward, stop that."

But, serious and inflexible, he stuck by his judgment. "I've never seen such a beautiful woman before."

When she was alone she, too, opened the albums secretly and looked at the pictures. In the course of these reveries, she felt moved to go to the storeroom and bring one special old suitcase down to her room. In some chain of associations or another she had recalled this light old traveling bag. And when she opened it she found inside—carefully packed and supplied with fresh mothballs every year—a light summer dress.

She had been weighed down with her thoughts when she opened this suitcase. Tears streamed down her face as she took the thin, simple dress out of it.

What times she had lived through. What had become of her. What had life done to her. Let those who will say that we determine our own lives and go our own ways. Gordon is right.

As she bends over the suitcase to put the dress away, the idea of putting it on occurs to her, an irresistible idea. She closes the door and puts the dress on. She looks at herself in the mirror with immense satisfaction, tingling with a sense of well-being.

She runs her hands over the cloth. The smell of camphor is strong. It doesn't bother her. It actually intoxicates her.

She sits in the dress for a while, sits catercorner to the mirror and casts an occasional glance of greeting at it. She basks in the feeling of happiness that flows through her whole body. She sits there, in that dress.

Now she takes it off slowly, and she has a lovely idea. Edward will come to see her in her room in the afternoon as he always does. She'll wear the dress for him. Wonderful idea! Oh, that one still has such ideas and can take such delight in them!

She hangs the light dress on a hanger and is about to take it outside to air. But then she thinks, before she opens the door: Why? Leave the camphor smell in it. It belongs there. It's good.

And when three o'clock came Alice was sitting on the sofa in her blue dress that was a bit too large for her—she had been heavier then—and turning a varnished Japanese parasol in her hand. She had found that in the suitcase, too. Edward stamped up the stairs, opened the door, and stood there, incredulous. She took his crutches and put them aside. (How good that you come on crutches. I bless your crutches. Because of them I can have you.)

He sat next to her on the sofa and played with her parasol. He was at no loss for words.

"We ought to have blazing sunshine. We ought to go for a walk. Where were we then, Mother?"

Her eyes shone. "At the shore. You remember."

"There were lots of people lying on the beach. You got into a carriage to go off swimming, and you stayed in the water a while. I wasn't allowed to swim. In the afternoon we went for a ride in an old one-horse carriage."

She nodded.

He: "You had the parasol opened up. All at once your lovely parasol was there above us. You've kept it."

She, softly: "The dress, too."

He: "Once we were home again, in the city, I never saw the parasol again."

"It's not right for the city. You were six or seven then, your first year in school. You had to take warm sea baths to build up your strength. You were very delicate. And you slept badly."

"I didn't sleep at the shore if you were out late. I stayed awake until you were home again."

"You sinner, only now you confess it."

"I could always hear you say good-bye to your friends in front of the house. Who were they?"

"Vacation acquaintances. It's dark in those small villages. I needed an escort. I didn't like to go home from parties alone."

"With one of them you always laughed and argued."

"Eddy, how can you say that?"

"Every time you came home with him I sat up in bed, ready to come help you. But then he would go away."

"Dreams, Eddy."

"You've forgotten. It's a long time ago. I called him 'Uncle.' He visited us in town sometimes, too. But he didn't like it at our house. He was very elegant and dashing, with a little mustache. In town he wore a navy uniform."

"An acquaintance from the shore."

"He gave you the dress you're wearing now."

She put her hand on his shoulder. "Eddy, my blond-haired boy, what are you dreaming?"

"It was a nice time, Mother. You were happy."

She let her tears run down on his face. She kissed him.

"And now here you sit, ill and thinking about old times."

"About happy times. That's why you put that dress on."

She didn't let him look into her face.

"I came across the dress by chance. What you can make out of the smallest things, Eddy. The things you drive me to."

"Then that man went to India. Perhaps with Uncle James."

She was staggered. "Who told you that?"

"You gave me the stamps whenever he wrote. I found my old stamp album in my room, the big red one. The stamps are pasted into it. They came for several years, judging from the dates on them."

"For heaven's sake, Edward, what is it you want?"

"Don't say: 'That doesn't concern you; it isn't something you need to know.' I want to know. You mustn't hide it from me." He shook his fists. "Oh, this house. Secrets upon secrets. Let me know something. You at least. Why send me to school and university when I don't even know what's going on at home?"

She sat at a table some distance from him, stood up, and was about to rush out, as she often did. He called, "Mother, stay."

She: "I want to change my dress."

"Keep it on."

She wept bitterly. "I don't want to. I don't want to wear it. Leave me alone. What are you doing to me?"

"Come, Mother, my little mother. Sit with me. I'm your son, your flesh and blood and a bit of your soul, too. Keep the dress on for a while, for me. You're enjoying it, too."

"Eddy, you're not a schoolboy anymore, and I—I'm your mother. Forget about these things from the past."

"I can't. I think there must be some good reason why I can't. I didn't hit on them by myself either. That's what they started right off with in the hospitals. And Mother, what is the present anyhow? Does the present fall out of the skies brand-new every day? A tree in the yard has leaves and branches and blossoms. Can every single leaf say of itself: I am a leaf and nothing but a leaf? It grows on a tree, and so much goes into a tree: the young and old roots, the trunk, the bark. Every leaf is also root and trunk and branch, the whole past."

"If you knew everything that makes up us human beings, my boy, you would leave well enough alone."

"You're crying again, Mother. I'm no child, Mother. Are you crying because of me, because I am hurting you? Or are you crying about things from the past?"

"Why should I cry because of you?"

"Because I hurt you. I didn't mean to. I'll leave you now."

She went to the door and then on down the stairs with him, forgetting that she still had the blue summer dress on.

But there was a spy in the house, Gordon Allison.

As the stamping from Alice's room came closer, heading toward the stairs, he glanced out at the two of them through his slightly opened door.

Edward had taken her arm.

She was wearing a dress, a light, blue summer dress, that he recognized.

Scenes from the Underworld

AND one morning she came out of her room on the second floor where the bedrooms were and was about to go downstairs. Edward was sitting there—she hadn't heard him come—on a chair in the hallway at the head of the stairs, deeply absorbed in the pictures on the wall there. She said good morning to him. He asked whether the pictures had come with the house or if she and his father had bought them.

Alice: "They're old pictures. Father hung them there."

"Father bought them?"

"Possibly. What about them? They're no treasures."

"The one is a print; the other, a photograph."

"Come along now," she said, taking him by the arm and leading him down the steps. They found Gordon Allison in the dining room. They breakfasted peacefully together; then she went with Edward to his room where she wanted to play dominoes with him. But he wouldn't be distracted.

"I remember seeing those pictures as a small boy. They always frightened me. I couldn't understand why you liked them. I was having another look at them this morning. At least I know now what they are. Before they were just weird, gloomy, scary pictures to me."

"One is a print of a Rembrandt painting."

Edward: "Pluto, the god of the underworld, has seized the young Proserpina and thrown her onto his chariot drawn by fiery horses. She is screaming and scratching at his face. They're about to descend into the earth."

"The old Greek myth."

He: "The photograph is of one of the Pergamon frescoes. The titans are fighting their hopeless, tragic battle against the gods. They tumble down and are buried under mountains."

"I know."

Edward: "Whenever I read in Father's stories or hear him talk or

261

when he tells a story on our evenings together, he is always cheerful and strong and sure of himself. There's no shadow side to him. He belongs to the upper world, to Olympus. What can these pictures mean to him? Why did he pick them in the first place, and why are they still hanging there? He used to look at them often. And he sees them every day now when he goes upstairs."

"He doesn't see them, Edward. I don't either. They've hung there for years. We leave them there for sentimental reasons."

Edward: "Something about them must have attracted him. An Olympian likes scenes of triumph. But the rape of a blossoming young woman and a descent into hell? What do you think, Mother?"

"I don't know," she said under her breath.

"You don't know. Maybe you've forgotten. You've packed your memory away with your summer dress. Call it up again."

"Why do you want me to do that?" She caressed him. "Do you really enjoy hearing about such bygone things? You're not a child anymore, though you are our dear patient, and sick people always have something childish about them. You liked my old summer dress, too."

She sat arm in arm with him and snuggled up to him. She dreamed at his side.

"You really liked it, Edward? I did, too. And everything from those times. Oh, what happy times they were. We didn't enjoy them anywhere near enough. Only when they're long gone do we realize what they were."

"What were they?"

Her eyes were closed. He looked down at her. There was a blissful glow on her slim face. Oh, how lovely she was. Her lips moved.

"The only thing in the world worth living for—apart from you children."

"You don't include Father?"

She let him go but kept his hand in hers. "Don't ask that, my child."

After she had sat in silence for a minute, she spoke again.

"And now about that picture. I'd like to tell you the story that Rembrandt painted, if you don't know it already."

"I remember it only vaguely."

He settled himself comfortably on the sofa. She sat by the window.

"You know who Pluto was, the god of the underworld. His realm was Hades. Neither the sun nor the moon shone there. No stars could be seen; no flowers grew; no birds sang. It was a joyless land, and Pluto was master of it."

"Was he a tyrant? Did he suppress joy?"

"There was no joy. He lived there."

"Can that be, without a tyrant who suppresses it? There's some joy in everything alive."

"Bless you for knowing that, my son. How grateful I am to you."

"So he wasn't a complete stranger to joy after all, this Pluto? And why didn't he want it around him?"

"He didn't even want any for himself."

"Why not?"

"The ancients saw him as the joyless god. That's why he was lord of the underworld, where there was no light and where no flowers grew. He had been given this underground cave that even moles spurned, and the shades of the dead, who could not defend themselves, were banished there. No light was granted them. They performed the tasks they were condemned to do, the same ones, for all eternity. Here the souls of the departed, the millions, the myriads, found a home after they had left the earth. They wandered about helplessly on earth for a while, then found asylum there."

"Do you believe that, Mother?"

She had been speaking bent over, both arms on her lap, crouching down near the floor. After a while she shook her head and said, "No."

She was silent a few minutes, then went on.

"I did a lot of reading and thinking about Hades after Father put that picture up."

"Didn't Father tell you about it?"

"I didn't ask him. I leafed through his books. I haven't forgotten what I found.

"Hades was a kind of abyss under the earth. The entrance to it was on the sea near a promontory. An underground passage led to it. Cerberus, a dragonlike creature, a dog with three heads, a living nightmare, guarded the entrance. His howling and barking which came up from the depths day and night and kept echoing on and on, this dreadful, hollow-sounding wail, frightened man and beast away from the entrance for miles around. Every now and then, who knows why, Cerberus doubled his cry. It cracked and became a squealing and whimpering, as if made by creatures being broken on the rack. Then even the primitive peoples who had settled in these remote parts of the earth took flight, and legend has it that even in later times it was fear of this hellish wailing, of these soul-rending plaints, that set the primitive peoples in motion from time to time. Panic came over them. They fled for their lives with their wives and children and everything they owned.

This is supposedly how the great tribal migrations began. That's why they penetrated into the territory of the wealthy and educated nations. Here they were far from that wailing. No sound reached them from the ends of the earth.

"But the ends of the earth were still there. And the abyss under the earth.

"There were rivers in Hades, rivers of two kinds. One kind rose in Hades and not high up in the mountains. They bubbled up from below through cracks in the earth, fed small lakes, and ran off somewhere into the ocean. No one had ever found their source. People thought they must come from groundwater, but it was hell that sent them to the surface. As if the barking of Cerberus were not enough, the water from these rivers has to pass into the oceans, too, and mix with the seawater there. That accounts for the horrid monsters that live at the bottom of the sea. Everything revolting and slimy, all that is deceptive about the sea springs from these poisoned waters, everything gelatinous, incandescent, attractive, deadly. Odysseus got to know it all."

Edward's voice: "Oh, Mother, I know it, too. I've experienced it."

"And then there are the rivers that rise in Hades but do not leave it. They are formed from the tears of the penitent who became wise too late and from the tears of rage and pain that the sinners and the impenitent, hardened criminals cry as they suffer their punishments. These rivers—oh, what a good thing it would be if they, too, could reach the surface of the earth to instruct the living. But the prince of hell prevents that. They run together into a single river called Cocytus. It flows around Pluto's throne in one small loop and in one large one. The water that feeds this river never stops flowing, for here the souls of the dead suffer punishment for wrongs done to others and to oneself. Here there is infinite suffering without hope. Here there is no mercy."

"The punishment will never grow lighter?"

"The ancients said no. It could never grow milder. There was no mercy, no one who could absolve men of their sins. There was only Pluto, nothing but punishment and pain. All the condemned could do was cry and shriek and curse, and that was the only mercy granted them. The whining and yelping of Cerberus carried the screams of the tormented out into the world. The saltwater river washed the foot of the throne where the mute king sat, his face glimmering a lemony green in the darkness. He made no sign of life, perhaps because in his heart he himself was suffering as much as they who wept and were able to weep. For he, Pluto, could not cry."

"Why should he cry, Mother? What could have happened to him? He was a god."

"It was his fate to be here, among evil and tormented souls. It was a curse. He was a god, but he suffered under the curse."

"Who had cursed him?"

"I don't know. He was good, just as everything is good. Even a criminal who does not, and never will, repent is good, without his wanting to be, against his will. But a will like that makes a man a criminal, and that is what Pluto has chosen, and so he has to sit here, as the god of the underworld, the most harshly punished soul in hell. Because his own pain is so immeasurably large, this kingdom has fallen to him as his lot so that he can see himself infinitely reflected there. It shows him himself in a million different forms, and that offers at least some assuagement of his torment."

She interrupted her story and held her hand in front of her mouth.

"What am I doing, Edward, telling you a horrible tale like this?"

"I'm enjoying it. Go on, Mother. You had mentioned the river Cocytus that flows around Pluto's throne."

"The river that formed the outer loop, a black, bottomless river that separated earth from the underground realm, was called Acheron. The rulers of the upper world, the Olympians, had insisted that it sink deep into the earth and form a definite border. There were to be no points of access from the one world into the other. The gods didn't realize it, but there were some access points nonetheless. I've already told you about the rivers. There are others you'll hear about later. What is infinitely evil and black cannot be restrained. It cannot be killed or restrained. It simply is, and that is why it is there.

"Any of the shades who could no longer remain on earth and so wanted to cross the Acheron—those souls who had no inkling what lay ahead of them in Hades where all their fellow dead were eager to go, too—anyone who wanted to cross the Acheron called for the ferryman, whose name was Charon.

"He came in a narrow, leaky boat that would not hold many souls. He was completely naked, a giant of a man covered from head to toe with black hair that grew like fur on him. The travelers saw his yellow eyes gleaming across the water long before they could hear the plashing of his oars. Once the boat had landed, they could take a closer look at this huge, animallike being. He was something between a man and a gorilla, perhaps he was a gorilla, with bowed legs strong as iron, legs he rocked back and forth on, with his bulging torso, his massive chest, with his totally receding brow, the restless, yellow eyes. He emanated a dreadful stench. That was enough to drive off many of the shades who wanted to cross. But still, the boat was full in an instant.

"At first he rowed without saying a word, without addressing anyone. But in midstream, when his sharp eyes, which were accustomed to the darkness, made out a yellowish green light that appeared to the others to be a grass-green moon in the night—it was Pluto's face—the beast began a fiendish howling, a blatting and mocking and puffing and a long, fitful 'ah, aaaah' that echoed back (they were alongside mountains and heading into a cave). Was that his laughter perhaps? Yes, that is how he greeted his master in the distance and announced the arrival of new souls.

"Sometimes Charon spoke and sang. When a crowd of poor, frightened souls had gathered on the riverbank, surrounded by darkness and weeping as they recalled the warm, colorful life they had left behind, sweet despite all its trials, at that moment Charon, who could hear them, should have set off instantly to fetch them over. But the harsh, unfeeling beast let them flutter about and whimper on the banks of this dreadful Acheron which they did not want to cross, no, did not want to cross but had to. And if it had to be, then why not be done with it and know what awaited them on the other side; yes, know what awaited them, what this new start would be like. Let's get it over with, they whined at the gates of the underworld, already tormented by memories, thoughts of what they would be called to account for. All that they saw clearly before them, and it grew and grew and flooded down on them. They had never known how great a torture guilt could be. They learned on the banks of the Acheron. And so Charon left them waiting.

"The poor souls gathered by the thousands. Their plaints swelled to a croaking and screeching of birds that wanted to fly across the Acheron. And when it grew loud enough the boatman on the far side pushed off at a signal from Pluto.

"And now they heard the beat of his long, heavy oars. It sounded as if the oars were striking stone or lead, a cracking sound. And his boat groaned, creaked, scratched its way forward. The water was not a yielding liquid but an obstinate mixture in which each particle grated against the other. Even water had lost its natural character here. They fell silent, the poor souls, recalling the sweetness of the earth. They were afraid Charon would break his oars and never reach them. Then he sang. They heard him bawling out his song.

*   *   *

How many are you?
Are you fifty? Are you a hundred?
Are you five hundred? Are you a thousand?
Squeeze together!
Squeeze together!
My boat is small.
If you can't get on, you stay behind.
Will have to wait a hundred years,
Will have to wait two hundred years.
Or a thousand.
How many are you?
How many are you?
Are you fifty?
Are you a hundred?
Are you a thousand?
Squeeze together. You're nothing but smoke.
Twenty can fit on the point of a needle.
That makes my job easy.
For it long ago ceased being fun to ferry the
   likes of you back and forth, back and forth.
When they've boiled you, when they've roasted
   you,
When they've strung you on a spit and frozen you,
When they've thawed you out again and torn you
   open
And ripped your guts from your bellies,
Then you'll be better.
That's what's coming; that's what's coming.
Squeeze together.
How many are you?
Are you fifty, five hundred, ten thousand?
Always a hundred on a thimble.

"They crowded together; they rushed onto the boat, the poor frightened souls. He struck out at them with an oar, and then he was off. Those left behind shrieked and wailed. The boat creaked and groaned as if it were rolling on stones. The bawling voice grew fainter.

    How many are you? How many are you?
    Are you fifty? Are you a hundred?

"Legend says that Charon had to take all the dead across, regardless of their rank. Well, it's true that he had no respect for rank, but he had a sharp eye for the obolus, the penny, that the pious put under the tongue of the dead.

"During the trip across the river, Charon tore these pennies from his passengers' mouths. They thought they could keep them to pay for some service or another on the other side, but he took them and threw them in the water. And it was from these coins that the water had gradually become so hard and firm. The boat shoved and cracked and ground its way through the masses of coins. Charon hoped he could fill in the Acheron with them and so rid himself of his onerous work.

"But the river of death was too deep. All the human piety in the world could never fill it up.

23 "OH, the fortunate dead who had put dismal Acheron and the bellowing of the ferryman behind them, the creaking of the boat, Charon's frightful laughter and the echo, the echo. Happy the man who was led to the river Lethe, the blessed Lethe. Whoever drank from its waters forgot all suffering—the pain of life on earth, the pain of leaving it, the pain of the crossing—and forgot himself as well. That was the ultimate happiness that the Lethe's waters gave him: release from the self. He existed no more. The water had freed him from himself.

"And so he could walk the meadows of bliss, the Elysian fields."

Edward: "They were there, too, in the underworld?"

"For most of the dead there was nothing but hell. Heaven, Olympus, was reserved for the gods. Not many entered the Elysian fields. Everybody had to stand trial, and only those whom the court acquitted were rewarded with the waters of the Lethe and could forget. From them, everything was stripped away, even the ego."

"Only those who had lost their egos could enter Elysium?"

Alice: "They alone."

Edward: "Oh, how sad, how awful, how hopeless."

Alice: "Three terrible judges stood next to Pluto's throne. They plied the defendant with uncanny questions. They inquired, but it seemed they already knew the answers to the questions they asked. They didn't want to hear anything themselves. It was the dead man who was to hear, hear himself repeating the words they drew out of him. There was no hiding or distorting the truth here. The questions were thoughts, and the answers were thoughts. Thoughts answered thoughts; everything was clear. And so the dead stood trial before their own consciences.

"The terrible judges led the dead before a huge, mute woman who stood there motionless, her eyes blindfolded, a sword in her right hand, scales in her left. The scales tilted back and forth continually, weighed thoughts, desires, dreams, feelings, and intentions. These things were no longer in the person. The dead man no longer carried them inside himself, hidden from others, his own treasure. He was broken open now. Everything he had ever dreamed and desired flowed around him and still clung to him. But when the judge made a motion with his hand, the poor shade felt happy in an instant, happy for a moment. All his feelings, desires, and thoughts had left him for this short interval of time. They had settled onto the mute woman's scale along with invisible pictures of all the things the dead man had ever done and all he had failed to do. The good deeds and thoughts were in the right-hand tray of the balance, the bad ones in the left.

"No word was spoken. The judgment was visible.

"The guilty—and they were guilty whether they repented or not (for what good does penance do when the deeds are there and cannot be imagined away or obliterated from history, when their consequences and the consequences of those consequences are there to see and have swelled the mountain of human crime)—the guilty shrank back from the judges. And a huge, moaning mob that was waiting for them received them. Oh, many were waiting here.

"Now a shrieking and hissing and clapping began, and before you knew it you were surrounded by those hellish females, the Furies. Some say they were old hags in whose gray, wild hair snakes writhed, dried-out witches with tusks. But there were many of them and different kinds. There were even male Furies. For these jobs Pluto had his pick of candidates. Those who had committed crimes on earth because they were oppressed and had not been able to fulfill themselves seemed to him best suited for this work. They were given sharp whips of wire and could indulge their need for vengeance all they wanted. Pluto knew they would do their work well.

"He employed young, voluptuous women here, too, who, in their lust, took pity on no one, beautiful women who delighted in their conquests and drove hordes of men to their ruin. Pluto gave them barbed whips, and they, too, could indulge their desires.

"All these demons slashed at their victims and drove them to a place where a yellow, biting, sulfurous smoke rose into the air, and the heat grew worse and worse and finally became intolerable.

"They had reached the fiery river Phlegethon and had to cross it—on foot. The jubilant women grabbed anyone who hesitated, dragged him to the bank, and shoved him in. Now the dead had truly set out on their

path of suffering. Their worst torment had begun. The path was without
end; it could have no end, for here there was a torment to punish every
crime. Past crime was present in the world; it could not be eradicated.
The sufferers could try to blot it out with their pain, could bring their
penance and agony to bear against it day after day, could hammer and
scratch at this block of marble, but it remained unchanged. It would
stand there tomorrow and the next day just as it stood today, as it had
stood yesterday. The poor souls shrieked and wept at it. They pleaded
in whining tones for a magician who could melt it away. They were
beggars in hell. But who in Pluto's realm would take mercy on them.

"But before those who were thrust before the judges could tear their
terrified gaze away from Pluto's throne, they saw there at the feet of the
mighty, green-faced tyrant three silent women, strange figures, draped
from head to toe in long robes. They squatted there together and were
doing something with quick, jerky motions, had a spindle among
them—sat there quietly with a spindle. The first one spun: She made
the life thread of someone, man or woman, who had just been born
somewhere on the earth. This human being, man or woman, just born,
did not know what had summoned him to life or what would become of
him. He would grow up, would think he existed; but the one strange,
silent woman, this Fate, she had spun the thread and drawn it out and
now let it pass into the fingers of her sister.

"This second sister took the thread and turned it first this way, then
that way, tugged at it and stretched it—all this in an instant, and anyone watching from the shadows would think it had taken only seconds,
but it really had been years, decades. Time passed differently here than
it did on earth.

"And any shade who passed by the three before he was taken in front
of the judges could hear the spindle making fine, distant sounds, a twittering music. Were there cicadas, mosquitoes, small birds in hell? No,
that was the sound the thread of life gave off when the second sister
turned it a bit to the left, a bit to the right. One minute she pulled it
tight; the next she loosened it—and it laughed and it sang and whooped
for joy, and then she pulled again, and it cried and groaned; then came
complaints and then wailing and then silence.

"The thread passed on to the third sister. She let it run through her
fingers for a second. She had a stubby pair of scissors in her hand,
scissors with strong jaws. She struck with them, ike a bird of prey, and
the thread, the short thread, the light wisp, fluttered to the ground. A
soul had ended its journey. It would arrive soon, be here soon. There it

is, see? On the banks of the Acheron. It is waiting for Charon, the ferryman."

Edward: "That's the way they saw life, the Greeks. How defenseless they must have been. Were those the aristocrats who had tens of thousands of slaves at their command and built the Parthenon? And who produced such beautiful statuary. Sophocles was one of them, and Sappho."

Alice: "I don't know, Edward. They seem to have suffered a great deal, suppressing their suffering, not letting it surface. They covered it over. Perhaps their sense of beauty was so highly developed because, wanting to see only beautiful things, they overcultivated it."

Edward: "And what about us? What is it we do? We don't suffer in the same way. And why not? What has changed?"

His mother sat with her head lowered on her chest. He didn't see her lips moving. She was calling on her heavenly father.

Edward: "Go ahead with your story, Mother. Don't worry about upsetting me. I've experienced a lot myself. Some of what you say sounds familiar."

"I don't want to say anymore. That's enough about that old picture in the hall."

"You're not paining me. You're helping me. You spoke of Pluto and how the Furies, after the judges' verdict, drive the condemned to the river of fire, and about the Fates who spin the thread of destiny. But why is there any punishment or judgment or any hell at all if the Fates sit there and everything depends on what they spin? That makes everything predetermined. We enter life ready-made. We don't act out our fates. We just experience them passively."

"That's what the Greeks thought. Oh, there's some truth to it, Edward. Our fate is much larger than we can imagine."

"So you believe in that kind of gloomy necessity, too, Mother? And you think we are nothing? Human beings are nothing?"

"I don't think that."

"And we're here just to want things but never to achieve them? Some goal is dangled before us—that's Father's idea—and we run after it and are duped and stumble over a stone?"

"I don't believe that, Edward."

"Tell me more. How Pluto snatched Proserpina away from the upper world. What do you know about her? Who was she?"

Pluto and Proserpina

    "SHE was the daughter of Demeter, the goddess of fertility and growth.

"Proserpina was a joyous creature of the upper world. She played with the nymphs of the forest and fields near the smoking volcano Etna on Sicily, where the fire from the center of the earth breaks out. She played there, and the land was rich. She didn't know where she was playing.

"And one evening at dusk Pluto's chariot, drawn by two black horses, rolled up from a steaming fissure in the earth. The horses trotted across the soft ground, and Pluto heard laughter somewhere nearby. When he looked around he saw nymphs dancing in a clearing, and Proserpina caught his eye.

"She was taller and more richly clothed than the others. She danced among them, gay and exquisite, unattainably exquisite. Her black hair flew as she danced; she turned, lost in herself, proud and happy. Her mouth was open as she danced. She emanated the joy of her youth.

"Pluto almost stopped breathing, so painful was the sight to him.

"He reined in his horses. The chariot stopped without a sound. The vapors of the volcano hid it from view. Pluto peered through the haze. He reached a decision.

"He let up on the reins. The horses trotted slowly on, right into the circle of girls. Shrieking with fear, they fled in all directions. But he kept his eye on Proserpina. He put on speed, leaned over, and pulled her into the chariot with his free left arm. And the horses raced on, striking sparks as they went.

"Pluto had to shift the reins over. He steered with his left hand now and hung on to the struggling young creature with his right. He clutched her to his chest. She squirmed like a cat. She scratched his face. She tried to get away by twisting, tugging, and thrashing about.

"While he subdued her but drove more slowly because she was blinding him with blows from her fists, the nymphs gathered their forces behind the chariot. Then they attacked, hanging on to the manes of the horses and getting soaked in the foam from their mouths. They swung up onto the chariot and leapt onto the back of Pluto's neck. With a shake of his head the powerful god flung them off. They wailed. They screamed for Demeter. The goddess could not be too far away. The nymphs jumped off, picked up stones, threw them into the chariot and at the horses. Pluto did not let go of his victim. He was aware of the danger. Demeter might hear them.

"Then, completely blinded—both of Proserpina's hands (she had already torn his lip open) were covering his eyes—he dropped the reins. The horses knew the way home. He yanked Proserpina away from his face and put her on the floor of the chariot. He forced her to kneel down and clamped her body firmly between his knees. Then he picked up the reins again.

"By now they were entering Hades. Here Proserpina could scream all she liked. No one would pay any attention to her cries. Ears here were accustomed to other sounds. He could open his legs and let her go. She sank forward on the floor and—in her pain and to keep herself from falling out—she held on to his feet. He observed that with satisfaction, drenched with blood though he was.

"He stood up straight. His face gave off its greenish light in the darkness. He rolled into his kingdom, passing Cerberus, who greeted his master with wild leaps and a hollow rattling in his throat. They drove into dim Hades. Proserpina had stopped screaming. She cowered in the chariot, paralyzed by fear."

Edward: "And lived with him from then on and became queen of the underworld?"

Alice looked up at him quickly. But his face was as serious and attentive as ever. She went on.

"The nymphs had finally managed to alert Demeter. But what use was it that the goddess searched for her child in the bright upper world? Night descended. Demeter went on searching with a torch. She shone its light into the abyss of Etna, hoping to discover the kidnapper there. She did not find him. Where had he hidden? Where was he? Where had he dragged her child off to?

"She stopped at nothing to solve this awful mystery. She asked the sun god, who illuminated everything and had to know everything. She implored him to say who had made off with her daughter and where the chariot had gone. The sun god could not answer. He had seen the chariot for only a second; then it had disappeared.

"'Disappeared,' Demeter laughed despairingly, 'disappeared from the face of the earth. How can that be?' And the sun god answered, 'Ask the moon; ask the stars.'

"She asked the moon, and she asked the stars. Both the moon and the stars shone more brightly when the great mother addressed them. They were honored that she had turned to them. But they had nothing to tell her. Demeter got nothing but polite phrases and flattery from them.

"Demeter wrung her hands. 'No one saw anything! Everyone went blind, everyone! Oh, the wretches!'

"All of them were conspiring against her. But why? What had happened?

"Then she threw herself down on the ground in an olive grove to weep, to weep. Nearby there was a brook; and when Demeter went on complaining day and night, Arethusa, the water nymph, rose out of it. And, lo, there was the glorious mother of all nature lying close to her brook. Demeter lay on the ground, crying and lamenting. And the grass around her had grown up to form a soft bed under her, and colorful flowers had sprung up, and the singing and twittering of the birds were so loud that they often drowned out Demeter's complaints, so joyfully did the birds call out to the great, the wonderful goddess.

"Surprised, Arethusa approached her. Because the birds were making such a cheerful racket, Arethusa bent over close to the goddess and asked why she was crying.

"Demeter: because she had lost her daughter. She was looking for her, had been looking for her for days but in vain, in vain. The sun had not seen her; nor had the moon or stars, nor any beast or bird or bat. She had even asked the fire and the black shadows of the earth's depths, but they were conspiring against her. Oh, what had she done to deserve this, she, Demeter, who makes everything grow and gives children to all creatures. Her child had been taken from her, her beloved child, her only child.

"'What is your child's name, great mother?' Arethusa asked.

"'Proserpina.'

"Then Arethusa hid her face behind her veil.

"And Demeter realized that the nymph knew something. And she got up and pulled the veil away. She made Arethusa speak and confess. 'My source rises deep in the earth, and down there many rumors spread among the waters. One spring passes the word on to another.'

"'And what do they say?' Demeter urged. 'What do they say? What, what?'

"'That Pluto, the god of Hades, has a queen. She sits on the throne next to him. He stole her from the earth.'

"'And her name, what is her name?' Demeter cried.

"'Proserpina,' Arethusa replied.

"Then Demeter fell to the grass unconscious. The birds thought Arethusa had killed her, and they attacked the nymph in dense flocks, pecking at her. Arethusa had to dive underwater to protect herself.

"And when Demeter regained consciousness and heard all the details, the news tore at her heart so that she threw herself down and begged everything around her, the grass and flowers and trees, to grow over her and enclose her in her grave, for she never wanted to see the day again. If her daughter had to perish in darkness, she, too, wanted to go to her death in black night.

"But what the gods decide, what they do and suffer, has consequences for the world. Demeter held a high office. She was in charge of the life of nature. And as she lay there lost in apathy, a victim of her grief, disorder crept into nature. The seasons shifted. Spring didn't know when it was spring and awoke too late. The summer, confused, rushed in to fill the breach and scorched the plants that had sprouted belatedly. And the fall, which was supposed to bring maturity, came out the worst loser, producing only dry, lifeless fruit.

"The clouds were in turmoil, too, not knowing when to rain, hail, or snow or when they should just cover the sky. And as the clouds swam about in their confusion beneath the feet of the gods, they cried out to Zeus and brought their complaints to him and told him what was happening and asked him to do something about it.

"He was the highest god of all. He had been spending his time feasting with Ganymede, the boy he loved, and had failed, once again, to notice anything at all. The clouds told him everything they knew. The birds had overheard Demeter's conversation with the water nymph. Zeus immediately summoned the nymph Arethusa to his throne, learned the rest of the details from her, and knew straightaway who had been at work here.

"He went about his task slowly. He could have issued a decree and set everything straight. But he didn't do that because he was ashamed that he had noticed nothing and had spent his time banqueting with that sweet boy Ganymede instead of seeing to it that the world was in good order. Perhaps, unbeknownst to him, other things had gone wrong, too. Perhaps the titans were rearing their ugly heads again. And then his brother, Pluto, the lord of the underworld, was involved. He had made off with a girlfriend for himself. It would be hard for Zeus to condemn that when all the world knew, his wife Hera better than anyone else, what his own habits were.

"He consulted with no one, thought the matter over carefully, and had all the witnesses appear before him once again, supposedly to clarify the matter even more. But his real reason for taking his time was that he, himself a philanderer, was finding increasing pleasure in the case: the prince of hell, the ruler of black Hades, bitter as gall and immune to temptation, mixed up in a love affair after all! Zeus liked that. It showed that Pluto put his pants on like everybody else. And now, at last, Zeus had caught this tyrant over the world's conscience, this judge of the public morals, with those pants down. He would enjoy this spectacle at his leisure.

"'Who,' the crafty, easygoing god asked, 'who is this Proserpina you're telling me about? I've never heard the name before.'

"The answer, which he already knew, was: Demeter's daughter, a young, simple, charming creature.

"'A farm girl you mean to say. Well, what else would a daughter of Demeter's be?'

"Now you have to understand that Demeter, because she managed the seasons, the harvests, and so forth, had the reputation of a peasant among the Olympians. That's why she was seldom invited to festivals at Olympus, the pretext being that she should not be taken away from her work. The gods declared her indispensable. Zeus laughed uproariously over the news. His brother Pluto had taken a little peasant girl to his heart, a gawky, stupid creature. But then what else could a sourpuss like him find, and how could he develop any taste, associating with his dreadful Furies and his judges over the dead? Such were the cohorts Pluto had chosen in the underworld. It was hard to believe that a being like Pluto could be his own brother. Zeus inquired again whether this Proserpina didn't have special charms after all. He would have liked to see her. But he wasn't ready to let his curiosity take him that far. That would look suspicious. He would have to summon the girl together with Demeter, her mother.

"Zeus shook his famous locks which had to be curled and hung with new thunderbolts every day. No earthly king wears his crown day and night. But Zeus, arrogant as he was, never put off his thunderbolts, the attributes of his power, not even in his happiest and most relaxed moments. Even in the winter he carried them, burdensome as they were to him.

"He wondered now how he could best draw out this Pluto-Demeter business and exploit it to the full. And since it was only Proserpina who interested him, he came up with the following idea, an evil, deceitful, cynical idea, the kind of idea one would expect from the soul of a professional tormenter and despiser of humankind (oh, how good that this era of criminal gods is in the past; how lucky we are that a benign divinity has come to free us from them).

"He ordered his gloomy brother, Pluto, this lord of the underworld, deprived of light and joy, to release Proserpina, the kidnapped daughter of Demeter, if she wanted to go. But to have a little fun and because this decision was much too just ever to have come from him or for him to feel comfortable with it, he added what seemed to be a trivial condition to the order. If Proserpina left, if she did in fact decide to go, she was forbidden to pick any fruit in the underworld. Nor could she turn around and look back when she left this dismal hell. What did Zeus mean to accomplish with these conditions? All he wanted, base wretch that he was, was to experiment. He wanted to see if she really was the child she had been described to be. His jaded brother's taste interested him. How does a prince of hell love? What does he love?

"Delirious, overjoyed, Proserpina sprang away from her gloomy husband. She ran as fast as she could, ran back, following the tracks of Pluto's chariot, ran toward the distant light. She was running in dusky semidarkness, but she could see well enough. There was a tree laden with pomegranates by the wayside. In her joy, she picked one. She remembered that she was forbidden to. But that was ridiculous. Besides, she was running away to her mother. And who could see what she had done anyhow, and even if this was a valuable fruit, her mother grew millions of others.

"The pomegranate tasted wonderful. It refreshed her, and she ran twice as fast, reveling in how she had outwitted this band of thieves. In her exuberance, she recalled that she was not supposed to turn around either. That had been another condition. But why not? Nonsense and more nonsense. Perhaps there was someone hard on her heels, intent on fetching her back. Oh, run, just run, and then when you're safe outside you can laugh at them and stick out your tongue: Yaahh, yaahh.

"And there it was, bright light, the light of the sun, the sun. And there, oh joy, a voice, the voice of her mother, her mother's dear voice: 'Proserpina, Proserpina, my child, my darling!'

"And the child, saved, stood still. She jumped in the air for joy. She turned around. She stuck out her tongue and cried, 'Yaahh, yaahh!'

"But silent shades had followed her, and now they rushed out of the night. They threw a noose around Proserpina's feet. With a single pull they yanked her slim white ankles together. Proserpina fell over. She tried to get up. Her feet were tied. She tore and yanked at the rope, trying to free herself from it. 'Mother, Mother,' she cried.

"A battle with slippery, cold-breathed, elusive shades.

"She struck out on all sides and hit nothing. She thrashed about in the sand like a fish, first on her back, then on her belly. She kicked and squirmed.

"This is how she had been carried into hell on Pluto's chariot. They had her in their rope. Now they wound it around her arms, too. She collapsed, helpless. A despairing sob.

"And outside, out there in the light, in the sunshine, Demeter, her mother, waited, knowing what was happening but unable to come closer or to interfere. Her daughter was being attacked; violence was being done her.

"'Treachery! Betrayal! Zeus, Zeus, hear me! See, Zeus, how your orders are carried out!'

"She did not see how Zeus on Olympus gloatingly stroked his thunderbolts, the attributes of his power, and how he laughed cynically about Proserpina and her, about his whole successful plot. He had his proof. It was plain to see. His grouch of a brother had taken up with a child, a peasant girl.

"The shades raced back to Hades with Proserpina. They moved so quickly that Proserpina, drawn behind them on the rope, never even touched the ground.

"The young queen sat rigidly on the throne next to the prince of hell.

"She was transformed, from one minute to the next. She heard the now familiar begging and whimpering of the arriving souls, the bawling and animal laughter of the ferryman, the shrieking of the condemned on their way to the river of fire. At Pluto's feet she saw the mute, horrible sisters with their spindle, saw the judges and the giantess with her sword and scales, saw her husband's whole grisly administration at work. She obeyed and stayed here and did not shirk and accepted what she had to and said to herself: Here I am, yes, here I am, Proserpina, Demeter's child.

"She repeated those words hour after hour and grew more and more rigid and became the prince of hell's mate.

"Demeter's mother did not give up on her child. And now Zeus turned serious and let himself be touched. He looked more closely and saw what was happening to sweet, delicate Proserpina at Pluto's side. No, she was not a peasant girl. When it came to women, his brother, the grouch, was a total nincompoop. Zeus had known that all along. But what he was doing here to this obviously childish but nonetheless delicate young woman, this slow suffocating and extinguishing of a fine young creature, that outraged Zeus and moved him to action. He wanted to do something; he had to do something. He would show his brother down there how powerful he, Zeus, was and let Pluto know what he thought of him.

"Zeus thundered his rage through half a winter, so loud it was that it was heard even in Hades, and Pluto leapt up from his throne, startled at first, then afraid that the titans had broken free again. And then a flock of vultures, sent down into the underworld by Hermes, Zeus' messenger, brought an order from Zeus: Things could not go on this way. A kidnapping, an out-and-out kidnapping, had taken place, of a woman no less, the daughter of a goddess. The gods, as Pluto well realized, were subject to the law, too. The very least that could be done in the way of reparation for this outrage was to return Proserpina to her mother—for half the year. And Pluto had better not think of hindering Proserpina's return with any of his chicanery. This judgment was, of course, the exact opposite of the earlier one. But Zeus was Zeus, master of the world.

"Gnashing his teeth, Pluto accepted this latest word, filing it away with past injustices.

"So it was arranged, and so it remained. Proserpina went to the upper world once a year. She did not need to run. At the appointed time, she stood up slowly from the throne and got into Pluto's chariot, which stood waiting for her, the same chariot that Pluto had used to bring her here. It pained her every time she climbed into this iron vehicle and saw the strong, fiery horses snorting in harness and thought back on the crime Pluto had committed against her, that crime she would never, never forget; and she swore as she took her place behind Pluto in the chariot, her head lowered, that she would avenge that deed and never let it fade from her memory. If there was anything she owned in this life, anything she clung to and regarded as her own innermost possession, it was that deed. And ineradicable would her hate remain for him who had committed it, and her abhorrence for the gods who had tolerated it. And so Proserpina gave herself up to gnawing rage and grief.

"Perhaps, she dreamed, this woe will consume me. Then it will possess me no longer, and I will dry up, an empty husk.

"— But that is not what happened."

Alice was silent for a long time.

Edward whispered: "Then what did happen, Mother?"

"The return each year—the greetings, the reunions, the talks with her mother—those things happened. And the games and songs with her friends, and the Sicilian spring and the summer and flowers and animals. That all came back and was not lost. And if it disappeared today, it would return tomorrow.

"At first her entire visit to the upper world stood under the cloud of having to leave it again. This cloud did not pass away until the day when the divine messenger that Zeus sent swooped down for her, took her by the hand, and led the trembling girl with downcast eyes away amidst the plaints of her mother and friends. That exquisite, innocent creature. Her mother looked at her and threw herself down on the ground in a frenzy—her child in hell! She could not grasp it. This world of Zeus—oh, he was not a good and just god; he was not her god. — Oh, I pray that he is not the last god.

"And Proserpina—she fought at these early partings; she struggled; she did not want to go. It was a pitiable spectacle. She called to her mother, her friends, for help. They had to stand there, their hands before their faces, and could give her nothing but their tears and their protestations of love. None of them dared attack the messenger of the gods. He took Proserpina gently on his arm. He had huge pinions. Dusk fell. He hurtled away with her. Tender words of parting followed her. Everyone felt at first that each parting was a repetition of that heinous kidnapping."

Edward: "What was it like for her in the underworld? How did Pluto treat her?"

"Like his wife, as well as he could, in his way. How was he with her? You know about Tantalus in the underworld, the man standing in the water yet suffering from thirst because every time he lowers his lips to the water, it sinks away from him. That's how it is between Pluto and Proserpina. He longs for the happiness, the innocence of youth, the gaiety that he doesn't have and the sight of which tears at his heart—he aches for those things, he thirsts for them. But when his lips come near her, then all those qualities leave her, the gaiety, the happiness. She doesn't understand what is happening to her. She gives up her own nature. At first she sat next to him stiff as a stick. She looked straight ahead. He looked straight ahead. Later, after the journeys to the upper world, her fear abated. She was familiar with everything. She knew

Pluto, she knew this whole hell he had built up around himself. And that is where she lived for half the year."

Edward: "She got used to it."

Alice: "What a way to put it, Edward. No, she knew it. She tolerated it."

"And then what happened?"

"She knew it was impossible to swim against the stream. What happens to a lump of salt that you throw in the water? It dissolves. The salt assumes a different mode of existence. The salt shouldn't have fallen in the water if it had wanted to stay the way it was.

"She became as he was. Hades rubbed off on her. Her mother and her friends in the upper world noticed it when she came back. And when she first fully grasped her situation in the underworld she picked up a pomegranate, the fruit that she had plucked and that had been her undoing, and held it in her hand on the throne as a symbol of her position as queen. Pluto allowed it; indeed, it pleased him. He thought she had submitted and accepted her fate. But she held the pomegranate as an accusation and as a reminder that she had sinned against herself, knowingly or unknowingly; for she herself was guilty of reaching for this fruit, not Zeus with his cynical judgment, but she herself. This was the kind of change her thinking underwent.

"When she sat on the throne next to her green-glowing, glistening husband, she had to carry a torch to light up a large circle around her. Her eyes, which now saw the light of the upper world again periodically, were poorly adapted to Hades. But so that she could see where she was and realize she was not dreaming—so that she would know who her husband was and what realm he governed—for those reasons Pluto had pressed a torch into her hand when he had seen her sitting there on the throne holding her pomegranate. He did it out of pride, for he was proud of his kingdom and of the awful justice with which he ruled it. He felt he governed over a model kingdom, a model world very different from the decadent, frivolous world of his brother, Zeus. He laughed only once. That was when Proserpina, with the torch in her hand, asked him if there were any love here. He didn't reply. He laughed, proudly, self-satisfied."

Pause.

Edward: "Did they have any children?"

Alice: "Yes!"

Edward: "And what else needs to be said about this picture hanging in the hallway, the one of Pluto and Proserpina?"

Alice: "Gradually, despite the torch, she reached the point where she didn't see anything anymore. The pomegranate lay in her hand. She knew what it meant, but it did not stir her anymore. What does she do? She sees the rigid, greenish-faced tyrant Pluto next to her. He delights in his possession and guards over her. She knows—though now the picture strikes her as romantic—that in the upper world, near Etna, people are flitting across meadows in the sunshine, and she hears the distant howling and snarling of Cerberus, the animal laughter of Charon, the whimpering of the souls who bring a faint breath of the other world with them. And the unchanging criminal trials, the Furies who hurl themselves at their new victims, the condemned. Their snakes hiss horribly. Oh, what evil, coldness, harshness. The judges, who want to know all, ask the same questions. These interrogations are enough to make ice melt.

"Proserpina no longer looks at Themis to see which way the scales tip. How she hates those scales. They think they can weigh such things here. They weigh guilt against innocence. But what is truly guilty is everything here, all of it, Pluto's existence, his hell itself. Screams from the river of fire. There's nothing I can do about them. You listen more carefully when the shrieking subsides.

"Pale and erect, Proserpina sits there. Her name is no longer Proserpina. She is Hecate, the queen of hell.

"She is pleased when he gives her this name. He was right. She is not Proserpina anymore.

"Who is she? Does she know? Does she still know?"

Edward Alone

SHE rejected him. He coerced her. He overpowered her. You can't say it any plainer than that.

Then she lived with him. She probably didn't have strength enough left to resist him after that. She accommodated—but didn't forget. She tried to remain true to herself. But he took his toll on her. She doesn't know her own name anymore.

Edward's hands began to shake. He pressed them down on his knees. His teeth chattered.

What a fate. And I'm sick and lie here shaking.

The shaking increased. He stood up, walked back and forth to try to control it.

Proserpina had children by Pluto, too. "Did they have children?" "Yes." She let him wring the answer out of her.

We are those children. What can grow from such roots? But she didn't think about us. Do parents think at all about the children born of their rutting?

She could have denied him children. But she accommodated. She became Hecate. Dark desire. That's the way it was. That's how I got here. And I still carry something of her history in me.

He gagged. The nausea passed. But he was feeling battered about so much that he had to take refuge in his bed.

And now he lost consciousness and lay there like a dead man. Then his face contorted in fear, pain. In fear of death, in rage, in the fury of his despair, he bared his teeth. He clenched his hands. He raised both arms in front of his face, as if expecting a blow.

When he woke, he was exhausted. He felt in his bones that "it" was there again. He knew what he was like in these fits. The doctor had told him. But he didn't dare come any nearer to the image that appeared before him. It exuded horror.

Edward noted with grim satisfaction that "it" was back again, brought up by the story of Pluto and Proserpina.

283

I couldn't ask for better proof that I'm on the right track. The *i*'s are dotted, the *t*'s crossed. Without my realizing it, my body has been acting out the sequel to Pluto and Proserpina's story.

The situation is not without its comic, its grotesque side. I've given up the role of the child in this affair. They are fighting out their battle. I just provided the occasion for the battle to begin. Now, in their eyes, I've been neutralized. They know they are guilty, but I'm of no interest to them anymore. They're opening up the flood gates. I'll be interested to see how far they'll go.

If everything was the way she represents it, I can't imagine how she could have children by him. They're both of them up to their ears in their own feelings and so they distort things. But one thing is clear: She "accommodated"; she took the name of Hecate; and that means I'm the child of a Pluto-Hecate marriage, and she has no right to ask me to take sides against him.

But his aversion for me, his hatred of me, remains. That is a fact. He has hated me from childhood on. I remember always being afraid of him. Why I don't know.

What could he have against me? What did I ever do to him? If I'm a symbol of Pluto's victory over Proserpina, he should have delighted in me and spoiled me. But he didn't like me. Obviously. The whole thing doesn't make sense. She's keeping something from me.

Or does he hate me because she took me over for her own? What's the answer? What occasioned his hatred for me? It must have been something bad. I can't be to blame myself, through anything I did, because I must have been a very small child.

And if it wasn't anything I did, then it must have been the mere fact of my existence. Why my very existence? Was I illegitimate? I know when they were married. I was born a year and a half later.

Why does my existence enrage him so much that I can still feel that rage today, so much that I've stored it up in me over twenty years; and now that I'm sick it's devouring me skin and bone. What is behind that rage? What evokes such hatred for me in him that even now he can't be friendly toward me, affectionate, the way he is with Kathleen? He tries, but he can't manage it.

The doctor is no help. Mother is no help. I have to break my own poor head over it. I have to be both patient and physician at once.

And I want to be both because they would just try to "cure" me in their fashion. But what I want is the truth. They're afraid. They can afford to avoid these things and let them rot. But the corruption is inside me. I want to, have to get rid of it. I'll kiss the knife that pokes a hole in me and lets me explode. I won't back off. I swear it: I won't let up.

Edward sat brooding.

James Mackenzie has an easy job of it, searching out his truth, his comfortable truth. He hasn't experienced anything. He takes his health and good spirits out for walks and feeds them. But what about him? Is he really healthy? I used to think Father and Mother were healthy, and Kathleen. You think people are healthy as long as things go smoothly between you and them. But when you get closer to them, you find out differently.

What a world, this "upper world." Is it the upper world? Is there such a thing as an upper world? The ancients wouldn't think so today. The upper and underworlds have merged. Cerberus is running loose among us, barking furiously. He's out of a job. What should he watch over now? Pluto and Proserpina have come up to the upper world. She could get away from him now. But it seems she doesn't find him as awful as she did in the old days. She has even had children by him.

And all their hellish machinery has come along with them, the Furies, who swing their whips on living flesh now, the judges, who hold their trials every hour and torment consciences. The scales rise and fall constantly, damning, condemning. We no longer need to cross Acheron and the river of fire. Modern progress has made hell much more accessible.

Salvation, salvation! How can anyone bear this?

Open Battle

AFTER her conversation with Edward, Alice surrendered. Up to now she had resisted. Now she let herself drift with the current.

One afternoon, as she was going downstairs from her room, the library door opened behind her.

She turned around. Gordon was standing in the doorway. He motioned with his head: Come in.

When he locked the door behind her, she asked, "Why are you doing that?"

Gordon: "So he doesn't follow you in. He's developed the habit of coming in without knocking."

He went to the window and looked out; then he sat down, not in his usual place but on a stool close to the door. He slumped down and spoke hoarsely. At table he hadn't said a word.

"What's going on in this house? How far do you mean to push me, woman?"

"What has come over you?"

Gordon: "Do you want to destroy us all? What is it you're after? Come out in the open with it."

Alice: "I won't answer that. What is it you want from me?"

"Wonderful, I from you."

Alice: "Open the door. Let me out of here."

Gordon: "We haven't had a talk in a long time, Alice. You're plotting something against me."

She did not answer.

Gordon: "I saw you going down the steps with him. Day before yesterday."

Alice: "Who is 'he'?"

Gordon: "Edward."

Alice: "Then say 'Edward.'"

Gordon: "You had a light, blue dress on. You went arm in arm, a lovely picture."

"I was helping him down the stairs."

"I laughed. A loving couple."

"Gordon, you disgust me."

"It's the truth. He's so intent on the truth."

Alice: "Edward."

Gordon: "Stop interrupting me. I think we can dispense with stylistic subtleties. You kept the dress, and you put it on in his honor."

"Edward saw it and remembered. He came into my room and saw it. He comes in like a child. And so I put the dress on."

"What did he remember? What does he know?"

"Nothing. Nothing that couldn't be talked about—summer vacations, walks, and so forth."

"Walks with whom?"

"I won't be interrogated. What's past is past."

Gordon: "But you haven't thrown that old dress away."

She pretended not to hear.

Gordon: "A souvenir."

"Yes."

Gordon: "At last an answer I can make sense of."

He stood up and walked heavily across the room. He sat down on his chair.

Gordon was gasping for breath. "What is it you're after? What's going on in this house? We're about to tear everything down around us, everything, I say, everything!"

"I can't do otherwise, Gordon."

"Say what you mean."

She was silent.

He repeated: "Say what you mean, Alice. What's happening with you?"

"I can't stand it anymore, Gordon. I'm getting old. When I was younger, I could bear it."

"And now?"

"I can't anymore. I can't anymore. I can't anymore."

"Can't what, Alice?"

"Go on living this way. It has to stop."

Gordon: "Why? What has happened? What do you want to do?"

"You can't go on asking sacrifices of me forever. You're no god. I'm a living being, too, you know."

"I've never denied that."

"Never denied that?"

She went toward him. He rose to his feet.

She: "How dare you say that to me, now, after twenty-five years?"

"I'm not aware that I ever denied that."

"You—I wish I could see into your heart. No, I don't want to either."

Rage on his face: "He's infected you with this stuff, that crazy man. But you're not going to get the best of me. I never should have let him into my house."

"It wasn't you who did. You held back. You dodged your responsibility from the first moment, just as you always do."

"I'll defend my home. I'm not afraid of him."

"Not of him, but of the truth."

White with rage, he shook his fists: "Come on, come on! You'll find who it is you're up against!"

She looked at him and nodded. "Thank God you're out in the open now. Lord Crenshaw has finally come to himself."

"Congratulations on your achievement."

"Now will you open this door for me?"

He let her out.

James Mackenzie had asked for an extension of his leave. Alice, sitting with him at the breakfast table, did not respond to his announcement.

Mackenzie: "That's of no interest to you?"

Alice: "James, of course it is."

Mackenzie: "I'm going to stay. I have the feeling I'm needed."

"I asked you to."

Mackenzie: "You've made little use of my presence, Alice. Things are not going well in this house."

She went to see if the door was closed, then sat down with him again.

She: "I'm an adult, and I'm aware of the consequences my actions have."

He: "I'm afraid you aren't. I can't imagine that it's your desire for things to take the course they are taking."

She: "It's not I who am acting, James. It's Edward. That's why we took him in. We wanted to help him regain his health."

"We. It was you, Alice. You told me yourself that you wanted to have him here to fight out what you called 'your battle.'"

"Mine and his."

"Alice, I've been trying to dissuade him of his ideas, this crazy search for the so-called truth. He is genuinely ill."

"Tell him that. He thinks otherwise. And ask the doctor."

James: "I haven't felt moved to do that yet. But it can't be his intention to conduct this kind of diabolical experiment. He hasn't taken in the whole situation. He's a physician who wants to bring about a cure, not a disaster."

"I don't see any disaster in the making. I'm emerging from disaster. The truth does not bring disaster. The truth brings happiness."

"Alice, you too! Now you're talking that way, too. This is horrendous. That's why I'm staying. You remember what our own home was like. We saw only the good, and we had a happy childhood."

"Yes. What did I do to bring this down on me?"

James: "If one of us had ever taken it into his head to poke around in our parents' lives and thoughts, what would have become of our inner peace?"

"What inner peace are you talking about? Inner peace in Gordon Allison and Alice Mackenzie's home? Edward grew up and became what he is here. I sometimes thought, as the years went by: Now things are in order; the worst is past. The storm has blown over; a merciful hand has smoothed everything over. I was even happy sometimes, before the war. I was deluding myself. That Edward was so quiet and went around locked up in himself and sulky—I thought that was just his way; we all have our eccentricities. Then he was drafted. I didn't find out until later that he had volunteered. That came as a shock to me, perhaps because I had an inkling of why he had done it. I couldn't get that thought out of my head afterwards, and how I worried about him. He was so far away. I prayed that nothing would happen to him. I don't know what I would have done if he had been killed. I called to him, I called. And then—this happened to him; and he came back, in this condition; and I asked myself day and night before he came: Who is this person they're bringing into my house? And how do things stand with me? My fate was so closely linked with his. And then, as you know, the first thing I saw of him was that frightful grimace, a grimace I'd seen before. Don't ask the doctor anything, James. I beg you. Let it be."

"I'll let it be. But you, you should let it be, too, Alice."

"James, it won't let me be. It's gotten out of my control."

"Then you'll have to accept the consequences. Have you taken any notice of Kathleen lately? You're surprised. You've noticed nothing. She should have taken up her studies again by now. The semester began a long time ago. But she stays here. Why? She comes to my room. She is upset. She wants something. She asks me questions. She, too! She is a good-natured soul. But now she can't comprehend things anymore. She told me lots of people were having this experience. When they came back from the war, they found they didn't understand their homeland anymore. That's the excuse she gives, but she's not saying what's really bothering her. The fact is that you're drawing her into your battle, you and Gordon. Her parents are beginning to frighten her. Can't you see that? She's fighting the whole situation. And she's angry with Edward, too."

"What can I do?"

"Can't you see the harm you're doing?"

She: "Don't keep harping on that. Edward has to recover. We owe him that."

"The truth that you'll find won't make him healthy again."

She stood up.

"Well, I'm not ill at least. Perhaps it would be a good idea to send Kathleen back to London."

James: "So you can be at each other's throats all the more. She won't go. She can't. She's a human being. Nobody would walk away from his home when it was starting to burn. It's still her home, too. I can't go either."

Alice, her brow wrinkled, walked about the room, put the sugar bowl aside, and carried the toaster back to the sideboard. Then she returned to James.

"That's what it was you wanted to tell me. You're welcome in our house as long as you want to stay. It means a lot to me that you stay. I'll speak openly with you anytime you ask me to. I have no reason to conceal what I'm doing. But Kathleen—"

"I'll say it again, Alice. She won't go. Won't you make a small concession to me, do me a little favor?"

"I don't know what you mean."

"For Kathleen's sake. You don't seem to realize, Alice, how you are these days, unapproachable, distracted. And Gordon, for his part, is having his meals brought to his study. That's a dreadful state of affairs. But perhaps it's reasonable and tactful of him. That way he avoids the grim silence at the table. But Kathleen is sitting there keeping an eye on you both. And sometimes Edward comes up to my room and makes a few mysterious remarks."

"What are you getting at? You're not equal to situations like this. I've been through worse ones."

"Be a bit more gentle, Alice. For my sake, too. Don't be so wild.

Imagine that our parents were here. The family meant everything to
Mother, and I'll be eternally grateful to her for that. And don't try to
tell me you're doing all this for the sake of your family. I'm a loner. I've
never had to worry about a family. All I had to do was think about
myself. Do it for me, please. You know me. I'm vulnerable and basically weak. All the vicissitudes of a marriage would crush me. My case
is so extreme—"(he smiled at her) "and I beg your pardon for this—
that I even have to meddle in other people's marriages occasionally,
especially if they concern me as directly as yours does. And so I ask you
now to spare me."

She smiled, too, and shook a finger at him. "You're a sly one. You
always were a flatterer. All right, what do you want me to do to help
you preserve your inner equilibrium?"

"Not much. Just show the world a little friendliness. For example, I
miss our evening gatherings where Gordon did such noble service and I
did my bit, too. We sat with others. You circulated among the guests
and had to fill your role as hostess. That had therapeutic value—for
you, too. Society is a great goddess."

She sat at the table, her head propped on her hand.

"The evening gatherings. Edward would be there. What's supposed
to happen at them?"

"The same things as usual. People chat, maybe tell stories."

"Who would tell stories?"

"We'd see. Gordon, or you. I'd very much enjoy hearing from Kathleen sometime."

She went to Gordon.

"Am I bothering you?"

Gordon: "Have a seat. There perhaps. I'll move those books."

Alice: "Are you starting something new? Something longer? Short
stories?"

"You think I should do something larger again? Not a bad idea."

"So I provide you with a little inspiration after all, Gordon."

"I beg your pardon, Alice, but you often provided it in the past.
Much more often than you realized. It was always a great help to me."

(She thought: Later, there was no admittance for unauthorized per-
sonnel.)

Alice: "Would it bother you, now that you're working so much again,
if you spent more time in our company? What I mean is how would you

feel about it if we started up our evening gatherings again? They were entertaining, and they seem to have interested you, too."

"With stories?"

"With or without, whatever turn things happen to take."

"What gave you this idea?"

"I thought we might be able to improve the atmosphere in the house. Besides, we're not alone. Kathleen is still here, and James, too, along with Edward. It bothers me that we're neglecting our home life."

"I can't tell you how delighted I am with your suggestion, Alice. I've had similar thoughts now and then. I thought to myself: Is this really all that's left between us? Am I dreaming? Do I not know you at all? Don't I know who you are?"

(How cowardly he is. How eagerly he clutches at this straw.)

He appeared for the noon meal that same day, and conversation flowed easily. When James got up to leave the table, he pressed his sister's hand.

Michelangelo and Love

THE evenings could not start up again right away. Dr. King had asked to be invited to all of them and reminded of them. Like it or not, the Allisons had to tailor their plans to suit him.

The first gathering was like an entirely new start. Beneath the bust of Socrates in the background, in the wings, so to speak, the chorus of rational men, the judge and the railroad executive, took up their hiding place again. They had much to say to each other about developments in the world, and they indulged in speculations on the changes that had taken place here in this house, with or without their aid, in speculations, that is, about Edward. The gray-haired teacher who had entertained the company with her heart-warming tale of the page who had given Mary his ring appeared again; and before she seated herself, she looked around her carefully. Of all the friends present, she was most involved with what occurred here. Edward's school friend, the abstract painter, had not been forgotten either. But who was not aware of what an inane babbler he was? People therefore drifted away to a safe distance from him. But despite this he always wound up near somebody.

All who entered the library ascertained to their pleasure that nothing had changed here in the intervening weeks when they had not come together, unless, of course, one counted changes for the better in Edward Allison, on whose account these gatherings took place. He came in on his mother's arm, using only a cane now. He stood tall; his color was good and his mood so friendly, indeed, cheerful, that everyone saw instantly that the worst of his illness was now behind him. The sight of him—if the guests recalled what a grim, oppressive presence he had been before, bedded down on the sofa, mute most of the time, his mother or the doctor attending to him occasionally—the sight of him now, as he let himself be led to a chair and sat upright in it, nodding to both left and right, could only be a cause for rejoicing that the stamping of his left leg in no way diminished.

293

The gathering had a remarkably festive atmosphere to which the refreshments contributed: sandwiches, cakes, bonbons, liqueurs. Yes, peace reigned. Everyone who approached this table of delights, set to one side in the room, beamed and said, "Behold, peace reigns."

And how lively Alice, Edward's mother, was. She, too, had completed her molt. On most occasions in the past she had been a silent presence, a hovering fay. Her son's recovery, which meant so much to her, had transformed her. She made herself heard. She laughed. She went from one guest to another, shaking hands and inquiring how everyone was.

The elegant James Mackenzie sat there, too, her brother, and was content and immediately made room for the young painter and lent him his ear.

The daughter of the house, however, Kathleen, of whom it was said that she was not attending university courses at the moment but was working at home to brush up on knowledge that had faded during the war—Kathleen looked pale and worn. She looked like someone who had been disturbed in the course of some strenuous activity or inactivity. Her mother had to step in often as hostess because Kathleen was too slow in serving their guests. The absence of the master of the house accounted for the one large gap in the scene. And in fact Lord Crenshaw in his familiar massiveness was not sitting in his chair by the fireplace. He was still working, the guests learned. He appeared later, coming in with Dr. King, whom everyone congratulated on his success with Edward Allison. He expressed his thanks but disavowed any responsibility. The cure here, as always, had to be ascribed to nature and, in this particular case, to the milieu, to the domestic circumstances. Like the giant Antaeus, Edward had regained his strength when he touched the ground, the ground of his home.

Oh, the elderly teacher said, that would make a wonderful theme rich in possibilities. Perhaps the doctor would develop it for their entertainment this evening. But he raised his hands. "Me, tell a story? Haven't you ever heard of professional secrets that mustn't be betrayed?"

Gordon Allison sat down. It was obvious that he was working too hard. Then, too, he must have been dealing with a subject alien to him; for the joie de vivre, the delight in the world his stories displayed, was usually reflected in his face as well, harmonizing with his burgeoning fat and the inexhaustibility of his production. But now that quality was absent from his expression. Now—everyone he shook hands with and greeted realized this—now something had hit him hard. The war that had come into the house with his son and that he had fled so far away from before had finally caught up with him. His son had come back ill. Lord Crenshaw, it seemed, had given way to Gordon Allison.

This change in him was obvious to anyone who recalled the earlier gatherings when Lord Crenshaw had enthroned himself in front of the fireplace and the play of the flames and had begun to tell his extravagant, sumptuous tale, sweeping his listeners away; and they had not known whether they would emerge from the cataract alive again or not.

Kathleen placed his chair for him. He sat there again, his head propped in the left corner of the armchair. Anyone who saw him there in his massiveness could well think again today: what a mountain, a living mountain of fat and meat and skin, apparently without bones. He was not wearing his blue bathrobe with the wide belt, nor was he wearing his blue socks and embroidered yellow slippers. He came in a regular dark gray suit with the jacket left unbuttoned. His cuffs and soft collar glowed white, and around his neck he wore a greenish tie held in place with a pearl stickpin. Anyone sitting near him noticed, too, that he had a wide gold bracelet around his left wrist.

His fat still encircled and surrounded him like armor plate, but Allison looked younger. Why was that? Only because of his more formal clothes? His face had, however, a grayish cast to it; his eyes looked small; his gaze, clouded, unclear. This Lord Crenshaw, everyone realized, could not be expected to spin any fantasies out of old troubadour ballads, if, indeed, he made any contribution at all. He soon assumed a different position in his chair than he usually did. His heavy head with the combed-back gray hair left its accustomed, lofty place in the left-hand corner of the wing chair and leaned forward. His upper body slumped comfortably. Lord Crenshaw looked around him and watched the proceedings unsmilingly.

At one point during tea as he bent forward, grasping his right knee in both hands, chatting with his brother-in-law, Mackenzie, and remaining in this pose for quite a while, only to straighten up and light a cigarette—Lord Crenshaw had never been known to smoke before; he pulled a slim, gold cigarette case from his vest pocket—at this point Alice had just picked up a plate of pastries from the table near him and was about to offer them around to her guests. She stood still as though transfixed. Her eyes, turning to Lord Crenshaw, opened wide. Her heart skipped a beat. "When I was young I traveled lonely paths. I lost my way once and was glad when a wanderer happened by—"

As she came closer, holding the plate in both hands and smiling warmly to the guests who made way for her, she spotted on his left wrist the wide bracelet he had worn in his younger years. She had meant to pass the plate around or give it to Kathleen, but she went straight over to Gordon. She had not intended to. It simply happened, and there she stood, Alice with her pastries, before her brother and Lord Crenshaw, who remained bent forward and drew deeply on his cigarette. Only when Mackenzie interrupted the conversation to take a pastry his sister had recommended did Lord Crenshaw sit up and look into Alice's startled, immobile face.

They exchanged glances.

His hand searched about on the plate and knocked a pastry to the floor. Kathleen leapt to the rescue, picked it up, and teased her father. She took the plate from her mother and laughed: "Father isn't supposed to have any of these anyhow. That's why this one fell down."

He: "That's right. Sweets are off-limits for me. But I had a sudden yen for one."

James: "Why did you come and hold them under his nose then, Alice?"

She: "I'd forgotten."

His gold bracelet held her in its spell. He knew that and understood why.

Finally she closed her eyes, turned her head away, and could then leave him and mingle with the guests again.

After conversation had gone on in the usual vein for a while, Virginia Graves—after a whispered conference with the railroad man, who had crept out of his Socratic corner—raised her timorous voice and drew everyone's attention to herself. Had they, she wanted to know, given up their earlier format for these evenings? For her own part, she found herself still preoccupied with their host's thesis that all-powerful fantasy subdues everything in its path, that human beings are possessed by certain ideas, cannot break free from those ideas, and so undertake crusades and, as troubadours, pay homage to ladies they have never seen.

She had then countered with the proposal that men do in fact play a very clear role in events and that their customs are more of their own making than they realize. And she had illustrated her point with the story of the page who had put his ring on the finger of a statue of Mary and could not get it off again; for love, genuine love for the Virgin, had seized him; and though he did not realize this at first, that is why Mary held on to his ring.

Edward praised the story, which he could recall in detail. He had thought about it often and reflected on it; but, he said, he had forgotten what conclusion she had drawn from it.

Miss Graves: "Simply that we have a hand in events. Whether we know it or not. We act. It is we who act."

Lord Crenshaw did not move.

Edward: "But how? The war swept over us like a natural event. You could take your umbrella and protect yourself from the rain. When the alarm sounded you could seek shelter in a hallway somewhere, privately, personally, as an individual. But the rain fell; the storm raged. But of course the war was no natural hurricane. It was of human origin."

Miss Graves: "We agree completely."

Edward: "But what people caused it? And why, for what reason? Who acted? We can go back now and study the beginnings of wars, from newspaper reports, for example. People at conferences disagree; somebody mistrusts somebody else; they negotiate; nobody wants to be taken advantage of. But who are these people who negotiate and mistrust each other? Who are these plenipotentiaries of humankind who, thanks to the joint efforts of mathematicians, chemists, physicists, technicians, and engineers, supported by industry and finance, now have horrendous weapons at their disposal and can bring down the deluge upon us, destroying us all? Us, who are in no position to act at all. Who are these people? Have we had a good look at them? Who has subjected them to close scrutiny before granting them their commissions? Hasn't anyone felt obliged to sound them to the bottom of their souls? We read about food shortages and that millions have no place to live because the war destroyed their homes. But whom are we tracking down as these representatives of mankind, as these guilty representatives who caused all this in the past and who, unbeknownst to us, are planning the same or worse right now? Because we don't know who they are and what principles they adhere to and what goes on in their minds and because we go on following them, we—in fact—do not act at all."

Mackenzie, in a soft voice: "Edward, why ask these questions? Humanity has never learned anything from history."

Edward: "Why not?"

Mackenzie shrugged his shoulders. "I don't know."

Kathleen: "That's no answer, Uncle James."

Lunn, the railroad man: "Kathleen, that is the answer of all answers: I don't know. Or do you think, Edward, that if we sent a different

delegation to the conferences or if we went ourselves we would do any
better? Every once in a while, under some benign star or another, mankind rises up out of its swamp and faces up to the big questions, but not
for long. Then it sinks back down into the swamp. There's something in
us that makes us that way, Edward. That's the way it is, tinker with
humankind as much as you will."

Edward: "So we're evil and lost, and that's that?"

During this conversation Alice sat at the buffet table, still frightened
of Gordon Allison—and of herself. So he, too, had fallen back into the
past. It had not died out in him either. They had both unearthed the
battle axe.

But I am to blame. I admit it. I wanted this. I wanted clarity, truth. I
wanted to claim my life at last.

Alice had taken a seat to the rear of the group so that she would not
be forced to look over at him. She fought against the temptation. But
she had chosen a place that allowed her to see him after all if she
looked diagonally across the room between Virginia and Kathleen.

She could not resist looking, had to look. What torture to have to
look at him again. And there he sat, his old self. Yes, she recognized
him. He had not shaken loose from it, the sin, the evil. He had not
fought his battle to the end any more than she had. But she had
dragged him down from his perch. He had understood the call and not
tried to avoid it.

She was deluged by memories. She stood up, left the room, and ran
up the stairs to her room (the rape of Proserpina), turned on the lights,
and locked herself in. She paced up and down furiously. She stood at
the window and looked out into the dark grounds. She was horrified,
filled with shame. Persistent voices argued in her.

— What is it I want, what is it I want? I wanted this. No, it was
Edward who started it all. I? No! I did it for him. No, it couldn't have
been avoided. Fate sent him home to me. It's too much for me.

Alice, what are you doing? This is too much for you.

Oh, how it still has hold of me, the past, what happened then, the
brutality, the lust, the desire. I didn't realize it was still there. I see him
all over again, in that suit, with the gold bracelet and smoking a cigarette, and I tremble when I think about it. That's how I fell into his
power. My skin crawls and my fingers tingle. That's how he looked
when he attacked me and dragged me into my room. I fought, I
scratched his forehead. He knows.

He put that suit on. He's wearing that bracelet. He's playing the victor. He's going to try his old game again and drive me back. That's his way of wooing. —

While she argued with herself, looked at herself in the mirror, and slowed her racing breath, she reached for her powder puff.

— He thinks he is the winner. That's his answer. He's taking up the challenge. He thinks the very sight of him in battle dress will instantly put me under his spell again. Does he understand me better than I realize? His ploy almost worked. (It did work? Lord, save me!) He'll find I'm ready for him. (Lord, where am I falling to? Lord, save me!)

She stood in front of the mirror without seeing herself, blind. She had run to her room to pray and to rescue herself from herself. Only now, as she was heading for the door, did she remember why she had come.

She took her small wooden crucifix from her drawer, kissed it, and kneeled with it on the throw rug next to her bed. All she could say, the cross clutched in her hands, was "Salvation, salvation." At the same time, horrible images flitted through her head. She moaned, tried to drive them away. "Salvation, salvation." She pressed the crucifix to her breast. As she put it back in its case and closed the case, she stood in front of her dresser a while and tenderly stroked the wood. Then she went back to the party.

Downstairs a lighthearted debate about love was in progress. The theme had suddenly popped up when it seemed that the gloomy thesis under discussion was about to triumph. Man and mankind, the argument went, were just plain rotten, and that's why human beings, subject to intellectual epidemics as they were, tore each other apart now and then. But at this point someone interjected: But what about love?

Who was this someone?

Lord Crenshaw.

He had not entered into the debate at all until then. Now, though, he uttered this pronouncement. "But there is still love."

His remark came as a small footnote to the discussion, tossed in between two puffs on his cigarette.

Its impact was considerable.

The Socratics in the background began an antiphonal song of praise to that philosopher and sounder of the human heart, Lord Crenshaw. They waxed poetic, and their old-fashioned metaphors ("the light that breaks through dark clouds") drew laughter from the others. They remained unperturbed. Next to speak was, of course, Virginia Graves; then, somewhat more cautiously, James Mackenzie, who wanted "love" understood in a precise way that he could not define very clearly. Then came Kathleen, who said "Yes," because she couldn't make head nor tail of anything at the moment. The chubby-cheeked painter sat there defiantly, his arms crossed. He was not going to have any of this talk, whether of evil or of love. And that Lord Crenshaw, of all people, had capitulated!

Edward could not recall ever hearing his father pronounce the word "love." He had tossed the word out in such a strange way, too, with a marked diffidence, like someone who has stolen a watch but can't keep it and slides it onto a table on the sly, then turns, picks up a newspaper, and reads aloud from it, perhaps about the most recent ambassadorial conference or perhaps, if he's in the mood, about a theft—the sublimity of love.

— Whatever possessed you to speak of love? How dare you let the word pass your lips? I'm sitting here watching you. I have plenty to say about you and your idea of love. I'd be more than happy to spill it all. You're sticking your nose out of your cave. I can wait. —

Edward glanced behind him. He had looked for his mother earlier. She had been gone, probably to give some order or another. Now she was back in her place. Would she have anything to say?

She smiled at him. Edward thought of the silent battle this woman had fought for years, for decades, against him, the tyrant, who sat there in his glory. How much she had suffered alone, without comrades in arms, without help; and out of shame, a feeling of humiliation, she had not been able to open her mouth in her own defense. Now she smiled at him, tenderly, resigned. No, that isn't the way it will rest, Mother. Weakness may to down to defeat, but against brute force and lies we can set truth and justice.

"But where was love, Father, in your own story of Jaufie and Petite Lay?" Edward began. (I want to bait him!) "Love had a place in it. In fact, your story dealt with practically nothing but love. But in what form? There were the courts of love, and the troubadours busied themselves with love professionally. But something was missing."

"What was missing?" Lord Crenshaw asked.

"Well, love. And there is still such a thing as love, you say. But in your story of the gray knight and his harsh wife and then in what the gray knight said and even in the story of Jaufie and Petite Lay love comes off badly. In truth, only one thing comes away victorious, and that is custom."

But at the very moment when he put this question to his father to bait him and challenge him, the question recoiled back on him, and he felt with a sudden pang: But where do I stand myself? Is there any love in me? And he knew: I have no love. He saw that all at once, for the first time. He leaned back. He took in his father's answer only vaguely, so dreadful was this discovery about himself.

— You have robbed me of so much. Because of you I've fallen sick. What have you done, you monster, you ravager. —

After speaking a few words Lord Crenshaw stood up and went to a small table in front of the bookshelves. He picked up a small book that was lying open there and returned to his chair. He nodded toward his son and said, "I owe you and the others who heard the Jaufie story an amplification of that story."

He leafed in the book.

"There is still love, I said. What part does it play in important matters?"

Edward thought: You're nodding to me. We're in the same boat, but neither of us knew it. But if that is my condition—if I know nothing of love and do not feel any, then you must be partially responsible for that, you monster. I see through you more and more. Why talk and defend yourself? Where is Mother? She's smiling. Let her. I won't smile.

Lord Crenshaw, slowly and softly:

"In recent weeks I came across a book I'd been looking for for years. That happens sometimes. Suddenly I found it again, and at just the right moment. It is this book here."

Mackenzie: "Gordon, you say you had been looking for that book you're holding for a long time, and it just fell into your hands?"

"Quite by chance. I bought it eighteen years ago, no, twenty; here's the date."

Alice held her hands over her eyes. So you've come to that, have you? You're standing at bay. And I've forced you to it.

Mackenzie turned to Edward—who looked back at him but did not hear him (You have robbed me of many things. My body is broken; my soul is broken; what have you done, you monster?): "My remark goes back to a conversation I had with Edward recently. I was telling him that we are so busy pursuing things that we don't give them a chance to come to us. We may desperately want the truth, but for the very reason that we besiege it, it refuses to surrender to us."

Gordon: "So how should we go about finding the truth?"

Mackenzie: "Through ridding ourselves of the will. You have just seen that yourself."

Gordon: "Through coldness? Through indifference?"

Mackenzie: "Through gentleness. Calmness, devotion. The truth will come, but we cannot go fetch it."

Gordon: "But I don't recall being in that state of mind when the book came into my hands."

Mackenzie: "You weren't aware of it, Gordon. You said you came across the book accidentally. Accidentally means that you didn't will it. It was when you were in this state of mind, in this attitude, that the call of the thing, the book, could reach your ear. And you found what you were looking for."

Gordon laughed in his old, cheerful way. "I plead ignorance, absolute ignorance. And I needed the book? What for? I didn't need it, and I wasn't thinking about it, and I hadn't missed it. I know your theory, James, and I promise you I'll convert to it if I see it really work. But now to turn to this book: It's a collection of the sculptor Michelangelo's sonnets. They're about love, about love among other things. Michelangelo was a great sculptor, perhaps the greatest, surely the most powerful sculptor Europe has produced in the post-Hellenistic age. What was his view of love? Let me read a few of these poems. Take these two lines, for example:

> *And in this wretched state it is your face*
> *That lends me light and shadow, like the sun.*

He does not say 'light.' He says 'light and shadow.'

> *When sometimes I'm beset by your great mercy,*
> *I fear and chafe no less than at your rigor;*
> *At one extreme or the other*
> *The wound from the blows of love is deadly.*

And this:

> *So eager is this my lady, and so swift,*
> *That she, at the same time that she would kill,*
> *Promises me with her eyes all joy, and still*
> *Can keep inside the wound the cruel knife.*
> *Thus both my death and life,*
> *Opposed, I feel within my soul concurrent*

During one little moment.
But still the fatal torment
Mercy can threaten, lengthening the pains.
For evil harms much more than joy sustains."

In the pause that followed this reading Kathleen said, "The poems aren't very pretty, Father. There's not much about love in them."

He: "So you think the book might better have remained missing."

Mackenzie: "Come on, Kathleen. We've heard very little so far."

Allison: "This next one is Michelangelo's response to an epigram that his friend Giovanni Strozzi had written in praise of Michelangelo's statue *Night*. Strozzi had written: 'The Night you see sleeping in such a sweet pose was carved by an Angel in this stone, and since she is sleeping she is alive; wake her, if you don't believe it, and she'll speak to you.'

"And Buonarotti responds:

I prize my sleep, and more my being stone,
As long as hurt and shamefulness endure.
I call it lucky not to see or hear;
So do not waken me, keep your voice down!"

There was silence in the room. Lord Crenshaw leafed further. Edward sat to the rear of the company with crossed arms. Alice's face was dismayed. Without realizing it herself she was breathing so loudly that it could be heard in the room.

Gordon:

"Since I have straw for flesh and my heart's sulphur,
Since I have bones consisting of dry wood,
Since my soul lacks a rein and lacks a guide,
Since I jump at desire, at beauty further,
Since all my brains are weak and blind, and totter,
And since quicklime and traps fill all the world,
It will be no surprise when I am burned
By a flash of the first fire I encounter.
Since I've the beautiful art, that those who bear it
From Heaven use to conquer Nature with,
Even if she can parry everywhere,
If I, not blind or deaf, was born for it,
A true match for my heart's fire-setting thief,
He is to blame who fated me to fire."

Alice's expression changed. Her forehead was furrowed with anger, her mouth ready for speech, but she said nothing.

"Now a gentler sonnet, if we can speak of gentleness at all in Michelangelo. You can't stop with just one of his poems and think you've seen him whole.

> *I am dearer to myself than was my habit,*
> *More than myself, since you've been in my heart,*
> *As a bare rock will get much less regard*
> *Than a stone with its carving added to it.*
> *Or, like a written or painted leaf or sheet,*
> *More noted as the more it's torn or scarred,*
> *Such I make myself, since I've been the target*
> *Struck by your face; and I have no regret.*
> *I go as one who bears arms or enchantment*
> *So that all dangers fall away from me,*
> *Made safe in every place with such a seal.*
> *Against fire, against water I am potent,*
> *All blind men in your sign I make to see,*
> *And with my spit all poisoning I heal."*

Kathleen: "At last a poem with some beauty in it. It offers a moment's relief. He seems to live in hell. Why? What happened to him? I wasn't aware of this side of Michelangelo. I always thought of him as the great, powerful creator of his *David*, his *Moses*, his *Night*. But then there's the ceiling of the Sistine Chapel, of course. There's his gruesome side again, a descent into hell."

Allison: "I've got one more poem to read yet.

> *My course of life already has attained,*
> *Through stormy seas, and in a flimsy vessel,*
> *The common port, at which we land to tell*
> *All conduct's cause and warrant, good or bad,*
> *So that the passionate fantasy, which made*
> *Of art a monarch for me and an idol,*
> *Was laden down with sin, now I know well,*
> *Like what all men against their will desired.*
> *What will become, now, of my amorous thoughts,*
> *Once gay and vain, as toward two deaths I move,*
> *One known for sure, the other ominous?*
> *There's no painting or sculpture now that quiets*
> *The soul that's pointed toward that holy Love*
> *That on the cross opened Its arms to take us."*

"Read that again, please, Gordon," Alice's voice said, "read it nice and slowly."

He raised the book and read the same lines word for word again.

"There's no painting or sculpture now that quiets
The soul that's pointed toward that holy Love
That on the cross opened Its arms to take us."

No, this was not the atmosphere that had prevailed on those earlier evening when Lord Crenshaw, telling of young Jaufie, his clever Petite Lay, and the courts of love, had reveled in the richness and delight of the world. "There's no painting or sculpture now that quiets the soul." Lord Crenshaw had sustained a blow. Where had he picked up this penitent's expression that was so ill suited to him? And Edward, the son, who sat there upright. He was no longer a sick man. Alice, who usually glided around the room like a fay and spread good cheer, in the background, in hiding. The formidable Kathleen (the only candid soul present) said in her pitiless way:

"The poems you read, Father, have precious little to do with love. They're not love poems in the normal sense. You surely could have found better ones than those."

Gordon: "I can see now it was no happy coincidence that sent them my way again."

Kathleen: "Tell us what it is, Father, that interests you in these gloomy poems. You said you had been missing the book for fifteen or twenty years, and now you've found it at the right moment. What moment is that?"

She plays the childlike innocent. But for weeks she has been living in a house befogged with an increasingly thick and heavy smoke. She feels caught in a net that is tightening around her, and she wants to break free.

Lord Crenshaw calmly puts his book down on the carpet next to him. "We live in a world full of tensions. Our initial question was: Where do wars come from? What sets them in motion? Who is responsible for them? Why can't people join together and live in peace? And at that point I remarked that in spite of everything we still have love."

Kathleen: "But there is not much about love in those poems."

Allison: "Not much about love. You have happy, fulfilling love in mind. You're thinking about the harmony of two souls, of a man and a woman, their joy at having found each other. That's what most love

poems talk about, and they may mention the usual obstacles and inhibi-
tions to love and the accompanying feelings. True enough, these poems
have nothing to say about that condition. But they do reveal knowledge
of love—and of how Michelangelo failed to find love. His relationship
to love was like Kierkegaard's to faith. He knew what it was, but he
couldn't find it. That happens a lot and follows from our nature. At any
rate, that's what love was like for Michelangelo.

"I'd like to tell you what I know about him.

"He was a lonely person from his youth on, and he was no different
at any other time in his life. His environment can't be blamed for this.
This is the way he came into life, the way nature, the creative force in
the world, made him. My sense of him, though, is that nature had not
let him fully out of her grasp, that in his heart he was not as separate a
being as most people are. They are complete in themselves and can play
and move about like birds and butterflies. He was like a figure by Rodin
that emerges only partially from its medium. He felt that, and he struggled to become a distinct, individual self.

"How could he be anything but lonely among young, ingenuous, fully
formed people, he, who was shaken by mysterious storms and knew
only fear, anxiety, and sadness along with envy and bitterness. He felt
excluded from the banquet table of the world.

"And since that was his situation and he had been created (actually
not created) this way, he saw men and nature with a clearer, sharper
eye than others did and knew what was to be found between earth and
hell and even had some inklings of heaven. When he was young and
studying in Florence, a fellow student, Torrigiani, had broken his nose
when the two of them were wrestling about in a chapel decorated with
gorgeous paintings. The blow squashed Michelangelo's nose flat, as if
putting a stamp on his strange and lonely nature. Torrigiani boasted of
what he had done, but the deformity worked little change in
Michelangelo. Indeed, it was a confirmation of his nature. And if he
sometimes could not understand why he was the way he was, all he had
to do was run his hand over his broken nose or look into a mirror.

"He did not remain imprisoned in seething darkness. When he set to
work on stone with his hammer and chisel, everything was different.
Human beings rejected him. They drove him into gloom and crippled
him. He was denied the sweet, soft, liberating warmth of human com-
panionship. What he yearned for, had to yearn for more than others to
whom it was granted, evaded him. He had to make do with hard, cold
stone. With hammer and chisel he struck stone to evoke from it what

was not human but was more than human, no playful tribe but something they would be forced to admire and that would fling them down onto the ground.

"Let other men embrace beautiful women and sire children that might die tomorrow or grow into this or that kind of adults. When he discovered this power in himself, he felt that he was working in a superior material, marble, and that he would still be speaking to future generations when all this soft flesh had long since decayed.

"What was love to him! The love he was capable of, ardent though it was, was not permitted to love anymore. His titanic powers had stepped to the fore and thrust love aside to complain and languish. His powers made him eccentric, lonely, and terrifying. And whatever of love dared raise its head in him was colored, shaded, hardened, by those powers.

"He struggled both against and on the side of this primal force that took possession of him, fulfilled him, made a master of him but did not let him become Michelangelo. He turned melancholy, and it is said that he inspired fear even in a pope who had commissioned work from him. His moods varied, but they often bordered on madness. The bestial power that had taken root in him and claimed him body and soul abused him dreadfully and would not even grant him the early death he yearned for.

"He lived to be over ninety and had to suffer the torments of Tantalus that long. He became like a blind man and could not see what he had, and in reality he had nothing, for he was incapable of enjoying anything. He once wrote to a relative that he had no time to eat, and he complained that he had been ruining his health with overexhaustion for years. He lived in misery and suffering.

"His relatives thought he was miserly, and in fact he did develop a kind of greed, clinging to money, loving money. At least he had money, the stuff with which other people could buy things but with which he could buy nothing, for what could he get that would ever satisfy him or delight him?

"Perhaps he would have been capable of pleasure earlier. But now his throat had closed on him. He could not swallow anymore. The only tie he still had to the world was money. The only other thing left to him was drudgery, barbaric work. And arrogance and scorn for humankind and his black conscience.

"Why that? He hadn't murdered anyone. Certainly not. But how many people had he beheaded, stabbed to death, tortured, with his hammer and chisel? And how often had he, in his hammering and chiseling, wooed, begged, worshiped, kissed, embraced, and been rejected? How often had he set himself up as a tyrant over his fellow men? They had to kneel before him and worship him.

"Never, when he was young and had been surrounded by beautiful women, had he ever approached one in the ateliers. He could not do it. And when he forced himself to try, the women could not understand what this strange creature that could neither laugh nor dance wanted of them. They were frightened; they turned cold and ran away. He soon understood. Actually, he had already known. He needed no mirror to tell him who he was.

"He cursed himself: 'How can I escape myself? Oh, see to it that I do not wake to myself again.' And so he cursed his desire to be like others. He gradually gave up on it altogether. All he did about love was to write poems about it. It was an abstract, intellectual entity for him. He made do with the money the world gave him as compensation. He crept back into his stone, the native stone from which he had only half emerged to begin with. Yes, he disappeared in it again.

"I said he had a bad conscience. He felt it to be a crime, a sin, that he had treated himself as he had and thrown both body and mind into his work this way. He could not resist his dark powers. He could not free himself of them. They infused his whole being, body and soul, robbed him of happiness. He fought and fought—finally he sold out to them. His sense of guilt assumed horrendous proportions. Look at his face. It is guilt, not Torrigiani's fist, that has left its mark there.

"Of his works that were to outlive the flesh-and-blood creatures he lived among and that relieved him of the duty to live and suffer with his fellow creatures, only a few have survived, as if to demonstrate that they originated in the underworld and that the underworld does not emerge victorious in the end. Many of his statues and sketches were destroyed. Much of his work remained only half-done. One of his bronzes, a statue of Pope Julius II, was melted down a few years after its completion to make a cannon. And who has loved the works that remain? Whom have they made happy? Have even those that do not inspire fear ever spread any joy? They have drawn admiration, the statues of David and of night. People have gazed in astonishment at the vast panorama of Judgment Day.

"And Michelangelo knew that."

A Discovery in the Attic

MACKENZIE's comment: "A sad story. But if I recall correctly, there was Vittoria Colonna. And he had some favorite students."

Gordon Allison: "Exceptions to the rule. Fate granted him some relief. Cavalieri is said to have been his best friend. He was over sixty when he met Vittoria Colonna; she was almost fifty. The yearning for love had not died out in him."

Kathleen said Michelangelo must have been an unusual case. (How confused she was. And no one came to her aid.)

Alice: You want to reflect yourself in the picture of this Italian. Don't paint yourself prettier than you are. You're a brigand, nothing but a brigand. You have never known what love is, and you still don't. It has not died out. Your love has not died out. Now, in your declining years, you're turning sentimental. Are you a coward to boot? You addressed this story to Edward. Just look how coldly he's sitting there. What Edward thinks of you. Do you think you've touched him with this grisly ballad of yours? You'll be unmasked yet. —

But as the conversation continued and she battled with Gordon in her own mind, she was drawn out of herself before she realized it.

Suddenly she saw Salome dancing.

Salome was dancing before King Herod on his birthday. Herod was pleased. He had taken Herodias, the wife of his brother, Philip, as his own wife, Herodias, Salome's mother. But John the Baptist had said: "It is not lawful for thee to have thy brother's wife."

How Salome danced, slim, brown skinned! Her curly hair flew. As she turned, she held her arms out, the veils held in her fingertips, and she let one veil after the other fall. Her body turned and throbbed, almost naked. She bent and stretched, child, virgin. And was the lust of the world incarnate.

The king sat there, and the matron Herodias sat there, and their eyes followed the twitching, whirling Salome. Their hands touched. They kissed each other on the throne.

The earth trembled at this time. John had foretold the coming salvation. He was the son of Zacharias. This was the fifteenth year of the reign of Tiberius. Pontius Pilate was governor of Judea, Herod, tetrarch of Galilee. In those days, when Annas and Caiaphas were high priests, the word came unto John in the wilderness, and he preached the baptism of repentance for the remission of sins. "Prepare ye the way of the Lord, make his paths straight. Every valley shall be filled, and every mountain and hill shall be brought low; and the crooked shall be made straight, and the rough ways shall be made smooth. And all flesh shall see the salvation of God."

John lay in prison. They had thrown the prophet of salvation into prison and made the earth to tremble; and sin, with cherry-red lips, danced before Herod and Herodias, who embraced on the throne. —

Alice shook herself.

Anxious, she stood up. What was this rising up in her?

Wearing her most cordial smile, she moved around the room, among her guests.

The name of Michelangelo was still being tossed about. Edward took no part at all in the conversation. He sat up straight in his inconspicuous location, acting—as he had in his first weeks at home—as if nothing happening here concerned him. His expression was so remote that Alice was afraid he had withdrawn completely. But when she moved close to him and tapped him on the arm, he gave her a clear, sure look. She could see he had just been thinking, reflecting.

Kathleen came up to them while her mother was standing next to Edward and tried to read Alice's expression. Alice put an arm around her daughter. They strolled about the room together, and as they walked, Alice thought about Salome and her dance again, and about the embracing pair on the throne. Alice dropped her arm from her daughter's waist.

Kathleen whispered, "Father is telling such dreary stories. We have to steer the conversation around to something more cheerful. Do you have any ideas?"

"Something more cheerful?"

While her mother was thinking, Kathleen went to a corner of the room. The first thing everyone heard was a roar of applause—all the guests looked over toward Kathleen, who was spinning the dials on the radio—then some light music floated into the room above the announcer's voice. Kathleen tuned the music in, lowered the volume, and presented her gift of music to the room with her childlike laugh.

Alice passed pastries and liqueurs around. When she neared Lord Crenshaw, who had taken up his old regal pose again and was looking at her as if nothing had happened, she grew angry and started to go on by him. He called her back.

She turned her head to him: "No sweets for you."

But he had snatched a piece of cake and bit into it, laughing.

He conjugated and ate: "I ought not, you ought not, he ought not."

James consoled his sister, "Let him have it as a reward for his Michelangelo story."

As Gordon gave her a broad wink, she saw his gold bracelet flash in the light, and she moved on quickly. You and Michelangelo. You are the monster, the wild boar, and you know it. You know that I'm hunting you and have to kill you. How you malign me, you despoiler.

Some of the guests couldn't let the story of Michelangelo drop. The icy quality it had didn't suit Gordon Allison. The men in the corner exchanged opinions on this matter.

The railroad man: "Gordon hasn't been himself since Edward's health has improved. Everything was fine, just like old times, as long as Edward was bedridden and couldn't get around. But now the boy is turning the family topsy-turvy. You can't convince me otherwise. No one speaks about it, of course. He's sick and lost his leg in the war as well, but he's exploiting the situation and pushing things too far. It's all perfectly obvious."

The judge: "Alice isn't her old self either."

"And Kathleen? That brick of a girl. Did you notice how she ran for the radio? She couldn't stand the mood any longer. It was touching to see. The only winner here is Edward. Just look at him sitting there with his arms folded. He hasn't said a word yet. I've never been very fond of the boy, you know. He was always standoffish. It was all one could do to lure him into conversation or a game."

They both looked over at Edward.

The judge: "He sits there like a district attorney at a cross-examination. I sometimes have the feeling that this soldier back from the wars has us civilians on the stand, as if we had to absolve ourselves of guilt for his wound."

The railroad man poked him in the ribs and laughed: "Did you see why Gordon brought up the subject of love? What he was driving at? An answer to the boy, a good answer. That's precisely what the youngster is lacking, love. It was almost painful for Gordon to relate Michelangelo's depressing history. Imagine him digging up something like that. But it's clear how Gordon's feeling. He's protesting, out loud, for all the world to hear. I feel sorry for him."

The judge: "A dreadful tale, this Michelangelo thing. It's hard to see how Lord Crenshaw could ever go for something like that. Someone ought to do something about it. Someone should speak up."

"Someone should. Someone really ought to. If somebody invites us to contribute, then perhaps we can put in our two cents' worth. These gatherings are no fun anymore. They're getting on my nerves."

The judge: "The boy should learn what people think of him in any case. With all due respect for illness and war wounds. But what is your sense of it? Does that allow someone to put unlimited demands on everyone else around him?"

The railroad man: "Extortion."

"My feeling exactly. Someone has to draw the line."

But they did nothing. It was enough for them merely to think about a plausible course of action. What transpired in their corner was talk and nothing more. They were quite content to be spectators and remain spectators. They sat in their box, opera glasses in hand. It wouldn't have taken much for them to start clapping and hissing, for they did find the show exciting.

Miss Virginia Graves, the teacher, made an effort to dispel the gloom that Gordon's story had introduced into the party (and that his strangely melancholy aspect helped maintain). Some of the guests were talking about the composer Richard Strauss, whose *Rosenkavalier* waltz had just been played on the radio.

Now more of his torrid, exciting music was coming from the radio. Alice, who was talking with the doctor, interrupted herself, coughed, and acted as if she had swallowed the wrong way. The doctor suggested she raise her arms. She took up his suggestion, smiling back at him, and sat there a few seconds in this odd pose.

Music from *Salome* was coming from the radio.

Alice stood up. She was still self-possessed enough to nod politely to the doctor, then she ran from the room and stopped for a minute on the stairs, frantic, frantic. It was incredible: *Salome* was on the radio. The music could be heard through the whole house. It followed her up to her room. She locked the door and fell down terrified on her bed.

What was happening? She sat up and looked around her anxiously: It's calling me. There's something calling me. We're being watched. I have to be careful. Oh, I have to be careful.

She ventured back out into the hallway. The radio was off now. She heard voices.

Will people notice if I don't come back for a few minutes? I want to go up to the attic. I have to.

She hurried up the stairs, opened the door, turned the light on.

What is it I want here? He was looking for his book here. I remember his putting it away years ago. Now he's poking around up here again. I want to look around. My God, *Salome* on the radio. How could that be? (She stood as if paralyzed.)

She wandered about in the attic. There was the children's furniture. There were the fairy-tale pictures from the nursery. The cupboard with his old manuscripts.

She tugged at the cupboard door. Locked, as always; locked, just like him.

I'd like to look around in there sometime, just to irritate him. She examined the lock. I'll try it with a key, or break it open.

She looked around her again. What is it I want here? I have to go back to the party.

And as she starts to leave, her eyes looking down at the floor (I'm dreaming Salome), she sees near the door just as she is about to turn off the light a strip of cloth, a rag. She bends down, picks it up. It is a light fabric. A shock hits her: her old summer dress.

She turns the light out, leaves, looks at the cloth when she is in the hall. Without thinking, she goes back to her room, opens the door.

The clothes in her closet are as she had left them. The summer dress is missing from her suitcase.

She stands over the suitcase, searches through it, looks at the small strip of cloth on the table again, and closes the closet and the suitcase.

He tore up her dress. He had gone into her room when she wasn't there. He'd never done that before, never. He had searched through her things and taken the dress. He tore it to shreds in the attic. Where is the rest of it? What did he do with the rest of it?

I can't go back downstairs. He did it in a fit of rage, that madman. He won't give me room enough to breathe. It's happening all over again. He wants to subjugate me. That's what he has decided. He's set on it. He's assassinating me. I'll expose him. "From my bones an avenger will arise." From my flesh and blood.

And while her guests chattered merrily and discussed Boccaccio she sat at her table and cried, and her fingers stroked the thin strip of cloth and pressed it to her mouth. She soaked it with her tears. She fell into a heavy sobbing. She cried like someone at the side of a corpse.

She washed her face and tidied herself up to go back downstairs again. I won't let on. I won't give him that pleasure. Things will take the course they have to take. I'll stay cold.

As she was going down the stairs she glanced at the Proserpina picture and felt it to be a humiliating insult. His triumph. I hadn't seen it that way before. As soon as I can I'll take it down.

When she reached the last step she heard radio music again. She had to stop. She covered her eyes with her hand. What is happening to me? Then she remembered: I haven't knelt down, haven't called on any heavenly being, not for weeks on end—because I haven't been able to. I'm evil, I know. I'm giving myself up to evil; I know that. I can't do otherwise. I don't want to do otherwise.

You in heaven, my guardian angels, forgive me. I can't help myself. You won't abandon me. I can't help myself. Everything is crashing down on me. He'll be sorry that he made me so evil.

Conversation downstairs had drifted away from the theme of love; but Miss Virginia, who was watching for her chance, was finally able to revive the subject again when the radio produced still more music from *Salome*. No one else was paying any attention to the music, but she drew attention to it so that she, following Lord Crenshaw's lead, could talk about love.

Richard Strauss, she said, had written *Der Rosenkavalier* as well, and the fresh, tender love depicted in that opera was reminiscent of the love cultivated by the troubadours. But all one needed to do was take a look at *Salome* to see how many kinds of love there were and what all went under the name of "love." King Herod "loved" Herodias, his brother's wife. And possessed by a wild, oriental love, Salome "loved" the ascetic John, who spurned her and thus—as a political prisoner he was at her mercy—moved her to demand his head. She wanted to possess him and take her sadistic revenge on him. This perverted love—which made no effort to disguise itself—was so revolting that the wicked king who had sworn to grant her whatever she wanted (he was himself in love with Salome, who represented the youth of his lover Herodias) did in fact have John beheaded but then was so disgusted by the obviously sexual delight Salome took in the bloody head that he ordered his soldiers to beat her to death with their shields.

"How awful," Kathleen said and then pressed her former teacher to go on (Kathleen felt particularly bad this evening. She was becoming more and more unhappy with each passing week. Such a dreadful silence surrounded her; it was closing in on her like the movable walls in Poe's story of the "Pit and the Pendulum"). "How awful. And then what happened?"

The teacher: "Nothing. The love of the page in the story I told was of a different order, the love that moved him to give his engagement ring to Mary. He found love, a real love that brought him peace."

"Real love," Kathleen said in astonishment. "What do you mean by that? That other 'love' you spoke of was certainly real, too, horribly real. What is real love?"

The teacher had struck a rich vein. Everyone was fascinated by this subject. She was sure of her ground.

Like the two gentlemen in the background, the two spectators and listeners, she realized that a battle was going on in this house, that there were attackers and defenders. She chose to fight on Alice's side. She knew too much to remain neutral.

"That's what was lacking in Michelangelo's case," she said. "I don't believe what he says in his poems. There was a Satan in him. I have the sense that he didn't even want real love, or if he did, then only on the side, as it were."

Gordon Allison: "Didn't he want to free himself from what you've called a Satan?"

The little teacher smiled skeptically: "Do you really think so, Mr. Allison? You're an artist. You can empathize with Michelangelo. I think he sold his soul to art the way Faust sold his to Mephistopheles."

Gordon: "Absolutely. That was foreordained. He had no choice. And why? He yearned for love. You can hear that in his poems. They strike me as genuine. Love was denied him—except in that one late episode and in the friendship of his students."

The brave Virginia did not yield: "He didn't really want it. Of course he suffered. Anyone without love suffers. If his hammer and chisel and his art had not come into his hands he would have become a fearful person, a criminal and murderer, a warrior." She smiled. "He reminds me a little—if you'll forgive me this somewhat far-fetched association—of Richard Strauss's *Salome*. Salome knows something of love, too. But it passes her by. She loves John, but wrongly. If that weren't so, she would have served him, no matter what, and helped him and sacrificed herself for him. Instead, she has her stepfather hand him over to her, and she kills him. She does not see him as a human being; she doesn't see him at all. When he falls into her hands, she can't think of anything

better to do with him than kill him. If she had really loved him, she
would have followed him into the wilderness. She would have demanded, and obtained, his release from King Herod. She knew that.
But she wanted something that she represented to herself as vengeance
but that was something else. Michelangelo suffered. Of course he suffered. Who does not suffer if he is without love? It's like the body
suffering hunger and thirst. Anyone who can't find food and something
to drink dies, or is somehow ruined. He doesn't become good. Michelangelo was persecuted. He had to strike back over and over again. As
Mr. Allison suggested, he had to create people out of stone because no
living human being could connect with him. I don't know his poems,
but I'd be willing to wager there are no Pygmalion sonnets among them,
no wish of Michelangelo's that one of his figures would become flesh
and blood, and he could love her. He created them proudly and defiantly, conscious of his powers. And that was that.

"In the Sistine Chapel he painted the Creation, Adam and Eve. But
he couldn't deny his dark side and had to turn it loose there; and in this
chapel dedicated to the teachings of Christ, to the salvation of human
souls, he felt compelled to paint his Judgment Day, this horrible descent into hell, this 'Dies irae, dies illa' in paint."

When Alice came in, she nodded to Edward, who fixed his eyes on
her. And when she looked over toward him again later, she noticed that
his gaze was still on her.

Gordon didn't notice her. He apparently hadn't realized she had left
the room. She held the blue cloth cupped in her hand:

You did this to me. You couldn't even leave me that much. You stole
my dress and tore it up. You suffer, you say. You are inconceivably
malign. I will not pardon you. Now that you have done this to me, I'll
accept none of your excuses. See there, Gordon, you've rejuvenated
yourself with your bracelet. And you're digging out your old books.
You don't want to write anymore. I've gotten that far. Now you're
ready to do battle. You'll find you're up against an opponent you never
dreamed of facing. —

"Isn't it your turn to say something, Mother?" she heard Edward's
calm voice say. "While you were out of the room we've continued the
discussion of love that Father began."

"Why should I have anything to contribute, Edward? I've spent my
whole life—most of my life—with you, with Father and you children, in
the family. Everybody knows about that kind of love."

I'm onto him. My face is giving me away. He wants to force me to
speak.

Edward: "We probably know least of all about this everyday kind of love. We feel it. We grow up in it. But nobody describes it. Michelangelo and Salome are far from the whole story."

At this point Gordon Allison stirred in his chair. He rested his left elbow on his knee, put his chin in the palm of his left hand, and turned his head toward her. She noticed a slight twitching at the corners of his mouth. She interpreted it as derision.

I didn't want to say anything. I didn't want to give you the chance to see my pain. But I'll answer, and you'll hear my answer. I'll wipe that scorn off your face. —

"What do you think, Mother?"

"Yes, tell us what you think," Dr. King encouraged. "Edward is right. We speak too little about the most important things. We come to take the ordinary, the essential things for granted. We don't notice them. We forget they exist."

How can he set such a trap for me! Is Edward doing this consciously? Is he against me, too? I'm supposed to talk about family life, now, posthumously. Perhaps now is the time to talk about it. I want to speak. I have to speak. I can't sit across from him without doing him physical harm (my God, it's all repeating itself. I'm in a rage, the way I was then, then. We're in battle. Will I be strong, this time? Who am I now? Who have I become? Don't fail this time. Do it right just one time, one last time before you die).

She nodded to the tall, warm-hearted physician. "Can I tell anything I like, whatever occurs to me?"

"But of course, Alice. First, it is not up to me to command; and, second, the life of a family extends over such a long period of time and takes in so many people that its history has to contain hundreds of incidents and stories. I think we would all be interested to hear what an authority on this subject has to say."

"I agree," Edward said.

She was determined to speak. She clutched the shred of cloth in her hand like an amulet.

She was asked to come in closer. While the chairs were being shifted around she was afraid someone would put her chair too close to Gordon's. But the arrangement fell out mercifully. She was seated not even across from him but at an angle to him. She could hardly see him, nor he her. But now Edward was only one chair away from her, and that was a comfort.

When Gordon had turned up with his old book of Michelangelo's poems that was all too familiar to her (he had not misplaced it; she had buried it herself as deep as she could under and behind his books, for she hated these poems he reveled in and exploited for his own self-aggrandizement. But how strange that he had found it again, an omen, an omen that inspired fear—like the music from *Salome* on the radio earlier), at this same time she had recalled that story she had read so often but could never read often enough. It had faded from her memory; but now, as he had told of Michelangelo, it had come back to her. (We are all sinking back into the past. Everything repeats itself.)

She did not begin with her story right away. She allowed herself a prelude, so to speak, to get up her courage. She knew, too, before she opened her mouth, that she would simply speak at first, let her voice sound in these people's ears, so that she could later load it with the burden she had in mind. It was like sizing up a stone with the eye before trying to lift it. Only when you actually lay hands on it do you know how big a task you've taken on.

Everything fell beautifully into place. Her voice, her mouth, did something different from what she had planned. Before Edward, her son, before Gordon Allison, gentle, friendly words took shape in her mouth. She was supposed to talk about love. And, indeed, she spoke about love. She didn't understand what was happening to her.

She directed her words to her brother, James Mackenzie, and reminded him of conversations that had taken place in their family.

Mackenzie had spoken about the role of women in earlier times and in the Orient. Women had not counted for much. The family was the man's possession. But the continuing existence of the family was held sacred. Ancestors were honored. The hearth was a holy place.

To whom was she speaking? To whom was she addressing these remarks? She squeezed the scrap of cloth as if to wring a new and different strength out of it, but it yielded nothing. She went on:

"Women had a wretched place in society in those days, and in the Orient they still do. We can count ourselves lucky that we don't live under those conditions. Men have their place in the world, and women have theirs." (Alice listened to what she was saying with astonishment and some strange inkling: Who is this who is speaking to me so gently? I haven't opened that case for a long time, haven't taken the crucifix in my hand.) "Woman is part of the eternal order. We see that from children. What is a child? A child does not arise from the flesh. It becomes a human being, a being informed with soul, that later seeks its happiness, suffers, struggles, and comes to terms with its fate just as its parents did before it. At first a child knows nothing. But as it grows, it feels what is within it. And what is that? An awareness that it belongs among God's children. Its father and mother do not instill that in it. That is beyond their powers. They cannot do it, even if they have retained that awareness themselves. And often they lose it."

Virginia's delighted voice: "Oh, that is lovely, Mrs. Allison. That is the truth."

But Alice had not spoken these sentences. Something had taken her by the hand and led her.

"Animals and plants arise from the flesh. Their spirit resides in the flesh. The spirit is not actually theirs. It is the spirit of nature. Nothing separates them from nature. We possess the spirit and are individuals and recognize our fellow human beings as distinct from us and are not at one with them. Mothers have been blessed with great good fortune, and that is why mother love is the greatest of all loves, the strongest and highest form of love, the most genuine. Oh, no other can compare with it. And the reason for that is that the child arises from it. I have often asked zoologists and physicians what their view of motherhood is, and they gave me all kinds of answers, some of them quite lovely, but none of them satisfied me. What did they say? Yes, there is something special about motherhood in humans. Why? A bird has to build a nest for its brood, and then it has to fly off to find food. A woman keeps the child with her. She carries it in her body until it has taken complete human form, and after she has given birth to it, it may be that she has to find food for herself in the outside world, but the mother provides for the child from herself. Her breasts produce milk; she presses her child to her; and it drinks.

"That's what the scientists said. And it is true, but it isn't the whole truth, and it isn't the most important truth."

Dr. King: "What is the whole truth, the most important truth, Alice?"

What answer shall I give? I want to tell a story; I'm supposed to tell a story. What am I finally going to say?

Alice: "The truth? There are different truths in the world. We've talked a lot about truth lately. The truth I have to tell is" (Alice took a deep breath) "that the body, our body, rests in the soul. That's the way it is. If that weren't so, children could not come out of us. When a child is created, is it the body that creates it? There is a mysterious love between this man and this woman. Can we know what it really is that has brought them together? People say it is 'love.' We have a word for everything. My brother, James, is right. It would be better for us and our understanding of things if we didn't have so many words. Then we wouldn't think, when we pronounce them or when we hear them, that we're really understanding something.

"When a woman holds her child in her arms she is amazed and senses something that goes beyond her. She senses what her love meant. Not reproduction. Not that. That's what animals and plants do, and they are driven to it, they whose bodies do not reside in the soul. The truth of human love, its mystery, everything personal about it, is linked together with hope, sweetness, guilt, and fear—and all those things lie deep within us and are hidden there. This young living thing, the child, oh, it is more than a continuation, a repetition.

"What is it then? Our inner being drawn out of us, given form in flesh, and more than the inner life I know and have to live. A new life is readied for its sweet and terrible passage on this earth. We do not come to an end. We can say what we like—we do not speak our last word. The soul, a larger, higher self, starts afresh. We give birth to the child, care for it, bless it, and give it all we have. How happy we are to sacrifice ourselves for it. And how blissfully happy we are when we feel and understand that in this new being we are completed and perhaps even justified."

Alice dreamed. She stopped speaking. No one interrupted her. Then she added: "I have heard some women say: Where is the dignity of woman? We have to find the dignity of woman. We have to create woman's dignity. It may be that there are still some areas left where that is needed. But the dignity of woman will be evident only to those who comprehend the mystery of feminine love. From her soul but in the flesh she gives birth to the child, and so she perpetuates the human race, our human race."

Now Alice looked up. Everyone realized she had finished what she had to say.

She had let this voice speak out of her, and now she looked around to see what it was she had said. She had become much calmer. She felt the cloth in her hand still, but did not think about the attic and what had happened to her there.

A much older story had come to her mind. It had announced itself to her as she had been speaking about the mystery of love.

Theodora

"NOW I'll tell the story of Theodora."

Her feelings overwhelmed her as she pronounced that name. It hadn't passed her lips for decades. What a rich name it was—filled with what? In earlier days she had not been able to separate it from her own. "Alice" and "Theodora" were fused together. Then, for some strange reason, the name faded. Only "Alice" was left. She began living her life under a new sign.

Now the name sounded as it always had, weighty, rolling, ringing, warning, like a bell that has been thrown down from its tower and is being winched back up again. It hangs in its old belfry, high above human heads, and rings out what it experienced, how things looked down on the ground, and who it is. (Theodora, I hear you. Hear me, too.)

"Theodora was a noblewoman. She lived in Egypt, in Alexandria, a long time ago. She was married. Her marriage had been arranged. It would be wrong to say 'against her will.' She had no will then, when she had married. She had no will for a long time later either. It was her nature to follow and to please people. She felt free when she served others and spread joy." (Oh, that's not who I am anymore.) "She had devoted her life to the service of Mary. Mary was her model.

"Then a rich and pious merchant in this luxurious city of Alexandria was chosen as her husband. She did not object. But she was afraid. She knew nothing of men. She would be thrust into a new and unfamiliar circle. That is what the law the world lived by required of her. She submitted to it, mindful of Mary's response to the angel's message: Be it unto me according to thy word.

"The law of the world was fulfilled in her. She was still very young and had just become a woman. Up to now she had seen human beings only from a distance, these poor prisoners of their passions. Now she moved among them. She became a prisoner herself, though hardly in a hard, harsh prison. Were there any walls, grates and bars, guards? On

321

the contrary. The walls had fallen in; the gates had burst open. It did not seem to her that she was a prisoner but rather that she was free. Yes, that's what Theodora felt. She fled into the wide open world, into this world without limitations. She was entranced, in bliss. When she found herself this way, she felt blissfully unblissful. She accused and berated herself, but she could not work any change in herself that way. A flood of dark feelings swept over her; her eyes were opened; she saw her husband next to her. The law of the world was fulfilled in her.

"He was a good and pious man. He was happy when she finally made her peace with him. And then she learned what marriage was. He took her in his arms. He eased her unrest. He kept her occupied and protected her. And then there was no more suffering or passion. The lions and the leopards lay down together and wandered around tame, as they had in paradise.

"Theodora's husband was named Philippus. He often sailed with his merchant ships and was gone from Alexandria for months at a time. Once he had been away for a long time, and Theodora had no news from him. During this time Theodora received a visit from Titus, a friend of Philippus to whom Philippus had entrusted his business affairs during his absence. She did not know that both men, Philippus and Titus, had asked her parents for her hand. Her parents had chosen Philippus who, though not particularly attractive, was solid and pious. Now Titus appeared on the scene and set his machinations in motion. Practiced as he was in these things, he had prepared his plot well ahead. He knew what a strong fortress he was attempting to overrun.

"At first he came with urgent business matters and wanted her approval on his decisions. Then he started dropping remarks, more and more often, that disturbed Theodora. He inquired, with no little astonishment, about Philippus—whether she had had any word from him at all, what this long absence without any news could possibly mean. He brought reports of storms and shipwrecks, made a concerned face, shook his head. He sat next to her to console her. The man who sat there with her in Philippus's opulent home and sighed often was a hunter, and she was the prey he was artfully stalking. That she had not been given to him before made her all the more desirable to him. Then he came to entertain her and distract her, bringing gifts. He dismayed her with his dreadful reports only to reassure her all the more earnestly that they were nothing but rumors and to encourage her to go out on the water with him to cheer herself up. She accepted his invitations, not on his account but so that she would not look bitter and ugly when

Philippus returned. She dreamed, too, of encountering Philippus's ship on one of these jaunts around the harbor of Alexandria.

"He did not come back. Titus dropped his mask. He was a practiced hand at this game. But with Theodora something happened that upset his balance. This Theodora was a beautiful creature, but there was also something about her that repulsed him yet at the same time attracted him all the more. She was a human being. And the more he saw of her, the more of an appetite he developed for this incredibly powerful mixture: female, beautiful, desirable female and human being. He had never encountered a human being before, neither man nor woman. He had gaming and drinking and sporting friends, but they were not close to him. And he was not close to himself. He knew himself only as one more of the sort of his fellow gamblers and sport enthusiasts. In Theodora, he sensed, he caught the scent of, a higher being. He knew he came off badly by comparison. And that drew him on all the more. And so we have to understand everything that happened next, everything he did to her, as an attempt on his part to raise himself up to her level.

"How should he behave? What would he do? It seems he had no choice. The decision that had been made in the depths of his soul took him by surprise. His situation is reminiscent of the old story of the king whose touch turned everything to gold. He wants to eat, but instead of a fruit he is holding a clump of hard gold in his hand. Such was the passion Titus felt for Theodora, who had thrown him into confusion. And he assuaged his confusion and finally rid himself of it by getting rid of Theodora herself. He could not do anything else. He didn't know how to do differently.

"Now he wooed her openly with a frantic passion that threw her completely off balance. She recalled the period of her own maturing, the dreadful restlessness, and she remembered how she and Philippus had made their peace together and how she had come to terms with marriage. She had felt herself lucky then that it was the earnest Philippus who had won her and that she had nothing to regret in being his wife. Now she felt sorry for Titus. She comforted him at first; finally she had to bar her house to him.

"He came back anyhow. It was obvious to everyone that he was pining away. Their meetings were an agony.

"She sighed and accepted his gifts again, putting them aside in an out-of-the-way room. If only Philippus would come back, come back soon. It was awful that he did not come. If he does not come I'm lost. I will not survive him. I do not want to survive him. She was afraid for Philippus and for herself.

"What is a child? I have to come back to my original theme. Our bodies rest in the soul. When a child takes form in a woman, is it the body that causes the child to grow? What is the love of a woman for a man? When a woman holds her child in her arms she knows what her love was all about. The child is the truth of her love. Yes, that is the mystery of love. And the dignity of woman consists in that: She bears the child from her soul and so perpetuates the human race.

"Theodora realized that. She and Philippus were linked together, but she had not borne his child. Now this intriguer had come into her life, this deceiver, this intruder. What did he know of the family, of marriage, of a woman and her child? Things had gone well for Theodora for a long time. Now misery rushed down on her.

"The ship Philippus had been on was reported definitely lost. The details were available. She could not deny it any longer. The news was crushing for her.

"Titus hounded her. She wept for Philippus, whom she no longer had. Titus lamented to her that he did not have her either. In the midst of her tears she admitted, 'We're like brother and sister. You're my second self.' In her grief she said that, scarcely realizing what she was saying; and the seducer, the despoiler, was delighted by what she said.

"Yes, he suffered. His passion had taken a terrible toll on him. Having begun as a lover and suitor, he was now so transformed that she was afraid of him. He seemed a madman with her. He begged for her favors. It was no act. She could see him wilt with delight if she gave him her hand and let him kiss her fingers. She saw how her touch ran through his whole body. She tore herself away from him. He disgusted her. She felt ashamed and humiliated.

"Nothing in her behavior toward him would have changed—the more often he came and the more often he lost control of himself, the more her antipathy for him grew—if she had not at the same time felt more and more sympathy for him. She would not have been Theodora if she had remained indifferent to that suffering. Could she let him suffer so? Could she herself torment him this way? Perhaps if she were ugly that would repulse him!

"She tried to make herself ugly. She put on her servants' dirty clothes. But this only increased his passion. Indeed, as she soon realized, it constituted some special charm. He encouraged her, he begged her in a transport of delight, to transform herself into a slave this way.

He implored her to wear this costume more often. She saw that she had unwittingly indulged some part of his evil, raging soul. He loved her when she was elegant and decorous, but if she slipped down into ugliness and filth, he thanked her for it, and his passion burned all the higher. His face glowed; she had subjected him completely.

"She gave up that experiment. But she had learned something. He had not closed in on her anymore, but he fascinated her. Fascination— what was it? He was Titus, a young, elegant seducer who was trying out his arts on her. A crazed man mad with love. But there was something frightening, terrible, painful, in his love. Perhaps he was not even aware of it. The devil had crept into him and taken up residence in his love. The devil was destroying this man with love and wanted to destroy Theodora, too. That explained this rage and the peculiar grimace Titus sometimes made when he was with her, a grimace that betrayed his delight in filth and in her humiliation. Such was her relationship with him. This is how she saw him. And yet she was fascinated by him. And could not free herself and heard things from her maids that cast a still harsher light on her picture of him, that, for example, he bribed the maidservants to let him into the house so that he could secretly watch Theodora in all kinds of different situations and activities. One of the maids, whom another had denounced, confessed that Titus had once overpowered her and raped her while Theodora had been in the next room singing.

"When things had gotten to this stage, Theodora realized she had to do some serious thinking. Pretending illness, she managed to keep him away from her for a while. Alone, she saw the image of her Philippus before her. What a pious man; what a warm, pure life he lived. But where was he, and why had he left her when she needed him most? What kind of test was this he had left her to face?

"She thought, she prayed. She prayed that she would be relieved of this trial and that Philippus would return. She prayed for the unhappy Titus, asking that he be freed from his demon. But in the course of her lonely prayers and reflection she felt growing in her the desire not to abandon Titus and leave him to himself, not to give up on him and reject him but rather to fight for him.

"And so she returned to her house in Alexandria—and to Titus's arms.

"He thought he held a lover in his arms, but she was a physician who did not give herself up to him. She came near a fire and thought she could extinguish it with love. He was a human being. She did not want to punish him for the fact that he was a man.

"She was taking a great chance. She took a great deal upon herself. Her piety and her prayers were her only supports in this secret and gigantic undertaking. She knew he would misunderstand everything, but that did not make her impatient. She wanted to tame him. She wanted to snatch his poor soul from Satan's jaws.

"Months passed. Titus came and went at her house at will. People began to talk. Theodora's parents reproached her; their disapproval pained her. She was unable to explain her actions adequately; her excuses were lame. Her parents, who were deeply attached to her, did not break with her; for they felt with growing certainty that her good husband Philippus, whom they had chosen to assure their daughter's happiness, was indeed lost. Perhaps Theodora was already a widow. They advised her to wait another year before thinking of another marriage— to this Titus, under whose sway she seemed to have fallen. Oh, what would happen if Philippus, poor man, should return and find his wife in this state.

"He did not come. But the helmsman and two sailors from his ship returned to the port after this long time. They brought the sad news of the sinking of his ship near Cyprus. They had stayed afloat for several days by clinging to some planking. Then a pirate ship had fished them out of the water and sold them into slavery in Morocco. They had escaped. Philippus and everyone with him and all his oarsmen had long since sunk to the bottom of the hungry sea.

"Titus did not see the widow for months on end. She was living with her parents. When she reappeared, she begged her friend Titus to leave her alone. Again she forbade him to enter her house. She cried and pleaded with him when he forced his way in. She was in despair, for the old game began all over again. Once again his frenzy, his obsession. It is my fate, she said, to do what I can with this man. I cannot evade this responsibility. She broke down. She could not stop her lamenting and crying. There was no help. She could not reveal her intentions to her parents. Now they themselves wanted her to marry him. He heard this. His dark face, swollen with lust, grew bright; his black eyes glowed; he was devouring her already.

"What a horrible fate God has visited on me. What have I done. I am condemned to throw myself away on him.

"And when she felt certain of this, she became calmer. She stopped crying. She did not beg anymore. She acquiesced. When she told Titus this one evening, he let out a whoop, spun about like a whirling dervish, kissed the sofa she was sitting on, slapped the walls, threw himself down on the floor and licked it, rolled around on it, and screamed and moaned. She ran to him and held his mouth shut as he lay on the floor. How fearfully he laughed in his satisfaction and delight. When he screamed once more, the frightening thought occurred to her that he was reporting his victory to hell.

"But she did not try to escape him anymore. Even before the wedding she had to put up with the terrors of his savagery and the humiliation of his embraces. What she experienced so disoriented her that on the morning after her wedding she lay in her room, looked at the ceiling, the walls, the objects scattered about the room, all of which had witnessed her disgrace and now reminded her of it, and she cried out to them, 'Behold me! You know what has happened to me. You emerge from the night. But I do not.'

"The ceilings, the walls, the statues, her clothes, did not bring her back to herself. Titus, her lord, and now the lord of the house, wandered around and enjoyed what he saw: Theodora, the woman, the human being, brought low. The human being no longer rose above him. She had become his tame, obedient woman.

"But that was not enough for him. He invented new games to play. I'll remain silent about what else hell devised to degrade her.

"And what happened next she had not expected: Theodora lost herself. How was that possible? She had taken on too much. She had made herself weak for Titus, had so totally subjugated herself to him that he could treat this beautiful human creature like a mere thing. It was too much for her. Her soul bore—no, could not bear it.

"After they had come home from an orgy he had taken her to, she tried to come to herself again but found she could not. She looked for herself in her room, among her jewels and clothes, then in the present, in yesterday, in the day before. She fell asleep in this process and thought to herself: Tomorrow, when the sun returns and reveals everything again, I will be there, too. But the sun came; her clothes were lying there, all her familiar things, also the reminders of yesterday. But she was not there.

"Theodora had stayed away. Theodora had died.

"But she was not even permitted to die. She lived—a creature resembling Theodora—at Titus's side, this Titus whom—she could feel it—she loved and of whom she was even jealous. Many women were devoted to him, vied for his favors, and who indeed was as charming, as

irresistible as he? Others had described him that way before, and now
Theodora, too, felt that he exuded some power over her. She complained to him about it. She was so much under his sway that she even
told him this. She was lying on his chest. He stretched contentedly:

"'You were a stupid, ignorant child. You knew nothing of yourself or
the world. I've opened your eyes for you.'

"'You are my teacher,' she sighed. 'Stay with me. Do not abandon
me, my Titus.'

"She blossomed. Her parents saw and were pleased. They said to
each other: 'She has become a woman. She will have a child. What a
happy marriage.'

"At that time Philippus was living only a few streets away from her.
He had quarters with an Arab boat maker who had known him before.
The barbarians had kept him as a slave for three years and some
months. Finally he had been able to escape and return to Alexandria.
Grim forebodings overcame him when he reached the harbor. He inquired here and there. No one recognized this man who had aged and
who now had a deep, red scar running diagonally across his whole face,
cheek, mouth, and chin, from his first unsuccessful attempt to escape.
He learned at the harbor that the Philippus he was inquiring after had
gone down with his ship years ago. His property had fallen to Titus,
whom his widow Theodora had married.

"Philippus remained at the harbor. He found the dark-skinned boat
maker, an old man, who took him in. He could rely on the boat maker's
discretion. Now Philippus often saw his wife, Theodora, as she was carried by in a sedan chair, usually at Titus's side. Philippus realized at a
glance what had happened: She had indeed become Titus's woman. The
world had taken a new turn during his absence.

"Philippus thought about this for a long time. He worked for the boat
maker and revealed none of his feelings. He felt compelled to go to his
old home often to reassure himself that he was indeed dead and that the
world had quickly forgotten him, a beneficent and pious man, after only
three years, three short years. Everything went its course. His business
was flourishing, and Theodora—she was carried by, a luxuriously
dressed, voluptuous woman with Theodora's features. She had been exchanged for someone else; she had been bewitched. I know Theodora.
She resisted becoming my wife, and now she is a jaded, lecherous creature with the dark circles of a whore under her eyes.

"Her litter bearers were carrying her through the narrow street of the black boat maker a second time. Philippus was hammering at his work in front of the door. It took a few seconds, but then the image 'Philippus' sprang up in her mind. She started; she was in doubt; she ordered the bearers to go back. But there was no one to be seen in the street. She didn't remember which house it had been. She must have been mistaken.

"The incident haunted her. She had changed so much that the only feeling the thought of Philippus awakened in her was fear, the fear that he could come and shatter her new life.

"She mentioned her fear to her husband. He laughed at her. But she saw Philippus again. He could not resist going back to stroll by his old home. She saw the utterly destitute man, the shrunken face, the dreadful scar that cut through his lips and twisted his mouth—but the face, the eyes, the posture of Philippus. She was certain that it was he. She sat in the sedan chair next to her mother. She fell silent. Now that she was sure it was he she did not order the bearers to turn around. She pleaded faintness. Her mother ordered the bearers to take them home. Theodora objected: not home. She didn't dare go back until later that evening when Titus picked her up.

"On the way home she told him everything and advised him to be on his guard. Philippus, perhaps in league with others, was watching her. There was no doubt he wanted to murder her and Titus.

"Titus laughed. But when he saw how certain and persistent she remained about her claim on the following days, how fearful she was, and how she didn't dare leave the house, he contacted an acquaintance of his, the centurion responsible for policing this part of Alexandria; and the officer sent out a patrol to arrest this easily recognizable man. His agents made inquiries and were soon led to the boat maker, who had gotten wind of what was happening. All the Arab could say, in full accord with the truth, was that the man was no longer working for him. To the best of the boat maker's knowledge, the fellow had been from Tunisia and had wanted to return home.

"Theodora's fears did not abate. She never left the house without armed guards; she kept looking around her. Her husband remarked irritably that she could think of nothing but Philippus. She threw her arms around his neck. 'Kill him, Titus. Get rid of him. That's all I ask.'

"He took her at her word and sent out men to whom Theodora had given an exact description of their quarry. Titus promised them a generous reward if they could catch this fellow, a man who had designs on

Titus's life. Titus whispered to them that they could make short work of the man. He would see to it that they had no trouble with the law.

"They did not find him.

"But Theodora did.

"He was sitting next to a fisherman's hut mending nets. This was outside of town and away from the port, a spot on the sea where Theodora felt she was safe from this ghost. She had left her sedan chair and companions behind. He looked up from his work as the elegant lady approached. She recognized him instantly.

"Her first thought was to call for help. But before she could open her mouth she realized how foolish the thought was. The presence of Philippus took hold on her, and that he was sitting there in the sand, poor, gray haired, mending a net, Philippus, that stabbed at her heart. She had to go to him and, unable to speak a word, stand next to him. And when he looked at her with his scarred face and twisted mouth, she burst into tears. Her arms hung by her sides. Helpless, confused, she wept without inhibition, wept for him, for herself, and over their common fate.

"He took her hands and drew her down on the sand. The beach was deserted. The sedan chair stood behind a dune. No one saw this pair, the elegant lady and the net maker; no one saw the woman weep her bitter tears of pain and regret, regret.

"He could not stem her tears. How could he. He was weeping himself.

"They sat together this way for a long time, unable to say anything but 'Philippus' and 'Theodora.' Then he noticed some people in the distance. He signaled to her. She stood up, whispered: 'Tomorrow at this same time,' and ran to the water's edge to wash her face. Her companions came. She laughed and greeted them with a dripping face. The net maker back on the beach went on working.

"That night she gave herself to her husband once more and bid him a silent farewell. In his arms she thought: I haven't been able to free you from your Satan, Titus. I didn't have strength enough. Lust cannot conquer lust. I went to my own ruin, almost. I violated my marriage with Philippus, and now I am violating it again with you whose neck I embrace, on whose mouth I press my own, because I want to be cursed and destroyed, because I do not want to be forgiven in the least. I want to be shattered to pieces. Yes, this creature that clings to your lips now, blissfully and for the last time, you sweet, cursed, unsuspecting man whom I ask eternal God to save, this creature will be torn to shreds by beasts in the wilderness. Since I could not save you and could not save myself and could only plunge us both into greater corruption, I want to be destroyed, eradicated. Theodora ought never to have been.

"Titus reveled in the body of his prey who was more delicious than ever.

"The next afternoon Theodora took the same walk she had taken the day before. She carried a bundle that supposedly held her bathing clothes. Long before she reached yesterday's meeting place she stopped and told her companions to wait for her there. She was going to swim at an isolated place, which she described in detail, beyond the fishermen's huts. And indeed she ran to the place, went into the water, and left her sumptuous dress on the beach. From her bundle she took a slave's old dress that she had snatched up at the house. She put it on and ran to Philippus.

"They sat hand in hand in his hut. She did not cry much today, and only at first. She knew what she wanted. In brief sentences, she told him everything that had happened. He told about his shipwreck and about Tunisia.

"She said, 'I'm leaving Alexandria.'

"He: 'We'll go together.'

"She hesitated, then accepted. They set off immediately. He loaded his boat with food, with bread and dried fish. The wind was favorable. They traveled along the coast for five days, sometimes stopping for the night and for some sleep. He rowed as long as he could, then let the boat drift; or they went ashore and camped on the beach. She was prostrate with fatigue. He traveled happily. She did him the kindness of looking happy.

"On the coast of X they left the boat. She took his hand and confessed that she was going off into the desert, and he mustn't follow her.

"'I wanted to cure Titus. I thought I could do it. But the doctor fell ill herself. I turned my back on God in whom you and I believe. I set myself against him. I served the prince of hell. I am lost, Philippus, my good Philippus. Do not touch me, or you will be infected by my evil.'

"To all his pleas and questions she said: 'My dear Philippus, do not follow me. Don't bring me to tears again. I have to stand before my judge and receive my punishment.'

"When she heard his loud laments, she came back once more. She implored him to be strong. Her face already wore an expression of uncharacteristic sternness.

"He did not row back to Alexandria. He stayed in X for a year, waiting for Theodora. Then, at last, he did go home, this time as Philippus, the shipwrecked merchant, who meant to reclaim his possessions and to punish those who had done him and his loved ones ill in his absence.

"When news of Philippus's return got about, Titus left his house and went into hiding; and from his hiding place Titus contested the identity of the returning merchant. Philippus proved it in court. His mother and his friends testified on his behalf. He tried to run Titus down and punish him. Word of Titus's crimes spread. Fiery coals were heaped on the head of the handsome despoiler.

"Philippus lived in Alexandria for a long time. He searched for Theodora. He searched for Titus, both in vain."

The scrap of blue cloth had long since slipped from Alice's hand onto the carpet. It lay next to her chair. Her voice had grown soft, then softer still as she spoke. Her thoughts led her off into soft, sad fields. Longing overcame her; longing drew her away.

Philippus, lost. Theodora, disappeared.

BOOK FOUR

A Play

LORD Crenshaw's birthday.

Guests were expected. The house was decorated. Garlands and lanterns were hung in the garden.

When it became known and spread about that Lord Crenshaw would have a birthday, all these things happened more or less of themselves. These actions followed on the letters and calls. The outside world wanted to invade the house. Behind Lord Crenshaw, the celebrated man, an invisible crowd gathered to congratulate him. They surrounded and protected him. His characters had conquered the hearts of many people. These figures preceded the visitors and escorted them into Lord Crenshaw's house. The people bowed, the characters bowed and shook their father's hand. Couldn't he see he had had an effect on the world? Couldn't he see he had played an active part? Or would he negate himself even now?

Cars drove up all day long. Strangers filled the house to the second floor with their laughing, talking, and calling. Everyone was decked out. Lord Crenshaw, fat, in high spirits, full of life, was wearing a long black frock coat. Edward had put on his uniform. He had resisted wearing it on earlier occasions. Now Gordon Allison had suggested the possibility to Alice. She agonized for half a day before she could bring herself to present the idea to Edward as her own. To her amazement, Edward did not object in the least. He was delighted with the suggestion and even wore his uniform the evening before. ("Quhy dois your brand sae drop wi' bluid, Edward, Edward? Quhy dois your brand sae drop wi' bluid?")

On the big day, his mother pinned his medals on him.

And so he came downstairs with his artificial leg, now using only canes, wandered through the rooms, threading his way between clusters of guests. Kathleen looked much prettier than she realized herself, a serious, quiet girl who represented the generation that had gone

335

through the war. Everyone who saw these two young people felt: We are saved, we have won the war and gotten over it; we have put it behind us. The young are alive. We are the survivors. And we will not forget the dead.

The elegant ladies. Their closets had yielded up the accumulated riches of the past, and the ladies had put those riches on, had draped and wrapped their warm, sleek bodies in them, layer after layer, like an onion: the underwear, the skirts, the blouses, the jackets and coats, the hairdos, the hats. Although they were unaware of it, they wore much more than their clothes, layer after layer, like an onion. The gestures of all the guests spoke of the society they came from, their native country, their homes, their pasts—is that what they were? The schools they had attended, their parents who had spoiled or neglected them, the battles they had fought to have their way, what they had achieved and not achieved. They were weighed down by the attire of millennia, centuries, decades. No matter how weak an individual was he had to carry this burden. It pressed down on them all. They had to cope with it. How much of it was dress, how much was they themselves?

The ladies and gentlemen sat at small tables, circulated in the house, walked about in the garden and admired the colorful, well-tended flowers over which Edward and James Mackenzie had watched the rain fall (and we should not ask anymore and not want; we should not speak, should only look at everything and open ourselves to it, let it enter into us; then, yes then, we will find ourselves).

They wore the coronation of Queen Victoria, who was old and grew older and was followed by King Edward, under whom the nation went through World War I. Perfume hung in the air: Oscar Wilde, his scandal, his miserable death in Paris. There were shawls because it was cool in the garden: Cardinal Newman and the Oxford movement. Shawls swung up and wrapped around shoulders: St. Bartholomew's Day. The landing of William the Conqueror ensued. They lifted their hands as they replied to a question, and winds from the Punic Wars and the destruction of Carthage passed through the room.

People talked and went up and down the stairs. They went from the house into the garden, Lord Crenshaw, Alice, Edward, Kathleen, and the pensive professor who knew everything and avoided everything, and the guests as they arrived—jovial, and each one dressed—or so it seemed to the professor—disguised, masked, covered with skin from which hairs sprouted, just as the past sprouted from them. They walked about in shining shoes and let their voices be heard. Their throats vi-

brated. Birds sang. Cattle bellowed. Generations of creatures were
alive, jellyfish, plants, coral reefs. Ancient eras and catastrophes in the
earth's history lived with them, the flood, the garden of Eden. In patent
leather shoes, in silk stockings the ladies walked, the gentlemen—dino-
saurs.

Although Alice looked young and elegant, altogether the fay with the
soft, full lips, she could not keep herself from glancing often at the great
sorcerer, Lord Crenshaw, found herself pulled into his orbit. He was
surrounded by guests and looked so staggeringly young. He blossomed
in this circle. His fat, his lard, had deformed him. But he was still the
old seducer with the tools of his magic, the bracelet and the pearl stickpin. She was drawn to him to sip, like a bee, from his honey.

Salome, Salome. She could not help herself. She danced around him,
before him, Salome, and, at the same time, sat on the throne as Herodias and embraced King Herod, to whom, in violation of the law, she
was wed. How her heart leapt whenever she saw Gordon, and what
shame she felt whenever she saw Edward's uniform coming her way.
She avoided him, she brought herself up short, she tried to distract herself.

The head of John the Baptist? She sighed in pain. She could not see
her way. My guilt about Edward. What path have I led him on.

But a half hour later, to the delight of her guests, she walked arm in
arm with him through the garden, my son, my support, my protector;
my son, my young, good self.

Sometimes the pair strolled near where Gordon was chatting among a
circle of admirers and London friends. Alice looked at her son because
each time he joined the circle for a few minutes and listened to the
conversation. "Do you want to sit down here, Edward? Would you like
to join the conversation?"

He shook his head; his face was troubled. "I've never seen Father this
way. We don't know each other. Each of us knows the other only in
certain roles. Have you noticed that, too? Was Father always like this?"

"He seems to be enjoying himself here." Alice drew Edward away
into the house. "Oh, of course people thaw out in company, Edward.
And especially on a high holiday like this."

Edward worried her. She left him in the house with Kathleen and
some young girls who were with her. They were searching through some
huge cartons and smaller boxes that contained an odd assortment of
things. The young visitors had brought some of the boxes and cartons;
Kathleen had supplied the others. The things in them, it seemed, were

to be used in a little evening entertainment about which the participants refused to reveal any details. Its purpose, however, was to salute and honor Gordon before dinner.

The plan was to present a theatrical version of his own story, "Lord Crenshaw." A section of the garden had been prepared for the show. There were costumes for some of the actors, a huge bell for the conductor, a mustache and saber for the policeman, and so forth. All these things were unpacked in Kathleen's room. The young ladies, the conspirators, were having a lot of fun with the project. Even the sober Kathleen was bouncing playfully about. Alice, who was quickly driven off, could leave her son there in good conscience. She had other duties, and she disappeared to attend to them. At one point Edward slipped off into the garden. He was drawn to the garden. He wanted to watch his father without his mother present. And there he stood behind a tree, unobserved by Gordon, and watched the cheerful, unconstrained fat man in his roomy wing chair which had been carried outside for him. Listening to him, Edward was astonished. That was his father. If he had been able to, he would have taken a seat close to him in the circle and taken part in the conversation.

Isn't this remarkable. I'm with him every day, but I've never seen him this way. This role! With us in our home he plays a different role; he plays that one only with us.

Gordon's listeners were laughing. Yes, it's a pleasure to see him and hear what he has to say.

And while Edward was standing behind the tree he thought of the line: "Quhy dois your brand sae drop wi' bluid . . ."

Edward shook his head. What's the point of that. — The young ladies had sent a messenger after him in the garden. She took him back inside.

And who was this walking about in the garden, alone much of the time, his hands clasped behind him, serious, indeed, gloomily pensive, joining first this group, then another, only to wander on in his pensive mood? No one asked what the learned James Mackenzie was thinking about. Everyone knew he was always preoccupied with deep and esoteric mythological problems. The distinguished gentleman had gotten himself involved in a dangerous business here. He had thought he could play the alert and moderate observer, standing on the outside as was his custom and able to withdraw from the game whenever he felt like it. But now he couldn't pull out anymore, and the situation troubled him. He had offered his knowledge to all concerned but still remained helpless. A disagreeable insight, a disagreeable possibility, had dawned on him: His ideas, tried and tested by old Indian teachers, could be ineffective. But why? Oh, if only his sister, Alice, had not drawn him into this mess.

Toward evening everyone was seated in the garden. The young people had prepared a "festive entertainment." They would play "Lord Crenshaw's Mysterious Metamorphoses." Alice saved a place next to her for her son. She had told him she would. But he did not appear to claim it. She looked around. She stood up because she was worried about him. People asked her what she was looking for. And then they laughed and pointed to the sheet, the curtain, that had been strung between two trees. "What do you mean?" — "He's one of the actors."

Incredulous, she sat down again. She put her hand on the empty seat of the chair next to her. What is this? What is he going to do? She was distraught.

Finally the curtain was drawn away from one side. There on the grass was a long, flat-bodied wagon with chairs on it, and three actresses and three actors were helping each other climb up on it, for the curtain had been drawn a minute too soon. The audience was not disturbed by this, nor was the cast.

An actor sat down on a chair at the front of the wagon and took the wagon tongue in his hand. He stretched out both legs, engaged the clutch with his left foot, put on the brakes with his right, and yanked and turned on the wagon tongue. He was clearly the bus driver. His intentions and those of his bus were revealed on a cardboard sign mounted on a stick above him: "Crenshaw Bus Line, Crenshaw-Wilshire."

Along the length of the wagon, facing the audience, sat three women passengers: an old woman with a heavy shopping bag; a slim, heavily made up, dubious creature in a short skirt; and, finally, an extremely elegant lady of high society. All three stared straight ahead. An ordinary fellow with a peaked cap and a change purse, the conductor, stood behind them and called out the stops. At every call the passengers started; the driver stretched out both feet forcefully and yanked at the brake lever.

A man in a summer coat sat with his back to the audience, his chin on his chest. He was asleep.

Next to him a young man who was apparently his companion.

The players acted and spoke the beginning of the familiar Crenshaw story, departing from the text in only one detail. Here, his lordship, the unknown man with his back to the audience, did not get out of the bus but, after some discussion with the conductor and driver, paid again and kept his seat. His companion did nothing. Now the sign was turned around and read: Wilshire-Crenshaw; and instead of the three ladies, the other passengers were now two crude-looking men and a little lady (whom everyone recognized immediately as the teacher, Virginia Graves).

The return trip; the man sleeps on. The conductor calls out the stops, passengers get off, the unknown man is wakened, discussion, he pays once more and slumps down into his seat again. Last stop. The conductor shakes him. Now the companion stands up, the young, slim figure, and asks the conductor not to make a fuss. Just let things take their course. They had not arrived at their destination yet. The other passengers, who have started getting off, overhear, turn around, and gawk in amazement. The companion, the young man, who has not turned around to face the audience yet either, explains: Certainly the conductor could not demand that he do any more than pay. A bus is, after all, a means of public transportation. Besides, he had just gotten on. Shaking his head, the conductor marches back and forth in front of the mute passenger. The companion turns with him, and now the audience can see him. He has thrown back his cape. He is not a youth but a gray-bearded man in chain mail, a sword at his waist, a black cross painted on his chest. The conductor cannot get over his surprise. He and the driver confer in whispers. From the driver's seat, they look back at the mysterious passengers. The driver says they must have been at a masquerade ball.

The companion has sat down again. "Go ahead. We're returning from a crusade."

The sign is reversed; the route is now Crenshaw-Wilshire. The first set of passengers, the three ladies, boards the bus again: the old lady with the heavy shopping bag, the painted lady, the distinguished society lady. As before, they all stare straight ahead. They ask about the stops; the conductor answers their questions; they pay; the bus starts up, stops. Last stop. The driver sticks out both feet, yanks on the wagon tongue, turns his head to the rear; the passengers get out. In the center aisle the conductor and driver turn their attention to the older gentleman and his companion.

The two passengers do not move.

The conductor, in a loud voice: "Last stop, last stop. Everybody out!"

The conductor, accompanied by the driver, goes up to the two: "Last stop, gentlemen. Everybody out!"

The two men do not respond.

The two working men and the little woman, the teacher, board the bus again. The conductor turns the sign around; the route is now from Wilshire to Crenshaw. The conductor swallows his irritation and collects fares from the new passengers. Then, outraged, he stands in front of the strange pair and yells in each man's ear: "Everybody out, gentlemen!"

The companion stands up. They have just gotten on, he says. He lifts his hat, revealing a small crown. The driver joins the conductor. Both of them circle this miracle that turns around with them: a red-cheeked, arrogant king, as can be seen from the scepter he holds in his hand. He repeats in forceful tones that admit of no back talk: "I am King Lear. We have just boarded the bus. Take my word for it."

The two bus-line employees exchange glances. With a shrug of his shoulders, the driver returns to his place. The companion pays. The conductor examines the money. It is proper, modern currency.

The bus sets off, makes stops. The driver often turns to look back at the conductor. They are keeping an eye on their unusual passengers. Last stop. The driver pulls on the brake and stretches out his legs. The passengers start to get off. The conductor and the driver go straight to the silent pair: "Everybody out, gentlemen! Isn't it about time?"

The two do not move.

When the conductor taps the companion on the shoulder, the passenger stands up and asks him what he thinks he's doing.

"You have to get off, sir. You have to get out of this bus. You've ridden back and forth twice now. What do you think you're doing?"

The companion answers calmly, "We haven't arrived at our destination yet. I've just gotten on."

"Tom," the conductor says, putting his hands on his hips, "this guy says he's just gotten on."

"I have."

They come closer to him, then jump back. The companion has turned to face them: He has a horrible, bristly wild boar's head; his hands have become hooves and are covered with bristles, too. But at the same time he remains a polite, elegant figure. He opens his fearsome jaws.

The conductor and driver flee to their places. In his haste the driver forgets to turn the sign. The passengers remind him to do it: Now it's Wilshire-Crenshaw again. The female passengers are on board again:

the woman with the shopping bag, the painted floozy, the distinguished lady from the best of all families.

But now the audience can see that these three have undergone some changes, too. The hour and all this nerve-wracking travel no doubt account for these changes. The simple woman digs around in her big bag and takes out things to transform herself with. The painted floozy becomes more vulgar than ever. She has taken off her shoes and is knocking her heels together rhythmically. The distinguished lady looks right and left and is thoroughly outraged. Something is about to give.

The bus moves on. The conductor calls out the stops in a shrill, ominous tone. The driver remains in the bus in case something should happen. The elegant lady has begun whistling, in outrage and protest against the floozy's heel tapping.

"Crenshaw," the conductor bellows, "last stop."

The companion has stood up and is wandering pensively through the bus. The lively floozy is clapping with her shoes. He nods; she jumps up, clutches his arms, and yelps gleefully.

The elegant lady starts back at the sight of him and covers her face with her hands. The simple woman has some butter in the paper next to her. She has smeared the butter over her wrinkled features and is powdering her face with some flour from a paper bag. Her mouth and chin are already white. Then she tosses the bag at the companion's feet and shrieks.

The companion looks horrible. The audience can see him now, for the conductor has seized him by the shoulders, spun him around, and is screaming at him in a rage: "Everybody out, everybody out! Crenshaw, last stop!"

The passengers are on their feet. The driver joins in the ruckus: "Last stop, everybody out."

The passengers don't want to leave.

Nobody wants to get off.

The companion, an ancient man with a broken nose, with a horribly bitter and tragic look, announces in peremptory tones: "I've just boarded the bus. Drive on."

"Your fare," the conductor yells. The old man takes a step back and punches the conductor in the chest. The conductor stumbles backwards and calls on the driver for help. The old man rushes past him, turns the sign around, and rings a bell that has suddenly appeared out of nowhere. He urges the male passengers, who are waiting outside, to board the bus.

"Everybody out," the conductor cries, "we have to clear the bus."

But the three men, powerful figures this time, ignore him and get on the bus. One of them has a big belly under his black robe and is wearing an academic mortarboard. Behind him comes a policeman with a child's toy sword. The last figure, dressed in bright red, leaps aboard with a yell. He is wearing red tights and has some heavy object with him, hidden in a sack.

At the sight of these three, the conductor, who has still not recovered from the blow he has received, throws his cap down on the floor, casts off his change purse, and takes to his heels. He leaps down the steps and runs across the lawn and into the bushes.

Chaos on the bus. The formerly modest old housewife with the shopping bag, horrible now in her mask of white powder, frisks grotesquely up to each of the three male passengers, puts her arm around his waist, and guides him to his seat, screeching, "Your Grace, Your Excellency, Your Lordship." The floozy, her shoes in her hands, provides a musical accompaniment to this greeting. She claps her shoes together like cymbals and spins around. Her stockings have begun to slip. She yanks them off and dances barefoot. The society lady jumps into the judge's lap. He does not object; they both seem content. Seated to the judge's right is the man with the sword; to his left, the figure in red.

The driver wants to escape, too, but the companion bars the way and shoves the driver back into his seat. The frightened man turns and asks: "Everybody ready?" The reply: "Yes." The driver looks at the sign. It is right. He reaches for the bell, stretches out his legs, releases the brake. They are off.

The passengers—they number six now—sit facing the audience. The companion has taken his place again at the side of the imperturbably silent and mysterious gentleman who never moves.

"Last stop," cries the desperate driver. It sounds like: Let me out of here! He tumbles out of the bus, picks himself up, and, like the conductor before him, races off across the grass.

The policeman takes charge now. "Wilshire. Hurrah! Everybody out who wants to get out."

Everybody looks at the slumped figure in black and his companion. The companion stands up and bows. "We have just gotten on."

He walks through the bus. He is a wonderfully handsome Greek youth. He enchants the ladies. The black-robed judge is instantly relieved of his feminine burden. The elegant lady seizes the youth's arm and gazes enraptured into his face. She lays her left arm across his chest to guard her catch.

The youth does not leave the other two women unaffected either. The situation looks serious. The housewife wants to yank the ecstatic woman away from the young man; and, oddly enough, the floozy has tossed her shoes, her cymbals, aside and is kneeling on her seat and looking with worshipful eyes at this male wonder.

No need to describe any more of this amateur production that lasted for over an hour. The main charm of it for the audience did not lie, however, in the little scenes just described but in the antics of several of the players while the bus was underway. Songs alternated with recitations from Gordon Allison's works. The boarding and disembarking scenes provided the framework for the revue. At the end of the play, the judge called on the mysterious gentleman and his companion to get up at last and leave the bus. And when the companion, now in still another mask, said, "The journey is not over for us yet," the blood-red executioner raised his axe, ready to kill the strangers at the judge's order. But the companion, a Herculean figure, tossed him and everyone else off the bus.

Soft music accompanied the close. The only two left on stage, seated side by side, were the mysteriously silent gentleman who had never turned around once and his magician companion.

The journey continued.

The curtain fell.

The Revelation

THE next day everything returned to normal in the house. Crenshaw and his guests rested and were not much about.

On one of the following days, Edward pressed his mother to come to his room. Then he asked her to tell him the end of Theodora's story. Alice had gone with him to his room only reluctantly and said she had had a bad night. She sat silent for a while at first; then she began. He had never seen her so downcast, tense, and distracted. Something was weighing on her.

She told how Theodora, after all she had experienced with men, and herself, renounced the world and cursed her sex. She cut off her hair and put on men's clothes. She did menial work at a monastery and chastened herself. Eventually, the penitent was accepted into the monastery as lay brother Theodore. There was more to be told about her, but little of it was worth the telling. Brother Theodore was later accused of having seduced a woman, and the woman brought a child to the monastery, claiming that Theodore was its father and that he had raped her. Theodore fell seriously ill at about this time, and it was obvious that he would soon die, perhaps from regret at what he had done. He was left to die unattended in his cell. But on the night of his death, the abbot dreamed that he saw a saint ascend from his monastery into heaven, and the angels welcomed the pious, penitent Theodora. Early the next morning, after relating his vision to his monks, he went with them to Theodore's cell and found him lying there dead. But his shirt was open over his chest. The monks examined his body more closely and saw that it was a woman's.

"And that's how Theodora died. That was her life."

"Didn't anyone show her mercy? Didn't she reveal her secret to anyone?"

"Mercy, Edward? There is none for the weak. It is the strong who triumph. Vengeance is all there is."

345

She was deathly pale.

"And you, Edward, what about you? Have you understood your life yet? What about you? How did you come to be in this condition? Why did you go to war? What do you think drove you away? Have you found out yet? He ruined you just as he ruined me."

Was this his mother speaking? ("Quhy dois your brand sae drop wi' bluid, Edward, Edward? — O, I hae killed my fadir deir.")

"Vengeance is all that remains. I know nothing else and want nothing else. All I'm living for is the day when I can avenge myself, and then I'll die. I don't want a new life; I'm too old for that. But I want to at least end this one in a way I can be proud of, with honesty, as you've said."

She couldn't stop talking. "Did you notice him during your play? You meant to shake him, to unmask him, the way Hamlet did with his vile stepfather, the murderer of his father. He sat among his admirers, and everything you played on the stage delighted him. Did you notice? He knew very well what you intended. He understood perfectly; you can be sure of that. He was pleased. Yes, he said, that's the way I am, if not more so, and the journey continues, and I'll wear more masks, the next worse than the one before, one abomination after another. Who can hold a candle to me? He went looking for you afterwards, but he couldn't find you. He wanted to congratulate you and thank you."

"What made you think of Hamlet, Mother?" (Nay, but to live in the rank sweat of an enseamed bed, stew'd in corruption, honeying and making love over the nasty sty,—") "I don't know why you're putting words like that in my mouth. I wasn't thinking of Hamlet. You're no Gertrude, and I'm not—"

He stopped short when he saw her close her eyes.

"I'm not," he repeated, "what is it I'm not?"

She pulled her hands away and stood up. "If things were only as simple as they are in *Hamlet*, then it would all be easy for us. But because they aren't, Edward, I cry out to heaven and ask for help. I don't want to drag you into this any further. The sins of the fathers have been visited enough on the sons. You are my only son, my beloved life. Let me be, Edward."

She was gone.

— Quhy dois your brand sae drop wi' bluid? I have to be patient. Then I'll know. I'll know how families are founded, children brought into the world, and fame and respectability increased. I read that we went to war against cruelty and dictatorship. We went at it all from the wrong end. What is it we are afraid of? They make films about it and show people its horrors. Who are they trying to fool? Or are we really so stupid that we don't catch on? You don't have to make any expeditions to foreign countries to fight this war. You don't even have to go to the movies. Everything's conveniently at hand right at home.

So there we had the explanation for wars. First it was supposed to be customs, styles, conventions, certain fits that overcame mankind from time to time. All obfuscation. Then it was supposed to be society. Who next, what next.

Everything, everything under the sun is responsible, everything except—me!

And we claim to be noble creatures! Why not stand up proudly and admit, Yes, it's me. That's the way I am, created this way by God the Lord. To hell with it. So it's not so lovely. But it's my nature. I can't change it.

Why doesn't anybody say that: I'm responsible, instead of pointing at somebody else or cooking up some abstract notion like custom, society? Or, when you come right down to it, it's all Adam's fault, and I can quietly go about my business. Cowards, weaklings, don't assume responsibility for anything, don't speak for yourselves and answer for yourselves. Fun, pleasure, peace and quiet, that's all they want, to feast at their ease—it doesn't matter at whose cost. A kind of bug, mosquito, fly, that buzzes around in the sun, takes a bite here and there, takes life easy. Tomorrow it's all over.

Hypocrisy, complacency, laziness, shoddiness, abysmal stupidity and dishonesty. Good for nothing, idiotic, and vile from childhood on and until they die. Can something like that even be said to have been born?

All I want is honesty. Nothing but that. I went to war because their society disgusted me and I couldn't find a spark of honesty or conscience in them. Not a single man, not a single voice on whose account I could say "Yes" to this world. Death didn't take me. He sent me back into this stinking cave that doesn't even deserve to be called hell. He took a leg as a token of good faith. Now I've got to earn the rest of my fare.

Wars? The reason for wars? What is it? The abyss of cowardice and mendacity.

So, how do things stand with me? It seems they brought me into the world in some strange way. I'll find out what it was.

The only other person in the house, apart from the parents, who had understood the burlesque performed on Gordon Allison's birthday was the elegant, troubled James Mackenzie. The very idea alone had been enough to upset him, and then this ghastly figure of the stranger, the eternal passenger who kept his back to the audience, this dark creature that revealed itself only in masks, savage, contorted, conceived in anguish. Why couldn't Edward let up? He was intent on following a madman's path, the path of a Hamlet who had no instructions from the ghost of a dead father but acted out of his own diseased, inner compulsion, his own awful need. The whole situation reminded Mackenzie much more of Oedipus, who, bent on solving the mystery of his own origin, destroyed himself.

In the garden Mackenzie had watched those horrible scenes, done up in clown's clothing, in which the red executioner had tried to lead the mute, immobile gentleman in the bus to the block. The executioner had argued cheerfully that all the play lacked was a beheading, which would provide it with a rousing finale. After the play the troubled Mackenzie mingled with the high-spirited company. He saw Gordon Allison, still in his same buoyant mood. Near him was Alice. Her mood had changed dramatically. She was with a group of women, laughing, talking, gesticulating. During the play she had laughed so heartily that everyone noticed her. Her laughter had been infectious. Now she could give her delight free rein. The play had been such a surprise for her and then such a great success on top of that. She congratulated the amateur actors and actresses who gradually began turning up to collect their accolades. Her son, yes, Edward (just thinking about it made her overflow with laughter again), had played the stranger beautifully, with such masterly muteness and such economy of gesture. — But then he had been the director, too. It seemed to Mackenzie that his sister was a bit tipsy, or her nerves were going to pieces. He witnessed a scene that drew the attention of the guests as well: Lord Crenshaw and Alice, each of them surrounded by guests, met after the play. Lord Crenshaw waved and offered her his hand. "Bravo, bravo! Congratulations! Who was the playwright, you, Alice, or Edward?" She took his hand. "It wasn't I, Gordon. You'll have to ask Edward. But it could have been me." And then he drew her to him, and they embraced.

Mackenzie's concern, indeed, his fear, did not abate. On that same evening he went to Edward's room and had a brief, painful conversation with him. He again asked two questions, a practical one and a theoretical one. The practical one: What was the purpose of his attacks on his father? Was he clear in his own mind about that, and about what their consequences might be? No answer. The second question: If it was clarity and honesty he wanted, how could he expect to find and grasp them if he was running amok through the streets? Edward replied as a high-ranking minister might to a petitioner: He would think the matter over, and he expressed his thanks for his uncle's message and visit.

On the afternoon of the day he spoke with his mother, Edward felt that peculiar unrest that everyone in the house had come to know so well by now, an unrest that went hand in hand with mild anxiety and prompted Edward to ask questions, questions, and more questions. Now he was afraid. He didn't dare turn to anyone. He set himself in motion and wandered about in the garden. Mackenzie had said, before he left him the evening after the party, that the best thing Edward could do for himself and his family was to leave the house and, if he still needed care, to return to Dr. King's clinic. Should he, or shouldn't he?

And as he walked and thought and debated with himself, he wandered back into the house and, without realizing it, climbed up to the attic. There, at a distance from everyone, he felt better.

And while he was looking around here amidst the junk, the locked cupboards and boxes, he was overcome by such a fit of weariness, such an irresistible, leaden-limbed exhaustion, that he felt it quite literally forcing him down onto the floor.

And clinging to a rafter as he looked about him helplessly (where could he sit, where could he lie down), he spied an old couch shoved up against the wall behind some cabinets. As he cleared the couch of the bundles of newspapers piled on it, his eye caught the label "1918–19, in chronological order" written on one of the bundles in his father's hand. Old truck like that they had piled on the couch. He stretched out and gave himself up to sleep.

Sleep, unconsciousness? He was aware of nothing. Then images began to form over the sleeper and to fly about like flocks of crows. New images came; they touched him the way a breeze does a field of grain. The stalks bent, swayed, righted themselves. The heavy, heavy sleep held him in its grip. The images fluttered on the wind, and voices rang out, calls. And suddenly he knew he was afraid and struggling with himself. Unreal events. No possibility of following and understanding them. And such an intense desire to be able to.

That's it. That's the mystery. Speak to me; tear me apart. I'm going to pieces anyway.

Words behind walls, behind doors. Loud voices, cries, whisperings.

It's going to happen. I'm going to find out everything.

He lay tied to a board in the water; the current drew him down; the board turned; he sank to the bottom.

A crashing. Words of thunder.

"So here we are. You've brought us to this."

"I'm glad. I've been waiting for this for years."

"You've stalked me like a cat. You hate me. You begrudge me my life. I know you, Alice."

"I'm glad."

"What do you want from me?"

"I want you to let me go. I hate you. I don't like you. I'm not for you."

"I know. You're for others."

"For others, as you say, you jealous beast. If you would finally come out of your books and show yourself for what you are."

"A wild boar, a murderer, a degenerate. I know."

"Isn't it the truth? Admit it, you kidnapper. Aren't you Pluto, hell itself? And haven't you said as much to me a hundred times and begged me to stay with you because you couldn't live if I didn't? And you devoured me, and now you strut and beam in front of everyone else."

"Pure fantasy. Your hatred."

"Then let me go. Give me my freedom."

"I won't, Alice."

"Why not, you bastard?"

"Bastard is a good word, an honest one. Because I need you. Because you belong to me. Because I love you. I'm going to keep you. You won't leave me. But go if you will. The door is open."

"You have to let me go."

"Why don't you go if the door is open?"

"You have to let me go."

"You can't go because you're attached to me."

"I to you, to Gordon Allison?"

"Just as he is to you. We are one. You're as much a beast as I."

"I as much as you?"

"Yes, little beast, that's why you're devoted to me. You're glad that I pulled you out from behind your mask. I freed you. Yes, I you, and don't stare at me like that. You were a fiction, a role you had condemned yourself to play. I gave you your life."

"I had none before?" she screamed.

"No real one. No honest, genuine, human one."

"For you, being human means being animal."

"We shouldn't deceive ourselves. There's nothing worse than a lie. Better the animals we are than the angels we are not."

"Then why don't you show people who you really are, Lord Crenshaw? Why do you keep wearing one new mask after another?"

"Because I enjoy it. And because I'm good at it."

"You cynic. I'll get you."

Silence. Sounds of struggle.

They are at each other. She scratches his face.

"I like you this way. It's like old times."

"Let me go, or I'll call for help."

"But I love you. I'm about to make love to you. And who will come anyhow?"

"You're tearing my clothes. Murderer, let me go. You don't own me."

"Who does then?"

"Others."

"Who?"

"Somebody else. You know who. That's why you tore up my old dress."

"Say that again."

"I'll say it again. Let me go. I'll scream."

"You slut, you whore. After all these years with me. — Say it again."

"Help! Murderer!"

A crashing. Words of thunder.

And then he came tottering onto the scene from behind a cabinet, his cane in his hand, and knocked over a bookshelf. His mother screamed when she saw him, her son, Edward. Delicate Alice's blouse is torn open from neck to waist. The right half is completely torn away. A piece of the sleeve is left on her elbow and lower arm. The other shreds of the blouse hang from her red belt. Her hair is disheveled from the struggle. Gordon is holding a clump of it in his fist. The dark mass of it hangs down over her face. She shoves it out of her eyes. She folds her arms over her naked breasts. She turns her slim body aside.

The fat, panting man, oblivious to the blood dripping from his forehead, ears, and lips, stares at the new arrival as if he were a ghost. He lowers the clenched fist that she has pulled away from. He lets out a wild laugh, more of a roar.

"There he is, lupus in fabula. There he is, the sick man, the malingerer. He's looking over the terrain, inspecting the battlefield."

And the more he looked at this distraught figure, the cane trembling in his hand, the more his hatred and rage grew.

"The sick, pitiful wretch, the monster, I'll kill him."

Edward takes in every word. He knows every word. He knows the tone, the voice, the expression. He has witnessed them a thousand times before, and they always meant one thing: murder. The fat, raving man has come toward him, his arm, the hammer of death, raised to strike. A clump of a woman's dark hair falls from his hand. Edward raises his free arm to protect himself, holding it in front of his face as he has a thousand times in his dreams. But Edward is not afraid. He feels no fear of death. He is standing on the ship's deck. The Japanese kamikaze plane straight down. It smashed, clattered through the deck, burst, and shattered the interior of the ship. The ship let out a horrible, animal bellowing. A geyser shot up, carrying planks, men, smokestacks with it, spun them together in a bale of black smoke, a stabbing red flame in its midst, shrapnel, bodies, torn limbs.

A choked "Ah" from Edward's open mouth. The cane in his left hand slips and skids backwards across the floor. His left knee won't support him anymore. Edward sways to the side, against his mother, Alice, who has thrown herself between him and the rampaging Gordon, ready to intercept any blow, and who is clinging to his shoulders and pressing her head with its mussed hair against his neck. She falls with him. She cries shrilly, his cold face against the breast that had once fed him.

Her arm broke his fall. She pulls it out from under his hard shoulder; she does not feel the pain. She kneels next to him on the floor and shakes him. She talks to him. Allison has remained immobile, not even lowering his heavy right arm, the hammer. Still half in the fury of battle, she glances up at him with a look of dark hopelessness—as one devil would look into the eyes of another—and hisses, "Go away. Go away. Go, I say!"

He stirs, lowers his arm.

He moves toward Edward. He has taken a step forward and is about to bend down when he is struck again by Alice's dark, terrifying gaze which seems to carry hell in it, and she whispers, "Get away. Away. Don't touch us. Don't touch my child."

He remains standing and sucks at the blood running from his lip. His face, bluish red and swollen a moment ago, has returned to normal. He stands there and mumbles something incomprehensible. She is talking tenderly to the mute figure on the floor. Gordon leaves.

*   *   *

As soon as Edward shows signs of consciousness, she rushes down the stairs to her room and throws a coat around her shoulders. On her way out again she snatches up a comb from her dressing table, runs it through her mussed hair, a few quick strokes to the right and left, without looking in the mirror.

She is crouching down next to Edward again. He is sitting up now. She coaxes him to his feet. "Come on. I'll help you."

She goes down the steps with him. They do not speak. He has a sleepy look on his face. When he reaches his room, he lies down.

Once she has left him and shut the door quietly behind her, she doesn't know what to do next, what time of day it is, whether it's a weekday or Sunday.

Footsteps approach from the side, her brother, James.

"Why do you have a coat on, Alice? Are you cold? Oh, you're bleeding. Your neck."

"Where? I must have scratched myself."

James: "Gordon has left."

"Oh?"

"With his suitcases. He took the car."

"Oh?"

James: "How is Edward? I'll send for the doctor."

"As you think best. Good night, James."

It was still broad daylight. But when she had wandered around in her room from one object to another for a few minutes—had picked up a hairbrush and put it down again and opened a box of powder and powdered her face heavily, had run water in the washbasin, washed her hands and dried them, looked out the window—she realized that something was intolerable and that she would have to take a sleeping pill. She swallowed it and undressed as if she were undressing someone else and put this strange body that was accompanying her to bed.

She waited for it to go to sleep and take her along with it.

The Long Night of Lies Is Over

THE family kept Gordon's flight a secret for a few days. It was even possible that he had just gone to London to gather material for a new project.

But when a few days became several, when publishers' inquiries had to be answered and checks signed, there was no hiding anymore that he had left without leaving a forwarding address.

Rumors began to circulate instantly in literary circles. Police agents appeared at the house to make inquiries. Alice turned away all speculations by pointing out that Gordon Allison would occasionally disappear without a trace because he wanted absolute peace. No one had taken much notice of that ten or twenty years ago when he had not been as much in the public eye as he was now. Alice's explanation fit in well enough with what everyone knew to be the situation in the Allison household, namely, that Gordon Allison was suffering from his wounded son's presence. He had yielded to his wife's wishes in bringing his son into his home, but the situation had proved more than he could tolerate.

The house was not the same after the scene in the attic. Alice locked the door to Gordon's study, drew the curtains, closed the windows. She didn't open the room up to clean and air it.

The next room she had to close up was Kathleen's.

When Kathleen returned home two days after that afternoon—she had been away visiting a friend—she stared up in amazement at the closed shutters of her father's study. Everyone was going around the house on tiptoe. The servants whispered that her father had gone away. Where to? They didn't know. This oppressive, anxious atmosphere in the house. Bitter and angry, Kathleen wondered, as she dropped her suitcase on the sofa, whether she shouldn't just turn around and leave right now. But her anger drove her upstairs to talk to Alice.

Kathleen found her mother's behavior unnatural and reminiscent of her mood early on in Edward's illness. But she spoke calmly and told Kathleen just what she had told friends who had asked about Gordon: Her father had wanted a change. He wanted to work alone.

"But why? What was bothering him?"

"I don't know, Kathleen."

"Did he leave a note?"

"Only a few lines."

"What is his address?"

"I don't have it."

"His address?"

"I don't have it, Kathleen."

"What has happened here? What have you done to him?"

"Kathleen!"

"You don't tell me anything. I've known for a long time that you've been nagging at him, attacking him, Edward especially. But you've been supporting him. What has he done to the two of you? He's our father."

"But Kathleen, we haven't driven him away. He'll write to us."

"He won't come back. I've seen it coming for a long time. This all started when Edward got sick. You can at least tell me what you have against him, you and Edward. I'm his daughter. I belong to this family, too, you know."

"We haven't done anything to him."

"You're lying, Mother. I won't put up with this. You're treating me like a child."

Alice was lying on her chaise longue. "Come back in an hour."

An hour later Alice heard Kathleen open the door. She turned to her and said nothing had happened and no one had hounded Gordon out of the house.

When Kathleen refused to believe her and pressed her for details, Alice broke down in disconsolate tears. Kathleen stamped her foot and insisted that she finally be given an answer. Alice had turned toward the wall again and was sobbing. Kathleen left in a rage, slamming the door behind her.

She hated her mother. She swore she would spare no effort to find her father and avenge him on Edward and her mother.

She stayed in the house a few days. Then Alice had to close up her room, too.

*   *   *

Crushed, Alice lay in her room.

Now and then she crept about the dismal house in her bathrobe and put in an appearance with the servants. She looked in on Edward, to whom James Mackenzie and Dr. King were attending. The two of them saw to it that Alice stayed in her room and calmed herself. They did not press her with questions. She was in a daze.

Dr. King kept an eye on her. Her brother came to see her. He told her he had good news for her. It was about a change in Edward's condition. That brought her out of her lethargy, and she sat up on the sofa as James began speaking.

"Alice, you'll be delighted with him. It's as if he had shed a skin. The butterfly has left its cocoon behind. I'm not exaggerating. He is calm, serious, content. He looks at you attentively but doesn't press you with questions. Before, he struck me as an adolescent. Now he looks at you like a mature man."

James Mackenzie did not tell her about the preceding days, the ones following on the unknown event in the attic. He did not tell her how, on that first evening, Edward had awakened from a deep sleep and screamed, screamed, rousing the whole house with his shrieks (Alice, still under the influence of her sleeping pill, was the only one who had not heard him). He acted as he had on the deck of the ship that had brought him home, only now he got up and hid himself in his room, first here, now there, to escape some invisible pursuer and attacker. James had called in Dr. King, who had left a young doctor with Edward for the night. Edward suffered another, similar attack early in the morning, but this time it was less severe.

And then Edward was worn out. Everything in him seemed to give way. He cried a lot, sobbed, and didn't know why. He just had to cry and cry. It seemed as if the last fragment of the stone he was carrying inside him dissolved in these tears. Afterwards he was freer, more open.

Alice asked her brother: "What is he talking about? What's on his mind?"

"We talk about themes of the day. I've brought him newspapers. We've talked about hunger in Europe, about how hard it is to resolve political crises. Edward is tending toward a view now that I find salutary. He says the war has had results that we mustn't ignore: It has to be seen as positive that among the people who have survived the war there are many for whom the misery they endured has been an education, one they are very grateful for and have learned more from than they could have from a book or from any other experience."

"And what is it that the war has taught him?"

James: "I haven't understood him altogether. He speaks very slowly, deliberately. He still hasn't clearly formulated what it is he really means. But isn't it remarkable, Alice, that someone like him, a young man who has suffered so much, feels a kind of gratitude toward the fate that has led him down this path?"

James did what he could for her, but there was little he could do.

He realized, when he saw her lying there as she was and wandering about the house, silent, sloppy, closed off to everyone, that something had happened to her. Oh, what had he taken on when he let himself be summoned to this house and taken into it. He was to have spent only a brief holiday here. Now he could not leave. His whole life, which had flowed by so comfortably, so sensibly, had taken a whole different turn. Yes, James Mackenzie, the epicurean, was suffering yet did not run away. He had asked his sister to control herself and not stir up what lay still and dead in her. But she had rushed on blindly.

Now fate had caught up with her. Gordon had fled. Kathleen had slammed the door shut behind her.

When James returned to his room with its balcony overlooking the garden—the room above Edward's—he felt a surge of anger toward the young man downstairs who had grown up in this house, been cherished and protected here. He was better now. Dr. King had made his experiment; it had proved successful. The doctor was rubbing his hands together gleefully: The cure was underway. But at what cost? Can anyone ask this kind of sacrifice from others? Without Edward and his illness Alice would have done nothing. The two of them, she and Edward, had struck an agreement to poke about in ashes that had grown cold long since. But there was a coal glowing there after all. She poked and scraped; she had to show that something had once been aflame there. She had to fan the coal until it became visible and no one could deny that there had once been a fire here, and then it flared up, leapt over the hearth, into the room, up to the ceiling, to the roof, and consumed the whole house.

The passion for honesty had triumphed, leaving corpses strewn in its path.

Dr. King was cheerful but only outwardly so. As the fruits of his "experiment" matured during these weeks, it dawned on him that it was already too late. He could not undo anything now.

He realized that Alice had exploited him. He visited her in her room, sounded her out, stood by her bed, and looked into her face. It became clear to him that she had played a game with him, this passionate person. She had finally satisfied an old desire for vengeance. Who was she? Proserpina? No, Medea. Or Dejanira, Hercules' sweet and crafty mate, who, to take vengeance for his faithlessness, had sent him the poisoned shirt. A woman's hatred—he was no stranger to it. A downtrodden sex that keeps battling to assert itself and, like terrorists, does not shrink from the most inhumane acts of violence.

Dr. King drove home in his carriage, back to his clinic from which he had discharged Edward. How motherly, how touching she was with me, leaning her head on my chest there in the hallway like a daughter— her son, her son. Women's hatred, insatiable malice. What can she have done to our decent Gordon who wants nothing but to write and make up stories. If you look carefully into a poet's life what misery, what grief you turn up. She laid her head on my chest and coaxed, begged, wept: "Give me my son, my poor son. He's my son, after all." And I fell for it.

She lured him into the house to work this deed. She is a criminal. This woman fills me with horror.

Gordon Allison's True Story

THE stupor, the awful feeling of being shattered, twisted, ground to dust, left Alice. She felt the need to move around. It drove her through the quiet house to Kathleen's and Gordon's rooms.

She stood still in front of Kathleen's door.

— To the left a row of windows. To the right several padded doors. The nurse opened a door. Kathleen slipped into the vestibule. He is lying with his back to the door. Now you look. In this room lay her son. It was a simple hospital room, but in it lay her son. He began to roll over. His face turned toward the door. Two wide-open eyes looked her way. She had dressed in girlish clothes: a wide straw hat, flowers at her breast. His lips moved; the corners of his mouth twitched. He was dreaming. The planes. Moaning. And now that awful expression, the fear, the unspeakable fear. Somebody wants to hit him. Somebody is out to murder him. He gnashes his teeth. He bares them. I fainted. —

She wandered upstairs to Gordon's door.

I was wearing the blue dress and was walking arm in arm with Edward (an eternity ago, in another life). Gordon was standing at the door, watching us.

Alice had to open the door and go into the big, stuffy, darkened room.

She stood in the middle of it. Then she went to his desk and sat down at it. She switched on a light. He had left everything just as it was. He hadn't even put away his manuscripts.

She didn't touch anything. A drawer on the left-hand side of the desk was open. A small box with the top open, red velvet, with something golden shining in it, caught her eye. She reached into the drawer. It was a ring, a smooth, heavy ring, a wedding ring. The box was standing on a piece of paper with some writing on it. She picked up the little box and read, in Gordon's handwriting:

Thursday afternoon. Alice, this is my wedding ring. You've got what you want. I'm leaving.

No signature. He doesn't know his name.

She took the ring and let it shine in the lamplight—round, warm gold.

I'm taking everything back, everything that's due me. He's letting me go. He's setting me free. He has set me free. I'm free.

And as Alice felt that, she let the ring roll into her cupped hand, and tears came to her eyes.

The ring. I still haven't quite taken it in. I'm free. He is setting me free. He's letting me go. Gordon is letting me go. Gordon is gone, gone for good. There is no more Gordon Allison.

She pressed the ring to her passionately. She stroked it and held it to her lips.

I hadn't known yet. I didn't know. Oh, how lovely, lovely, lovely.

She jumped to her feet. What am I thinking? Where is my head? He's letting me go. He's gone. Gordon Allison is gone. There is no Gordon Allison. The devil is gone. The tyrant has disappeared. I've won the war. I've won the war. She clapped her hands. She kissed the scratches that were still left on her hands from the struggle in the attic.

She looked at her own ring. Ecstatically, slowly, centimeter by centimeter, she slid it off her finger. When she set it down on the top of the desk, the empty space on her finger left her speechless. She licked the finger all around. The chains are broken. She raised her left hand and turned it this way and that. She showed her naked finger to everything in the room. Laughing, happy, light as a feather, she went about the room, waving her left arm like a flag.

Then she sat at his desk again and bedded her ring down next to his in the box. She closed the lid and put the box into the drawer. She took a red pencil and wrote on the paper under his note:

Tuesday morning. And this is my wedding ring, Gordon. Here they both are together. I thank you with all my heart. I'm leaving, too.

And as she was about to sign, she had the same experience that he had had. She hesitated. She shied away from writing her name. She thought of writing "the late Alice." She threw the red pencil down, put the paper under the box, and left the drawer open, just as he had.

Then she stood up and stretched. She turned the light out and left the dark, silent room. She rushed upstairs to her room and washed her hands, her left arm up to her shoulder. And went into the bathroom, lit the gas, undressed, and climbed into a warm bath.

She washed her body from head to toe and then showered. For the rest of the afternoon she lay on her chaise longue in her bathrobe and slept, slept until evening when she appeared for dinner and surprised Edward with her fresh appearance, with her strangely beatific gaiety.

During the long early morning hours when Alice lay in her bed before tea was brought to her, she thought that now she had to fulfill her obligation to Edward—had to tell him the truth, the whole truth.

Will he condemn me?

He has come this far with me. He is an adult. He is a human being. I won't keep anything from him. I mustn't hide anything; I don't want to hide anything.

The long night of lies is over.

She dressed carefully. Before her mirror, she practiced a smile that quickly gave way to a tender, pensive expression. And so she went to visit her son in his room. She felt ashamed and afraid at the prospect. He had witnessed that dreadful scene in the attic. But she had to appear before him, in person, to receive her sentence. (But she had already granted herself absolution; she was not wearing her ring anymore.)

He was glad to see her. He was sitting at the window, and when she came in he went to her and embraced her. He held her warm and close and did not let go of her when she sobbed.

"Don't worry, Mother. We'll stick together. I'm with you."

"You can't stay here, Edward. You have to leave. Believe me."

"Mother, what are you saying?"

She was happy beyond words, sitting with him this way, hand in hand. (She thought: If Gordon could see us, he would make snide remarks and begrudge me this. I'm happy. The long night is over.) Tears came to her eyes again.

She looked at her son: "And you, how are you? Uncle James brought me good news of you."

She took note of his calm, clear expression. He has become a man; James was right.

"I feel good. I sleep well. The doctor says, 'Bravo, we've done it.' It was, after all, a bold experiment of great interest for him, too. He wants to write it all up for the medical journals some day. A case of dramatic self-analysis he calls it. The interesting thing about it for him is that it ran its course without a doctor's help or guidance. What use would his guidance have been to me anyhow? What good would his couch have done me? I told him: 'Wars are fought face to face with the enemy, not in the general staff's quarters.'"

"What did he say to that?"

"Oh, you know: Things might have gone this way instead of that. Unexpected problems might have turned up, and so on. As far as I was concerned, I had to work it out myself. It was my business, not any doctor's."

"And so you feel better."

"Absolutely, Mother. I'm completely clear. I'm completely free."

There was a lull in their talk.

"Just in the last few days I've started to think everything through, Mother. I feel like a new man, as if I had just come back from overseas on my ship. I haven't been able to focus on details before. Now I'm able to bit by bit."

"And what is it you're thinking about?"

He looked at her, took her right hand, and examined the scratches still visible there.

"You had blood on your arm. On your neck, too. Your blouse was torn."

"Yes."

He rested his chin in his hand. Her dear son, her judge. I know. You'll start asking questions now, and I'll answer them. I can answer them, freely, as freely as I can do everything. I'm not wearing my ring anymore.

He whispered, his eyes toward the floor.

"Father has left. He hit you. He felt a blind rage toward me. I know he has always had something against me, something verging on hatred. He wanted to get rid of me. What did I ever do to him?"

She bit her lip. "You didn't do anything to him"

"Now that you're sitting here so calmly with me and I'm so pleased you're feeling better, Mother, could you do me a favor? Will you tell me, in plain language, without any images or similes, how all this came about? Some things you've already told me. He kept you captive. But you're a free person, and he is no jailer—why didn't you just leave? I've just realized now that when I was sleeping there in the attic, you were standing there fighting with each other. He was bleeding, and you were calling for help. What was that all about?"

"Is there anything else you want to know?"

"I experienced all this as a small child. It stayed with me and became a pillar in my body, and I grew up around it. Will you explain this to me, Mother? Can you?"

She held his right hand in both of hers, stroked it, held it to her cheek, and kissed it. "My dear son, what you're saying makes me so happy."

"Will you tell me, Mother?"

"Yes, I will." She lowered her head. "I wanted to before."

She looked around the room. "Do you mind if I lie down on the sofa? I'm a little tired."

She lay down so that she would not have to look at him as she talked. She wanted to bring everything (everything?) she was thinking and carrying around inside her out into the open, make it visible for him and for her as well.

For things had taken the course they had to take. She was not at fault. And there was no one in the world who could pass judgment more fairly than her son Edward, for he had shared her fate; it had been his own, from his birth until the moment the war broke out and he fled into it. He had had to risk body and soul. As Alice laid her head on the pillow and looked up at the white ceiling she felt her son across from her in the room.

How glad I am that I'm a mother. I have given birth to my helper. She gathered her thoughts, and she felt wonderfully at ease. Now she was ready to speak.

"You'll get the explanation you want. I hope it won't upset you. I couldn't give it to you before.

"But now he is gone from this house I built with him. Our family is dissolved. You and I will still stick together.

"Edward, let no man hold together those whom God hath put asunder. Love stories and plays are usually about men and women who want to come together and are kept apart by their parents or by circumstances. Just the opposite occurs more often, Edward.

"I was a young, cheerful, and naive girl, like the daughter of the goddess Demeter, like Proserpina, whom Gordon Allison later discovered in me."

(Is that true, Alice? You know it isn't true. Now you know that for sure. But go on.)

"You never knew my father and mother. Uncle James and I had a happy childhood and youth. Father owned a large printing company and was very wealthy. I could study anything I liked. I traveled a lot with my mother and my chaperone. Uncle James took me along on his second trip to India. Yes, I even went to India."

"You never told me that before."

(You're hesitating, Alice. You wanted to tell all, remember?)

"I put it off. I meant to tell you when you were grown up, and then I forgot about it. I had other things on my mind. And I have to tell you,

Edward, that things happened soon enough in our house and in the world that we could not talk about. There are some names that can't be mentioned lightly, and here in our house there are certain other names that could not be mentioned at all even though they were constantly present to us. Why not? Was some crime connected with those names? No, it was happiness, but a happiness that someone else hated. And because he hated that particular happiness, it gradually became impossible to speak of any kind of happiness at all. There could be no more happiness, not even the appearance of happiness.

"I had friends, men and women. My parents' house was an open, sociable place. The atmosphere was cordial and frank. Nothing remained hidden. We wouldn't put up with secrets. And if it looked as if someone were carrying some burden around inside himself, someone else stepped in immediately and helped and refused to let things go on that way. We didn't want to lead separate existences. We were a family. 'Secret love that no one knows of'—that may be all very exciting. But to keep silent about what one loves, without which one cannot live, to have to attach a stigma to it, to brand it with a mark of shame—that is humiliating. But I'm getting ahead of my story.

"There was no Gordon Allison in our circle. I would have called anyone crazy who had told me I would someday suffer a slave's fate.

"But I did suffer it, and I assure you, Edward, I still can't explain even today just how it all happened.

"Who was he? He recently represented himself to us as Michelangelo. But now let me tell you the story of Gordon Allison, the man I married and lived with up to now. His story is also partly my story and yours. What you're about to hear is no ballad, no Celtic fairy tale, no saint's legend. It's as real as your enlistment in the army, your landing in France, your voyage across the Pacific, and the explosives that destroyed your ship.

"Allison is his real name. He took the first name of Gordon later on, as a young man, because he read a great deal and once happened on the story of Charles Gordon, the hero of Khartoum. He came from a poor family. His father called himself a shipper. He owned a few carts, sometimes only one. Like many men in his trade, he drank. He was a crude man. I met him a few times, but I never once saw him completely sober. He neglected his family and often left them without money. His wife had to work hard. There were three children. The eldest was a daughter I never saw. I think she was crippled and mentally retarded. Then came Gordon and another daughter, a quiet, timid, pathetic creature. She couldn't work hard, not, in any case, as hard as she was expected to work. I used to visit the family often later just to see her. She wound up on skid row. She knew what was in store for her. She always had the expression of a drowning woman.

"Charles, who later called himself Gordon, was robust and did what he could for the family. He sacrificed himself, but under protest. Because of his neat hand—there were still no typewriters then—he had gotten an office job with a big firm. Soon he was writing for local newspapers, reporting on fires in London, sports events, fairs, and so on. It brought him a little extra money and gave him practice in writing. It also expanded his horizons and drew him out of his dismal family situation.

"Then he got a job as a reporter for a suburban paper and managed to scrape by as a journalist. Things got worse in his family, and the fact that Gordon was earning more money made things even worse. Now his father thought he could play the suffering old man, and he was the first to profit from the family's improved circumstances. He expanded his sheds and stables and took on new employees. While his son slaved and allowed himself no pleasures at all and did nothing but chase down news, the old man played the grand gentleman.

"Gordon had taken it for granted that he would be enslaved. But he grew resentful when he saw what was going on: His own life was being crippled while his father was off having a good time. His father, who exploited him like a beast of burden and at the same time called him a bootlicker, sometimes took his son along to 'cheer him up.' Gordon realized he was out of place with these gamblers and drinkers. He was too plodding, too serious, and, later, too bitter.

"He sometimes had to skimp on his noon meal so that he would have enough to take home and, of all things, to be able to support his father in the manner to which the old man was accustomed. Finally things came to a head in a London bar where Gordon was supposed to do a story commissioned by a whiskey manufacturer. And whom should he encounter partaking of the whiskey he was supposed to praise? His father with a young soubrette.

"The rampaging reporter is tossed out of the bar. He winds up at home with his clothes torn and a spinal contusion. He feels so depressed and hopeless that he doesn't tell his mother and younger sister what happened. He doesn't keep his silence to protect his father but because he feels nothing but disgust for his own way of life.

"And now comes the first episode the later Lord Crenshaw let himself in for in his struggle to escape his situation.

"As I mentioned, he said nothing at home about the incident in the bar, and his father was amazed to see that no one reproached him, that the bootlicker had not squealed on him. He interpreted that according to his own lights. He praised and thanked his son the first chance he got, and he encouraged him to join him in more escapades. After some thought, Gordon agreed. As far as women were concerned, he had the advantage of youth over his father, and he meant to exploit that advantage. He made up his mind to lure away the soubrette he had seen with his father. He struck up an acquaintance with her, and she shared her charms with both father and son.

"This depraved woman was his first love. Gordon was very young, just twenty. She pretended she was going to drop his father, but the fact was she liked them both, each in his way, the old drunk and the young lover.

"Because he wasn't earning enough as a journalist, Gordon worked on the side as a waiter in bars and at weddings and parties. One time somebody brought the elder Allison into one of the bars where his son worked. The old man, accompanied by the soubrette, greeted Gordon jovially. The son did his job and served them without blinking an eye. Every time Gordon filled their glasses, the old man gave him a little tip—from money that Gordon had earned.

"But when the party broke up, the old man realized—out on the street—that his soubrette was missing. He suspected she had stayed in the bar and was still drinking there. He went back alone. It was late at night. The bar was closed. He pounded on the door and was let in. And there he found his son cleaning up the bar, lovingly aided by the soubrette.

"She fled from the drunken man and locked herself in a back room. Gordon tried to restrain him, but his father struck him down with a bar stool and broke his arm.

"The old man wanted to teach the soubrette a lesson. Passersby who came in from the street overpowered him while his wayward lady took his son to the hospital. Gordon spent two weeks there. Then family life resumed its old course."

"A martyr's existence," Edward said when Alice paused briefly. She had thrown her blanket back partway.

"It was indeed," she replied; then she continued:

"Those were his early years.

"Then he met Hazel Crocker. His journalistic work, his depressions, his stubbornness and bitterness, or simply his fate, his stars, brought him into closer and closer contact with society's outcasts. Hazel Crocker had quite a reputation in her day. She had tampered with the will of an old man for whom she had kept house. The circumstances of his death were never fully cleared up. It appeared that he had died of poisoning, but the autopsy turned up no conclusive proof. Hazel Crocker had been lucky, this time. But her doctoring of the will was discovered, and she served a few years in prison for that.

"She was still young when she got out, in her thirties, still young enough to pick up where she had left off. Much was written about her later, but she's been forgotten for a long time now. Others like her have come along to take her place. She's been described as a serious, likable woman who inspired confidence in people. The policewomen who guarded her when she was held on suspicion of murder were all convinced she was innocent. Incredible as it may seem, it was through the good offices of one of these policewomen that Hazel got some of the positions she later held.

"Hazel Crocker operated within the sphere of middle-class respectability. She was apparently born on the fringes of middle-class society, that is, in some corrupt milieu, but I don't know the details of her background. She had a compulsion to enter into society, but only to defile it. Her ability to play the respectable middle-class lady made her job all the easier.

"She chose as her next victim a real-estate broker to whom she revealed the full details of her past (we know this from his letters) and who, in the incredible blindness of his infatuation, married her. She seems to have been very sure of him, so sure that she could afford to tell him everything about her past. Either he did not believe what she told him, or (who can understand what people will do) he was fascinated by it. She maintained her friendship with some women she had gotten to know in prison. After a brief period of marriage she delivered her husband, the real-estate broker, into these women's hands. She could easily prove that she was not personally involved in this murder, which was committed in some woods near her home. On the days in question she had been visiting relatives in London. It was clearly not her doing.

"Those present when she was brought back from London and confronted with the strangled man report that her reaction was moving to an extreme. It seems as if she had two or three totally different and unrelated souls. It would have been impossible for anyone to fake the performance she put on. She did not indulge in any mere tears and sobs. It's hard to imagine what was going on inside this creature who was, after all, still a human being. Here she was, a widow now, who had been brought home and told nothing. When she entered the living room where the dead man was laid out, she uttered a slightly astonished 'Ah.' According to the reports, what followed was horrible.

"She stroked the dead man's face, his shoulders, arms. She covered his hands with kisses and kept looking into his bluish, swollen face (he had been strangled) as if she expected something of him. The witnessess pulled her away, but she rushed to him again and held him tightly to her, once, twice—then there was no further need to pull her away. She seemed to understand now that he was dead, and his death horrified her.

"So far she had not uttered a syllable. Now she went to this person and that in the room and tried to hide behind them. She asked what had happened, how anyone could have done this, what harm he had ever done anyone, and so on. She refused to turn toward the dead man again. When someone tried to force her to, she screamed. When she was released, she ran to the door and stayed outside in the hall, deathly pale and with the same dazed expression as before.

"The case was not solved until much later. It turned out that she had incited the others, who managed to go undetected for a long time, while she, Hazel, inherited the dead man's money (at least until she was caught) and paid the others generously. She was put in prison, though there was no evidence of her complicity, and held for a few weeks. Then the authorities let this mystery called Hazel Crocker go, a creature—or so many people claimed—pursued by misfortune. That is when Gordon Allison got to know her. He had reported on the murder in the woods and had been present when Hazel was confronted with the strangled man. He interviewed her when she was released from prison and became attached to her. She became a student of criminology. The papers carried a lot about this turnabout in Hazel's life. There was no doubt that she had committed one crime, the falsifying of that will. But people were ready to forgive her that dereliction, explaining it away in terms something like this:

"An old man hires a young woman of questionable background as his housekeeper, and there is reason to believe that they became intimate and led a happy and dignified life together. She sacrificed her youth to him and no doubt expected some reward in return. In tampering with his will, she translated that expectation into a reality, crudely, naively, and, of course, illegally. She was punished for that. When she was released from prison, she married. This man died, too, murdered soon after the wedding. How awful, how unfair! Were fate and the world intent on driving her mad? The newspaper reports evoked sympathy in their readers: Hazel Crocker, sorely tried by life, has decided to study criminology, hoping to find clarity about herself and her fate.

"Gordon Allison joined her in her studies. This was a peculiar constellation indeed for the man who would become the later Gordon Allison. He spared himself no trouble later in life to cover up this chapter in his past, and his efforts were successful.

"I know the whole story in detail. He confessed it all to me not just once but often after we had first gotten to know each other and when he was courting me. It was the awful bait he dangled in front of me."

"Bait? Why do you say 'bait'? Why was it bait?"

"That was the effect it had. It both repulsed and fascinated me. It frightened me, terrified me. It was ghastly, awful, mysterious. He never spoke of it to anyone else. It was only with me he dared talk about it. I couldn't get it off my mind."

"It was his way of wooing you."

Alice: "I didn't understand what was happening. What he told me frightened me, but I couldn't stay away from him. I couldn't refuse to listen to him. I saw what he said as his confession. There was no one else he could turn to.

"But it was bait. He had singled me out. I was his target.

"What did I know of the world? Or of people outside my own circle? He initiated me into his secrets. It was my fate that the first person to ever speak to me about himself this way was him. He came ostensibly to unburden himself to me, but his real purpose was to make me his accomplice. I soon grasped that, and it frightened me. I lay awake nights and had to keep what I knew to myself. At that point I was already half lost. He asked my advice, even in horrible matters. That was his way of wooing me and corrupting me. For unless he could corrupt me, he could not be sure of winning me.

"What I am going to tell you is the history of his crimes against me. But, Edward, the fact that I am here, complaining and accusing, shows that he did not subjugate me and drag me down among those creatures of the underworld he associated with.

"He did to me what Hazel Crocker had done to him. He passed on what he had learned from her. He was her apprentice. He wanted to avenge himself for his terrible background and past history. I, a young girl, became his victim." And she added: "I know he was striving to leave his awful life behind him."

Edward: "That's right." He listened. He did not hate his father. He followed him on his old paths.

"He was a frequent visitor at our house, a young journalist whose name one often saw in the papers, at the same time he was connected with Hazel Crocker. He led a double life. I never knew what he had been up to just before he joined us for tea or a boating party. He was sent on trips to the Continent and wrote the first travel reports that displayed his distinctive style. He wrote some short stories, too, first experiments that he was not yet ready to publish. He read his work to me, including his first short stories. They were strange, grotesque things, and I didn't know that he and Hazel had written them together during the same period that he was calling at our house. She inspired him. She was his lover and muse, this Hazel Crocker."

Alice burst out laughing. Edward thought: She's still jealous of that woman.

"He couldn't stay away from her, and she kept a firm grip on the young journalist. How she lived her life fascinated him. He admired the uncomplicated way she went about her business. He thought it possible that she had committed the murders she was suspected of, but that didn't bother him. That was all part of her character. She simply did everything she fancied doing, and whatever she did turned out just fine for her. What a blessing for her that nature had given her that innocent-looking, middle-class face!

"Now in the course of one of her intrigues she ran across a plainclothes policeman who, for some reason, took her fancy. But he was engaged and planned to be married. That was just the kind of situation that whetted Hazel Crocker's appetite. She could interfere, intrigue, torment. She was in her element. Chaos and tension were the only things that excited her. She was otherwise a cold fish. Only in a situation like this did she catch fire. And the climaxes she prepared and then watched come about were what made her games worthwhile.

"That is how she had worked out her earlier schemes. But as time went on she began to operate more boldly, quickly, and impatiently. Earlier, she had taken pleasure in seeing things develop slowly, in the careful planning of her intrigues, in the clever execution of her plot. Each phase had held its particular pleasure for her. But now, after her past successes in which she had gotten what she wanted and come away scot free, she threw herself recklessly into her enterprises. In Estelle Stoyten's case, all she had wanted to do at first was cause some trouble. She begrudged the young woman her plainclothes policeman. Estelle was a robust, lively person of lower middle-class background, the daughter of a butcher. Hazel had gotten on well with Estelle at first. But the closer the wedding day came, the more often she found some trivial reason or another to clash with her. Hazel meddled in all the wedding preparations, finally pushing things so far that she had to be put in her place.

"And indeed she had been more attentive than ever to the groom, whether out of real feeling or sham would be hard to say. Her purpose was to raise doubts in his mind, make him uneasy, make him indecisive and unsure. At the same time she duped Estelle, threw herself at her, and acted as if she were terribly fond of her. She spread warm feelings to all sides, and no one knew how to save himself from her. The only person enjoying herself, no doubt, was Hazel Crocker. Gordon stood on the sidelines and admired her. He was not jealous, or if he was every now and then, that was part and parcel of his feelings for Hazel. That simple, basic human tie we call love was as foreign to him as it was to Hazel.

"She went the whole hog. At the wedding she set up a lascivious scene between herself and the groom. Everyone had been drinking, and she meant to show that the groom really belonged to her. It was an outrageous, scandalous performance. The groom and Hazel sat next to each other and began kissing and embracing in front of the bride. Hazel sat on his lap. The assumption was that she had had too much to drink. Estelle did not react.

"The drinking and dancing continued. As is customary, the newly married couple were supposed to disappear shortly after the ball had begun. The groom disappeared, but alone, leaving Estelle sitting there in her white veil. She danced with one guest, then another. She danced most with Gordon, who kept talking intently to her. Everyone present knew that something was in the wind. Finally, Estelle disappeared, too.

"The wedding party was being held in a mediocre hotel. The inevitable explosion came. Chaos broke out, men and women screaming and yelling. There was a crash, the sound of blows, someone slamming against a door, calls for the police, then the horrifying cry: 'She's stabbed me!'

"Estelle had found the two of them, her bridgegroom, now her husband, and Hazel Crocker, in one of the hotel rooms. It was Hazel's last adventure. This time she was the victim. It came out later that Estelle, who had been drinking heavily, had found a long, pointed butcher knife in the hotel and had stabbed Hazel with it. Hazel Crocker bled to death before she reached the hospital.

"And that was the end of Gordon's girlfriend, the notorious Hazel Crocker, who later became the heroine of the popular ballad."

Edward: "He came to you after this?"

Alice: "No. I said that before. He was a guest in our house when all this was going on. He told me everything. I was such an innocent creature. He confessed everything to me. He kept me posted."

"But he had no part in the murder. No charges were brought against him?"

"No, he had no part in the murder. Of course not. He kept company with Hazel. No charges were lodged against him. But he lived in the same atmosphere of murder that she did."

"And you?"

"What do you mean: 'And you'?"

"Why did he tell you everything? Why did you let him?"

"I had the feeling that I had a mission to accomplish with him. That's why he had come to me. It seemed to me that I could not turn my back on him. I had to save him."

"And he wanted to be saved? You say that's why he came to you."

"Absolutely. If you like, if you want to see him that way, he wanted to be saved, though his salvation was not as urgent a matter for him as it was for me."

"Or not as conscious a one. He wanted it, though. Otherwise why would he have come to you?"

"So that he would not have to leave me as I was. I had caught his eye. He couldn't let me be the person I was. He had to corrupt me."

"It can't have been that way, Mother. He came to you. He entrusted his secrets to you. You could see what he was. You wouldn't have had anything to do with him if there hadn't been something else to him. It's impossible that you would have put up with all that for so long, that dark and terrible side of him, if you had not felt he wanted something completely different from you."

"What would he have wanted from me?"

"Love."

She threw off her blanket and sat up.

"That's just what he was saying the other evening." She sat there with a hard expression on her face.

"Perhaps that's what he wanted, in his way. — We'll talk about it some more tomorrow, Edward, in my room."

Alice and Franklin Glenn's Love

JAMES Mackenzie sent him a note that afternoon, but Edward avoided seeing him.

I don't have time. I can hardly take it all in. What is all this I'm hearing. I have to be careful not to hear too much. Honesty, truth—you can get too much of them. He wandered about restlessly in his room. He didn't know what to do with himself. He sighed, sighed.

He didn't leave his room, despite the beautiful weather. He drew the curtains and made it night in his room. He wanted nothing to come in from outside.

What kind of house am I living in. I wouldn't have thought it possible. So that's what my family background looks like. I'm gradually beginning to make out details. I'm gradually extricating myself from that background. I lost my leg and fell ill because I remained stuck in that dark background. Nature has forced me to play Hamlet. I can understand now why Uncle James didn't want to tell me Hamlet's story. He left it to me to act it out. No, he saw that it would have been idle to talk about it. It was incumbent on me to live Hamlet's role.

You've put the first stage of the journey behind you, Edward. You thought the play was over. It's not. I'm in for more discoveries—*Hamlet,* Part II—without having to lift a finger for them. Revelations are hot on Hamlet's heels, Hamlet on the run from revelations. This part is called *Hamlet, or Curiosity Punished.*

What's going on? What has gone on? Among what kind of people? What does Mother have up her sleeve? I thought I could help her now that I'm better. But she has something else in mind.

What kind of people am I living with. What kind of people are these I'm living with and calling Father and Mother! And the others are just like them. Why haven't I seen that until now? I had to have my nose rubbed in it. I couldn't see anything before. My eyes have been opened. That's what's called society. It converses intelligently, plays music,

373

reads noble stories, raves about Milton, Swinburne, and Shelley. It smiles, sits together and drinks tea, and in the background—

Perhaps some horror haunts them just as one haunted me. They carry it around inside them, but they can't pin it down. They try to struggle out of it, to free themselves from it, but it sticks with them. They carry it firmly rooted in them. Not only they do. I do, too. You're caught in it. You thrash about helplessly.

They remain what they are.

That's the way they are, and they continue on their way. They can't stand themselves. But instead of wiping themselves out, they wipe other people out.

That's what Hazel Crocker did, and that's why Father came to Mother. But he knew how bad things were with him. He suffered. He wanted to be eradicated, by her. And what was the upshot?

One person turns to another and asks the other to take away his baseness and degeneracy and forgive him for them. And what happens? I don't know what happened between them. But I did see a scene from the Hazel play, saw it with my own eyes in the attic when they were about to kill each other.

Who was he? A poor slob who clung to Mother. He carried something horrible about inside him, something awful from his childhood. He felt it. He felt himself to be some kind of reptile, some cold, slippery lizard, a whole swamp.

He attached himself to her. He wooed her in his way. He dealt with her in the only way he knew. When Hercules patted a child on the head, he crushed its skull. He couldn't help it. He didn't mean to.

She accepted him. He had hopes. She was willing to associate with him. He didn't let go. He wouldn't let her shake him off. But then she couldn't bear it after all. She didn't have the strength. He heaped more on her shoulders than she could carry.

Their marriage. Now he's out of the house. Mother has won the field. She's done it. Kathleen is gone now, too.

He stamped around his room, moaning.

— What else does Mother have to tell me? She has failed, failed, failed! I can see that already. What else is there to say? I can do without further details. Their marriage can't have been nothing but one unending battle. Proserpina had a child by Pluto. I was born. Kathleen was born. Why can't I be spared this?

He stood staring out the window a while longer. Then he went to his bookshelves. All lies, smoke screens, obfuscation. He took out a book, one on natural history. He opened it. It was about spiders.

There is a spider called the malmignatte that lives in Mediterranean countries. Another, the black wolf, occurs in Asia and Russia. Anyone bitten by a black wolf becomes paralyzed, and death follows on shivering, cramps, and delirium. And here is the katipo. What a name. But the worst of them all is the black widow. It lives in California and Hawaii. The female is gray to black and three-eighths of an inch long. If you're bitten by a black widow, you become feverish. You lose your memory, become confused. The black widow kills more people than the black wolf and the katipo. In the dunes near Los Angeles there's a spider only a millimeter long. The female bores into the egg sack of the black widow and lays its eggs there. When its larvae emerge, they eat the eggs of the black widow.

Edward turned the pages and read, amazed.

There we have nature, marvelous, innocent, wonderful nature that we all worship because, working by her miraculous laws, she produces so many beautiful things, blossoms, snowflakes, for us to adore, just like the handsome clothes our ladies and gentlemen wear. Just like the fine words they line up one after another. One thing lives on the destruction of another. Jaws, teeth, are part of nature. Death, no, murder is deeply rooted in the world.

And we sense that. It soaks into us. We mistrust ourselves. Yet there is something in us that wants to escape this deadliness. It torments us. We try to resist it. Whose trail am I on here? We want to get away from it and can't. We struggle, and we try over and over again. Why does a man born in darkness seek the light? He turns to this gentle, delicate woman. Why? He tells her about himself and Hazel and the whole abominable business. Why? Just to drag her down, too? There is something of that in it, but what he really wants is to complain and to have her relieve him of his complaint. She is to play an active role, as a physician.

I see Father, Michelangelo. That's how he came to her. That's the guise he took when he knocked at her door, perhaps as dirty and confused as I was when I came back from the war.

He brought her a task.

It appears she understood what that task was.

It appears.

But not completely.

The result? —

Edward threw the book down. He brooded the rest of the day away and then slept.

He didn't leave his room.

In the evening he started thinking again.

— that she play an active part. — But she wasn't supposed to be just the physician alone who would diagnose his illness and cure him of it. She had a mission to accomplish with him. And there we have the result, the result. She was not his doctor. The patient infected the doctor.

He took Shakespeare's *Hamlet* from the shelf and started leafing through it.

Why did he want to strike me down? What have I ever done to him?

Their quarrel was between them.

He never liked me. I can remember how he wanted to hit me once when I was a small boy. I dodged him. He flew into a rage, ran after me; I locked myself in my room; he pounded on the door. Mother interfered. He surely would have beaten me up. Why? What have I ever done to him?

What could I have ever done to him? He hated me. I said it to his face another time when Mother had come between us. He shrugged his shoulders. He didn't know what to say, and he went away. He didn't dare to say it wasn't so. I'd taken the wind out of his sails. He couldn't deny it was true.

It says here: "Ghost: Ay, that incestuous, that adulterate beast, with witchcraft of his wit, with traitorous gifts,—o wicked wit and gifts, that have the power so to seduce!—won to his shameful lust the will of my most seeming-virtuous queen." My most seeming-virtuous queen—a good phrase. The beast made your "royal bed" into "a couch for luxury and damned incest."

He hung on to her. She didn't want him. But maybe she did want him, too. I came onto the scene. Then he hit me.

What does Mother want to tell me? What else can she tell me?

The next morning he reluctantly went up to her room. Just before he went, he gulped down another passage from *Hamlet:* "But to persevere in obstinate condolement is a course of impious stubbornness; 'tis unmanly grief; It shows a will most incorrect to heaven, a heart unfortified, a mind impatient, an understanding simple and unschool'd."

He would tell her that. Oh, if only I could put this chore off on somebody else.

He stood on the stair landing in front of the darkened picture of Pluto and Proserpina. Why, for heaven's sake, doesn't someone take that picture down? It's a good thing that it's getting darker all the time. People shouldn't make either pictures or statues. They use them to try to hold on to things that can't be held on to, shouldn't be held on to.

I swear that before I leave this house I'll tear that picture off the wall.

He was still holding on to the rounded banister post. I've thought of leaving this house. The thought just came to me. I want to leave, it seems.

Unhappily, reluctantly, anxiously (and now he knew: with fear), he looked down the hallway toward Alice's door.

If only I didn't have to do this. What's happened to me?

I've always gotten on so well with her. What is it I'm afraid is going to happen?

Her brows drawn together fiercely, her head propped up on her pillow in an attitude of challenge, Alice lay on her sofa, her arms raised and her hands behind her head. Her gray-blue eyes wide open and lively in their expression.

What is sin? Salome danced for the head of John. Sin? I see the deceiver who stole my life away from me. Under my pillow I have the letter he left me among his old papers, a short letter. I like this letter. It pleases me and picks up my spirits. It restores me, his letter:

"I was a fool. I hung on to you. I couldn't help myself. My old life, with which you are familiar, drove me to it. I clung to you like a leech. I sank my claws into you and wouldn't let go. But no more. Now I know you for what you are. Since Edward has been back. Now you can go. I'm sending you away. Edward, too. My house is closed to you."

That's Gordon. He didn't finish the letter. He has run off. That's good. Yes, he has seen me for what I am. I'm free now, for sin, for anything I like. I could even become a Hazel Crocker. I could turn up in his life as a second Hazel Crocker. I bless him for going. I would have preferred it if he had driven me out.

Your refined Alice, your society lady, exists no more. I'll take a broomstick and fly out the chimney like a witch.

Edward went out looking for the real Gordon Allison. I joined him on that hunt, but what I found on it (I laugh, I'm happy) was myself. Edward doesn't know that. Perhaps he's guessed it. He intuits so much. His illness has made him so perceptive. He's always fancied himself Hamlet, whose task it was to uncover a dreadful crime: "That incestuous, that adulterate beast won to his shameful lust the will of my most seeming-virtuous queen."

Oh, virtuous queen! Oh, my desire to be virtuous no more. No, I've put that behind me. Yes, we lived together incestuously, Gordon. I know that now, because we're brother and sister. I'm like you, and you (how could I save you) are like me.

Edward came in. She lay on the sofa, her hands behind her head, her eyes half-open. Her tongue played on her upper lip.

My mother—what manner of creature.

She was in a triumphant mood.

I wish I'd never come into this room.

On the carpet next to her couch was a pile of old newspapers. Edward recognized the yellowed paper instantly. The papers came from the pile he had pushed off the couch in the attic, the one he had gone to sleep on before witnessing everything between Gordon and Alice and learning about himself as well.

His mother pointed at the papers.

"The reports about Hazel Crocker's trials are in them, and some commentaries reporters wrote about her death. Some of them wrote that she had always eluded the law but that justice had finally caught up with her in the end. Justice! She got what she wanted. When the trial was over, Gordon went off traveling. Her death left him no peace. He said to me once he felt as if he had been murdered himself. He traveled, changed his name, and then his rise in society began. He didn't cut off his connections to the underworld. I met this Estelle woman, who had murdered her rival, Hazel, ten years later when she was released from prison. She had not known that Gordon Allison had married in the meantime. He had made no mention of it in his letters to her.

"So she turned up at our house once. You children had both been born. An incredible situation—the underworld makes its appearance in untrammeled everyday life. The ex-convict wanted to visit her old friend. And what did she find? A heavyset, dignified gentleman living in an elegant house. She apologized. How embarrassing it was. I left them alone. He soon called me. I understood. We drew a curtain on the past. We shoved it off onto another stage. He left it up to me to give her the help she needed."

As she related these memories, expressions of pleasure played over her face. Edward looked down at the floor, ashamed.

I'm not in the room. She doesn't know I'm here.

An old woman was standing on the steps. It was in Paris, the sun beating down on the stone steps of Montmartre leading up to Sacré-Coeur. The heat was oppressive. There were not many people going up the steps. I'll stand there after the war, my son, and wait for you. She could go to the railroad stations. A lot was happening at the stations. And the officials sit in their offices. Office hours are posted on the doors. There is hope that news will come later.

What point is there in taking up that post, day after day, for months at a time? What is it she thinks will happen?

But what can ever separate a mother from her child? They are one. And no more than your heart can fall out of your chest can a child be torn away from its mother.

And when the cease-fire came and the long war was over, lots of people started picking up their lives again. Some decided to raise flags and celebrate first; others wanted to get right at repairing their houses. Some came back from abroad, looked over the damage, climbed around and cursed. But there were many, too, who were searching.

Alice, on the couch, continued.

"Franklin Glenn Washtrook. His name was never mentioned in this house. But wherever I am his name is, too. This man, deported for life, has been rehabilitated now. This man, ostracized and exiled, is coming home. Alien rule has been broken. I can set out my flags. I did not do right by him. I disgraced myself, but I have fought my way clear now.

"I can't tell you much about Glenn. It's easy to say a lot about suffering and misfortune, not so easy to talk about happiness. We were for each other what people should be. We were friends, comrades, lovers. I loved him from the moment I saw him, as he did me. We were born for each other. When I saw him I swore we would never be parted. I knew I had reached my life's goal. We lived innocently together. Neither he nor I was conscious of sin. We saw ourselves in the old love stories we read. But none of those stories were as sweet, as heavenly, as the one we were living.

"Once I knew Glenn the world acquired meaning for me. I met him on that trip to India with my brother. I traveled with him, and we searched out new landscapes. We carried our love to snow and ice, to seacoasts drenched in sunlight, to broad gravel beaches—why? To see ourselves reflected there and to find a change? No, to find and know ourselves, for that is what fog and storm and snow and the heat of summer taught us.

"When I was alone, apart from him, when he was alone, apart from me, then we sighed and felt weak. 'Paradise lost, where will we ever find it again?' we complained. Then we called out to each other and rushed back together. The archangel at the portal made room for us.

We took each other's hands, we fell into each other's arms, guiltless, ecstatic.

"I did not give him up after I had fallen into the hands of the other one. I could not tear myself away from the other one. He had me and he held on to me. But he couldn't keep Glenn from existing or keep me from him.

"I had clothes he had given me. He brought them to me from his trips. He traveled to India and the Far East. The last place you were heading was the Far East, Edward. When you left I had the sense that you felt something and had to follow where it led you. You were drawn to follow on his path. He brought me dresses from the Orient, from China. I wore them. Gordon could not prevent my wearing them, except by tearing them up. What I wore, what I felt on my body for a long time, he had selected piece by piece. I may not have been in his house and with him, but I was still surrounded by him. And so I gave him everything I had and was.

"That blue dress was the last he gave me. You saw Glenn, too, on our vacations at the shore."

— The sea was smooth. We were making good progress. If they'll only leave us in peace. The sea, oh, I can't stand the sea: the glitter of it. I feel sick. We're going to Asia, Jonny. We're leaving wretched old Europe behind. It's agreed. Do you swear it? I'll swear it to you. We'll stick together. We'll stay in Hong Kong or Shanghai, or we'll go to Mandalay. Do you swear? Under the table, his uniform. He was supposed to stay below. I'm lost. You've left me alone, Jonny. Don't leave me alone. Where will I go? —

Alice: "You can be hungry, but after a while you forget your hunger and get over it. That's what I did. It wasn't hunger I was feeling anymore but a deficiency. It gnawed at me. Something was tormenting me. I felt this great longing."

— Why is she talking to me this way? She's unburdening herself. The time when people talked to me to entertain me is over. They don't want to distract me anymore. She feels free. I've helped her reach this point. But is this what I wanted? I wanted truth, honesty. They've misused me. I went to war for a cause I was unaware of. — I wish I had never entered this room.

And this is a defeated country. The Cathedral of Naumburg. She has been standing for such a long time. Now she is sitting on a bench, her scarf tied on her head. Why is she sitting here, the mother? Who will lure them home? Who will bring them back? They will not return. They were all taken to Russia, to France, to Italy. They will not return. They will stay where they are. Lucky them. They were captured, beaten to death, drowned. They were taken to Africa. They were left lying in the sand, dead of thirst. They have stayed. Lucky them. But why were they sent off to such wars? Whose idea was it? Can you tell me? Perhaps they went of their own accord. They'd had their fill of all of you here. Reverend, you stood up there and preached war to us. You're responsible, too. Get out of here. That's one way to deal with me. And what does the mother do? She knocks on the door. Let her knock. I'll hold my hands over my ears. She stands at the church door and starts banging on it with her fists. And cries and sobs. I hold my ears shut. That's what Dr. Martin Luther did. He nailed his theses on the door, one, two, three, four. Let them hear. Those whom it concerns should hear. She pounds on the door with her hands. She kicks at it with her feet.

She screams for her son. She protests. She cries for justice, for truth. —

"I'm not trying to justify myself in your eyes, Edward. But I want you to see everything, know everything. Without you I never would have come this far. I knew you would help me. Without you I would not have been saved. Yes, now everything is all right."

She said loudly, toward the ceiling, "Glenn," and once more loudly. She was letting go. The brakes were giving way. It was the first time in decades that she had spoken freely. She felt better than she ever had in her life. To say openly to another human being what she had endured and enjoyed. Living with Glenn, in those days, was heaven, but there had been a curse on it. Now, before all the world, she felt her love again and was proud of it.

It swept over her like a flood.

Saint Anthony drove me away from him and into my cave. But I didn't want to go into it. I won't go in. I can't go in. Please stay with me. — Get away from me, temptress! — I'm no temptress. I'm a human being. You should become one, too. You should know what a human being is. You should lead a reasonable life, not the kind I had to lead. Come, see me dance.

I'm Salome, and I'm Herodias, too, that lecherous woman sitting next to the king on the throne, drinking with him, and kissing him in front of everybody. That's who I am. I won't deny it anymore. I'm free. I've won my right to that; I've earned it over these long years. There's no greater thing in the world than freedom, say what you will. That's how God created us, and that's how we ought to be. How else do you explain the happiness that comes over us when freedom opens up before us? — Oh, don't torment yourself, Glenn. Why all this human pain? God is not evil. He has not put us in a prison but on his earth, under the sun and benevolent moon, under the sky and the happy stars, among the gentle plants and animals, and no one torments and tortures us—only man himself does that, because he does not feel free and so he strikes out around him and is condemned to violence.

I embrace freedom. It is sin. I embrace sin. I pray to the great power of sin.

There is Edward. He is my son. I called him back from the war so that he would help me and hear me. He is my brother. How glad I am that I bore him, Edward, my son, my brother, the troubadour, yes, the young, innocent troubadour with his cockle-hat, his staff and sandals— and so he went across the fierce sea to the princess who awaited him. But with me he will regain his health. He has already. I am leading him down from his ship to my castle.

Edward did not move. Where guilt is, there the axe should fall.

— Glenn, you have waited for me. You will see me. My intoxicated head, my blossoming, bleeding mouth. My tongue is dry, like that of a panting hound. My teeth hurt. I am turning myself loose. I care nothing for the houses with or without people in them. They run around me; they cannot catch me. The houses sob for me and beg and mourn for me. I lived with them for a while. I can't any longer.

And if you cannot forgive me, then fall upon me and beat me to death. King Herod's shields upon Salome's head.

A lure was thrown to me. I bit on it. It hurts me. It tugs and tugs. Is that sin?

Sin—it blossoms and showers fruits down upon me. Precious, opulent sin, a queen that has been represented as a slave. See who she really is. She pours her fruits out on the grass. All I need do is collect them, gather them in a basket for myself, so many. I'll never go hungry again. And the yellow moon rises and gradually turns white. What a blinding light. You night of magic. Its glow falls on my face. My temples pound. My shattered heart, my heart now whole again. Leopard skin on my shoulders. Salome dances. The houses, sobbing, dance with me.

Alice squinted over at him through half-closed eyelids, saw him sitting there.

— I still haven't shown him that other picture, the one next to Proserpina in the hall. It belongs together with the rape, is the true sequel to it, for she does not sit on the throne afterwards with a pomegranate in her hand.

The bacchanal. The crazed men and women.

The heavy, voluptuous women, their flesh rounded like grapes about to burst, the bulging breasts and bellies and thighs.

And children and goat-legged fauns and satyrs. And out of the trees leap the tender nymphs that have hidden there, some of them shyly, others boldly.

And there are panthers and lions in the procession. Even snakes wriggle out of the brush and crawl along with it, their sly black eyes glistening in their raised heads. The snakes have crept onto the dancers' thyrsi and let themselves be carried along, happy as children. They wind themselves around the tips of the staffs, proud as victors, as if this celebration were in their honor, the snakes, yes, the notorious snake. And why not? It leads the procession, hissing and rattling while the people laugh and sing and play the pipes and the bells ring.

Dionysus, the savior, is out front. The whole world, the fields, the forests, all are his. The waters of the lake rush toward him and after him. Into the dark, sacred grove the procession goes, to life, to death, who knows, and who cares?

I'll show the picture to Edward. It has grown dim with time.

— I have to help Mother. Now I am the healthy one. Why can't she let the past be? Now she is the way I was. The game is reversed. She is under a magic spell. I can see that. I have to help her. She has lost all control. I'm afraid I'll become sick again myself.

"Mother, I'm very grateful to you. You have helped me. Now think of yourself."

She smiled at him. "But I am, Edward. That's exactly what I'm doing. For the first time in many, many years. You are free and calm now, and so am I. I am not complaining anymore, not anymore. And you were my helper, Edward. Heaven sent you to me."

It's a kind of madness. How can I save her?

"Here, look at my hand. I've taken off my wedding ring."

"I don't want to see, Mother."

She is mad. I don't recognize her.

"I put it in his desk, in Gordon Allison's desk, right next to his ring. He left his behind for me."

"You're both mad, both of you."

"I've struck the wild boar down." Her face glowed fiercely. "Now the criminal has taken flight. He is wandering about somewhere. We have driven him off. Fate will catch up with him. There is justice. If I had a church, I would set all the bells ringing."

"Mother, I can't bear hearing you speak of Father this way."

"Of whom?"

"Of Father."

She stood up and came over to him. She laughed into his face and raised her arms (a chill ran down his spine).

"Your father! Gordon Allison, your father! Edward, you didn't know how truly you spoke when you compared yourself with Hamlet. My brother told me about it. But I kept him from telling the story of Hamlet, of the old and the new king and of the queen. It was too early then. But now you can know. You can celebrate with me. We have succeeded in our revenge."

He stammered: "What is this, Mother? For God's sake, what are you talking about? I can't understand anything you're saying."

"You have avenged me and your father, your real father. You don't know your father. Gordon Allison didn't poison him, but he had to wander around as a ghost, a ghost among the living, like me. He did not appear to you as a ghost. But he urged you on and called to you, just as he did to me. Perhaps he really is dead, and his ghost really was calling you and driving you on."

"If you lie to me, Mother, I'm going to scream for help."

"I don't want to hurt you, Edward, my dear son. We're celebrating. This is our great moment."

He was trembling. He sat there with his fists clenched.

"What about Father, Mother? Answer me! And don't tell me any fairy tales. I want a clear, straightforward answer."

"Gordon Allison is not your father. Sit still. I beg you, sit still. So you'll at least know everything there is to know. Why did he hate you? Why did I have to protect you from him? He wanted to strangle you. He would have knocked you down. Why? Because he knew and because I never denied that you aren't his son. No, you aren't. Kathleen is his daughter, but you are not his son. That is one triumph I've managed to win for myself in this marriage. I had you—by Glenn. That's why I took you to the shore when I met him. So we could both enjoy you, your real father and I."

"He is not my father?"

"Why does that shock you? You ought to be as glad as I am. This is a gift I'm bringing you. — Or isn't it a gift? Aren't you devoted to me anymore? Couldn't you see how I was suffering? Do you understand now how fate ordered things, kindly, mercifully for you and me? That he hated you and that you came here? The ghost drove you, and you couldn't give any peace and had to stir everything up and see what was there—and free yourself and me at the same time."

Edward trembled. He hung on to his chair.

"I didn't want this, Mother. I didn't know that. Don't touch me. No, don't touch me." (Whore, adulterate beast, the royal bed of Denmark a couch for luxury and damned incest!)

He turned to face her. She drew back from his distorted face (will it come over him again; his gaze is so horrible). "Edward, listen to me. Stay here. Don't leave this way."

The terrible expression of hate was on his face.

He bared his teeth—at her.

She screamed. He wanted to go but couldn't. Finally his artificial knee bent.

He stamped out, slamming the door behind him.

She stared at the door. She listened to the sounds coming up through the house. His pounding footsteps faded away. She didn't dare follow him. She sat down on her bed and pulled a scrap of blue cloth from under the pillow.

She trembled. She kissed it. Her fingers were icy cold. "Glenn."

She soaked the blue cloth with her tears.

Alice Leaves

SHE did not get a chance to show Edward the picture of the Dionysian procession. When she finally went downstairs to see him in the course of the day, his door was locked. She heard him crying softly, but he did not respond to her knock.

Noises in the house woke her early in the morning. But, having once noticed them, she dozed off again.

And later in the morning when she rang, the old housekeeper came to her bedside to report, with no little trepidation, that Mr. Edward's room was empty. He was gone. The gardener had come and told her that Edward had waked him early in the morning, saying he had to leave immediately. They drove to the station, Mr. Edward with two suitcases. He had taken the first train to London.

The little woman stood nervously by the bed. Alice said, "Well." Then: "Thank you."

The servants reported the news to Professor James Mackenzie, Alice's brother. Receiving the message in his room, he immediately left it to go find Alice. But he stopped on the stairs and crept back to his room. What did he have to say? He had warned them. Now things had come to this pass. He was thoroughly shaken, more so with each passing minute. He sat down but could not calm himself. He reached for his papers.

He read: "When a traveler returns home from a long journey to distant lands, his friends and relatives welcome him. Similarly, when a man who has lived a just life travels from this world to the next, his own good deeds receive him there just as friends receive a beloved friend on his return home."

So they had accomplished what they had set out to do, she and Edward. It had kicked back at Edward. It would come down on her, too. The world chews with slow, iron jaws.

He read: "Blessed the detachment of the enlightened man who knows the lesson and has learned to see. Blessed the freedom from desire. Blessed the state of being without passion in the world. Blessed the overcoming of sensual desire, the mastering of pride."

They wanted to know. Do they know now? What do they know? They run into the woods to look for herbs. They look and look and rip things out by the roots and eat them and poison themselves.

He read: "But there is a not-having-been-born, a not-having-become, a not-having-been-created. If that did not exist, then we could find no way out of having-been-born, having-become, having-been-created. There is a realm where there is neither earth nor water, neither fire nor light, neither this world nor any world, neither sun nor moon. This I call neither coming nor staying nor dying nor being reborn. It is without supports, without development, without things. — It is the end of suffering."

How could he have left without my noticing it. I must have been sleeping soundly. The gardener helped him. He shouldn't have let him go. He ought to have known what condition Edward is in. No, he couldn't know. Where do you suppose he's wandering about?

He read: "The state of illumination. The state of unity. Each of us is identical with universal life. Each of us lives face to face with holiness. Each of us receives the overflowing mercy of holiness. Life is not a sea of illness, birth, old age, death.

"Life is not a vale of tears but a land of bliss. In it my spirit is fully turned around, transformed, free of envy and hate, anger, ambition; it is no longer overpowered by grief and despair."

That's what I am myself, "overpowered by grief and despair." I couldn't prevent it from happening. I didn't prevent it. And how could I? What use can I be to them? I can't calm myself.

He got up to go and see Alice. He felt like a peddler about to offer some second-rate wares.

Alice was standing at the mirror opposite the door when he came in. She put down her powder puff and gave her brother a nod and small smile in the mirror. She reached for her lipstick. She was carefully dressed, her hair carefully combed. Her thick, graying hair had a wave in it and covered the tops of her ears. Her slender face was firm and unwrinkled. She opened her mouth and ran the lipstick over her lower lip. When she had painted in the corners, she called out to him, "Sit down, James. It's good of you to have come. How are things with you?"

As she worked with the lipstick, she turned her head to the right and the left, raised and lowered it, and cast occasional glances at him, which he picked up.

She was wearing the same light green summer dress she had worn when she had gone to the sanitarium with Kathleen. Edward had come back from overseas. She was going to visit him for the first time. He had not been taken away from her; he was alive; she had been expecting him; the time was ripe; he was alive; her savior was coming. The wide straw hat lay on the stool next to her.

He sat there, surprised, uncertain. She repeated her warm greeting. "A nice idea to pay me a visit, James. You've no doubt been working since early morning. Did anyone bring you your tea?"

He was no longer thinking of offering his poor wares. He asked if she needed his help.

"Oh," she said, "that's not a bad idea. But I don't know to what extent I can rely on you."

He bowed in his chair: "There are no limits, Alice."

She gave a short laugh. "I won't overburden you. Just a brief errand. I haven't seen the gardener recently, and I've neglected to go look for him. Perhaps he's ill."

"I'll be glad to go check, Alice."

"If he isn't sick, ask him to get the carriage ready for me. And I'd like his wife to come over and help me pack some suitcases." She took her two white, elbow-length gloves from her dressing table and ran them through one hand.

I was wearing these gloves when I looked through the little window into his room. The nurse was standing next to me. He looked awful. He turned his face toward me, the fear, the unutterable fear. His rage, despair, gnashing of teeth. He covered his face with his arms. He bared his teeth.

She sat down on the bench in front of the mirror. I protected him, and he has left me. I saved him, and he condemns me.

She felt tears coming. She leaned her head back. Her face was freshly powdered.

James: "You're going to look for Edward?"

"What a silly idea."

Strange, what other people think. That never would have occurred to me.

"What are you going to do, Alice?"

She's still pushing. How she torments herself. She wants to rush away into some new disaster.

"My dear, wise brother is worried about me. I'm most grateful to him. You'll no doubt tell me I have to face up to the consequences of what I've done. That's just what I'm doing. Now will you go find the gardener and give him my message about the carriage, and tell his wife to come up and help me?"

He stood up. Awful, to see fate running its course and not be able to intervene. Reason is of no use. Perhaps one would have to speak with angels' tongues. I don't have any.

"You're unable to make up your mind, James? I'll go myself."

"Oh, stop it, Alice. I'm going."

I'm abetting her in her madness.

She's having the same experience that everyone does: The ceaselessly raging sea of illness, age, and death keeps rocking her little boat until the boat finally tips over.

They ate lunch together. The gardener had already taken her luggage to the station.

Alice walked through her room with her hat and coat on, brushing dust off her. She had been up to the attic again, had touched first one object, then another, and had sat on the couch where Edward had been sleeping during the final battle between Gordon and her. It was a good battle for Edward. It cut the Gordian knot for him, and then she had wanted to tell the story to its end, and it turned out that he did not understand at all, that she was his mother but he was not her son, not her friend and helper. He hadn't understood anything. She meant nothing to him. He cursed her.

Don't cry, Alice. You've waited all your life for this moment. For this moment, yes, for this moment. Do I deserve this hatred? Why have I been cursed? Why is fate doing this to me?

The gardener came back from the railroad station. Madame would do well to postpone her trip to London. She could not get a connection to London today. Something had gone wrong somewhere on the line.

Tomorrow then. One more day here. Something wants to tie me down so that I'll register clearly what's happening to me.

She returned to her room.

You're alone, poor, dumb, little Alice. You were dreaming. You had the wrong ideas about people. No one values what you have given him. They take it for granted. No one thinks as you do. No one pities you and stands by you. They abandon you as if you were some beast.

James surely thinks I'm the beast now, the wild boar from his *King*

Lear. Oh, what a pathetic boar I am, a little mouse looking for a hole, a mouse in a trap.

In the course of the day Alice opened her door a dozen times, stepped out into the hall, and listened to what sounds the empty house had to offer. Who might come? Who? She heard James's footsteps, heard someone working in the kitchen. She might as well let the help go. I could close the house up.

Late in the afternoon she took a chair out into the hall and took the two old pictures off the wall, the rape of Proserpina by Rembrandt and the bacchanal.

She took the two pictures, one after the other, into her room, leaned them against two chairs so that the light fell on them, and looked at them from the sofa, closely and for a long time.

Then she walked around them. She had finally made them prisoner. They had done enough damage, for years and years. She took a pair of large scissors from her closet and stabbed them furiously into the two pictures. She stabbed again and again, and when she was done she tore the shreds of canvas out of the frames and crumpled them together. She took the wads of canvas up to the attic and stuffed them into a box between the packing straw and the cover. She went back to her room for the frames and smashed them to pieces in the attic. The splintered wood went into the box, too, and she closed the lid on it. May you rest there till Judgment Day.

She could not sleep. She cried all night and wandered around. She blamed herself and others and despaired. She felt nauseous.

She sat at her desk, exhausted, the next morning, her picture of Saint Theodora before her. You will not abandon me. You led me onto this path. I called on you when they brought Edward home, called on you. You didn't warn me. Oh, it doesn't matter.

And then she was suddenly so weak, so weak that she lay her head on the desk and slept soundly for an hour. And afterwards she felt sick at her stomach again. She gagged. She thought: It must be because I haven't been eating. And she decided to go down to the kitchen. The maid asked, as she served her, if she shouldn't call a doctor, for Alice was deathly pale and unsteady on her feet. She sat at the kitchen table a while after eating a few bites. Then she wanted to go back upstairs, but she was so weak and unsteady that she had to lean on the maid's arm.

When she was stretched out on her sofa again, she felt calm and care-free (the wind had changed). Now everything has fallen away. Alice, Little Alice, has no more worries. Alice, Little Alice, has gone for a walk. Where has she gone? She's rolling a hoop. She's at her lessons. She has to learn things. We should let her play in the sun

The nausea increased, and as she thought about it, she had a sudden realization. She ran from the room; the nausea overcame her; she vomited. An old memory had come back to her.

Something from the distant past, when she was still at home. It was her Greek teacher, who gave her private lessons. They talked a lot together; he liked her; she was unsuspecting; they kissed; he made sexual overtures to her. No one ever knew, but Miss Virginia had her suspicions, and the tutor was fired. Then Alice was sent to the country because of her anemia and nausea.

I remember that if that young teacher had stayed with me any longer I would have killed myself. I couldn't stay away from him and felt nothing but disgust for myself.

Why did I remember this? I'm like Edward. There's something buried in me. It lies farther back than the story with Glenn and the shore.

What are you thinking about, Alice?

You've been waiting for this moment your whole life. You're free. This moment.

A wave of pain flooded through her chest. It became intolerable.

And as she moved to try to shake off the pain, bending over her dresser, the pain burst like a cloud; and something frightening mixed with the pain, something she had felt coming for a long time, and split her from head to toe, from the tip of her tongue to her inner depths— lust, raging lust, an ineffably, intolerably sweet feeling.

It flowed through her like a command. For the moment, she was its servant, prostrate before it, begging for mercy.

And as she felt herself physically possessed by that power and as she bent her knee and knelt down on the carpet in front of the dresser (dragons coil their long, scaly bodies; Saint George swings his lance down from his foaming mount; and strange, brightly colored birds flutter up into the air), her white mouth opened in a moan, but into her open, hungering mouth, into her throat, into her open breast raced the triumphant image of Salome.

Salome threw herself upon her. Let me ge! Gordon ruined, degraded me completely, the barbarian. — Salome invaded her, disemboweled her. Salome made a shadow of her, her arms and legs raised like a doll's, her limbs screwed together.

And so Alice was caught up in the dance and let herself be caught up and taken away. Sweetness encircled her, embraced her, seized her breast and neck, her back and limbs, like a long, soft cat.

Alice stood up and stretched when the soft, hot cat left her. She took a few steps and tumbled onto the couch with her legs drawn up.

An hour later she was cool and certain of herself. Everything is clear, she thought.

Time to leave. She wandered through her room. Alice Allison lived here for a long, long time. Alice Allison lay here and dreamed. Alice Allison waited here for many years.

She isn't here anymore. She had fled without saying good-bye.

She looked at the case with the religious symbols in it. She stared at it from a distance. She felt nothing. They have abandoned me. Abandoned me and betrayed me. They have turned away from me.

I hate you all. All of you.

She picked up her small parasol and her handbag.

She turned at the door and looked back into the room: a monster with its mouth open, its teeth bared. And now that everything was clear to her and there was nothing more to grieve about, she opened the door.

She looked down at her brown shoes and her feet in them. At the threshold she was stepping over, she set one foot on one side, one on the other side. Her body swayed over. There is nothing more to feel here.

She tripped over a fold in the carpet. She lay on the floor for half a minute, not moving. Then she pushed herself up, brushed herself off, and reached for her parasol and handbag. Somebody tripped me up. Nobody should get the bright idea of coming after me.

James was standing at the foot of the stairs.

"Come on," she said, taking his arm.

He looked at her. "Did you fall? I heard a noise."

"I stumbled. The carpet's coming up."

"The house will go to the dogs even more when you're gone."

"Oh?" she said, and gave him an empty smile. She apparently hadn't understood him.

They waited on the platform for the train. Her face was expressionless, and she made inconsequential talk. Uneasy and depressed, he stood next to her. She said good-bye to him in a calm and friendly tone. She boarded the train.

The train rolled out of the station. The tracks flashed in the sunlight; the black coaches thundered along them. The two bright metallic lines converged behind the train and eventually came together.

*   *   *

James stayed on in the empty house, wandered through the halls, and climbed up the stairs.

He went to the attic. This is where "the truth" had done its work. It had made short shrift of things. Something had needed to be cleared up.

Now it's done and over. Now we've got it, the truth.

He sat alone under a tree in the garden.

To look at a tree, to leave the ego behind—they can't do it.

I can't either.

No, I can't do it either.

I don't want to.

He looked at the mute house, the closed shutters.

He felt something contract inside him.

From whence can help come?

Gordon's Confession

IN a room at the house of old Ken Farley, his friend and first publisher, Gordon Allison sat heavily in a spacious wing chair, his head leaning back into the left-hand corner as far as the bulging fat of his short neck permitted. His legs set wide apart, he was talking to the small, agile man with yellowing, wrinkled skin who strode about the room with his hands in his pockets and laughed his crowing laugh now and then.

Gordon was relating details from his and Alice's past. He had come to that. His visit had proved no easy task for Ken and his warm, shrewd wife. In his first weeks with them, Gordon had not wanted to talk. He behaved like a madman, sat rigidly for hours at a time staring into space, groaned a lot, avoided people, rejected everyone's overtures, called himself a plague. Fearing he might harm himself, Ken had hired a nurse to stay by him.

He had turned up at Farley's house one evening in a sad state of array, filthy, without a suitcase, looking like a tramp. The butler did not want to let him in. And in addition to looking like a tramp, the man at the door was drunk. Farley was familiar with escapades like this from Gordon's past. But that all lay many years back. The next day at noon, Gordon had asked that absolutely no one be told of his presence in Farley's house. And then he sank into his disturbed state.

Inquiries at Gordon's house revealed that apart from the gardener, the only person still there was Professor James Mackenzie, Mrs. Allison's brother. The rumor was that disagreements having to do with the son, Edward, had split the family and driven them all out of the house.

Now Gordon was at the point where he could talk. The fat, heavy clump of flesh he was emanated a totally different spirit. Ken, clever and interested as he was, drew him out. Gordon started to speak, to threaten, to complain, and, finally, to boast. And with that, it was clear that his crisis was over. He began, in his old style, to wax epic and tell about himself. The publisher regretted that he could not take short-hand. The yarn was fascinating and in part, of course, improbable. Gordon was obviously embellishing his tale as he always did.

He drew a portrait of Alice Mackenzie.

She was (as he saw her, in the past) a figure of total fantasy, the opposite of a real, natural creature. A common denominator that would explain her behavior at different times simply could not be found. She was something like a cloud with the sun shining on it. It swims across the sky, dissolves, takes on new forms. Anyone interested in making fresh discoveries got his money's worth and more with Alice.

"She was a constant surprise to me. All my knowledge of nature and human beings failed me. The Bible speaks of angels that came down to earth (excuse me if I'm getting this a bit wrong) and mated with the daughters of men, and from this union came the powerful, the tyrants, of earth. Alice is descended from that race. Take my word for it. I have an eye for things like that. I'd run into strange people before, border-line cases, people who live on the fringes of society, people society can't cope with. As you know, I was a student of criminology, a reporter—I even wrote for your paper. You probably can't recall those cases any-more, ones from my earlier years. But what I saw then was nothing compared with the mixture I encountered in the Mackenzies' solid, re-spectable, upper middle-class household. And Alice was a particularly perfect representative of her class: rigorous, elegant, gracious, proper. I soon realized that she was afraid of herself. She was ashamed of her nature, her origins, her membership in that half-human, half-divine race, so she exaggerated, emphasized, the borderlines so that no one would guess her secret. But she betrayed it to me despite herself."

He laughed. "How afraid of me she was—but couldn't resist me either. What a wonderful, exciting time that was. How grateful I am to her for it and to the great being who dreams the world, for I was cut from the same stuff as she, in part anyhow. But she was perfection.

"Can you believe that her family sometimes forced this creature to recite lines from Milton? She could do it. She was amazingly talented, but what idiocy to have her recite someone else's version of what she in fact was. All she had to do was open her mouth to ask for the time or to offer you a cigarette and she outdid Milton."

Gordon licked his lips with satisfaction.

"It's quite an experience to encounter a creature like that. How afraid I was of her at first—I can still remember it. It was a great inspiration on my part to decide I had to have her. It surpassed all my other poetic ideas, both before and after. It was a—"

He searched for the word. Ken encouraged him: "What was it?"

Gordon (a shadow flitted across his face): "A challenge. An incredible one, young as I was. But it seems I was clear about myself early on in life."

The publisher sat with his dreaming guest and poured him another glass of liqueur. He was pleased to see Gordon dreaming out loud. Things were falling into place.

"She was a divine but difficult creature?"

Gordon laughed.

"She couldn't put up with anyone for long. Special rules applied at her court of love, and it was she who wrote the rules. Ha, ha—she put many a man through his paces. I can think of a dozen men in high places right now for whom she remains the one great experience of their lives. I was no troubadour like the rest. When I turned up, the game was over, the masquerading, the accepting, the rejecting, the worshiping, the emoting, all that was over. A new chapter began when I came on the scene, and she saw that immediately. She wanted it and didn't want it either. A battle began in her, and it never stopped. It's no wonder. Why are you shaking your head?"

"Then you should be glad—however painful this may be and however long it has dragged itself out—that it's finally over. After all, you're still young, and somebody who still has a future and should look out for himself. The last thing you need is a marriage out of a Strindberg play."

Gordon made a sweeping gesture with his right arm.

"You're missing my point. You still haven't understood what I'm saying. I haven't expressed myself clearly."

He let his arm drop on the table so heavily that the glasses rattled.

"You have to understand what I'm saying when I talk about battle. You forget who she was, who she is, a being of another order."

"Oh, come on, Gordon."

"Of another order. You have to accept that on faith. I was the only one to see it. I saw her for who she was. Without me she would have consumed herself. With me she found her proper place, and I saved her. I tore her out of her isolation. That was possible only for me. Only someone with a special kind of vision and someone a bit like her could do it. She resisted. As I said, she was afraid of herself. She knew what was at stake. It's true, of course, that she had something sunny, gay, childlike about her—she had practiced that role, had convinced herself that she was the delicate Proserpina, the daughter of Demeter, and that I was the malevolent Pluto. That's why I bought that picture of Rembrandt's. You know the one, that wonderful painting where Pluto in his chariot makes off with the little tigress Proserpina. She had leapt on his chest and is scratching his face. Marvelous, the expression on his features. What could she do against him? But it was different with us. She came to me. She flew to me.

"I lured her out and drove her out. I smoked the vixen out of her den. And of course she bit back. I had my hands full, Ken. If you only knew how much of my energy this woman, this female of all females, has absorbed. You weren't aware of that. And no wonder. It was between her and me, and it was such a personal business that we couldn't let anyone else in on it. Neither she nor I could; neither of us turned to a third party. There was no flight from this battle, no breaking it off. Neither of us would have gained anything from that. All that you noticed, Ken—and I remember your remarking on it—was that I gave up traveling and changed jobs, as it were, switching over from journalism and travel reporting to books, novels, short stories."

"And only then did you start to become what you are now."

"So now you know to whom I owe that and who my muse is. I couldn't travel anymore. I was indispensable at home. My friends and acquaintances began to make fun of me, saying I'd gone in for a cottage industry. It was a more dangerous business than sailing the high seas. I was so absorbed with her and myself from that time on that I stopped traveling. But I was actually making more dangerous journeys than I had before. I traveled incessantly—in circles around her—and I had to lay the tracks myself, in my imagination, in the realm of so-called fantasy, which still remains more real (I'll never stop saying it and preaching it) than the supposedly sole reality our senses reveal to us."

Ken agreed. "I know. But fortunately you have not become a fantast in the process."

"But my dear friend, my good friend Ken, fantasts have no fantasy. To have fantasy, to have imagination means to experience reality whole.

"She could sit in front of me or walk next to me and turn her head to me or clasp her hands over her knee or run both hands up the back of her neck, tossing her brown hair, her masses of hair, upward. To free myself from the excitement those gestures evoked in me, to translate that into words, I had to write for days on end, day after day. It was enough to fill whole chapters. I never exhausted that material."

*   *   *

Ken understood what his job was here. He let Gordon talk. Gordon was clearly trying to buck himself up and defend himself, to justify himself. He kept inventing one new tall tale after another, spreading them out in front of him to hide behind, using them to help him cope with what had happened. He once came up with the statement: "Alice was the sun; I, the planet." It sounded pitiful, plaintive. He so much wanted his listener to believe it.

"Oh," he sighed once and hummed a song (it was Schumann's "Mich hat das unglückselige Weib vergiftet, mit ihren Tränen"). "Yes, I've been poisoned. Who will make me healthy again? Where can I find an antidote?"

Again restlessness and trembling seized him. He threatened harm to Alice and shifted to a new theme (but not a word did he say about the horrible scene in the attic; he did not mention Edward; he did not say that it was he who had run away): He spoke about human loneliness; individualism and the ego were nothing but delusions. He praised Alice.

"I often sat near her and stared at her and had to struggle with myself not to fall down on my knees in front of her. I couldn't believe that it had been granted to me to meet such a—well, as you put it—such a 'divine' creature."

"It's true, Gordon. People were saying then that you were fatally in love with her."

Gordon raised his hand in a conspiratorial gesture.

"She was a sign for me. Has a sign like that ever been given to you? It comes to some people only once. To others it comes more often, with varying degrees of strength and clarity. There are philosophers and pessimists who have made whole theories out of the human being's supposed isolation. But every sunbeam would be more justified in feeling lonesome than we. I have no illusions in this respect: I've never yet struck on anything I could call my ego. People have called me Lord Crenshaw. We are all Lord Crenshaws. We all carry multitudes inside us, a whole menagerie; and from time to time we stick the label of 'self' first onto this animal, then onto a different animal or shape, and let it stand for and represent the whole. We have within us—no, we are—a whole people, with a bourgeoisie and a proletariat, with a nobility and parliamentary chambers, with a house of representatives, with a king. With revolutions, too, many revolutions, depending on our age.

"And then there is eros, a chapter for itself. As long as Alice was with me I always came back to the same thought.

"We all have in us the inclination described in the passage from Genesis that says, 'It is not good that the man should be alone; I will make him an help meet for him.' And it goes on to say how God made every beast of the field and every fowl of the air and brought them to Adam. And whatever Adam called each creature, that would be its name. And Adam gave names to all the beasts of the field, all cattle, and all fowl of the air. But for Adam there was no helpmeet. Then comes the passage that tells how God caused a deep sleep to come over Adam and how he took a rib from him, from his own body, and the Lord God made a woman of the rib he had taken from Adam, and he brought her to Adam, and Adam said, 'This is now bone of my bones, and flesh of my flesh; she shall be called Woman, because she was taken out of Man.' And the story closes with the sentence: 'Therefore shall a man leave his father and his mother, and shall cleave unto his wife; and they shall be one flesh.'

"Those are profound words, my old friend Ken, deep as a well they are. You have to admit it. Man does not find himself in the animals, in nature. Nature takes its names from us. It has to come before us. That was the Creator's will. But in woman man sees himself; she is meant for him; he accepts her and gives her his own name.

"That is eros: man and woman, made of one flesh, made for each other from the beginning, yearn to come together. That brings happiness, bliss. Every generation learns that and celebrates it. Now it's certainly true that there are many of us humans, many men and many women, and how can anybody find his particular flesh and bone in that confusion? But that isn't how the Bible story is meant. We mustn't read it too literally. Every human being yearns to become a single, a whole Adam. And that's why I sing this woman's praises and remain her troubadour and call her the only one for me, the highest there is."

"As you know I've always held Alice in the highest esteem. And how I feel about you I needn't say. Both of you would get along fine with any number of people. I mean you could fit in with this person or that one without difficulty. It was chance that brought you together. Just look at nature—"

Gordon interrupted him. "Nature is just where I won't look. If I look at nature I see nothing of myself." He struck his thighs and screamed angrily, "Leave me alone with your nature. I have nothing to do with nature, no more than anyone else. I've shown that I don't have anything more to do with it than anyone else. I'm no animal, no King Lear.

I'm no wild boar that has to be hunted down. No, that's precisely what I am not. Nobody and spin fables out of me."

He stood up but only to shake his fists (Ken understood nothing of what he was saying), then murmured, "I beg your pardon." Ken was afraid his visitor would lapse back into his old state, but he sat down again (apparently after a wild, mute, accusatory speech addressed to an invisible party) and again leaned his head to one side in his proud attitude. The attack had been beaten off. A few ritual curses followed.

On another occasion he had this to say:

"I sing this woman's praises. She made me what I am, and if you want to use that word I don't much care for, the word 'poet' (but not some long-haired poet standing by a duck pond, in the woods somewhere, hungry, stupid, and hypocritical), then it was she who made a poet of me. She engrossed me totally. Ever since I met her I haven't been able to give another woman any serious attention at all. She made me monogamous. For a while, I resisted that. In vain. I wanted to topple the idol. But I couldn't. And I helped her to find herself, too. She came out of me. I could see in her who I was and what I wanted. My dream image and a rib from my side.

"At first she tried to get away from me. I dug into her tooth and nail and hung on. The struggle ground me down, and her, too. But I knew what I had to do, and I didn't weaken. I behaved strangely during it all, like a drowning man. And she, to bait me and to separate herself from me, often told me—and she did just recently again, too—that Edward is not my son but someone else's, a fellow I knew, a naval officer she used to meet a lot even after we were married, in spas and other places. She carried around in her the image of a strong, cheerful, light-hearted man, a not very masculine man. She tried to get away. I hung on to her." (Crazy the way people dredge up ancient stuff, after such a long time. It was as true and alive as ever.)

"Even now, during our last fight, she had the nerve to throw her old litany of 'Edward isn't your son' into my face again. The boy turned up on the scene as he had once before (what a horrendous coincidence). I was on the verge of striking him dead. She thought she was going to get away from me yet, put me out to writer's pasture in my old age, and go her own way."

He fell silent and chewed on his lip; he didn't know what to say next.

"Gordon, you should have talked to me long ago. I could have advised you. This is all crazy."

"Ken, in some situations you can't turn to anyone else. Fate puts its seal on your lips. You're delivered up to your fate."

"Gordon Allison."

"Yes, delivered up. The one along with the other. You're on the edge of the abyss. You struggle together. You know you're going to fall. It can't end any other way. You've got to fall. And you do."

"Suicide, plain and simple."

"That's just a word, Ken. What do we know, my friend, of life and death. Death is part of our lives, but we realize that only in those situations that touch on the whole truth of our lives. I've always seen my relationship with Alice in that kind of context."

"I don't understand you. This fate you're talking about is one you've brought down on yourself. I repeat: You should have talked the whole business over with someone else long ago."

Gordon lifted his arm in a sign of resignation. "Well, now I have talked it over with someone else. What's happened has happened. Now we'll just have to wait and see what happens next."

He stood up and looked at the chair he had been sitting in. "Strange. I've been talking. I'm still talking. That's not a good sign."

Ken took his hand. "It's the best. Believe me."

"You're my friend, I know. — That I'm talking about this belongs in the same sad chapter as my letting her go. It's weakness. I'm falling apart."

"It was good, admirable. It was a positive action."

Gordon put both his heavy hands on Ken's shoulders.

"I can tell you right now, Ken, that she'll ask me to come back."

She did not ask him to come back.

He waited for two weeks. He sent a messenger to the house with a letter for James Mackenzie to give to her. She did not come. He became alarmed. He left, to go to her.

"Take me along," Ken asked him. "I don't want to leave you alone these days. I may be old, but I can't let you go off in the shape you're in. I beg you."

"Why, for goodness' sake? She's sitting there at home. She can't explain things to Edward and Kathleen. I can feel the dismal atmosphere in that house, and it's my fault. And who knows how Edward is. I lost control of myself completely with him when she came with her old story that he isn't my son. We behaved like tigers."

"Take me along."

"She'll be waiting for me. All of them will be waiting for me. I've been owing them my return for a long time now, and it pains me that I didn't realize that long since."

So all the old publisher could do was to invite Gordon to come back for another visit as soon as he could arrange it, alone or with Alice, or, indeed, with the whole family, so they could all spend a few happy days together, just like old times.

Gordon Allison's return.

James Mackenzie meets him at the door.

"You're back at last."

"Where's Alice?"

"You didn't meet somewhere?"

"Where? When?"

"I thought maybe you would. She's been gone a long time. I've had no word from her."

"Where's Edward? Where's Kathleen?"

Gordon is standing in the front door of the house, his bags behind him.

Mackenzie shrugs his shoulders. He pulls Gordon inside and puts the suitcases in the hall. The maid appears in the kitchen doorway. "Oh, Mr. Allison."

Happily, without being asked, she picks up the suitcases. "Do you have the key to the library, sir?"

Gordon stands there, dazed. "I don't have the key."

The maid looks at Mackenzie.

James: "Ask the gardener. He can open it for you."

They remain standing in the hallway for several minutes. Gordon keeps his hat on. They don't speak. The gardener comes in with a cheerful greeting. He has a full set of keys. Gordon and James follow him up the stairs. When the library door is open, the maid goes in first, pulls back the curtains, and opens the windows. She leaves the suitcases at the door and disappears along with the gardener.

James: "Can I help you in any way, Gordon?"

"No, thank you."

Gordon stands there in his hat and coat, his stick in his hand. James can't decide whether he should leave or not; then he does go out but stands waiting in the hall.

Gordon closes the door behind him and crosses the large room. His papers are spread out on the desk. He sits down. A drawer is open.

James hears him groan: "What have I done? What have I done? What have I done?"

James opens the door.

Gordon's hat has fallen from his head. The hat is lying in front of him on the papers, the stick on the floor next to his chair. James has to step over it when he goes to help his brother-in-law sit up. Gordon moans: "Where is she? What have I done? What have I done?"

James manages to get him sitting upright. He brings him a cognac from the sideboard. Gordon swallows it in one gulp.

Then Gordon sits there absolutely mute. James and the maid have helped him out of his coat. He lets them do with him as they will. He sits there, crushed. James looks over his shoulder and reads the note:

Tuesday morning. And this is my wedding ring, Gordon. Here they both are together. I thank you with all my heart. I'm leaving, too.

Finally Gordon gets up from his desk. He says he wants to go lie down. When James offers to go with him, he declines the offer.

He lies down on the bed for an hour. Then he wanders around in the house, opens the door of Alice's room next to his, and stands there a while. He goes up to the attic. He sees two picture frames right next to the door. He looks at them, has an inkling, goes back to the upstairs hall: two bright rectangles in the darkened wallpaper.

She destroyed the pictures, Gordon says to James, who has followed him. "They were my wedding present to her, those pictures."

James doesn't know what this is all about. Gordon is crying and lets himself be led into the living room. Then he sobs: "She shouldn't have done it."

To Mackenzie's pleasure, Gordon stayed in the house for another week. They had quiet talks together. Gordon even laughed and behaved in his old way. For the most part he was serious and pensive. He said often, in a questioning tone: "Then we'll just have to make the best of things." Finally they agreed they would both leave together, Gordon to go back to Ken's and James to return to his work. Without exchanging all that many words, the two men had come closer together in that one week than they had in all the years before.

But when James called from his university town and asked to speak with Gordon, he learned that Gordon had not arrived at the Farleys' house. And he did not arrive the next day and had still not arrived a week later.

The War Was Long Since Over

THE war was long since over. Anniversaries of the major landings, the battles in Normandy, the dropping of the atomic bombs on Nagasaki and Hiroshima were observed. The war took its place in the history books. Had it really taken place at all?

Delegates took part in peace conferences to push the war as far as possible into the past.

But in a run-down London hotel, the dismembered body of an old prostitute was found. The murderer was not found. And a month later in a nearby hotel, the body of a girl turned up in similar condition. The police had stuck a Negro in jail at first. Then they caught a white man who confessed he had followed both the women into the hotels. He had been drunk, had gotten into arguments with them, and had drawn his knife just to frighten them. And then he had gone berserk, possessed by a madness he could not explain.

A bewitching film star, Lupe Velez, thirty-four years old, lived in Beverly Hills in a luxurious house. While she had been making the film *Frenchman's Creek*, she had become acquainted with a French actor. That was all years ago. She had recently told her friends that the liaison was over now. But he had been the only man she had ever met who really understood her. She became restless and depressed but did not confide in anyone. So what happened next? She was found dead one morning, lying in her bed in her blue silk pajamas. There was an empty bottle of strong sleeping pills on her bedside table. The police came. A doctor came. The rich, charming Lupe Velez was dead. On her dressing table was a note in her hand.

"May God forgive you and me, yes, me, too. But I prefer to kill myself and our child rather than bear it in shame. How could you pretend to such great love for me and our child, Harald, when you really didn't care for us at all the whole time? I see no other path for me to take. Good-bye, and the best of luck to you."

Her mother came from Mexico. Her sisters with their fine faces came. They cried. It was love, it was the world, it was humankind.

In X, Mr. Meadow, the father of young Jonny, who had been torn to pieces next to Edward on the cruiser, came to Edward's car and helped his guest, who was using a cane, get out. He embraced him for a long time on the street. He took him by the arm and led him into the house and up one flight of stairs. A small, frail woman, Jonny's mother, whom Edward had never met before, came into the room, too. She took his hand and held it to her mouth for a long time. She sobbed and left again without having said a word.

Edward had sent a telegram from London announcing his arrival. He had not, as the servants at home had assumed at the time, gone to the train station. Afraid of himself, he had made a last-minute change in plans and put himself in Dr. King's care. The doctor kept his whereabouts secret.

Here Edward could scream and rage. The doctor did not try to calm him. He let him scream.

Why did Edward scream? So that he could not hear. To shut his ears. To drown out what his mother is saying. He stands at the window in front of a little shelf with plants on it and stares wide-eyed at a cactus and buries himself in picture magazines to obliterate that scene from his eyes, to cancel it out—his mother lying there, raising her hand, glowing with pride: Look at my hand. I've taken off my ring. Now that criminal is on the run. How she gloated and smiled: He's roaming around somewhere. This is our great moment. He is not your father.

Edward screams; all he hears now is his screaming. Later, he apologizes to Dr. King. "I wasn't as strong as I thought I was, Doctor. I couldn't stand it at home after all."

The doctor gives him time. He urges him to say anything he wants to say. Edward cannot come out with it. Dr. King does not press him.

Two weeks of complete rest and isolation and a few brief, superficial consultations are enough to dispel fears of a relapse.

Now Edward was living with Jonny's parents. He settled here, a bird driven out of his own nest. Here he was the friend of the family's dead son. He was not Edward, the son of a cursed race, a bastard who had to go into hiding.

He stayed in Jonny's room. Jonny's parents were happy to have him use the room, to have him in the house. It was as if Jonny had somehow come back.

A bright, narrow room; on the bookshelves the classics, adventure stories, travel writings, atlases along with the Bible and a hymnal.

Edward lay there for hours at a time, lost in thought, unable to get hold of himself, often plagued by slight anxiety.

They took the trouble to heal me of the terrors I had experienced. They succeeded. Then they waited for the right moment to hit me with a second blow. I want to read, read.

And he began to read, Kipling. But his mind kept churning and pushed through and beyond the print.

To think that she is my mother. She waits for me when I'm wounded. She calls to me. I heard her calling. She quite literally brought me back from across the sea. She didn't abandon me in the clinic, and then at home she went to no end of trouble for me. That's the way she is. She did all that for me.

All that—and why? Because I'm her son, but also because I'm the son of someone else whom she loves, whom I don't know, whom I detest, who disgusts me, her Glenn. I'd like to kill him.

He threw the book down on the table. He got up and took the Shakespeare from the shelves.

I thought of myself as Hamlet. It was my task to uncover a horrible crime and to punish the criminal. Here it is: "Something is rotten in the state of Denmark. — I am thy father's spirit, doom'd for a certain term to walk the night, and for the day confin'd to fast in fires, till the foul crimes done in my days of nature are burnt and purg'd away. But that I am forbid to tell the secrets of my prison-house, I could a tale unfold whose lightest word would harrow up thy soul. . . . If thou didst ever thy dear father love—O God!—revenge his foul and most unnatural murder."

And where is Father? He left the house. I hadn't known everything yet on that day. They argued. She told him everything, clearly and without shame. What a woman, a maenad. Then he left. I can understand his wanting to strike me down. He didn't mean the blow for me. He meant it for that other man—and that woman, his two murderers.

What a storm is brewing in me. Oh, if only I don't go mad again. I want to read something, Kipling. That's good.

He read a page of Kipling.

I'm lying here, and he's wandering around somewhere. "Quhy dois your brand sae drop wi' bluid, Edward, Edward? Quhy dois your brand sae drop wi' bluid? — O, I hae killed my fadir deir." That's what she wanted to drive me to. I was at the point of avenging her because he had driven away her noxious lover.

A woman, a mother. That's why she had a son. I was to be her son to that end. She has exploited me shamefully, horribly, outrageously. She drove me like a dog, and only after I had torn out the hare's throat could I see what was lying there. And she stood by and celebrated her triumph.

"Murder most foul, as in the best it is, but this most foul, strange, and unnatural. . . . but know, thou noble youth, the serpent that did sting thy father's life now wears his crown. . . . O Hamlet, what a falling-off was there! From me, whose love was of that dignity that it went hand in hand even with the vow I made to her in marriage, and to decline upon a wretch whose natural gifts were poor to those of mine! But virtue, as it never will be mov'd, though lewdness court it in a shape of heaven, so lust, though to a radiant angel link'd, will sate itself in a celestial bed and prey on garbage."

I have to find him. He is wandering around. He'll have to see me. I have to tell him everything.

"If thou hast nature in thee, bear it not; let not the royal bed of Denmark be a couch for luxury and damned incest. But, howsoever thou pursuest this act, taint nor thy mind, nor let thy soul contrive against thy mother aught. Leave her to heaven, and to those thorns that in her bosom lodge to prick and sting her."

The anxiety that troubled Edward and reminded him of that old scene of terror did erupt and overcome him. He saw everything in the bright light of day. He went through things point by point, tirelessly. His mind kept to its task and left no stone unturned.

Jonny's parents came to his room more and more often to chat and bring him books and gifts. He went on short drives with them. Another world. He had been out of touch with this world for a long time. He had been playing on a different stage.

(Once upon a time there was a certain Lord Crenshaw. He was the wild boar in King Lear, rooted in his Celtic heritage. He also lived at the time of the Crusades, the time of the young troubadour Jaufie, and he left his beautiful Provence and gave up his family and spent the rest of his life among Arabs in a hot desert country.)

I'm changing scenes now, too. I lived here once, too, studied here, planned to finish my degree. The war came. A restlessness came over me. I was like an old warhorse that responds to the bugle call. A new stage. I put on a uniform, the landing on the Continent, Normandy, Belgium, Holland, the march on Germany, always together with young Jonny. I chummed with him in the army. We decided to go to the Far East, to India, to Burma.

Then, on the Pacific, the kamikaze plane. The curtain drops for Jonny. For me, another call.

A new act. I hobble around on one leg. I'm at home. I discover what my "home" is. New scenery, a new act: I want honesty, truth. I have them. The act is over.

Is it over? The act, yes. The play goes on. I remain Lord Crenshaw's son. He is changing costumes now.

There was much talk of young Jonny. His parents could not hear enough about him. Everything new that Edward told them about him they took back to their room like a present and used it to recreate their son. They wept and mourned less and less. A new Jonny was growing up in their home. They cared for him tenderly.

The faces of statesmen, artists, film stars, and criminals stared out of the newspapers at the readers.

There was the sad, worn face of Mrs. Lilian Smith, a fallen cleaning woman, an ordinary, pathetic creature with plaintive eyes. For a few shillings, she followed a tough into a hotel and was massacred in the most horrible way imaginable. Who made her so poor and let her sink so low and left her without help?

And because no one else would help them and they didn't know what else to do, several hundred people in London took things into their own hands because they and their families had no place to live and because, for one reason or another, some large buildings stood unoccupied, and they took over those buildings, and there they sat, and the public, the greater part of it anyhow, cheered them on, and another part of it, which was worried about its property rights, debated the legalities of the situation and called on the authorities to take drastic action, or otherwise where would we wind up and so forth.

Edward (should he call himself Allison, or what should he call himself?), Edward took all this in.

War guilt? That's where it all began. I asked about war guilt because I had lost a leg. I wanted, as it were, to catch the guilty party, in my own country, who had torn off my leg.

There had to be villains and profiteers at work, I thought. We just have to get our hands on them. But I don't think we'll get control over things that way. What have we conjured up? What have we destroyed? Has it left any impression on people? The despair? No. It seems they can't behave differently. It all just drives them on to fresh deeds.

Is there such a thing as a human being—a free, thinking being?

I know for a fact, I've experienced it myself, that there is something in us or behind us that motivates our thinking and directs our actions. In my case, for example, there was this old fright left in me from a time I had long since forgotten, and it drove me to act. Was I present? Free, responsible? Was I at fault? I moved like an actor on the stage, following a text I didn't know, but a prompter whispered to me what I should say and do.

A supervisory council over my rational powers, a council behind, beneath, my rational powers, which, oddly enough, I had thought were my own.

And Mother must be driven the same way. In her, too, this dark subrationality and superrationality. And in Father, too. All of us led against each other—Mother against Father and Father against me.

What is it? What is this dark "rationality"? Is it reason at all? No, it's something else. I don't quite know what yet.

Dr. King's Regrets

EDWARD wrote to Dr. King. He had not given the doctor his correct address when he had left the clinic. He wanted no ties with
home. Now he wanted to see him. As soon as Dr. King received the
address, he went to Edward.

Edward was amazed at the rapidity of the doctor's response. "How
did you manage to come so soon, Doctor? Do you have some extra help
at the clinic? Or aren't you terribly busy right now?"

Dr. King: "Every bed is taken, and I'm as shorthanded as ever."

"Then I'm doubly grateful to you for coming so quickly."

The tall, white-haired man looked tired and worried. They went to
Edward's room. Now the former patient took a close look at his physician.

"You're exhausted, Doctor. You shouldn't have made this trip on my
account."

"I came on my own account as well, Edward. I've been waiting for
some sign of life from you. You know that your father has left the
house, and no one knows where he is. Now your mother is gone, too.
James Mackenzie took her to the train."

"Where did she go?"

"Nobody knows. Kathleen is gone, too, and you are gone. I was glad
when your card came. And so here I am."

"I'm very grateful to you, Doctor, and I appreciate your concern for
our family."

"I'm here on my own account, Edward."

And the doctor began to speak. He began with his last visit at the
Allisons' home. He had found James Mackenzie living alone in the
house. Finally he left, too. The house was standing empty.

"I didn't assess the situation properly. I took it all too lightly. I
shouldn't have let you leave the clinic, Edward. I let things slip out of
my grasp. That was wrong in every respect, worse than wrong. I

thought: He wants to go, so why not? The patients usually know better than the doctors anyhow. That's why. And I also thought I'd have you close by and could keep an eye on the whole process, the self-analysis you wanted to undertake and that you finally carried through successfully. I gave you and the experiment this kind of scientific consideration, superficial as it was. But I neglected everything else around it, the circumstances, the effect you would evoke. I didn't take all that into account, and that wasn't just a mistake on my part. It was a crime."

"Doctor, you're being too hard on yourself. Do you think you did real harm?"

"*Quieta non movere*. That principle holds true for all human relationships. We all have our weaknesses. We all hide things from each other. We all carry sacks of secrets on our backs. We get used to carrying them, however curious we may be to know what the next man is carrying in his. It lightens our load to know that others are carrying theirs just as we are. So there was nothing special about the fact that your parents had their secret, Edward. Granted, it was a special secret, but I know—because I've known them both a long time, ever since your father bought the house—that their secret weighed a little less heavy on them with each passing year."

"So what you're saying is that I broke up our family?"

"Edward, please. It's not you I'm talking about."

"Why not, Doctor? Who else disturbed the family peace?"

"I did. It was I who put you back into the nest. I gave in to your mother. She implored me. She pushed me. I let myself be exploited. I knew long before you were wounded, before you even went into service, what your mother was after. She was seeking a confrontation. She wanted to get away. Unlike me, she wanted the result she got, and she could see in advance that she would get it."

Edward shook his fists. "She exploited me just as she did you."

"Things were bound to take the course they did. It was an obsession with her. Your father didn't know how things stood between him and her. I sometimes think things would have taken this same course no matter what. Your mother was determined to be done and finished. In recent years she used to come to my house for a few weeks' rest every year, and every time she came I had to do battle with her. Then, when you came home, the die was cast."

"Then you shouldn't have let me go home. Then you did commit a crime, Doctor."

Dr. King sat quietly, his hands folded on his knees.

"That's what I keep reproaching myself with. Don't be too harsh, Edward. I blame myself enough. I was thinking about you, only about you, about your recovery. The path your mother suggested was viable. You were to assume responsibility for your own cure. I didn't expect that it would end as it has." Dr. King wrinkled his brow. "It's as if everything had been arranged this way in advance. The only hitch is that I come out the guilty one."

Edward: So the doctor sees it that way, too. He uses the word "arranged." I see a script behind my words, a supervisory council above and below our human reason.

Edward reached for the doctor's hand. "Let's put all this aside for now, Doctor. You played the role of Providence a bit for us. Now I'd rather hear what has become of Father. Where is he?"

"I've come because of him, too. I thought you would have his address. There are some business matters to attend to. He has appointed an attorney to manage his affairs, and the lawyer came to me for your address. He wanted to let you know he is administering your father's bank account and that you should turn to him with any financial questions you may have. I'm supposed to give Kathleen the same message."

"Thank you. But where is Father?"

"I don't know."

"Is anyone looking for him? Have the police been notified?"

"What on earth for? He's chosen to go off by himself for a while. The lawyer received a card from him just five days ago, from Scotland."

"What did he write?"

"Just a request for money. He's traveling around. He's gone into hiding somewhere. — It's hit him hard. That was to be expected."

"And me?"

"What about you, Edward?"

"Hasn't it hit me hard, too?"

"You'll come to terms with it. You're young."

Edward sat down next to the doctor and whispered, "Did you know that my name is not Allison?"

The doctor shrugged his shoulders.

"Did you know that I'm not his son?"

"You're dreaming, Edward. Where did you get that idea?"

"Mother told me."

"What did your mother tell you?"

"That I am not the son of Gordon Allison, in whose house I was raised as his son, but the child of another man she had a relationship with earlier or at the same time."

"She told you that?"

"Yes, at her moment of triumph, when the family fell apart. She couldn't keep it to herself any longer."

Dr. King: "She never said anything of the kind to me. I knew that your father was not overly fond of you as a child. But that's common among jealous fathers if mothers are excessive in their affection for a child. Your father was quick-tempered, too. There were scenes between your parents, some of them in your presence, when you were younger. It's possible that in a fit of rage he lost control of himself to the point where he might have attacked you. But I can tell you, too, that not long ago—it was when the news came that you had been wounded—that he came to me in the clinic with tears in his eyes and told me what he had just heard. He wept real tears. It's the only time I ever saw Gordon cry. He feared the worst for you and asked me what I thought your chances were. He said to me, and these are his exact words, that he had to make a confession. He had sinned against you gravely. He had been insanely jealous of you and behaved very badly toward you. There was nothing he wished for more than your recovery so that he could be reconciled with you and receive your forgiveness."

"And then I came home and attacked him and drove him out of the house. — But she says I'm not his child. She did not have me by him."

"A fairy tale she made up in the heat of her own emotions."

"I'm a bastard. I won't call myself Allison anymore. I won't take any money from him."

"You're crazy. Your mother made that up to use against him, either to provoke him or to take you away from him altogether and win you over to her side."

Edward stretched his arms out: "What has she done to me, to us all!"

But after Dr. King had left, Edward wrote to the lawyer, gave him his address, and asked that he be sent a certain amount of money each month. He meant to resume his studies. He also begged, in this and later letters, that the lawyer tell him where his father was. It was urgent that he get in touch with him.

The lawyer replied several times that he could not tell Edward where Gordon Allison was. Postcards came from him occasionally from different parts of the country. The last had been from Ireland.

Edward stayed with Jonny's parents a little while longer. He owed it to them that he was calm and capable of working again. Grateful to them, he left their home. Mrs. Meadow kissed him when he left. She cried very little this time. He promised to write and to come again as soon as he could.

He went to London to brush up on his academic subjects, also to look up Kathleen, who was now engaged to a veterinarian. He found her in exaggeratedly high spirits. She wanted to drag him to all kinds of parties he did not want to attend.

At their first meeting he had been struck by something about her that he couldn't quite put his finger on. At the second and third meetings he solved the riddle: She was acting like their mother. Her gestures were similar; she laughed and smiled as Alice did. He looked at her uneasily, this sister of his. The resemblance was even more pronounced when she visited him in his hotel room for the first time so that they could speak undisturbed. She spewed out her outrage and defiance; then came a paean to freedom and independence. Edward withdrew into himself.

Kathleen wanted no further contact with her parents. She looked on her brother as a fellow sufferer. He noticed the way she treated her fiancé. He took her to see Shakespeare's *Taming of the Shrew* and said afterwards as he held her strong hand in the restaurant—head over heels in love as he was, and blissfully ignorant—that he was better off than the hero in the play. His "shrew" had not caused him anywhere near so much trouble. She took hold of his shoulders, hugged him, kissed him on both cheeks, and laughed brightly: "Yes, that's because you're a real man." She gave Edward a little glance that said: I'm fond of him, but he is something of a dope. Chills ran down Edward's spine.

Edward resumed his studies. Letters went back and forth between him and the lawyer, between him and Dr. King. Where was his father? And then he began to ask, too, with growing concern: Where was his mother? Had no one heard anything from his mother?

But she had faded out of sight.

BOOK FIVE

The Virgin Persephoneia

⚜ "VIRGIN Persephoneia, you found no way to escape marriage. You were wedded to a dragon when curly-locked Kronion, his face transformed, an alien serpent, invaded the dark ground of the maiden's chamber. Thus was born Dionysus, who dared to sit on the throne of Zeus."

Under the bright sky, in the near-African climate, under cork trees and palms walked Alice, who used to be called Alice Allison, walked in the hot, dry landscape of the troubadour Jaufie Rudel de Blaia.

A noble knight loved the Princess of Tripoli. He loved her because of her great youth. All the pilgrims returning from Antioch spoke of her. Jaufie sang of her. He so longed to see her that he took up the cross and boarded a ship. On the way to her he became ill. On the verge of death, he was carried to an inn in Tripoli. The princess came and took him in her arms. He could see and speak again. He praised her and glorified her and died in her arms.

She buried him in the Templars' residence in Tripoli and took the veil that same day.

— I have not lived the days of my life.

A vulture visits me and sinks his talons into my body. He wants to carry it away.

Transform yourselves. Save yourselves.

She wandered through the narrow streets of the old French city.

The houses sob around me. The trees follow me and bend down to me.

A girl fled from a hunter, and when it was clear she could not escape him, she turned into a tree. To turn into a tree, to cover oneself with bark, wood, roots, branches, and leaves and stand there, mute, in one place, to grow slowly, to become rigid and more rigid still until an axe you don't feel anymore comes and cuts you down.

417

She climbed up to the famous old castle, sat on the edge of the wall, and looked out onto the hilly plain.

She had gone to Scotland at first, to the small city where Glenn had lived.

She already sees and knows everything before she arrives. But she yields to the impulse, as one lets a child have its way, and she looks for Glenn, afraid of the crushing blow she is expecting. And if what she wants does not come to pass, if he is not there, if he no longer exists (but did he exist?)—then, well, what then? (But don't think about that, not yet. Everything, everything will be as it should be—why shouldn't he be there?)

A brightness grows in her the closer she comes to his town. She feels an ever greater longing. She is completely immersed in longing. A miracle will happen.

No miracle happens. She hesitates for a moment, then gets up her courage to go into the small town church and pray for the miracle to happen. But she does not find him. He is not there. No one knows anything about him. The ground is giving way under her feet.

When she hasn't found him after a week, she begins to freeze in her room even though it's summer. This icy sensation creeps up her body. She goes to bed and stays there for half the day.

She begins holding mute conversations with Glenn. She begs him to come and take mercy on her.

I wanted to come to you, to bring our child to you, our son; you don't know him yet. I bore you a son. No, you haven't misunderstood me. He is your son, even though I bore him in a marriage with another man to whom I didn't belong. I carried him for you, in your name, and I raised him in memory of you, consecrating him to you, to us. He is not here. He abandoned me. Everyone has abandoned me, because of you, because of us, Glenn. But I am true to you. Glenn, my Glenn. I'm not myself anymore, from longing for you. I'm nothing more than your shadow. And if you don't exist either, Glenn, then what am I? They say I'm dreaming. They say you don't exist, you didn't exist, no, you never did exist! Don't kill me, Glenn. Come, be alive, give me your hand.

She had sent him a letter from home, to his old address, and to play safe she had sent another letter to his mother (but was she still alive?). She received no answer. The answer was to be sent to her here at the local post office. She doesn't go to the post office anymore.

He holds her right hand in both of his and thanks her for getting in touch again.

"Had you expected it, Glenn?" She listens: She is speaking to a living man called "Glenn." He: He had not expected to hear from her after all this time. The years have a way of passing. People drift apart and then lose touch altogether: "I heard years back that you had married Allison. He is a famous man. Good of you to think of a poor mutt like me."

(She dreams and dreams.)

He tells about his life, how he gave up the sea, went back to school, and became a forester. As he spoke, she played with the carnations he had brought. Now and then she would take a careful look at him. He was a tall, bony, serious man with sad, loyal, brown eyes.

What does Alice do when she doesn't find Glenn? She leaves the British Isles. She travels across the canal to France.

She wanders through the narrow streets of the old French town.

How Gordon deceived me. Perhaps I could have been happy with the man who called himself Glenn. I don't know. I have to realize that the chapter in my life called Glenn is done and over with. No "if"s can help me anymore.

Who will help me.

Alice wandered through the quiet, winding streets of the old city—

Alice, the daughter of Albert and Evelyne Mackenzie, wandered—

the wife, the runaway wife of the roaming Gordon Allison, alias Lord Crenshaw, wandered—

the bride, the dream bride, of the young naval officer Glenn wandered and looked around her (but there is nothing down there but the old French city; no one will come after you, for how can he rise up and follow you; he has been lying at the bottom of the North Sea for a long time now, his body has fallen to pieces, been picked away by the fish).

And why do you long for him, Alice? You never even kissed each other, you only held hands and gazed blissfully into each other's eyes, and that seemed like heaven back then, summer days at the shore.

When will the dream let you go?

Who is this woman who walks through the quiet streets of the French city and has left her own country behind?

Alice, really Alice?

*   *   *

I have not lived the days of my life. A vulture has come to me and sunk its talons into me.

The houses sob around me.

I have been cast out. Because I am true to myself, I have been cursed. The mother rescues her son and helps him to find himself; the son breaks with the mother when it's time for her to find herself. I called him back from over the sea. I cared for him and saw him through. I showed him the way. I knew what he was suffering from; he did not know. We both suffered from the same disease; the disease is called Gordon Allison. I've pulled through. And if I am still covered with boils from head to toe, like Job, I want to wear those boils like medals of honor and show them. Look at me, you clouds and hill, you old walls below me. I'm not going off on any crusade to rescue the Holy Sepulcher from the Moslems. I'm fighting for myself alone.

The blue sky stretched out tight over her. Not a cloud in sight.

I don't fear death. Let them try to strike me down with their shields. Salome dances; Salome remains a dancer. She whirls about the head of John the Baptist, that strict, imperious John. Oh, heavenly Salome, my joy. See how she whirls. She pulls me along with her.

John curses and accuses from his prison. "You generation of vipers, do you not feel the earth tremble?"

The earth trembles, and death comes near. And yet Salome moves and turns. He who is coming has the power to abolish all laws. But she whirls and turns. She has gotten up from her chair next to Herod and Herodias and come down here, and in her dance she is standing trial and defending her rights against the world.

People cry out: "Woe to you, you sinner!" The one promised to us, the savior, is coming. She knows that is true. But she dares to dance anyway. Hell opens its jaws to snap her up. Her hips sway, her feet dance.

She dares perform her monstrous dance before the eyes of heaven, and she demands the head of John, and she goes to her death under the shields of the mercenaries.

When Alice woke up one night—she shrank back from wakefulness, slipped deeper and deeper into dream, clung tighter to her dream, and begged it not to leave her—when Alice awoke one night—she found herself hot and trembling; she had abandoned herself to voluptuous imaginings—the ice had broken in her. The floes were in motion, sliding over each other and crashing into bridge pilings.

There was no flesh, no bone left to her. All of her had become fluid, melted, and throbbing.

The wild water from the mountains rose in foaming waves. Fish shot back and forth in it. The rivers overflowed their banks.

The dream had devoured her completely. The view from the house into a new, sweet, frightening, painful, blissful land, the only land, a longed-for land, a murderous land. Persephoneia-Dionysus, who dares usurp the throne of Zeus, is born.

Transformation comes amidst flame and chaos. How does transformation come? Amidst flame and chaos.

What shall I do. She sighed. She covered her eyes.

Wherever she looked she saw sensual images. Crawl away and hide. Become a whore. Is that what's coming to me?

The truth, honesty. What is there to keep me from it? Should I keep myself from it?

She had intended to travel. She wanted to go to North Africa, Egypt, and—after long absence—back to India again, wanted to celebrate a reunion; a new and grateful human being greets the old earth again. She abandoned her plan. She didn't want to travel. The voluptuous images flooded over her. There were no dikes to hold them back. It was as if all the debauched creatures of this love-crazed landscape, men and women, the dead, everyone between heaven and earth, everyone on the ground, hidden in the trees, in the sand, and in the clouds, had gathered to descend on her from time to time and celebrate orgies in her.

She ground her teeth together. What kind of life is this? Am I nothing but a beast in heat?

She touched the cold wall, the wallpaper of her room, with her hands and laid her face against the wood of the furniture to find relief. But instead of drawing the heat from her, the stone glowed hot and transformed itself into flesh. It responded to her touch. Yes, everything responded.

The landscape, even the landscape transformed itself. I'm wading in my own blood. What was the hot föhn saying? The olive tree, the palm? Long, thin tongues leapt out from the leaves, and the branches trembled in their excitement. The fronds of the palms spread out longingly.

Alice locked herself in her room. She struggled with herself.

Glenn had disappeared. I'll never find him. I know I've passed everything by and let it slip through my fingers with my waiting and hoping, my squabbling and yearning. How can I find a life for myself now without him? I have to take charge of my life without him. How can I sacri-

fice myself up to you, Glenn? How can I find you? Your bride—
wherever you are, won't you take me—at last, at last?

And then, just as suddenly as the storm had broken over her, a calm
set in, following on a sentence she had come across in one of her books:
"But those who sin and do wrong are the murderers of their own souls."
The evening before, when she had read that sentence, her eyes
slipped over it without taking it in. But the next morning when she was
combing her hair in front of the mirror, when she looked into her own
eyes (saw this half-dressed, fleshly creature, this seething kettle), the
sentence came back to her.
She was astonished by this alien, half-naked, fleshly creature, this
female, whose image looked out at her from the mirror with a familiar
yet shameless, vicious little smile and look in the eye. What kind of
figure, human being, animal, plant, is this? What is this thing that clings
to us, accompanies us like a shadow, doesn't even let go of us at night,
lies down with us and moans and writhes when we embrace a lover? A
dog, a domestic animal. This beggar we can't get rid of, this beggar who
knocks and rings the doorbell and has to be fed. What can we do with
him? And if we do nothing to silence this creature, we sabotage ourselves; it snuffles at us, scorns and mocks us—a creature that never
gives a moment's peace and that we can never get clean. We can change
its clothes as often as we like and powder it and perfume it. It has no
shame.
But for all that it's still acceptable enough on the outside. But on the
inside, the intestines and lungs and all, the guts, like a butcher shop,
bloody red, slippery, revolting, wormlike, ugh. And the innermost interior, the inner core that hauls all the rest around with it, the heart, the
feelings, the drives, the soul: What about that?
And as Alice sat eye to eye with her evilly smiling mirror image,
thinking about these things, her mind went back to the sentence: "But
those who sin and do wrong are the murderers of their own souls."
She put down her powder puff. I read that.
Murderer? I haven't murdered anyone. People accuse me of having
lost my soul.
A brightness, a clarity in her. A leap.
Yes, I have lost my soul. What a wonderful sentence. I have lost it. I
have no soul left. I've killed it off with sin. For I have left Gordon, my
wedded husband. I was not married to him at all. In my heart, I deceived him and betrayed him year after year; and I have put my son

away from me. Do I still have a soul? That rotten limb, my soul, has been torn from me, burnt away. Sin has amputated it.

I don't have a soul anymore.

She looked into the mirror: the white neck, the lace blouse, her bare breasts, her slim, naked arms, the astonished, pellucid gaze and the smile, no longer malicious but tender now.

My comrade, my friend, my strange companion, you, my sweet little brother, you don't hold it against me that I, like everyone else, was stupid and ungenerous in my dealings with you. I won't belittle you anymore. I will be kind to you. I will honor you and love you.

I be ashamed of you? I want to wrap myself up in you. You are my new, my true self.

And as she sat there half-naked at the dressing table, a sensual enchantment came over her, a feeling that was not of this earth flowed through her and seemed to lift her into the air.

Ah, look there. Satan, the devil, the evil one, is entering into me. Welcome. Will I submit to you? I am in your power. I am yours from head to toe.

Do as you will with me. I am your possession, your animal.

I am doing this to myself.

May this be inflicted upon me.

May it come down upon you, Alice, with knives and hatchets, with shields, with boulders and with bliss. This is my gift to you. This betrothal.

Her eyes were opened as if by magic, and she knew: This is my fate.

She sat down on her bed and covered her face with her hands to let the storm pass.

The decision throbbed in her.

If the count would like to dance and play then let him but say, and I'll strike up the tune.

—What will she do after this? Finish getting dressed?

She did not get that far. She lay back down, obediently, in the still-warm bed and reached for a jar of cold cream on the nightstand, and she began to rub the cream slowly onto her face, like a black tribesman or an Indian who puts on a mask before approaching a demon. Or like someone who puts on an amulet to make himself immune to danger. Or like a recruit who gets a tattoo when he joins the service. And we embalm the dead, too.

She lets her hands drop, pushed the jar aside, closed her eyes. Sleep instantly swallowed her up.

The Witches' Kitchen, Modern Style

SHE went into the Beauty Institute in Paris, a witches' kitchen, modern style. She went there for treatment. Along with the lower-level, female professional staff, there were also doctors. Alice underwent the ministrations of this clinic, which went beyond the merely cosmetic. The institute housed a cult of the body, and that was precisely what Alice wanted.

A new world, a new sun in the human sky, a bright, cheerful moon after the pale one of yesterday. What a wrongheaded view of things people have taken in the past. They neglect the body, the root of human life, and then are surprised that they languish, that the leaves turn yellow, and that no blossoms form; and they feel that, and finally they lose heart and wish they had never lived. But why must that be, you foolish gardeners? Don't you see how you are mistreating your plants?

Alice took care of her body; she pampered it and toned it up. She did for it and let be done to it anything that would help it forget the past years that had wearied it so much. She did not let her thoughts dwell on things that pained her. She locked up the past in herself more securely than she had the broken, useless things in the attic and the rags in the trunks and cupboards there.

The youthful-looking, charming, elegant woman who was the institute's director and who could speak so intelligently and knowledgeably impressed one thing very clearly on Alice:

"We won't get anywhere, dear lady, if you give in to your troubles. Fretting disfigures. It works against all the procedures you will undergo here. As a client who left our course of treatment prematurely once remarked to me, our institute is less a physical plant and a set of rooms than it is a conviction. If you have that conviction, the cure will succeed. If you don't, it will fail."

"I think I'm on the way to reaching that conviction. And I promise you—or myself—to do everything I can to suppress harmful thoughts and feelings. But if you, Madame Suzanne, are the high priestess of a doctrine or a professor, tell me—since I am an absolute neophyte—what else I have to think and do to attain the whole truth that you possess. You laugh. You laugh as you would at a child. Well, I am one, and I'd like to be treated as one."

"Dear lady, what you said struck me so funny: the 'truth,' and me a professor or high priestess. Our institute is not a church. We want to help you and promote your well-being, on a psychic as well as a physical level. You'll find a small library here, books we suggest you read. Later I'll ask you to join us for our lectures and social evenings."

"You offer that kind of thing, too?"

"You really are a child. Where do you come from anyhow? What has your life been like? Why does that please you so?"

"It just does, Madame Suzanne. I thought I was—lost." (She did not say: an outcast.)

"Lonely?"

"Lonely, too."

"And you so beautiful and fascinating! You haven't been kind to yourself, Mrs. Mackenzie."

She whispered: "I know, but it's not too late."

Alice stood up. The gracious woman went arm in arm with her into an adjoining room.

"You have to avoid everything that smacks of strictness and harshness. 'The truth,' 'high priests'—what use do you have for such things, Mrs. Mackenzie? We are easygoing and cheerful because we know that no one can flourish without joy and love, especially not we women. You can learn to take things lightly."

Alice sat with Madame Suzanne in the tea salon of the institute, and while they were enjoying the fine pastries and sipping their dark, aromatic drink, Madame Suzanne tapped Alice's little finger with a spoon and said, "What a sweet little finger, bent just like a question mark. I can assure you that whenever you see a little finger bent like that the answer is already there. But why does the little finger keep on asking its question? You still have memories in your head? But those are someone else's memories. We aren't that person anymore."

Oh, how much this little Suzanne understood! No wonder she had been made the director of the institute.

Alice glanced at the newspaper on the coffee table in front of her. Suzanne pushed the paper aside.

"Someone left that paper lying here. I'll find out who it was. Surely some visitor. I don't permit newspapers in the institute. The maid should have picked up more carefully."

"And why are you so dead set against newspapers?"

"We shouldn't occupy ourselves with things that upset us."

"You mean we should not know what is going on in the world around us, Madame Suzanne?"

"Anyone who takes it seriously has no choice but to lock himself in his room and weep."

"But if what the papers say is true?"

Madame Suzanne gave her a reproachful look. "But whether it is true or not depends on you."

Now Alice laughed. "You're quite wonderful."

Madame Suzanne, her eyebrows raised, was rummaging in her handbag. "You doubt that? It depends on you how close you let things come to you. What doesn't touch us directly . . ."

"Doesn't exist?"

Suzanne found the flat, gold case she had been looking for. She laid it on the table and ran her hand over the cover.

"It took me quite a while to understand that it does not exist. We have to deliberately decide that it does not."

As Madame Suzanne lit a cigarette and blew out the match she was holding close to her mouth, Alice saw that she was older than she appeared to be.

"I enjoy my work. I studied medicine, but I found the clinics boring. It was impossible for me to spend my time that way. I wasn't willing to sacrifice so much just to earn my keep and to watch myself shrivel up a little more each year. You cut yourself in half, throw half of yourself away so you'll be able to 'live' later on? I took the opportunity that offered itself."

Suzanne and Alice

GORDON Allison's wife, Alice, had been slim and elegant when she was in England. Now she wore her reddish brown hair in an upsweep and held in place with a silver comb. She wore high heels, moving about with a proud, elastic step. Her face was ingratiatingly wistful, her smile so enchanting one might think she had been sent out from the witches' kitchen for the very purpose of seducing whomever she met. Her large eyes had retained that deep look they had always had.

She spent several hours every day on her chaise longue. She didn't read. She chatted with this person and that and looked at pictures in albums and books. She felt good. Each passing day added to her sense of happiness and well-being. No more bad thoughts: That was—as the clever Suzanne remarked (she often sat with Alice in the hotel)—the first expected result of the cure, which, with the aid of baths, massages, shots, and pills, restored the body to health, gave back to the body what was the body's due. The cure worked no magic. It simply made available to the body the youth and joie de vivre that were already present in it and waiting to be awakened. "We are locksmiths in this institute. We open locks that the client can't open for herself. We make a new key, and the client can finally claim what she already owns."

"I'm well-off, Suzanne. I would gladly give you some of what I have if you needed it."

"Do you have the feeling, Mrs. Mackenzie, that I lack for anything? I have to earn a living. But it is not difficult for me to get what I need. My profession is not hard on me."

Alice had already met a friend, an admirer of Suzanne's (or one of her friends), a lawyer no longer in the bloom of youth, who treated her like a queen. It was obvious that Suzanne was using the Beauty Institute only as a springboard. Alice took great pleasure in her looks, her conversation. Suzanne was an attraction the institute offered its clientele.

They talked about money. Suzanne gave the subject a great deal of thought. Alice learned a lot from these talks, in which Suzanne revealed a remarkable side of herself and developed her own special theory. She observed once, for example: "Money is essential to everything. That sounds crude. But you know my position: If you work to earn money in the usual way, you first make yourself poor and weak so that you can become rich and powerful at some later time. But if you're rich then, who are you rich for? There's no one left to possess that wealth."

Alice looked off into nowhere.

Suzanne: "You're financially independent, Mrs. Mackenzie, and understand what I'm saying. You wouldn't have come to us otherwise. You want to enjoy life. I don't have the impression that you're out to be extravagant, but you want the freedom to do what is in keeping with your nature, and you want to be able to hold your head up. You can't do that unless you have some wealth."

"You don't think we should be moderate in our way of life?"

Again Suzanne made a gesture that dismissed this suggestion. "We should be moderate about work, but that's all. Why moderate? What should we deny ourselves? And why? Most people have to live under the curse: 'In the sweat of thy face shalt thou eat bread.' It has held true from earliest times."

Alice admired her teacher; she asked anxiously, "But how do we escape that curse?"

"How? Most people never do escape it. Do you still not understand? Ah, you never had the need to think about these things. People are horribly content with that curse, and there's no reason why we should do anything to change that. We're giving them a gift; we're giving them the possibility"—Suzanne laughed impudently—"to see how happy we are."

Alice was studying the lines in her hand.

"And these other people who allow us to be happy—they really don't want happiness themselves?"

"Read the newspapers. Go out on the street, and answer that question yourself. I sometimes let myself be dragged to gatherings of one kind and another. There are political debates; people talk about peace all the time. They come up with one plan after another. But in their heart of hearts," she whispered in Alice's ear, "they are afraid of peace. For them, it's like a Sunday afternoon with nothing to do. Where peace is concerned, they are impotent. You have to have a talent for peace, just as you do for joy. They don't have that talent. They have a 'desire for progress' instead. Progress is the promise of happiness tomorrow. So, if they want to leave today's happiness lying by the roadside, we'll pick it up."

Alice, after a pause: "And you yourself, Suzanne?"

She gave the Englishwoman a playful tap on the tip of her nose. "I— I'm not cursed. I wouldn't go so far as to say I am blessed either, but I'm in possession of my five senses. It seems to me, too, that we women are cleverer than men. And you, Mrs. Mackenzie, do you agree with me?"

"It seems to me that we're sisters."

Suzanne threw her arms around Alice's neck.

The Pictures

ALICE looked at pictures. They appealed to her more than poetry. Suzanne had recommended them as a way to avoid overtaxing the mind.

Alice surrounded herself with handsome Corot reproductions. The colors had a magic effect on her, warm, brilliant, scintillating colors. The stage on which Alice was acting underwent a transformation. What kind of human creatures were these coming toward her now?

"I am fully involved," Alice thought. "This is just what I need. My mind and my thoughts are so worn out and dried up. There's no strength left in them. Do they exist at all anymore? My inner life—I feel I'm discovering a new inner life. The path to it is by way of the eye, the ear, the emotions."

Yes, it seemed to her that she was growing a new inner life and that she had to watch over it the way a pregnant woman does. Avoid thought. Isn't that what her brother, James, had preached, too?

The picture was called *The Torso*.

A mature woman sat there, a mother. She had let her blouse fall down below her breasts. She wore her dark hair parted in the middle, the way a peasant woman does. She was holding on to her blouse with her work-hardened right hand and looking down at the wrinkled breasts at which her children had nursed. Her expression had a touch of melancholy—her thoughts slipped back into the past, to springtime, blossoming, embraces. She said something to herself and pulled the blouse up over her shoulders.

When Alice, who now called herself Sylvaine, emerged from one of these long, profound, hypnotic contemplations, which were just the opposite of ascetic meditations, she felt she had merged into this human figure and it into her; she had let it come to her. She had been emptied out inside, it seemed to her, and now this emptiness was being repopulated with new images and forms. She could not articulate this experi-

430

ence, but then she did not even want to convey to anyone else what concerned her alone. A new grammar and a new physics would have to be invented to explain it.

Suzanne congratulated her on her progress. Sylvaine seemed to be a new human already. And Suzanne was not one to bandy compliments about. What a light touch Sylvaine-Alice brought to things, even in the process of her cure. How deeply the flowers that were brought up to her from the hotel moved her. It was as if she had come from another planet and had never seen flowers before. Everything was new to her: the carnations, their color, their fragrance (the carnations Edward brought her). They seemed to intoxicate her. Bedazed with wonder, she once held an ordinary orchid with yellow spots on it in her hand, passed it over her face, and sighed: "Oh, oh."

Alice once seized her maid's hand, asked her to forgive her, then had the girl sit down in front of her in an armchair and let Alice stroke her arms and hands.

"Forgive me, forgive me," the foreign woman begged, "everything about you is so lovely."

"But you are much more beautiful than I am, Madame."

"Not at all. Let me hold your hand."

Sometimes, when she had invited some guests from the hotel to join her, she sat among them drunken with happiness. Some people found her ridiculous, of course. Others thought she was hysterical.

And more pictures.

Henriette Stoffels by Rembrandt. A strong, intelligent, trusting face, an able woman. She takes a firm hold on things; she digs right in. The way she folds her arms and looks at me. Here I am Henriette. I used to be called Alice, but now I'm Sylvaine. The painter preserved you so that you would continue to exist past your lifetime. There are so many illnesses that can strike us down. Welcome, dear girl, don't be afraid if I look at you like this. How thick your hair is, falling down over your face. But I can see your face. You are here. Your face is here. Henriette is here, in me.

We were both dead, Henriette and Alice. But I am holding you. We are both here.

And then she had a picture by Delacroix before her: *Furious Medea*.

Her mouth is open. She seems to be saying something. The upper part of her face, her eyes and forehead, is in shadow. It is a strong, grim face, not what you would call a beautiful woman's face. But the painter

knew more about her than most writers know. This fierce, suffering face
of a hate-ridden, mature woman rests on a bulging, a spongy soft
female body. The fat, plump, overly heavy arms and shoulders, sagging,
hanging—they don't know yet what they want. Medea has been
wronged. She has been humiliated. — The colossal domes of her two
breasts. And from beneath her right breast peers the unknowing face of
a curly-headed child.

She sees something: what? She is plotting: what?—with that sweet
child's face under her arm.

Edward speaks:

Mother, you have told me some long stories, the last about Pluto and
Proserpina. Now I want to tell you one.

Medea, do you see her? This picture did not hang in the hallway in
our house, next to the Rembrandt.

Some men wanted to win a golden fleece that promised happiness and
riches, and they traveled far across the sea to find it, just as Jaufie de
Blaia, the young troubadour, did to fetch the Princess of Tripoli. These
men were called Argonauts, and Jason captained their ship. The fleece
was in Colchis. But in Colchis, Medea, the sorceress, the daughter of
the king, saw Jason and fell in love with him. She helped him gain the
treasure.

And when Jason and Medea sailed away on the *Argo* and her father
pursued them, Medea had her little brother with her. She seized him
and killed him and cut him to pieces and scattered his limbs on the
shore so that her father would give up his pursuit and look for her
brother's small corpse.

She was nothing but love for Jason; love was a ferocious fire in her.
There was no Medea apart from that love.

And when they came to Corinth, this fierce woman, this female demon (she was no sweet, complaining Proserpina) bore her beloved husband children.

But then he abandoned her.

And what did she do? Did she awaken from her madness?

She, the sorceress, made Jason's new bride a wedding dress and gave
it to her. On the wedding day, it ate away the bride's skin, her flesh, her
entrails, and she died, writhing in agony, before Jason's eyes. Then
Medea let fire rain down on the dead woman's house; that death was
not enough to satisfy Medea.

And when Jason returned to his palace, weeping, the two children
Medea had borne him lay on the threshold. They, too, had been murdered.

And she stormed away through the air overhead in a chariot drawn by dragons, back to her gloomy homeland of Colchis. Medea, Medea—

Alice-Sylvaine took the picture, tore it up, and had the shreds taken out of her room.

For hours horrible screams were tossed up to Alice from an abyss. She sat motionless in her room until the screams stopped.

Others in the hotel took note of the incident.

That was just the way she was.

At the Shore

23 FREEDOM lay before her.
Boundless the sea she drove out to, the gray, ancient ocean, ancient and gray, an elephant that was kneeling down and switching his back and legs with his tail.

The broad surface—the saltwater—reached down into the depths and was host to the fish and the mysterious mollusks of the blackness. It rolled upward and surged higher. It wanted to come up on the shore, wanted to spread out. It washed up over the land but had to retreat again, condemned to stay behind the barrier of the shore, and storms whipped it into a frenzy, and it tossed ships about and smashed them to pieces.

No matter how high the sea tossed up its waves, it could heave them only so high. The air remained empty, unattainably high the sky and the stars, the glorious, numberless stars that laughed down and watched the spectacle below, and in their midst the moon and the sun. All the sea could do was reflect them and rock their images as in a cradle.

The white gulls soared above the heavy sea that was condemned to eternal rest. They whistled and shrieked and fluttered and used the water as an eating dish. They sailed above it happily and arrogantly, above the shackled, sunken titan who had grown used to his misery. He played castanet music for them. He plashed, gurgled, clapped, as best he could. They understood what he meant. They were pleased. Now the old ocean lay still. From far away it voiced an uncanny roar, a rumbling from deep in its throat, this tongueless being.

At the shore and in the city Sylvaine met a lot of people who acted the way Suzanne had described. They had not emerged from the most rudimentary stages of life and remained caught there. What depressed, encrusted shellfish.

Sylvaine moved among them and celebrated life and freedom, while in back of her someone raised a megaphone to make an announcement.

434

A barker touted the secrets of his show. He wore a not quite clean suit, held a bell in his left hand, the megaphone in his right. Next to him stood a clown who did not move, his face white—the features black lines—like a death mask. In his eyes sockets little animals ran from right to left, from left to right. Between the barker and the clown was a monkey climbing around on a bar above their heads. Now a hurdy-gurdy started to play inside the tent. The barker rang his bell and put down the megaphone. He passed out tickets. The customers lined up at a table where an ill-humored woman in a black pelerine collected their money.

One after the other they handed over their tickets and disappeared inside the mysterious tent.

Alice had what she wanted. She had become Sylvaine. She was young; the years had been swept away. She was beginning again as if nothing had happened, could do as she pleased. She did just that.

She had bathed in the fountain of youth and had a beautiful, a different body. She was no longer that delicate, discreet Alice with the regular features and the open, deep, and penetrating gaze, Alice who sometimes pressed her lips together into a thin line and who had run up the steps to Dr. King's clinic so lightly to greet the wounded, delirious homecomer, her son—Sylvaine walked proudly and lithely on high heels, wore the face of a contented woman, an ingratiating, languorous face that could smile bewitchingly.

Was she choosing her path? Did she want to start over again? Before she could reach a decision she had already made her choice. What path had Theodora taken, and didn't she want to and have to follow the same one? The moment she had entered Suzanne's sorcerer's workshop it had been clear to her that she wanted not only a cure and rejuvenation but also something else that she said "Yes" to and swallowed down, hook, line, and sinker.

At parties at Suzanne's she had met a young man, a navy officer wounded in the war. She didn't know at first what it was that drew her to him. And he did not understand what this beautiful, wealthy woman, surrounded by suitors, wanted with a sporty type like him. But she soon realized and understood, to her dismay, how external circumstances and her inner needs were conspiring against her. He, this particular man, had been put in her path. And she had not been thinking about Glenn at all. — He belonged to the early phase of her life; now his chapter had to be written out to its end. She dreamed and was amazed at what she dreamed. What is happening to me? Fate wants to remind me of Glenn? Should I go searching for him again?

The young officer saw that she had fallen for him. He was dazed. She never let him out of her sight. She went out for rides with him and dined with him. Everyone thought they were lovers. But she made no advances. She enjoyed his company and kept him on tenterhooks. When he could bear it no longer he fell at her feet in her room and begged her to let him at least kiss her feet.

"Kiss them," she said nervously.

He took her shoes off and kissed her feet. In an instant he was standing up and embracing her. She turned pale and weak in his arms. He was shaken. He tried to arouse her with kisses. She burst into tears, sank down on her knees, and lay sobbing before him on the carpet. He had no choice but to leave.

He couldn't stand it with her anymore. She asked, "Why are you leaving me?"

"I can't just live next to you like this, Sylvaine."

"It's so lovely to have you here. Isn't it enough if I just kiss you?"

What a way to treat him! She was teasing him as a girl would. The young man thought he had to put an end to this business. There, in her room, he drew her forcefully to him and threw her onto her bed. A blow from her fist against his temple sent him reeling back, dizzy. "Get out!" she screeched at him.

He cursed and left.

That was how she dealt with the navy officer, Glenn's ghost. She lived aimlessly, made no demands on herself. She moved like a sleepwalker on the new stage onto which she had walked.

She had become a field of blossoms over which the bees hummed in droves. It was more than a yielding of self—it was self-surrender, a dissolving of self, when the first man took her in his arms. She was only an element with the woman's name "Sylvaine." She did not hold on to any man and didn't let any hold on to her.

Men were ecstatic with her. But they discovered that she did not love.

This was a period of clarity and calm for her. Suzanne accompanied her a lot as a kind of tour guide and steward. Suzanne was always drawn to money. She gave up her job in the witches' kitchen. Her friend Sylvaine supported her. Alice-Sylvaine was living from her bank account, her inherited capital, which was dwindling, however. She didn't keep accounts. She didn't let Suzanne look into the state of her account, and she didn't look into it herself. She behaved as if her resources were endless.

Then came a second period. She had lain there like a field of blossoms and let the bees play. They took pleasure from her. Now she felt torn, tense, and irritated. A hunger set in with her, a hunger for people, men, pleasure.

I'm missing something. I can't put it out of my mind.

She felt like a drinker who can never satisfy his thirst.

She complained to Suzanne. "I don't like myself. I'm exhausting myself, ruining myself. There's something wrong with me."

Suzanne laughed at her. People need alternate periods of repose and activity, she said.

Sylvaine covered the black rings under her eyes with makeup and obediently drank the tonic Suzanne gave her.

"Am I really free, Suzanne? Is someone who has a fever free?"

Suzanne, her doctor, her sly doctor, laughed and reassured her. She sensed that Sylvaine-Alice feared the end of the magic spell. Beyond it lay only emptiness and more fear.

When Sylvaine was lying in the arms of some man once she dreamed: I'm dead. If only somebody would put an end to me.

The Hunt for the Destroyer

THAT was the sea, and that was the ballyhoo of the barker in front of his show. He urged people to step right up.

She lay on the edge of the abyss and was staring down into it.

I, my self, Alice, Sylvaine, one mask after the other falls.

This is just what Lord Crenshaw must have experienced.

The morass. I'm bogged down in the morass. When will I suffocate. How long does it take for a person to die. We ought to be able to stop breathing voluntarily. We shouldn't have to wait for death.

The hunt for the destroyer.

She flogged what she called—to Suzanne, who remained as cheerful and skeptical as ever—her "corpse" and kept on the lookout for the one who would kill and bury her along with her corpse.

Suzanne realized that the rich Englishwoman was about to run out of money, and she prepared to deliver the coup de grace. She exploited Sylvaine's apathy and indifference to "borrow" a large sum to found a beauty institute. If she had asked Alice to hand over her entire account, Alice would have done that, too. She lay on the edge of the abyss and wished that someone would push her over.

Then Suzanne disappeared.

The next to take her up was a shrewd and cynical young banker, a womanizer. He traveled from Paris to Cannes with her.

He was stronger than she was. She had to make herself conform to his tastes. He almost succeeded in selling her to one of his friends in Cannes, for money. He came home late one night, having lost a great deal in gambling. He didn't tell her that but disappeared for a few days, and then a small, mustached, unappealing Polish man appeared. After some small talk, he explained to her the deal he had made with her friend. She managed to hold the man off. He came back again, enraged, and repeated his attacks. He felt he had been cheated. When the banker reappeared, he was delighted with his Sylvaine. The Pole's failure amused him. He had swindled the man.

438

On a soft summer evening they sat with a glass of wine on the hotel terrace overlooking the sea. The conversation came around to problems of the times. The banker said:

"Human beings are capable of anything. We're living at a time in which laws are losing their force. And why? People have seen through them. Science has revealed what gives these so-called laws their character. A word, spoken by someone who had power, called them into life and gave them force. Laws are mere commodities, deterrents for those who let themselves be deterred."

Alice-Sylvaine: "It's a sign of progress, Raymond, that people can see through the hoax."

"Laws are tools of enslavement."

Alice: "And what about money, Raymond? Some people work; others have money."

The banker, flattered: "That's another whole story. Nobody can do everything at once. Someone who thinks and makes decisions can't work hard at the same time, and someone who works hard can't think and make decisions. Take the railroad and locomotives. Coal produces the steam. The train can run now, true enough, but where should it go? Tracks have to be laid; there have to be switches and switchmen, and somebody has to say where the train will go."

"Please, Raymond," begged the tall, pale young man next to him, "since when have you talked such nonsense so seriously?"

Sylvaine: "And what is your opinion, Hippolyte?"

Hippolyte: "I'm of the same mind as Raymond, but he seems reluctant to express his true opinion today."

The banker: "Why should I always stick to the same opinion? I'm not sure what my opinion really is. First I try this one, then that one."

Sylvaine: "What about money? Is it good not to have money? Should we try not to have it?"

"I've never met a woman as deeply skeptical as you. Well, then, if we have no money we should at least know why we don't want to have it. Why do you or why should anyone not want to have money? The way I see it, most people don't have money anyhow. So why should they feel a need to not have money?"

He waited for her answer. When it was not forthcoming, he continued.

"There are two things characteristic of the average person: fear and imagination. The two things go hand in hand. Fear inspires fantasy. Fear and fantasy keep the average person from achieving existence, and they cripple him so much that he is bound to fall into the hands of others who then exploit him. Anyone in a position of power knows how obedient the average person is. In the twinkling of an eye he leaps out of the real world to wallow and delight in fantasies. Fear is a leftover from our animal past; and now, even though we have no more need for fear, people still cling to it and indulge in fantasy. Clever people make use of this phenomenon. Average people, given the opportunity, will give themselves up to dreaming and sell their reality and themselves along with it. Politicians, businessmen, financiers, and crooks are the only people who have raised themselves up out of animal existence and who prefer to deal in facts. I can't include scientists and scholars in this group because I've found that in everything except their work, they're average people, too."

Sylvaine: "And how does your politician or your crook make use of his sense of reality?"

Raymond: "Just look at the way you live yourself. How? Reasonably. We have, by the way, a little imagination ourselves but not enough to do us any harm. And what we have we use for speculation, putting it in the service of our reason so that we can expand our power over other people. We enjoy life, and we call the shots. A clergyman who didn't like my views and wanted to talk up his god to me to scare me once told me that for his god thought and reality were one. In other words, there was no gap between his thoughts and their realization. He was so powerful that his thoughts were immediately translated into action. Now granted, we haven't achieved that level of divine power; but, in our way, we're approaching that ideal."

Hippolyte: "Since you're so big on theory today, tell us something else. What does democracy have to say about your ideas? How does it feel about your godlike way of doing things?"

"The institutions of one political system or another have no influence on reality, my dear friend. Reason remains reason, and fantasy remains fantasy. Democracy requires a lot of propaganda and intelligent, well-paid people like yourself. It's particularly important in a democracy to offer people a lot on the imaginary level because you can't offer them much of anything else. On the contrary, you want to take a lot from them or prevent them from getting it. But as a rule people are grateful for the smallest favors that authority chooses to deal out to them."

The banker laughed heartily at his own remarks and added for the benefit of his poetically inclined secretary:

"That's why poets are most at home in a democracy. There's a con-

stant need for novelty and bright ideas, which are everyday commodities in a democracy. You have to watch out, of course, that no
single idea wins the upper hand. Every citizen has to have the right to
choose among ideas. He can pick whatever he likes, but then he has to
stick with it." He interrupted himself here with a loud laugh. "Which is
to say: He can choose what he wants to get drunk on."

Hippolyte bowed: "The Greeks had very different ideas. They were
no strangers to the imagination either, Raymond, but think what fantasy meant to them. Did they consider their gods products of the imagination, mere fantasies? They had no truck with our separation of facts
from imaginings, ideas, phantasms. Indeed, they saw things just the
other way around. A fact, such as a tree or an animal, took on 'reality'
only through—what shall I say—only through the imagination, only if
something like a god or a nymph was alive in it. They populated heaven
and earth with gods and goddesses, with demigods, nymphs, nixes,
fauns, just the way we keep discovering more and more new stars,
nebulae, hot and cold celestial bodies that form, fall apart, and basically
mean nothing to us. If I were a Greek, I would say our modern reality
is deaf and dumb, born with a congenital defect. All the Greeks,
whether aristocrats or plebians, believed firmly in their gods and
nymphs, although no one had ever seen them. For the Greeks, everyday life was permeated with heavenly and hellish creatures. But for us,
God, if he exists at all, is a god of nature, above nature, certainly the
creator of it all but at such a great remove that he is more a theoretical
necessity than anything else. What effort religious people in our society
have to expend to reach him with their prayers. And who knows if they
ever do reach him. There's surely a lot of chance involved. The Greeks
lived with their gods, for better or for worse."

The banker, in a mocking tone: "What was there then for you poets
to do in Greece?"

"Not much. We really didn't have to do anything at all. But even so
there was a great demand for fantasy. Then, too, we had special access
to genuine reality. We took ourselves seriously. Back then, art, which
does nothing but decorate the living rooms of the wealthy now, had
dignity. It was a link with reality, with the divine."

Sylvaine: "You're getting carried away, Hippolyte. We can thank our
stars that your age of the Greeks is over. Ours is more humane, and we
are freer. There's nothing greater we can ask for than freedom, no matter what its consequences. What do we amount to among gods and

demigods, nymphs and satyrs? I must confess that our one god is one too many for me."

"Bravo, bravo, Sylvaine." The banker clapped his hands.

Sylvaine, with a smooth, cold face: "Just imagine, Hippolyte, where we would end up if it were true that there was only one single god, one who, as we learned in school, created heaven and earth and all the animals and plants and us as well? Would you like to live at his mercy, under his care and supervision? Would you call an existence like that life? On the day that someone could convince me that such a god existed, I would commit suicide. I would not yield my freedom to any god and allow him to guide me and either praise or punish me. I would immediately make use of the freedom I have by removing myself from his paternal care."

"Well, then," asked the expansive Raymond, turning to the champion of the Greeks, "what does the ancient world have to say to that?"

Hippolyte gave Sylvaine a supplicating look. "May I speak, lovely Madame Sylvaine?"

The banker: "And you should add: my Pythia."

"Thank you. You have spared me that trouble. I'll stick by the Greeks. If I knew how to conjure up the gods, or even how to conjure up God, I would do it."

The banker raised his hands in an imploring gesture.

The secretary: "Madame Sylvaine, just look at our world of 'facts.' What a structure! It is not a house we can live in. It's a storehouse for furniture. There's a lot in it, every day a little more, but we can't get at any of it. Under these conditions, it seems to me, knowledge doesn't exist anymore. So it's a genuine blessing that we still have fantasy, that we at least have the power of imagination left. If we had the gods, we wouldn't need that. But we don't have them. Fantasy is our only refuge. It's the retreat humanity has reserved for its old age. We flee to a little cubby we've fixed up for ourselves in the attic."

Sylvaine: "Do you have anything else to tell us about the Greeks?"

Hippolyte: "You want more?"

She nodded. He looked at her. Half of her face was lost in shadow, the other, rigid, haunted.

As he spoke, he lost himself in this strange face.

"They had the tragedies we are familiar with, but after the tragedies came the satyr plays. And then, to celebrate life and lighten it up, they invented bacchanals and celebrations of Dionysus. And don't forget the legends about their melancholy god of death. What marvelous stories.

We could almost say that they shaped their death god for the treatment Offenbach would later give him. For example, the old, ponderous, jaded Pluto climbs into his chariot because he's had enough of judging and punishing. He wants a breath of fresh air. The Greeks realized that Tantalus, Sisyphus, and the rest of that hellish mob got to be too much for him in the long run. They granted him some relief. They thought of their gods in human terms. And so Pluto climbs into his chariot and happily rolls out of hell and finds himself a sweet, crisp little Proserpina."

I know, Sylvaine's eyes said.

"That, you see, is how the Greeks made sense of their world and demonstrated their understanding of life. They knew that not even a god could put up with life in the underworld without a sweet little thing to cheer him, and so they let him have her."

The banker: "Their hearts were in the right place. Sylvaine, I'd like to propose an idea. I find what Hippolyte has been saying convincing to some extent, and he has given me an idea. You are experienced, Sylvaine; you are clever, energetic, and—last but by no means least—beautiful, a woman. No one can put anything over on you, and you know your own mind. You should plead the case of Greek lightness to people. You should bring them to the point where they can laugh about Hippolyte's retreat to the attic. Life is what it is, but we need our fun. Where would we be if we couldn't have any fun? The only truth would be Don Juan's lines: "Let the earth shake. Slaves tremble at the sound of thunder." You should go out among people as a missionary and bring this comforting message to them. You can do it, Sylvaine, if you want to. You could even manage to lure old Pluto out of his moroseness and inspire him to a little dance."

Sylvaine: "You think I can make a Pluto dance?"

Both: "No question about it."

"If I were young—I admit it—the prospect would tempt me. Unfortunately, there's no Pluto anymore. Otherwise I'd have a go at it, try it again."

The banker: "What's this I hear?"

Sylvaine, unmoved: "I tried it once before."

Hippolyte: "To what effect?"

"I was probably too young. Perhaps I went about it the wrong way."

Hippolyte: "You obviously didn't have your heart in it. You were too young."

"I had too much of my heart in it."

"Oh, no," the banker said, full of admiration, "he would have swallowed you up whole."

She yawned and suddenly turned the table lamp out.

"Human beings are not born free, as the American constitution says they are. They become free only gradually. How do they go about it? Let me ask my question again: Shouldn't we try not to have money? You're a millionaire, Raymond. Can you throw your millions away? Shouldn't you? You aren't free. I can do that. I can throw away every last thing I have. What can't I do? Tell me. Shoot myself, drown myself, poison myself? I can do anything I like. Hippolyte, you had dinner with me last night, and afterwards, when the music was playing, we looked up at the same dark sky, the same stars we can see tonight. You were moved by that sight and quoted Kant, who said that nothing filled him with greater awe than a star-filled sky above him and the moral law in his breast. I let you talk. But I want to tell you now that neither of those things moves me. I can gawk at the sky, now or any other time. When the moon and stars shine into my room, I usually pull the curtains and let them do their shining outside. And as far as that noble law implanted in my breast is concerned, I belong to a different breed of human being than the philosopher did. I can say here categorically that I don't find any law inside me, and if I did find one, I'd certainly get rid of it. I don't want any stowaways in my boat."

The banker rewarded this speech with copious praise and ordered champagne. The cognac that Sylvaine drank down glass after glass did not agree with him.

She touched glasses with him and pronounced judgment on herself:

I've died. Alice Allison is dead; Alice Mackenzie is dead; Sylvaine and any of her successors and any executor of her estate is dead. The only remaining question is whether there is still something there in the place where she used to live, sitting in her skin, something that hates her or curses her or weeps for her.

She creamed her face. She tried to call up the old magic spell again. That path was behind her. Her cold fingers ran over her temples.

"Woe unto you, scribes and Pharisees, hypocrites! for ye are like unto whited sepulchres, which indeed appear beautiful outward, but are with in full of dead men's bones, and of all uncleanness."

An Experiment

ALICE's mention of her attempt to make the god of death dance had roused the banker's curiosity. She had to tell him her story, and she spoke coldly and frankly about herself, as if about some figure from the past. He found her wonderfully cynical, flesh of his flesh, blood of his blood. He had tried everything there was to make his life palatable. This elegant Sylvaine promised him all manner of new experiences.

Raymond sat on the hotel terrace with her.

"Sylvaine, you're so undemanding. You run your affairs like an adolescent or a young girl. You're out for pleasure. You think you have to take love in stages, the way someone catches a fish or kills an animal first, then dresses it out, then cuts it up, then fries it, then finally eats it. But in love, you have to eat the fish alive."

"Explain that to me, Raymond."

"For love, you have to have knowledge and philosophical seriousness to tranform it from a natural process into an experience."

"What you just said sounded more like cannibalism."

"Why put it in such crude terms, Sylvaine? Love can be a great thing, a truly great thing."

"Are you unwilling to share your secret?" (He is as lost as I am. He has some plan up his sleeve for me.)

"What is it that you find exciting in life, Sylvaine? What helps make life palatable for me? I've been well-off from childhood. Most of what I have I inherited. I was able to study and travel. When I encountered high-class prostitutes in Rome for the first time, whores who looked like society ladies, I realized something about human beings—I should say: about us. It was an illumination like the one young Buddha had when he left the palace of his father, the king, and saw illness, old age, and death for the first time. After that, he gave up everything he had."

She looked at him. For the first time she felt a twinge of real feeling for him.

"And what did you do, Raymond?"

"You can see that, Sylvaine. I didn't become a Buddha. I stayed in the world, learned, earned money. I wanted to experience myself fully among human beings who were, after all, my own kind. I wanted to live a genuine life. I saw so much lying and falsehood that I came to the conclusion that it was absurd to speak of truth and honesty among humankind."

(She held a hand in front of her eyes. Where had she heard that before? Lord Crenshaw was sitting in his chair: There is nothing but fantasy. From time to time illusions take possession of people; then they go to war. — And Edward with his book in his lap: I want honesty, I want honesty.)

Raymond: "Lying was one thing I saw, and along with it came the masks, the games, the roles we take on."

(Oh, Lord Crenshaw—)

"Lots of people know this, Sylvaine. But to live with that insight and not to run away, not leave the world and become Buddha, that is more than they can bear. What else can we expect of men but conflict, revolution, and war? I saw this bank of dark clouds in my sky; and no star, not a single star, glittered there. That was one thing I grasped. The other was animality."

"What do you mean by that?"

"The truth. The truth about the human creature is that he is an animal. He has bones, flesh, insides, skin, and hair. He knows hunger and thirst. He eats and digests. He is a thing that belongs to the earth, the air, the water. All that is straightforward. There's no lie about that. But as soon as man starts to think, truth evades him. He looks down on the animal."

"What does he have against the animal? Animals are beautiful, noble."

"We can't manage it, Sylvaine. Believe me. Noble, beautiful, lots of people have used those words. Our minds won't accept them. It's our arrogance. We have to go about it differently."

"In a practical way?"

"Yes, we have to reduce man to the animal. We have to bring him to the truth by relieving him of his brain. Listen to what I'm saying, Sylvaine. It may sound banal, but there's something behind it. Let's stay with the subject of love. I have a Socratic method in mind. Just think how delightful the seduction of a so-called innocent, virginal person is. Such a person resists the animal, resists animality. He wraps himself up in emotions, illusions, that seem to him to be truer than animality. Like an endangered octopus, he gives off black, inky clouds to hide in. He saves himself by way of the lie. He 'thinks' to protect himself from the truth. That is the birth of idealism. The same pattern is repeated time and again, but every individual thinks he is finding his personal, private self in this process."

"A comedy, if that's the way you see things."

"The next step is not one that everybody is willing to take. Most people cling to their illusions. It takes courage to break through to the truth. But before that, of course, comes disgust, insight into the lie and disgust for it."

"You want honesty, openness?" Sylvaine said, laughing.

"Why are you laughing?"

"I've heard the same thing before, in a different context."

"In what context?"

"Let's not get into that now. Go on with what you were saying."

"The breakthrough takes you into an ice-cold realm. You come to Buddha's nirvana by another route. And it isn't exactly his nirvana that you reach."

She whispered: "The route to bestiality."

"The route to the truth. Rousseau minus the sentimentality."

Sylvaine: "Awful." (He is a degenerate. A criminal. That's the way it looks.)

"Silly, that's what man is, just plain silly. He doesn't follow through with anything. There's nothing he really wants, neither insight nor the inevitable consequences of insight. Man is an animal and a dreamer. The animal possesses the truth and the sensuality; the dreamer, the arrogance."

"Say more, so that I can understand you better."

"What I'm saying makes sense to you, Sylvaine? It speaks to something in you?"

"It is not new to me."

"Oh, that's good. Come to me."

In his room she took his hand. "Make an animal of me."

He: "You'll risk it?"

"Help me. I offer myself. I've tried so many things already."

"You've traded in one mask after another."

"There is no animal, Raymond."

"What?"

TALES OF A LONG NIGHT

"I offer myself to you. And I bet that you will not be able to make an animal of me."

She proved to be more determined than he had thought she was. She revealed all her thoughts to him, as if he were her father confessor. But at the same time she mocked him.

"All I want to do is go to sleep," she confessed to him at one point.

"Should I kill you then?"

"Do as you like. There's nothing I can do with myself anymore. I have no will. Put an end to this."

Fear ran through him. What emotion, what seriousness. A warm feeling for her sprang up in him. She was good for him; she helped him. For if he killed her, he would be making a bit of an end of himself, too. No woman he had ever known before had ever meant so well by him.

He took her at her word. But she drew back later. Death, real death, frightened her. He persisted with the idea. Finally she agreed.

She sat at her desk and wrote what he dictated to her:

"I, Alice Mackenzie, formerly Allison, now known as Sylvaine, separated from my family in England, hereby declare that I will take poison this evening. My motives are of concern to no one else."

She signed with a firm hand, feeling more strongly than before: I don't want this.

She lay down on the sofa to take the first sleeping pills. Trembling and blissful, he watched her. He kissed her dress and said how fortunate he had been to have met her. He was ecstatic. This was real seriousness. He had tears in his eyes. She took the second dose calmly in a glass of water. He could not stand it anymore. He embraced her and broke away from her. He said good-bye. This event, his happiness, exceeded his strength. He behaved like someone who has been thrown in the water, who has struggled for his life, lost hope, and considered his life finished. Then he is pulled into a boat. Incredulous, full of fear, he asked: "You'll carry it through?"

She swore she would.

He listened for a while outside the door, then ran off. He could not calm himself and had to go out on the street and blow kisses at the hotel in which she lay and in which she was now dying, for him—in which he now lay and in which he was dying. He loved her as he had never loved another human being before. He had to leave the city instantly. His feelings were too strong for him.

She locked the door after him. Thoughtfully, she read over her note and crumpled it up.

When will the time come for me? This is not it. It is not yet time.

She slept for a long while.

The Animal Trainer

THE banker had disappeared. She was passive. She remained passive. She returned to Paris. The bank advised her that her balance was low. She had used up all but a little bit of her money. She panicked when she received the letter. This was the end.

A few days later she took action. She called Suzanne up. Suzanne came, took one look at her former friend, said she was sorry but she was low on money herself, and disappeared.

Sylvaine changed hotels. She kept her head above water. She was not yet ready to admit to herself that she was doing this as penance. She deserved (she told herself) the life she was leading.

She sank still further. In a moment of weakness, she made one attempt to save herself. She took a job in the cosmetics section of a department store. Things seemed to be going well. But she was not serious about the work and quit after a few weeks. The department head, who had some idea what she had been up to in the past months, called her into his office when she said she wanted to quit and offered her a raise, larger commissions on her sales, more time off. She said she would think it over and then never returned. She didn't want to be saved this way. She condemned herself. Even if her way led her into the swamps, it was a way, and her way. Deeper into disgrace. She did not want to avoid the sinkhole.

She thought of Edward, of Hamlet, who had exposed his parents' lives to the light.

"A bloody deed! Almost as bad, good mother, as kill a king, and marry with his brother." — With his brother, what do you mean, "brother"? With anyone and everyone, with Tom, Dick, and Harry, with cats and dogs.

She had the rigid features of a doomed person. She had to wear a lot of makeup, and she drank.

449

In Salida, Colorado, there was a woman who lived like a wild animal in a cave in the Methodist Mountains. The authorities arrested her. She was wandering around naked from the waist up and wore men's pants. Her name was Editha Garson. She was forty years old and had lived in Denver and Buena Vista in quite comfortable circumstances. She carried a long hunting knife in her belt. She wanted to experience the depths of poverty, and that's why she lived like a wild animal of the forest. She escaped from prison. The authorities could not catch her again.

What prompted Alice to read English newspapers? She brooded a lot, in the cafés and in her room. She reached for newspapers. What had happened to her was so improbable. That was her life. A whole life lay behind her, with the Mackenzies, her parents; with Gordon Allison; with Edward and Kathleen, whom she had borne in her own body; and now this. That was all behind her. She looked out over it, onto the broad plains on which mists rose up, fantasies, ideas; and things became visible, facts, events, people.

Have I been dreaming? What's going on with me? What has happened to me? Lord, my God, give me clarity.

Have I done nothing but live in fantasies? That's what they told me. Why did I do it? What blinded me so? In that case I wronged them, Gordon and Edward and all of them, acted like a devil. Am I a devil? Am I possessed? What is wrong with me?

These thoughts overwhelmed Alice and locked her breast in an iron grip.

But she could not cry.

She met a man in a café. He sat down next to her and looked over her shoulder at her English newspaper. The man asked if she was English. They began to talk. The man took her to his room.

She had begun wearing a veil. And as she took it off and the man was about to kiss her, he began looking carefully at her face, and it seemed to him that he had met this woman before. He asked her if she had ever heard of the writer Gordon Allison.

Dismayed, she said, "No."

He noticed her distress and held on to her when she tried to get up. He kept after her until she admitted that she had been—occasionally, not too long ago—a guest at the Allisons'. Then (he squeezed it out of her, for he had heard that Mrs. Allison had left the house and her husband) she admitted, too, that she was Mrs. Allison, the writer's wife, she, whom he held in his arms here.

No, she did not escape him. And after he had overcome her resistance—she wanted to get away at first, she was ashamed—she experienced the very embrace she had been seeking: Yes, there she stood on
the street, cheap, naked, wild, an animal, a street cur. And everybody
should look and see who she was and what she was making of herself.
And if that's the way things were, well then, she would own up to them.
She challenged everybody, God and the devil alike.

For men are blind and foolish. They don't see that you can do things
this way or that way, and whichever way you choose is all one. We're
all lost one way or another, and we let ourselves be duped with pleasure
and society and a high standard of living. The banker is right: We
should hit anyone in the face who claims there is something we can hold
on to. And so all the questions about guilt and responsibility are pointless.

For we can do whatever we like. We can make war. Why not? We
are smoke, a ball to be tossed about. And we can be rulers, too, tyrants, beasts.

(I'm suffocating. The muck is up to my mouth. If someone would
only strangle me.)

She clung to this stranger with her utmost passion. She practically
clawed him to pieces. She gave herself up to him as a building yields to
a bomb, apartments, stairways, walls, all crashing down into the cellar.

She made a burnt offering of herself.

Now she was ripe to fall into the hands of a man who realized more
clearly than the banker had what could be done with her. This was a
man who kept a stable of women who worked for him. He appeared on
the variety stage and trained women to perform with him in mind-reading and clairvoyant acts, for example, which he then presented in little
nightclubs and in traveling circuses.

Alice still had some elegant clothes and moved like a lady. She
seemed to have a past in keeping with her clothes, he thought (but
better not delve into it; she made a mistake somewhere, out of prison
now, fraud, con games, something like that).

She trained for a clairvoyant act; and, as was always the case with this
fellow, who called himself MacSeecy on the posters, the training called
for innumerable blows and every conceivable humiliation. He was utterly brutal with her. He had never had such an apt pupil and partner.
If the poor creature only weren't so melancholy and evasive. She was so
cringingly obedient that it irritated him and brought out the worst in

him. Try as he would, he could never overstep the limits of her subjugation.

"I have no will of my own, Henry. Believe me. Why don't you want to believe me. Kill me or let me live, as you like."

"Kill you. That would suit you just fine. Bring the police down on my neck. Have you always been this way, you slut?"

"No."

"Well, since when? Who broke all your bones for you? Who was my predecessor? Out with it! I want to thank him."

She stared in front of her without saying anything.

"Did you run out on somebody? They threw you out? Did you steal something?"

"Yes."

She sat there, hunched over.

"Were you married? Did you have another man? Younger, handsomer? Huh? Is that the kind you are?"

"Yes."

He laughed and gave her a punch. "At last an answer out of you. Why can't you open your mouth? Do you still have another lover now?"

"No, Henry, no."

"Because you're afraid, right? And with good reason, slut. Nobody fools around with me. You better not skip off on me with those clothes. If you fool around with anybody else, you'll wind up with a knife between your ribs before you know it."

Love Never Faileth

ON a rainy evening James Mackenzie's doorbell rang. The housekeeper opened to a drenched man with his collar turned up. The water ran from his sodden hat brim onto his shoulders and chest and on down his black leather coat. The man asked for James Mackenzie and apologized for crashing in this way unannounced. Mackenzie came into the hallway. But only after the housekeeper had taken the stranger's hat and coat—he put his suitcase in front of him and would not let her take it—did James recognize this man with the long, plastered-down hair as his brother-in-law, Gordon Allison.

He started and went quickly to greet him. He had his guest take a chair. The housekeeper helped him take off his wet shoes and brought him some slippers. Gordon snorted and grumbled but let her have her way. He also let her rub his wet head dry and give him a warm bathrobe.

This man who had once been grotesquely overweight had shrunk away to almost nothing. The housekeeper brought him hot tea and rum.

"I was traveling through, James," he repeated. "It's late, and I didn't want to go looking around for a hotel. I thought you might be able to put me up for the night."

The housekeeper put a large plate of cakes and jam on the table. He stared at it and shook his head.

"Sometimes I don't eat for a whole day, sometimes longer. It just doesn't occur to me. I could break the habit of eating altogether."

James pressed him to take a bite. Gordon nibbled gloomily at it.

"Where have you come from, Gordon?"

James was shocked.

"I went to Y from X. I stayed there for a while. Then I went from Y to Z. And then—I've forgotten what comes next."

He put down his cake and looked at the red stripes on the palm of his left hand. "I've started writing again. I'm trying. I'm making slow progress."

And he pointed to his wet suitcase standing by the door.

"My manuscript is in there. I don't have any more ideas. It can't be forced. Gordon sits in judgment on himself. He should. But his pen won't go along. It's not used to this kind of thing. And then it isn't essential to write down everything anyhow. For whom? At best only to justify myself before—"

He didn't say before whom.

James: "If you don't want to go home, Gordon, you can stay here with me and work as you please. You know the room upstairs. You'll have peace and quiet and be comfortable. The library is close by if you want to look anything up, and you can help yourself to my library, too, of course."

Gordon stared at him.

"I'm the wild boar, you know. You told a story about him, King Lear, the dragon that ravaged the fields. That's me. I don't need any material. I'm not writing. No, I'm not practicing my trade. — Have you had any word from Alice?" He looked at James hungrily.

That's why he had come.

"None at all. I've found out, though, that she has been drawing on her bank account."

That news upset Gordon a great deal. "Why? What does she need the money for? What bank did she transfer it to?"

"The account is drained. She's taken every last bit of it. She can't have spent it all at once, of course. She probably didn't want anyone to be able to trace her."

The man in the flower-print bathrobe swung his arm.

"And why? Why that? What are we plotting against her? Are we murderers she has to hide from?" He panted for breath, embittered. "What now? What is she doing? I have to talk to her. I travel from city to city, and she hides. She's playing cat and mouse with me. She must be living somewhere under an assumed name. Is that decent behavior? What do you say to that? It cries out to heaven. She'll get her comeuppance for it."

He suddenly fell back in his chair. "I'm tired—this wild goose chase she's leading me. We're not young anymore. Soon it'll all be over. She should consider that."

What confused, troubled talk. James poured some rum into his tea. "Take a sip, Gordon. I'll have something to eat taken up to your room. You'd best lie down a bit."

He took his guest's arm, helped him sit up straight. Gordon swallowed the tea and got up. He leaned on James as they went out of the room. At the door he looked down at his suitcase. "I keep dragging that thing around with me. It can stay here for now, if you don't mind. I won't take it upstairs with me."

And he bent down and petted the suitcase. "Poor beast, poor master."

The next day he wanted to go into town. James knew he wanted to search for Alice. He had interrogated the housekeeper and even snuffled around in the apartment for clues to her whereabouts. James held him back.

After the noon meal—Gordon barely touched his food—James took him into his study and had him stretch out on the sofa. He lay there gratefully, a refugee, a hunted man. Rest during flight. He still hadn't shaved. James considered sending someone up to tend to him, a nurse perhaps, to help him wash. James sat near a window with his newspaper.

"Have you thought much about people?" Gordon began. "Have you ever asked yourself how it is people come together, why this person stumbles on that one and that one on this one?"

"Coincidence, Gordon. It can't be anything else. We live among thousands of people. We walk on by most of them. Some come close to us. We choose."

"How is it that we choose? Who chooses? I have the feeling it's not all a matter of chance. We have some predetermined, primal link to the people we select."

"A primal link." (I know what it is he's driving at.) "We mustn't be superstitious, Gordon. That deprives us of our independence. What kind of link do you think there is? Who does the predetermining? All sorts of things pass before us. We select what speaks to us, what pleases us, and what enriches us. You stand on the shore of a pond, toss your line in, and fish."

"So it seems. That's the outward form things take. But it all looks different after the fact, James. You are intelligent and cautious. You love your books and your studies. You can't come close to things that way."

James agreed with him.

"You're absolutely right. It's my own conviction—which I've expressed to you before—that our ideas form an iron curtain between us and reality. Our thoughts, which tear at things so frantically, do not bring us closer to reality. They only lead us away from it. We imprison ourselves. We move among mere phantoms. It is a remarkable phenomenon. But once you grasp it, you'll run your hand over your eyes and find that you can see better. And you will be less tormented."

He had said all that often enough before. But it did no good. He lacked the courage of his convictions.

"I know that's what you think, James. And I've propounded the thesis myself that there's nothing but poetry, fantasy. You remember that when Edward was plaguing us with his questions about the war and war guilt I told him that from time to time people are possessed by an urge, a madness, a drive, to make war. They develop plans appropriate to their times, and then they conduct wars that are supposed to bring about some kind of progress or another. You remember all that. I spoke about fashions and custom."

"You told that wonderful story about the knight and troubadour Jaufie. I haven't forgotten it. Jaufie was on the verge of giving up his love for the little peasant girl, whom he really loved, because of the fashion of his times."

"You mustn't think that was my real view of things. What if I had just made it up, for whatever reason? I even remember why I did it, what I wanted to achieve with that story. I wanted to protect myself from Edward. And I was taking aim at Alice, too—at her fantasies. I could see what was coming at me. My story didn't help at all. Things took their course." Gordon fell silent, then began again.

"My imagination has been hunting me down all my life, like a mortal enemy. It has ruined my life. But who can live without it? Just look at me. It drove me toward what you have called 'things,' toward real, genuine life in the raw. And what I encountered first was the bad, dangerous types, the criminals. That was reality. And then I met Alice. You know what she was like. And I thought: reality, the good reality. But then she began to dream, to fantasize. She dreamed herself away from me under my own hands. She didn't see me. She drew a false picture of me. She transformed me. She drove me out of existence."

This is what Gordon Allison said as he lay on the sofa. He did not direct his words toward James, who sat leaning forward, his elbows on his knees, listening. He was talking to himself.

"I'm not going to write anymore. I can't do it. Something is telling me that I have to reorder my life. And that's what I mean to do. I'm going to resist. No one should think he can simply ruin me.

"I'm a Christian. I've been baptized. I have to fight for my salvation. Each of us has to fight for himself. That necessity comes to all of us,

one way or another, whether we are aware of it or not. I wasn't aware
of it for a long time either. Then I tried to postpone and shove it out of
sight. But then it grows, assumes gigantic proportions, and throws itself
on you, and you have to meet the test, and it seizes you by the throat,
the way it's doing with me now.

"And you find yourself in a pit and you look up where the light
should be to see if there is any light. You walk through a tunnel, you
wander, wander day and night, trying to find your way out. There's no
end to it. You're trapped. You pound on the walls, scream. Somebody
has to hear you.

"It seems that she was able to climb up out of the pit. She wanted to.
I know that. But, James, she's deceiving herself.

"She can't do it without me, James!"

He sat up on the couch.

"Do you hear me, James? Don't, for once, just go on thinking your
own thoughts. They aren't getting you anywhere anyhow. She thought
she could fight her own fight apart from me. She thought: The old play
is a failure. We're not going anywhere. We're stuck in a blind alley. So
I'll pull out and start over again and leave all the old, dead past behind
me, leave it and run away. Those are Alice's thoughts. Begin a new
play without having finished the old one. And without me. Put Gordon
Allison on the scrap heap. She thinks the way you do. People meet;
they live together for a while; chance has brought us together; then we
tip our hats and say, 'Adieu, have a good trip, sir. Have a good trip,
madame.'

"There is a tie, James. We don't meet by chance. Not we human
beings.

"It's built into you that you'll meet whom you do meet. Our ideas of
an isolated ego are wrong. There's no such thing as that 'I' without a
'you,' no such thing as that great, empty abyss. You're gradually lured
out of yourself. Gradually you emerge, or you try to isolate yourself.
Something in you calls out. You're still unaware of it. It's not until you
hear the answer that you realize it's beginning to come to you. You and
the other belong together. And gradually the two of them battle out
their fate, their salvation, together. They rise up, or they plunge down."

James let him talk, just as the publisher had done before. James was
pleased to see Gordon make himself at home, take books to his room
occasionally, primarily picture collections, and leaf through them, indul-

ging his old liking for landscapes and portraits. He seemed to have
calmed down some.

When James was sitting with him once, the two of them going
through a collection of Delacroix prints, Gordon drew his attention to
The Death of Sardanapal, the original of which hangs in the Louvre.

Just as a voluptuous odalisque has shed her last garment, the bearded
king pulls her backwards toward him and, with his powerful hand,
plunges his dagger into her breast.

"What is the truth here?" Gordon asked, looking the elegant, intelligent, and attentive professor in the eye. "Look at each figure, the
woman, a hot, mute lump of flesh, and him, the way he kneels there on
the cushions and delights in the knife's passion, and soon he'll be intoxicated by a stream of blood as thick as your arm. Step before them, step
into this scene with your questioning after the truth. Truth? A washed-
out word.

"And look at this picture, *The Battle of Poitiers,* this seething, raging
turmoil, blows, screams, men and horses, the living and the dead all
tangled up together.

"What meaning does the word 'truth' or 'fantasy' have in the face of a
fate like this that does not say 'truth' but moans 'murder.'"

"I see," James Mackenzie said, nodding and covering his eyes.
"People shouldn't paint pictures like that."

"Why not? But then who sees them correctly? For most people this is
a marvelous picture, somewhat gruesome, of course. But then people
love gruesome things. The truth is always what happens to somebody
else."

When Gordon didn't appear for breakfast one morning James found
him dressed in his room, his suitcase ready before him. He had been
waiting for James to appear. He was short of breath and spoke very
softly.

"The way she has treated me, your sister. This concerns you because
she is your flesh and blood. What she's done—this running away—is
nothing new to me. Her son, who is supposedly not mine, helped her.
Who was I after all? There was something malign about her from the
very beginning. Even if I came to her with my hands in the air I was still
a murderer in her eyes. Did I want to write? Was it money and then
more money I wanted? I earned enough. Did I want a name for myself,
fame? I would have given it all up for one single word of love from her.
I wasn't as black, as lost to the underworld, as she thought I was.

"But behind those delicate, virginal features of hers was a hunger for the underworld. She drove me into it, amused herself by tormenting me, and felt nothing but scorn for me, the destroyer she was. She exiled me to my study. I had to be satisfied with merely existing.

"I did my best to give her presents so that she would give me her favor in return. For her I sat there and made up my stories. The outside world would grant her glory, and then she would be merciful to me.

"And then it seemed that everything was easing up. The picture of Pluto and·Proserpina still hung on the wall, but it grew darker and darker and hard to see. She seemed not to notice.

"Then the war came, and Edward came back with his demands and still more demands, digging and digging, egged on by her! He burrowed and rooted, egged on by her. She knew what the untrue outcome would be, and she wanted it. At first I couldn't believe that's what she was really out to do when she brought Edward into the house, after all the ground we had gained together, and at what sacrifice. She could see well enough what sacrifices I had made. I was hardly a human being any longer, that creature sitting there in his fat in his study, lying in a grave of fat that was gradually burying him alive."

Gordon groaned loudly, an awful sound. Then he went on talking.

"I couldn't offer her the tender love that she had perhaps come to know before, when and from whom I can't say. But since I could not offer her a sweet, gentle love, why could she not see that what I offered her was love, too, a different, stronger, much stronger love, a painful love that perhaps even tasted of blood, of the blood I had sacrificed for her.

"I did not have an easy time with myself. I couldn't battle my way out of myself. She was to save me from myself. I knew that she was the way to myself, my way to myself, and then she slammed the gate shut. I had to climb over that gate or break it down.

"It's her fault that hate and anger and contention crept into our love then. I sank my teeth into her and would not let go. I admit that and take responsibility for it. I was determined to crush her resistance. I would not be turned away."

Gordon stared into space and nodded.

"And then she began to take pleasure in all this. She developed a real appetite for it. She toyed with me. I had wakened a dormant streak in her character. She saw me suffering, and she consoled me but only to make me suffer some more. She found me amusing. It was not my fault. The rest was not my fault."

James: "What wasn't your fault?"

Gordon: "That she lived a life without love. I tried to give her love; I came a thousand times and offered myself to her. She didn't want me or my love. She scorned me, she roused me, she teased me, she drove me to rage only to calm me down again. She wasn't happy unless she could make me frantic. Oh, what has she made of me, transforming me into something I was not. It was often a relief to me to go back to my desk and collect my thoughts again and ask: Who am I after all? Am I really what she is making of me?"

James: "For heaven's sake, Gordon, if that's the way it was, if you lived in that kind of hell, why didn't you just leave?"

"Because deep in her heart she knew . . ."

"What?"

"That she was misusing me and that she was meant for me. She suffered, too. And now she has gone, has just picked up and left. After so many years, so many sacrifices. But that's her style. And if I bleed to death, well, that's just too bad. That's what she has done. That's what your sister has done to me.

"And now she's off somewhere 'in freedom' and is dancing. I guarantee you that: She is dancing."

James could offer no reply.

And why the suitcase? What did Gordon mean to do? Go off hunting for her again?

"You're ill, Gordon. You're feverish, believe me."

"She has humiliated me. She's pushed me too far this time. I—"

He closed his fists and raised them as if ready to strike someone down.

James, devoid of hope, sat with him through the morning. He could not bear this any longer. He wished himself that Gordon would leave. After the noon meal Gordon was calm again but at the same time quieter, serious. He said he wanted to leave. He thanked James for his hospitality.

"Where are you going, Gordon?"

Gordon put a hand on his shoulder and gave him a resigned smile. "You don't believe in preordained ties. You've avoided such things. But I'm sure they exist, between her and me. If she doesn't realize that yet, she will realize it soon."

James looked long and sadly into his eyes and stroked his hand.

Gordon: "You think I'm going to do something crazy, take vengeance or something like that. Whatever I do I'll do for her, too. You won't understand it. I think I'm a few steps ahead of her."

A Visit

SHE went to the country and stayed in his empty house, dimly aware of a need to act, called, like a migratory bird that receives a signal from the air and flutters around, feeling out that signal, until he is certain of it and it has him in its grip and he can become one with it.

On one of these short, questioning, listening days Gordon received a visitor, a man he had traveled with many years ago. The man had remained a travel writer, and since he was passing through the area, as he said, he had come to see Gordon Allison and share a whiskey with him.

It turned out that this quiet, friendly man knew nothing of Allison's "disappearance." On the Continent, where he had spent the last few years, little note had been taken of the incident; and the few, spare newspaper reports that had been written about it—addressed as they were primarily to the literary world—had apparently escaped his attention.

It turned out in the course of the conversation, to which Gordon, nervous and distracted as he was, contributed only a few sentences, that Wescott, the visitor, was familiar both with this country house and with Gordon's former home in London and had been a guest at parties in the Allison home before the war. Gordon found himself in the uncomfortable situation of having to make some kind of accounting of his domestic and family situation. Wescott had a remarkable memory and recalled, at least superficially, every member of the family. They were all in London with friends at the moment, Gordon said brusquely, meaning to cut further inquiry short. He did not like this interrogation. Perhaps the man had assumed this role of old friend simply to get an interview with Allison that otherwise would have been refused.

But the man blithely drank another whiskey and said that he had a greeting to convey to Alice, from a French woman who was born English and had known Alice years ago when she had still been Alice Mackenzie.

Who was this woman, Gordon wanted to know.

Wescott mentioned a name that Gordon could not place.

"It was a long time ago," Wescott granted. Could he not convey the lady's regards to Alice in person?

"I just told you: She's in London."

"At your house? I had heard your house was badly damaged."

"She is staying with friends of mine. I'll pass your message on to her."

The guest had lit a cigarette and remained unperturbed by his host's reticence. He had a slender, intelligent face; his eyebrows grew together over his nose; he smiled a lot, a friendly, engaging smile, showing his large, white, slightly protruding front teeth.

He had not forgotten that evening in a run-down Paris café where he had sat next to a woman who was reading in her newspaper and had long since finished her aperitif. He had glanced at the paper and seen it was the *Daily Mail*. He asked her if she was English. They began to talk. She wore a veil over her face. She let him take her to his room. But when she was sitting next to him on the sofa and lifted her veil, it struck him that he had seen her face somewhere before. She had been upset at first but had eventually admitted that she was Gordon Allison's wife. It was an encounter he did not forget. He had to return to England for business reasons, and because the image of that woman haunted him, indeed, because the farther into the past the incident moved, the more disturbed he was by it, he resolved to find out how things stood between Allison and his wife and what it was that had driven her away. But he yearned, too, the moment he touched English soil, to return to her (even though the whole incident had been no more than a brief adventure, the magical excitement of a single hour).

Wescott, Gordon's annoying visitor, then began, quite out of the blue, to inquire about other visitors to the Allison home, about James Mackenzie, for example, Alice's brother. Gordon found the interview exceedingly painful.

Then Wescott said, "So I was right. It was Mackenzie, the Celtic scholar. I wasn't mistaken after all. A while ago in Paris, I was out for a stroll, gathering impressions—unfortunately I'd left my little Leica at home—when I happened on a poster way out in the outskirts of town. That was the name on it. Mackenzie."

"And so?" Gordon asked, bored. "What does that have to do with my brother-in-law? He hasn't been away from England for years. I don't think he's giving lectures in the outskirts of Paris."

"I thought of him because there in big black letters on a yellow poster stood "Alice Mackenzie, Mind Reader," or something like that, a magic act in one of those little variety shows where you don't have to pay any admission but have to drink a lot."

The birds rose up into the air. In the heights they sought the fine strands of air that would guide them on their long flight.

"In Paris, in Batignolles." (Just look at the change that has come over you. I remember you as heavy, downright fat. What happened between you? Now you're frightened.)

"Did you—go into the variety?"

"Yes, once. I was sorry that I couldn't go again. But I had to come back to England."

"This Alice Mackenzie—did she dance? Or what did she do?"

"I told you. Magic. Guessing what you have in your pocket, how many buttons are missing on your coat, and so forth. She sits on the stage with her eyes blindfolded, and the manager moves about in the audience."

"I know the kind of show you mean."

Gordon was sitting up straight and breathing heavily. Now he leaned forward toward his visitor. "Did you speak with this woman? Did you have a chance to ask how she happened to pick that name?"

"To be perfectly honest, I didn't think much about the name. Mackenzie is a common family name, and Alice is quite common, too. And she spoke with an English accent. But that doesn't prove much either. Variety artists are an international lot and like to present themselves as foreigners wherever they appear. The exotic element helps draw customers."

"Batignolles, you say, near Paris."

He fell back in his chair.

A lull in the conversation.

She could have gone to France. I thought about that for a while. Batignolles, *varieté,* Alice in a mind-reading act in a variety show on the outskirts of Paris?

Gordon felt a sudden rush of feeling in his chest, stormy, overpowering. It's she, it's she. Something awful has happened to her, to me, to all of us.

He groaned. "You can't, of course, having seen this woman only on the stage with a blindfold on her, you can't describe her to me, can you?"

(I could. If I could only tell you. I know her every line and feature, the way a painter knows his model. And I know her with more than my eyes. My mouth knows her mouth, my tongue her tongue, my face her face, my arms and legs her arms and legs, my body, my loins, her body and loins. And I know how she gives herself. She is Helen, and I'm Menelaus, who has succumbed to her and could start the Trojan War for her sake. And I can see that you know her, too, Gordon Allison. Do you want to fight me for her?)

"Unfortunately, I can't tell you how she looked. The hall was dimly lit, and her act did not last long. At the end of it, when the audience was clapping, the manager stood next to her" (a vicious type, *un filou*), "took off her blindfold. She beamed at him. The spotlight was trying to find both their faces, but by the time it finally reached the right spot, she had already left the stage, probably at a signal from the manager, and he took his bow alone. He had trained her. It was his act."

"Trained her?"

"Yes. It's all a fake. Every word is agreed on beforehand. The crudest kind of hokum. But for the simple people in an area like that it has a lot of appeal."

Gordon: "What are your travel plans? You'll be traveling to France again soon?"

"In two, three days."

"Would you show me where this variety show is?"

"It interests you?"

"I'm—looking for my wife. Please don't ask any questions. When will you leave?"

(I'm looking for my wife. — The sentence had a dreadful ring to it. It hit Wescott like a thunderbolt. I'll take him there.)

Drum Rolls

THE days until he came to pick Gordon up.
Gordon waited.

The earth takes the dead to herself. The earth is faithful. She expects us. We can entrust ourselves to her. She is faithful; she means well by us.

What a good thing it is that the earth exists. She takes everything we have, our smiles and our weeping, our dancing and our warring, our battles and our struggles, the colors, she blots them all out and takes them to herself.

I hear march rhythms, drum beats, drum rolls, each just like the next.

But above them slowly, solemnly, horribly, stretches the long, long drawn-out melody, the murderous, all-consuming melody. It burrows into the brain. It empties the soul. It steals consciousness away. A crater opens up. It swallows us. The beats, the rolls, the march.

Gorgons, harpies, sirens, we know them all. And yet we still let them rend us. —

This is not a story. This is the truth. There is a steel blue little beetle with short wings. In May the female's lower body swells up with thousands of eggs. The male is dead by then. He dies right after mating. The female digs pits in the ground in May. In June the larvae crawl out, six-legged, like their parents, and with three claws on each foot. That's why they are called triangelines. They crawl out of the pits. They live on dandelions and yellow camomile and wait for the bees, the wild bees.

And when the wild bees buzz and settle on the blossoms, the little larvae leap onto their hairy bodies and cling there with their claws—for that is why they were given the claws, but they have no consciousness—and they let the bees carry them from blossom to blossom until their time comes, the time when the bee builds its nest, fills the combs and cells with honey, and lets an egg fall on the honey and float there.

Then the triangeline's moment has come. It leaps onto the egg. The

465

bee seals off the cell, thinking its work, its maternal work, is done. The egg swims on the honey, and when the egg has matured, the young creature that emerges from it will find sweet nourishment at hand. But triangeline is rocking on that sweet sea in its little boat. Triangeline has teeth and eats its way into the egg. It eats everything but the shell, and then it has eaten enough to undergo metamorphosis.

And it is transformed into a larva that is designed to live in honey. It slurps up the honey and grows and changes its shape once more and becomes a pupa and eats its cupboard empty and is a blue oil beetle that breaks out of its cocoon.

There is still another beetle, a handsome beast, that loves corpses, and whenever it smells a corpse, a rotting bird, a lizard, a mouse—they all die, just as people die, and sink into the earth—then five or six of these beetles gather and dig the dirt away around the dead animal, they dig and dig, and the corpse sinks deeper and deeper into the ground.

And when it is deep enough in the ground they have a wedding on the corpse, these grave diggers, these handsome beasts, and they mate, and the females lay their eggs in the corpse, and it provides a banquet for the brood, the beetles' progeny.

And then there is, there is—

The march rhythms, the drum beats, the drum rolls, regular, each like the last. And above them, slow, solemn, unearthly, the drawn-out melody.

The Black Death. They run from it. They fear death. A mother abandons her child. Women run into the churches, bring their jewelry with them, throw their gold at the priest's feet, at the altar.

Drunks wander through the streets, men and women, sing and topple over dead wherever they happen to be standing.

Some of them scream: Repent, repent! Repent your sins!

The black monks sing. Death makes his rounds. The earth swallows people up. Dust thou art, and unto dust shalt thou return.

The flagellants, half-naked, on the streets. And everywhere the dead sink into the ground, back into the earth, the good earth.

There Sat Alice, the Daughter
of the Mackenzies

▟▜ THERE she sat, Alice, the daughter of Albert and Evelyne Mack-
▙▟ enzie—

there sat the bride of the missing Glenn, who was long since dead, long since on the bottom of the North Sea, rotted to pieces, carried off by the fish, this sweet, childlike Glenn, who had never touched her—

sat the mother of Edward, the mother of Kathleen, the wife, the runaway wife of the dissolute, subdued, wandering Gordon Allison, sat—

sat in a small, cold hotel room with a cracked ceiling, tattered wallpaper, sat at a white wooden table, bent forward on a kitchen chair—

sat and beat her breast and sobbed deep down in her chest and didn't dare speak:

O God, almighty God, what have I done to myself, why did I have to do it, why did I have to punish myself this way, why didn't someone hold me back and shake me before I did this to myself, before I degraded myself so, twisted myself so, sullied myself so, threw myself away.

It was not the right thing to do. Alice, you did not do the right thing.

Alice, you cannot justify what you have done.

Alice, admit it. You have brought this curse down on yourself and are accursed, and you deserve to be thrown into the pit where there is nothing but wailing and torment without end.

And that's what's before you, and that's where you're heading straight as an arrow, look around you, look at yourself, just listen to yourself, just feel yourself.

What have you done to yourself, Alice, why did you do it? What drove you to this? Who drove you to it?

Oh, I don't know. I thought of Glenn. It was when I was young. I loved him. Did he even know it? I couldn't stop thinking about him. I

467

should have torn my eyes away from him. I should have freed my heart from him. I should have forbidden my thoughts to wander back to him. I yearned to be with him. We loved each other without ever saying so, and then he was gone.

Now I torment myself and can't find peace, and I want peace. And I don't want to be unhappy anymore and castigate myself when I wake up in the night and everything is still, and I'm lying in the pit on the bottom of the black, dreadful pit that I am, that is my self. — I, alone with myself, alone in the world.

All of life, all that I know, is my own floundering, tormented self. And I have to torture myself in the morning when daylight appears at the window and the first traffic starts moving, and I had dozed off a bit after all, and several hours were obliterated, but I was not to be allowed real peace. I was thrown back, delivered up to myself again, to my hangman and to my tireless torturer.

And when I want to pray and drive them off, to shove their hands away from my door, I find only words. I do not find prayer.

My prayer stays outside the door. It rejects me. It does not accept my invitation. My invitation does not tempt it; and the hangmen and the torturers, the big ones and the small ones, they know that moment, and they grin and come in and are there. They know I belong to them.

Oh, what will become of me?

Oh, what will become of me?

Why do I have turn and roast myself on the spit this way?—

There sat Alice, the daughter of Albert and Evelyne Mackenzie—

sat the bride of the ghostly Glenn, abandoned by her, long since missing, long since dead on the bottom of the salty North Sea, fallen to pieces, dissolved, carried away by the fish, Glenn, who had touched her life like a dream (perhaps his restless spirit was searching for her, his spirit searching for happiness, searching happiness, just as she was)—

sat the mother of Edward, whom she had summoned to obtain justice for her—but what justice was it, justice against whom? Against her dream which she loved, then pillaged?—

sat the mother of Kathleen, who had fled her parents' house with bitterness in her heart and whose children would inherit her melancholy, questioning gaze—

sat the wife, the runaway wife of the wandering, moaning, mortally wounded wild boar Gordon Allison, sat at the bare, battered wooden table and froze and laid her head on the tabletop.

The hard, smooth wood, once the flesh of a birch in a distant wood, consoled her. The wood was softer than the linen of a pillow. Alice laid her hand on the wood.

I'm so lonely, so abandoned, that I have to lean my head on a table-top instead of on someone's shoulder. I would be grateful if an executioner came, raised his axe behind my back, and cut my head off with all its thoughts, so that the thoughts would run out with the blood and sink into the ground where they could do no more harm, so that my breast would grow cold, empty, and hollowed out, like one of those bombed-out houses where only the frame is left standing.

How I long for peace. Is it possible that there is such a thing as "peace"?

When have I ever known peace? With the children when they were young. But that was not true peace either. It was a peace troubled with weeping because the children were not his, not the children of the man I loved, because it was not he who kissed them and picked them up and rocked them in his arms.

Peace—why could it never be mine? Why is it forbidden to me?

Oh, I want to know bliss. I am a human creature and sinful; but, like everyone, I have an angel in me that wants to play and fly.

Show me how. Fly for me. Oh, my cramped, frozen, dreadful heart, free yourself.

Have mercy on me, my fearful, frozen heart, my strict, pitiless judge, release me from my chains.

Fall out of my breast, my heart.

Heavenly Father, father of mercy, I am contemptible and deserve nothing. Because I am so sinful I hardly dare turn to you. I know that I shouldn't. And that's why my lips shut tight, even though they want to pray, and I know there can be no mercy for me.

But have mercy despite that!

Have mercy! Have mercy anyhow!

Heavenly Father, see what has become of me. Have mercy. Come to me.

Say something to me.

Even though I am crushed underfoot—remember that it was you who created me—perhaps you can spare a syllable for me, too.

The Mid Reader

23 THE day after they arrived in Paris, Wescott, without making any
explanations, took Gordon Allison to the little café where he had
first seen Alice. Wescott harbored a dim hope that they would find Alice there. Desire for her was strong in him. The fire that had burned in
Alice during that hour had spread to him and was still burning. He tried
to put it out, but he couldn't. He trembled just thinking about what
would happen if he saw her.

He took Gordon to the building where the variety show was playing.
When Wescott saw how the man ran his hand over the poster and
pressed his face against it where her name was printed, he fled.

Evening. A stuffy, smoke-filled room. People were sitting around at
small tables. The place was full. First there was a snake charmer, then a
dance act, then acrobats on bicycles.

Then the lights dimmed.

The manager, the trainer, led Alice Mackenzie in. She wore heavy
makeup and a tight-fitting black dress. She sat right down on a chair.

The musicians blew a fanfare. The medium's eyes were covered with
a black blindfold. The manager invited members of the audience to
come forward and convince themselves that the cloth was opaque and
completely covered the medium's eyes. A young man, then—amidst
much laughter—a young girl, went up on the stage, put on the blindfold, and assured the others they couldn't see anything. Then they
checked to see that the blindfold was firmly tied around Alice's head
and extended both above and below her eyes.

Another fanfare. The manager went from table to table and asked
people to give him or show him whatever they liked. One man gave him
a wallet. He took some bank notes out of it and asked, "How much
money am I holding here?"

She answered in a monotone. He asked question after question. She said how many buttons one man had on his jacket, what color the neck-tie of another was.

The manager came up to Gordon Allison. He asked Alice Mack-enzie, "Tell me, what is this gentleman like? Tall or short, heavy or slim? Quickly now."

She answered, "A heavyset man."

"Young or old? What color is his hair?"

"His hair is streaked with gray."

He took hold of Gordon's tie. "I am looking at the gentleman's neck-tie. The tie is embroidered. Tell me quickly what the embroidery on the tie depicts, a plant, a bird, a wild animal? Quick now, what's the an-swer?"

Up to now the woman on the podium had sat up straight and an-swered like a robot. Now she raised her hands as if to take off the blindfold, but then she lowered them again, leaned her head back, and trembled.

The manager turned toward the stage. "Well, Alice, come on, quickly now, tell us what's embroidered on the gentleman's tie. Is it a flower, a bird, an animal? Say what you see."

She said under her breath, "A wild boar with two tusks."

The manager glanced over at her, bent down to the man, and looked closely at the tie. Then he bellowed out into the room, "Would the ladies and gentlemen at this table care to see for themselves, and you folks at the next table? A boar's head embroidered in the middle of the tie, the gentleman's coat of arms apparently, or a sporting emblem. The gentleman is no doubt a hunter? The two tusks can be seen only from up close. Step right up and have a look."

With broad gestures he urged the people at the neighbouring table to come closer. The man wearing the tie, his face immobile, let all this roll over him. In the meantime the manager took a few steps toward the stage and looked suspiciously at his medium. He went up to the stage, stood in front of her, and whispered, "Sit up straight. Fold your hands."

She obeyed, sat stiff as a doll. But tears were running down both her cheeks, rolling visibly over her makeup.

The manager, who had turned back to the hall, could not tear himself away from the man. He was uneasy, on edge.

"And now," he went on in his sharp barker's voice, "now pay atten-tion carefully, Alice, and tell me what the gentleman here is wearing on his left arm."

She wept. She sat there with her blindfolded eyes and her head sunk down on her chest and wept.

The manager waved his fat arm in the air. "That happens with her. She's in a trance, and sometimes she cries. It doesn't mean anything. Afterwards she won't even remember it. Pay attention now, Alice, and tell me quickly what the gentleman is wearing on his left wrist. Is it a watch, a bracelet, is it made of cloth, of metal?"

"Of gold. A narrow gold bracelet."

She sobbed loudly and stammered on.

"And there are letters on it, a G and an A, his initials. He hasn't added any others. But this can't be."

The audience was suddenly restless. Voices cried out, "Turn on the lights," "Stop the show," "It's a hoax."

On the stage Alice went on speaking haltingly. Was she awake or dreaming? Her heavy tears fell onto her hands. It was difficult to understand what she was saying.

"Gordon, it's you. I know it is. You're looking for me. Gordon, Gordon—help me."

"Stop the show. A put-up job. A cheat. Turn on the lights."

The hubbub drowned out the voice of the man with whom the manager was still standing and whose left arm he still clung to.

"Let go of me, man. Let go of my hand. Alice, Alice."

She cried, mumbled, and stammered.

The lights had been turned up. The director of the show had come onstage and signaled to the little band down in front. The musicians started drumming and tooting away.

The manager leapt up onto the stage without a word and grabbed his medium by the shoulders. He shook her and took off the blindfold. Behind him the crowd was hooting and yelling. "Crook, con man!"

He yanked her out of her chair and dragged her offstage by the hand. They took refuge in the director's room, where they could still hear the audience's catcalls and the voice of the stranger whose screams of "Alice, Alice" drew laughter from the rest of the audience.

When the short, fat director, outraged at this scandal, came into his room, he saw the manager punch the woman in the face, then seize her by the throat and try to strangle her. The director had to tear him forcibly away from her.

The Reunion

THE manager lived a few blocks away. Alice tried to get away from him on the way home. In the apartment he took out his rage on her. He beat her during the night and the next morning. She was so weak and limp that he could leave without fear of her running away on him.

He came back in the evening and looked around the apartment suspiciously. She was still lying on the bed. The director had told him not to come back. In his rage, he had gone out drinking. Now he wandered about the room. He shook Alice. She should get up. She should make him coffee.

The apartment was on the ground floor in the back of an old building. High stone steps led from the dark, narrow courtyard into the rotting building. The iron railing on the steps was broken and hung at an angle to one side.

Alice had made the coffee and put it on the table in front of the man when someone felt his way up the stairs in the dark. The man listened, set his cup down, and threw a glance at the woman, who went and stood next to the wall.

Someone knocked. Someone pounded on the door. The woman didn't move. The man didn't either.

The visitor outside went on pounding. "Open the door," she whispered.

He: "Why? Who is it?"

The visitor went on pounding. The man slowly drank the rest of his coffee, said, "Well," and went to the door.

The minute he opened it he was pushed back into the room, and the man from yesterday, Gordon Allison, was standing in the room in which only one small lamp was burning on the table. He looked around wildly. "Where is she?"

"Who?"

"Alice, where are you?"

She was standing in the shadows by the wall, and she could not speak.

"Who is Alice?"

"My wife."

The manager laughed coarsely. "He's come to get his wife."

"My wife."

"Coming up, my boy."

The manager seized the other man by the shoulders, kicked the door wide open with his foot, and, with a powerful shove, pushed the heavy man out. Gordon Allison stumbled sideways for two or three steps, then lurched backwards through the door and onto the top step where he crashed through the hanging railing, fell head first onto the stone courtyard, and lay still.

The man above him slammed the door shut.

Alice ran past him and opened it again, without any interference from him, and listened. She took the lamp from the table. He didn't stop her. Moaning, she went down the steps, shining the light to one side, then the other.

She set the lamp down on a step. He did not move. She cried loudly and piteously. She called his name. He didn't move.

The man in the apartment was becoming alarmed. He cursed, said, "Shut up!" and came down the steps. He bent over the prostrate man. And when his victim showed no signs of life, he ran up the steps in a few leaps, thumped about in the apartment for a few minutes, then reappeared with his hat and coat on and a suitcase in his hand. As he ran past her, he said, "I'm taking off."

There Lived a Singer in France of Old

ALICE at Gordon's bedside in the hospital.

His head, his neck, his chest in bandages. A broken vertebra and a concussion.

The earth is faithful. She expects us. She takes the dead to her. But is the thing we call death really death?

Alice had a room next to his. She could not be dissuaded from that. She was the wife of the Englishman, a rich man who, like her, had gotten mixed up with some criminal types. She had gone to the dogs and looked like a worn-out whore. In the course of an argument, a thug, a pimp, who also dabbled in variety show numbers, had knocked him down some stairs.

He lay unconscious for two days. Then he began speaking thickly. Then he recognized her.

She prayed and wept day and night.

She prayed and implored. That he be saved, pulled from the jaws of death. She tormented herself. She offered herself as a sacrifice: She would not live, not an hour longer, if he could not live. She saw him wake up. When he recognized her, she could not control her feelings. She cried out at his bedside, in penance, pain, joy, hope, faith, doubt, gratitude. The nurse came and led her out of the room.

When she had calmed herself in her room, Alice closed the door and kneeled down at her bed. She pleaded with God and all the divine powers and helpers to save Gordon. She included thanks and words of love in her frantic prayers, words of contrition and bliss. When she got up again, she was calm. I will save him. It will be given to me.

Then sitting quietly at his bedside for hour after hour, and then two days of talk.

Alice talked to Gordon for the first time. For the first time Gordon talked to Alice. They left nothing unsaid.

We were standing on either side of a door.

We pounded on the door. We heard the other pounding, but the door did not open. It was made of iron, heavy, immovable.

We couldn't open it, not we. Now it is open, and we have each other—in this condition, but we have each other, and it is not too late.

And if our lives should last only a second longer, they will have fulfilled their purpose.

"Why didn't we come together, Gordon? Because I didn't want it."

"Now there is peace, Alice. Peace at last, at long last. Oh, Alice, I'd like to live. I have to talk with Edward again. I have to tell him that I never hated him. I want him to forgive me. If he will only do it. Oh, Alice, you know how to pray. Pray that I can see him again and give him my hand and tell him that I love him. I'm so ashamed of myself."

"Don't torment yourself, Gordon. He'll be so happy to hear that. I know him."

"He is your son."

"Yours, too, Gordon. You know that. I did a bad thing. I wanted to have him all to myself."

"Even if he did not have my blood in his veins, he would still be my son. He is my son, and he knows that, and that's why he attacked me at home, and that's why I want to tell him, at least once, that I love him and always did love him. And I probably won't get a chance to say it."

The days passed. Gordon lay in his bed of plaster. The doctors came in more often. He had a fever. She understood. But she did not give up hope for him. She stayed awake and prayed. She would not let herself cry.

"Come, pray with me, Gordon. Fold your hands, and pray with me. — We regret the way we were. From the bottom of our hearts we regret how we have lived our lives. — Come on now, leave your hands together, dear, and say with me:

"Our Father, which art in heaven. — He is our father. He knows all about us.

"Hallowed be thy name. Thy kingdom come. — Yes, let it come. It will come when we have purified our hearts, when we have become his children again.

"Thy will be done on earth, as it is in heaven. — We want to see his will done and to submit to it. We want to place our bodies and our souls in his hands, whatever he chooses to do with us. We will accept everything, everything. We can do that because he is our father.

"And forgive us our debts. — Oh, I pray for forgiveness, we pray for it, we beg for it. Forgive us our dreadful debts. He will forgive us our debts. How could he be our father otherwise? He will do it. And, Gordon, to bring us his mercy, he sent his only son, our savior, the sweet fruit of Mary's womb, and Jesus sacrificed himself on the cross for us, for you and for me. Can you imagine anything grander than that? Won't you accept that gift, Gordon?

"As we forgive our debtors. — You can say that. You forgive me. I can see that. I feel it, Gordon; and I—I forgive you everything, though you did me no wrong, you did nothing to me, no, never wronged me. And because God will forgive us our debts and because we pray for it, Edward will forgive you, too, and he will forgive me. God will see to that.

"And lead us not into temptation, but deliver us from evil.

"Pray with me, Gordon. Move your lips. Do you understand what I'm saying? It makes me happy when you speak the words with me."

And because she persisted he spoke the words with her. And afterwards she wept uncontrollably at his bedside and then ran from the room.

He stayed awake for a long time that evening. Perhaps it was the fever. He brought the conversation back to Edward again and to how much he wanted to see him. He felt so burdened with guilt. He reminded her of those long evenings when they had told Edward stories to entertain him, but Edward knew how to interpret those stories, and no one had been able to evade standing trial.

"He was Hamlet, and I was the king. You were Gertrude. 'O, my offense is rank, it smells to heaven; it hath the primal eldest curse upon't, a brother's murder!' "

The patient was dreaming to himself.

" 'For thou dost know, O Damon dear, this realm dismantled was of Jove himself; and now reigns here a very, very—pajock.' "

She touched his hand and called him back.

He began talking about his long troubadour story.

"What a wonderful poem, Alice, that one by Swinburne:

> There lived a singer in France of old
> By the tideless dolorous midland sea."

"I know."

"He loved a woman he had never seen, Alice, never seen."

He squeezed Alice's fingers. He had to look straight ahead. His bandages would not let him move. She laid her face on his hand. But he murmured:

"And it so happened that the troubadour was overcome by a powerful longing, an irresistible yearning, to see the princess. And he took up the cross and traveled to her. But fell ill on board ship."

"Don't speak, Gordon, dearest. I know the poem."

"You know it. — And he was carried to an inn in Tripoli. He lay there unconscious in this strange room, far from home. But the princess he had never seen came to him. He saw her."

Alice: "I know, Gordon. It's true. Then she took him in her arms, as I'm doing now, and touched his lips with hers and held him to her."

And she did it.

And when she stood up, his mouth was open, and the light had left his eyes. She had known it when she came close to him.

She sank down on the floor next to his bed.

A Farewell Across the Channel

COMPLETELY calm, she took care of the necessary formalities in the next few days. He had wanted to be buried in England, in his home soil. She arranged to have his body shipped home. She sent her brother, James, a telegram, telling him that Gordon had died in an accident and that his body was being sent to England. James was to receive the body at the port and arrange for burial. She asked him to pay for the shipment and also inform the children. She would write soon.

Wearing a black dress and a heavy black veil, she accompanied the coffin to Calais. She even went onto the ferry and went below with the coffin. She lay on it until someone lifted her from it. The ferry was about to leave.

In Paris she wrote to her son, Edward.

"My son, my dearly beloved son, heart of my heart, love of my life, my child, my dear friend whom I will never see again.

"I'm writing to you. I'm writing to bless you and, in spirit, to hold you to my breast and cuddle you the way I used to when you were small.

"Forgive me for what I have done to you and Kathleen. Both of you please forgive me, just as your father did, whose eyes I—poor, wretched, lonely woman that I am—have just closed.

"He died from a fall. He fell down some stone steps in the city, suffered a fractured skull, and could not be saved. I was with him every day in the hospital. I stayed in the room next to his. I talked with him, with your father, Edward, your good, departed father. I was able to ask his forgiveness for everything I had done to him and to you in my blindness and madness. He forgave me. He took me back. The mother of God, the heavenly Virgin, stood by me. And so he left this world reconciled and in peace, and I pray ceaselessly for him.

"He spoke of you in his last days, Edward, on his very last day, spoke of you with love, with great love and in pain and still in the hope that he might take your hand and tell you how much he loved you and always did love you and that any ill he may have done you was not directed at you.

"Oh, Edward, how unexpectedly good and happy the end of my life is now that reconciliation with him has been granted me. I kiss your face, my dear child. You hear my grief; you know how repentant I am. Please think kindly of me, too, for all the love I have shown you during my life. I am your mother and remain your mother, and you will mourn for me.

"Eddy, dear son, you will not hear from me again. I cannot return to the world of men. I can never make good what I have done, not on this earth. I'm remembering those days long ago when we were caring for you in our country house and I began telling you the story of Theodora. It was the story that was always with me in my youth. Do you remember? I told you how Theodora had lived in the world, and then later, how she escaped that life and left the world. Now I want to tell you the conclusion. And I won't change a word of it. I'm telling you the end of the story, Edward, and I'm telling it to myself as well. I think about it every day.

"Theodora had fled from Alexandria with Philippus, her husband, who had returned and to whom she had been unfaithful during his absence. They sailed in a small boat for five days. Then they put ashore and left the boat.

"She took his hand and confessed to him. She said she wanted to go into the desert, and he mustn't follow her.

"'I wanted to cure Titus, that handsome, dissolute man, that degenerate and seducer. I thought I could do it. But the physician fell ill herself. I turned my back on God and made him my enemy. I sank to the point of serving the prince of hell. Now I am lost, Philippus, my husband, my good Philippus. Do not touch me, or you may be infected with my evil.'

"To all his pleas Theodora replied:

"'My dear Philippus, stay here. Do not follow me and bring me to tears again. I do not have much time left for crying.' Once again she turned and came back to him because he complained so loudly. She urged him to be strong. At that moment her face took on a firm expression. He stayed on the coast for a year, waiting for Theodora, but she thought only of doing penance.

"Theodora hired herself out to a farmer in the area. She cut her hair short and wore men's clothes. The farm was eight miles from the city, but on the road to the city lay a monastery. She begged to be admitted to the monastery. The abbot fulfilled her wish. She called herself Theodorus and performed menial household chores.

"And once again the world came to tempt her. She was leading her camels into the city on the road called Peter's Martyrdom. And there on the roadside stood her husband, Philippus, who had dreamed that he would meet her here.

"She recognized him and lamented in her heart: Woe unto me, my Philippus, that I have to disappoint you.

"She passed on by him, saying, 'May the Lord bless you, sir.' He thanked her but did not recognize her.

"Another time she saved a man from a lion and became stronger in her resolved and holier, so that even the devil, who saw her slipping out of his grasp, had to yield to her. Then he played her a nasty trick.

"She had to travel across country to a rich man's lands, and because it grew late she spent the night in his house. The man's daughter saw the handsome young man from the monastery, Theodorus, and went to him in the night to lie with him. He refused her gently. Enraged, the daughter left him and slept with another man.

"And when she became pregnant, she went to her father and said, 'Theodorus, the young man from the monastery, lay with me.' The father took the infant in his arms, went to the abbot, and showed him the child.

"The outraged abbot called all the monks together and said to Brother Theodorus, 'Wretch, you have disgraced us all.'

"Theodora fell on her knees before him. 'I have sinned, Father. I have sinned. Punish me.'

"The abbot laid the child in his arms and sent him away from the monastery.

"Brother Theodorus wandered around with the child and found a place nearby where the people let him stay. He begged alms at the monastery gate. Farmers in the fields gave him milk for the child. He suffered patiently and welcomed any pain that came to him and thanked God.

"A devil plagued her often. He urged her to go back to the man who had been her husband in the world, for the child's sake and for her own sake. That devil came in the guise of her husband's messenger. She struggled with herself, prayed, made the sign of the cross—and the devil disappeared.

"Seven hard years she lived this way. Then the abbot came from the monastery to see Theodorus and asked him to come back. He heard his confession and absolved him of his sins. He took Theodorus and the child into the monastery. And then Theodora's measure of earthly penance was full. Theodora knew she would die soon.

"The abbot had a dream in the night. He dreamed about a wedding, and he saw many angels, saints, and prophets. And then one beautiful woman appeared. An ornate divan was brought to her. She sat down before all the others, and they were all friendly to her and greeted her and bid her welcome.

"And as the abbot was wondering who this beautiful woman was, a voice said, 'That is Brother Theodorus. He has done his penance.'

"And in the morning, when the abbot got up, he called his monks together. And they went to Theodorus's cell. And when they opened the door, he was lying there dead. But the abbot wanted to know the whole truth, and he ordered them to bare their brother's breast. And they saw that he was a woman.

"She had taken a heavy penance upon herself. Her hunger for penance was insatiable. But now she had done enough. The Lord in heaven had accepted her.

"And so ends my prayerful story of Theodora, Edward, a story that runs like a thread through my own life.

"Don't say, Edward, my son, let that be enough. You do forgive me. I know it, and I kiss you for it. It would make me happy if I knew you could pray, and also pray for me. Do it, Edward, help me.

"Help me today and tomorrow and when I am no more, my beloved son, my only son."

Alice did not have much longer to suffer. She left Paris, but no sooner did she arrive in the country than a terrible weakness came over her. She couldn't walk anymore. She could not move her arms. Cups, spoons, slid out of her hands. She was succumbing rapidly to a general paralysis. She couldn't even lift her eyelids, and she had difficulty speaking. The wild life she had been leading was taking its toll. She realized that and suffered it gladly. She spoke with the nurses in the hospital she was taken to and asked for a priest.

She made her general confession. She hadn't spoken with a priest since her childhood. Tears streaming down her face, she told all there was to tell. The divine words fell on her withered soul which soaked up the balm in deep draughts.

The next morning she was as if transformed, lying calmly and peacefully in her bed, smiling at the nurses. She had tasted bliss. It even seemed in the next few days as if she were getting better. But one afternoon, just as the priest was about to visit her again, the respiratory paralysis the doctors feared set in, and the end came quickly. The priest found a dying woman.

She attempted a smile and reached for his hand.

Her face lit up when the oil touched her forehead.

The priest and the nurses, acting on Alice's request, wrote to Edward and Kathleen, reporting what details they could of her last illness and death. They mentioned, too, that she lay buried in consecrated ground in France.

Kathleen did not receive the nurses' letter. She was in Scotland, recovering at her fiancé's parents' house. When the coffin containing the body of her beloved father, Gordon Allison, arrived in England, she had been the only person on hand to receive it and had behaved like a madwoman in the chapel at the cemetery. She couldn't understand what had happened, and she even went so far as to claim that her mother had killed him.

When Edward went to the Continent to bring back his dead mother, it was the first trip he had made since the war and since his long, disastrous voyage to the Pacific. In the same ferry in which Gordon Allison had returned home, lying flat and mute in the hold, some months before, Alice Mackenzie now returned, too, accompanied by her son, her calm face still wearing the radiant expression of her last hours.

James Mackenzie was waiting for her at the harbor in Plymouth. He insisted on helping to carry his sister's coffin to the train. But in the train compartment—Alice rode farther back on the train—he broke down in a paroxysm of sobbing, and all his limbs started twitching convulsively. He had to lie down, and a doctor had to be summoned to the station in London to attend to him.

That was the end of the life of Gordon Allison, known as Lord Crenshaw, the well-known writer, and of Alice Mackenzie.

They did not lie in the same cemetery. Alice's place was in the consecrated ground she desired, in London near the ruins of her old home. The brother and sister, the heirs, soon sold the country house near Dr. King's clinic. Edward drove out to it one last time before the sale to pick up some mementos. In going through his mother's belongings he came upon the small, medallionlike picture of Theodora that Miss Virginia had told him about, a colorful but darkened picture of a woman, executed on a gold background. He took it to his room and hung it near his desk.

The End of the Long Night

23 IT had come down on the Allison family like an avalanche. There were deaths. One family member was missing, Edward, the son, Hamlet. In the dueling at the end of Shakespeare's *Hamlet,* the prince of Denmark is mortally wounded and then dies. What became of Edward after all the details of his parents' lives had been cleared up? Old Dr. King, once he had recovered from his own shock, wrote first to the scholar James Mackenzie, Alice's brother, who had not wanted to tell Hamlet's story at the evening gatherings. Dr. King asked where Edward was and what he was doing. Instead of a letter in reply, he received a personal visit from James Mackenzie; and after an initial exchange of their impressions, they got into the doctor's comfortable car and drove to the family's old home in London to which Edward had withdrawn. The town house with its large grounds made a dismal impression. An elderly woman appeared at the door when the two men rang. She wanted to send them away, thinking they were journalists, a breed of which she had seen more than enough in recent weeks.

Even after the two men straightened her out on that point she still refused to invite them in but explained that Mr. Edward Allison was not in. He had gone into town with his male nurse—an announcement the visitors were not inclined to believe—but finally she asked them to come in and look around the living quarters and bedrooms. After that they sat nervously in the garden and waited until noon. Then there was a sign of life at the house, and Edward appeared on the steps, supported by his male nurse, a robust young man. Yes, it was clearly Edward, smoking a cigarette. The two visitors restrained themselves for another half hour until the housekeeper appeared and led them into the house.

Edward was waiting for them at the door. They begged his pardon for crashing in on him unannounced; then the three of them sat in Gordon Allison's former study. Dr. King, at Edward's invitation, had to take

Gordon's chair. The preliminaries over, a silence set in. Standing at the window and looking back into the room only occasionally, Edward asked, "What do you gentlemen have to tell me?"

Dr. King: "How are you? That's all I have to ask."

James Mackenzie: "I've come just to see you and talk with you."

Edward: "I walk and ride around in the city with my male nurse. When I first arrived here, I thought nothing could touch me. I was lying in the grave but wasn't yet dead myself. My first experience here was seeing June bugs in the garden and watching them. They ate and flew around and didn't worry about anything. And I thought to myself, why can't I be just like the June bugs? They act as if nothing had happened. And that's when things started to change for me. Remember when we all came together to celebrate Father's birthday? It was I, me myself, who put on that play, worked out the production that you both saw, the story of a man who got on the La Brea bus in Los Angeles and kept riding around in a circle and never arrived at his destination. As far as I am concerned, I retract that play. We do not just ride around in circles, no, we do not ride in circles."

A long pause. The two visitors didn't dare put in a word. Now Edward's eyes settled on his uncle. "I'm not going to play *Hamlet* either and wait for a Nordic King Fortinbras to overrun my Denmark with his powerful army. And then there is the picture of Theodora hanging on the wall in my study. And though it is only a picture, it engaged me in steady conversation and, in my first days here, often didn't let me sneak a word in edgewise."

Uncle James: "And now?"

Edward shrugged his shoulders, and the visitors saw him smile for the first time. "Now the picture is a picture. The June bugs were dead during the winter. Now they crawl about and eat the green leaves. And day after day, Dr. King, I asked myself whether I wouldn't do better to purify myself and go into a monastery instead of into your sanitarium. For I have already experienced everything that can happen to a person in the world. But then what does a monk do? Why should I spend the rest of my life in a cell, praying and singing? To purify and prepare myself—but I'm still not anywhere near arriving at my destination. What I have to digest I will digest, and I'll manage that better in the outside world than surrounded by four walls."

Then Edward invited his guests to join him in the dining room across the hall; he was hungry. They sat together at table until Dr. King stood up, looked at his watch, and said he had to be heading home. Neither on this day nor on the following ones was there conversation of any consequence between James Mackenzie and his nephew, who appeared to be avoiding the older man. Finally, one morning, Mackenzie held Edward back before he had gotten out of the house.

"Will you tell me how you are spending your days?" his uncle asked.

Edward: "I have no reason to hide from you what I am doing."

They were standing next to the breakfast table. Edward's male nurse had knocked and appeared at the door with Edward's coat and cane in hand.

"Sit down for a minute, Uncle. You have seen the letters I've received, and you know our family history better than anyone else. I'm ready to let it rest. I have no further part in the play." He slammed his fist down on the table. "I am not in the play, I tell you. If this is supposed to be a drama that represents the fates of human beings, then mine is not among them. Or if it is, then only as that of a man who was run over in the course of the play. But I am still alive. I'm still in a developmental stage. I'm a fetus that hasn't learned to speak yet. That's why I'm going out into the world now, to discover myself. I had thought everything would be fine after the avalanche and after everything that had been obscure had been clarified; I thought my hands would be free. But in fact nothing has changed. I'm like a new Columbus who has come upon a previously unknown continent, and I'm just about to go explore it."

The scholar: "And what do you call this new continent? Are you sure it is one and not just another fog bank?"

"I'm positive it isn't that. I'm meeting people, sharing in their concerns and learning that their concerns are mine, too. I haven't yet assumed my legacy. I can see that I have, or had, arms and legs, but nobody taught me much more than that. I thank heaven that I was able to learn more. This immense life, this mass, at one with me, with others, with itself. At last I'm catching sight of it and facing up to it, as someone who is part of it."

The scholar: "You've found your homeland?"

Edward reached out both his hands and pressed his uncle's firmly. "Thank you for asking that. You will be a great help to me. Speak to Dr. King, too, and put this Hamlet business to rest for good. Now come join me on my drive."

And as they rode through the city, he told his uncle that he had given his father's entire, vast estate to medical charities for the poor, keeping out only the bare minimum he needed until he could support himself by his own efforts.

And so they drove into the teeming, noisy city.

A new life was beginning.